THE FUTURES

THE FUTURES

Anna Pitoniak

MICHAEL JOSEPH

an imprint of

PENGUIN BOOKS

MICHAEL JOSEPH

UK | USA | Canada | Ireland | Australia
India | New Zealand | South Africa

Michael Joseph is part of the Penguin Random House group of companies
whose addresses can be found at global.penguinrandomhouse.com.

First published by Lee Boudreaux Books,
an imprint of Little, Brown and Company 2017
First published in Great Britain by Michael Joseph 2017

001

Set in 13/15.75 pt Bembo Book MT Std
Typeset by Jouve (UK), Milton Keynes
Printed in Great Britain by Clays Ltd, St Ives plc

A CIP catalogue record for this book is available from the British Library

HARDBACK ISBN: 978–0–718–18456–8
OM PAPERBACK ISBN: 978–0–718–18457–5

www.greenpenguin.co.uk

MIX
Paper from
responsible sources
FSC® C018179

Penguin Random House is committed to a
sustainable future for our business, our readers
and our planet. This book is made from Forest
Stewardship Council® certified paper.

For Andrew

PROLOGUE

Julia

It was a story that made sense. An old story, but one that felt truer for it. Young love goes stale and slackens. You change, and you shed what you no longer need. It's just part of growing up.

I thought I had understood. It seemed so simple at the time.

We moved in on a humid morning in June. Our suitcases bumped and scuffed the walls as we climbed three flights of stairs, the rest of the boxes and furniture waiting unguarded in the foyer. The locks were clunky and finicky, resistant on the first few attempts. Sunlight streamed through the smudged windows, and the floorboards creaked beneath our weight. The apartment looked smaller than it had before, on the day we signed our lease. 'I'm going down for some boxes,' Evan said, holding the door open with one foot. 'You coming?'

'I'll be there in a minute,' I said. I stood in the center of the room, alone, finding that I couldn't breathe.

What else was I going to do? He had a job and a place

to be. I didn't, but I had him. I could feel the tremors of change even before we graduated, growing more pronounced as the date approached: time to get serious. We'd been dating for more than three years, and we loved each other, and my friends already had roommates, and I couldn't afford to live by myself. So we signed a lease. We packed our things in shared boxes. It felt sensible and grown-up. And maybe taking this plunge would repair whatever hairline crack had already appeared between us, in the late months of senior year. Double or nothing.

In New York, we settled into a routine along with our friends, accruing habit fast. We all endured the same things: shoe-box apartments, crowded subways, overpriced groceries, indifferent bosses. What kept everyone going was the dream: store windows on Madison Avenue, brownstones lit golden in the night, town cars gliding across the park. Imagining what it would be like when you got there, someday. Manhattan was like a dazzling life-size diorama. A motivation to work harder, stay later, wake earlier. Fantasy is the only escape valve – what's all the pain worth without it? But not for me. I'd screw my eyes shut and try to imagine it, what the future would look like, what alchemy might transform our current situation. But nothing came. There was no thread of hope. Who was this man next to me, his body curled up against mine? What was this feeling of vertigo that sometimes came with the blurry edge before sleep? I realized that I had made a mistake. Evan wasn't the one. We weren't meant to be.

And so my life in New York grew smaller and smaller, a thorny tangle of dead ends. I rattled around in the tiny apartment. I hated my job. Evan was too busy. My friends were too busy. I was lonelier than ever. The problem was obvious. I was trapped in an airless bubble, with no plan to get out. My life lacked any escape.

Until, against my better instincts, I went looking for it in the wrong place.

PART I

CHAPTER 1

Evan

I could hear footsteps and murmurs from the other room. The creak of the door opening finally dissolved the last shards of sleep. When I opened my eyes, there was a pale face peering through the crack.

'Who is *that?*' somebody whispered.

The door slammed shut. The alarm clock said it was a little past 9:00 a.m. It took me a minute to remember where I was: on the third floor of an old stone building in New Haven, still wearing my clothes from the night before. I found a half-melted stick of gum in the back pocket of my shorts, tugged my T-shirt straight, and pressed my palms against my hair. When I opened the door to the common room, a plump woman was surveying the scene with a look of dismay. Empty Bud Light cans were scattered across the floor, and dirty clothes were heaped in one corner. She started fanning the stale air toward an open window. It was move-in day, late August, the first real day of college. This had to be my assigned roommate, Arthur Ziegler, and his family. I'd meant to clean up that morning, but I'd forgotten to set the alarm last night when I stumbled into bed.

Arthur was crouched in the corner, fiddling with a nest of wires. Arthur's father, a bald man in a polo shirt and khakis, was humming to himself as he peered down at the street. Arthur's mother was sniffing the air, her frown deepening. The room was quiet except for the car honks and shouts from outside. I cleared my throat. The three of them turned in unison.

Arthur's mother forced a smile. 'Well – hello,' she said, stepping over. She was small, round and doll-like, with a tartan headband and sensible shoes. 'I'm Elaine Ziegler, Arthur's mother. This is Gary.' Gary waved. 'And this is Arthur. Arthur, what – what are you doing?'

'Hang on,' he said, peering at a plastic box. A row of green lights blinked to life. 'Got it.' He stood up, dusting his hands on his jeans, then he followed my gaze. 'Oh. The router. Setting up the wireless connection. Figured it was the most important thing to start with, right?'

'Yeah. It's, uh, nice to meet you all.'

Elaine Ziegler kept staring. Maybe she was trying to reconcile it, the polite young man suddenly emerging from the shell of a passed-out lunk. Then she clapped her hands together. 'Well, let's get to work. Gary, you make the bed. Arthur, why don't you start unpacking those suitcases? And I'm just going to . . . here we go.'

She shook open a black garbage bag and bent over, reaching for the empty beer cans on the floor, crinkling her nose at the smell. I felt a hot bubble of guilt.

'Mrs Ziegler, I'm sorry. Let me . . .' I hurried to start gathering the cans.

'Well . . .' She paused, then handed me the bag. 'All right. Thank you, dear.'

When I was done, I announced that I was taking out the trash. Elaine and Gary were absorbed in a discussion with Arthur about where to hang a poster. The door creaked on its hinges when I opened it, but they didn't notice.

The captains had given us the morning off from practice. There was a diner on Broadway that I'd passed before, a place that served breakfast all day. The room was packed and buzzing, new students chattering excitedly with their families, utensils ringing against china while waiters wove through the crowds with plates aloft. I was about to give up when the hostess finally caught my eye and led me to an empty stool at the counter.

After, while I was waiting to pay at the register, a girl walked in. Other heads turned too, taking in her tanned legs, her cutoff shorts, her scoop-neck T-shirt. She had a blond ponytail sticking out from a faded Red Sox cap and a freckled nose. She leaned into the counter and said something inaudible in the din, and even that – the shape of her mouth forming silent words – carried some kind of promise. I tried to edge closer, but it was too crowded. A waiter handed her two cups of coffee. She pushed the door open with her shoulder. I craned my neck but lost sight of her on the sidewalk.

I wandered for a while, only returning to the dorm when I knew Arthur and his parents would be at lunch. I changed and jogged up to the rink for afternoon practice. I was the first to arrive, which was what I'd been hoping for. The burn of the laces against my fingertips as I tightened my skates, the smell of the locker room, the wet reflection left behind by the Zamboni, the sound of the blade carving into the ice, the wind and echo of the empty rink – it was like slipping back into a native tongue. This was the best part. It only took a second, in that first push away from the boards, to feel the transformation. From a bulky heaviness to a lighter kind of motion. The friction of the blade melted the ice just enough, sending me flying forward on threads of invisible water. I was in a different country, a different side of the continent, but in those moments at the rink, home came with me. The ice was a reminder of the world I had left behind just a week earlier: long winters, frozen ponds, snowbanks, pine trees. It had always seemed like a decent enough reward for life in a cold, forbidding land: the gift of speed, as close as a person like me could come to flight.

I grew up in the kind of small town that isn't easy to get to and isn't easy to leave. It started as a gold-rush settlement, and while no one got rich from the land, a handful of prospectors liked it enough to stay. It's in a mountain valley in the interior of British Columbia, surrounded by wilderness, defined mostly by its distance from other places: seven hours to Vancouver, two hours to the border, an hour to the nearest hospital.

In a small town like ours, where there is only one of everything – one school, one grocery store, one restaurant – it's expected that there is only one of you. People aren't allowed to change much. I was held back in kindergarten – I'd had some trouble with reading comprehension – and it marked me well into the next decade. I was big for my age, always a year older, and I think people liked me more because of it. It made the picture snap into focus: I was a hockey player; I was a born-and-bred local; I was a hard worker even if I wasn't the brightest. An image easily understood, one as solid and reliable as the mountains in the distance. I grew up with boys like me, most of us hockey players. We were friends, but I sometimes wondered how alike we really were. The things they loved most, the things that made them whoop and holler with glee – keg parties and bonfires, shooting at cans on a mossy log, drunken joyrides in a souped-up F-150 – only gave me a vague, itchy desire for more. I could imitate easily enough, like following an outline through tracing paper, but it never felt like the thing I was meant to be doing. I got good at faking laughter.

Maybe the girls at school sensed this difference. It happened fast: one day puberty arrived, and they all started paying attention to me. From then on, there was always someone waiting at my locker when the last bell rang, twirling her hair, holding her textbooks tight to her chest. I genuinely loved those girls, loved that they banished the loneliness, but it was a generalized feeling; it didn't matter who was next to me, whose bed or musty basement carpet we were lying on. I had sex for the first time with a girl a year older than I was, eleventh grade to my ninth. After she had coached me through our first short but glorious session, she started telling me her plan. She was going to drop out at the end of the year and move to the Yukon, where she'd work as a chef at a logging camp. The pay was good, and the setting was wild. She propped herself up on one elbow, resting a hand on my bare chest. She hadn't told anyone, but she was telling me. She kissed me in conclusion. 'You're a good listener, Evan,' she said, then she moved lower beneath the duvet.

A pattern emerged from the filmstrip of tanned faces and soft bodies. All the girls liked to talk dreamy – about the jobs they'd get, what they'd name their kids someday. We became blank screens for each other, desire reflected into a hall of mirrors. It solved a problem for me, but sometimes it left me wondering if that was it – if love was always so easily caught and released. I realized after a while that I gave these girls something very specific. They knew it even before I did, that I would be gone someday. I wouldn't be there to hold them accountable when their dreams eventually fell short. I wasn't like everyone else, wasn't meant to stay in this town.

Not that people didn't attempt to leave. They'd go for a few years of community college or university, but a small town like ours possesses a strange gravity, and they always came back. A few of my teammates were going to escape by leaving school early to play hockey in the Major Juniors, a path that would lead some of them to the NHL. I might have done the same. But I'd heard about someone from town, a decade ago, who'd played for an American college instead. He was rich and successful and living in New York by that time. He came back occasionally to visit, and I glimpsed him once at the gas station, filling the tank of a shiny high-end rental car. Even in that split second, I saw that he carried himself in a different way, and something within me latched on. I'd known that the world was bigger than Carlton, British Columbia, but I'd never really thought about just how big it was. I was fourteen years old, and I made up my mind. I played in Junior A and kept my college eligibility. Despite my reputation, I was smart, or at least I wanted to be smart, and I studied hard in school. In spare hours I shot tennis balls into the street hockey net, did squats and flipped tires and jogged the dirt roads around our house. On a Saturday morning, I drove two hours to take the SATs at a town on the border. In the fall of senior year, I finally got the call. The one I'd been hoping for. A new door, swinging wide open.

On the afternoon before my flight east, I stood with my parents in the driveway as the sun slipped behind the mountains, casting an early twilight over the yard. My parents owned the town's grocery store, and they couldn't afford the vacation time or the cost of the plane tickets. My mom would drive me to Vancouver, where we'd spend the night in an airport motel before my flight the following morning. My dad was staying at home to work. I'd said good-bye to my friends at a party the night before, truck headlights illuminating the clearing in the woods where we always gathered, squat kegs and foamy cups of beer clutched in the semidarkness.

It was quiet during the car ride out of town. 'Music?' my mom asked, and I shook my head. The trees along the highway blurred together.

'Evan,' she said after a long silence. 'It's okay to be nervous.' She looked over at me, her face tanned from the summer. A long salt-and-pepper braid fell down her back. Her bare arms were lean from years of carrying boxes from delivery trucks to the loading dock. It was her hands on the steering wheel, their familiar age spots and creases, her thin gold wedding band, that made me understand that I was really leaving.

But I shook my head again. 'I'm fine.'

'Well,' she said. 'I guess you're probably pretty excited about it.'

I was. I still was. But the anticipation had been building up for so long, and now that it was actually here, the moment felt disappointingly ordinary. We could have been driving anywhere, on a family trip, or en route to some hockey tournament. I had the feeling that eventually we'd turn back in the other direction, toward home. It seemed impossible that this was how life transformed itself: a drive down a road you'd driven so many times before.

'Only a hundred more kilometers,' she said an hour

later, as we whizzed past another road marker. I felt like I should make conversation – it was the last time I'd see her for months – but I couldn't think of anything to say.

'Checking in?' the clerk at the motel asked.

'The reservation is under Peck. Two rooms,' my mom said, digging through her wallet. I raised my eyebrows at her, my eternally frugal mother. Only when we were wheeling our bags down the hallway, away from the lobby, did she lean over and whisper: 'You're a grown-up now, honey. I think you deserve your own room, don't you?'

I was on campus early. Every year a rich alum from the hockey team paid for the team to have use of the rink for one week in late August. The captains would run the practice, skirting the NCAA rules that prevented us from officially beginning practice until October. Most of the players lived off campus and could move in early. After my flight – the longest I'd ever taken, the first one out of the country – I caught a shuttle bus to New Haven. I was going to crash at the hockey house for the week, along with the other freshmen. The door was unlocked when I arrived.

'Hello?' I called into the empty living room. I followed the sound of voices to the back of the house, where I found two guys sitting in the kitchen, eating dinner.

'Hey. I'm Evan Peck. I just got here.' I held out my hand.

'Hey, man. I'm Sebi. And this is Paul. We're new, too.'

'Where are you guys from?'

'Medicine Hat,' Sebi said.

'Kelowna,' Paul said.

Our team was mostly composed of guys like that, guys like me – Canadians from the prairies and the western provinces, some New Englanders, a few boys from Minnesota. It made settling in easy. The routine was familiar, the intensity turned up: twice-a-day practices, runs and lifts, team dinners. I was exhausted, not so much falling asleep every night as passing out, too tired to feel homesick. On the second-to-last day of that week, toward the end of afternoon practice, I noticed a man sitting in the stands, watching us scrimmage. He wore a crisp suit and tie, which seemed incongruous with both the August heat outside and the manufactured cold inside the rink.

'Did anyone else notice that guy?' I asked in the locker room.

'The guy in the stands?' one of the seniors replied. 'That's Reynolds. He's paying for all this.'

The same man was waiting outside the rink when we emerged in the late afternoon light. He wore mirrored sunglasses and leaned against a bright yellow sports car. One of the captains went over and shook his hand, and they spoke briefly.

'Guys,' the captain called out to the rest of us. 'We're going over to Liffey's for beers. Mr Reynolds is treating.'

'I still don't really get who this guy is,' I said to Sebi as we trailed the group down Whitney Avenue. At the bar, quiet on a weekday evening when the campus was still empty, Reynolds took off his jacket, rolled up his sleeves, and slapped his card down to open the tab.

I thought of the dwindling contents of my wallet as I reached for the pitcher. I was planning to find a job on campus, but until then, I was spending the last of the money saved from my summer job. At least the beer was free. A little later, Reynolds came over to our table and pulled up a chair. 'You're all new, huh?' he said, reaching to pour himself a beer. 'I don't recognize any of you from last year.'

We nodded. 'Yes, sir,' I said.

'Well, this is my favorite time of year, getting you guys together for the first time. The main thing is you get to know each other. These early days are the best, let me tell you. When everything's still up for grabs.'

Reynolds had the build of an athlete in retirement, muscles gone soft, a cushiony midsection. His mirrored sunglasses shone like an extra pair of eyes from the top of his head. He squinted at us. 'Not that I don't expect a return on my investment.' He laughed. 'I'm paying for this because I expect you guys might be able to bring home a national championship in your time here.'

We sipped beer in silence. 'Did you play at all after college, Mr Reynolds?' Sebi finally asked.

'It's Peter. No. No, I wasn't good enough to go pro, never expected to. But there's another game, you know. It pays better and it lasts longer.' He laughed again, his teeth glowing white. 'Moved to New York, started in banking, and now I'm running a hedge fund. You know how hedge funds work?'

He talked and talked, going into more detail than any of us could absorb. I tried to pay attention, but I kept drifting, noticing instead the embroidered monogram of his shirt, the gold wristwatch peeking from beneath his cuff. His accent still had the last traces of a childhood spent somewhere in Canada's sprawling interior. He was rich and young. He'd done everything right. But he looked tired beneath it all.

The sky outside had darkened. Reynolds waved down the waitress to close out his tab. 'Have to head back,' he said, draining his beer. He passed around business cards. 'I know you guys are good, but odds are you're not going to the pros after college. Call me if you ever want advice.'

Earlier that day, before afternoon practice, I'd finally moved my things into my dorm room. The other students would be arriving the following morning. That night, after Reynolds left, I wanted to forget what I was about to face: the people who had earned their place at this school through different means – through more *legitimate* means. I'd spent the previous week pretending that this place belonged to me, but it was only that – pretending. After leaving the bar, a few of us picked up a case of beer and a handle of whiskey and brought it back to my room, drinking until late. By the end of the night, it had done the trick. I'd almost forgotten. I kicked the empty cans aside and collapsed onto the bare bed.

★

In the dim basement of a frat house, in a room that smelled like beer and dirt, a girl pressed her body against mine. She kept laughing at everything I said. It was that first night after everyone arrived, the first real night, and my teammates and I ventured in a pack from party to party. I moved my hand down her waist, over her T-shirt, and she drew closer. *Okay,* I thought. It still worked. We danced for a while, and then we were kissing. She tasted like tequila and salt. A few songs later, she pushed closer with impatience. She was cute, with a great body, and both of us were the right amount of buzzed. But in that moment sex seemed only marginally appealing, not worth all the trouble. I felt a little melancholy. My teammates were scattered throughout the room, distracted by other girls or games of beer pong, so I extracted myself and left the party unnoticed.

Back at the dorm, the light coming through the door to my entryway caught a figure in silhouette. It was a girl, tall and long-legged. Blond. She looked familiar. As I got closer, I recognized her from the diner that morning. Her hair was loose and long, and she'd changed into a dress. She was looking for something in her purse and didn't see me until I was right behind her, reaching for my key card.

'Oh! God, you scared me,' she said.

'You need to get in?'

She laughed. 'I think I managed to lose my card already.'

'You live here, too?'

'On the fourth floor. I'm Julia.'

'I'm Evan. Third floor.'

I stepped aside to usher her through the open door. 'After you.'

'Oh – thanks.'

The door fell shut with a loud bang.

'So, Evan.' She smiled. 'Where are you from?'

'Canada.'

'Really? That's cool. Where in Canada?'

'The middle of nowhere. You've never heard of it.'

'Try me.'

'Carlton. It's in British Columbia, the interior.' She shrugged, and I laughed. 'I knew it. What about you?'

'Boston. Well, just outside Boston. Brookline.'

I was tempted to say something about the Red Sox, remembering the hat from that morning, then I reminded myself that she didn't know I'd been looking.

'Did you go out tonight?'

'Yeah, with my teammates. Hockey,' I added.

'That explains the Canadian thing. You must get that a lot. Or you will.'

I laughed. My beery buzz had vanished. The way she was looking at me wasn't the way the other girls looked at me back home. Her face was like an image firmly fixed on canvas where the other girls' had been slippery glass. Right here in the present, breathing the same air, not off in some imagined future. Midnight wasn't late. The night was just starting. 'Hey, are you hungry?' I asked.

'Starving, actually.'

We walked to the pizza place on Broadway. Up at the counter, she reached for her purse, but I waved her money away. I could give her this, at least. On the way home, we sat on a low stone wall, waiting for the pizza to cool. I watched as she plucked a piece of pepperoni from her slice. Her kind of beauty snuck up on you. You had to look a little closer to really get it. Someone called her name from across the street. She waved back at him.

'That was fast,' I said.

'What was?'

'You made friends already.'

'No, we went to high school together. There are a bunch of us here.'

'Oh. That must be nice.'

'I guess. What about you? What do you think of it so far?'

'This place?' I swiveled, taking in the panorama. 'Just like the brochure. But more drunk people.' She laughed. 'It's about what I expected. Or not. I don't know. I'm still taking it in.'

'Different from home?'

'Are you kidding?'

She smiled. 'It must be an adjustment.'

'That's an understatement. What about you? What do you think of it?'

'It's just like the brochure.'

'Touché.' I laughed. 'So, Julia. How was your summer?'

She blinked once, staring down at the sidewalk. She blinked again.

'I'm sorry. Wrong question?'

'No, no, it's just – long story. I don't need to burden you with it.'

'You can tell me.' A beat. 'People like to tell me things.'

'You'd better be careful. I might never shut up.'

Eventually she took the last bite of her pizza, and then she held the crust out toward me. 'Do you want it? I never eat the crust.'

'Sure?'

'I wouldn't offer it to just anyone,' she said in mock solemnity. 'But I can tell we're going to be good friends.'

Back in the dorm, we stood in the hallway outside her room. It was late, 3:00 a.m., then 4:00 a.m. Other students tripped up the stairs to bed, but we kept talking and talking, and whenever I thought maybe the conversation had reached its natural end, one of us fired off in a new direction, bringing the other along. She didn't invite me inside. Mostly I was glad for that. Finally, when she started yawning uncontrollably, I said that I should probably get to bed.

'Yeah. Me, too.' She paused, hand on doorknob. 'Thanks for the pizza, Evan.'

'Anytime.'

She smiled. 'See you in the morning?'

Julia had a boyfriend. Of course she did. A guy named Rob, from her boarding school. They'd been together for almost two years. But by mid-September, she was barely mentioning Rob. Usually I was the one to ask about him, as a way of making sure he did in fact still exist. I wondered how much she and Rob actually spoke, how much she told him about her new life at college.

It turned out to be easy enough: making friends, fitting in. It didn't seem to matter how different two people might be or how different their lives had been before college. That was true for me and my roommate, Arthur. We fit together like puzzle pieces, a big one and a small one. And it was true for me and Julia. She took my hand at parties, leading me through the crowd. She came and went through our unlocked door like another roommate. She helped me cram for midterms; she read my papers. I needed the help. That was what surprised me most – how hard the work was. It was like the other students saw English where I saw hieroglyphs, even in the most basic, introductory courses. Maybe that hometown feeling had been right all along; maybe I *was* the same as the Evan Peck who'd failed kindergarten way back. I couldn't admit this to anyone, not even to Julia, although she probably saw it anyway. She saw everything about me.

One night in late October, coming home from practice, I passed her in the courtyard, where she was on the phone, pacing back and forth. I pointed to the door, but she shook her head. Then she snapped: 'Rob, listen to me – no, just listen. Why are you so pissed? Seriously? What do you want me to say?' She rolled her eyes at me and mimed holding a gun to her head. She cupped her hand over the phone. 'Sorry. He's ranting. I'll see you up there in a minute.'

I spent Thanksgiving with Arthur's family in Ohio. On Sunday afternoon, we got back to campus. Every time I heard footsteps on the stairs from the other students trickling back, I wondered whether it was Julia. We hadn't spoken during the weeklong break. I fiddled with my cell phone – I'd finally gotten one, after a few months of working on campus – but something stopped me from calling. The neediness of it, maybe. Later on Sunday night, Julia's roommate, Abby, knocked on our door. They had liquor leftover from before the break and were having people over that night.

My stomach twisted as we climbed the stairs. There were about a dozen people crammed in Abby and Julia's small common room. Julia was across the room, talking to Patrick, another guy from our entryway. She looked different, but it was hard to say why. She tossed her head back when she laughed and kept resting her hand on Patrick's forearm.

'Evan,' Abby said, pulling me aside. '*Evan.*I have to tell you something. She might kill me for telling you first, but I don't care.'

'What is it?'

Her eyes sparkled. 'Julia and Rob. They broke up.'

The rolling eyes, the mimed pistol. Julia had started to hint that the end was imminent. Abby laughed. 'Oh, come on. Don't act like you're not totally overjoyed.'

'I'm not. I mean, I am. But –'

She shoved me. 'Go.'

The mantelpiece served as the makeshift bar. I went over and poured myself a drink, willing my heart to slow down. I glanced at Julia, but she was still talking to Patrick. She hadn't seen me, or she was pretending she hadn't. It seemed strange.

'Hey,' I said to Arthur when he wandered over. 'Hey, Arthur, guess what.'

'Julia and her boyfriend broke up. I know. Abby told me, too.'

'Yeah. Big news, right?'

'So this is it, then? You guys are gonna be together now?'

I shrugged, but I liked the suggestion of inevitability. Julia. It *did* seem inevitable. It always had. 'I haven't even said hi to her yet.'

'You sure it's such a good idea?'

'What do you mean?'

But at that moment, an arm slipped through mine. 'Hey, stranger,' Julia said, kissing me on the cheek.

'Hey, you,' I said. Arthur was slinking away toward the door.

'How was your first-ever American Thanksgiving?'

'You people really like your football.'

'Do you want to know how mine was?' Her cheeks were flushed, her eyebrows arched. She was drunk.

'I do. You wanna get out of here?' I slipped my hand into hers, which was warm and familiar, and it flooded me with hope. 'Let's get something to eat.'

'No.' She pulled her hand away. Yanked it, almost. 'Come on, stay! Don't you want another drink?' She started to refill my empty cup. Then Patrick called her name from across the room, asking for another beer.

'You got it,' she called back. She handed me my cup and went back over to Patrick, who ruffled her hair. She avoided me for the rest of the night. When the last of the liquor was gone, Julia and Abby announced they were going to the deli on Broadway for sandwiches. Julia didn't seem to notice or care when I didn't come along.

But I wasn't tired yet. Back in our room, I stared at a muted rerun of *SportsCenter*. I couldn't make sense of it – of her. What explained her sudden distance, her caginess? Julia didn't bother playing games, not usually. I liked that about her.

Later I felt a hand on my shoulder, someone saying my name. I opened my eyes, and Julia was standing in front of me.

'You came back,' I said.

'I'm sorry,' she said. 'I got this for you.'

She held it out like an offering: a sandwich from the deli. My favorite kind, the one I always ordered. I never realized that she'd been paying such close attention. The heft of the paper-wrapped mass in my hand sparked the strangest feeling, or, really, two feelings at once. A home-sickness I hadn't realized that I'd been feeling all along, and a sudden cure for it. 'Can I sit?' she asked.

I patted the couch, and she folded herself around me, resting her head on my shoulder, draping her legs across my lap. She was always so at ease in the world. Taking my hand at a party, resting her head on my shoulder: those gestures made the world feel big and small at the same time. It was just me and Julia, but what lay before us stretched so far you couldn't see the end.

'How was your Thanksgiving?' I said. 'I never asked.'

'Abby told you, right?'

'Yeah. Do you want to talk about it?'

'Not really. There's not much to say.'

She lifted her head to look at me. The sparkle and flush I'd seen earlier that night were gone, replaced by the old steadiness. 'Abby went home with that guy,' she said. 'Patrick. That guy I was talking to. She's not going to be back until morning.' She took my hand and led me upstairs.

One week later, we were walking back from dinner, Julia's hand in mine. It was a cold December night, our breath clouding white in the air, and she slipped our twined hands into my jacket pocket for warmth. I'd been thinking about it all week, and I wanted to say it.

'Julia,' I said. I stopped and pulled her closer. 'I love you.'

We stood together for a long time. She wrapped her arms around me inside my jacket, my chin resting on top of her head, the night dark and still. She was silent except for the sound of her breath, dampening my shirt. It had been only a week. Maybe this was too soon, too fast. Maybe I was alone in feeling this way.

But then: 'I love you, too. Evan. I love you.'

The heavy certainty of it, like a smooth stone in your pocket. We stood there for a long time, rooted to the ground by what we'd just said. When we started walking again, I realized my toes had gone numb from the cold.

———•———

The years went fast. We had our separate lives, but they were lived in parallel, and we ended every day the way it began: together. I couldn't untangle the feeling of my new life – the one I'd always imagined having – from the feeling of being with Julia.

Spring of our junior year, Julia went abroad, to Paris. She said that she'd always regret it if she didn't. And, she added, it might do us good to have some time apart. To become our own people. I didn't disagree. Occasionally I wondered whether there was some chance I was passing up in being with Julia, some mistake in committing to one person so early on. I missed her when she was away, but the hockey season didn't give me much time to be lonely. And it wasn't loneliness, in any case, that I felt in those rare moments of quiet. I didn't feel particularly different when Julia wasn't there – but the world felt different. The horizon drew nearer, the colors grew paler. That semester was when I realized how much I needed her.

'I can't wait to see you,' she said, her voice scratchy over Skype. It was late May; I hadn't seen her since January. 'I miss you.'

'Me, too.'

'I'm going to meet you at the airport, okay? Right near baggage claim.'

The crowds ebbed and flowed beneath the bright lights of Charles de Gaulle Airport, and then I saw Julia. She wore a loose black dress that skimmed her tan thighs, a bright scarf, her hair in a bun. She looked older, and more beautiful. That summer we traveled across Europe, living out of our backpacks and surviving on bread and wine. It was my first time abroad, and I was self-conscious about my unstamped passport. Julia had traveled a lot on family trips to London, Paris, Venice, Barcelona, Athens. She knew her way around these cities intuitively. One afternoon in Rome, she led me to the top of the Aventine Hill. 'Where are we going?' I asked.

'You'll see,' she said, walking with purpose.

At the top of the hill was an orange grove overlooking the city. The sky was soft and golden, and couples took turns posing for pictures in front of the sprawling sunset view. I figured this must be the place she'd meant to lead us. But Julia kept walking. She led me past the grove, down a paved road, to a plain-looking green wooden door. 'What is it?' I said.

'Okay.' She pointed at a small keyhole. 'Look through that.'

I found out later that it was a famous thing to do: to peer through this keyhole and see the framed view of the basilica in the distance. But at that moment it felt like she was giving me something just discovered, something I never would have found for myself. A new way of looking at the world. There was a stillness as the image came into focus.

We got back to campus senior year, and it was different. It was better. We were happy. I felt more certain about all of it. It made sense to me, for the first time, how one thing flowed into another; that there was a logic to the way life unfolded. We never did wind up winning a national championship, the one Reynolds had hinted at back in freshman year. I was a solid player, up and down my wing with discipline, but I wasn't good enough to play forever. Gone were the days when I'd cram my hours with extra squats and lifts and sprints. It didn't matter anymore, because that wasn't what I wanted. I was done with hockey. What I wanted was a life with Julia.

I still had one of the business cards from four years earlier. Reynolds must have passed out hundreds of those over the years. Finance was a well-trod path for other guys from the hockey team. *I could do that,* I thought. And it felt in keeping with a certain vision, an answer to the question that I'd been chasing ever since I was a kid. The jobs in finance flowed through campus like a wide, swift river. I wound up getting an offer from the most competitive place I applied to – Spire Management, a hedge fund in New York.

And when I asked Julia to move in with me, she said what I knew she would say. She smiled and threw her arms around me. 'Yes,' she said. 'Yes. I will.'

CHAPTER 2

Julia

Abby and I were at a party at Jake Fletcher's apartment on the night of the opening ceremonies for the Beijing Olympics. The flat-screen TV in the living room showed a massive stadium filled with glittering lights. Jake shared this apartment, at the top of a high-rise building in the financial district, with three of his friends from Dartmouth.

'Holy shit. Look at that view,' Abby said. The Statue of Liberty was visible in the distance, through the window. 'How much do you think they're paying?'

'A couple thousand each.' The wraparound terrace, the sunken living room: Jake and his roommates may have been pulling down banker salaries, but this was above and beyond. 'Right? At least. I'm sure they're getting help from their parents.'

'You think any of them are single?'

I grimaced. 'Ugh. Don't even joke.'

'Hello? You've seen my shit-hole apartment, right? It might be worth it.'

She turned, expecting a laugh, but instead she saw me scanning the room again, frowning at my phone. She waved her hand in front of me. 'Earth to Julia?'

'He's two hours late. He hasn't even texted.'

'Oh, don't be such a mope. Come with me.' She grabbed my hand. Abby always knew how to turn things around. She was the youngest of five, and the Darwinian pressures of a crowded childhood had made her resourceful. She was like the stone soup of friends. Give her twenty bucks and a room and you'll get a great party.

'Hold this,' she said, handing me her cup. We found an empty corner on the terrace, forty stories above the street. A constellation of cigarettes moved through the night air. Music thumped from the built-in speakers.

'Where'd you get that?' I asked as she lit the end of the joint.

'Here. We're splitting this.'

'I haven't smoked since graduation.'

'That's no way to live,' she said in a choked voice, holding the smoke in her lungs. Then she exhaled. 'See? This party is awesome.'

We'd smoked half the joint when I saw Jake Fletcher across the terrace. I waved him over.

'Hey, Jake,' I said. 'This is my friend Abby. My roommate from college.'

Abby held up the joint, but he shook his head. 'I wish. They drug-test us at work.'

'Where do you work?' Abby said.

'Lehman.'

'Oh, well, sorry about that,' she said. 'Great party, by the way.'

Abby got even friendlier when she was high. She and Jake started talking. My attention slipped loose, which didn't take much to happen these days. There was a pause in the music, and the next song that played was one of the big hits from the previous summer, a song I'd heard a million times on campus in the past year. I leaned out over the railing. We were at the edge of the island, where the East River curves into the harbor. The shorter, darker skyline of Brooklyn sat across the water like another city.

I could close my eyes, and the sounds of the party weren't so different from those in college, but I wasn't tricking myself. The feeling in the air had changed. There was a whole world out there, beyond wherever we were gathered. It didn't matter whether it was a cramped walk-up or a tar rooftop or a weedy backyard strung with lights. How you spent your time was suddenly up to you. There were other options. Infinite, terrifying options opening up like a crevasse and no one to tell you which way to go. I think everyone was wondering, through the haze of weed and beer pong and tequila shots, whether this – right here, right now – was in fact what they were supposed to be doing. I suspected I wasn't alone in detecting a desperation in the muggy air, people laughing too loudly, drinking beer that hadn't been chilled long enough.

My reverie was interrupted by the sound of my name. I turned and saw Evan pushing through the crowd. Evan, who was more than two hours late, his tie in a straggly knot and dark circles under his eyes.

'Nice of you to join us,' I said, more sharply than I'd intended.

'I'm sorry, Jules. I got held up at work. There's this big new project, and –'

'It's fine.' My cup was empty, and that suddenly seemed like the most pressing thing. I pointed at the kitchen. 'Let's go get a drink.'

We took a cab home that night, up the FDR. The old Crown Vic groaned as the driver hunched over the wheel, his foot pressed down hard, swerving between lanes and urging the car to go faster. The meter ticked higher, and I felt a prick of guilt for taking a cab instead of the subway. I leaned my forehead against the cool glass of the window and saw the Pepsi-Cola sign glimmering up ahead like a lighthouse. I'd been unfairly terse with Evan all night. We both knew what he was signing up for when he took the job at Spire. I turned back toward him, intending to apologize and to ask him about the new project he'd mentioned. But his eyes were closed. He was already asleep.

———

I guess I'm having trouble knowing where to begin. It's true, that summer was when the feeling descended. Those hot, humid New York City days and nights when I was nervy and jumpy all the time, a constant thrum underneath ordinary movements, a startled sensation like taking one too many steps up the stairs in the dark. It seemed obvious enough, the source of it. I had just graduated. I was trying to become an adult, trying to navigate the real world. Trying to find an answer to the question of what came next. Who wouldn't be made anxious by that? The problem existed in the present tense. But sometimes I wonder whether I got it all wrong. I wonder how far back it really goes.

Junior year of college, Christmas break. I was home earlier than everyone else because I had a light exam schedule that semester. My parents were out, and I was wandering around the house with nothing to do. I pulled out an old hardcover copy of *The Wapshot Chronicle* from one of the bookshelves in the living room. A frail, yellowed photograph slipped from the pages. It was a picture of my mother as a young woman, wearing a loose paisley dress, her long hair parted down the middle. She was sitting on a flight of steps with a group of girls flashing peace signs at the camera. On the back of the photograph, in her delicate handwriting, was the inscription: REPRODUCTIVE RIGHTS RALLY, WELLESLEY COLLEGE, 1975.

I shivered. Her hair, her smile: it was like looking at a picture of myself dressed up as a tourist from another era. I closed the book, put it back on the shelf. Then I took the book out again, removed the picture, and put it in my pocket. I kept thinking about it, all through that week, that month. How different my mother looked back then. She was the exact same age in that photograph – a junior in college – as I was in that moment. She never spoke about college. When she occasionally talked about the past, the stories always began in law school, never further back than that. Law school was where she and my father met. Both of them graduated near the top of their class and took jobs at high-powered firms before my mother left to raise me and my sister. I don't think she ever stopped comparing herself to my father, who is a senior partner and a widely admired attorney. She excels in other ways instead: charity boards, meetings and lunches, a perfectly slender physique. Her energy is always channeled to productive ends. But maybe that wasn't how she originally intended her life to turn out. Maybe there was another trajectory, one she'd been careful not to reveal to us.

But how would I know that? She doesn't complain or wax nostalgic. She doesn't tolerate moping – not in herself and certainly not in us. She was too busy shaping us into the best versions of ourselves. That was her job, and she was good at it. I turned out right. I fit smoothly into the world around me. My teachers liked me. I fell into a comfortable position within the social hierarchy: near the top of the pyramid, but not so high as to wind up a target of scheming usurpers. I never had a problem getting a date. I checked every box there was to check: friends, boys, sports, school.

It's only now I see the red flags along the way. Cracks in the armor. I remember a writing assignment in English class, the year before I left for boarding school. Our class filed outside, notebooks in hand, and sat down on the grassy hill behind the gym. Our teacher told us to describe the scene around us in any way we wanted – to be creative, to free-associate. I never liked English as a subject. I never got what was so great about it. Still, I was surprised to find a bright red C on my essay and a note from the teacher asking me to come see him. He inquired, eyes full of concern, whether I'd understood the purpose of this assignment. I'd always done okay in his class before, even though I hated it. I could string together insightful statements about *Hamlet, Lord of the Flies,* you name it. But somehow, I couldn't manage such an open-ended task. I struggled to fill those two pages. I had described the sights, the sounds, the smells. What else was I supposed to do? My stomach roiled with humiliation. What else did he want me to say?

But that was just one essay. One bad grade evened out by many good ones. The next year, I went away to boarding school, and I had never been happier. I started dating Rob. I played volleyball in the fall and lacrosse in the spring. I snuck cigarettes in the woods on Friday nights and sipped spiked hot chocolate at football games on Saturday mornings. I got straight As. Rob was recruited to play soccer at Harvard, and I was going to Yale. We agreed to try long distance, although I think both of us knew it wouldn't last. And it didn't matter, because on the very first day of school, I met Evan.

Three weeks after I found that photograph of my mother, I left for a semester abroad. She had been the one to persuade me to go. I'd lamented the idea of leaving, of missing Evan, of missing Abby and my other friends. 'Don't be silly,' my mother said. 'They'll be there when you get back.' She framed it as a decision to be made for practical reasons. When else would I get the chance to live in Paris? Why wouldn't I take advantage of this opportunity? She was right, of course, but I had different reasons for going. Sophomore year had been a difficult one, a bad year capped by a particularly bad incident. I needed a change. I sent in my application the first week of the new school year.

That January, I flew to Paris on a red-eye and took a bleary taxi ride to a crooked street in the 11th arrondissement. That old picture of my mother at Wellesley came with me in my suitcase, and I tacked it to the wall above my narrow bed in my homestay. My host was young and gamine, with bad teeth and great hair. She was a costume designer for the national theater. She hosted students in her spare bedroom to make extra money, she explained, so that she could spend her summers traveling with her boyfriend. Her hours ran long and late, and I rarely saw her, but the apartment always smelled like her – strong coffee and clove cigarettes.

Except during our weekly Skype dates, I didn't think about Evan much. I was too consumed by what was in front of me: the bottles of wine on the banks of the Seine, the afternoons in the Luxembourg Gardens, the yeasty scent of the bakeries when we rambled home from the clubs at dawn. I sank into it, like a deep bath, and I felt myself letting go of something for the first time. Evan and I planned that he would meet me in Paris after the semester ended. But when that day arrived, on the Metro ride to the airport, I felt sweaty and nervous. What if, these past months, I had changed – or he had changed – so much that we wouldn't have anything to say to each other? I scanned the crowds at baggage claim, anxious not to miss him; he didn't have a phone that worked in Europe. We'd spent time apart before, the previous two summers, when he'd gone back to Canada and I'd gone back to Boston. But this stretch was different. I'd learned to live in another country. He'd learned to live without me. Suddenly our plan – traveling through Europe for two months before senior year – struck me as foolish. What if he arrived and everything was all wrong? What if it was over?

Then I spotted him, towering above the rest of the crowd, in a ball cap and T-shirt. He saw me and smiled. I'd forgotten what it felt like to be wrapped in his arms, to feel the vibration of his laughter in his chest. Things did feel different. Evan felt like an old friend, an old lover, one whose reappearance in my life was sweeter for giving me a link between past and present. I was known; I was remembered, even far from home.

We flew back to Boston in August, pausing for a night, and then we got on a plane to British Columbia. It was my first time out there, my first time meeting his parents after more than two years of dating. His hometown was tiny, like a grain of sand on the map. That first night, in Evan's childhood bedroom beneath the slanted rafters, in the modest house tucked among the tall pine trees, I realized that I had never experienced so much quiet in my life.

'Have fun, kids!' His mother saluted us with her thermos as his parents drove to work the next morning. She leaned through the window as they backed out of the driveway. 'Oh, and Julia, my bike's out back if you want to borrow it.'

We rode through town that first day, Evan pointing out the landmarks of his childhood: the high school, his first girlfriend's house, the hockey rink where he'd spent so many hours practicing. Weeks, months, years of practice. Someone called his name as we were pedaling away from the rink. 'Peck? Is that you?'

'Coach Wheeler?' Evan called back. The two of them hugged, the coach clapping him hard on the back. 'Julia, this is my old coach, Mr Wheeler. Coach, this is my girlfriend, Julia Edwards.'

'Where are you from, Julia?' He knew right away I wasn't a local.

'Boston,' I said. 'Evan and I go to college together.'

'How is it out there? Been meaning to ask your folks how your season was. He was the best player I ever had.' He winked at me. 'No one ever worked as hard as Evan Peck. I knew this guy would go places.'

Evan beamed from the praise. They talked for a long time, catching up on Evan's college career, on how close Yale had come to winning the championship that year. His coach asked whether he knew what he was going to do after graduation. 'You going to try and play in the minors, maybe?' he said. 'Or you could go over to Europe. You're good enough for it.' Evan shrugged, his smile slackening, the light dimmed. I couldn't read the expression on his face.

The next day, we biked over to the river to meet up with some of his friends. Most of them had stayed put, working construction or other odd jobs in town, still living in the houses they grew up in. They brought along beer and a waterproof boom box, and we went tubing down the river. It felt like something out of a movie. We floated with our inner tubes lashed together, our toes trailing in the cold water, the beer light and fizzy on our tongues. Evan traced circles on the back of my hand. He tilted his head back to look at the summer sky, a bright blue banner framed by the soft green fringe of the pine trees. 'God, I love it here,' he said.

'Why did you ever want to leave?' I asked, with genuine curiosity. He seemed so happy, so comfortable.

'I don't know,' he said. 'I guess it never seemed like enough.'

His mother picked us up downriver, and we strapped our bikes to the roof rack of the car. Evan offered me the front seat, but I shook my head and slid into the back. His mother turned around. 'What did you think?'

'I loved it,' I said, and I meant it. We were silent for the rest of the ride home. I could see where Evan had inherited his tranquillity, the ease he could find in just about any setting. I imagined car rides from years before, his mother shuttling him to early morning practices, each of them silently content in the other's presence. The landscape out here had a way of shutting your mind off. We were all tired and happy, warm from the sun, hungry for dinner, and that was all that mattered.

The two weeks went quickly. His parents hosted a barbecue the night before we left. Nights there were cold, and by the time the burgers were sizzling on the grill, everyone had donned sweaters and sweatshirts. I borrowed an old crewneck emblazoned with Evan's high school mascot. 'Look at that,' his dad said, pointing at the sweatshirt with a pair of tongs when I approached the grill. 'Julia, you could be a local. You fit right in.' Evan's mother leaned over and said, 'He means that as a compliment, hon.'

The next morning, on the bus that would take us back to the Vancouver airport, I waved good-bye to his parents through the window with a dull ache behind my eyes. How was it possible to be homesick for a place that I couldn't call home, a place I'd only known for a handful of days? The previous two weeks had felt like an escape, different in aesthetic but not so different in essence from the way I'd felt in Paris. I realized, at that moment, that I had no idea what I wanted. There was so much out there. The bus shuddered and heaved into motion, and I blinked back a few tears. I was going to be okay. I had Evan, no matter what happened.

By senior year, my commitments had dwindled. Club sports, volunteering, writing for the magazine: the extra-curriculars I had taken up with such diligent dedication as an underclassman were finally finished. I was working on my thesis, about Turner's influence on Monet, and Monet's London paintings. Other than that and a few seminars that met once a week, I took it easy – everyone did. Abby and I went out almost every night; someone was always throwing a party. The nights we didn't, we smoked pot and ordered Chinese and watched bad TV. Things didn't matter so much. The hurdles had been cleared, and we'd earned our break.

One night during the fall of senior year, I was sitting on the futon in our common room when Evan let himself in. He slept in my room almost every night.

'Hey,' I said, muting the TV. Then I looked up. 'Hey. Whoa. What's with the suit?'

He tugged at the cuff. It was short on him. 'I borrowed it from one of the guys on the team.'

'Yeah, but why are you wearing it?'

'Oh. I went to a recruiting session. Didn't I tell you?'

I had become vaguely aware of it a few weeks earlier – the flyers and e-mails from the finance and consulting recruiters. They made it easy, hosting happy hours and on-campus interviews, promising an automatic solution. I hadn't pegged Evan for this path, and maybe that's why it caught me so off guard. I thought I knew him too well to ever be surprised. That night, when he showed up in his borrowed suit, I didn't say anything more. This phase would pass. I couldn't imagine him actually going through with it.

But a month later, he told me he'd gotten called back for several interviews. We had just had sex, and we were spooned together in bed. He mentioned it in the same tone he might remark about the weather, but beneath that was evidence of a certain pride. Validation at being selected to interview. The thrill of success, even if it wasn't permanent yet.

'That's, um, great.' I hoped I sounded normal.

'Jules, I'm really excited. I think this might be what I'm meant to do.'

'When's the interview?'

'And you know the best part?' He hadn't heard my question, or didn't care. 'A job like this could get me the visa I'd need to stay after graduation. Wouldn't that be great? To know that I could stay and not have to worry about it?'

In January, he had an interview with Spire Management, the famous hedge fund in New York. Even I had heard of Spire. Evan kept insisting it was a long shot, it was too competitive. People *killed* for jobs at Spire. But he got the offer in March. Suddenly he had an answer to that question everyone was asking: *What are you doing next?* Evan, working in finance in New York City. I don't know what I'd imagined for him, exactly, but it wasn't

44

this. Evan, who was so old-fashioned in his decency, who was so patient and kind. Maybe he'd be a teacher, or a hockey coach in some small town. Or he'd start a company, or he'd go to grad school – but this? It almost gave me whiplash, but I seemed to be alone in this reaction. Evan was happy. Our friends were happy for him. I was the only one who struggled to adjust to this new idea of him.

'Julia,' Abby said a few days later. We were sitting around watching reruns of reality TV. 'You know what? We should throw a party. For Evan. Tonight.'

'Don't you have that essay due?'

A long bleep obscured a string of cursing from the real housewife on screen. Abby shrugged. 'The class is pass-fail.'

'Okay. I'm in,' I said. 'What else do we have to do tonight?'

But as we lugged cheap booze back from the liquor store, a nasty voice in my head, dormant for so long, started to resurface. *What are you doing, Julia? What do you want? Why don't you make up your mind?* I had made absolutely no plans for the future, and that seemed okay, as long as I wasn't alone. But as I looked around the party, I realized that I was the only person left. The only one without a job. Abby was going to be a teacher. Evan's roommate Arthur was working for the Obama campaign. And Evan had secured one of the most competitive jobs in finance. Only then did I see it clearly: everyone was figuring it out. Everyone except me. I had no passion, no plan, nothing that made me stand out from the crowd. I had absolutely no idea what kind of job I was supposed to get.

Later that night, at the party, I overheard Evan talking to a friend of ours, Patrick, a tall guy from Connecticut who rowed crew. The guy Abby had slept with, freshman year, expressly to give me and Evan the room. Patrick still pined after Abby, but she had long ago moved on. She never kept a guy longer than a few weeks.

'You followed the news about Bear over spring break?' Patrick asked.

'Yeah,' Evan said.

I was standing several feet away, but they didn't notice me.

'That was nuts. Feel bad for all those guys who got their offers rescinded.'

'I know. Jesus. What a mess.'

'Close call, too. My dad works at a hedge fund, and he was jumpy as hell. You know I was interviewing with Bear back in the fall? I'm so glad I didn't go with them. Shit. Can you imagine?'

'Seriously. You're going to Goldman, right?'

'Yup. By the way, congrats, man. You must be stoked about Spire.'

Evan's eyes suddenly lit with anticipation. 'So stoked.'

That expression on his face: a huge, satisfied grin. He didn't know I could see it from where I stood. He had big plans for the future. He was going places. The system had deemed him exceptional. Why shouldn't he feel a little

46

cocky? When he told me about the offer earlier that week, he had insisted it was just a job like any other. 'The main thing,' he said, 'is that now I'll be able to stay. Isn't that great?' He didn't want me to feel bad. And I didn't. I didn't really care. It hadn't sunk in that there was something I had forgotten to do.

But when I saw that expression on his face, talking with Patrick about their jobs and the money and the city and the future, I realized that the way he was looking at me was different from the way I was looking at myself. Evan saw someone who wasn't keeping up. Someone he had to tiptoe around. I felt a shift that night, when I overheard their conversation. It was also the first time I was aware that Evan had concealed something from me, that he had been anything less than totally honest.

A week later, he asked me to move in with him.

We didn't bring much with us when we moved to New York: clothes, books, lamps, my futon and coffee table. It all fit into a handful of boxes and suitcases. We unpacked everything that first day. I even managed to hang our meager art – a few prints I'd gotten in Paris, my favorite Rothko poster from MoMA – strategically covering up the cracks and stains that showed through the landlord's cheap paint job.

'Wow,' Evan said, grinning as he surveyed our tiny apartment, our new home. 'This is awesome. I can't believe we're *unpacked*.'

He went into the bathroom to brush his teeth before bed, and a sob caught in my throat. The only thing that had kept me from losing it that day was the relentless distraction of unpacking. I caught a glimpse of myself in a window turned mirrorlike by the darkness. This was where I was: in a shitty fourth-floor walk-up in the shitty part of the Upper East Side. Tired, sweaty, dirty, and what was the point? Why was I even here? I didn't have a job. I didn't even have prospects. Evan and I would both wake up in the morning with nothing to do, with a day to spend however we wanted. Evan could enjoy it because it was sanctioned, an acceptable length of idle time before his job started. But this freedom, for me, came with a different weight. With the knowledge that every moment I wasted was another moment I wasn't looking for a job. My breath grew fast and short. What was I *doing?*

Evan emerged from the bathroom, wiping away the remains of toothpaste. He saw me frozen in place. 'Jules?' he said. 'Jules, are you okay?'

'I'm fine,' I said, but the tears had started spilling over. 'I'm . . .'

Evan led me to the futon, where we would sleep that night; we'd chosen the cheapest possible delivery option, and our mattress wasn't going to arrive for another week. 'Hey,' he said, rubbing my back. 'Julia. Hey. What's wrong?'

'I don't know,' I said, tears flowing, trying to choke back the waves I felt rising through my chest. 'It's just – I don't know – I'm tired, that's all.'

We sat in silence for a long time. That's one thing I'd

48

always loved about Evan. He knew when it was enough just to be there; when nothing had to be said or asked. Several minutes later, my pulse slowed down, my breathing steadied. I felt like such an idiot. What was I crying about? If I didn't have a job, that was my own fault, and it wouldn't help to sit there and whine about it.

'Well,' I said, finally. 'I bet you're regretting this, huh? Asking me to move in. You're stuck sharing a lease with some blubbering crazy person.'

I thought Evan might smile or laugh. The call-and-response of our relationship. But his eyes were sad. It was a pity I'd never seen from him before.

'Julia,' he said quietly. 'Don't say that. Don't even think that, okay?'

Later, I got up to brush my teeth in our closet-size bathroom. Evan had kept an extra toothbrush in my room for years, but when I lined mine up against his that night, it felt different. A permanent version of what we'd only been pretending to do before.

By late June, three weeks into my joblessness, my mother was ready to intervene.

'Julia,' she said, already sounding harried and annoyed, even though she was the one who called me. 'I only have a few minutes – we have to make this flight – but listen, sweetheart. I'm calling about the job situation. There *has* to be something more you can do. I can't bear the thought of you just sitting in that apartment all day.'

Which was pretty much what I'd been doing that summer afternoon. I'd been feeling okay about the day up to that point – I'd already sent out applications for assistant openings at a small museum, a PR firm, and a publishing house – but my mother's words punctured any feeling of progress. I was standing directly in front of our newly installed air conditioner, enjoying the luxury of the cold, and I reached out to turn the air up a notch, in a gesture that felt like spite. My mother, father, and sister were all flying to Nantucket that day. This was the first summer I wasn't invited on the family vacation. My mother thought my finding a job ought to take priority.

'Mom,' I said with a sigh. 'I get it.'

'Have you thought any more about what we discussed last week?'

'You mean taking the LSATs?'

'I'm not saying you have to *go* to law school, Julia. It's just not such a terrible idea to have that in your back pocket.'

'*Mom.* I'm trying, okay? Trying isn't the problem.' That was true, but it was an aimless kind of trying. I had applied for all sorts of jobs, anything that seemed remotely likely, but there was no unifying theme. The HR departments could probably sense the dispassion in my cover letters. That feeling had set in, and I couldn't shake it: *What was wrong with me?*

My mother called back the next day, the roar of the Atlantic in the background. She told me that she had spoken with Mrs Fletcher, a friend from Boston. The

Fletcher Foundation was looking for an assistant, and I should send my résumé right away. 'I don't think it pays much, but Julia, you should take this job if it's offered to you. I mean it. You really need to get going.'

The next day, I was in the office of Laurie Silver, the president of the Fletcher Foundation. 'So you're friends with the Fletchers?' she asked, peering at me over her glasses. She was small and birdlike, dressed in black, with silver jewelry that jangled and clanked every time she moved. 'Yes, that's right,' I said. 'My mother and Mrs Fletcher are involved in some of the same charities in Boston. And my father is one of Mr Fletcher's attorneys.' Laurie nodded, scribbling a note in the margin of my résumé. I had also entangled myself, briefly, with their son Jake Fletcher the summer before freshman year of college, but that wasn't a topic for discussion. The Fletchers were extremely wealthy – he made a fortune in venture capital, and she came from an aristocratic southern family – and their foundation provided grants to artists, museums, and other worthy recipients.

'Well, Julia,' Laurie said. 'You've come along at a good time. I'm in need of an assistant rather urgently. It's paperwork and record keeping, running errands, basically pitching in wherever you're needed. Does that sound okay by you?'

'Absolutely.'

'Then I'd like to offer you the job. We'd need you to start next week. The salary is twenty-five thousand dollars, plus health insurance.'

I nodded vigorously. 'Thank you, Laurie. Yes. I'd be thrilled. Thank you.'

She stood up and shook my hand. 'You can find your way out okay?'

It was the lunch hour, and the office was abandoned. I wound up looping the perimeter of the floor before eventually finding my way back to the elevator. I was dizzy with relief. Someone was willing to pay me for my time! No matter how paltry the money, no matter how humble the work might be – this was exactly what I needed. Balance had been restored between me and everyone I knew.

On my first day at the Fletcher Foundation, I found a list awaiting me, sitting in the middle of my new desk. The list, from Laurie's former assistant, outlined in neurotically perfect handwriting all the tasks I would have to, in her words, 'learn how to perform immediately.' By the end of the first day, I had them down pat. I wondered whether my predecessor was just not very smart. Maybe she had been fired, based on how challenging she seemed to find these tasks.

On my second day, I had an early morning e-mail from Laurie asking me to brew the coffee when I arrived. There was a small kitchenette with a sink and a microwave and an old drip machine. It seemed easy enough. When Laurie arrived twenty minutes later, I delivered a mug of coffee to her desk with two Splendas, as requested. She was on the phone. A minute later, she called for me to come in.

'Julia, thank you for the coffee, but I'm afraid – well . . . you didn't use soap on the machine, did you?'

I had to think about that one for a minute. Soap? 'Oh – oh, I'm sorry, Laurie. I washed out the basket in the sink and I used the sponge on it. Maybe the sponge had soap on it. I thought I should clean out the basket, and –'

Laurie sighed. 'Yes, you're right, you *should* clean it, but don't use soap on it. Just use very hot water to rinse it, then dry it off with paper towels. You see, it makes the coffee taste like soap. I can't drink this. Why don't you ask Eleanor to show you what I mean? And if you wouldn't mind making a new batch.' She slid the mug across the desk.

I rinsed the basket several times with near-scalding water. I wasn't going to ask Eleanor for help. I had met Eleanor the day before, and she scared me. She was the foundation's one-woman publicity department. She had red hair and a porcelain complexion and dressed like a *Vogue* editor. She had started five years earlier as Laurie's assistant. I was sure she didn't have the time to help me with coffee brewing. Meanwhile, I began to reevaluate my feelings about my predecessor. Maybe she hadn't been fired. Maybe she had gotten fed up and quit.

Eleanor walked past the kitchen as I was very, very carefully drying out the filter basket. She stopped and stared at me from her towering stilettos.

'Oh, no. Let me guess. You used soap on the machine.'

I laughed nervously. 'Yeah.'

'Don't worry. It's just one of her pet peeves. How's it going otherwise?'

'It's good. I think I'm getting the hang of –'

'Good,' she said, then glanced at her watch, which was large and gold and glinted in the light. 'I have to get on a call, but why don't we have lunch sometime? We should get to know each other. Next week, okay? Let's say next Friday at twelve thirty.'

'Sure – yeah – yeah, twelve thirty is great,' I stammered.

'See you then,' she said.

That week and the next passed uneventfully. I kept minutes at the meetings: the fall deadline for grant applications was September 15; plans were on track for the gala in November. I answered Laurie's phone, filed her paperwork, made polite small talk while I waited to use the copy machine. On Friday morning, at the end of my second week of work, the phone rang. 'Julia, it's Eleanor.' Her voice crackled from a bad connection. 'I'm off-site this morning, so I'll meet you at the restaurant, okay?'

The maître d' sat me outside. Eleanor arrived ten minutes late. She tossed her long red hair over her shoulder and dropped her bag onto the seat next to her. She kept her sunglasses on. I wondered how she managed to afford all of it, the watch and the bag and finely made clothing. Surely the foundation didn't pay her *that* much. She waved to get the waiter's attention. 'Iced tea, please. Julia?'

'I'm okay with water.'

'And an ashtray, too. Thanks.'

She pulled out a pack of Camel Lights and a silver Zippo. 'So,' she said, leaning back in her chair, directing a stream of smoke from the side of her mouth. 'Laurie tells me you're friends with Henry and Dot.'

'I guess so. Really it's more my parents. They're friends with the Fletchers.'

'Close friends?'

'Kind of. My dad is one of Henry Fletcher's lawyers. They go way back. My mom is involved in some of the same organizations as Dot. You've met the Fletchers, too?'

She smiled, like she knew something I didn't. 'Oh, of course. Henry and I do a lot of work together. I do all the publicity – which I guess you know by now – so I'm really the gatekeeper when people want to talk to Henry. We're very close. And they are quite involved in the event planning. This gala might drive me mad, actually. Henry is as sweet as they come, but Dot can be a total control freak.' Eleanor ashed her cigarette. 'She's so *stubborn*. I swear, everything I suggest, she wants to do the opposite of. I don't know what it is about her. You know what I mean?'

So this was why she had asked me to lunch. Even behind her sunglasses, I could see the hunger for gossip. Truth be told, I didn't really know much about the Fletchers. Not at that point, at least. I'd said hello to them at parties for years, but that was it. They were rich, that was the main thing to know. I mumbled some assent, and Eleanor's gleam faded to indifference, as fast as a scudding cloud. She glanced at her watch, calculating how much longer she'd have to endure with me.

We passed the time with empty back-and-forth. She perked up when I mentioned that Evan worked at Spire. 'Oh, they're great. Their CEO, David Kleinman, he bought a table at our gala last year. Those guys are legendary.' She laughed. 'So I guess you're doing well for yourself, then.'

After our plates had been cleared and we were awaiting the check – she kept looking over her shoulder to hurry the waiter – someone called her name from down the sidewalk. She pushed back her sunglasses, and she smiled for the first time.

I turned in my seat. Then I went cold, despite the sunshine. I turned back, and reached for my water to erase the dryness in my throat, my hand shaking. The person waving at her was Adam McCard.

Eleanor kissed him on the cheek. He turned to introduce himself to me just as I was standing up and trying in vain to smooth the wrinkles from my dress. Before I could remind him who I was, his mouth fell open.

'Julia Edwards!' he shouted.

He remembered me. Of course he did. He laughed, then hugged me. 'I can't believe it! It's been – how long? Two years?'

'Something like that.' I smiled. Then I exhaled. My nerves were already fading. I felt shy, empty of anything to say, but a little part of me felt an old comfort return. Adam could always make me feel like I belonged, which in those tricky months after graduation was the most important and elusive feeling of all.

I saw Eleanor watching us – watching me – with unconcealed disdain.

'How do you two know each other?' she said.

'Wow. I can't get over it.' He shook his head. 'El, Julia and I went to college together. We both wrote for the same magazine on campus. Shit, we go way back. Wait – how do you guys know each other?'

'We work together,' Eleanor said. 'Julia's an assistant at the Fletcher Foundation.' She pronounced the word *assistant* with a distancing sneer.

'Man. This is crazy.' Adam looked at his watch. 'Shoot, I'm actually late for something. Jules, I'm so glad I ran into you. I didn't even know you were in New York. I'll give you a call, okay? Eleanor, beautiful, you look as amazing as ever.' He walked backwards down the sidewalk, waving before he continued on his way.

'Well,' Eleanor said, donning her sunglasses again and reaching for the check, which had arrived at last. 'You just know *everyone,* don't you?'

CHAPTER 3

Evan

'Do you want to ride in together tomorrow?' Julia had asked the night before. We were lying in bed, her blond hair fanned out across my chest. It was the first day of work the next morning, for both of us.

'Nah, that's okay. I have to get there early.'

'Evan.' She turned to look at me, like she could sense the anxious jump in my stomach. 'You're going to be great. You know that, right?'

I drank my coffee too fast on the subway ride down and burned my tongue. My pace quickened on the side-walk in midtown, to keep up with the other workers hurrying toward their air-conditioned refuges. Outside my building, I caught a glimpse of my reflection in the glass and started – I wasn't used to seeing myself in a suit. Up on the thirty-ninth floor, a receptionist typed rapidly behind an imposing front desk branded with Spire's logo. She sized me up in one glance. 'First day?' she said.

I'd gone through several rounds of interviews back in the spring. My third and final interview had been with

Michael Casey, the second in command at Spire. Back in March, he'd come to fetch me himself from the thirty-ninth-floor lobby, jerking his head for me to follow. He was on the short side, and his hair was going salty from gray. Other people stepped back as Michael walked past with an impatient stride, giving him a wide berth. In his office, he pointed for me to sit. He looked pissed off. He hadn't even shaken my hand. He must hate this part, I thought – sifting through résumés, trying to discern some difference among us. It was all a big waste of his time. The interview was doomed. It was stupid of me to ever think I'd get the job. But then Michael picked up my résumé, and at that moment his expression changed. Softened. He looked up at me, back down at the résumé, and nodded carefully.

'You're from Canada,' he said.

'Yes, sir.'

'British Columbia – near Vancouver?'

'In the interior, actually, about seven hours away.'

'Small town?'

'Yes, sir.'

Michael crumpled up the résumé. 'Tell me about yourself.'

I launched into the routine I'd been perfecting the previous few months. My experience was thin, with none of the internships that everyone else had done, but I had other talking points. An economics major interested in the efficiency of the free market. A varsity athlete who knows the value of teamwork and discipline. So on and so forth. But Michael interrupted me before I was even halfway done.

'No, no, I already got all that from your résumé. Tell me more about where you're from. Your hometown. How's the economy doing out there?'

'My hometown?' I said, scrambling to rearrange the words in my head. Michael nodded. 'Well. It's really small. There's not much to do. We like to joke that there are more bears than people.'

Michael smiled. He nodded again for me to continue.

'Everyone who can plays hockey. That's the main source of entertainment.'

'You played? You must have been pretty good to get to Yale.'

'I'm all right.'

Michael barked a short laugh. 'You're all right,' he repeated. 'That might be the first humble sentence ever spoken in this office. What do people do for work?'

'My parents run a grocery store. There's some tourism a few towns over, so some people commute to that. And logging is pretty big in the region.'

We went on like that for a while. To my surprise, Michael seemed engaged. Some transformation had happened. Maybe my lack of experience wasn't such a bad thing.

They didn't seem to think it was, in any case. Two days later, I got the call from Spire. The job paid more than any of the others I'd applied to, a six-figure sum that I couldn't quite believe. I accepted on the spot. I'd be the only person from Yale joining Spire that year. I was certain the old small-town Evan Peck was gone, once and for all.

I was assigned to sit next to Roger, another analyst, a former tight end at Stanford with a thick Alabama drawl. We didn't have much to do early on. When we weren't in training sessions, we wasted a lot of time on ESPN or skimming the news, only jumping into action when the higher-ups staffed us on something. But it looked bad to leave before 10:00 p.m., so none of us did, no matter what. There were five analysts in total that year, all of us men, which wasn't that remarkable – Spire overall was mostly male. Roger was our ringleader, the one who stayed latest and arrived earliest and generally assumed authority. He led the charge every night for postwork drinks at a bar called McGuigan's near the office, and already it felt like a mandatory part of the routine.

'So how was the first week?' Julia asked. This was Saturday morning. We'd brought bagels to the park along the East River. Every night that first week, Julia was already asleep when I got home. It annoyed me a little, that she couldn't bother to stay awake. Her job ended many hours before mine did. This was the first time we'd really seen each other since the weekend before.

'Good,' I said. 'I think. I don't know. It's hard to tell what it's really going to be like. It's all just training sessions for now.'

'What about that guy – Michael? The one who interviewed you. Have you seen him yet?'

'I passed him in the hall, but he was talking to someone else. We didn't say anything.' Truthfully, I wasn't sure whether he even recognized me.

Julia nodded. She was quieter than usual. She seemed to be gazing at the buildings across the river in Astoria, but her eyes had that glassy quality of staring at nothing in particular. There was a poppy seed stuck to the tip of her nose. I leaned over and brushed it away. She turned and then smiled. Back to normal.

'Everything okay?'

'Fine,' she said. 'Just distracted. Thinking about work.'

'What's up?'

'Nothing worth talking about. Tell me more about your week.'

It was a relief to have Julia there, to have a partner in the minor struggles: how to decipher the Con Ed bill, where to find the nearest Laundromat, what to do about the noisy neighbors and the leaky faucet. She always knew exactly what to do. I was acutely aware, that summer, of how alone I was in the world. My parents had gone back to Canada right after the graduation ceremony, and I wouldn't see them again for months. This never bothered me in college, when the proximity of your family only mattered when it was time to travel back and forth. But being in the real world seemed to emphasize how far I was from home – something I hadn't felt in a long time. And moving to New York had highlighted certain differences between me and Julia, too, things I'd never noticed before. The advice and money and connections she took for granted. How she was never limited to this place. She could always take the train to Boston, or hop on a plane to Nantucket. Even though she made less than a fifth of what I did, she had money from her parents. We'd agreed to divide the rent in line with our salary discrepancy, so I paid two-thirds, although sometimes I wondered how fair that was. My money came like water from a pump, flowing only as long as I kept working. Hers came like a spring whose source was bountiful and deep. We never talked about this.

The truth was that I missed my friends, my teammates, the ones who hadn't come to New York. I especially missed Arthur, who was working in the Obama campaign's field office in Ohio. We'd traded a few stiff e-mails since graduation, but I couldn't say what I was really thinking, not in stark black-and-white text. I didn't even *know* what I was really thinking. And we hadn't acknowledged the fight we'd had right at the end. I wondered if we ever would.

The shower was already running when my alarm went off on Monday morning, at the beginning of the second week of work. Julia's bathrobe was hanging on the hook, the steam drifting through the open door.

'You're up early,' I called into the bathroom.

'I figured we could go in together,' Julia said over the weak sound of the shower. Our water pressure was pathetic. 'You have to be in by eight thirty, right?'

We walked to the subway hand in hand, stopping for

an iced coffee at the cart on the corner of 3rd Avenue. The train was packed, and I got on last. Julia was crammed next to me, the front of our bodies pressed together. I felt an incongruous longing for her in the chaos of the train car. The smell of her perfume, the tender paleness of the part in her hair. We hadn't had sex all week, not even on the weekend; I'd been too exhausted. I was an idiot for not appreciating what was right in front of me. I slipped my hands down her waist, pulling her closer, and kissed her on the forehead. She smiled up at me. She seemed to know what I was thinking.

We commuted together all that week. I liked the routine. Alternating turns in the shower, Julia drying her hair while I shaved in front of the speckled mirror. The coffee cart, the descent into the hot subway, the kiss good-bye. On Thursday night of that week, Julia had plans to get dinner with her parents, who were passing through town. 'Bummer you have to work so late,' she said as we walked to the subway on Thursday morning. 'They'll miss you.'

'Your parents? I doubt that.'

She laughed. 'You know what I mean. Their version of missing.'

Later that night, as I was riding the elevator down to the lobby to pick up my dinner delivery, I thought of Julia and her parents. I pulled out my phone and texted her: Sorry I couldn't make it. Tell them hi.

She texted me back a few hours later. Just finished. I'm nearby. Meet me outside your building in a few?

It was almost 10:00 p.m., and the office was dead.

There was no one left to impress. I stood up and turned off my computer. Roger raised an eyebrow. 'No McGuigan's tonight?'

'Nah, not tonight. Other plans.'

Julia was waiting outside. She was more dressed up than usual, probably for her mother's sake. Had she been wearing that dress this morning? I couldn't remember. She was clutching a funny-looking silvery thing.

'What is that?'

'Leftovers,' she said. 'It's for you.'

'Weird-looking leftovers.'

'You've never seen this before? No, see, look. It's a swan. See? That's the neck, and those are the wings.'

It was made of aluminum foil. 'That's a thing?'

'I ordered the biggest steak so I'd have extra. My mom almost had a fit – she thought I was going to eat the whole thing. Oh, and guess what else I got?' She opened her tote bag and pointed inside, but it was too dark to see. 'Come on, I've got a plan.'

We walked up Broadway, the crowds gradually thinning as we left behind Times Square. Julia was chattering happily with news from home, from work. She was having lunch the next day with her coworker Eleanor. She was hopeful that they might become friends. This stretch of midtown at this hour was strange and abandoned, like the aftermath of a hurricane. Julia tugged me across the intersection. We stopped, and she swept her arm across the mostly empty plaza. 'Voilà. It's like our very own Campo de' Fiori.'

'Columbus Circle, you mean?'

'Come on, play along. You remember that night, right? It was almost a year ago exactly.' She sat down on the stone steps next to the fountain and pulled two cups from her tote bag, then a half-empty bottle of wine. She split the remaining wine between the two cups, handed one to me, and stashed the empty bottle in her bag.

'Where'd you get all this?'

'We got the wine to go with dessert, but we couldn't finish it, so I took it with me. And the cups are courtesy of Starbucks.'

We touched the paper cups together. 'What are we toasting to?' I said.

She tilted her head, her blond hair catching a shimmer from the lamps at the edge of Central Park. The stoplights changed from red to green, and the yellow taxis swept forward in unison, peeling off at various points around the traffic circle. If you squinted, the color blurred into one mass, and it looked like the same ring of taxis going around and around, forever. Julia smiled at me and said, 'Whatever we want, I guess.'

I wanted this feeling to last. To fix it in place.

We kept commuting together. On Wednesday morning, our third week of work, the subway was messed up, even worse than usual. Several trains went by, the doors opening and closing on packed cars from which no one disembarked. It was hot and sticky, and frustration was mounting on the platform. People jostled, leaning into the tunnel to look for the next train. Someone stepped on Julia's sandaled foot. 'Ow!' she said. 'Fuck. That hurt.' When the third and fourth and fifth trains passed by, Julia muttered, 'This is fucking ridiculous.' The sixth train pulled up, and she said, 'I'm getting on this one, I don't care.' We both squeezed ourselves in, but Julia slipped farther into the train than I did, finding a pocket of space in the middle of the car. She gave me a halfhearted shrug, then looked away.

It was a strange thing to watch her from this distance. To realize what a difference a few meters could make. The way she glanced at her watch, as if to make the train move faster; the way she stared vacantly at the ads for dermatologists and vocational schools. She seemed frustrated and grumpy, but underneath was something harder. An irritation that had nothing to do with the sick passenger or the signal malfunction or whatever had caused this train backup. Something that had been there before we'd even left the apartment that morning. It was like I was looking at Julia from a different angle and seeing something I hadn't seen before.

The next morning, she was still asleep when I left for work.

———————

August arrived, and the city grew quiet. Our neighborhood was a ghost town on weekends. It had become a way of marking time, the Hampton Jitney pulling up on Sunday evenings, the seep of sunburned passengers back to the crosshatch of numbered streets. Everyone who could afford to had fled for the beach.

Work was quiet, too. I checked everything two or three times, guarding myself against boneheaded mistakes. The bosses accepted the work I was doing with a clipped thank-you. I tried to see this as a positive – the models and decks must have been good enough to make it across their desks without comment – but I felt a crackling undercurrent of worry. The sluggish market, rumors about layoffs. There were still long stretches of hours, sometimes days, when I didn't have much to do. Maybe it had been rash to jump at this job. Maybe I should have thought more about trying to play hockey after college – in Europe or the minors. My life at that moment would have been totally different.

Until one Friday night in early August, when my luck changed.

It was early evening. The higher-ups had left around lunchtime to beat the beach traffic. The other analysts were already at McGuigan's. I was getting ready to leave when my phone rang.

'Could you stop by?' Michael Casey asked in a flat, untelling tone.

When I arrived, he looked up from a stack of papers and gestured me inside. I hadn't been in there since the interview back in March. His office was bare of decoration except for a few pictures of him and a younger blond woman who had to be his wife, the two of them smiling against Caribbean sunsets and snowy ski hills.

She looked a bit like Julia, though not as pretty. No kids, I noticed. Michael was unsmiling. 'So, Evan. How have things been? What are you working on?'

'Good. Great. Things have been great. I've, um, been working on a few projects for Steve. He's had me run some models for the macro group. And, uh . . .'

Michael nodded briskly. 'Fine. And are you liking it? Is the work engaging?'

'Well, um, yeah, I would say it is.' Shit. This was exactly what I'd feared, coming across as some inarticulate hick with nothing to say. 'It's been really interesting, learning about these new markets, and –'

'All right. It's okay, Evan. Relax. We don't have to skirt around this. I know what it's like, your first month on the job. It's boring. You can admit that, okay?'

I laughed. I hoped it sounded confident, not nervous. 'I guess.'

'I was impressed with you in our interview, Evan. I was. I admire your ambition. It's not easy to get yourself out of a small town. Trust me, I know. What I want to know is what you're looking to get out of this. Don't get me wrong. Some people just want to do their two years, go to business school. They'll do fine for themselves. Dip their toe in, then do the next thing. For some people, that's just fine.'

Michael leaned back in his chair, his evening stubble catching in the light.

'You know, I grew up in South Dakota, on a farm in the middle of nowhere. Where I came from, people never left. You understand what I'm talking about.'

I sat up a little straighter. 'I do.'

'People like us, we actually have an advantage. We remember where we came from. We work that much harder. Now, Spire gets its pick of who to hire. The best and the brightest. But it's not often I have the chance to hire someone like you. Someone who reminds me a little of myself.'

A few blocks away, my coworkers were already drinking and laughing, off duty for the night. I felt a buzz and pop of adrenaline near the point where my spine met my brain. Just like at the beginning of a game, right before the puck drops.

'Evan. I think you're smart. I think you've got huge potential. My question is, what are you looking for? Do you want to try for something bigger?'

'Yes,' I said. 'I do.'

The tone shifted. Faster, more relentless. I was trying to keep up.

'I'll tell you, first of all, there are no sure things. We always have to bear that in mind. Nothing is certain. But this is the closest thing to certainty that I've ever seen in this world. So. What's the most important thing you learned about hedge funds when you decided you wanted to work here?'

'How to – how to exploit inefficiencies in the market?'

'That's one thing. And some people may agree with

you that it's the most important thing, but that's not the answer. The *most important* thing you need to know is the art of timing. Being first. Knowing when to get in and when to get out. Knowing the inefficiencies does you no good if you screw up the timing.'

'Right. Timing. I see.'

'And what does the right timing allow you to do? What's the primary rule of arbitrage?'

'Buy low, sell high?'

'Exactly. If you can get it cheap and find a market for it at a higher price, then that's all there is. Simple, right? And if you can time it perfectly, then you're golden. So what's the cheapest thing you can buy right now in this country?'

'Well, um . . .'

'You read the news. You see what's happening with the housing market. We're right on the edge of a complete collapse.'

'Housing? So buying up cheap housing? And then find –'

'No. Right track, though. Break it down into components, make it liquid. What do you need to build houses? What's in demand when the market is booming? I'm talking physical resources. Something you can count and measure and ship.'

'Lumber?'

'You would think this would be a terrible time to bet on lumber, with the housing market cratering, right?'

'Right.'

'No one is going to touch it. No one with an ounce of sense. People go looking for an ark in a flood. Who goes looking for more water? So what does that mean, Evan?'

'It's cheap.'

'Dirt cheap. And that's where we come in.'

'You guys celebrating something?' Maria asked as she brought over another round, later that same night. We were at McGuigan's, at our usual booth in the corner. Maria, our regular bartender, was just a few years older than we were. 'The weekend,' Roger said loudly. 'Why don't you join us for a round, gorgeous?' Maria smiled with cool tolerance while she stacked our empty glasses. Roger had been leering at her for weeks. 'That one's mine, fellas. I call dibs,' he said when she was barely out of earshot.

I felt my phone buzz with yet another text from Julia. I was supposed to meet her at a party downtown, and my time was up. I went to the bar to pay for my drinks. Roger often laid down his card at the end of the night, picking up the tab like he was some big shot, but I didn't like the feeling that I owed him something.

'Leaving already?' Maria said. She counted out my change, but I waved it away.

'Yeah. A party downtown. I'm already late.' I wondered why I didn't mention anything about Julia – that I was meeting my girlfriend at the party, that my girlfriend was the one pestering me to get going. I hadn't yet found a way to work Julia into any of my conversations with Maria. I wasn't sure I needed to, or wanted to.

'Have fun, Evan,' she said. 'See you next week, right?'

I called her name from across the room. Julia was out on the balcony, staring at the Brooklyn skyline with that same vacant look I'd noticed her slipping into on occasion.

There was a pulse of relief across her face when she saw me, and then her expression clouded back into annoyance. Maybe it would have been better to make up some lie about work and skip the party entirely. But she had insisted I come along. 'Jake Fletcher is having a party for the opening ceremonies tonight,' she said that morning, calling after me as I was about to leave. 'We have to go. Remember? It's his parents' foundation I'm working for, after all.'

The television in the corner showed a massive stadium filled with flag-bearing marchers. I squinted and moved closer through the packed living room. I thought of Michael's abrupt departure a few hours earlier, and it finally made sense.

A ding had sounded from Michael's BlackBerry as we were talking. He glanced at the screen and stood up sharply. 'I have to go,' he said. 'I've got a flight to catch. I had one of our researchers pull this material together' – he indicated a blue binder on the desk – 'and I want you to get up to speed. We'll convene when I'm back.' He started down the hallway, and I had to jog to keep up.

Before Michael stepped into the elevator, I asked where he was going.

He looked up from his phone, brow furrowed. Then he smiled. 'China.'

'Oh,' I said. 'That's great. For business, or –' but the doors slid closed.

I'd forgotten about the Olympics until then, but the scene on the TV explained it. He and his wife were probably reclined in their first-class seats at that moment, en route to Beijing. I still hadn't quite absorbed it – Michael, the legendary and fearsome Michael, had just handpicked *me* for this big new project. At the party, I tried to pull Julia aside to tell her the news. But she kept shaking herself free of my grasp. She knew everybody there: friends from Boston, from prep school, from college. Most of the time she remembered to introduce me – 'Oh, do you know my boyfriend, Evan? Evan, this is so-and-so' – and I'd nod and they'd continue talking. Anyway, I suspected that I had served my purpose the moment I'd walked through the door. I'd proved to Julia that I was a loyal boyfriend who would answer her call, and Julia had proved the same thing to her friends. A lot of them worked in finance, like me, but it didn't give us anything to talk about. Everyone worked in finance.

As the party ended, I climbed into the cab while she was saying good-bye to someone on the sidewalk. I closed my eyes, and when I opened them we were almost home. Julia was at the other side of the backseat, legs crossed, staring out the window. I felt a jolt at that moment.

Annoyed with how the night had gone, with this sour distance between us, that stupid party. Things were about to change for the better, beginning right then.

'Leave it off,' I said, when Julia went to turn on the lights in our apartment. I kicked the door closed and pushed her up against the wall. She tasted like sweet white wine, and that made me even harder, knowing that she was drunk. She snaked her fingers through my hair. She was yanking loose my tie, unbuttoning my shirt, unbuckling my belt. I hitched up her dress and we had sex against the living room wall, her legs wrapped around me. 'Oh, God, Evan,' she said, her fingertips digging into my scalp, our bodies slamming into the wall. 'Oh, my God.'

We collapsed on the bed afterward. We hadn't had sex like that in a long time. Later, I realized that I never told Julia what happened at work. It was the whole reason I'd been trying to get her attention, but when I finally had it, I'd completely forgotten about it.

The blue binder from Michael was waiting right where I'd left it the night before. I'd woken up without an alarm that morning, showered, and gone straight to the office. While I was waiting for my computer to warm up, I pulled out my cell phone and flipped it open and shut, considering whether to call Arthur. Maybe I was making too big a deal about our fight. But it wasn't even 10:00 a.m., and Arthur liked to sleep late. I put the phone back in my pocket and opened the binder.

It contained a massive sheaf of information about the state of the North American lumber markets: quarterly reports, stock trends, charts and graphs of historical data, analyst predictions for the coming years. The recommendation was unanimously bleak. The rest of 2008 into 2009 and 2010 and beyond was terrible. In our conversation the night before, Michael had hinted about a new source of demand, but what new source of demand? I couldn't see it. My optimism started to evaporate. Suddenly someone was paying attention to my work. This might be the thing that exposed me as a fraud once and for all.

Roger sauntered in later. 'Whatcha working on there, Peck?' he drawled.

'Just something for Michael,' I said. The last thing Michael had told me was to keep quiet about this new assignment, for the time being. Roger stared for a beat before he sat down. He made a point, later that day, of not inviting me to lunch. He didn't say good-bye that night, either. But I didn't care. I was going to have bigger problems than Roger if I didn't figure this out fast.

It was only at the very end of the day, when the office had emptied again, that I finally saw it. The page was headlined BRITISH COLUMBIA PRODUCERS − PACIFIC WESTCORP. The number I'd been focusing on was 'Growth Forecast 2009.' It was a useful indicator, and for the most part that number had been negative, often double-digit negative. Flat at the very best. But Pacific WestCorp was predicting 200 percent growth for the next fiscal year.

Two hundred percent growth. I reached for a highlighter.

There was a line in fine print that broke out the predicted revenue for 2009 in terms of North American versus international markets. Nearly all of next year's revenue for Pacific WestCorp was predicted to come from international markets. And below that was an analyst's note: *Pacific WestCorp predicts exports to China in FY 2009 will increase tenfold, to $500 million CAD.*

I sighed in relief, letting the yellow highlighter bleed through the paper. But a series of questions sprang to life in the back of my mind, like popcorn popping in the microwave. Why weren't these predictions making news all over the Street? Why wasn't everyone lining up behind this company? If this held true, it would be the easiest decision anyone ever had to make – Pacific WestCorp was going to make a fortune. But the answers sprang up, too, like echoes to the popping questions. Investors were often skittish about exports to China. It was a risky game, and the taxes and tariffs and unpredictable barriers to entry were enough to dissuade most people. There were far saner ways to make money. The Chinese didn't always play by the same rules as we did, and that was a dangerous proposition when hundreds of millions of dollars were at stake.

'China,' Michael had said with a smile, just before the elevator door closed.

As the market sunk deeper, the numbers that had been hovering in the back of my mind started to loop obsessively: my student loans and my share of the rent on one side, the comforting and hefty regularity of my paychecks on the other. I couldn't admit my worry aloud. No one at work talked much about the crisis as it escalated. It was too big to put words to; too abstract, too unknown, but mostly too frightening.

But, finally, on the morning of Monday, September 15, our CEO, David Kleinman, summoned the entire office to the fortieth-floor boardroom before the markets opened. Lehman was about to go under, and Merrill was on the edge. What Michael had been talking about was finally here, the water lapping at our doorstep.

Roger hummed the death march as we walked up the fire stairs. 'A hundred bucks says at least ten people go home today,' he said.

'Jesus, Roger, don't say that.'

'Is that a bet?'

'Hell, no. If I'm fired, I'm gonna need all the money I can get.'

'*You're* not getting fired, teacher's pet.'

We continued trudging. I'd been wondering when Roger was going to say something. There was no way he hadn't noticed my increased tempo, the early mornings and late nights and busy weekends, all of it because of the budding WestCorp deal. But he'd kept his mouth shut over the previous month, concealing what was almost certainly jealousy.

Kleinman walked into the boardroom. 'Everyone here?' he asked. His bald pate shone under the lights. Michael, to his right, nodded at him. 'Good,' Kleinman continued. 'The reason I've called you here this morning – well, you know the reason. It's a shitstorm out there, and today's only going to get worse. Now, let me make this clear from the start. Spire is healthy and profitable, and we are well equipped to weather this. No one is being let go. I repeat, no one is being let go. Not today, not for the foreseeable future.'

He paused. 'You can all relax, you know. Christ. Loosen up, people.'

Someone laughed, then another person. Someone started clapping.

'See, that's what I want.' Kleinman smiled. 'We're smarter and faster and better than the other guys. I'm not saying this isn't serious – you all know people who will lose their jobs, people whose companies might even go under. But if you keep doing what you're doing, you can sleep at night knowing that your future at Spire is secure.

'So. That begs the question: Why am I taking up your very valuable time? Right now there's a helicopter sitting on the roof of this building that will take me to Teterboro, where I'm getting on a plane to DC. I'm joining the government advisory team until we get through this crisis. I got the call early this morning, and I wasn't given much time to decide. But it was clear to me what I had to do.'

Kleinman glanced around the silent room for reactions.

'This means that for the next few weeks or the next few months, or however long this takes to settle down, I'm handing over the reins to Michael Casey. Michael will lead you through this just as well as I could myself. And we didn't get to where we are today by caving under pressure. So don't fuck this up.' Another small wave of laughter, and he smiled again. 'I'll see you all on the other side.'

Kleinman stood up. The rest of the executives followed suit, nodding at him crisply, ready to do battle. He turned on his heel and strode out of the room, his secretary chasing him with a pen and one last piece of paper to sign. Everyone started to file out. Only Michael remained seated. Running his hands over the finely grained wood of the table, and smiling to himself.

CHAPTER 4

Julia

I'd taken to having the news on in the background while I got ready for work to dispel the constant quiet. Since he'd started working on this WestCorp deal, Evan had been out the door before my alarm had even gone off, every day for weeks.

I was clicking through channels while I brushed my teeth and stopped on CNBC as it returned from a commercial. I sat down on the futon, the minty toothpaste tingling in my mouth. It was Monday morning, and a situation that had looked uncertain before the weekend had exploded into full-blown apocalyptic chaos. Weeks earlier, Evan had explained to me how the housing slump would actually help Spire's position on this WestCorp deal – the further the market sunk, the more Spire eventually stood to gain – but at that moment, even he seemed worried about how fast it was happening. We had watched the news the previous night: enormous firms shuttering, thousands of people losing their jobs, billions of dollars vanishing overnight. Friends of ours saddled with apartment leases they could no longer afford. I knew I shouldn't enjoy it too much, but I couldn't help it: part of me felt a weird thrill at our positions suddenly flipping. I was employed while they were adrift.

Evan had been pacing in front of the TV the previous night, Sunday night, worrying about what might happen. This panic was new; I'd never known him like this. 'But Spire's going to be fine, right?' I said. That's what he'd been saying to me all along. 'They're not going to fire you. Right?'

'They're not going to fire you,' I'd said with more conviction earlier that summer, before either of us had started work. We were standing in the Brooks Brothers on Madison Avenue, the afternoon sun flaring through the windows. I was drinking a Pellegrino and watching Evan in the mirror in the fitting area.

He laughed. 'I hope not.'

'So why worry whether they're returnable? You'll be wearing these for years.'

He adjusted his tie. 'Habit, I guess.'

'You look great. I think you should get both.'

He'd never owned a suit before. That morning in early July, he had been looking up the address for a discount retailer downtown. 'You still have all of your signing bonus?' I'd asked, and he nodded. 'Okay. Come with me.' There was a Brooks Brothers near our apartment. He'd guffawed at the price tag on the suit I pointed out, but I pushed him toward the dressing room. 'Could you help us?' I asked a salesman. 'He's probably a forty-two long. He needs one in blue and one in gray. And some shirts and ties.' When the salesman went to get his pincushion, Evan looked at the price again, whistled, and wondered out loud whether he could return them.

But I think he knew, even then, even if they were nicer than what he needed, that he looked too good not to keep them. When he stood on the raised block to let the salesman adjust the hem of his pants, it was like a time-fuzzed image snapping back into focus. I could appreciate just how handsome he was, as I had at the beginning. His sandy brown hair, his light blue eyes. Wearing the trappings of adulthood like a natural. Our gazes met in the mirror, and he smiled at me.

'I'm glad you made me get them,' Evan said. We were walking back to the apartment, a bag with his new shirts and ties swinging from one hand. He'd pick up the altered suits in a few days. He kissed me. 'I don't know what I'd do without you.'

I was proud of him. Really, I was. He was a boy from the middle of nowhere who had gotten himself to Yale. He was working at the most famous hedge fund in New York, leaving for work every morning in his finely made suits. He'd said it to me more than once that summer. *I don't know what I'd do without you*. I knew he meant it as a compliment. But Evan was always better at taking direction from others than he was at taking direction from himself. It could have been anyone prodding him to get a better suit, and his gratitude would have come out sounding the same. My being the prodder was only incidental.

I suppose, at the time, I didn't understand how rapidly my feelings toward Evan were evolving. Maybe I didn't want to admit how little it took to dismantle what we'd built. It wasn't that our relationship had been perfect before. We'd fought in college, but those fights always felt specific: fireworks that faded into smoke as fast as they arrived. But in New York, in the real world, every annoyance and disagreement felt like a referendum on our relationship. The bitterness started to linger. I was seeing growing evidence of why this was never going to work. A sickening suspicion that Evan and I were, in fact, all wrong for each other.

On the surface, my life seemed normal enough. I went to work, I jogged in the park, I saw my friends at crowded bars and brunches. Evan and I would try to have a late dinner on Friday or Saturday, compressing a week's worth of intimacy into a few hours, but more and more often he didn't even have time for that. Every night, I came home to a quiet apartment. My brain crackled with excess energy. I'd pace. I'd toss aside books, unable to concentrate. I'd sit in silence, ears pricked, hearing every flush of the toilet and clacking of heels echo through our building. Sometimes I'd try to stay up late for Evan, but those were always the nights I fell asleep with the lamp burning. Or, instead, I'd decide to go to bed early and wake up for a long run before work. Those were inevitably the nights I tossed and turned in our too-hot bedroom, unable to sleep, and when the alarm went off at 6:00 a.m., I'd rise like a zombie and jog through the empty streets.

What had happened? Looking back at those early weeks in New York, as we were wading into the shallows of our new lives, I realized that everything had changed so quickly. Earlier in the summer, things hadn't been perfect, but they'd been okay: late nights out, long walks home, lingering over the last glass of wine. But something had changed soon after we started working. I was plagued with a new dissatisfaction. Was this it, was this everything? Was this my life from now on? Something was wrong, but I couldn't put my finger on it – until suddenly, it seemed obvious what the problem was.

One August weekend, Evan and I were having a hurried brunch before he went back to the office. He had a new habit of keeping both his phones, flip phone and Black-Berry, on the table while we ate. I was telling a story when his BlackBerry vibrated. He picked it up immediately and started reading the e-mail that had just come in. 'Oh, man,' he said loudly. I couldn't tell whether it was good news or bad. Then he smiled at the screen. A big, wide, face-cracking grin. 'Jules, this is awesome. Oh, man. So I was telling you about this WestCorp deal, right? Well . . .'

And he launched into the details, forgetting entirely that I'd been in the middle of a story. But I wasn't listening. Instead I was thinking that I was such an idiot. It was so obvious – how had I not seen it before? That night in March, when I'd overhead his conversation with Patrick. That smile, that big grin. It was the exact same grin he was wearing at brunch, chattering away about the WestCorp deal. It was the blossoming of the seed I'd first glimpsed months earlier. Evan was more excited about his future than I was about mine. He had been all along. More alive with energy, with possibility, thinking about a million things other than me. I'd seen it before, how Evan threw himself into something he cared about. It happened in the most intense parts of the hockey season, back in college, and it was happening now, only now it wasn't finite. This wasn't just a season. This was real life. Our life – my life.

I had a suspicion. I started administering silent tests. Evan would get home, dropping his briefcase to the floor with a sigh. 'You wouldn't *believe* what happened at work,' he'd say, flopping down on the futon. He told me everything about Michael Casey, about the WestCorp deal. On and on and on. I'd keep perfectly quiet, waiting for him to finish, to turn his attention to me – to anyone but himself. Waiting for him to ask how my work was going, what I'd eaten for dinner, the people I'd been hanging out with in his absence. Anything. But he never asked, not once.

This new Evan didn't have anything left for me. Evan needed me to affirm his existence, to nod and smile and say the right thing at the right time. He failed the test, and my suspicion was confirmed. He wasn't really thinking about me. He never was. *I don't know what I'd do without you.* He seemed to forget that it was supposed to be reciprocal.

At work, later that September day, there was nervous chatter in the hallways. I imagine that was true everywhere in New York that afternoon – watercooler speculation about how far it would go, if we were witnessing the end of one era and the beginning of the next – but we had particular reason to be concerned. Organizations like ours formed an appendage to the financial industry, rising and falling along with the market. It was symbiotic, our minnow cleaning the gills of the whale that swam around lower Manhattan. We relied on the largesse of the Fletchers and others like them to keep us alive.

Had I started thinking of the foundation as *ours?* Had I started thinking of myself as *us?* I guess I had. I was beginning to understand why people sometimes stayed in jobs they hated. It wasn't just about the paycheck. It was about the structure, contributing to the hum of civilized society. My own contribution was almost invisible, but I liked the accoutrements. The nameplate on my desk; the security guard in the lobby who knew me by sight. Even if the job wasn't much, it was something. I'd complain about it to Evan, but all he said was how lucky I was to have such easy hours; cutting, even if true.

I thought of Evan pacing the apartment the night before, of what he must be going through at work. After lunch, I sent him a text. He didn't respond until hours later, when I was getting ready to leave. All good. Probably gonna be here late.

Can you take a break for dinner? I wrote.

I'll go out around 6:30 to get something, he replied.

I glanced at my watch – it was approaching 5:30 p.m. I thought of one night from earlier that summer, from better days. This was a chance to get back what we'd lost track of. I walked north from my office and found a deli a few blocks from Evan's office. His favorite sandwich, the same since college: a chicken cutlet with mozzarella and bacon. I took two sodas from the cooler, draped with strips of dusty plastic that reminded me of tentacles at a car wash.

I thought about calling, but I liked the notion of surprising him. Maybe it was the air of doom making me alert, but I felt optimistic. Renewed with hope. I leaned against the side of his building, my eyes closed against the sun, two sandwiches and two cans of soda in hand. Maybe we both just needed to try a little harder. This was a phase, and it would pass. I checked my watch. It was 6:30, then it was 6:45, then it was almost 7:00 p.m. Well. I couldn't be upset with him. He didn't know I was waiting.

A group finally emerged from the building, spit out of the revolving door like pinballs. Evan came out last, jogging to catch up with his coworkers. They all had their jackets off, their sleeves rolled up, and they were laughing about something.

'Evan!' I called, waving at him.

He looked confused when he saw me. The group kept walking, slower now, giving him the chance to catch up. A few of the guys stared at me.

'Hey,' he said, walking over. 'What are you doing here?'

'I brought dinner.' I lifted the deli bag. 'I thought we could eat together. Like the old days, you know.'

'Oh. That's nice of you, Jules.'

'I got your favorite. Chicken cutlet with bacon and mozzarella.'

'The thing is,' he said, glancing over his shoulder, 'I was going to get dinner with the guys. We're going to this new Indian place on Ninth. You understand, right?'

I squinted. I couldn't see. The sun was right in my eyes.

He laughed, then took the sandwich from me. 'I can have it for lunch tomorrow, okay? Don't worry about it.'

'But what about – how was your day? I was watching the news at work.'

'We're fine. Our CEO had to leave for Washington. He's joining the government advisory team. So Michael's in charge now. Acting CEO.'

'Is that a good thing?'

'It's a great thing. It means the WestCorp deal becomes a top priority. Pretty cool, right? Hey, I should really catch up with the other guys.' He rested his hand on my shoulder for a moment. 'Thanks again, Jules.'

'You're welcome.' I didn't mean it.

He started to walk away, then paused. 'Oh. I forgot to tell you. Guess whose byline I saw today?'

'*What?*' A truck was rushing past, blaring its horn.

'I said, "Adam McCard."'

My heart sped up. My hands went clammy. I was suddenly glad Evan was already several feet away. My brain couldn't think up a reply.

'He's on the business beat at the *Observer*. He was

writing about the crash. Small world.' Evan smiled. This time, he walked away for good.

Was it possible that he knew? Through the rest of that week, I waited for Evan to bring up Adam's name again. I was certain he was going to test for my reaction, to watch for the fluttering pulse in my neck or the nervous twist of my hands – damning proof of how much that name still meant to me.

But that wasn't Evan. I was the one who thought like that, not him. I could never decide whether Evan sensed those concealed parts of me and chose to leave them alone, or whether he thought that what he saw was everything there was to see. And the harder problem was – I could never decide which of those possibilities I wanted to be true.

———

A memory, from freshman year, from the time when Evan and I were just friends. A few months, that's all it was, a ratio that diminishes as the years go by. But those days were intense and heady, when our affection was waxing like the moon, when the uncertainty electrified the air between us. In an odd way, those feel like our purest days. When we were truly ourselves, before we started bending and changing to accommodate each other.

But that's not quite right. Because even then, even before we were together, I was hiding certain aspects of myself from Evan.

That night, in early October, we were on the couch in Evan's common room. Evan was sitting upright at one end, and I was lying with my head in his lap, the TV low in the background. Evan would occasionally brush a piece of hair from my forehead, but he couldn't see the expression on my face from where he sat. At the time, I was still dating Rob, my high school boyfriend. Evan didn't mind talking about Rob, which surprised me. Maybe he knew it was only a matter of time before Rob would cease to be an obstacle.

'So you and Rob,' he said. 'Do you ever worry that he might cheat on you?'

'Not really. We have too many friends who could report back to me if he did.'

'Even if he was secretive about it?'

'Rob thinks too highly of himself to cheat. Like, he doesn't see himself as that kind of guy. He's too proud.'

'Do you think he worries about you? That you might ever cheat on him?'

'I don't know. Maybe.'

'Were you guys always faithful to each other?'

My face must have tightened when Evan asked that last question, but he didn't notice. He just kept running his fingers through my hair, tracing the ridge of my ear. I thought before answering. This was the second time a chance had arisen to make my confession. The first had been the very first night of school, while we were eating pizza. He'd asked me about my summer, and I'd almost said it – the look on his face had been so warm and trusting, and I wanted to tell him everything. He was just a friend at that point, and there was no reason not to be truthful. But even at that first moment – and at that second moment, too – I wanted Evan to think of me a certain way.

'Yes,' I lied. 'I mean, I always was, and he was, too, as far as I know.'

'Mmm,' Evan said. 'Did I tell you about what happened at practice? So one of my teammates said . . .'

It never came up again. He never knew the difference. Perhaps he hadn't been administering any kind of test, or perhaps he had been, but only unconsciously. As the night wore on I began to feel a certain relief – that I had passed – but there was guilt, too. Did I think it was okay to lie because it was never going to happen again? Or did I know, even then, that it was an error destined to be repeated?

I tried not to think about Adam. I really tried. Our encounter that summer had lasted barely two minutes, capped with an empty promise to stay in touch. How many times did that happen in a given day in Manhattan? Hello and good-bye, a hundred heartbeats. I did everything to force Adam McCard out of my mind. I focused on whatever was in front of me: Evan, work, friends. But there was too much time in between. Too many empty hours, alone with nothing but my thoughts. I scanned the faces of everyone I passed in the street. I jumped every time my phone rang. While I was waiting for sleep, I found myself thinking about him. Adam McCard, Adam McCard, repeating billboards at the side of the highway. It seemed impossible he wasn't thinking about me, too.

And then, just as September was about to turn into October, I heard my phone ringing over the weak dribble of our shower. How did I know? But somehow I did: I knew that this time it would be him. His voice on the message was deep and smooth, an answer to an unasked question.

'Julia, gorgeous, it's me, Adam. If you're screening my calls, I don't blame you. God, I was so happy to run into you this summer. My only excuse for not calling is how busy work has been. Original, huh? But let me buy you a drink some night and tell you all about it. Please. I'd love to see you. Call me back. Same number.'

We planned to meet for drinks the next night at a bar downtown. From the outside, it looked like a very Adam place. A wooden door, no visible sign. The kind of place easily passed without notice. I'd dressed carefully, pulling my hair back and putting on lipstick, and earrings that dangled against my neck. My palms were sweaty, and my mind was jumbled. I had to remind myself it didn't matter. He was the one who called me. There was nothing to lose. I walked into the bar a few minutes late and didn't see him. Lots of young men with dark hair and deep voices, but no Adam. Maybe he was standing me up. Maybe it was for the best. Maybe it was better to go back to my own life and listen to that instinct flaring in the back of my mind – to stay away.

Then I felt the hand on my shoulder.

Adam kissed me on the cheek in greeting, the scent of his aftershave something that I'd never realized I'd memorized.

'Julia. You look amazing.'

'Thanks.' I tried not to blush.

We found a small, rickety table next to an open window at the front of the bar, where the breeze from the sidewalk drifted in. It was still warm, the last of an Indian summer. Adam picked out a bottle of wine for us to share. A Friday night, and the bar was full of people laughing off the week with pints of beer and platters of oysters on ice.

'This place looks great,' I said.

'It used to be a dive bar. We'd come here sometimes in high school. You could bribe the bouncer to let you in without ID.'

'Doesn't seem like that would work anymore.' There were exposed bulbs, framed prints, cocktails, craft beers, the prices high enough to make me wince.

He lifted his glass. 'Then it's a good thing we're so old,' he said. 'Cheers.'

It was like days had passed, not years. Adam's voice had that unchanged quality to it, a baritone depth that made me feel like we were actors on a stage, exchanging lines. Something about the way he leaned forward and cocked his head: it was like a cue, and the words that emerged from my mouth were more eloquent and interesting and right. The evening light came in at a low angle, casting a long shadow behind my wineglass on the table, warming my shoulders. I crossed one leg over the other, and my sandal dangled from my big toe.

I had a second glass of wine, a third. I'd been nervous and hesitant walking into the bar, but even an hour with Adam put me at ease. I was more relaxed than I'd felt in months. I was flirting, but just a little. I was still waiting for a signal that it was okay to keep going down this road.

The sun finally slipped behind the building across the street, and Adam's face sharpened in the dimmed light. In the previous few years, since I'd last seen him, he'd acquired an appealing patina of experience. The conversation lulled, and in that moment I felt the night changing cadences. A deepening, the wine sinking in, the dinner hour upon us. The silence flustered me, and I didn't know where to direct my gaze. A long second ticked by. When I looked up at Adam, his smile had disappeared.

This was it.

'Jules,' he said. He took a breath. 'I can't – I feel like I have to say something.'

I shook my head. I wanted – needed – this moment to happen, but I wanted the outcome without the procedure. Wake me up when the surgery is over.

'About last time, I guess. It was a long time ago. But I was a jerk. It was totally inappropriate. I should never have said or done those things. I'd like to think I'm a different person now, and I want to say –'

'Adam, it's okay. We don't have to talk about it.'

'No, I want to say it. I'm sorry, Julia. It's been

weighing on me, especially since – I guess that's the real reason I never called. I was worried you wouldn't want to talk to me again. I wouldn't blame you for that.'

'It was just a misunderstanding.'

He tilted his head and smiled sadly. Apologies didn't come naturally to Adam. 'I'm not sure I deserve to get off so easy.'

'It's fine. We're fine.' A pause – could I say it? 'I missed you.'

We talked about my job, about the last two years of school. Adam was the first person since graduation who actually seemed curious about my life. I didn't realize how much I'd been holding back until he started asking questions.

'Well, she sounds like a character,' Adam said after I told him about Laurie's soap-in-the-coffee bit. 'I know the type. Probably spent too many years living alone.'

'It's so strange. She's smart – I can see that. I respect her. I want to like her. But it's like I'm not there. It's like she doesn't even see me as a real person. I don't get it.'

'That's her mistake, Jules. It sounds like you're too good for that place.'

I'd forgotten how much I loved the sound of Adam's voice. 'I guess I should stop whining,' I said, reaching to refill my glass. 'At least I have a job, right?'

'What about Evan?' he asked. 'What's he up to these days?'

'Oh.' I was surprised that Adam had even remembered Evan's name. 'Evan.'

'You guys are still together?'

'Yeah. Yeah, he's working at a hedge fund. Spire Management.'

'Spire? That's a tough place to crack. He must be good.'

Relief washed over me. Back in college, Adam usually dismissed guys like Evan, if he noticed them at all. But now he was genuinely interested in Evan, in what he was working on. There was a warmth to his questions. Adam *had* changed. He wasn't the same person he'd been the last time we'd seen each other. Evan was my boyfriend, and Adam respected what I'd chosen. It felt good. This, maybe, was the signal I'd been waiting for. I nodded vigorously when he suggested a second bottle.

'So you're a reporter?' I said later. 'How long have you been there?'

'It's boring. You don't want to hear about it.'

'No, I do.' He grimaced, and I laughed. 'Come on. It can't be as bad as my job.'

'About a year and a half now. I started as a stringer, and then they had an opening on the business desk. The editor said he would move me to politics before the election.'

'That sounds promising.'

'He changed his mind. Once the housing bubble started heating up, he decided he needed me to stay where I was. So.' He sipped his wine. 'It's annoying. I don't like what I'm writing about. It's the same news

97

everyone else is reporting. I'm putting out feelers for other jobs.' He shrugged, looking resigned. 'Not much else to say about it.'

In the following days, this gave me comfort. Even *Adam* didn't have everything figured out? Unfathomable, a few years earlier. In college I was certain he was going to be famous. Adam McCard – people would know that name.

We knew each other from the campus magazine at Yale. In the first weeks of fall, freshman year, I crammed into a musty old office with two dozen other freshmen, lured by the promise of free pizza. The editors of the magazine made their pitch, telling us that joining the magazine would be the best decision we ever made. I thought I'd never go back. Me, the girl who hated English class, the girl who still recoiled from the memory of that bright red C on that stupid essay? But the next week, I returned. Already the people around me were finding their niches: Evan with his hockey, Abby with her volunteer work. I knew that I needed to hurry up and find my thing. I was assigned to write a short profile of the new football coach. I didn't know the first thing about football. 'I'm sorry. This is probably awful. I'm a terrible writer,' I told my editor, an older girl named Viv, when I turned in that assignment. 'That's okay,' Viv said. 'That's what I'm here for.'

My next assignment was to review a new show at the campus art gallery. 'Julia,' Viv said as she read my draft.

'This is really nice. Your descriptions are great. You must know a lot about this stuff.' The rest of my assignments from Viv were, thankfully, in that vein. I wrote several more pieces for the magazine that year. I wasn't gung-ho about it, wasn't angling to be an editor. But I liked walking into the office and feeling that I belonged. I liked the satisfaction that came from Viv telling me I had done a good job.

As a sophomore, I wrote more. I had a regular beat by then, on the arts and culture desk, and I was getting ready to declare an art history major. Those moments when I was starting a new piece – blank document, blinking cursor – were a rare reliable pleasure in my life. Writing for the magazine was one of the only things I had control over. Sophomore year was proving to be strange. Bad strange. Compared to freshman year, everything felt precarious. The landscape of friendships had shifted, thrown off by different dorms and new roommates. Classes seemed harder. Parties seemed duller. Everyone was sinking deeper into their own worlds. Evan was consumed by hockey and didn't have much time for me. When we were together, we bickered frequently. Our relationship didn't seem so fated or so satisfying anymore. I felt restless, in search of something new.

'I've noticed you around a lot,' Adam said, dropping into the chair next to mine one midwinter afternoon. He extended his hand. 'Remind me of your name.'

'Julia Edwards.'

'Nice to meet you, Julia Edwards. Adam McCard.'

I knew who he was, of course. He was the editor in chief, a senior. Adam had never before paid attention to me.

'Are you new?' he asked.

'I'm a sophomore. I wrote a few pieces last year. I'm doing more this year.'

'What are you working on?' He peered at my computer.

'Oh,' I said, tempted to cover the screen with my hands. 'It's just a little thing. It's stupid. A review of a new show at the Center for British Art.'

'Aha. Julia. Of course. You're the genius art critic. I love your stuff.' Someone called his name, and he stood up. The issue was about to close, and the editors would work well into the morning hours. Before he walked away, Adam put his hand on my shoulder. 'Hey, Julia. Let's grab coffee this week. Get to know each other. Sound good?'

A few months later, in the spring, I arrived at the magazine offices one night, ready to go over an article with Viv. But I was told she was sick, at home in bed. We still had a few days before the issue closed, so I put my laptop back in my bag. Adam spotted me just as I was about to leave. We had been having coffee every week. I'd admitted to Abby that I was developing a little crush on him, but it was innocent. It was nothing compared to what I felt for Evan, obviously.

'Julia. Leaving already?'

'Yeah. Viv's out sick.'

'I have half an hour until my next meeting. Why don't we give Viv a pass on this one? I'll edit it for you.'

My hands were shaking as I pulled out my laptop and opened the file. This was a terrible development. I had written this piece quickly, to meet Viv's deadline, and it was full of holes. Viv was exacting, finding the flaws in my work with merciless rigor, but she actually made me feel okay about that. It was never going to be right the first time; I knew that by now. I was fine with Viv seeing a rough draft of my work, but not Adam. I liked Adam, I liked spending time with Adam, but I wasn't ready for him to see an unedited version of my thoughts. This was going to be a disaster.

'Let's see,' he said, squinting as he read. A few minutes later, he looked up from the laptop. 'This is great.'

'Really?' I thought he was joking, but then he nodded. 'Wait, really? Do you think so? I know I need a better opening, and –'

'No, it's great. Yeah, the lede could be punchier, but once you've nailed that I think you're basically done.' He leaned back in his chair, hands folded behind his head. 'So. What should we do for the next twenty-four minutes?'

I laughed, closing my computer. 'Did you turn in your thesis? Or theses, I guess?' Adam was a double major in English and history. He'd spent the previous year writing about the Weimar Republic for the history department and working on a novel to fulfill the requirements for his writing concentration in English. His novel was also about the Weimar Republic. I'm not sure the English and history departments were, respectively, aware of this.

'I handed in history last week. And I'll hand in the novel next week.'

'And that's it, right? You're done? I'm so jealous.'

'Don't be. You're the lucky one. Two years left until shit gets real.'

I rolled my eyes. He knew my complaints. Adam often took the train into the city on weekends, forgoing campus parties for the more glamorous options of New York, where he'd grown up. I was envious. Did he not get how constricted, how stifling this life felt? Class, study, party, Evan. Over and over and over.

He smiled. 'You know I'd take you with me if I could. Start our own magazine or something.'

'Ha. I'd just be deadweight.'

'No way. I'm going to miss you, Jules.'

'Shucks.'

'I mean it.' He nudged my foot with his. 'I really like you. You're special.'

That was the thing about Adam. You believed everything he said. He said that he was going to be a writer after he graduated. I never imagined that he wouldn't succeed. He would go to New York after graduation and find a job at the *New Yorker* or *Harper's* or the *Paris Review*. In a few years he would have published his novel, and his picture would be gracing the cover of the arts section in the *Times*. There was no question about it. Adam would succeed at whatever he chose to do.

I took the subway home that night, after Adam and I said good-bye. The man sitting next to me on the uptown train was flipping through a copy of that morning's *Observer,* scanning each page for a few seconds before moving on. Until he stopped and pulled the paper a little closer. Adam's byline. The man read Adam's article slowly, nodding to himself. The train reached Grand Central. The man stayed in his seat, eyes glued to the page. It wasn't until the car had emptied and refilled that he looked up and jumped to his feet, elbowing his way out before the doors closed, sprinting to catch the late train back to Rye or Greenwich.

I'd wanted to lean over and tell him: I know Adam McCard. More than that: he's my friend. He'd liked me, once upon a time. He told me I was special. That night was the very first time, that year in New York, that I felt like I knew something that the people around me didn't. That I felt like I had a reason to be there. I sat back in my seat, flooded with a warm feeling of satisfaction.

He called me again the next week and the week after. October dawned chilly and clean. The whole planet was tilting on its axis in a new direction, a better direction.

The New York I'd been living in went from dull sepia to vibrant color. As Adam and I spent more time together, I felt a distant pity for Evan, for the narrow constraints of his world. In Chinatown Adam and I ate strange, spicy food in fluorescent-lit dives. We drank wine at sidewalk tables in SoHo. We went to gallery openings, to readings, to jazz shows in West Village basements. Adam took me to secret bookstores; he lent me his favorite novels. He was so confident, so comfortable. He wasn't running around in search of an identity, the way so many of my classmates were. He already knew who he was, and that was intoxicating. Adam would sometimes slip his arm through mine as we walked, or place a hand on my shoulder as he stood behind me at the museum, or brush a stray leaf from the sleeve of my jacket when we sat in the park. Women looked at him with envy. I craved the intimacy, every little touch. I so badly wanted more.

One night, at a French bistro in the West Village, the remains of steak frites on the table between us, he asked me the exact question I'd avoided asking myself.

'So what does Evan think of us spending all this time together?'

I toyed with my napkin. 'He doesn't mind. He's working on this deal all the time, anyway.'

He sipped his wine, watching me. He must have realized the truth, that I hadn't said a word about this to Evan. Adam always knew how to read me.

Evan was still a factor in this equation, much as I wished otherwise. We kept up the charade at our weekly dinners, when he talked in a monologue about work. He'd seemed tired lately, worn down by the demands of the deal. For some reason, Michael wouldn't staff anyone else on it. It was Evan and Evan alone. 'But,' he said in early October, his voice straining with a forced optimism, 'it's really starting to come together. Michael had me run a model this week. The numbers are dynamite. You wouldn't believe how huge the upside is.'

Evan's hours only grew more extreme as the fall progressed, and our date nights became rarer and rarer, until eventually I was left with the life of a single woman. The turning point came when I started taking advantage of this instead of resenting it. It was a new stage in our relationship, that was all; a phase where I could be more independent than ever before. A weight had lifted from my shoulders. I was free. There was a different kind of sadness in my life now, but it was a sweeter kind of sadness, easier to bear, because I had never accepted that falling for Adam was in fact such a hopeless mistake.

'What did you do?' Abby squinted at me. 'Did you change something? Your hair?'

I shook my head. Nothing had happened between Adam and me, but still, I didn't know what to say about it. Even Abby's sympathy only went so far. For the time being, I kept my mouth shut.

It was a Saturday night in October, and we were at her apartment in Harlem, a run-down and homey old railroad setup she shared with a friend. Her super had turned on the radiators early, so Abby kept the windows open to let out the heat. She used the gas burner on her stove to light the end of a joint. We smoked it sitting cross-legged on the living room floor while we waited for our Chinese food.

'Don't you miss this?' she said, exhaling. 'It's almost like we're back in school.'

'You never told me who you've been getting this from.'

'Why? Are you in the market for some? Evan need something to take the edge off?'

'It just seems so *real*. Buying weed from a real drug dealer.'

'A *drug* dealer!' She yelped in laughter, collapsing to the floor. 'You sound like Mister Rogers. No. No. Actually, I just got it from another teacher.'

'That is terrible.'

'Where the hell is our food?' She stood up and wandered into the kitchen, opening and shutting all the cabinets. 'I'm starving.'

The end of the joint smoldered like a jewel. I slipped a bobby pin from my hair to hold the burned nub. 'You're done?' I asked Abby. She waved, and I pulled the last of it into my lungs. It was pungent and stronger than what we had smoked in college.

'How were your parents?' I said. They had visited her the week before. Abby wandered back in, eating Froot Loops from the box. 'You know dinner's going to be here in, like, five minutes.'

'Appetizer. They were good. We went to Ikea, and I talked them into buying me a nightstand, so success.'

'Had they seen your apartment yet? Did they like it?'

'They did.' Abby paused, her hand full of brightly colored cereal, and tilted her head in contemplation. 'They did, except my mom got sort of teary. I don't know. I think it was too real for her. Seeing me all grown up and everything.'

I threw a pillow at her. 'You are *not* that grown up.'

'Well, my mom cries at everything.' It was true. I'd taken a picture of them at graduation, Abby and her parents, and her mother had been sobbing before I even turned on the camera. She was sentimental. Their other four kids were already grown and scattered, with careers and marriages and children and at least one divorce. But Abby had always been the baby, and suddenly she was gone, too.

After dinner, when we had devoured the sesame beef and kung pao shrimp and cold noodles, I felt myself sliding into a familiar jelly-limbed mellowness. Our thoughts were moving slowly enough for us to observe them, like glassy orbs in the air.

'Do you know that feeling?' Abby said, her voice thin and distant. 'When you wake up in the middle of the night and don't recognize the room you're in? Like, the shadows on the ceiling are all weird, and you're like, where the fuck am I?'

'Yeah.'

'I hate it.'

She was lying on her back, arms and legs splayed out, gazing up at the ceiling. She was quieter than usual. I nudged her with my foot.

'You okay?'

She rolled to her side and curled into a fetal ball. 'It was sort of weird. When my parents visited. I couldn't figure it out. And then my mom told me, on their last night, when the two of us went to get ice cream after dinner. It's my dad's job.'

When I got high, my emotions always felt slow to catch up, thickened like honey left in the fridge. 'What happened?' I said, belatedly registering the heaviness in Abby's voice.

'Nothing. Nothing yet. But you know, he works at a bank. This year has been brutal. He thinks he's going to be laid off soon. Which explains – well, like, every time we went out to eat, he'd sigh and roll his eyes at the prices. He and my mom got in a big fight, I guess, and he told her she needs to go back to work. But I mean, who the hell is going to hire her right now?'

'Oh, Abby. That sucks.'

'The whole thing is a disaster.'

A few days earlier, the president had signed a massive bailout into law. A few weeks before that, the Republican nominee had suspended his campaign, announcing that he had to return to Washington to address the crisis. I followed the developments with a shallow curiosity, but lately I'd been caring less about all of it. Maybe this was going to be the headline for the era when the historians had their turn. Maybe the market crash would emerge as the defining moment of the year, of the decade. But I'd been thinking about other things. I'd been thinking about Adam, the sound of his voice, the color of his eyes. Talk of the NAS-DAQ and the Dow was so abstract. The world still looked the same. The sun still set and rose; the moon still pulled the tides in patterns around the globe. My mind was aloft, scattered among the stars. I squeezed my eyes shut and tried to snap out of it. Other people were hurting, even if I wasn't.

'I'm so sorry,' I said.

'At least I'm off the dole, right? Last kid. No more tuition.' She tried to smile. 'I don't know. I mean, maybe he won't even lose his job. Maybe everything will be fine. But it's so weird. These are my parents. It's weird to have to worry about *them*. Aren't they supposed to worry about me?'

I lowered myself to the floor and curled up behind Abby, a big spoon to her little one. It was rare for me in our friendship, offering comfort to her. To Abby, who always knew what to do. 'You want to sleep over?' she said. I had started spending the night occasionally, when the quiet of my apartment was too much. I texted Evan to tell him. We lay in her bed, talking until late, when we finally drifted off.

The next morning, we went to the diner on the corner for breakfast. I emptied the tiny plastic cup of cream into my coffee, watching it swirl into spidery threads. I still felt a little high. Abby scrolled through her phone while eating a piece of buttered toast. She had cheered up considerably.

'Guess who texted me last night,' she said. 'Jake Fletcher.'

'You guys know each other?'

'Remember? You introduced us at his party. I've bumped into him a few times. He asked for my number last week.'

'Wow. Small world.'

'I think I'm gonna do it. I have gone *way* too long without any action.'

I laughed weakly, signaling to the waiter for more coffee. Abby looked at me.

'Wait. Wait — what is it? Do you guys have a history?'

'No! God, no. I've just known him since forever. I still think of him as, like, the bratty five-year-old he once was. That's all.'

She raised an eyebrow. I wasn't sure whether she bought it. But that was the nice thing about us. Abby knew the difference between big lies and little ones. She might guess at what I was leaving out: a game of spin the bottle in middle school, or maybe a tipsy kiss in the backyard during one of his parents' big parties in Boston. A stupid kid thing that wasn't even worth the energy to mention. Something you could skate past because you were so certain it was meaningless, that it had nothing to do with what you were actually talking about.

CHAPTER 5

Evan

'What the fuck, man?' Roger said, shaking his head. 'It's a bloodbath out there.'

Despite Kleinman's rousing speech that morning, there was not much to be done that day. The top executives were in damage-control mode, on the phone with our investors, conveying to them the same confident lines we'd just heard. But everyone else had too much time on their hands. Taking slow walks around the floor, calling their wives in the middle of the day. Roger staring, slack-jawed, at the computer screen. The eerie quiet was only punctured by his occasional declarations of disbelief, which I did my best to tune out, because I was the anomaly. I actually had work to do. This lumber deal was taking up every second of my time.

Roger noticed me studying a model and chewing on a thumbnail. 'What is that?' he said. '*Peck*. Are you actually working right now?'

'Just something, um, something leftover from a few days ago.'

Keep it light and vague, those were my orders. 'Not till we're ready to push the button,' Michael had said. 'Soon. I know how hard you've been working on this, Evan. I've seen how late you're staying and how early you're coming in. I'm impressed. You're handling this very well.'

This was the previous week, in Michael's office, the beginning of September. I had stopped by to go over the latest numbers. I'd been working up the nerve to say something to Michael about the workload, which I could barely handle. In a bathroom stall that morning, I practiced the sentence in a whisper. My stomach was a watery mess. *Michael, I wonder whether we want to think about bringing someone else on board. Couldn't the deal use a fresh pair of eyes?* That seemed a fair enough rationale.

But Michael had preempted me with praise before I had a chance to open my mouth. It was a cornering tactic. A dare. What was I going to do, tell Michael that his confidence was misplaced? That I actually *wasn't* as capable as he thought I was? And risk getting kicked off the deal entirely? So instead I mumbled a thank-you.

'And I appreciate it,' Michael went on. 'How discreet you've been. That's the best way to handle a deal like this. Stay quiet. Just focus and do what you're doing. Keep up the good work, Evan.'

So that was it. I was just going to put my head down and get through it. Just as I'd done in the past, taking it one predawn practice at a time, inching closer to the end. By eleven that Monday morning, the morning of

Kleinman's departure to DC, I had finished the latest component of the model. I walked the papers over to Michael's office. There was an assumption in the formula that needed clarifying, the one part of the deal that still didn't make sense to me. I was a little worried, actually. It was the last factor that seemed liable to screw everything up.

Michael's secretary, Wanda, halted me outside his office. She was all sassy middle-age curves: blown-out hair, chair-wide hips, bright red lipstick. 'Uh-uh,' she said in her Jersey accent. 'I don't think so, honey. You're not getting in there today. You wanna give that to me, I'll try to get it to him.'

I peered over Wanda's shoulder, trying to see through the open door. She'd been with Michael for years, and she could be excessively protective. 'What's he doing?'

'Trying to run the company – what do you think? He's been on the line all morning.' The phone on Wanda's desk rang. She tapped her Bluetooth headset and jerked her head to dismiss me. 'O-*kay?* Stop by tomorrow. Maybe I can fit you in.'

I couldn't go any further on this model without Michael answering my question. So I spent the rest of the morning as Roger and the other analysts did, trolling the Internet for updates, killing time in an uneasy boredom, the same things I had done at the beginning of the summer. The TVs in the lounge were tuned to CNBC and Bloomberg Business. People lingered there, watching, looking for any excuse to stay away from their desks. Late in the afternoon, I walked past and found myself hypnotized by the mounting intensity of the coverage.

WALL STREET'S WORST DAY SINCE 9/11

DOW DOWN OVER 500 POINTS

LEHMAN DECLARES BANKRUPTCY

MERRILL BOUGHT BY BANK OF AMERICA

IS YOUR MONEY SAFE?

FORCED LIQUIDATION — HISTORIC VOLUME

EVERYTHING CALLED INTO QUESTION

One of the managing directors, a petite brunette woman, had her hands steepled over her mouth and tears in her eyes. Another woman put her arm around her shoulders. 'Her husband works at AIG,' I heard someone whisper. 'Three kids. Just bought a house in Quogue.'

Roger, standing across the lounge, caught my eye and waved me over. 'Let's go to the roof,' he said.

'What? Now?'

'Come on. It's dead. No one's gonna notice.'

We took the elevator to the top of the building, where Roger propped open the door with a loose brick. It was a beautiful day, a bluebird September sky. The city stretched out far below us, metal and glass glittering in the sunlight.

'Holy shit,' I said.

'You never been up here?'

'I had no idea we could get up here.'

'We're not supposed to.' Roger pulled a crumpled pack of cigarettes from his pocket. 'You want one?'

'I'm okay.'

I wandered out toward the edge. The roof was covered with tar paper and gravel. Only a low wall and a flimsy metal bar stood between me and the sixty-story drop. On the other side of the roof was the area where David Kleinman's helicopter had taken off that morning.

From this vantage point, life down below was proceeding normally. Taxis and trucks flowed up 8th Avenue in waves. Tiny pedestrians drifted down the sidewalk, their motion smooth and toylike. Sounds echoed up from the street: honking horns, a jackhammer, the rattle of a loose manhole cover, a siren in the distance. I could almost pretend the crisis was contained within the walls of our building, the babble of the TV irrelevant beyond its perimeter. The numbers were plummeting, the market was in a frenzy, but for the moment, it didn't result in any visible change. No fires, no earthquakes, no violence or bloodshed. But it would take time for the real world to catch up to what was happening on our screens, and in a situation like this, the worst lay ahead. I understood that.

That woman downstairs, trying not to show her panic: her husband would lose his job, and she would probably keep hers, but it didn't matter. The balance would be upset. I knew that feeling, of living exactly within your means. Their life was fancier than mine – children in private school, a second house in the Hamptons – but that feeling didn't change. The precarious flow of incoming and outgoing gave you a toehold in this world, but it was one that would vanish if the paychecks stopped. Numbers had always felt realer to me than anything else. Days like this reminded you of that.

To the rest of America, to the rest of the world, I was indisputably one of them, even if I hadn't been pushing shady CDOs. A bad guy. A practitioner of the dark arts who had suddenly lost control of his slippery magic. Why didn't this bother me more? In the past, I think it would have. But my mind kept going back to the numbers. You could talk in generalities: Wall Street *bad,* Main Street *good.* It didn't really mean anything. I liked the economy of action. A goal scored before the third-period buzzer, a clean and precise pass, an airtight model. You didn't need words to complicate it. There were winners, and there were losers. The game bore it out. At first this job seemed more practical than anything else: a way to stay in New York with Julia, to make money and pay off student loans quickly. But it had transformed into something else. The thing I was *meant* to be doing.

I shoved my hands in my pockets and turned, taking in the panorama. The city was sparkling and alive, taking up every inch it could. I looked back at Roger, leaning against the wall. He was moving his lips as he read something on his BlackBerry.

'What is it?' I asked, walking over.

'Shit. This is crazy.' Roger thrust his phone toward

me. 'You see that picture? No, scroll down. There. That short guy in the blue tie? That's my old roommate from Stanford. What are the odds, man?'

'What is this?'

'He works at Lehman, I guess. The little shit is famous.'

'Actually, it looks like he just got fired.' I scrolled to the top, where the headline read: LEHMAN GOES UNDER. It was from the *Observer*. The picture showed several bewildered-looking young men standing on the sidewalk, clutching cardboard boxes while pedestrians streamed around them.

'Whatever. He was a tool.'

'How did you find this?'

'I always read the *Observer*. Just for their finance guy. He's good. You never read him?'

'What's his name?'

Roger reached for his phone, checking the byline. 'Adam McCard.'

'Adam McCard?'

'What, are you deaf?'

'No. No, it's just that I *know* Adam McCard.'

Roger raised an eyebrow. 'How?'

'He was a friend of Julia's in college. Really? Adam McCard?'

'He's a good reporter. Better than anyone else. He actually seems to get it.'

'Shit. If you say so.'

Roger took a final drag of his cigarette. Adam McCard.

I hadn't thought about him in months – in years. 'Ready?' Roger kicked the brick away and held the door open.

'Right behind you,' I said.

Sophomore year, Julia dragged me along to a party off campus. I was hungover and stiff from the night before, from the hockey team's end-of-season rager, but Julia insisted I come. She was in one of those moods. The party was on a dark, tree-lined street, in a crumbling old Victorian with a sagging porch. She had given a vague explanation of the occasion – for the magazine she worked on? Something like that – but when we walked through the front door, I saw the real reason.

Adam McCard was leaning against the wall, arms crossed, one foot hitched up. He waved at Julia, then shook my hand, gripping it too tightly. He told us to help ourselves to the beer in the kitchen, *his* kitchen. I realized belatedly, stupidly, that this was his house. Julia had been mentioning Adam's name a lot in the preceding weeks. I'd decided, a while earlier, that I hated him.

We joined a group in the kitchen gathered around a keg. They gave me curious looks. 'Are you an *athlete?*' one girl asked. She was scrawny, black-clad, with a cigarette smoldering between her pale fingers and an expression of surprised wonder.

'I'm on the hockey team.'

'Oh,' Julia said. 'Oh, that reminds me of something. So last night . . .'

I tuned out quickly. I was thinking, mostly, how hungry I was. Maybe I could slip out for a slice of pizza and get back before she noticed. But a minute later, Julia said my name. I turned to face her. She leaned against me, briefly, in recognition.

'So Sebi finally finishes the bottle,' she continued. 'We're upstairs, in his room, and he goes over to the window. Then he pulls down his pants and starts pissing all over the crowd at the frat next door. Just, like, so casual about it.'

The group laughed. Julia's eyes were glittering.

'Some of the guys from next door get really mad. They come over, trying to start a fight. They're threatening to call the cops, all that stuff. We're downstairs at that point, too. Sebi had passed out in his bed. They keep asking who it was, who did it, no one's going to tell. But then Sebi strolls up to the front door himself and asks what the problem is. And he's totally buck naked.'

They laughed louder. 'So funny,' the scrawny girl said flatly.

'So the frat guys are backing away, they don't know what to think, and Sebi offers to walk them home, throws his arms around their shoulders, being all friendly. He was completely blacked out at that point. He tried to pull one of the guys in for a hug, and that's when they all finally ran away. No one wants to fight a naked dude.'

Julia was grossed out when this happened the previous night, at the party at the hockey house, grimacing at the sight of Sebi's bare ass. But not anymore. She was beaming, clearly thrilled with the story's reception.

Later, when we were finally alone, I asked her what that had been about.

'What the hell, Jules? That was embarrassing.'

'Oh, come on. It was hilarious. You're never going to let Sebi live it down.'

'Yeah, but we're his friends. These people don't know him.'

'Relax.' She rolled her eyes. 'It's not a big deal.'

Relax? She wouldn't even look at me. I felt a smoldering curl of disgust. 'What's with this attitude?' I snapped. I wanted to grab her by the shoulders, shake her until she listened. How did she not get it? 'Jules. Why are you being like this?'

'*God.*' She rolled her eyes again. 'Whatever. I'm going to the bathroom.'

She walked away. In those days our fights seemed to come out of nowhere, and with more and more frequency. They were about stupid, meaningless things, but Julia could so easily turn vicious, like an animal baring her teeth. I never knew what to say. I just wanted it to be over. It always seemed easiest to concede before things escalated. I was good at apologizing, even if I didn't know what I was apologizing for.

I pushed through the living room, which was tight with bodies. The bathroom door was locked. When the door finally opened, some other girl emerged, her expression smeary with drink. She gave me a hazy smile. I went back to the kitchen, then to the backyard, then again to the living room. Julia was nowhere. I pulled out my phone and texted her, then I opened the front door to check the porch. Nothing. I called, but she didn't pick up. Five minutes passed, then six, seven. Ten minutes. Fifteen. Where was she? Maybe this was some kind of punishment, forcing me to navigate this awful party alone. She probably enjoyed the thought of it.

Then, just as I was about to call again, I saw her coming down the stairs from the second floor. She pushed her way past the crowds. Her cheeks were flushed, her hair messy. She was staring straight ahead. She noticed me and came over, but she was still avoiding my gaze. 'Had to use the bathroom upstairs,' she muttered. Then I noticed Adam McCard behind her, bouncing down the stairs two at a time.

She walked several paces ahead of me the whole way home. She wouldn't even let me come close. As good as an admission of guilt, in my mind. When we got back to the dorm, I was going to tell her that I'd sleep in my own room that night. But outside her door, when Julia turned to face me and looked up at me for what felt like the first time all night, her eyes were brimming with tears. Her lower lip quavered, and she burst into a sob. 'I'm sorry,' she gasped. 'I'm sorry, Evan. I'm so sorry.'

I checked my cell phone when I got back to my desk that afternoon. Julia had texted, asking me how my day was. It was sweet. I smiled to myself.

We usually ordered dinner from a regular rotation of

places in the neighborhood: Italian, Chinese, Thai, Vietnamese, Turkish. Roger always took charge, dictating what everyone was going to order so we could share, and he calculated the tab ahead of time so that we could maximize our thirty-dollar per diem. That night, around seven, he threw a balled-up piece of paper at my head to get my attention.

'Peck,' he said. 'Let's go. We're going out for dinner.'

'Picking up? Or out out?'

'Out out. It's deader than a doornail around here. Hurry up,' he drawled, standing. 'I made a reservation. A new Indian place on Ninth.'

My stomach rumbled as we walked to the elevator. Roger had that slightly satanic ability to discern your desires with perfect accuracy. Going out for dinner, eating at a table with real tablecloths, hot and spicy food washed down with frosty beer – it was, in fact, exactly what we needed in that moment. And so, by the time we emerged into the last of the day's sunlight, I was actually in a pretty good mood.

'Evan!' I turned and saw her squinting against the lowering sun. Julia.

'Hey.' I felt the guys staring as I walked over. 'What are you doing here?'

She lifted up a plastic bag, a logo I recognized from a deli around the corner. I went there for lunch when I was too impatient for delivery. 'I brought dinner. I thought we could eat together. Like the old days, you know.'

'Oh. That's nice of you, Jules.'

'I got your favorite. Chicken cutlet with bacon and mozzarella.'

Which I'd ordered many times before. The bread was usually stale. The chicken cold and tough. That sandwich was always a last resort. Roger and the others were walking away without me. I just needed a break. The thought of it was unbearable, eating that terrible sandwich, forced to talk about my day, to fake it with Julia. I just wanted to *be* for one minute. With people who understood. I told her the truth, partially. 'The thing is, I was going to get dinner with the guys. We're going to this new Indian place on Ninth. You understand, right?'

She was quiet, the bag drooping from her wrist. But just because she could saunter out of her job whenever she liked didn't mean that I could. I was annoyed. I was a little pissed, actually. She could have called ahead. Roger had made a reservation and everything. Her mopey silence was unfair. This didn't seem like it could be *my* fault.

After I took the bag from her, promising I'd eat it for lunch the next day, but already planning to let it molder in the refrigerator until I was forced to throw it out, I thought of something. I'd meant to text her earlier.

'Oh,' I called as she walked away. 'Guess whose byline I saw today?'

'Another round?' the waiter asked. The empty beer glasses were speckled with our greasy fingerprints from the paratha.

'Absolutely,' Roger said. I still had an inch of beer left, which Roger pointed at. 'Keep up, Peck.'

We went out together a lot. Dinner, the bar after work almost every night, clubs on the weekends. In better moments, it reminded me of the hockey team. It was something even more comfortable than friendship. I drained my glass and handed it to the waiter.

'Who was that?' one of the other analysts asked me.

'Who was who?'

'That girl you were talking to back there.'

'Oh,' I said. I'd already forgotten. 'Right. That was Julia. My girlfriend.'

'What was she doing here?'

Roger laughed, reaching for the last piece of paratha. 'You didn't know?' he said loudly. 'Peck is completely whipped. Does whatever his girlfriend tells him to.'

I rolled my eyes. 'She was just saying hi.'

'Hey, Roger,' one of the other analysts said. 'So what happened to that chick from Saturday night?'

'Which one? Can't keep track.'

'The blonde. The one from the club.'

'Her? She won't stop calling.' He gestured at his phone. All of us kept our BlackBerrys faceup on the table, alert to the buzz of incoming e-mails through dinner. He tipped back in his chair. 'She was all right. I'm worried she's gonna be a clinger.'

The waiter delivered our entrées. Roger made another lewd crack about the girl he'd brought home on Saturday night. I ate my lamb curry and let myself dissolve into the banter. Something about that time of year had been making me homesick. Fall had always meant a turnover in routine, a new year of school, the beginning of the hockey season. I missed it, even the miserable parts: muscles that screamed in pain, bruises blackening under pads, sticks slamming into legs. Maybe *homesick* wasn't the right word. It was more like a part of me had been put away in a dusty old box, and I missed it. But moments like this were a relief. Another beer, and another. In those moments, I'd forget.

At McGuigan's later that Monday night, I slipped out of our booth while Roger was in the middle of a story, and waited at the bar for Maria to look up.

'Hey,' she said, finally. She smiled. 'How long have you been sitting there?'

'Busy night?'

'You have no idea. Hang on a second.' She delivered a brimming tray of bourbons to a waiter, who carried it over to a table. Not our table, but it might as well have been. You could tell they were bankers from a mile away. Almost everyone in there was. Young guys in loosened ties, getting bombed with an end-of-the-world abandon.

'That'll keep them busy for about five minutes,' she said. 'The usual?'

After several weeks of going to McGuigan's almost every night, I had befriended Maria. She felt like someone I'd known for a long time. In a strange way, even longer than Julia. Like someone from back home. I liked her company, especially when I'd had too much of my coworkers. One night she let me buy her a drink and told me her story. She was putting herself through law school at Fordham with loans and bartending wages. As a girl, she had dreamed of becoming a ballerina, of studying at Juilliard. Her teachers at home all said she had the talent, and she'd moved to the city for it. When I asked what happened, she shrugged. 'Flat feet.' She was tall and gorgeous, had thought about modeling, she said, but realized that if her body could let her down once, it could do it twice.

'So why law school?'

'I want to be taken seriously, I guess. I find it interesting. Mostly I don't want to end up like my mom.' She paused. 'I sound like an asshole.'

'Not an asshole. I get it.'

'Well. You're nice, Evan. You're not like those other guys, you know?'

Guilt twinged in my chest occasionally during those hours we spent talking, sometimes till the end of her shift. Hours I should have been spending with Julia. I worried Julia could smell the bar on me when I got home, stale beer and smoky whiskey clinging to my shirt before I stuffed it into the laundry pile. I found myself daydreaming about Maria. It reminded me of high school – a girl waiting by your locker after the last bell. Consistent pleasures: the same familiar face, day in and day out.

Maria drew a Guinness for me. 'What's going on tonight?'

'What do you mean?'

'You guys are all worked up. All of you.'

'Oh. It's the market. This could be the end for a lot of companies.'

'Okay, but you'll be fine, though.'

'But that's the thing. Nobody knows. There's never been anything like this. Nobody knows what could happen to Spire.'

'Well, I don't mean Spire. I mean *you*. Say you get fired, go bankrupt, whatever. *You* aren't going to have a problem getting a job. I mean, look at you.'

I raised an eyebrow.

'Not like that.' She laughed. 'I mean you're smart, you're polite, you look like a guy anyone could trust. You fit right in. Guys like you don't stay unemployed for long.'

Someone was waving her down. She rested her hand on mine before she walked away. Maria was good at her job. 'Don't worry too much about it, Evan. You're just one of those people. It's all going to work out, you know?'

'Evan. Come on in.'

This was the following evening, Tuesday night. It was the first time Michael's door had been open and unguarded in almost two days.

'Is this an okay time?' Michael was typing fast, glancing over his shoulder at a chart, ignoring the blinking messages on his phone. His office looked like a war zone.

127

'Fine, fine. I sent Wanda home. What do you have there?'

'The WestCorp models. They're almost finished, but I need to check an assumption with you before running it.'

'What is it?'

I took a deep breath. 'The exports to the Chinese market. I wasn't sure what tariffs they're subject to and how much that's going to affect us. I've done some research, and there's a lot of variation in the taxes on lumber exported to China, so I thought I'd go with a rough average, something like –'

'Zero.'

'Pardon?'

'Your number is zero. The WestCorp exports won't be subject to any tariffs or taxes. Is that all?'

'Well – yes. Yeah, that's it.'

'Good.' Michael turned back to his computer. I started toward the door, but I couldn't help myself. It had been puzzling me for so long. And it still didn't quite make sense.

'Michael, just want to be sure – no tariffs or taxes at all for these exports, none? It's just that I've seen a lot of –'

He spun in his chair and stared at me, anger flaring in his eyes. 'No,' he said sharply. 'No tariffs. *None*. Put that in the model and run it. E-mail me the numbers when you have them. Then go home.'

Back at my desk, as I plugged the last numbers into the model, I felt a hot flush spread under my collar. I shouldn't have questioned Michael like that. In all my research, I'd never seen a scenario in which the trade barriers had been dropped completely. But he was the boss after all. Maybe I hadn't looked hard enough.

After the model was finished, I checked everything over slowly. The papers were still warm in my hands when I walked over to Michael's office, a stupid-big grin stuck to my face. Assuming we took even a conservative position on WestCorp, the money we stood to make was staggering. I had to read it twice, three times to be sure. This kind of good news ought to be delivered in person. When I got there, the door was nearly closed. Michael was on the phone. I almost didn't recognize him – his voice was strange, different. It quieted. I edged a little closer.

Then Michael spoke again. Another language. It sounded familiar.

Then I remembered: in his usual overly ambitious way, Arthur had decided to take up a new language junior year, even though he already spoke French and Spanish. He stayed up late every night, practicing his tones and inflections. This was the fluent version of those efforts. Michael was speaking Mandarin.

A prickle ran up my spine. Odd. Michael had always asked one of the third-year analysts, a Princeton grad who spoke flawless Mandarin, to translate on conference calls with the Chinese. Michael never spoke on those calls, not once.

It went silent again. I was about to leave the model in

the in-box on Wanda's desk, but I hesitated. I'd e-mail it instead. Better not to have evidence that I'd been hanging around. Overhearing things that I strongly suspected I wasn't supposed to overhear.

The apartment was dark when I got home. It was early for me, just past eleven, but Julia was already asleep.

I sat on the futon and opened my computer. I found myself typing Michael Casey's name in the search bar. Strangely, it had never occurred to me before, to do this. I didn't even know what I was looking for. Maybe an explanation for what I'd overheard. The creepy feeling that I couldn't shake.

I hit Enter.

The top search results were from Spire's website, Michael's official company biography. Undergrad at South Dakota, wildcatting for oil in West Texas for a year, MBA completed in 1983. He started at Spire in 1986. Michael never said anything about working any-place but Spire. I wondered about that three-year window after his MBA.

I kept clicking through the results. A few pages in, there was a link to an archived article in the *New York Times*. A profile from the business section, dated 1985. There was a grainy photo on the page. I squinted. It was Michael, twenty-odd years earlier.

I scanned through the article. Michael had worked at another hedge fund called Millworth Capital. In the summer of 1985, he made upwards of $400 million for

Millworth, shorting foreign currencies. The profile described his unlikely success: a farm boy, the first in his family to go to college, a rising star on Wall Street at age twenty-six. The reporter asked Michael what he thought he could attribute his success to.

Mr Casey tilts back in his chair, resting his feet on the desk. There are no traces of his former life in his office: no family pictures, no college diploma.

'I don't think there's any one way to answer that question,' he says. 'You could point to any number of things. But I think there was a moment when I got hooked on this. My first big trade. I cleared $50 million in one day. I was twenty-four years old. I wasn't going to look back after that.'

'Evan? Evan? Hello?'

Julia was standing in front of me, hair rumpled and eyes scrunched against the glow of the computer screen. I twitched, my hand slamming the laptop shut. 'Oh,' I said. 'Hi. I didn't hear you get up.'

'I said, what are you doing? Work?'

'Uh, just some e-mails. I'm done now.'

She padded over to the kitchen sink, her bare legs sticking out from beneath her T-shirt. She took a glass from the cabinet, turned on the tap, held her finger in the stream of water, waiting for it to get cold. Mundane gestures I'd seen a hundred times before, but at that moment, they felt too private for me to witness. Part of a separate life. I wanted something from Julia that it felt impossible to ask for. A silence different from the one that had grown between us.

'I'm coming to bed,' I said. She waved a hand to show that she'd heard before disappearing into the darkness of the bedroom.

CHAPTER 6

Julia

I looked up from the donor database I was updating to see Eleanor march into Laurie's office. Others maintained a certain deference around Laurie, asking me in a whisper if she was available before approaching her door, but not Eleanor. Not this day, not any day. She slammed the door shut behind her, but her voice vibrated through the wall.

'Laurie, I don't know how you expect me to pull this gala off. Not with this shitty budget. This is pathetic.'

'It's the best we can do. You know things have been tight around here.'

'But this is *ridiculous*. This is less than half our budget from last year. Do you expect me to cook the food myself? There's no way this is going to work.'

This conversation kept repeating itself. Each week, Eleanor secured a few more dollars for the November gala. Then she turned right back around and cajoled Laurie for more. And, strangely, Laurie never lost her patience with Eleanor. It was clear that the crash was creating a strain. Laurie had taken to sighing a lot and rubbing her temple. She grew brittle with the rest of us. But never once did she shout back at Eleanor. It baffled me, but then again, almost everything about Laurie baffled me. I answered her phone and kept her schedule, but I had no insight into what she was thinking. Her remove seemed deliberate. She must have seen me as just one more link in a chain – another assistant, another year. I wondered if I could ever prove I was different. But then what? I didn't want to work there. I didn't want to be Eleanor in five years. Eleanor, who breezed in and out of the office when she felt like it, who threw temper tantrums, who'd barely spoken to me since our lunch over the summer.

In late October, Eleanor declared that she would be leaving town to 'recharge' before the gala. She would be unreachable for the next five days, on some tropical island. The following day, a Thursday, Laurie told me to get Henry Fletcher on the phone. His secretary said he wasn't available, but she could pass along a message. 'I don't want to leave a message,' Laurie yelled from inside her office. 'I'll try him this afternoon.'

He remained unavailable that afternoon, and Friday morning, and Friday afternoon. Laurie swirled around her office, slamming file drawers, throwing out papers, rearranging furniture. I wanted to help – it was distressing to witness – but I wasn't going to put myself directly in her line of fire. She seemed ready to snap at any moment. And as much as I disliked the job, it was still the only job I had.

★

I wonder. Could I see it at the time? My life crystallizing into a new pattern. Evan and I drifting, each of us caught in different currents. Adam and I had grown closer, and I contemplated what I had ever done without him. I was never good at skepticism, at questioning what was happening to me. And besides, nothing had even happened – nothing that couldn't be explained away in innocence. Until one specific night, the weekend at the end of October. When imagination hardened into reality.

Abby called me that Saturday afternoon. 'Come to this party with me,' she said. 'I'm schlepping all the way to Brooklyn. I need a buddy for the subway.'

The party was in the garden-level apartment of a brownstone near Prospect Park, hosted by a girl from college, someone Abby knew better than I did. She and her roommate both worked in publishing. We picked up a bottle of wine on the way over, and when I set it down on the kitchen counter, I saw that someone else had brought the same bottle of wine, down to the identical $8.99 price sticker on the neck.

Tall bookshelves, track lighting, dusty Oriental rugs. It was a nice party. Lively, not too crowded, the conversation earnest and serious. A lot of the parties Abby and I went to that year felt like an ardent imitation of college: twenty-two-year-olds spending their salaries on light beer, blasting hip-hop, puking out the cab door. This pulled in the other direction: people acting older than they really were. It surprised me how rarely those two worlds ever overlapped. There wasn't any middle ground.

'So Jake's coming by,' Abby said as we helped ourselves to the wine. 'Later. Is that weird? I'm not sure he's ever been to Brooklyn before.'

'Wow. So are you —'

'Kind of. I don't know. It's nothing serious yet.'

'But you like him?'

'I like him enough to sleep with him.' She shrugged. But she was blushing a little.

I finished my wine and had another, then another, drifting from conversation to conversation. The night passed easily, without friction. After a while, Jake arrived. I saw Abby kiss him and lead him to the kitchen. I turned back to my companion, who was critiquing a recent article in the *New York Review of Books*. Out of the corner of my eye I saw Jake slip his arm around Abby's waist and draw her in.

Stop it, I thought. I had no right to be jealous. In fact, I should have been happy for them. That would be definitive proof of just how meaningless my own encounter with Jake had been.

The drink crashed over me like a wave, stronger than it had been a minute earlier. It was past midnight, and the group I was standing with was gone. The party had thinned, and the music was louder without the muffling of voices. Jake was kissing Abby, pulling back to whisper in her ear, making her laugh. I had to admit he was cute. And Abby looked so happy. He tugged her closer. I could tell they were having great sex, probably twice a day.

And I felt like I was going to be sick. I went outside to the garden and sunk into a dented plastic chair, lowering my head between my knees. Then I noticed another couple in the corner of the patio, snuggled close, sharing a cigarette.

'Fuck,' I said. They looked at me, startled. Couples everywhere, reminding me of what I didn't have. It was horrible. For so many years, I'd been one half of a whole. I knew that the wine was making it worse, but I couldn't help it. All this affection, this electric desire zipping through the air – it made me feel unloved and worthless. I was twenty-two years old, for God's sake. When was the last time someone had kissed me like that?

On Thursday night, two nights earlier, Evan had gotten home just after I'd returned from dinner with Adam. He dropped his briefcase and coat on the floor, went to the kitchen, opened the door to the refrigerator, and stared into the chilly blue light.

'We have nothing to eat,' he said. That was his greeting. 'What did you eat?'

'I, uh, picked up a slice of pizza on the way home.'

He sighed and shut the refrigerator. Then he collapsed on the futon next to me.

'Is everything okay at work? You're home pretty early.'

'Fine. Things are slow this week. Should be back to normal soon.' He stared at his hands, picking at a cuticle. He didn't know what to do, or where to look.

'Okay. Well, I'm going to go to bed.'

Eventually he slid into bed next to me. I switched off my lamp, and we lay there in the darkness. It had been nearly a month since we'd had sex. Evan's leg brushed against mine, and he left it there. My pulse accelerated. A minute later, I rested my fingertips on the back of his hand. He was perfectly still, and then he rolled over, away from me. From his breathing, I could tell he was already asleep.

Maybe that was the power Evan wielded in our relationship. I was so used to his presence that when he pulled away, it left me spinning. I took it for granted, like the subways running regularly or the water coming out of the faucet. Even then, even with everything, Evan gave me what I hadn't yet learned to provide for myself.

—◆—

Sophomore year, one rainy night in March, Adam and his housemates threw a party. I was insistent that Evan come, which should have been a red flag. I'd gone to plenty of parties without him. Was I trying to protect myself from what awaited? It seems obvious now.

'Jules, seriously. I don't want to go.' Evan was slumped on his couch, playing a video game. 'Just go by yourself. It's not like I'm going to know anyone there. And I'm still beat from last night. And it's pouring.'

'I don't care,' I said. I felt like stamping my feet. He'd been consumed by the hockey season for the previous four months. He needed to care about *me* for a change. 'Evan, *come on*. You said last night that you would.'

'*Fine.*' He tossed aside the controller. 'I don't remember saying that, though.'

Adam was in the foyer when we arrived. A fizz of excitement: I'd never been inside his house before. In the kitchen, I stood where I had a view of the living room and the rest of the party. I hoped that I'd catch Adam again later in the night. The beer had already loosened me. I just wanted to talk to Adam: that was it. Nothing was going to happen.

'Are you an athlete?' one girl was asking Evan.

'I'm on the hockey team.'

'Oh,' I said, thinking of something. 'Oh, I have to tell you guys the funniest thing. So last night –' I looked over at Evan, but he was staring off, not listening. Evan's teammate Sebi had made a fool of himself at the party the previous night, pissing on the crowd next door from an upstairs window. Everyone laughed uproariously at the end of the story. I couldn't help laughing, too. It was funnier in the retelling.

Later, as the group disbanded and I started to wonder where Adam was, Evan grabbed me by the wrist.

'Ow. Jesus.'

'What the hell, Jules? That was embarrassing.'

I rubbed my wrist, though it didn't hurt that much. It was more the surprise. Evan had a look on his face. Not anger – disappointment. Scolding. *What the fuck is wrong with him?* I thought. After months of ignoring me, this was what I get? I snapped at him, then pushed through the living room. The bathroom door was locked. I made my way upstairs instead and found another bathroom door ajar. I locked it behind me, lowered the toilet lid, and sat down, pressing my palms into my closed eyes.

The night before, at the hockey party, Evan left me with his teammates and said he was going to get us another drink. That night they had played the last game of their season. Toward the end of the third period, Evan swooped down the wing and scored the winning goal. The team never got as far as the preseason polls had predicted, but the season ended on a happy note. They piled on Evan, thumping him on the back. He was only a sophomore; there was always next year.

In the living room of the hockey house, I glanced at my watch. He'd been gone for a while. It was late, hours after the Sebi incident, and the party had died down. I made my way into the kitchen, which led to the back porch, where they were keeping the keg. Someone had propped open the back door. A strong breeze swept through the kitchen, making music of the plastic cups scattered across the floor. Outside, the porch light illuminated the keg like a piece of scenery on a stage.

Evan was standing there, talking to a girl I didn't recognize. She wore a low-cut tank top, her blond hair dark at the roots. Trashy. Maybe she went to one of the community colleges near New Haven. Sometimes those girls crashed our parties. She was shivering. Evan removed his sweatshirt and draped it around her shoulders. She pulled it tight and smiled at him. He smiled back. She reached out and touched him on the forearm, and then –

'Evan,' I shouted from inside the kitchen. They both jumped, like they'd been caught at something. 'What are you doing?'

'Hey. Um, Julia,' he said, floundering. 'This is –'

'Are you ready to go? Let's go,' I said, turning on my heel.

Later, while we were lying in bed, he asked me why I was so mad. They had just been talking. She was dating another guy on the team. She had forgotten her jacket. Et cetera. He gave me an opening to explain myself. 'Jules, are you jealous? Is that it? Because –' But I cut him off. 'I'm not *jealous*,' I snapped. 'Of her? Please.'

I opened my eyes. I was in the bathroom in Adam's house, the sound of the party thumping below. Why was everything so difficult? One party, another party, and things kept going wrong between us. What gave Evan the right to be so judgmental, so *disappointed* in me? His teammate was the one who had acted like an idiot, who had broken at least one law. All I had done was repeat what I had witnessed. 'Tell the truth,' Adam liked to say at the magazine. 'The truth always makes for a more interesting story.' I looked in the mirror. Screw it. Maybe I didn't need to care so much about what Evan thought. What did he really know about me?

When I opened the door, there was another girl waiting outside. One of Adam's cooler, older friends. Probably an art or theater major. A messy bun atop her head, willowy limbs, a small tattoo inside her wrist. She winked at me like we were both in the know, using the upstairs bathroom.

'Julia?' Adam was down the hallway, pulling a door closed. His bedroom, I guessed. Probably where the other girl had just come from. 'Is everything okay?'

I wanted to cry, but didn't. 'Yeah. Everything's fine.'

He kept his hand on the doorknob, watching me carefully. I felt like he understood everything I was thinking, everything I yearned for. He had all the answers to all my questions. Adam pushed the door open and gestured at the room behind him. 'You want to come in for a minute?'

———

At the party in Brooklyn, I went back inside, in search of my coat. But when I turned into the hallway to leave, I slammed directly into the one person who could fix this black mood. The person who always managed to find me at exactly the right moments.

'Hey!' Adam said. 'Julia. Are you leaving already?'

'I was thinking about it.'

'Have a drink with me. Come on, I just got here.'

I let Adam lead me back into the kitchen. Abby shrieked when she saw him. They had been friends in college, too – she was friends with just about everyone – but she hadn't seen him since he graduated. 'Where have you been hiding?' she said, hitting him on the shoulder. Adam just winked and slung his arm around me. She raised an eyebrow at me. I shook my head: *just flirting,* nothing more. Abby knew that I had had a little crush on Adam in college, but I never told her what had happened between us that night. We chatted, and they caught up. Adam kept handing me drinks.

Little things. New intimacies. Slipping his hand down my back, pressing his hip against mine. Adam was debating with Jake about some recent development in the Lehman bankruptcy. They kept talking, talking. I couldn't follow the conversation, but it didn't matter. Adam was at my side, and I was certain I was the only thing he was thinking about. He never even bothered to say hello to the girls hosting the party.

After a while, Abby rested her head against Jake's shoulder. 'What do you think – should we get going?' she said. 'We have to get up early tomorrow.'

She said to me and Adam, 'We're meeting his parents for brunch.'

I raised my eyebrows. *We?* Parents? Brunch?

She shook her head to dismiss my implication, but again – that blush. They were a couple. A real couple, no matter what she said.

'Oh, shit,' Jake said. 'I forgot to tell you. My dad canceled. My mom thinks we should wait till he's back. She said maybe in a few weeks.'

Abby's smile wilted. 'Why?'

'Some business meeting, I guess. He's off in the Caribbean for something.'

I coughed, almost choking on my wine. It finally added up. Eleanor's rocketing ascent at the foundation.

Her power over Laurie. Her possessive smile at the sound of Henry's name. *We're very close.* An image of Henry and Eleanor under a dark sky and a tropical moon. Drinking Champagne, sex on smooth white sheets, the ocean crashing against the shore outside their villa. Tall palm trees dramatically lit from below. Each one of them an aphrodisiac to the other.

'Tough life,' Adam said heartily.

'Well,' Abby said, more subdued. 'We should go, anyway. It's late.'

The black mood descended again, magnified by the fact that I was by that point blazingly drunk. I couldn't believe it – *this* was what my life looked like? My best friend was sleeping with my secret ex, whose father was sleeping with my coworker. My boyfriend was ignoring me, in love with his job instead. And I was treading water in a pool of dead-end nothingness. What the hell had happened? When did it all go so wrong?

Adam got us a cab and told the driver to stop at my place first. It was the gentlemanly thing to do, but I knew what it meant. Adam lived alone. If he wanted to sleep with me, he would have brought me back to his place on the Upper West Side. The flirting meant nothing at the end of the night. I wasn't pretty or cool or charming or sophisticated enough. Everyone was moving forward, and I was getting left behind.

I was quiet and sullen, finally too drunk to conceal it. Adam noticed.

'You okay, Jules?'

'I'm *fine*. It's just . . . I don't know. Ugh.'

'What is it?'

'I don't know.'

'You can tell me.'

'God. Adam.' I snapped. 'This sucks. I'm all by myself. Completely alone. Everywhere I go.'

He reached for my hand. 'Don't say that. You have me. I'm right here.'

'I *don't* have you, though. I have this lousy boyfriend who doesn't give two shits about me because he's too busy with this fucking lumber deal.'

'Maybe it'll be over soon,' Adam said carefully. It wasn't the first time I had complained about Evan's devotion to his work. 'It can't last forever.'

'I mean, Jesus, the way he talks about it. It's like the universe revolves around this fucking middle-of-nowhere Canadian lumber company. Pacific WestCorp. It's so *important*. They're gonna make so much *money* off it. They're gonna be rich and famous. You know, I can't remember the last time he even asked me how my day was. How work is. None of it. He's an asshole. He doesn't think about anyone but himself.'

I was ranting, but I couldn't help myself. Abby and Jake, Henry and Eleanor. I couldn't complain about any of them, so my anger funneled toward Evan instead. *'WestCorp Timber is gonna make Spire more money than any deal on Wall Street.'* I imitated Evan's voice in a snide tone. *'People's heads are gonna turn.* Him and Michael Casey, at the top of the fucking world. Fuck all of it.'

The lights of Manhattan glittered up ahead. We were zooming across the bridge, the East River rippling below like black velvet.

'It's disgusting,' I added. The torrent wouldn't stop. 'They're so fucking arrogant. He's saying this trade is foolproof. It's like they didn't even notice what's been happening. How fucked up everything is. How screwed the rest of us are.'

Adam was silent, probably dreading the rest of the ride. Even through my drunken haze, I saw what an idiot I was, complaining about my boyfriend, like *that* was a turn-on. Great. He was never going to call me again.

But then he slid close and put his arm around my waist. I closed my eyes and turned my face away, trying not to cry. The cab accelerated into a curve on the FDR, pulling me into the corner. 'Jules,' he said softly. 'Jules, it's okay.' Adam took my chin in his hand and turned my face toward him, and then he kissed me.

We broke away a moment later, pausing. Then we kept going. He slid his hand under my shirt, and I felt him go hard through his jeans. He kissed my neck, ran his fingers through my hair. The solid heft of his body, the pressure of affection – I'd been missing this for so long. The feeling of someone else's hands showing me what to do next. My body had almost forgotten how to do this.

Too soon, the cab had stopped. 'Miss?' the driver said.

'I –' I stopped, looked at Adam. Both of us were breathing hard.

He glanced down at his lap. 'You should go in, Jules. It's late.'

'I don't have to. You know.'

'Let's just say goodnight for now. I'll call you in the morning, okay? I promise.'

He kissed me good-bye, less urgent and more tender. Then he reached across the seat and opened the door. I watched the cab pull away, heading west toward the park. I shivered and pulled my coat tighter around me.

When I lay in bed that night, next to an already sleeping Evan, I was aware of something. After Jake Fletcher, I had been racked with guilt. It had happened the summer before freshman year of college, while we were on Nantucket with our families. Rob was my boyfriend at the time. I didn't have to face him for another two weeks afterward, which gave me time to collect myself, to replay the memory – Jake and I, high and drunk, sneaking down to the nighttime beach, him tugging down my shorts, me not wanting him to stop, so helpless in the face of his attention – over and over and over, until eventually it became something that happened to a different version of me. I decided, on the ferry ride home, letting the wind tangle my hair and the salt spray sting my eyes, that I didn't have to tell Rob. It was a stupid mistake, but it was just sex. As soon as it was over, when Jake rolled away from me and I was aware again of the cold sand sticking to the back of my legs, I realized that it was never going to happen again. The guilt formed a high wall in my mind, and the memory lived behind it, drying and shriveling with age. Sometimes I almost managed to forget it entirely.

But this, with Adam. The feeling that washed over me as I lay there next to Evan – it wasn't guilt. It was more like a beginning than an ending. A book cracked open to the very first page. How could I feel guilty about something that was so clearly meant to happen?

PART II

CHAPTER 7

Evan

In mid-November, Michael stopped by my desk.

'You're coming with me and the rest of the team to the conference in Vegas. The flight is at five. Go home and get your stuff and take a car to the airport, terminal four. Travel is e-mailing your ticket now.'

I glanced at my watch – 2:34 p.m. – and started shoving things into my bag. 'So I'll see you –' I started to say to Roger, but he had his headphones in and refused to meet my eyes. Uptown, I packed as fast as I could, then sprinted down the stairs to the waiting town car. I called Julia from the car and told her I wouldn't be able to make dinner – it was her birthday that night, but she seemed to understand, which was a relief. They were calling my name on the PA when I ran up to the gate.

'Right over there, Mr Peck,' a chirpy flight attendant said, pointing at the remaining empty seat in the business-class cabin, next to Roger.

'Too bad,' Roger said without looking up from his

BlackBerry. 'Thought this train was going to leave the station without you.'

'Sorry to disappoint you.'

'Sir?' the flight attendant said, offering a tray with a flute of Champagne. 'Just let me know if I can get you anything else. We'll be taking off shortly.'

The flight attendant was cute and perky and available, exactly Roger's type, and I expected him to make some crack about it. But he kept his eyes locked on his phone, his mouth shut. Roger had been bragging about this for weeks. Spire was sending a small team to a global investing conference in Las Vegas, and Steve, the head of our macro group, had been so impressed with Roger's work that he invited him along, too. A first-year analyst had never gone to one of these conferences before. You didn't get to jump the line like this, not unless you were exceptional. My stomach had churned at the thought. Well, I was working on a deal that would dwarf a trip to Vegas soon enough. Let Roger brag all he wanted.

But there I was. Ruining Roger's week, to boot. I counted six people from Spire, scattered through the cabin: Steve, Brad, and Chuck, all from Spire's macro group, plus Roger, Michael, and myself. This had nothing to do with my work, but I supposed that Michael would fill me in eventually. I finished my Champagne, settled in, and closed my eyes. Business class. I could get used to this.

★

A hand on my shoulder shook me awake, and Brad's face came into focus. I'd only spoken to him in passing before. He was Korean American, in his thirties, had a PhD in applied mathematics from MIT, a mind like a thousand-horsepower engine. He'd made the company an enormous amount of money over the years.

'So here's the deal,' Brad said, addressing me and Roger while he scanned his phone screen. 'Travel tried to get new rooms, but the hotel is sold out because of the conference. So Evan, you're going to be in Roger's room.'

'The hell?' Roger snarled. 'Are you serious?'

'Suck it up, sweetheart. Chuck and I have to share a suite, too. Michael took Steve's suite, and Steve is taking mine.'

'There better be separate beds,' Roger said. When Brad left, Roger finally snapped. 'What the fuck, Peck? Why are you even here?'

'I don't know. You heard it. Michael only told me a few hours ago.'

Roger looked like he wanted to punch me in the face. The plane's engines hummed in the background. 'Whatever it is y'all are up to,' he said, clenching his fists on his armrests, 'you sure have a way of pissing other people off.'

———————

More than a month earlier, as the market panic was reaching its climax, I'd put the final touches on the WestCorp deal. The numbers were dazzling. Michael had said it right: this was a check just waiting to be cashed. Early one October morning, after working straight through the night, I was finally done. The very last piece was in place. This was the deal that would permanently cement Spire's dominance, during the most volatile moment of our lifetime – and I was right in the middle of it. I left the folder on Michael's chair and went for a walk in the cool dawn, stopping at a bench in an empty Times Square with a coffee and Danish in hand, watching the city wake, the taxis and pedestrians flowing up and down the streets, the conclusion vibrating through me like a note struck on a piano.

Back in the office that morning, I shaved and changed into the spare shirt I kept in my desk drawer. I sat, calmly, waiting for the call from Michael. But morning passed, then afternoon, without a word from him. I went past his office around 8:00 p.m., but his door was closed.

Nothing the following day, either. Or the day after that. When I couldn't stand it any longer, I went by his office. He ignored me while I hovered in the doorway. I cleared my throat. 'Michael. Just checking – what's the latest on the WestCorp deal?'

That got his attention. He turned to look at me.

'Something's come up,' he said. 'It's on hold until I iron out a few more details.'

'Oh. Okay. So –'

'So I'll let you know.' He turned back to his computer.

Panic rose as I walked back to my desk. What did he mean? Iron *what* out? But there had been a finality in his tone. I was just a low-level analyst, after all. He didn't owe me any explanation. These kinds of things happened. Deals were called off all the time, for all sorts of reasons.

But it made me feel sick, physically sick, the thought of so many days and nights disappearing with nothing to show for it. Who was I? What was I doing there? I'd always had an answer before. I was a boy from British Columbia. A student. A hockey player, most of all. When graduation erased that, I found a new scaffolding. I was an analyst at Spire Management; that was the life I was building for myself. Everything else that was fading into the background – Julia, my friends – was made bearable by this. The sureness of my work and the nearness of success. Without that, I started to come loose.

My solution: I'd keep busy, so busy I wouldn't have time to think. I jumped at every assignment, tried to fill the hours, insurance against the worst outcome. Roger and the other analysts must have sensed the change – my constant volunteering, joining them for lunch when before I'd been too busy. Julia could sense it, too. She was cooler and quieter than ever in the moments we overlapped at home. She sat there looking at me, but her mind was somewhere else. It was like she could tell how desperately I was faking my way through it, and it disgusted her.

Until just a few days before the trip to Las Vegas, when something had changed. I got home early and found Julia standing at the stove. Stirring a pot, flipping through a magazine, one bare foot lifted to scratch the back of her calf. 'It smells amazing,' I said. When she turned, it was the old Julia who was looking at me: the spill of blond hair over her shoulder, her eyes crinkled at the corners from her smile. 'There'll be enough for both of us,' she offered. After we ate, I led her into the bedroom. The sex was good, not the best ever, but it was what I had needed: the two of us, finally in the same place again. It was so sad that this tiny moment of tenderness was even worth remarking on.

The next night, I stopped by McGuigan's with the guys after work. Just for a drink, one drink. It was a weeknight, and I wanted to get home early again. To get things back on track with Julia. I sat at the bar, waiting for Maria. I was going to end this flirtation, or whatever it was, before it went any further. I'd slip in a mention of *my girlfriend,* which would do the trick. A clean break.

Maria came over and drew a pint of Guinness without needing to ask. Part of me wished that we'd gotten our chance – that I'd made a move one of those late nights, saying good-bye on the sidewalk outside the bar, a one-time slip that could be forgiven. I sipped my beer, feeling nostalgic. I'd finish the drink before I said anything.

Another man came into the bar and sat a few stools down, a tanned guy in a leather jacket. Maria said something to him, then poured him a generous whiskey. I lifted my glass to get her attention. She came back over and placed another pint of Guinness on the bar, then said,

'This is it for me tonight. Cathy'll take care of your tab.'

'Where are you going? Actually, I wanted to talk to you about –'

'I'm off early,' she said. 'I've got plans.'

A minute later, she emerged from the back with her coat on. The guy in the leather jacket stood and gestured at her to go ahead. They passed me on their way out, and as an afterthought, Maria turned on her heel.

'Oops. I should introduce you. Evan, this is Wyeth. Wyeth, Evan.'

I was used to towering over other people, but Wyeth was the same height as me. 'Hey. Maria's favorite customer,' I said, extending a hand and forcing a smile.

'Hey. Maria's boyfriend,' he said.

Maria smiled, then tugged on Wyeth's sleeve. 'See you later, Evan,' she called over her shoulder. Through the window, I watched them pause on the sidewalk. Maria stood on her toes and kissed him, for a long time.

I sat back down, disoriented. Cathy, the other bartender, came over a few minutes later. 'Another?' she said, pointing at my empty pint glass. I shook my head. 'I'll have a Scotch. Straight up.' The other analysts were going out to a club in the Meatpacking District where Roger knew the promoter, and I went along. We got a table and ordered bottle service. A group of lithe, glittery women floated toward us. I poured myself a vodka on the rocks, one after another. This feeling could only be scoured out by something strong. Music – deep house with a thumping beat – vibrated through every pore. After a while I looked up and realized a petite Asian girl was sitting on my lap. She leaned in and said something inaudible. *'What?'* I shouted back, over the music. She leaned in again and this time licked the edge of my ear-lobe, and finally – finally – my mind went empty. We wound up pressed against a wall at the edge of the room. Her tongue in my mouth, her tiny body, my hands sliding up her sequined miniskirt, it was all I was aware of. I wanted this nameless girl more than anything I'd wanted before. I'd fuck her right there in public if I had to.

The next day, I got up from my desk several times to go retch in the bathroom. *You asshole,* I thought, staring at my sweaty and sallow reflection under the fluorescent lights. I'd managed to tear myself away from the girl and get a cab before any of my coworkers noticed. I passed out on the futon at home. At an early morning hour, I dragged myself to the sink for a glass of water and took a scalding shower. Eventually I crawled into bed next to Julia, my hair wet, feeling like a teenager sneaking in after curfew.

Two black town cars were waiting for us at McCarran. They whisked us straight to the expensive steak-and-red-wine restaurant in the hotel, our luggage sent up to our rooms without us. A private room in the back of the restaurant was walled in by ceiling-high racks of wine bottles. Chuck and Brad and Roger started getting drunk and rowdy. Steve was supervising in a bemused way, and I was just trying to roll with it. I drank my wine slowly, still feeling my bender from a few days earlier. Michael was distracted, answering e-mails, stepping out to take calls. When he left the room to take his third call of the night, Chuck rolled his eyes and said, 'Why the hell is he even here?'

Roger shot me an accusatory look.

'I mean,' Chuck continued, looking at Steve for an answer, 'doesn't he have better things to be doing? Like running the company?'

Steve shrugged. 'He's the boss. He can do what he wants.'

'Probably just wants to get laid,' Brad said sullenly. Chuck hooted in laughter, and Roger joined in. Chuck was slightly older, had a fiancée, owned rather than rented, but in every other way, he and Roger were practically twins. They were, of course, hitting it off.

Michael walked back in, eyes still glued to his screen. In that moment, between songs on the restaurant speakers, the clicking of Michael's BlackBerry keys was the only sound to be heard. Chuck, in a fit of flushed boldness, balled up his napkin and lobbed it across the table at Michael's shoulder.

Michael looked up, as surprised as the rest of us.

'Hey, Michael,' Chuck said. 'I know you're the CEO, but you're in Vegas, man. Drink up. We're going out tonight.'

Michael stared at him. 'What did you say?'

'I said, "Drink up."'

Silence. Then Michael broke out in a smug grin. 'You're right,' he said finally. 'Someone get me a real drink.'

Chuck hooted again, calling for the waitress to bring a bottle of their best Scotch, and I relaxed a little. Michael drank a double in one smooth swig, then another after that. A limo was idling outside, waiting to take us to a high-end nightclub where Chuck had reserved a table. In the limo, I sat next to Michael, who kept refilling my glass and clapping me on the knee when I downed my Scotch straight, in one macho gulp.

Liquid courage helped. I was careful to keep my tone light, not ruining the mood. 'Michael,' I said. 'I just wanted to ask, before everything starts tomorrow – what's, uh, what's the agenda for this weekend?'

'Oh, you know. Keynotes and panels, networking, the usual. Most of it will be interminably dull. These things always are.'

'Right. So I've heard.' I nodded. 'But the focus is on global macro, isn't it? I'm just wondering if there's anything you wanted me to – or what the angle . . . or I guess takeaway, you could call it –'

Michael clapped me on the knee again, refilling my glass. 'Evan, don't worry. You're asking why I invited you, aren't you? Just watch and listen, and you'll see. You could learn a lot these next few days.'

We pulled up at the entrance of another hotel-casino

monolith. Chuck led the way down the long, plushly carpeted hallway toward the club. The Scotch in the limo had been too much for me. The night began to blur and spin when we entered the club. The whole room seemed to rattle from the collective frenzy: drinking, dancing, snorting, vibrating. Women in thongs and pasties shimmied on platforms around the dance floor. High up in his booth, the DJ lifted his arms, and the crowd responded with a deafening roar. Smoke and confetti poured from the ceiling. Our waitress was wearing a tight scoop-neck minidress that displayed her cleavage, which bounced vigorously whenever she mixed a drink in the cocktail shaker. I had shot after shot handed to me. I was drunker than I'd been in months, drunker even than a few nights ago in Meatpacking. I had long slipped past the point of enjoyment. What time was it? Would this night ever end? Nothing seemed to exist except for this club, the gyrations of the people around me. A slow-motion orgy: Michael getting closer and closer to a blond woman on the banquette, Chuck kissing a woman — then two at once — sitting on his lap. Steve had turned in earlier, his wedding ring glinting in the strobe lights. Brad had his hand at the small of our waitress's back, his eyes traveling toward her chest. Roger was off somewhere else.

Our limo driver was, miraculously, still outside when I got up to leave. I pulled the hotel-room key card out of my pocket, where the room number had been written on the card's paper envelope: 3605. Back in the hotel, I stumbled toward the elevator bank and leaned my forehead against the cool marble wall while I waited. It felt so good. I could have fallen asleep there. I found myself wandering down a long hallway, red carpets and golden wallpaper. Such a long hallway. How had I gotten there? I studied the paper envelope again: 3605. I looked up, and there I was – our room at last.

I swiped my card, and the light turned green, but the door banged abruptly and wouldn't open more than an inch. I pulled the door closed and tried again. The light turned green, and I pushed the door open, but again it banged up against something. I squinted, trying to right my vision, and saw that the security flip bar had been latched into place.

I propped the door open with my foot and shouted through the opening, 'Roger. Roger! Come on, it's me.'

Silence at first, and then came the sounds of female giggling. 'Ocupado, amigo,' Roger said from within the room.

The door closed with a bang, and I slumped against the wall, my legs splayed out across the floor. Sexiled. I needed some kind of plan. Focus. I closed my eyes. My head jerked up – had I fallen asleep? – and I slapped my forehead several times. I hated being this drunk. I couldn't stay out in the hallway. Everyone from Spire was staying on this floor. I couldn't let them see me like this. No way.

Back at the elevator bank, I pushed the Down button. I'd explain myself at the front desk. Maybe they'd had a cancellation. Or I'd take a cab to one of the motels I'd seen between the airport and the Strip. They had to have something, a bed where I could sleep for a few hours before morning came.

A small ding sounded as the car arrived. I kept my eyes down and didn't see the dark-suited figure striding out until we nearly collided.

'Evan? Whoa, what are you doing?'

It was Chuck, looking rumpled and sweaty but in better shape than I was, and thoroughly pleased with how the night had gone.

'Yeah. Hi – hey, Chuck. How are you?'

'How are *you*? What, you didn't get enough? Going back out for more?'

'No.' I shook my head with effort. 'I'm locked out. Roger is – he has . . . company.'

Chuck laughed. 'Shit. Well, come on, you can crash in our room for now. Roger's gonna be done soon. Trust me, he's paying her by the hour.'

I followed Chuck to his suite at the other end of the hallway. Even through my blurring vision, I could see that it was enormous. Bigger than any New York apartment I'd ever seen. Steps led down to a sunken living room with floor-to-ceiling windows. The skyline sparkled against the desert night. I could make out a bar on one side of the living room and a huge soaking tub on the other. A spiral staircase, half hidden in the darkness, twisted up to a second floor.

'Nice, huh?' Chuck said, his voice echoing in the room. 'Would've had the place to myself, too. The beds are spoken for, but I think there's a foldout in that corner near the kitchen. Brad's still out. He'll be back soon.'

Chuck's footsteps retreated up the spiral stairs. I found the bathroom, flipped on the light, and hurled the contents of my stomach into the toilet. I paused, gulping for air, then puked again. After the nausea receded, I splashed water on my face and rinsed my mouth. I felt better. More in control. I'd sleep a little, get back to my room, be fine in the morning. Hungover, but fine.

Something woke me. The sound of the air-conditioning turning on or off. I'd passed out on the couch without bothering to unfold it. I was shivering, and I had a kink in my neck.

It was tempting to stay there, to close my eyes and let the drunken fog tug me back under. I knew I ought to get up, go back to my room, get some real sleep. In just a few minutes. My mind swam with the soothing hum of the AC.

Then, how much later I didn't know, there was the sound of laughter and high heels on the marble floor. The high-pitched, breathy voice of a woman.

The lights went on. Suddenly I was wide awake, my heart hammering and blood rushing to my head. Brad was back, with company. I felt a preemptive embarrassment at being discovered here.

There were more than two voices. One woman and another. Brad muttering something. Then:

'I'm going to have a drink. Ladies?' Michael.

The two women chorused a yes.

The sound of liquid splashing into glasses, bodies sinking into leather sofas. I turned onto my stomach and peered over the arm of the couch. My view was mostly obscured by the dining table and the oak-paneled bar. They hadn't seen me, and the window for making myself known without humiliation was closing rapidly. No, I realized. It had closed already.

Brad was on one couch, Michael and the two women on another. One woman, the blond from the club, was hunched over the glass-topped coffee table. When she sat up, she handed a rolled-up dollar bill to Michael.

'This is good shit, Brad,' Michael said, wiping the coke from his nose.

Brad was silent. It looked like he was reading something on his phone.

'So,' Michael said. 'What do you ladies think of my friend here?'

The second woman – a redhead – giggled. 'I think he's handsome.'

'I think *you're* handsome,' the blond purred, nestling up to Michael.

'I think you have better taste than your friend.' He ran his hand up her bare arm. I grimaced. She was at least thirty years younger than he was.

The redhead stood up, dress slipped off her shoulder to expose a lacy black bra, and went to the other couch. She snuggled up to Brad, but Brad just kept his eyes on his phone.

'So what do you guys do?' one of the women asked. 'You must be big shots with a room like this.'

'You should see my room, honey. We'll take a field trip later.'

'We're in finance,' Brad said abruptly. 'Hedge funds.'

Silence, then one ventured, 'Hedge funds. What does that mean?'

'It's a way of investing designed to mitigate risk,' Brad said, alert again. 'Hedging your bets. At any given point in time, we're betting on a number of different scenarios, so no matter which way the market goes, we're protected. So an example would be – if I met a woman out at a club, but I wasn't sure how she felt about me, maybe I'd bring her friend along, too. See? I've hedged my bets. In case one says no, I have a backup.'

Michael snorted. 'Brad's a nerd, in case you couldn't tell. Don't get him started. But this is boring. Let's talk about something else.'

'Actually.' Brad's voice was rising. 'Actually, I don't think it's boring at all. It's interesting, in fact. I was going through the books this week, and there was some *fascinating* stuff in there.'

'Not now. We have company.' Michael slid his hand up the blond's skirt and kissed her neck. She was giggling and blushing. Her friend attempted the same with Brad, but he pushed her away impatiently.

'I think we do, Michael. I think we want to talk about this right now. We can do it alone, or we can do it in front of these two. Up to you.'

Michael laughed. 'Ladies, I'm sorry. I apologize for him. No manners at all.' He tucked several crisp-looking bills into the blond's dress. 'Some other time.'

The high heels obediently clacked their way back across the marble foyer, and the doors opened and closed a moment later. Michael turned to Brad.

'You mind telling me what the fuck that was about?'

'I need to talk to you about this, Michael. Right now. We have a big problem on our hands.'

'What? For God's sake, what is it?'

Brad took a deep breath. 'I was looking at the books, getting ready for the conference. I noticed something wasn't lining up. So I went deeper into the numbers, and I saw we have a lot of exposure – a *lot* of exposure – in one particular area. Which I'd heard nothing about. The lumber markets.'

'And?'

'Do you know about this? All the money we have tied up in lumber futures?'

'Of course I know about it. I'm running this company. It's my deal.'

'Well, then explain it to me. Because I'm sure as hell not seeing it. The housing market is the worst it's ever been. And yet we're betting that the demand for lumber is going to go *up?* For there to be massive, imminent *growth?*'

'Correct.'

'What the hell, Michael?' Brad stood up and started pacing. 'This isn't some murky situation where we don't know what the economy is going to look like next year. We *do* know. No one in their right mind is going to be building.'

'In North America, maybe. But before you get any more worked up, Brad, I suggest you look at the bigger picture. We're not betting on there being demand here.'

'Where, then?'

'China.'

'*China?* Are you serious? We have no idea what the Chinese are going to do *tomorrow,* let alone next year. Since when do we make predictions about their market with *any* kind of confidence?'

Michael chuckled. 'Brad. Are you sure this isn't some kind of personal animosity? I know the Koreans aren't big fans of the Chinese, but –'

'Stop. Just stop. Does Kleinman know about this?'

'It doesn't matter. Kleinman put me in charge, and frankly it would look bad for him to be overseeing every little deal while he's in Washington.'

'Every *little* deal? Michael, are you even listening? Our exposure on this is *massive.* If it goes the wrong way, we are totally fucked.'

'You're getting hysterical about something that's going to make us a lot of money. Will you listen for a minute, *please?*'

Brad stood in place, quivering with anger. He seemed on the verge of shouting, but he clamped his mouth shut and crossed his arms over his chest.

'Thank you. Sit down, too. You're acting like a lunatic. We've been working on this position for a long time. Months and months. Demand from the Chinese market for North American lumber has already gone up this year. Every single one of our predictions has played out, and I guarantee you that demand is going to continue to skyrocket in 2009. Our calls on WestCorp are going to make you a very rich man.'

My mind was racing. So the deal wasn't dead. Not at all. It was very much alive.

'What I don't get,' Brad said, 'what I don't understand, Michael, is that if this bet is such a sure thing, why isn't everyone else all over this? We don't specialize in this. There are a dozen shops that know lumber better than we do.'

'Because it's impossible to make any real money selling anything to the Chinese, that's why. You know that. The tariffs and taxes eat into your profits like a parasite. It's byzantine. The only way to make money is to find your way through that system.'

Brad started pacing again. Michael sat back on the couch calmly, waiting.

Brad wheeled around to look at Michael. 'Your trip to China in August. For the Olympics, right? Did you go to a single event? Or was that all just a cover?'

'Of course I did. Swimming, rowing, whatever. Let me tell you, you meet all sorts of people at the Olympics. All sorts of politicians and government flunkies who are just so *eager* to rub shoulders with us Americans. The people in that country love us. They finally got a taste of capitalism, and now they can't get enough. They know how much better things are over here. They'll do just about anything to catch up.'

'Jesus Christ. Are we talking bribery, Michael? Did you bribe the fucking Chinese *government?*'

On the plane ride that day, we had encountered a particularly nasty bout of turbulence. I gripped the armrests, my jaw clenched. I *hated* turbulence. I kept counting to ten, over and over, waiting for the plane to steady again. Surely it would stop when I got to ten. That's exactly how I felt at that moment.

'Give me a little credit,' Michael said. But before I could exhale, he continued. 'Bribery. It's such an unsubtle word. You can wipe that sneer off your face. I didn't *bribe* the Chinese government. We worked out an arrangement that was mutually beneficial.'

'What arrangement?'

'Sit down. You're making yourself all agitated.'

'*What* arrangement, Michael?'

'The appropriate Chinese authorities are now inclined to look favorably upon lumber imports from certain Canadian companies. Those imports won't be subject to the usual taxes and tariffs. When WestCorp sells their lumber to Chinese buyers, they'll keep one hundred percent of the revenue.'

'And what are they getting in return?'

Michael sighed. He seemed bored by the conversation. 'WestCorp wanted the Chinese to drop the trade barriers.

The Chinese wanted a few favors that some highly placed WestCorp executives were, luckily, able to grant.'

'*What favors?*'

'Like I said. The Chinese love us. They love our lives. They love North America. They want to come here, to live here, to buy homes here – well, not *here* here, not Las Vegas, this place is a hellhole. But Vancouver? Toronto? That's a different story. These businessmen and bureaucrats, now they've got money to spare, but the one thing they still can't buy is a normal life. They want their kids to be like ours. To go to Ivy League schools. To have good careers. They need visas. And Canadian immigration moves like molasses. WestCorp was able to help them out. Speed things up through back channels. They have something we want. We have something they want. It's really not so complicated.'

'And you went to Beijing to make this happen. You decided to put the entire company at risk for this deal. I can't *believe* this.'

'Yes, I did. And I would do it again. I don't need to tell you how dismal things are. How pathetic our returns are this year. How much worse it's going to get. Do you really want to go back to New York and tell half the company that they're going to lose their jobs? China is booming. They need lumber, and the Canadians have a glut they need to unload. We're just providing liquidity. We're making a market. We applied a little pressure to make it happen, but it's happening, and it's working.'

Brad was silent for a long time.

'You're not going to be able to keep this quiet much longer, Michael,' he said at last. 'Pretty soon someone else is going to notice it, too, someone besides me, and they'll start asking questions.'

'Maybe. But what they'll notice is how much money we're making. And what they'll ask is why they didn't think of this earlier. Does anyone really care how you get from point A to point B? Did you hear a single complaint from a single banker cashing his checks during the last five years? And we're not stupid. We've been discreet for a reason. When people finally notice, the proof will be there. The profits will be there. I'm not going to apologize for doing my job.'

'You keep saying "we." Who is we?'

'Me and Peck, the analyst. That's it. A few people have pitched in occasionally, but they never really knew what they were working on.'

'And does Peck know about the arrangement you have going?'

I closed my eyes and felt an insane rage – all of it directed at Roger. Most of me realized that this was ridiculous. Roger was the least of my concerns. But were it not for him, I would have been asleep and blissfully ignorant. Yes, I'd had my suspicions along the way. The trip to China. The overheard phone call. But I'd decided, a while earlier, to trust that Michael had a plan. He was the boss. He wasn't going to do anything *illegal*. I kept my head down and did my job. It had worked, up until that moment.

'He knows I went to China,' Michael said. 'He doesn't know what I did there. I picked him for a reason. He keeps things to himself. And he's ambitious, too. He wants it to succeed. I can tell. He's perfect for this.'

'Michael, come on. He's – what? – twenty-three years old? These analysts go out drinking every night. They can't keep a secret.'

'He's different. And we have an insurance policy on him.'

'How?'

'He's Canadian. Which the WestCorp guys loved, by the way. But his visa is contingent on his remaining in our employ. If he puts this deal in jeopardy, we'll be talking layoffs. Visas don't come cheap. He'd be the first to go. So it would behoove him to keep his mouth shut.'

I could make out a green pinprick of light from the smoke detector on the ceiling above me. The rage had turned into panic. A stinging rash spread across my chest, down my arms, and under my shirt. Breathe, I reminded myself. Breathe.

'Fucking hell, Michael. This is your mess. Okay? I don't want anything to do with it. And I'd like you to leave now, if you don't *mind*.'

'You're the one who brought this up,' Michael said, standing from the couch, tugging his cuffs straight. 'I didn't ask you to get involved. And Kleinman didn't ask you to be his watchdog. I'm going to bed.' The door opened, there was a pause, and Michael said: 'And I hope you don't have trouble sleeping, because I certainly won't.'

★

'All right, Peck?'

Chuck cuffed me hard on the back. We were at the breakfast buffet outside the conference room, where the day's first panel was about to begin. Chuck popped an enormous strawberry into his mouth and winked.

When I finally returned to my room, I'd lain in bed for the next three hours, jittery and unable to sleep, while Roger snored loudly on the other bed. I'd taken a long shower, had already drunk several cups of coffee, but it didn't help. My mind was like a helium balloon. I tried to concentrate on the men on stage who were holding forth on the euro. A glossy pamphlet promised several more panels like this one before the day was out. The bland normalcy of it contradicted everything that had happened the previous night.

The conference broke for lunch around noon. On my way out, I felt a hand grab my elbow.

'I need you to do something for me,' Michael said.

Did he know? But how would he know? I followed him out of the conference center, back to the hotel elevators. Up in Michael's suite, I had to shield my eyes from the sun, blasting in full strength through the wide windows.

Michael disappeared around the corner. This room was even bigger than Chuck and Brad's. Plush cream carpeting, a dazzling glass chandelier, an urn on the hall table overflowing with tropical vines and flowers. Michael returned holding a slim leather briefcase. Black, brand new, with a small combination lock built into the top. He handed it to me. It was surprisingly light.

'I want you to walk this over to the Venetian,' he said. 'Bring this to a Mr Wenjian Chan. He's a guest there. Walk, don't take a cab. It's important that you hand it to Chan directly. Not to the concierge. Tell him you're there on my behalf. Okay?'

What had I been thinking, trusting Michael all this time? Of course he didn't care about me. He didn't give a shit.

'It's a short walk,' Michael said. 'You'll be back in time for the next panel.'

He turned and disappeared around the corner. I stood there, unsure what to do. I wanted to shout after him, tell him that I knew. Drop the briefcase and walk away forever. But I'd never do that. It must have been why Michael picked me. He saw it from the start – from the very first time I walked into his office. I wasn't brave. I never was. Obeying orders was just about the only thing I knew how to do.

At the Venetian, a young Asian girl opened the door. She inclined her head and gestured me inside. She spoke in Mandarin but stopped when she saw the look on my face.

'Michael Casey?'

'No. No, I'm Evan Peck. I work with Michael.'

'Ah. Mr Peck. My mistake. Please, come this way.' Her English was smooth and flawless, with no more of an accent than mine. She had a round and dewy face, and couldn't be more than a teenager.

I followed her down a hallway to a large sitting room.

An older man with silver hair gazed steadily at the view of the desert through the window, indifferent to the luxury of the suite, to the Champagne chilling on ice, to the mirrored walls. He turned toward me.

'Michael Casey?' He had a thick accent.

I shook my head. My shirt, soaked with sweat from the walk under the scorching noonday sun, started to chill in the air-conditioning. The girl cut in, in rapid Mandarin. The man kept his eyes on me while they spoke, then he smiled. The girl turned back to me with a respectful tilt of her head. 'This is my father, Wenjian Chan. He was expecting to speak to Mr Casey. He has asked me to stay and translate.' She paused, waiting for me to nod. I did.

'Thank you,' she continued. 'Forgive our urgency, but he asks whether he may please have the briefcase you are delivering on behalf of Mr Casey now.'

She took it from me and laid it gently on the coffee table. Her father put on reading glasses and spun the combination lock. It opened with a pop. Chan removed a slim manila folder and scanned each page in the folder carefully. Several minutes later, Chan looked up and spoke to his daughter. It was clear from his tone that he was satisfied.

The girl smiled at me. 'Thank you. My father is very pleased with this. Please convey our gratitude to Mr Casey.' She held out her arm and started to lead me to the door when Chan interrupted, barking at her.

She stiffened and turned red, then shook her head at her father. Chan was pointing at me, his voice almost at a shout.

She started speaking, but he cut her off, insistent. My heart started thudding like a muscle gone loose. The daughter drew a deep breath, glancing sideways at her father.

'My father is very pleased with the help you have offered to us. And now that you have helped us with these papers' – she was so quiet I could barely hear – 'he wonders if you might offer us help in the future, too.'

'I'm sorry?' I said. Chan was chattering excitedly. My mouth had gone dry. Michael hadn't said anything about this.

She turned a deeper shade of red. 'I'll be applying to college next fall, here in America. My father is aware that you might have useful connections. You went to Yale, yes? You know many people there?' She took another breath and added, 'He says that he would like to – as you say – keep in touch.'

The words echoed through my head. *Keep in touch.* I began walking back to the hotel, then I broke into a run, sweat dripping down my forehead and into my eyes. I had to talk to Michael. So they knew where I'd gone to college. What else did they know about me? Just exactly how far did this thing go? What were they expecting from me?

But at the conference, Michael was nowhere in sight. I ducked into a corner and dialed his number. It went directly to voice mail. I sent a frantic e-mail. I tried calling again, but his phone remained off. I refreshed my e-mail. Nothing.

The afternoon panel was about to begin, and the others were drifting back into the ballroom. Chuck waved me over. I was the last one to file into our row and wound up sitting next to Roger. He didn't seem affected by the night before. Bright-eyed, cleanly shaved, popping a stick of gum. His collar crisp and perfectly white. He raised an eyebrow, taking me in. 'You look like shit,' he said.

The panel was about to begin. There was an empty seat in the middle of the row, where Michael was supposed to be. I craned my neck, scanning the entrances to the ballroom. I had a sudden, dizzying fear.

'Oh,' Roger said. 'Who are you looking for? Michael, your boyfriend? He had to leave. Just went to the airport. He's flying back to New York right now.'

Chapter 8

Julia

I was standing in our tiny kitchen, humming to myself, stirring a pot of pasta and a bubbling skillet of sauce. It was Adam's recipe. He was always giving me things like this – scraps of knowledge, bits of adulthood. I wanted to make it just so I could tell him later that I'd done it.

I heard the door open, then the jangling of keys and the thunk of a briefcase dropped to the floor. 'What's this?' Evan said. He was home earlier than usual. I don't think he'd ever seen me use the stove before. 'Are you making dinner?'

He looked so disbelieving that I smiled. 'Pasta. There'll be enough for both of us.'

'It smells amazing.' He hovered a few inches away. A year earlier, he would have slipped his arms around my waist. 'I'm starving.'

We ate together on the futon. When I finished my pasta and looked up, Evan was watching me. He took my hand and pulled me to my feet. I let myself follow him.

What I felt for Adam was spilling over into the rest of my life, like some blissful pharmaceutical. When Evan was on top of me, I stared at the ceiling. I didn't want to have sex with him, but I also didn't mind. I felt easy and calm about it.

After, as Evan was catching his breath, he turned to me.

'It's your birthday on Thursday,' he said.

'Yup.'

'We should go out.'

I'd been counting on Evan having to work, leaving me free to do something with Adam instead. 'Oh. Okay,' I said.

'Unless you already have plans?'

'No. Uh, no plans. That sounds good.'

'I'll make a reservation somewhere. I'm glad I remembered.' He kissed me on the cheek, then rolled over and fell asleep.

This was part of the problem. Evan remembered my birthday; he stayed faithful to me; he paid his share of the rent on time. There had been no dramatic betrayals. Instead there was a long stretch of absence. Where I saw an accumulating string of rejections, lonely nights and questions unasked, Evan probably saw a normal relationship. He upheld his end of the bargain. He checked the boxes required of him. And if there were no further boxes to check, he probably assumed he'd done everything he needed to do.

On Thursday morning, two dozen red roses awaited me at the office, with a card that read: 'Thinking of you today – Adam.' I propped the card next to my computer. Laurie saw the flowers when she came in, paused briefly, but didn't ask about them. My phone rang later that morning, my sister calling.

'Julia?' Elizabeth said. 'Hey, happy birthday!'

'Why are you whispering?'

'I'm in the library. Studying for midterms. How's the day been?'

'Pretty good. I'm at work, so . . . you know. Boring old Thursday so far.'

'Are you and Evan going out tonight?'

'Yeah.'

'Somewhere good?'

'I hope so. He was supposed to make the reservation.'

'How's he doing?'

'He's fine.'

She was quiet for a moment. 'Jules?' she finally said. 'Is everything okay?'

'It's fine. I don't know. Yeah.'

'What's wrong?'

But that was the thing. I didn't want to talk about Evan or what was wrong; I wanted to talk about what was finally *right*. Having to muffle the good news – Adam, this new turn my life had taken – was so annoying. I couldn't do or say what I wanted, not even on my birthday. I inhaled the thick, sweet scent of Adam's roses. What was wrong with this picture? I hadn't heard a thing from Evan all day. Evan, the one who was supposed to be my boyfriend.

'Is it Evan?' she prompted, interrupting my silence.

'Kind of.' I sighed. 'Things aren't great.'

'Oh, shit. What's going on?'

'Well, for one, he works all the time. I barely even see him.'

'Poor guy.'

I laughed bitterly. 'Don't feel bad for him. He loves it.'

'Okay, then. Poor you.'

'I guess it's okay. I've been spending a lot of time with' – I came so close to blurting out Adam's name, so incredibly close – 'with, um, friends. Keeping busy, you know.'

The rest of the afternoon passed in tedium, with Laurie dropping off files and marked-up memos on my desk. Her eye kept catching on the roses, but she seemed strangely determined not to comment. Near the end of the day, my phone rang again.

'Jules,' Evan said, his voice heavy. 'I'm so sorry. I'm on my way to the airport right now. Michael just told me. Spire's sending a team to this conference in Las Vegas, and he wants me along, too. I'm there all weekend. I feel terrible.'

'A conference? Why?'

'I'm not sure. It's global macro, stuff I don't even work on. Michael said he'd fill me in later.' A loud honk sounded. I had to hold the phone away from my ear. 'Shit,' he said. 'This traffic is insane. I'm sorry, Julia. I really am. I'm on the red-eye back on Sunday, so I'll see you Monday, okay?'

'Whatever. It's fine,' I said. Evan, once again relegating me to second place, proving how little I mattered to him – a fact that was equal parts upsetting and liberating. I felt a weird mixture of anger and relief. It *was* fine. In fact, maybe it was better than fine. I'd be spared from dinner at some overpriced midtown restaurant, with mediocre food and nothing to talk about. The weekend was all mine. I put a smile back into my voice. 'See you in a few days.'

———

I began running longer, farther that fall. I could go for six miles, eight, even nine or ten without tiring. Far north along the river and back down to the Queensboro, or in long loops around Central Park. I thought maybe I'd train for a marathon. Or at least a half marathon. The miles flew by while my mind was lost in daydreams, breath steaming in the cold morning air, the rhythmic crunch of gravel under my shoes. I felt my body growing lighter, stronger. For six months my imagination had been starved of oxygen, but I was breathing at last, enormous gulps of air.

For the first week, after that kiss in the cab, Adam and I had studiedly sober interactions: brightly lit coffee shops, a walk at lunch, a gallery opening in the evening. Testing the water. That deliberateness seemed so grown-up, part of the reason I was sure it was the right thing to do. We didn't talk about what had happened in the cab, but it saturated our relationship with a new intensity. Adam would e-mail me at work to tell me a funny thing he'd overheard or share a link to a story he thought was interesting. He'd ask how a meeting went, how my day was going. Things he hadn't done before. It thrilled me, the knowledge that Adam – Adam McCard, the most dazzling man I'd ever met – was thinking about me all the time.

We made plans to have dinner on a Saturday night in early November – a week after the kiss – then stop by his friend's party afterward. Evan would be working late, as usual. We met at the restaurant, a small place in the West Village. He was waiting for me at the bar, and I could taste the liquor on his breath. I knew this was it, the night when things would go one way or another, once and for all. I was nervous. The way I imagined an actor might feel before the curtain rises for the first time.

We had a drink before dinner, then shared a bottle of wine. Adam greeted the maître d' by name. The sommelier, too. He was a regular. It skipped across my mind that he had probably brought other women here before, other girlfriends, but I didn't care. It was my turn. There was candlelight, thick linen napkins, leather armchairs. The menu, tiny type on creamy paper. Jewel-like coins of tuna tartare, halibut crusted in a bright green sleeve, a tangle of golden pasta. The wine was a rich, deep Burgundy – at least that's what Adam told me – and I was tipsy by the time we stood up to leave, my nervousness forgotten. Adam helped me on with my coat. He was so handsome up close. The dark hair, the cheekbones. He leaned forward to kiss the tip of my nose.

'Come on,' he said. 'Nick's place is right around the corner.'

The doorman nodded us inside a stately brick building on Christopher Street. Adam held my hand through the crowded apartment to the bedroom, where we added our coats and scarves to the pile heaped on the bed. It was a big room, an adult-size bedroom, with a proper four-poster, a woven rug, art on the walls, floor lamps. It looked like a room Nick must share with a girlfriend, one with good taste and plenty of money.

These were all Adam's friends. He was a few years older than me, and he ran with a crowd a few years older than him, so these people were miles beyond anyone I knew: journalists and editors and lawyers and producers, people who no longer had *assistant* in their titles. Adam steered me through the party, introducing me to everyone he knew. At one point, he bumped into a woman smoking a cigarette next to an open window. He turned to apologize, and I watched both of them light up with recognition. 'Sara,' he said, kissing her on the cheek, then tugging me forward. 'Hey. You two should meet.'

She was Japanese, her hair like a long curtain framing her face, her clothing artfully draped, her build slender and delicate. Her silhouette was like an old Al Hirschfeld sketch. 'Sara, this is Julia Edwards. She was at Yale a few years behind us. Jules, Sara runs a gallery in Tribeca.'

'Hey,' she said. Her voice was smoky and cool. 'Nice to meet you.'

Adam cast his eyes across the room. 'I just have to say hi to somebody. I'll be right back.'

I was nervous again without Adam there as a buffer. Surely Sara would dismiss me out of hand: a ditzy girl who didn't belong, too young, too naive. She'd only talk to me until she could find an excuse to leave. But after he walked away, she smiled at me. She was less intimidating when she smiled.

'When did you graduate?'

'Just this year. In May.'

'Tough year. What are you doing in the city?'

'I'm working at a nonprofit. The Fletcher Foundation. I'm just an assistant, but –'

'But you have a job? Hey, that's great. That's more than a lot of people can say.'

I laughed. 'I guess.'

'Most of my friends had to intern for, like, years before they found jobs. You're doing fine.'

'It doesn't really feel that way.'

'It will, eventually.' She had a knowing glint in her eyes. A lot of the people in this room did. I wanted that – the knowingness – more than anything. An understanding of the world and where I fit in it. Sara told me about her gallery in Tribeca, some of the artists she represented. She was going to Art Basel in Miami Beach in a few weeks. We talked for a while about the recent Turner show at the Met and the new Koons installation.

I was surprised to find I was actually having fun. Sara made me feel like myself.

'Here,' she said as she lit another cigarette. 'Here's my card. Call me sometime. We can have lunch. And if you're ever interested in leaving that job of yours, the gallery might be hiring next year.'

'Really?'

'Really. We could use someone like you. You seem smart. And nice, too. Too nice for Adam.'

She exhaled a plume of smoke. I laughed nervously. *Too nice for Adam?* I glanced down at her business card. A simple square with her name in raised black type. SARA YAMASHITA.

'There you are,' Adam said. 'Come on – let's say hi to Nick.'

'It was nice to meet you,' I said to Sara, slipping the card into my purse. 'And thank you, really. I appreciate it.'

'No problem.' She smiled serenely. 'Keep in mind what I said.'

Nick had a real kitchen, too, a separate room with marble countertops and oak cabinets and a stainless steel range. He was holding court, in the middle of some story, and he turned toward us at the sound of his name. He was just like Adam, I could see – brimming with the same confidence, tailor-made for this kind of life. Nick stepped forward and reached for my hand. 'You must be the famous Julia,' he said. 'What can I get you guys to drink?'

He was tall and tanned, with very white teeth and a

shock of blond hair. He wore a navy blue cable-knit sweater and khakis and soft brown loafers. He seemed to match his apartment: old money, old-money taste.

'I'll have a bourbon,' Adam said, 'and she'll have a vodka soda.'

'With lime, if you have it,' I added. Adam always forgot the last part.

While Nick was fixing our drinks, Adam nudged me. 'So what do you think?'

'This kitchen, holy shit. Is this guy a millionaire or something?'

'You were talking to Sara for a while.'

'Yeah. I like her. I can't believe she runs her own gallery.'

'Don't be too impressed. It's all her family. Their money, their connections. Nothing she got on her own.'

'What, are you not a fan?'

'No, nothing like that. Sara's a good person for you to know. But her dad is one of the biggest art dealers in the city. How hard do you think she had to work to get that gig?'

'She seems to be doing what she loves, at least.' I wished Nick would hurry up with the drinks. But he was distracted, greeting more people in that clubby way.

Adam laughed. 'Sara's not like that. I'm not sure love is an emotion she's capable of.'

I tried to read his expression. For Adam to criticize someone else's family connections seemed unfair. He had grown up in a Central Park West penthouse, his father a real estate mogul and his mother a society type. Adam was as privileged as they came. So what if he hadn't chosen to follow his father into real estate? It was still strange for him to belittle Sara for doing something that almost anyone in her situation would have done. It stung, too, realizing that Adam could have said the same thing about me. The job I had, at a foundation run by our family friends – nothing I got on my own.

A thought occurred to me.

'How do you know Sara again?'

'Hmm?'

'Was she in your college, or what?'

'No. We dated for a while.'

'Oh.'

'It was freshman year. We met through the magazine.'

The same way that Adam and I had met. Adam's reputation was well known. He'd slept around, a parade of flings and hookups, often a few at the same time, many drawn from the ranks of the magazine. This party had to be populated with other past conquests besides Sara. But weirdly enough, I wasn't jealous. Maybe because I had no real claim over Adam. Being with Adam had become a way for me to step outside the bounds: a minor rebellion, leaving behind the boring life I had before. This was a different world, one of sommeliers and marble kitchens and doormen. It was a world where you could be blasé about the past and the consequences of your actions. A world where envy was what other people felt, not you.

'What, are you going to Russia for that vodka?' Adam said to Nick, raising his voice over the chatter.

'Hey.' Nick flashed his white-toothed smile, cutting a lime into wedges. 'You want your drink or not?'

He handed us our glasses a moment later. Heavy cut-crystal tumblers. My hand dropped under the weight. I felt like I was at a party at my parents' house.

'So, Julia,' Nick said. 'Tell me about yourself.'

'Oh.' I hated that kind of question. What the hell was I supposed to say? What were the things that made me interesting or special? 'Well, right now I'm –'

'Nick. There you are.' A brunette woman in a red dress appeared next to Nick. She laid her left hand across his chest, and an enormous diamond flashed from her ring finger. 'Sweetheart, pass me the seltzer? Someone spilled in the living room.'

She noticed Adam and me standing there. 'Hi,' she said, turning to offer me her other, ringless hand. 'I'm Megan. Nick's fiancée.'

'Julia. Thank you so much for having us.'

'You go with him?' She pointed at Adam.

'She's my date for the night,' Adam said. 'We're old friends from college.'

'Well.' She smiled tightly. 'Welcome.'

Fiancée? I thought as Megan walked out of the kitchen. *Engaged?* I didn't know anyone who was engaged. When I saw that diamond sparkling on her finger, I felt the gulf that separated me from the rest of the partygoers crack wide open. It made sense. She and Nick had to be in their late twenties. Their kitchen, their artwork, their furniture, their clothes. Poised right on the cusp of bona fide adulthood. Only a handful of years separated us, but I felt further away from them than I did from my childhood self. I was about to turn twenty-three years old, and I couldn't even begin to imagine it, real adulthood.

The thing was, it hadn't always been so impossible to imagine. We had never actually talked about it, never said the word *marriage,* but that summer Evan and I spent in Europe – hot nights walking around Rome, sunny days on the Greek coast, afternoons in Paris – I thought about it more than once. I held his hand in mine, wrapped my arms around his neck, and felt myself consumed by love. A love that could endure anything. A love that had changed me. I grew dizzy from it sometimes. Of course we would be together forever. Of course we would get married someday.

But then everything changed. I regarded the Julia from a year and a half earlier with pity. That girl had known so little about what was to come – had been so naive about what it took for a relationship to work in the real world. I could never marry Evan. Never, ever. Evan wasn't someone I could have a life with. We were too different, and he didn't care about me. That's why it felt so natural, sliding into this new thing with Adam. Evan and I were clearly headed for a breakup. It was only a question of time.

So why didn't I rip the bandage off? Why keep living with someone for whom I felt nothing? Ending things would have kept me from cheating on Evan. It would have prevented so much of the collateral damage. But that decision would have taken conviction. Planning and execution. And, frankly, it would have required that I find my own place to live, which was annoying and prohibitively expensive. And in that moment, I liked the *doing*. Abandoning myself to impulse. Besides, I thought. The coming holidays might precipitate a breakup. They always had a way of throwing gasoline on the fire. Evan wasn't any happier in this relationship than I was. If I waited, he might just do it himself.

'Let's mingle a little longer, and then we can go,' Adam said.

We talked to more of his friends. They were so different from the people at parties I'd gone to with Abby and Evan. A filmmaker working on an indie documentary. A consultant traveling four days a week to Omaha. A literary agent who had just sold a novel for seven figures. But even in this crowd, I could sense that Adam was exceptional. People were drawn to where he stood like iron filings to a magnet. He was as charming and commanding as he'd been in college. In this apartment, in this room full of people, Adam was still the brightest star in the universe.

And he had chosen me. In the cab afterward, he took my hand.

'You're so beautiful. You know that, right?'

'Come on. Stop.'

'I mean it. I adore you.'

He leaned over and kissed me. We were sailing up 8th Avenue, no sign that the cab was going to go across town. Adam must have given the driver his address. My heart sped up. This was it. We stopped at a brick building at the corner of 80th and Riverside Drive. 'You have to come up for a drink, at least,' Adam said, giving me an excuse that I didn't need. 'I have a great view.'

Adam's apartment was on the twelfth floor. He tossed our coats on an upholstered chair in the foyer and led me to the far end of the living room. Family money: there was no way he could afford this on a journalist's salary. He steered me to the window and slipped his arms around me from behind. The Palisades looked dark and velvety across the river, and the lights of Weehawken and Hoboken sparkled in the southern distance.

'Amazing, right?' he said, brushing his lips along my neck.

'Mmm.'

'I've wanted you to see this for a long time.'

'It's beautiful.'

He turned me around, sliding his arms down my back, keeping me tight against him. He kissed me, and for a second it ran through my head like a siren, the last time we'd been here – but then it disappeared. I wanted this. There was no hesitation this time.

Afterward, we lay facing each other. Naked, sweat cooling, the room dim except for the glow from the streetlamps outside. He had one arm behind his head, and with his other hand he traced a line along my waist.

'I can't tell you how long I've thought about that,' he said.

'Me, too.' I moved closer and buried my face in his chest, breathing him in.

'We fit together,' Adam said. 'Look at that.' And it was true. Our bodies were made to be in this very position. He kissed me on the forehead and said, 'Do you want to stay over? I make a mean breakfast.'

'I think I'd better get home. What time is it?'

'A little after one.'

'Can I use the bathroom?'

'Out the door and to your left.'

I showered, my hair pulled back in a bun to keep it dry. I opened my mouth and tipped my head back, letting the hot water run in. I had to stifle a laugh. Adam McCard. It had finally happened. The steam drifted through the bathroom, and the glass door of the stall fogged over, and everything else disappeared.

Monday, more than two weeks later. A few days after my birthday. I went for a particularly long run that cold November morning. As I came down our block, I remember thinking it strange that there was someone sitting on our stoop. Who had time to linger at this hour? It might be one of the homeless men who sometimes slept in the alcove outside the drugstore. I dreaded having to squeeze past him on my way inside.

As I got closer, I felt a prickle on my neck. It was Evan.

Sitting there, on the stoop. How had I not recognized him sooner? He was staring at his phone and jiggling his knees in a fast bounce, his duffel bag beside him. I'd forgotten that he was getting back from Las Vegas that morning. Adam and I had spent the weekend at his apartment, which was the best birthday present I could have asked for. He cooked, we listened to jazz, and I sat on the couch reading and watching the Hudson flow past. 'Evan should go out of town more,' he said when I emerged from the shower wearing one of his button-downs. 'Where did you say he was again?' He was in bed, shirtless, wearing his reading glasses. He looked like Clark Kent. It was a Saturday night, and we were staying in. I slid under the covers. 'Some conference in Las Vegas. It's weird. Michael wanted him to go along at the last minute. It has nothing to do with what he's working on.' Adam nodded, his brow furrowed. Then he relaxed. 'Well, it works for me.' I'd finally gone home late on Sunday night. The creaking floorboards in our dark apartment filled me with a wretched loneliness.

I stopped a dozen yards short of our door. Evan still hadn't seen me. He stood up, picked up the duffel bag, then put it down. He tilted his head to look up at the sky. He checked his watch, then paced a few yards before reversing course. Something was off. I suddenly saw him as any stranger might: unshaved, tired, puffy, anonymous. It's an odd trick, to consider how different someone looks when you strip away the forgiveness of familiarity. I had always known Evan up close. I encountered him all at once, and that's what I had always liked about him: no hidden tricks or trip wires. But right then, that November morning, I had the feeling of traveling back in time. Evan was becoming a stranger in front of my eyes. This man sitting on my doorstep was someone I had never met before.

I shivered. This was how bad it had gotten: I considered turning around to do another lap in the park, waiting for Evan to leave for work. But then he finally looked up and saw me.

'Julia,' he said, springing to his feet.

'Hey. How was the trip?'

He glanced over his shoulder, then up the street behind me. His eyes, when they landed on mine, were brimming with a new emotion. Panic? Fear?

'I have to tell you something,' he said, and he pulled me inside.

The long-awaited Fletcher Foundation gala had been the week before. I got there early, in charge of checking guests in upon arrival. I peered through the doors into the ballroom, which glowed softly, with white roses and candlelight on every table. Up on stage was Eleanor, clipboard and BlackBerry in hand. She wore a long black gown. Her skin had the slightest dusting of a tan.

Laurie arrived, looking exhausted. I had overheard snatches of her conversation with Henry Fletcher earlier that day. She was explaining that the gala had cost more than anticipated. Donations had dried up, returns from the endowment were down, and we were tight on cash for the rest of the year. The conversation seemed to go badly. 'Yes, of course,' she had said, raising her voice. 'Of course I *know* how bad the market is right now. But I'm telling you that we're at real risk of –'

She paused, apparently listening to him. She spoke more quietly, and I couldn't make out what she was saying. She sighed after she hung up. Then she shut her door, and it stayed shut for the rest of the afternoon.

'Oh, hello, Julia,' she said distractedly. She dumped her bag and coat on the check-in table. 'Can you find somewhere to put these?'

The guests started arriving in a trickle, then all at once. I kept a smile plastered on my face, answering questions, directing traffic. A corner of my mind worried over Laurie's mood. If things were as bad as she said, I wondered whether my job might be in jeopardy. A little later, Abby and Jake walked through the door. 'Julia!' Abby said, coming over to give me a hug. 'Holy crap. Woman in charge.'

'Hey,' Jake said, jerking his chin in greeting.

'Hi, guys. Let's see . . . you're at table one. No surprise there, I guess.'

'You look great,' Abby said.

'Stop. *You* look great.' She did, too. I had never seen her so radiant. 'Hey, Jake, are your parents here? Laurie is eagerly awaiting them.'

'Yeah,' Jake said, rubbing his chin and looking bored. 'They're outside. My dad got stopped by some reporter.'

Adam, I thought, and my heart fluttered.

'Are we sitting together?' Abby said.

'What? Oh, no. Laurie is probably at your table, though.'

Abby and Jake drifted toward the coat check. There was a lull in the arrivals. I took the chance to scoot out from behind the table and survey the red-carpeted sidewalk. Henry and Dot Fletcher were talking to the reporter, a man in jeans and a parka. He held a recorder up toward Henry Fletcher. The parka man turned, catching the light on his face. It wasn't Adam. Of course it wasn't. I went back to the table, smoothed my skirt, and resumed my smile. The Fletchers approached the table. Dot, to her credit, remembered who I was.

'Julia, dear! It's so wonderful to see you. How are you?'

'I'm well, thank you. I'm so –'

She clutched my hand to cut me off. 'I was just talking with your mother the other day. You look lovely. So grown up. Doesn't she, Henry?'

He turned, distracted, rubbing his chin. He and Jake were so much alike.

'Of course. Nice to see you.'

Dot smiled sweetly at me, waving her fingers as they walked away to join the party. Henry, I noticed, had a tan, too.

★

Eleanor swept through to check on me as the guests started filing into the ballroom for dinner, after the cocktail hour ended.

'What time is it?' she said.

There was a clock on the wall. 'Ten past eight.'

'Good. Stay here till eight thirty, in case anyone trickles in.' She tossed her hair back over her shoulders. 'Oh, and Julia, I forgot to say. Laurie doesn't like junior staff to drink at work events. It's always been her policy. So just be aware of that.'

She emphasized the *junior* in 'junior staff' with particular care. I gave the finger to her back as she walked into the ballroom. The event had started at 6:30. Nobody else was going to show up at this point. This was pure spite – Eleanor wanting to remind me that she was the one in charge.

I texted Adam. How's the deadline coming?

It was quiet in the entrance hall, just the muted sound of traffic on Park Avenue and the occasional clatter of silverware from the ballroom. I started counting the number of no-shows for the final tally when I felt my phone buzz.

Still trying to get this piece done. I don't suppose you have any comment on the AIG bailout? Or insight into what the Fed is thinking?

I laughed. No comment. And no insight. Sorry, I'm useless.

A minute later, another buzz. Not useless. You're my motivation to get this done. Meet me later for a drink?

★

I found my seat in the back as the waiters were delivering the entrées. Everyone was already paired off in conversation, raising their voices against the echo of the big room. My arrival went unnoticed. I cut my chicken and asparagus into small, careful bites, taking up as much time as I could. I buttered a roll and ate it, then buttered and ate another one.

Thank God, I thought when the waiters cleared our dishes and Henry Fletcher approached the podium on stage. He cleared his throat, and the microphone screeched with feedback. He rattled off a list of thank-yous, then droned on about the importance of supporting young and emerging artists. That during these trying economic times, it was crucial to ensure that arts programs retained funding. It was very dreary. Half the room was checking e-mail by the time he was finished.

At the end of his speech, Mr Fletcher paused. He folded up the piece of paper he had been reading from, removed his glasses, and returned both to his pocket. Then he cleared his throat again. 'And now, before I turn it over to the formidable Laurie Silver, I'd like to make an announcement.'

This was a surprise.

'I'm pleased to say here, for the first time, that Dot and I are making a donation of ten million dollars to the Fletcher Foundation to establish a new series of grants for next year and future years. And for all donations made in the next six months, we will personally match your gifts dollar for dollar.'

The room erupted in applause. Mr Fletcher smiled a stiff smile.

'We want to show our commitment to the vitality and endurance of the great achievements of the foundation during the past decade, and we hope you'll join us in doing so. And, without further ado, Laurie Silver, president of the Fletcher Foundation.'

The room rose to its feet, the applause swelling as Laurie ascended the stage. I was relieved. Even if I hated it, I would be able to keep my job until I found something better. Laurie and Mr Fletcher embraced. She was smiling, but she looked less exuberant than I expected. From the snatches I'd overheard, Laurie had asked for another three or four million to keep things running. Henry Fletcher had just thrown us a lifeline above and beyond what we needed, I was sure of it.

After Laurie's speech, I found Abby and Jake by the bar. I ordered a double vodka on the rocks. Eleanor's rule probably wasn't real, and I didn't care. Something about the news of the donation, and Laurie's reaction, had unsettled me. I suspected that I had very little understanding of what was really happening. It was all occurring under the surface, where I couldn't see. But a minute later, after the drink, I felt better. Calmer.

'That was nice, right?' Abby said to Jake. 'It's great that your parents are doing that.'

Jake shrugged. 'Yeah. It's good.'

'Did you have fun?' Abby asked me.

'Sure. It was fine.' I tipped back my drink, the ice rattling in my glass.

'Let's get you another one of those.' She waved at the bartender.

'We're going out after this, right?'

'Not me. My alarm is going off tomorrow at six whether I like it or not.'

'What? Abby!'

'Do you know what it's like teaching kindergarten with a hangover? Fucking miserable is what. I learned my lesson the first time. Sorry, Jules, I can't.'

'It's just been so long since we went out together.' I sounded whiny.

Jake faked a yawn, slipping his arm around Abby's waist. 'Yeah. I've got an early day tomorrow, too. Should we go get a cab?'

'Sorry, sorry.' Abby hugged me. 'You look great, though, you really do.'

When the bartender came over, I ordered another drink. The ballroom was emptying fast, the guests bolting for the coat check and their black cars. I noticed Laurie and Dot Fletcher by the side of the stage. The vodka emboldened me. I ought to go and thank Mrs Fletcher for the donation. Laurie sometimes seemed to forget that I was a real person, equipped to handle more than the most basic administrative work. This — a chance to sound articulate and thoughtful — might help remind her of that. I was smart, I was interesting, I was capable of intelligent conversation. I deserved more than I was getting. Maybe I just had to take it for myself.

I touched Mrs Fletcher on the elbow. She looked startled to see me. 'Oh, hello, Julia. Laurie's speech was wonderful, wasn't it?'

'Yes, it was. Mrs Fletcher,' I said, glancing over at Laurie. Her lips were drawn in a tight line. 'I just wanted to say thank you, so much, for your and Mr Fletcher's show of support tonight. It was inspiring, really.'

Dot and Laurie made brief eye contact, something passing between them. 'There's no need to thank us, dear. We see this foundation as our responsibility. It bears our name, after all.'

'Of course. Well, I thought it was very nice.'

'Yes,' Laurie said. 'In fact, we were just talking about what this donation is going to allow us to do in the upcoming year.'

Laurie looked more annoyed than anything else. She and Dot tilted their shoulders to indicate I was no longer welcome. But I was distracted anyway by the sight, behind them and out of their field of vision, of Henry and Eleanor.

It looked innocuous enough. Their heads were awfully close together, but it was noisy in the ballroom. I stepped aside and took my phone out, pretending to check something. Then I glanced back up at Henry and Eleanor. He slipped his hand to the small of her back, leaning in closer. She looked over her shoulder, then nodded. From my pretending-to-be-on-the-phone post a few feet away, I heard Mr Fletcher approach Laurie and Dot. 'Honey,' he said to Dot. 'I just got a call from the office. I need to go in tonight. Something urgent's come up.'

'Now? Henry, it's so late.'

'Turmoil in the Asian markets. I should only be a few hours. You take the car, and I'll see you back at the hotel.' He exited the ballroom with long and loping strides. Eleanor had already disappeared.

Outside, the sidewalk held a few lingering couples. It was a little after 10:00 p.m. I was less than twenty blocks from our apartment. I could go home, wash my face, put on my pajamas, and wake up early and fresh the next morning. Be responsible. It didn't sound so bad. I started walking north on Park, past the empty office lobbies strung through the night like square golden beads. Some of the lobbies had oversize sculptures in the center, like exotic flowers suspended in a high-ceilinged terrarium. They looked so strange, alone in the night, on display for no one.

I was getting closer to home, and Park had gradually turned residential, the big glass lobbies replaced by solid limestone and brick. I felt my phone buzzing and saw Adam's name on the screen.

'Hey. Where are you?'

'Walking home. I just left the gala.'

'I'm only going to be a few more minutes. Meet me at my place?'

'Well . . . I really am almost home. It's getting kind of late.'

'I have a good bottle of wine. I've been saving it. In the cabinet next to the fridge. The doorman will let you in. I'll be right behind you.'

This was my fourth visit to Adam's apartment in as many days. Upstairs, I flipped the lights on and wandered through the living room, running my fingertips along the spines of the books on his bookshelf. It was the first time I'd been alone with Adam's things. I went into the bedroom. He had a desk at one end of the room. I noticed the bookshelf next to his desk was filled with books on finance. Histories, economic theory, *Barbarians at the Gate, When Genius Failed, Liar's Poker*. Curious. It was his beat at the *Observer,* but he'd always described it as a way station. Not something he was genuinely interested in. I pulled the copy of *When Genius Failed* from the shelf. The pages were dog-eared and bristling with Post-it notes. I fanned through it. There were pencil marks and underlines on nearly every page. It had the look of something obsessive.

I jumped when the door slammed. 'Hello?' Adam called. I shoved the book back onto the shelf and hurried out to the living room, where he was shrugging off his coat. 'There you are,' he said.

'How was work?'

'I'm glad it's over.' He ran his eyes over me. 'That is one hell of a dress.'

'You think so?' I glanced down, tugged at the fabric. 'I was just about to take it off, actually. But if you'd prefer I keep it on . . .'

Afterward, in bed, he rolled over and pulled a pack of Marlboros from his nightstand drawer. He lit the cigarette, inhaled, then exhaled with a sigh. He always looked more pensive in profile.

'You smoke?'

'Sometimes.'

'I don't think I knew that.'

He blew a smoke ring that floated briefly in the air above him. The room was almost unnaturally quiet. The constant thumps and squeaks and rattles that I'd come to expect in our walk-up apartment were absent here. Thick walls, double-glazed windows, the rugs and the floor-to-ceiling bookshelves: we were in a womb of money and culture. 'There's a lot you don't know about me.' Then he laughed. 'You want one?'

'Sure,' I said. I didn't want it, not really, but it felt like the right thing to do.

In our apartment, that morning of his return, I sat on the futon while Evan paced.

Back and forth, back and forth. I'd never seen him like this.

'Evan, what is it?' I said. 'Just tell me.'

He stopped abruptly. 'Michael. It's Michael. The thing has been rigged all along. And he made me deliver the papers, so the blood is on my hands, too. They trapped me. I can't go anywhere. It's totally fucked.'

'Slow down,' I said. 'What? What are you talking about?'

'The WestCorp deal. It's fixed.'

'What do you mean?'

He took a deep breath. He started talking about the mechanics of the deal, Spire betting that WestCorp was going to skyrocket because of their exports to China. I nodded. I knew all that. Then he explained that China had agreed to loosen the trade barriers, to drop the taxes and tariffs. Again, old news.

'Evan,' I said. 'I don't —'

He held up a hand, kept talking. He'd gotten locked out of his hotel room by his coworker. So he'd crashed on the couch in another suite. Michael and someone else from Spire came back to the room in the middle of the night.

'Did they know you were there?' I interrupted. Evan shook his head. 'Why didn't you say something? Like, hey, guys, I'm right over here?'

'I couldn't, Jules. I just couldn't. It was too late.' There was a sheen of sweat on his forehead. The other person in the room confronted Michael while Evan was listening. He'd spotted something in the books. Michael admitted that the deal was rigged. Michael and WestCorp had arranged for immigration papers for the Chinese officials and their families. The next day, Michael asked Evan to deliver a briefcase to a Mr Wenjian Chan at the Venetian.

'And you did it? You agreed to deliver the briefcase?'

He nodded, looking pale and sick.

'Evan. You had just overheard all that and you *went along* with it?'

'What else was I going to say? He didn't know that I'd overheard them. So I deliver the briefcase, and Chan seems happy. But before I walk out, his daughter stops me. Translating what her father's saying. They want to keep in touch, she says. She's applying to college in the States, and they want my help. They seem to think I have the right connections. Like, she can blackmail her way in through me.'

'Did you tell Michael this?'

'He was already gone by the time I got back. I haven't talked to him yet. I don't know what to do.' He stopped his pacing and sank down onto the futon next to me. He dropped his head in his hands. 'Jesus. What the fuck am I supposed to do?'

I was silent. I waited for him to look up at me, but he wouldn't. He kept his palms pressed up against his eyes, like a child willing a monster to disappear. After a minute, he said it again. 'Julia. What should I do?'

He finally looked up. I flinched when he reached for my hand, when his gaze locked on mine. My heart was hammering. Evan had been ignoring me for so long. He hadn't asked a single question in all that time. How was I? How was my day? How was I feeling? What was I thinking? And, finally, this was what he came up with. He wanted my help. I was only there to solve his problems, and then he'd go right back to ignoring me.

I was also thinking: how had he not figured this out? His pretending at innocence made me queasy. He *wasn't* innocent. He'd done this, too. He let himself become

208

blinded by it. *We're going to make billions. Spire is going to crush the rest of Wall Street.* But when the truth finally became too uncomfortable, he wanted out. He wanted an escape. I was angry, but part of me felt relieved, too. Validated. I wasn't the one who had fucked up our relationship. I'd been duped. Evan had betrayed me – had betrayed us. And whatever was happening, whatever person Evan was becoming, I wanted no part of it. This was a waste of my time. I was done.

'I don't know, Evan.' I stood up, walked over to the kitchen. 'I don't know what you should do. You need to figure this out on your own.'

'What do you mean?' He looked confused. He hadn't even considered that I would be anything but sympathetic. That confirmed it. He really *wasn't* thinking about me.

I reached for a glass and filled it with water. I was just realizing how thirsty I was. 'I mean that I don't have the answer for you. This is *your* problem. You need to fix it.'

He said nothing for a long minute. My pulse was pounding in my ears. I hated this person in front of me, hated what he made me feel. I felt it boiling up, the blood in my body primed for a fight. Shouts, slammed doors, permanent words. *Get out. The end.*

But he just said, quietly, nodding to himself, 'Okay.'

'Fine,' I said. 'I'm late for work.' I put my glass down loudly on the kitchen counter and went into the bathroom, slamming the door behind me. The shower took a long time to get hot, and as it did, I felt the sharp edge of my anger dulling. This was how it always went. Evan was always waiting for me to cool down, to come to my senses. He never let our fights escalate, never shouted back. His patience knew no bounds.

It didn't have to be this way. Our relationship deserved a better ending than this. I wrapped myself in my towel and opened the bathroom door. I could apologize, tell him I was sorry for snapping like that. I would.

But Evan was already gone, his duffel bag left behind on the floor, the imprint of his body slowly fading from the cushions on the futon. I was too late.

CHAPTER 9

Evan

Paranoia was a disease whose symptoms I didn't recognize right away. Or maybe that's the essence of it: nothing is as it seems. The world rearranges itself while you aren't looking. You never know you're suffering from it.

'Evan? Honey, are you there?'

'Yeah. Yeah, sorry, Mom, I'm here.'

My parents often called to catch up after their workday ended. I'd stepped outside the office to take the call, pacing for warmth in the chilly November night. Until I noticed a dark figure sitting in the front seat of a car parked down the block. Just sitting there, unmoving. He'd been there for at least fifteen minutes. Watching me.

'I said, how was your weekend? It was Julia's birthday, right?'

'Yeah. Um, it was good.'

'I hope you two did something nice.'

I hadn't told them I'd gone to Las Vegas. It felt like a jinx, telling them even that, spreading any aspect of the story further than it needed to go. A family of tourists was walking down the block in an unwieldy ameba, arguing about the best way to get back to their hotel. I ducked behind them, trying to blend in and get a better look at the figure in the car without his seeing me. We got closer and closer, and finally I could see clear through the window. It was a chauffeur, his cap pulled low over his forehead. Asleep.

'Hey!' One of the kids glared at me. I'd stepped on his heel.

'Shit. Sorry,' I said.

'What?'

'Nothing, Mom. I should go.'

The same thing kept happening all week. The towel hanging crooked when I was sure I'd left it straight. My desk chair spinning in slow circles when I returned from lunch. And a hot flare of panic until I eventually realized the explanation. Julia wiping the toothpaste from her mouth in the morning, leaving the towel askew. Roger pushing past my chair on his way to the bathroom. Chan and his colleagues were businessmen, not thugs. They weren't going to corner me and press a gun to my head in some dark alley. Whatever they did was going to be more subtle than that.

—————

We got to the airport in Las Vegas on Sunday evening for the red-eye home. I stood in front of the departures board. The destination cities were organized alphabetically, and near the end of the list was Vancouver. The flight was leaving a few minutes after ours.

I could do it. I could afford the ticket. I had my passport with me as ID – my British Columbia license had expired a few months earlier – and I had my duffel bag in hand. I'd arrive near midnight, get a room in an airport motel. There was a Greyhound that headed east out of Vancouver in the morning. My hometown sat near the end of the line. I imagined walking into the grocery store, near where the bus dropped me off. Finding my parents in the back, doing inventory or reviewing the accounts at the end of the day. They would be surprised to see me, but maybe not that surprised. I could sleep in my own bed, with the familiar rush of wind through the tall pine trees outside. I could be doing all that *tomorrow*. It was right within my reach – a chance to run away and pretend this never happened.

'Evan?' Chuck emerged from the airline's first-class lounge and caught me staring at the board. 'They're calling our flight. Come on, let's go.'

———

'I'm sorry, hon,' Wanda said. It was Monday morning. I'd gone home to change after the flight, then went straight to Michael's office. Wanda could probably tell that I was underslept and in desperate need of a shower. I hadn't had time to wait for Julia to finish hers. 'He's completely jammed today. I can't fit you in anywhere. You want me to get him a message?'

'You can just tell him that I'd like to see him. *Need* to see him.'

'What's it regarding?'

I shook my head. 'He'll know.'

I tried again on Tuesday, on Wednesday, on Thursday. It was the same story. Door shut. Wanda shaking her head. It had been almost a full week since I'd found out, and the knowledge was starting to solidify within me. Telling Julia had done no good. I knew I owed her the truth – I couldn't just flee to Canada, if only for that reason: the thought of telling her what I'd done over the phone or in an e-mail had made me too sick to go through with it – but she seemed utterly uninterested in it. The sting of her cold reaction only lasted for a few moments. So Julia was in a bitchy mood – I still had bigger problems. I decided to try to use this mess to my advantage. There was more than one way that I could have theoretically discovered the truth. Maybe Chan had let something slip, and I'd put two and two together. I'd show Michael that I knew exactly what he was up to. Show him that I wasn't so easily duped after all.

Late on Friday afternoon, I tried one more time. Wanda sighed. 'I'm sorry, Evan, but you'll have to wait until Monday. Mr Casey is about to leave for the weekend.'

'Who is that?' Michael strode into the hallway, pulling on his coat. 'Oh, Evan. Wanda, you know you can always send Evan straight in.'

'That's okay.' I stepped back. 'I don't want to interrupt.'

'I have an appointment, but we can talk along the way.

That'll be better, in fact. Get your coat and meet me at the elevator.'

Downstairs, Michael and I climbed into the back of a town car idling by the curb. It sped off, heading west. 'Just give me another minute,' Michael said, his thumbs punching the keys of his BlackBerry. Then he glanced up, saw the look on my face, and grinned unnervingly. 'Relax, Evan. This is going to be fun.'

The car came to a stop.

'My favorite place in the city,' Michael said, climbing out. We were out past the wasteland of 11th Avenue, in front of a nondescript building. The elegant silver lettering above the door was so discreet that you had to know what to look for.

'Mr Casey,' a voice boomed as we walked inside. A man in a dark green suit shook Michael's hand. He had slicked-back hair, a signet ring on his pinkie, a big barrel chest, and spindly legs. Like a toad with a very good personal shopper. 'We're so glad you could make it in this evening.'

'Bruno, this is one of my associates, Evan Peck.'

He extended a hand. Soft, pink, recently moisturized. 'Bruno Bernacchi. It's a pleasure to meet you.'

I glanced around the room. The cars gleamed under the bright lighting like sleeping animals. Maserati of Manhattan. It was empty except for the three of us. Bruno noticed me looking. He had a quick, darting gaze that didn't miss a thing.

'We normally close at five o'clock,' Bruno said to me in a conspiratorial tone. 'But we're always open for Mr Casey. One of our very best customers.'

'Your message said it was delivered today?'

'Just this afternoon. It's the newest model, a beauty. They aren't officially available until next year. There's a waiting list already, but you're at the top of the list, of course, Mr Casey.'

'I'd like to take it for a test drive.'

'Of course. I have in mind a route through Westchester. Wait until you see how this one handles the curves.'

'Actually, I'd like to take Evan along. This is the only time I can give him all week. So the two of us need to talk during the drive – multitask, you know what I mean?'

Bruno's smile wilted. His pink hands fluttered, his fingertips pressed together.

'I know you have your rules,' Michael said. 'But Bruno, I've given you a lot of business over the years. Surely we can take it out for a spin.'

I could see the calculation ricocheting through Bruno's eyes. Michael was smiling, but he was dead serious. A man whose wishes were dangerous to deny.

'You'll be here when we get back?' Michael said through the open window on the driver's side. It was a two-seater sports car, as precise and elegant in design as a piece of sculpture. I was in the passenger seat. For the first time, I understood why people liked to describe an engine as purring. The vibration felt like a warm heartbeat. 'We'll be a few hours.'

Bruno started to open his mouth, then swallowed. He looked severely pained, but he nodded. 'Of course, Mr Casey. I'll be here.'

'Ready?' Michael said after he'd rolled the window up. 'Don't forget to buckle up.'

We drove in silence for a long while up the West Side Highway.

'I'm going to take us over the bridge,' Michael finally said. He glanced over his shoulder, pulling into the right lane and then onto the exit for the George Washington Bridge. 'You can't really get a feel for it in the city. What do you think so far?'

'It's . . . uh, nice.' *Nice?* That was a stupid thing to say. But I was silently panicking, and it was making me dumb. We were headed to New Jersey. The Pine Barrens. Michael was taking me out there to kill me – or worse. It was insane, but it was all I could think.

'Wait until you see it on the open road.'

Friday evening, and the bridge was predictably jammed. Michael answered e-mails on his BlackBerry, glancing up whenever the traffic inched forward. I stared out the window, frantic but numb. Trapped. It was winter dark outside, and the caramel leather interior of the car was lit with a golden glow. What was I going to do, get out of the car and make a run for it? That seemed like the stupidest option of all.

Finally we made it off the bridge and into New Jersey. Michael turned onto the Palisades Parkway. There was a physical relief when we accelerated onto the highway, the engine finally flexing its muscles, opening up the way it was intended to.

'So Evan,' Michael said. 'I have good news. We're going live with the WestCorp deal.'

'That's – that's great.'

'I've reallocated the fund's capital, and I'm doubling our position on WestCorp. This is going to be one for the books.'

He looked at me. The speedometer was steadily climbing. He was weaving from lane to lane without signaling, and I felt my pulse accelerating along with the car. 'You should be proud, Evan,' Michael said. I wished he would look at the road. 'It's extremely rare to work on a deal like this. At any point in your career. You've done a stellar job. The fact that you're so young only makes it more impressive.'

He glanced ahead. 'That's our exit,' he said. 'Next one.'

The sign said we were entering Alpine, New Jersey. We swung around the bending off-ramp, the car handling the curves as beautifully as Bruno had promised. The busy highway vanished, and moments later we were driving down quiet streets. There were high, manicured hedges and towering old trees, wrought-iron gates at the end of every driveway. You couldn't even see the houses. These were rich people. I wondered if this was where Michael lived.

We came to a dead end, a cul-de-sac. Michael stopped the car in front of a gate, one even higher and grander than the others we'd passed. 'We're here,' he said, turning off the engine. 'Get out of the car.'

My legs were shaking as I climbed out. Michael stood in front of the gate, hands in his pockets. It was dark – cloudy, no moon, no streetlights – but Michael seemed to know what he was looking at. I stood next to him, and after my eyes adjusted to the darkness, it materialized. The shape of a house in the distance, down the long driveway.

'A few years ago,' Michael said, 'my wife told me she was tired of the city. She was sick of all the noise, the honking, the traffic. She wanted a yard. She wanted to be able to go outside in the morning and look at trees and flowers. She said she missed having nature around her.'

He shook his head. 'I grew up on a farm. You knew that, right? In the middle of South Dakota. You want nature? That's all there is out there. I had to get up every morning at dawn. Milking the cows, shoveling manure, waist-deep in shit before the sun came up. And after school, there was more. There was always more. It was mud and dirt and hay and shit everywhere. This' – he gestured at the boxy hedges and clipped grass – 'isn't nature. Not to me.'

'But my wife . . .' He laughed, shook his head again. 'My wife grew up in the suburbs. This is practically the wilderness to her. Me, I like the city. I like taxis and elevators and restaurants. But she wanted to move. She said she wasn't going to raise our kids in some *apartment*. So we bought this place a few years ago. Renovated, fixed it up, redid the yard. You want to see it?'

It took me a second to realize the question wasn't rhetorical. 'Oh, um, sure,' I said.

Michael punched a four-digit code into the keypad next to the gate. A moment later, it opened with a mechanical screech. He'd left the keys in the Maserati, in the cul-de-sac. I guess the chances of it getting stolen were low in this neighborhood. People here already had their own fancy sports cars. Michael kept talking.

'When she first raised the issue, I shut it down. I told her no: it's my money, I'm going to spend it the way I want. And we have a penthouse, for Christ's sake. It's not like the kid would be deprived. But she pushed and she pushed. And then I realized – it's like when you have something and it doesn't mean too much to you. But it means a lot to the other person. It means an enormous amount to them. And if you give it to them, maybe it's a little sacrifice for you, but they are going to owe you for the rest of your life. You let them have their way now, and you'll have the upper hand on everything else. Leverage, right? So I told my wife okay. Let's pick out a house.'

We were finally there. The house was enormous: a circular driveway with a fountain in the middle, a grand entrance flanked by tall columns. It looked like one of the old French castles that Julia and I saw during our summer in Europe – the same kind of expensive-looking stonework and old-fashioned architecture. But the fountain in the driveway was empty and dry. Every window in the house was dark.

'That's the thing, Evan.' Michael turned to face me.

'Sometimes you have to do things in life that you don't really want to do. But you have to bear in mind that there's a bigger picture. Do you understand what I mean?'

I was newly aware of how quiet it was. How we hadn't seen a single person since we exited the highway. At least the dark concealed the nervous swallow in my throat. But if Michael was going to do something to me, I realized, he would have done it by then. 'Yes,' I said. 'I think I do.'

He gestured at me to follow him down a path around the side of the house, which opened out to the backyard. Actually, it wasn't a backyard. It was more like the grounds of a country club: tennis courts, a pool, terraced stone patios. The yard was immaculate, but it was obvious that no one was living there. There should have been some sign of life. A chair on the patio, a toy or a ball left in the middle of the lawn. A smudge on the windowpane from a curious hand pressed against it. Anything.

'What do you think of it?'

'It's really nice.'

'I never even spent a single night out here. My wife didn't, either. It was a good thing we didn't sell our place in the city.'

'Why didn't you move in?'

He shrugged. Michael looked human-size, for the first time, like an ordinary man. One whose life contained mistakes, maybe even regret. 'Like I said. She wanted to live out here to raise our kids. When that didn't materialize, we didn't have any reason.'

He stared at the back of the house. A long moment

passed. The wind rustled the nearly bare branches of the trees. It felt like we were a thousand miles from Manhattan. Then Michael smiled that disturbing grin of his. 'Well, I got my way in the end.'

As we skirted the side of the house, back toward the driveway, I slowed my pace to look through one of the windows. Gradually the room came into focus, like a darkened fishbowl. It was completely empty. The walls blank, the floor bare and uncovered. There was one lonely drop cloth in the corner of the room. A ladder and a bucket of paint. It looked like the job had been abandoned halfway through. Like whoever it was couldn't get out of there fast enough.

Back at the car, I moved toward the passenger side. Michael put his hand on my shoulder.

'Why don't you take over for a while?' he said. 'You ever driven a Maserati?'

This was the old Michael, back again. The Michael whose orders you obeyed without question. He opened the passenger door and climbed in. 'Come on, Peck. It'll be fun. You don't get to do this every day.'

My knees were shaking again as I walked to the driver's side. I turned the key in the ignition, and I remembered that my driver's license had expired. Test-driving a car like this without a license seemed idiotic. I wondered if I should tell Michael. But he interpreted my pause as something else.

'You *do* know how to drive stick, don't you?'

'Yes.'

'Good. Let's go. Take us back the way we came.'

I'd only driven stick in my parents' old truck, the one they used when our newer car was in the shop. This was nothing like that. But soon enough, I got the hang of it. All you needed was a light touch. Not to control the car but to meld with it. Feel the acceleration and the curves within your own body. Trust that it was going to be okay. From the corner of my eye, I saw Michael smiling.

'Feels good, doesn't it?'

'Yeah, it does.'

'They're addictive. I have two already. Never get the chance to drive them. Just don't have the time. But I felt like we needed to celebrate. It's been a big couple of weeks. Take a right up here. We want to head back to the bridge.'

I nodded.

'So Wanda said you were trying to get an appointment all week. What did you want to talk to me about?'

I was trying to merge onto the southbound Palisades Parkway, glancing over my shoulder for an opening. It was one thing driving the Maserati on the empty streets of Alpine, New Jersey. It was another driving it in thick highway traffic. A single scratch on this car would probably send me into bankruptcy. I hadn't really been listening. 'I'm sorry, Michael. What did you say?'

'What did you want to talk to me about?'

'Oh.' The steering wheel went slick under my palms. 'The, um. I wanted to talk to you about the Las Vegas trip.'

'What about it?'

The traffic was even heavier than it had been an hour earlier, coming out. I could feel the Maserati bucking underneath me, growling at the speed I was forcing it to hold to. Part of me wanted to drop this, move on. But I couldn't. I had to do it, now or never. I took a deep breath. 'Well, when I delivered the papers –'

'Yes, Chan was very happy with them.'

'Well, as I was about to leave, he told me that he wanted to stay in touch with me. Chan's daughter was there, too, translating for us. She's applying to colleges in the fall. I think they want my help with it. They know I went to Yale.'

Michael laughed. 'Typical. Greedy bastards.'

'I guess I'm just not sure what I'm supposed to do. Or what they're expecting me to do. I don't have connections like that.'

'Of course you don't. You can't buy your way into Harvard or Yale.'

I felt a surge of relief. 'Exactly.'

'Listen, Evan. These guys think everything has a price tag. They want more, more, more. We've held up our end of the bargain. It's done. Anything else is icing on the cake, and they'll have to pay extra for that. So Chan's daughter will apply next year. By that point, this deal will be wrapped up. There won't be anything they can do.'

I was processing. 'So you want me to –'

'No. Evan. I don't *want* you to do anything. I'm not

asking you to do anything. Do you understand? You handle this as you see fit. Right?'

A low-riding Camaro swerved in front of me. I slammed on the brakes.

'Jesus,' Michael said. 'Be careful.'

I could feel the sweat gathering between my shoulders.

'Listen,' he said. 'Evan. You know how to play this game. That's one of the reasons I hired you. You've got the right instincts. You're sharp. You see things clearly. I don't have to tell you what to do. You were *made* to do this kind of work. And there's no higher compliment than that.'

We drove the rest of the way in silence, down the parkway, back across the George Washington Bridge. I thought about what Michael was saying. The confidence he'd had in me all along. He'd said as much to Brad that night in Las Vegas. Ambitious. A hard worker. Perfect for this project. He had no reason to lie to Brad, no way of knowing I was listening. He was telling the truth that night. Michael really did see something in me. And maybe it was something that I was only just starting to see in myself.

We drove down the West Side Highway, approaching midtown. The sign for West 54th Street loomed in the distance. I signaled and started to move into the left lane.

'No,' Michael said. 'Keep going.'

'Isn't the dealer on Fifty-fourth Street?'

'You're going to drop me off downtown first. Take it to West Twelfth Street.'

Michael was back on his BlackBerry, squinting at the screen and responding to e-mails. As we passed the Lincoln Tunnel, his phone rang.

'Babe,' he answered. 'Yes. Yes. I'm almost there. Ten minutes, okay?'

He had me take West 12th to Bleecker, then hang a right and loop down to West 11th. Finally, on a street lined with town houses and trees, Michael had me pull over.

'Up there, on the right,' he said. 'The house with the green door.'

Before he climbed out of the car, he leaned over and pressed on the horn. The sound blared through the quiet. Michael paused outside the car, one hand on the door, then ducked through the frame to look at me. 'Good talk, Evan,' he said. 'See you on Monday.' The door closed with a satisfying thump.

The door of the town house swung open. A figure, silhouetted by the light from the front hall, moved out on the stoop. She was petite and curvy, with wavy hair. Brown hair. I remembered the pictures of his wife from his office: a cool blonde, sleek and slender. Michael kissed this other woman, reaching down to grab her ass. She smiled and swatted his hand away, a joke they shared. Then they stepped inside and closed the door.

CHAPTER 10

Julia

'Is Evan going to join us this year?' my father asked. He and my mother were on speakerphone in the car, driving back from an event in Boston. It was the week before Thanksgiving.

'I'm not sure.' Evan had spent the previous three Thanksgivings with us, so it was only natural they assumed he'd come this year, too. 'He's been so busy. He might not be able to take the time.'

'Julia,' my mother chimed in. 'We really need to know. Jasmine is planning the menu and doing the shopping now.'

'Yeah, I know, but his schedule is so unpredictable.'

'We understand, sweetheart,' my father said. I could picture him shooting my mother a look. She didn't understand the world of men and their work, and the precedence it took. Lately, strangely, Evan's stock had gone up with my parents; he had a job at Spire, therefore he was a person of substance. 'Evan has to do what he has to do,' my father said, respect in his voice. 'Good for him. Give him our best.'

'Ask him again tonight, Julia,' my mother persisted. My father sighed in the background. 'This makes things complicated.'

Didn't I know it. The truth was I hadn't asked yet. To not invite Evan seemed cruel, but having him there seemed even worse. I hoped, in the days leading up to the holiday, that the obvious solution would present itself. Evan would preempt my question and tell me he had to stay in New York and work. I just couldn't get up the nerve to ask. We'd barely spoken since his return from Las Vegas. Our silences had grown denser, colder. I'd been surprised it had gone on so long – a day or two, maybe, for Evan to gather himself and save face, but a whole week? I had underestimated Evan. Or maybe I overestimated him. Why should I have been surprised that he had a breaking point, just like everyone else? A point at which he no longer wanted to bother – a point at which he stopped caring, as I already had, weeks earlier?

On Monday night, four days before Thanksgiving, Adam cooked dinner for me at his apartment. I had stopped being coy, stopped pretending at early mornings and other excuses. I wanted him all the time. It was the best sex of my life – in the shower, on the dining-room table, in every corner of his beautiful apartment. Sometimes I worried about the loss of control. I was in too deep; I was getting sloppy. Making all the clichéd mistakes that people make when they have affairs. But then I fell for the biggest cliché of all: I thought I was different. It was going to be different with us. What Adam and I had ran deeper than the physical, I was sure of it. I felt like I was finally beginning to understand myself, that I was finally seeing in myself what Adam had seen all along. Potential. Something bigger and better. A chance to live a different kind of life.

I got home around midnight on Monday, figuring I had a few hours to spare. Evan didn't usually leave work until two or three in the morning. But as I approached, I noticed the light shining from beneath our door and the dull garble of the television coming from inside. I smoothed my hair, tugged my clothes straight, wiped away the last traces of lipstick. I'd been putting more effort into my appearance lately, but Evan didn't notice.

He was sitting on the futon, staring at the TV. Among the beer cans dotted across the coffee table, there was a plain manila envelope. Evan reached for the remote to mute the TV. Then he turned to look at me, like an afterthought.

'Where were you?'

'Out with coworkers.' I hung my coat on the back of the door. I'd had the excuse ready to go for weeks. It was the first time I'd had to use it. 'We got a late dinner afterward.'

The room smelled like beer. Evan shifted forward in his seat, tenting his fingertips over his mouth for a moment. Then he reached for the envelope on the coffee table and held it between his two hands.

'What is that?' I asked, my curiosity getting the better of me.

He cleared his throat. 'Michael and I finally talked about Vegas.'

He turned the envelope over, examining the other side. There was no postage, no writing or marking on it. I wondered what he was looking for.

'No one's getting bonuses this year,' he said. 'We'd all known that for a while. Some of the guys were pissed. They were counting on it. But it wouldn't look right, not in this economy. Bad optics, you know.'

Optics. This was not the Evan I knew.

'Michael reiterated that today. No bonuses. But, he said, he wanted me to have this. As a token of his appreciation. He said he was proud of the work that I'd done on this WestCorp deal.'

He handed me the envelope, nodding at me to open it. Inside were several stacks of crisp new hundred-dollar bills wrapped in paper bands.

'How much is this?'

'Twenty thousand dollars.'

'Jesus. But Evan, what are you – you can't keep this, can you?'

'I don't know.'

He stood up, taking the envelope back. On his way to the bedroom, he dropped it on top of the bookshelf, like he was tossing aside a pile of junk mail. A gesture of indifference that both frightened and disgusted me. Evan couldn't feign innocence any longer, not like before Las Vegas. He knew exactly what Michael had done – what he *himself* had done. They were breaking the law. And this time, he hadn't asked my advice. He was acting like this was the most normal thing in the world. The Evan I knew was never coming back. So then what was his deal? It was so obvious he didn't care about me anymore. Why was he still here?

Later, in bed, wide awake. 'When are you leaving for Boston?' he asked.

'Oh. Uh, Wednesday afternoon.'

He was silent. I wanted to sit up, turn on the light, ask him what the hell he was thinking. But we were past that point. Whatever words we might once have said had nowhere left to land.

'Are you . . .' I started to say. 'For Thanksgiving, are you –'

'I'm staying here. Work.'

'Right. That makes sense.'

He rolled over, away from me. Our cheap mattress bounced and sagged from the shift in weight. 'Goodnight,' he said. A few minutes later, he was asleep.

Elizabeth was waiting for me at the train station. It was colder in Boston than in New York, and she wore a huge parka with a fur-lined hood. She was the small one in our family – a delicate build, a foxy face – and the parka made her look even tinier.

'This is weird,' I said, climbing into the front seat of

her old silver Saab. Hot air blasted from the vents. I kicked aside the empty Dunkin' Donuts cups rolling around in the footwell.

'What?'

'I should be the one driving. I'm your big sister.'

She laughed. 'You're a bad driver. I wouldn't let you.'

'You got home today?'

'Yeah. The roads were terrible. It snowed last night. Can you believe that? In November.'

Elizabeth went to a small college in Maine. She had been at the top of her class in high school and would have had her pick, but she decided to forgo the most competitive schools – no Ivy League for her. She was majoring in studio art. She wrote poetry on the side, and she developed her own photographs. My parents had expressed concern about the path she seemed to be headed down, but Elizabeth kept telling them this was what she wanted to do. Eventually it sank in, and for the most part, they left her alone.

'Plus I barely slept,' she said. 'I was in the studio until four in the morning. So how's New York? No Evan this year?'

I grimaced inwardly at his name. 'He couldn't take the time.'

'Are things any better between you guys?'

'Actually, there's this guy I sort of reconnected with. From college.'

'What?' She whipped around to look at me. 'A guy? Like, romantically?'

I saw the disapproval written across Elizabeth's face,

and I changed tack. The urge to confess came so strongly, but the lie came easily, too. 'Oh . . . um, no. Not like that. We've just been spending time together. Friends. I don't know what it is.'

Elizabeth nodded, turning back to the road. She had always liked Evan, and I felt bad dumping this on her. But she was also my sister, and she knew me better than anyone did. She may not have liked what I was saying, what I was implying, but I think she understood what lay behind it.

After a long silence, she piped up again. 'Hey, can you let Pepper out? Mom asked me to walk him.'

'So why don't you walk him?'

'I'm just dropping you off. This girl from school is having a thing. Mom and Dad are at that party at the Fletchers'. I didn't know I was going to have to pick you up.'

'Well, thanks for squeezing me in.'

'I'm just saying. I have other plans.'

'Yeah, well, so do I.'

'Really?'

'Really.' Well, I had the option to have plans. One of my boarding-school friends had started an e-mail chain suggesting that anyone in Boston for the holidays meet up at a local bar on Wednesday night. It seemed better than sitting alone in our empty house, waiting for everyone else to return. I'd been doing that too much this past summer in New York. 'I'm meeting up with some Andover people at Finnegan's.'

'Finnegan's! Yikes. Have fun with that.'

Elizabeth dropped me off, and I found the spare key under the planter. Pepper, our black Lab, was in his crate in the mudroom off the kitchen. His tail thumped as I fiddled with the latch, then he burst out and collided with me. He nuzzled his wet snout into my palms.

'I love you, too, Pepper,' I said. 'Let's go outside, okay?'

Pepper had been my and Elizabeth's dog. When we were younger, we alternated taking him on short, lazy walks. Suddenly I was thirteen years old again: the cold air, the sparkle of the stars overhead, the warm glow of windows in the dark, walking Pepper between home-work and bed. Running through dates of battles or lines of Shakespeare or base pairs of DNA. Worrying about grades. Worrying about getting into a good college. I had never bothered to worry about what came after that. No one *told* me to worry. Surely another rung on the ladder awaited, and wouldn't that next part be just like every other part? Pepper sniffed around the base of a tree. He didn't tug at his leash the way he used to. He was an old dog, I realized, almost ten. He only had a few good years left.

Tears pricked the corners of my eyes when we got back inside. I'd been feeling strange all week. 'You want a treat, Peps?' I said, brightening my voice. He wagged his tail. The clock on the microwave in the kitchen said it was just after 8:30 p.m. The group had planned to meet at Finnegan's by eight.

My parents had taken my dad's car to the party at the

Fletchers', which left me with my mother's Volvo. I wondered, for a moment, whether I wanted to do this. Drink bad beer and eat greasy food with people I didn't really care about. Maybe for once I'd be better off at home, by myself. Put on a pot of tea, curl up with a book, run a bath. Embracing instead of fleeing the solitude. I hesitated, about to switch off the ignition. Then my phone buzzed with a text from one of the lacrosse girls: Great! See you in a few! I put the car into drive and headed for the bar.

———————

I thought things at work might have improved after the gala, but the only person altered by the news was Eleanor. She floated in late every morning, smugger than ever, leaving for lunch and often not returning. But Laurie was the same as always. A heavy cloud trailed her as she passed back and forth in front of my desk.

Laurie was on the phone around ten days before Thanksgiving. It was a quiet afternoon, and if I stopped the clatter of my typing, I could just make out what she was saying to the person on the other end.

'Well, I can't get in the middle of this. It's not my place.'

Silence. I squinted at my computer screen in case someone walked by.

'I'm trying.' She was nearly whispering. 'I'm just trying to keep this place running. What else can I do?'

Laurie hung up, sighed loudly, and walked out of her

office. She flung her coat over her shoulders. 'Julia, I'm leaving for the day,' she said. 'If anything comes up, call my cell.' When she disappeared into the lobby, I reached for my wallet. I still had Sara Yamashita's business card from the night of Nick's party. I ran my finger along the edge of the thick card stock, thinking.

'Are you kidding?' Abby said to me. This was a few days later, the weekend before Thanksgiving. We were at a Mexican place on the Upper East Side. She swiped a tortilla chip through the guacamole. 'You should call her. Absolutely.'

'It doesn't seem too pushy?'

'Jules. She wouldn't have told you to call unless she actually wanted you to call. Come on! Quit that miserable job of yours. It's what I keep telling Jake.'

'Things are still bad?'

Abby rolled her eyes. When Lehman went under, Henry Fletcher called in a favor with a friend at Barclays, which was absorbing certain Lehman assets. He ensured that his son would have a place in the new organization. But it had all been a waste. According to Abby, Jake's grumpy dislike of the work had morphed into outright hatred.

'Poor guy,' she said. 'He's miserable. I mean, he never liked banking to begin with. The Barclays people are assholes, apparently. He wishes he'd just been laid off, like everyone else. He's going to take the GMAT next year.'

'Wow. Has he told his parents?'

'Hah. You know what they're like. He can't talk to them about this stuff.'

She went quiet, staring down at the table. A week earlier, Abby's father had finally lost his job. She delivered the news with a shrug, a what-can-you-do resignation, but there was a catch in her voice. The value of their house had plummeted by half. Her mom had started looking for work. They were pretending that everything was going to be fine. But Abby, as the youngest, had spent many years learning to decipher the language of her parents. She saw right through them.

'I'm sorry, Abby. That's really shitty.'

'Oy vey,' she said with a sigh. Then she tried for brightness again. 'Hey, could we get two more margaritas? And some more chips?' she said to our waiter as he walked past. She picked up her fork and scooped a bite of guacamole. 'This stuff is seriously like crack. So wait a second: how do you know this girl again? This Sara girl?'

'She went to Yale. She was a few years ahead of us.'

'Funny. Her name doesn't ring a bell.'

'Well, actually – I met her through Adam. Recently.'

'Adam?' She raised one eyebrow. 'Where was this?'

'Some party. He used to know her from the magazine. We sort of hit it off.'

The waiter arrived with a fresh basket of chips and two new drinks. After he took our order, Abby lifted her margarita toward me.

'I think this is great, Jules. Do it. Call her. To new

beginnings.' We clinked our glasses, and I took a sip of my drink – the salty and sweet tang of artificial lime. The restaurant was loud and chaotic, with colorful Christmas lights strung across the mirrored walls and pocked wooden tables. Saturday night in New York City. Moments like this I felt lucky, almost happy.

After dinner, Abby headed toward the subway, and I pretended to walk back to my apartment. But I pulled out my phone and called Adam instead. He was at a dinner party that night hosted by a classmate of his from high school, a downtown party girl who lived in an enormous SoHo loft. 'She's a brat,' he'd said. 'Trust fund when she turned eighteen. Never had to lift a finger.' Adam's critical streak was something I was still learning to navigate. He was suspicious of people who had it too easy, but at the same time he seemed suspicious of people who hustled too hard for their success. That's what I thought at the time, at least. Although later I realized I was wrong about the latter: it was jealousy, not suspicion.

I did sometimes wonder why he acted so friendly toward the people whom he claimed to dislike. I'd asked him why he was going to the dinner party if he hated this girl, and he shrugged. 'She knows a lot of people. Her parties are good for networking.' He grazed his hand along the back of my head. 'I'd have more fun with you, though.'

When he picked up the phone, there was a swell of sound in the room behind him, conjuring a picture in my mind: the beautiful people, the expensive clothing, the perfect decor. I felt a sharp pang of loneliness. 'Hey, you just finish dinner with Abby?'

'Yeah. You're still there?'

'They just cleared the main course. Maybe another hour or so?'

I took a cab to his apartment. The happiness of dinner with Abby had vanished, and I was in a maudlin mood. I wandered around Adam's apartment with an enormous glass of red wine, tempted to let it slosh over the rim onto his pristine carpet. But Adam hadn't done anything wrong; there was nothing I was allowed to be mad about. At some point I lay down on the couch and later woke to the sound of the front door opening. The glowing read-out on the cable box said it was 2:00 a.m. I'd been in his apartment for more than four hours.

'Where were you?' I said, rubbing my eyes.

Adam sank onto the couch, slung his arm around me. 'Sorry. It went later than I thought. I called. Your phone must be on vibrate.'

I rested my head on his chest. He smelled like bourbon and a sugary dessert. The faint scent of tobacco, which I had gradually grown to like. I ran my hand over his shirt, down to his belt buckle, and turned my head to kiss his neck. My addiction was kicking in despite my bad mood, despite the beginnings of a red-wine headache. I pulled him toward me. We had sex on the couch, my dress hiked up and his pants tugged down, fast and hard and mechanical. But something seemed different in Adam. He hadn't needed this the way I had. He was going through the motions, sating my hunger without needing to sate his.

Afterward I told him what Abby and I had talked about over dinner.

'I think I'm going to call Sara. You know, Sara Yamashita, from the party. I'm going to ask her to lunch.'

'You are?'

'She told me to keep in touch.'

'Sara's a lot of talk. I wouldn't get your hopes up.'

'But it's worth a shot, right? It can't hurt.'

Adam reached for my hand. 'Trust me, babe. I know Sara better than you do. It might not be such a great idea. All I'm saying is don't rush into it. You want to be deliberate about your next move, right?'

'I guess.' I glanced again at the cable box – it was almost 3:00 a.m. I started gathering my things, the scarf and boots and coat I'd scattered around the apartment like an animal marking its territory. 'I should get going.' Adam sat back on the couch, taking a beat too long before he stood up to walk me to the door. I wondered how much longer we were going to have to do this – saying good-bye in the middle of the night, sneaking back to our own lives. I was already getting sick of it. In the cab ride home, I checked my phone. There were no missed calls or texts from Adam, despite what he'd said – nothing, from anyone, all night. I was annoyed all over again.

When had I lost the power to control my own moods? I felt so porous that fall, so absorbent of whatever the people around me were doing. There was nothing to keep me tied to the earth. I scudded in whatever direction the wind decided to blow. My mistake was that I kept interpreting it as a good thing, confusing that lightness for spontaneity.

———◆———

'Julia! Hey!'

Someone waved at me from the sidewalk outside the entrance to the bar. It was Camilla, a girl from the lacrosse team. We had lived in the same dorm for my three years of boarding school. She had arrived at school with glasses and curly hair and prissy sweater sets. But after a few months around the older girls, she'd learned the ways of experience – hair straighteners, tight jeans, push-up bras, contact lenses. She started sneaking boys back to her room in the middle of the night. She was legendary by senior year. Camilla stubbed out her cigarette as I approached and gave me a hug.

'Oh, my God, I am *so* glad you came. It's fucking freezing. How can you stand this place?'

'Yeah, sorry. Not exactly sunshine and palm trees. When'd you get home?'

'I flew in on Sunday. I decided to make a week of it.' Camilla had gone to USC and was working as an assistant to some big-shot movie agent in Los Angeles. She had a tan, and her hair smelled like coconut oil. I was vividly aware of how different her life was from mine. 'Let's go inside,' she said, tugging my hand.

I followed Camilla toward the corner of the bar where the other lacrosse girls were standing. Most of them worked in consulting or in finance or as paralegals. A few of the finance girls joked blackly about how much time they had left – the bosses were just waiting for the holidays to pass before they brought down the ax. There were one or two outliers who, like Camilla and me, had found low-paying assistant jobs in more 'creative' industries. 'That sounds . . . interesting,' one girl said after I told her about my job at the Fletcher Foundation. She was an analyst at Goldman Sachs, and we quickly ran out of things to talk about. I was about to use my empty glass as an excuse to leave when I felt a hand on my shoulder.

'Julia?' he said. The dark wavy hair; the aquiline nose. His voice.

'Rob,' I said. 'Wow. Hi.'

'It's been a while, huh?'

'Wow. What, like, four years or something?' But, really, I knew: it had been almost four years to the day since we'd broken up at Thanksgiving, freshman year of college. We hadn't seen each other since.

'You look great.'

'So do you.' He did. Energized, happy. Rob at his best. 'I was just about to get another drink. Do you want to . . . ?'

After we got our drinks, he pointed at an empty booth. 'You want to catch up for a minute?' he said.

In the booth, our knees touched for a brief moment. 'Wow. It's so strange. You look the same,' I said.

He laughed. 'In a good way, I hope.'

'Where are you living?'

'Here, in Cambridge. I'm applying to med school. Working in one of my professor's labs for the year.'

'Med school! Right. I'd forgotten about that.'

'You thought I'd changed my mind?' He smiled.

Later, a waitress came by and brought us another round. Rob could still make me laugh. He was still that boy he'd been in high school, the one who made the younger girls blush when he talked to them in the cafeteria. Whose confidence and affability extended to everyone. He would make a great doctor. For the first time in four years, I found myself thinking about him as a real person. Not as a footnote to my history, a static piece of the past. As a living possibility, right in front of me.

'Are you still with that guy?' he asked. 'What was his name again?'

'Evan,' I said. I could feel the effects of my two and a half drinks. A looseness in my limbs, a narrowing of my mind. 'Evan Peck. Yeah. I mean, sort of.'

'Sort of?'

'Things aren't great. I'm not sure how much longer it's going to last.'

'Really.' His leg brushed against mine. 'That's too bad.'

'What about you? Girlfriend?'

'There was this girl, but we broke up at graduation. It wasn't going anywhere. Honestly, of all the girls in college, I'm not sure any of them really came close to you.'

He moved nearer, resting his hand on my knee. I was almost overwhelmed by nostalgia, by the rush of memories: fall afternoons on the sidelines of the soccer field, cheering for Rob after he scored a goal. Study hall, kissing in the dusty back corner of the library. The way he would sometimes catch my eye in the middle of class, backlit by the morning sun, and wink as our teacher droned on about mitochondria. Life opening up before us. That moment bursting with possibility – a feeling that now seemed light-years away. I never thought things could get so complicated. I didn't think I was capable of feeling so uncertain, so confused. Rob leaned closer, and so did I.

'Julia!' Camilla was yelling from the bar. 'Get your ass over here!'

The spell broke. We took a group picture. The band, back together again. Camilla ordered a round of tequila shots, but I demurred. I had to drive home. On my way out, I waved good-bye to Rob. He mouthed, *I'll call you*.

The next morning, I went downstairs and found my mother in the kitchen, hands on her hips, staring at a casserole dish. The turkey was already in the oven. The pies were lined up neatly on the counter. Jasmine, our housekeeper, had made everything days in advance.

'Well, there you are. Happy Thanksgiving, sweetheart.' She kissed me on the cheek, then resumed staring at the casserole. She poked it and frowned. 'I can't for the life of me understand what Jasmine did to these potatoes.'

'The same thing she does every year?'

'She's trying something new. That's what she said. It smells' – she leaned forward, sniffing – 'I don't know. It smells *off*.'

'I think that's just garlic.'

'Garlic.' She sighed. 'Why does everything need to have garlic in it?'

She came and sat next to me at the kitchen table. She was wearing what she called her 'work clothes' – faded jeans, an old cardigan – what a normal person might wear to the grocery store but what my mother only wore within the confines of the house. She wouldn't be caught dead looking like this in front of her friends. She was sipping her coffee and watching me while I peeled a banana.

'Mom. What?'

'Your hair is getting so long.'

'I haven't found a place in New York yet.'

'Why don't you just get it done while you're here? I can call. I'm supposed to go in tomorrow.'

'How was the party last night?'

'Oh, it was nice. The Fletchers are doing some landscaping, so their yard is a complete mess. Your father is actually on the phone with Henry right now.'

'Is something going on?'

'Everything's fine.' She set her coffee down and rubbed at an invisible scuff on the table. 'Did I tell you? I've been asked to join the board of that new women's clinic. You remember, the one Mrs Baldwin is involved in?'

'Is that why we had to invite the Baldwins to Thanksgiving this year?'

She pursed her lips. 'We invited them because they're our friends. You've known them a long time. Don't you remember how much you loved it when Diana used to babysit for you? Anyway, it's a wonderful organization.'

Charities and nonprofits sought out my mother for many reasons. My father's firm was a generous and reliable donor; she was a lawyer herself and could perform certain legal functions; she was smart and asked the right questions. Her days had long ago become full with assorted obligations, as full as they would have been with a normal job. When I was younger, around eleven years old, she'd considered going back to work. She mused about it out loud, asking me and Elizabeth whether it would be okay by us. Until, abruptly, those musings stopped. Then she'd been brittle with us in the weeks that followed, losing her patience and snapping at us more than usual. It didn't seem fair; it wasn't our fault. I knew the reason – I'd overheard the argument – but something drove me to ask the question. Maybe I wanted her to finally lose it, to admit her anger. I felt an anticipation of shame, and a sick curiosity, as I said it: 'Mom, why *didn't* you go back to work?'

Her cheeks reddened. But that was all I would get. She had too much control.

'Because, sweetheart, I want to spend time with you and your sister. *That's* my job. That's the most important thing to me in the whole world.' She smiled, her face returning to a normal hue.

But I knew the truth. A few weeks before that, the night of the incident, I'd been setting the table for dinner when my dad got home. My mother poured a glass of wine and slid it across the kitchen counter toward him.

'I have good news,' she said.

'Oh?' My dad took a sip of wine. 'This is excellent. Is this the Bordeaux?'

'James. I got the job.'

He took another sip, slowly, then set his glass down. 'You did.'

I'd rarely seen her smile like that. Goofy, giddy. 'They met all my terms.'

'Julia,' my dad said, 'why don't you go see where your sister is?'

I held up the forks and knives, bunched in my hand. 'But I'm setting the table.'

'It can wait. Go ahead.'

As I walked out, I tried to catch my mother's eye. But she was staring at my father, and her smile had disappeared. I ran up the stairs, then along the second-floor hallway to the top of the back staircase, which led down to the kitchen. I climbed down the back staircase as quietly as possible, stopping just before the kitchen came into view. I held my breath and listened.

'But you knew this wouldn't work, Nina. I told you that *weeks* ago.'

'No. No. You said you had some concerns, and we

agreed that we'd discuss them when the time came. Okay, so now's the time. James, I had to work my *ass* off to get this job. This is an incredible opportunity. It's the best class-action group in the country.'

'This is a terrible idea. The girls need you at home. And we don't need the money.'

'I don't care about the money. It's important work. A third of my cases are going to be pro bono. Do you know how hard I had to push to get them to agree to that? Do you know how unheard of that is?'

'It's a massive conflict of interest. That firm has multiple cases pending against my clients.'

'So I recuse myself from those cases. We put up a Chinese wall. Plenty of people have done this before. You think we're the first pair of lawyers to ever run into this?'

'You cannot do this. You will not. You'd be working for a bunch of glorified ambulance chasers. You'd be embarrassing me in front of everyone we know. You'd be embarrassing *yourself*.'

I flinched at the sound of glass smashing against the wall.

'Nina, stop it.'

'It's my turn, James.' She was shouting, her voice high and hoarse.

'You're not thinking straight. You don't want this.'

'Fuck you. Don't tell me what I want.'

Shortly after that, my father came upstairs and told us that we were going to McDonald's for dinner. Elizabeth was gleeful – we never ate fast food – but the whole time I felt a sad lump forming in my throat. Those french fries were bribery. My mother's car was missing from the driveway when we left, and it was still missing when we got back from dinner. Lying in bed that night, I tried to make myself cry, but I couldn't.

In the morning, my mother was back, smiling tightly as she waved us off to the school bus. There was a ghost of a red wine stain on the kitchen wall, scrubbed but not quite erased. The next week, she announced that we were renovating the kitchen, a project she claimed she'd been thinking about for a long time. The contractors sealed off the doorways with thick plastic. They let her do the honors. She picked up the heavy crowbar and swung it against the old walls and cabinets, smashing them into dust.

———·———

The Baldwins were friends of my parents from the neighborhood: the husband a surgeon at Mass Gen, the wife on many of the same committees as my mother. I was seated next to Mrs Baldwin, whose earlobes were soft and stretched from her heavy pearl earrings. She took tiny, precise bites of her food and dabbed her lips with her napkin between every bite. 'So, Julia. How is life in New York? What an exciting time this must be.'

'It's good. A lot of friends from college moved down, too, so it's been fun.' I took a big swallow of my wine. 'But tell me about Diana. What's she doing in Paris?'

Mrs Baldwin beamed. She loved nothing more than talking about her perfect children. 'Oh, Diana is just wonderful. She *adores* Paris. I'm not sure she'll ever come back!' She laughed in high, tinkling tones. 'She's fluent in French – did you know that? She's working at the American Library. She has a little apartment in the Seventh. One of her best friends is the niece of the ambassador to France, so she's become friends with everyone at the embassy through her. Isn't that marvelous?'

'It sounds great,' I said, reaching for the wine.

'You studied in Paris, didn't you, Julia?'

'Yes. Spring of junior year.'

'I remember that. Your mother told me how much you loved it.'

Well, of course she did. My mother had studied in Paris during her Wellesley days, too, and she laid out the reasons why I ought to go; she was the one who pushed me from hesitation to action. At first it felt like I was just doing the sensible thing, following in her footsteps, making her happy. But I had loved it – that was true. Not instantly. It was a love that came gradually, and it felt sweeter for it.

I went in armed with a plan. My first week in the homestay, before classes began for the semester, I'd get up early and make an itinerary for the day: museums, scenic routes, famous patisseries. My hostess encountered me on one of those mornings as I was scrutinizing a guidebook over breakfast. She looked baffled when I explained: I had a long list of sights in Paris that I wanted to see. I'd use this time, before school started, to knock out as many as possible. She stubbed out her clove cigarette and sat next to me at the kitchen table.

'Julia,' she said in a thick accent, preferring her bad English to my even worse French. 'This is not what you do. You come to Paris to live. *Alors.*' She closed the guidebook firmly. 'You do not use this. You walk the city and you see it. You understand, yes?'

I took her advice, and I walked through the city for the first time with no plan and no guidebook. It was a cold, miserable, wet January day. I'd worn the wrong shoes, and my feet were soaked and freezing within five minutes. I went into a café for lunch and ordered an omelet, and the waitress smirked at my pronunciation. The food sat strangely in my stomach, and jet lag trailed me through the afternoon. When I was waiting at the crosswalk on the Rue de Rivoli, a bus roared past and soaked me with puddle spray, and that's when I lost it. I was homesick and lonely and I missed Evan so much, and I was crying, and all I wanted was to go curl up on my narrow bed in the homestay. But going back felt like admitting defeat. So I kept walking. I crossed the Pont Royal and wound up at the Musée d'Orsay. My feet were still soaked, and my clothes were, too. My eyes felt gritty and puffy, and I was so tired I thought I might pass out. This was distinctly not how I'd imagined it – my first week in Paris, my first visit to the famous Orsay.

I sat on a bench up on the fifth floor and let the crowds

slide past, obscuring then revealing the artwork on the walls. It felt good to stay in one place, to sit and get warm. The light grew dimmer from the afternoon sunset – January in northern France. I'd been sitting on the same bench for at least two hours. Eventually the crowds thinned, and I had my first uninterrupted view of the art in front of me. There was a Monet that I recognized. The Parliament building in London, silhouetted against a reddening sky, the sun reflected in the water. A painting I'd studied before, in class. That day in Paris, I stared at it for so long that it changed into something else. No longer a specific building in a specific place but a mixture of color and movement that the eye could interpret any way it wanted. It was like when you say a word over and over and it becomes strange and new, a collection of sounds you'd never thought to question before. When you learn that there is something to be gained by examining what's right in front of you.

I lingered until a security guard told me to leave. I bought a postcard of that painting in the gift shop, and when I got back to my homestay, I tacked it up on the wall next to the photograph of my mother, the one I'd found a few weeks before. My mother as a younger woman, before her life had solidified onto its current course. Every morning during that semester in Paris, those images were the first things I saw when I opened my eyes. I began to think of them as a pair, as a symmetry. The past, the present. They reminded me of the gift I'd been given: time. Time to do nothing, or time to do whatever I wanted. I didn't need to have it all figured out. The uncomfortable feeling that had plagued me through sophomore year, that had made me feel strange and restless – it had taken a while, but it had finally evaporated. I was okay, right where I was.

Mrs Baldwin was regarding me with a quizzical expression.

'I'm sorry?' I said, emerging from the undertow of memory.

'I said, you're living with your boyfriend in New York, isn't that right?'

'Right. Right, yes. We went to college together. He works in finance.'

Those data points rendered him acceptable. Mrs Baldwin didn't need to know any more. She started telling me about her son's wedding over the summer – it was just the loveliest wedding, they were married at the Cloisters, the bride's parents were famous-ish, and the mayor came. I refilled my wineglass again, then again. The memories of Paris had made me melancholy, had reignited a longing for some vanished chapter of my life. It was a feeling too big to hold on to.

'You okay?' Elizabeth said between dinner and dessert, after we had gotten up from the table to load the plates into the dishwasher.

'I had too much wine.'

She snorted. 'Sitting next to Mrs Baldwin? Next time I'd go for something stronger. Heroin, maybe.'

'How was your end of the table?'

'He kept touching my hand. Like, to make a point in conversation. But he was leaving it there a little too long.'

'Dr Baldwin? Ugh. Creepy.'

My parents waved good-bye to the Baldwins as their car backed out of the driveway. When the front door closed, I noticed a slump in both of them. The mask dropped, the smile loosened. They didn't particularly enjoy the company of the Baldwins any more than Elizabeth or I did. But they did see the utility of their company. The Baldwins were the right kind of people with the right kind of connections.

'Just leave it,' my mother said when Elizabeth and I started clearing the dessert dishes from the table. 'Let Jasmine get it in the morning. I'm going to bed.'

She trudged up the stairs. My father retreated to his study off of the kitchen; always more work to be done. Elizabeth shrugged and went up to her room, too. Pepper had been in his crate all through dinner, and no one made a move to let him out. So I unlatched the door and fed him a scrap of piecrust from Mrs Baldwin's plate, then took him for a long walk through the dark and sleepy neighborhood.

Chapter 11

Evan

Roger caught me earlier that day. 'Trouble in paradise?' he said, clapping me on the shoulder.

I jumped in my seat and exited the browser where I'd been looking at apartment listings, but I felt the heat rise in my face. Roger sat down across from me, grinning with glee at his discovery. 'The wife mad that you've been spending so much time in the office? She kicking you out?'

'Shut up, Roger.'

'Oh, wow. Did I hit a nerve?'

Several hours later, Roger was gone. Everyone was gone, except for me. The streets were quiet when I finally left the office around midnight. The scattering to home had begun that afternoon. The only signs of life in our neighborhood were the divey Irish bars jam-packed with city kids who were home for the holidays from college, drinking with friends.

In the bathroom, brushing my teeth, I heard a strange noise. A mechanical chirp. After a minute of confusion,

I finally saw it on the ceiling: the smoke detector, flashing a yellow warning light. I dragged a chair over and disconnected it, took the battery out, and it went silent. It was too late to go out and buy a new battery. I'd have to survive a night without it.

But I couldn't fall asleep. The whole apartment felt unsettled — it had ever since I'd gotten back from Las Vegas. I'd taken to lingering longer and longer at the office to avoid it. At least I could still feel normal at the office. Even when she wasn't around, the feeling of Julia clung to the apartment. I'd started checking online apartment listings in my spare time, furtively, clearing my browser history afterward like I'd been watching porn. The options beckoned: sexy, seductive, a fresh start. Rents were loaded with incentives, post-crash. The new glassy, high-end buildings on the far West Side were perfectly affordable for a young finance bachelor. Then I'd shake my head. I wasn't a bachelor. Julia and I were still together, after all.

I kept tossing and turning that night, thinking I was hearing the distant chirp of the dead smoke detector. I finally drifted off, but I woke a few minutes later with a start. I thought I smelled smoke, but I knew it was nothing.

The next morning, as I passed the diner on the corner, I stopped and peered through the window. A TV in the corner showed the crowds at the parade. It looked cozy inside. The jingling bell announced my arrival, and a sullen waitress showed me to a table. 'Happy Thanksgiving,' she said, slapping the laminated menu on the table. 'You want coffee?'

The coffee was sour and burned, and the eggs were runny, but it didn't matter. I'd passed the diner every morning, and I'd always wanted to stop there. When the man at the next table departed, he left behind his copy of the *New York Observer*. I grabbed it, straightening the crinkled pages. There was a story about the war in Iraq, the troops celebrating Thanksgiving in Baghdad and Basra. An item about the Detroit bailouts. At the bottom of the front page was a teaser for a story inside:

HEDGE FUNDS DOWN IN 2008
Results show steep drop in earnings across industry. A12

I flipped to page 12. It was Adam McCard's byline.

'More?' the waitress said, not bothering to wait for a response. She tipped the carafe and let the coffee splash over the sides of the mug.

I skimmed the story. Manhattan, Greenwich, Stamford – everyone was having a bad year. Negative returns, investors yanking their cash, waves of layoffs. Hundreds of funds had shut down already, and more were on the brink of collapse. Sometimes you had a bad year, everyone knew that. But this looked to be something bigger. A bad decade, or more. Even at Spire, money was tight, and there weren't going to be any bonuses that year. People grumbled, and Roger let slip, bitterly, that he'd been counting on a bonus to make up for the money he'd been wasting on bottle service. But I think most of us knew how good we had it. We still had our jobs. Spire was the one hedge fund in the industry that hadn't laid off a single person since the downturn.

The WestCorp deal had finally gone live earlier that week, on Monday, a few days before the holiday. Michael had called me into his office that morning. He gestured at me to sit, then he shut the door. He didn't mention the car ride on Friday night, what had happened, or what we'd discussed. And that was okay – I didn't need him to explain anything. I finally felt like I got it. Like everything made sense.

'Evan. I realized I never actually thanked you for coming on the Las Vegas trip the other week, on short notice. You were immensely helpful. So thank you.'

'Of course. I was glad to.'

He searched, it seemed, for a crack in my expression, a sign of sarcasm or timidity. Finding none, he reached inside a drawer and withdrew a manila envelope.

'This deal is going to make history. And 2009 is going to be a record-setting year for us because of it. But you probably know that things are tight in the interim. I debated whether I ought to give this to you. But I wanted you to have it as a token of Spire's appreciation. Of my appreciation.'

He slid the envelope across the desk. 'I doubt I need to say this,' Michael said, 'but it would be best if you kept this quiet for now.'

After I left his office, I went into a bathroom stall and sat down on the lowered toilet lid. I paused, for a moment, to make sure I was alone. I ripped open the envelope. Inside were several stacks of crisp hundred-dollar bills. I counted them slowly. It took a long time. I counted them again, to be sure.

Twenty thousand dollars in cash. There was no note.

———————

I spent Thanksgiving Day at the office. I deleted old e-mails, checked over some models I'd been working on, read a backlog of market reports. I was already impatient for the holiday moratorium to be lifted, for work to resume. Around midday, my cell phone started vibrating. I smiled when I saw the name on the caller ID.

'Arthur!'

'Hey, Evan! Happy Thanksgiving.'

'You too. Jeez, man, I thought you were dead. How are you?'

Arthur was even busier than I was, and I figured my unreturned e-mails and calls were a symptom of that. A funny reversal of roles had happened by the end of college. Freshman year, Arthur lived in my shadow. Physically and metaphorically – being an athlete came with a certain amount of built-in respect. I was the one who knew about the parties on Saturday nights, whose name was recognized by other people. But by senior year, Arthur was the bigger man on campus. He'd grown into himself. He was president of the debate society, elected to Phi Beta Kappa, tapped for one of the elite senior societies. Arthur Ziegler was going places.

The noise of a full household echoed from the other end of the line. I remembered the Thanksgiving I'd spent with him, freshman year, all the cousins and aunts and uncles. The cramped dining-room table groaning under the weight of too many dishes, voices shouting to be heard over the Buckeyes game on TV. Four years had gone by: was that possible? He surely must have noticed the comparative silence coming from my end. It was the first time that day it occurred to me how depressing this must look to someone else. And then he asked:

'Hey, so where are you today? Are you up at Julia's?'

'No, actually – no. I couldn't get away from work.'

'They don't even let you have the one day off?'

'It's been crazy lately. But it's all right. You know how I feel about her parents.'

He laughed. 'How is Julia? You guys are still dating, right?'

Did he know how close to the truth he was cutting? 'She's fine.'

'Just fine?'

I felt something tightening inside. To be honest, that was the real reason Arthur and I hadn't talked much since school ended. The night before graduation, we'd run into each other at the pizza place on Broadway. We got our late-night usual: one slice of cheese for him, two pepperoni for me. We wound up in my bedroom, talking, reminiscing. I was sitting in my desk chair, and Arthur was perched on my bed, swinging his feet above the floor. I was halfway packed, posters stripped from the walls and the closet rattling with empty hangers. The next morning, in a few short hours, we would don our caps and gowns and assemble for the graduation procession. Arthur was talking about the Obama campaign, how his work would put him on the front lines of history. He sometimes turned a little grandiose when he was drunk.

'Are you nervous at all?' I asked.

'No. This is what I'm meant to be doing. I know it.' He drummed his fingers against his thighs and nodded, lost in his own thoughts. Then looked up at me, his eyes narrowing. 'But what about you?'

'What about me?'

'Are *you* nervous?'

'For what?'

'Well.' Arthur swept his hands across the room. 'Everything. New York. Your new job. But mostly, *dun-dun-dunnn* – moving in with your girlfriend.'

I laughed. 'Nah. Not really.'

Arthur went quiet. A heavy expression descended on his face.

'Well, maybe you should be.'

'What does that mean?'

'I just mean,' Arthur said, 'it's a serious step to take. Moving in together. Are you really ready for it? Sometimes I wonder whether you've thought it through.'

'Wait. Wait, what? I don't remember you saying any of this when I was actually making this decision.'

'Well, honestly, I kept hoping you'd see it on your own.'

'See what on my own?'

'What a colossal mistake this is.'

I jerked my head back and laughed. This had to be some kind of joke.

But Arthur took a deep breath. 'She's just – well. Look, I'm not trying to offend you. Maybe I shouldn't have said anything. But Julia can be difficult, right? I know how it's been with you guys. And I worry that without some space between you, some breathing room, she could drag you down into the morass with her.'

My hands were gripping the back of the desk chair. So hard that I thought the wood might splinter. 'This is my girlfriend you're talking about,' I finally said.

'I know. But I've known you a long time, Evan, and I've known her a long time, too. And she can just be so . . . well, self-pitying. You've seen what she's like when she's in a bad mood. And I know she's had a hard time finding a job –'

'Oh, come on,' I snapped. 'That is so petty. She'll get a job.'

'Right, well, that's not exactly the point. The point is whether it's a good idea to be moving in with someone so self-centered.'

'You're calling her self-centered?' I shouted.

He stared back at me. 'Yes.'

'What the fuck is your problem?'

'I wouldn't be telling you this if I didn't think it was for your own good.'

'Oh, well, in *that* case.'

Arthur sighed. 'Forget it. Forget I said anything.'

I stood up and opened the door. 'It's late. I think you should go.'

The next morning, we managed to act like nothing happened. These would be the pictures printed and framed, to be looked at years later: graduation day, all of college reduced down to a single snapshot. Julia had her camera with her, and she made us pose together, two roommates with their arms slung around each other. Still best friends, four years later, amid a sea of black polyester robes fluttering in the May breeze.

My mind snapped back to the present. The glowing, blipping computer monitor in front of me, the hum of the lights overhead. Arthur on the other end of the line.

'Julia? Uh, no, she's good. I don't see that much of her. I'm barely ever home. But she seems to keep busy.'

'That's good.'

There was a long pause. Arthur cleared his throat. 'Well, they're about to carve the turkey. I'd better get going.'

We hung up and promised, emptily, to talk again soon.

———•———

I had chalked it up to jealousy at the time. Arthur never warmed to Julia. When I was with her, I wasn't with him. Simple as that. I suspected that they were too much alike. Not superficially, but underneath they had that same quality. A watchfulness, a gaze that never missed a thing.

It was why I liked them both so much. They took me in whole without my needing to explain myself.

So that's all it was, I told myself while Julia and I drove a rented U-Haul down I-95 to New York the day after graduation. Arthur's words had been humming through my head since our fight. He was jealous. He thought I was picking her over him. Those nasty things he'd said – it was just envy. In our tiny new living room that first night in New York, I looked over at Julia. She had her hands on her hips, head cocked to one side, deciding where to hang the pictures. I felt such a rush of love at that moment, watching our new life become real. It wasn't a fluke, the way I felt about her. We were meant to be.

But Arthur's words were back again. Fresh and whole, like a submarine breaking through the surface. Had he been right all along? Self-centered. Self-pitying. Julia had an independent streak that I'd always liked, but since graduation, it had hardened into something else. A life so separate that I wasn't even part of it.

Had I known it, too? Julia was flawed, like anyone else. Sometimes she could be selfish, it was true. But she had so much that transcended it. When things were good, the selfishness disappeared completely. And for most of our time together, that's the way it was. I'd had glimpses of how it might be different. Our fights. The way she could snap like a sprung trap. One weekend sophomore year, when her friends from boarding school were visiting, I watched her turn into this other version of herself. They were catty and cruel, making fun of old classmates on Facebook, getting more vicious with each bottle of wine. 'Look at her dress!' Julia shrieked, mouth stained red with drink. 'God, she looks like a Russian prostitute.'

But those moods passed quickly. Mostly, college had been good to us. Julia's arc bent toward a happier version of herself. Senior year, after we got back from our summer abroad and our visit to British Columbia, she was more comfortable and relaxed than I'd ever seen her. There was one night in particular that sealed it for me, that seemed like definitive proof of the kind of person Julia had become. A Saturday in early September, near the start of senior year.

'You sure it's cool if I don't go?' I said. Abby's society was throwing a big party that night. A fancy one, with a dress code and bartenders. I sat on her bed as Julia was getting ready.

She caught my eye in the mirror. 'Of course. You already had plans.'

'It's just with the guys. I could cancel.'

'I don't mind. Hey, how do I look?'

She spun in her dress and heels. I smiled. She didn't even need me to say it.

But later that night, when I was hanging out at the hockey house, plans shifted. One of our teammates was also in Abby's society, and he texted me and some of the other guys around 11:00 p.m., begging us to come to his rescue at the party. It was a question of loyalty; we couldn't leave a teammate twisting in the wind like that.

When we arrived, ten minutes later, I saw what the problem was. This was one of those parties where the main form of interaction was conversation. The lights were too bright, the music too quiet, the whole vibe too stiff. He stood in a corner, eyes wide and terrified. Making friends with new people, especially nonathletes, was not his strong suit. The poor guy. When he saw us, he practically shouted 'Thank God.'

A few heads turned at his outburst. Julia was one of them. I felt immediately guilty. So I hadn't been willing to come to this party for her, but I had been willing to come for my friend? We lumbered in like a bunch of cavemen. I was still wearing a baseball hat and hadn't shaved in more than a week. There was no way this wasn't embarrassing for her. She spotted me and walked quickly across the room. I braced for impact. I deserved whatever I was about to get.

But instead she threw her arms around me. 'Thank God is right,' she whispered. She turned to my teammate and added, 'I am *so* glad you told them to come.'

'You're not mad?'

'Why would I be mad? This party is dead. You just saved my life. Come on, let's get a drink.'

Julia got the bartender to pour a dozen shots of whiskey. She raised her glass for the first toast. 'To bringing home that championship,' she said, and everyone cheered. One of my teammates nudged me after Julia threw her shot back without a grimace. 'She's a keeper, man.'

It was one of those long, meandering nights, the

best kind, when you don't need a plan. By senior year, all of us finally understood that we did, in fact, belong there; that we were no longer faking it. We ended the night, many hours later, lying in Julia's bed in the darkness.

'I'm so happy,' she said. 'Evan. I want you to know that.'

'I'm happy, too.'

She was quiet for a while. Then her hand drifted over, her fingers intertwining with mine. 'I'm just so glad we made it. You know?'

I leaned over and kissed her on the forehead. 'I love you, Jules.'

'Mmm,' she said, yawning, curling up in sleepiness. 'See? You always know exactly what to say.'

This was the Julia I loved the most, the person whose love meant more for having been tested, for having endured. But in the months between graduation and late fall, the story had changed. The arc I'd seen over the previous four years had vanished. Her outlying behavior became the new normal. She was spikier, crueler. Harder in every way. I considered the question from different angles. Had something happened in the world, an outside shift that set her in a new direction? Or was it inevitable, an uncovering of the person she'd always been? Maybe it wasn't that her flaws were balanced out by the good. Maybe it was that the flaws were merely one side of a two-sided coin. What made a person good also made a person bad. Confidence could easily become arrogance.

A sense of humor was only ever a few rungs away from cruelty.

<hr/>

Things were back to normal by late afternoon. E-mails started flooding in, and my BlackBerry resumed its regular buzzing. Michael told me he wanted to review the WestCorp numbers first thing the following morning.

As the sky darkened and night fell, I felt better. It was weird, actually. It was the opposite of that sick Sunday night dread I'd sometimes felt in college, the looming threat of classes in the morning. I was already thinking happily about the next day, about the office coming alive again with the sounds of work, the way it was supposed to be. I had told Julia about my bonus earlier that week, but I hadn't told anyone else. I'd stuffed the money into my sock drawer. I liked the idea of it tucked away, secret proof. On the walk home, I decided to stop for a drink. Maybe I ought to celebrate. It was Thanksgiving night, and Michael was right, after all. This was a historic deal. I ought to take a moment to savor it.

It was a cold, clear night. Along Central Park South, I passed families bundled up inside horse-drawn carriages, the hooves clopping loudly on the pavement. Christmas lights laced the awnings along the street. I saw the Plaza Hotel up ahead. I'd been to the Oak Bar once before, with Julia. We came into the city one weekend senior year to have dinner with her parents. We'd gone for a drink at the Oak Bar afterward, then caught the last train back to New Haven. At that hour, 5th Avenue had been so peaceful, just the two of us for blocks at a time as we walked down to Grand Central, the passing whoosh of a street sweeper and the silent drift of steam from an open manhole.

When I walked in, the bar looked just as I remembered – dark wood and leather and a soft glow from the chandeliers. I ordered a martini, and it slid down my throat, cold and bracing and wet. I ordered a second one. The bar was half full, a murmur of conversation and clinking ice cubes occasionally punctuated by the cocktail shaker. There was a beautiful foreign-looking couple at a table, the woman's neck dripping with diamonds. Another young woman in a black dress, a few stools down, glancing nervously at the door. A mother and father and two little boys, the parents drinking their nightcaps while the boys munched on peanuts. It was comforting, being alone in a room with other people. A floating island where we'd all happened to seek refuge in this eerily quiet city.

The door swung open, letting in the cold. A man in a dark coat and cream-colored scarf came in, peeled off his leather gloves, and ran a hand through his hair. He turned, and I felt a pulse of recognition ripple up my spine. I knew him from somewhere. He scanned the room, and his eyes landed on me.

He recognized me, too. He smiled and strode over.

'Hey – it's Evan, right? Evan Peck?' He extended his hand.

'Yeah. Hi.' I squinted. 'God, I'm sorry, you're so familiar . . .'

'Hey, don't sweat it. Adam McCard. We met a few times through Julia.'

Of course. That grin, the too-strong aftershave.

'Right. Good to see you, man.'

'You, too. You're in the city these days?'

'Yup. Yeah, Julia and I live together.'

'Oh, no shit. You two stay in town for the holiday?'

'Just me. I couldn't really get away from work.'

'So you wind up here on Thanksgiving night. Hey, things could be worse.' He laughed, showing teeth like white coins. There was something different about him. The few times I'd met Adam in college, he'd always looked past me. Always scanning the room for something else. But that night his eyes were fixed directly on mine.

'So where do you work?' he said.

'I'm in finance. Spire Management – a hedge fund, actually.'

'Wow. They're huge. You liking it there?'

'Yeah, I am.'

'Rough year to start a career in finance.'

'We've been lucky. No layoffs, knock wood.'

'Amen. What are you working on over there?'

The bartender swooped over. 'Another martini, sir?' I shook my head and asked for the check. When I turned back, Adam was still staring. 'Oh, the usual stuff,' I said.

'You know,' Adam said, lowering his voice, 'I saw that

Spire's taking a big position on some lumber company up in Canada. Some really ballsy play. You work on that?'

Part of me wanted to take credit for it, just to shut Adam up. *Yes, I did, and what the hell have you done lately?* But I was skittish about saying too much. The deal was public news, but it was habit by then, keeping it close to the chest, need-to-know. 'Not really,' I said lightly. 'But what about you? I've seen your articles. They're good.'

He stared for a beat longer. Then, suddenly, the old Adam was back. His gaze slackened and his eyes surfed across the room. 'Thanks,' he said in an empty tone. 'Glad you're a fan. Hey, great running into you. I'd better go join my date.'

The woman in the black dress at the bar lit up with a smile at Adam. 'See you around,' Adam said to me. He slid on the stool next to the woman and pulled her in for a long kiss. She had transformed from her nervous self and was suddenly playful as a kitten, kissing his neck and snuggling against him. Adam snapped his fingers at the bartender. I drained the last of my martini and stood up to leave, feeling slightly sick.

Chapter 12

Julia

The forecast called for snow – up to ten inches in the city, the first blizzard of the season. A few flakes were starting to fall when I went out for lunch that Friday afternoon in December, for a chicken-salad sandwich and a Diet Coke from the deli around the corner, where the cashier had finally started to greet me as a regular.

Laurie had spent most of the day with her door shut. Was there something unusually tense in her mood, in her heavier footsteps and louder sighs? I didn't notice it at the time. I was daydreaming about the weekend. Abby was throwing a holiday party on Saturday. I had Christmas shopping to do. For Adam, in particular. I'd saved a few hundred dollars during the previous months, bits and pieces from my paychecks. It was a good feeling, having money I had earned and could spend any way I wanted. It was the first time I could say that. I wouldn't be able to impress Adam monetarily, but maybe I could impress him with a gift that proved just how well I knew him.

Something small and perfect. More evidence that we were, in fact, meant to be together.

'Julia,' Laurie said, startling me from a consideration of whether I could afford one of the first-edition Updikes I'd seen in the window at Argosy. 'Come in and talk to me.'

She shut the door and lowered herself into the chair behind her desk. This was bound to be something annoying. We weren't just going to chitchat, that was for sure. I'd long since given up hope on that. Laurie only called me in to give dull, impersonal, demanding instructions. A new workflow procedure that needed enacting, a problem that needed fixing. I had forgotten to bring a pen and paper. *Pay attention,* I thought.

'So Julia,' she said, sweeping the papers on her desk into a neat stack, squaring the edges. 'We have to let you go.'

I waited. I wasn't even sure I'd heard her right.

Laurie cleared her throat, her eyes still fixed on her desk. 'The donation promised to us by the Fletchers has fallen through at the last minute. It's been a difficult year, you obviously know that, and with market circumstances changing so rapidly, the Fletchers didn't feel they could follow through on their initial commitment. And so without that, we have to cut costs. We're letting others go, too. I'm afraid today will be your last day.'

I blinked like a dumb animal. *Say something,* I thought. *Don't just sit here.* But I couldn't. My mouth was dry and hot and cottony. The room was too warm, the radiator groaning and clanking with steam. Laurie should open a window.

'You're awfully quiet,' Laurie said. 'Do you have any questions?'

I tried to think of something, anything, to say. This might be my only chance. 'How many others?' I managed.

'I'm not at liberty to discuss that. You're the first person we've told.'

She finally met my gaze. Didn't she feel an ounce of pity for me, the person who had sat right outside her office for the past five months, answering her phone and making her coffee every goddamn morning? Didn't she feel *anything?* I wanted her to explain it, to apologize, to lessen the blow somehow. To say *something,* anything. It's not personal. We're so sorry to do this. Why me? Why not somebody else? Questions? There were a hundred questions swirling through my mind, but I didn't know how to articulate them. So when Laurie said, 'Is that it? Do you have any other questions?' I just shook my head.

'You'll be paid through the end of the month. You can leave as soon as you've gathered your things. And we'd appreciate your discretion for the time being. Please don't say anything to the others just yet.'

The phone started ringing. 'I should take this,' Laurie said, visibly relieved at the interruption. 'Could you close the door on your way out?'

I sat down at my desk. I heard the printer humming, the phone ringing in the lobby. The office was unchanged from a few minutes earlier, except for the silent bomb going off in my brain. A half-written e-mail floated on my computer screen. It was a summary of Laurie's expenses for the month of November, for accounting. A rote, routine e-mail. Anyone could do this after I left. But why not just finish it? All I had to do was attach the statement and click Send. I was numb.

It was as I started typing that it hit. My hands shook. I was aware of the smooth plastic keys against my fingertips, the too-loud clacking, the strange way the words emerged on the screen, like someone else was writing them. The last e-mail I'd ever write from this desk. Finally it exploded, flooding my mouth with a sickly iron-tinged flavor. I had just lost my job. I was unemployed. *Unemployed.* I turned off the computer, gathered my things – an extra pair of shoes, a coffee mug, a spare sweater, that was it – and waited for the elevator. Unemployed. Unemployed. It ran through my head like blinding ticker tape.

Outside, the snow was starting to thicken. Fat, lazy flakes drifted heavily through the air, coating the pavement in white. There was the sharp piney smell of Christmas trees for sale down the block. I tried calling Abby, but it went to voice mail. I tried my parents next, but they weren't there. Then I called Adam. He picked up right away.

'They fired me,' I said, my voice splitting in half, tears springing unbidden.

★

I used to wonder, those months I lived in New York, about the women I saw crying in public. Usually they were on the phone, sobbing into the mouthpiece. It was always women. What was it? I wondered. What bad news were they delivering or receiving? It was so disturbing, one red crumpled face in a sea of blank expressions. Did they know something that the rest of us didn't? Was this the first wave washing ashore with news of some global tragedy, something we'd all hear about in a matter of minutes? In this city, privacy was a luxury. You shared the sidewalks and subways with strangers, heard sirens through the windows, your neighbors through paper-thin plaster. What you did – what you *had* to do – was erect invisible walls to protect yourself. A stranger sobbing on the street, a dirty hand holding out a cup filled with change, an elbow digging into your back on a crowded train. The person in your bed whom you haven't really talked to in months. Look forward, breathe in, shut your mouth, think about other places. Think about anything except what's right in front of you. It's a way of staying sane in an unreasonable place. But at that moment, I saw the downside of this careful indifference. Even in the cab I wasn't alone, though I might as well have been. I hiccuped and cried, and the taxi driver kept his gaze straight ahead, the scratched plastic barrier between us.

Adam gave me the name of a hotel bar in midtown, said that he was on his way. I stopped in the bathroom to clean myself up. I looked awful. I splashed cold water on my face, dropped Visine into my eyes, reapplied lipstick and mascara. I missed Evan suddenly. He'd seen me like this before, crumpled and exhausted and freaked out: our fights in college, the moments of bad news, the disappointments, the long four years. He never cared how I looked. And he wouldn't try to stop it; he wouldn't tell me to snap out of it or calm down. He was quiet and steady, always ready with just the right thing to say. This vanity was stupid. It didn't matter how I looked. And yet there I was, fixing my hair and makeup like someone about to embark on a blind date.

Adam wasn't there yet, so I found a seat at the bar with a view of the TV in the corner. The bartender came over, and I ordered a vodka soda with lime. The TV was tuned to CNN. A reporter in Kabul was describing a recent spate of fatalities. I knew I ought to feel lucky. I could have been born in war-torn Afghanistan, every day fearing for my life, and instead my biggest problem was losing a job I didn't even like. I had no right to complain. This was my mother kicking in, her voice in my ear. *Don't be a brat, Julia.* I finished my drink and waved to the bartender for another. I was glad that my parents hadn't picked up the phone, actually. Their sympathy would be brief, and then they would immediately embark upon the project of Fixing My Life. But I wanted a few dark hours to dwell in my resentment. I wanted to get really, really drunk. I wanted Adam to fuck me and then hold me while I fell asleep. I didn't want to go back to my shitty apartment on the Upper East Side, my shitty life.

I realize now: that should have been another clue. I had just lost my job – I *hated* the sound of those words – but I didn't want the encouragement of my parents. I didn't want the genuine sympathy of Abby. Even though part of me wanted to call Evan, I didn't, I couldn't – I couldn't go back to that old life. I didn't want anything useful from the people who'd known me the longest. What I wanted was Adam. He offered me an escape. A new situation entirely. I couldn't see it at the time, but Adam was always the easiest way out.

When I was halfway through my second drink – where was he? – the CNN anchor switched to coverage of the Bernie Madoff scandal. Madoff had been arrested the day before. They interviewed one of his victims, a sad old man in Florida with eyes like a basset hound. I fiddled with my phone, wondering if I should call Adam. Abby had texted. Saw your call, what's up? I had started typing out a reply when I heard my name.

He ran over. He *ran*. That's how much he cared. I dissolved. 'Oh, Julia,' Adam said, kissing my forehead. 'Babe, babe. It's okay. I'm here.' He was the only one who understood. He put his arm around me and steered me toward a booth in the corner. I hadn't wanted to cry in front of him like this, but maybe it didn't matter. If Adam and I were going to be together, really together, I had to trust that he wouldn't care about a few tears. He went to the bar and returned with whiskey for him and a vodka soda for me, with a wedge of lime floating on top. A little part of me wondered whether he'd finally remembered my drink order or whether the bartender had corrected his mistake.

'Do you want to talk about it?' he asked. He held his glass up, clinking it against mine. 'Or should we just leave it at "Fuck them, they're idiots"?'

He wanted me to laugh. I did, and he smiled.

When I told him what happened, I found that a story emerged. A narrative with a satisfying arc. It was so obvious when I traced it from beginning to end: I was the victim. *I didn't deserve this*. So what if I'd hated the job? That wasn't the point. The point was that it was unfair. I had worked hard, never made a mistake. I'd been fucked over, and I was angry about it. I had every *right* to be angry. It had taken the firing for me to see that. I was angry at Laurie and the Fletchers and Evan and everyone who had been treating me like shit for the previous six months. The floodgates were opening.

'So wait a second,' Adam said. 'Laurie said that the Fletchers had to cancel their donation for financial reasons, right?'

'Yeah. Apparently they're having a bad year.' I thought of my father, on the phone with Henry Fletcher every day over Thanksgiving weekend. It made sense. The Fletchers were running out of money.

'Did she say specifically that they were strapped for cash?'

'I don't really remember. It happened so fast.' He was staring at me. 'Why? What is it?'

279

'It doesn't add up.' Adam pulled his phone out, typed something in, then handed it to me. 'Look at this.'

'What?'

'It's from today's *Journal*. Just read the first paragraph.'

ForeCloser, a company that tracks upcoming foreclosure auctions within a given geographic range, announced today that it has raised $20 million in Series B financing. The round was led by Fletcher Partners and included founding investor Henry Fletcher. ForeCloser will use the financing to aggressively increase the scope of its geographic coverage, which is currently limited to California, Washington and Oregon. In the announcement, the company outlined a goal of covering all 50 states by the end of 2009.

I looked up at him.

'Do you see what this means?' he said. 'The Fletchers are fine. They have plenty of money. Maybe they withdrew their donation, but it wasn't because they didn't have the cash for it.'

'So they still could have donated the – then what?'

'I'm sorry, babe. It isn't right.'

Something turned. Darkened. 'What the fuck, then? Why would they do that?'

'I don't know, Jules. These people play by a different set of rules. Henry Fletcher isn't thinking about what's fair or not. Maybe when things were flush, he was happy to toss a little aside to make his wife happy. You know, give her a charity to play with. But now that the market's bucking, he has to stay lean. You see what he's doing, don't you?'

Adam finished his drink, held up two fingers at the bartender. His eyes were hard, shining, in pursuit of something. I'd never seen them like that. Or at least that's what I thought, in the moment. I *had* seen that gleam before. I knew what it meant. But I'd suppressed that memory with remarkable success.

'I mean, look at this company he's investing in. People want to snap up these foreclosures while they're cheap, and Henry Fletcher is going to get rich by helping them do it faster. They'll make money flipping these properties, and he'll make money giving them access. These guys just drove the economy off a cliff, and now they're trying to suck more money from the corpses. They're actually profiting from all this. It's more than unfair. They should go to jail, if you ask me.'

The alcohol made everything swirl together. Evan always at work. Tossing aside the manila envelope, like it was nothing. The arrogance, the indifference. Why did no one ever care about right or wrong? Why did no one ever care about *me?* Adam slid a new drink in front of me.

'It's fucked up, right?' He held my hand tenderly. My mind was going fuzzy, the radio signal growing faint. 'They shouldn't be allowed to get away with these things. None of these guys should.'

★

The spark had been lit. I'd succeeded at one thing, at least: getting really, really drunk. I was aware, in a detached way, of the rising pitch of my voice, of my frustration releasing in a continuous vent. Everything came spilling out. Adam kept signaling to the bartender, never letting my glass sit empty. What was I saying? I lost my train of thought. He mentioned Evan's name. I shook my head. I hated Evan; I hated everything that Evan made me feel. Evan, who reminded me of everything that had gone wrong, of every disappointment.

I felt myself curling in at the edges, growing blacker. Evan. It spun together into one theme: Fletcher, Spire, Madoff, all of it. I grasped at it through the vodka, the point I was trying to make to Adam. How had I never seen it before, the way the world worked? I described the strange identification I'd felt with Madoff's sad, gray-haired victims on TV. We were casualties of the same greed-fueled catastrophe. Adam nodded vigorously. He understood. *Don't we have to do something about it? Don't we have a responsibility to stop these things?* He asked me about Evan again. What had I meant about Spire? What was going on there? *You don't have to protect him, Julia. You need to let these things out. You can't carry this around by yourself.*

The afternoon plunged into darkness.

At some point I got up to use the bathroom, wobbling in my heels. In the hotel lobby, people came and went. It was nighttime. My head spun as I sat down on the toilet. I propped myself up with one hand against the stall. Later, minutes later, hours later, in front of the bathroom mirror, I tried to fix my reflection in one place, but it danced and wavered no matter how hard I stared.

I spun around and stumbled back into the stall and threw up. The bile came in miserable waves. With one hand on the toilet, then one on the stall, I pushed myself up like a fever-weak patient. I rinsed my mouth in the sink and hunched over the basin, watching the water swirl around the white porcelain before vanishing down the drain, wishing I could follow it down there, away from all this.

In the time that has passed since that day, I've asked myself, over and over, whether I was aware of what I was doing. Aware of what I was setting in motion. Did I think it was the right thing to do? Did I know the impact it would have? I ask myself now: is guilt determined by outcome or by intent?

I woke up the next morning in Adam's bed, and I knew this wasn't a regular hangover. The headache and dizziness and dry mouth were compounded by a nagging awareness. I had done something wrong the night before, something not on a continuum with the cheating and the white lies. But, amazingly, I got up and went about my normal routine. I drank two glasses of water, took a long shower, dressed. I pushed the previous night to the back of my mind and I walked out the door. I didn't even say good-bye to Adam, who was sleeping soundly. Outside, the sidewalks were white from the blizzard. The doorman hailed me a cab, and we flew across the silent snowscape of Central Park. It was early, and the snow was pristine, unmarked by footprints and sled tracks. I had no idea – no conscious idea – of the turning point I had just passed. One chapter of my life over, another about to begin.

Time has made it worse. It isn't just regret for that afternoon, for the things I shouldn't have said to Adam. It's the bigger realization that the entire thing was a mistake. Last year is like a movie starring somebody else. It's a scene in time lapse, sped-up and frantic, everything moving too fast to grab hold of. That girl, the girl who existed from July to December – she wasn't the person I had been before. She tricked herself, twisting the reality around her into something different. She was looking at it all wrong: like it was a plan finally coming together. She should have known better. The signs were always there. But there was something narcotic about the fantasy I was living, the idea of becoming someone else. No one had told me that doing these things could feel so good. They could feel so good that they blocked out everything else. They put to sleep the part of me that should have been watching.

The afternoon plunged into darkness.

'Jules, babe, it's okay. Shh.'

I was crying again.

'I'm sick of it. I'm sick of him. He told me all this like

it was *my* problem, too. He dumped it on me, and I've been carrying it around for weeks.'

'What is it? What did he tell you?'

'Spire. It's this deal they've been working on. It's messed up. It's rigged. They've been lying about it the whole time.'

'Who has? People at Spire?'

'His boss, Michael. Evan is part of it, too. He went along with it.'

'Michael Casey, you mean? Shh, Julia, it's okay. I'm here. I'm here.'

I was still crying, hot and angry tears.

'I'm so si-si — sick of him. He's an *asshole*.'

'Tell me what Evan told you. How was the deal rigged?'

'It's Michael. He knows people. Government officials in China. He bribed them to let them import from the Canadians, to get around the taxes.'

'How did he bribe them?'

Did I notice Adam reaching for the notepad in his pocket? Did I register his one-handed scribbles under the table? Did he even do this, or am I trying to rewrite the past, to insert a screaming siren for my former self, to make her sit up and notice what she was doing?

With his other hand he held mine, rubbing his thumb across my palm.

'Jules. Did Evan say how they bribed them?'

'Immigration. Canadian immigration paperwork. Spire and WestCorp helped the Chinese get their papers.

That's why they went to Vegas. I could kill him. He's such an idiot.'

'They got papers for the Chinese, is that what you're saying? In exchange for getting them visas, these officials are letting them export their lumber to China? Jules? That's what you're saying, right?'

'I hate him. Hate him.'

'Julia?'

———•———

Saturday, the day after. There was a feeling clinging to me that refused to be brushed away. A hammering in my heart. In the cab across Central Park, from Adam's apartment to mine, I texted Abby. My phone buzzed with her reply a minute later. Oh, Jules, I'm so sorry. Are you okay? Can you still make it tonight? I'm so sorry.

The cab let me out. I brushed the snow from our stoop and sat down. My dad picked up the phone. My mother was out, walking the dog. How was I? What was going on? I told him everything, including what Adam had said about Fletcher Partners' investment in the new start-up. When I finished, he sighed heavily. I could picture him in his study, the leather-bound books and diplomas lining the walls. Leaning into his elbow on the desk, rubbing the bridge of his nose where his glasses sat. Finally he said:

'Sweetheart, obviously I'm sorry to hear about this, but I hope you understand how complicated it is. The Fletchers have many factors to consider. It hasn't been an easy year for them. I'm sure they were very unhappy to have to do this.'

He'd used this voice on me before. A voice with an unbearable weight to it. My father wasn't someone to whom you talked back. His lawyerly gravity made you so painfully aware of your shortcomings: your irrational emotions, your unthinking reactions, your taking things personally when nothing was personal. The world wasn't against you. Stop indulging yourself. Why had I expected this time to be any different? But part of me had hoped for that, for some rare tenderness from my father, and I felt a doubling of the heaviness. A deflating of that hope and an awareness that I should have known better than to harbor it. He was taking the side of his client over his daughter. It shouldn't have surprised me.

An ache in my throat made it hard to swallow. 'I know, Dad.'

We hung up. The sky was clear blue, and the sunlight reflected off the snow. It was still early for the weekend, and Evan would probably be home, not having left for work yet. I could have lingered longer at Adam's, stayed for breakfast, but a voice in my head had propelled me out of his apartment. But now, at home, something kept me stuck to the stoop, just shy of the threshold. Evan probably wouldn't ask where I had been, or care. He'd keep assuming whatever he'd been assuming all along. But he would notice the redness in my eyes and know that I'd been crying. Over the previous few months, I'd built such a careful distance between us. He went to his office, I went to mine; he had his life, I had mine. I had Adam. There was barely anything left. But Evan would ask what was wrong, and I would start crying again, and I knew, just knew, that he would comfort me like he used to. He would remind me that everything would be okay, like the good boyfriend he always was in times of crisis. That careful distance would disappear, and I didn't know what would happen next. I wasn't sure I had the courage to find out.

When the door behind me opened with a suctioning whoosh, I stared straight ahead, ready to avoid eye contact with whichever neighbor was coming out. It would be easy; I knew no one in our building.

'Yup, yup, I'm on my way in now. I'll be there in ten minutes,' the familiar voice behind me said. I turned around.

'Julia.' Evan looked surprised. He bounced down the steps to the sidewalk, where he stood and faced me. 'Hey. I was just on my way to the office.'

I had to shield my eyes to block the sun. It was too bright. 'Hey.'

'That was Michael. He needs me to come in for something.'

'Oh. Okay.'

He seemed at a loss for words. 'Hey, are you going to Abby's party tonight?'

'I think so.'

We were a pair of strangers.

He looked closely at me. 'Is everything okay?'

'Oh, well . . .' I was so tired. I couldn't keep doing this. My voice cracked. 'It's work. I got laid off yesterday.'

He stood perfectly still. 'Shit. Julia. I'm sorry to hear that.'

My eyes hurt from the sun. I glanced down at the sidewalk for relief, at the snow and my salt-crusted boots, and then looked back up from under the hood of my palm. Evan was regarding me quietly, like a hunter watching a wild animal. Getting no closer than he had to. Eventually he reached out and put his hand on my shoulder, leaving it there for a moment. That was all he would give me.

'I'm sorry,' I started to choke out, the tears returning to my eyes. And I was – all of a sudden, I was sorry for everything. I wanted to rewind to six months earlier, when we stood on this stoop in the June humidity with our boxes, when we opened the door for the first time, when we hadn't yet started down this path.

But at that very same moment, he said, 'I have to get to work.' I don't know if he heard me. When he removed his hand, then removed himself and walked down the street toward an available cab, I felt the imprint of him linger on my skin, like a memory pressing itself to me one last time before it vanished forever.

CHAPTER 13

Evan

'Where the hell is he?' Chuck said, craning his neck toward the glass walls of the conference room. The meeting had been called for 9:00 a.m. sharp, and it was 9:06. 'He's keeping half the company waiting.'

Roger took a swig of coffee. 'I don't think Michael's real concerned about how busy the rest of us are.' He jiggled his knee, knocking against mine on purpose.

This was the weekly Monday status meeting, the last one before the end of the year. An empty chair awaited Michael at the head of the table. Roger and the other analysts and I sat around the perimeter of the room. Chuck, seated at the back end of the table, turned his chair around to talk with Roger. Most of the higher-ups at the table were in a sedate Monday mood, chatting about soccer practice and piano recitals, plans for Christmas in Aspen or Saint Barts. Chuck's wedding was fast approaching, and his fiancée spent most of her weekends in Connecticut ironing out the wedding details, which left Chuck by himself in the city, enjoying one final run of debauchery. Every Monday morning, he and Roger traded stories from the weekend.

'A model? I don't believe you,' Chuck was saying.

'For real. Apparently she's the next big thing out of Croatia.'

'Did you check your wallet before she left? Or maybe you just paid her up front. I know some of them won't have it any other way.'

'Fuck you, man. I'm not washed up like you. I don't have to pay for ass.'

'Bullshit. What about Vegas?'

'That's different. That's Vegas. Even *Evan* was paying for it in Vegas.'

Chuck raised an eyebrow. 'Evan?'

'Our first night there. He didn't come home until the morning.'

Chuck threw his head back and laughed. 'You think our little Evan was out with a *prostitute?*'

I felt the heat rising under my collar. I should have said something, changed the subject. But in the previous few weeks, I'd learned it was better not to draw attention to myself.

'Well, where was he, then?' Roger was acting like I wasn't right there.

'He crashed on our couch that night, in my and Brad's room. After you and your hooker locked him out.'

Brad, sitting across the table, glanced up at his name. He froze, thumbs hovering above his BlackBerry keyboard. He looked at Chuck, but Chuck had already moved on. Then Brad shifted his gaze to me. I could see the rapid realization in his stare.

The room went quiet. Roger's knee stopped jiggling. 'Finally,' Chuck muttered, spinning around to face the table.

'Morning, everyone,' Michael said, and the room murmured in response. He took his seat at the head of the table. 'Steve, why don't you start us off?' Steve nodded and launched into an update, doing his best to make the macro group's weak results sound palatable. Michael watched him with his hands steepled together, like a villain out of a movie. He did look the part: steely gray hair, a face carved with deep wrinkles, a skeptical squint. People still feared Michael, as they always had, but now the fear was earned. He was in charge; he'd saved the company. Things were going exactly as planned on the WestCorp deal. The rest of the world had noticed West-Corp's growing exports, and their stock was rising rapidly, just as predicted. There were whispers that Kleinman was going to stay in DC and angle for the top job at Treasury in the new administration. That would mean Michael was permanently in charge, and that my trajectory at Spire could continue unchecked. Michael hinted at a raise and a promotion on the horizon. I couldn't really believe how lucky I was.

But I had miscalculated what would happen after the deal went live. The rest of Spire didn't want to see that the firm's survival hinged on this one specific deal. The only thing they saw was their exclusion from it. We were the competition. Roger confirmed it for me a few days earlier. I bumped into him as I was leaving Michael's office. 'Shit, sorry,' I said, bending down to help gather the papers he'd dropped. While we were crouched, our faces close, Roger snarled: 'You think you're real hot shit, don't you?' People stared at me pointedly in the hallways – others, not just Roger, had noticed how much the newly powerful Michael had taken me under his wing.

I thought they'd be happy about the success. I thought I had finally proved that I belonged in this world, too. But I wouldn't make that mistake again.

A parallel had become clear to me. For a long time I'd hoped that things would get better, at home and at work. That the small daily miseries – jealous glares from co-workers, stiff silences from Julia – would eventually prove temporary, if I worked hard enough. But it was Julia, the previous weekend, who finally made me understand. I'd been hurrying out the door on Saturday morning, and Julia was sitting on the stoop, her eyes red and puffy. She told me that she'd been fired. I felt a pulse of sympathy for her, and then – nothing. I was struck less by the news than by my own lack of reaction. It was like hearing about a minor plane crash in a distant country. Sad, but not sad for me. On the way to work, I wondered whether it was a delayed response. Maybe the feeling would come later, the feeling of watching a loved one suffer. But it never did. I didn't love her anymore: that was the answer. Simple and clear. I was relieved to realize this, actually – it was about time. I shouldn't have kept loving Julia for so long after things had turned so bad. And I shouldn't have expected that Roger and the others at Spire would see me as anything but the competition. It wasn't worth it, caring about people who didn't care about you.

The droning at the front of the conference room stopped. Wanda was waiting for Michael in the doorway. He gestured at the person talking to continue. On the other side of the glass wall, Wanda fluttered her hands as they spoke. She looked nervous.

Michael stuck his head back in. 'I have to take this,' he said to the room. 'Finish without me.'

In the silence, Steve cleared his throat, said we might as well keep going. But I wasn't listening anymore. I leaned back to watch Michael and Wanda retreating down the hall toward his office. Michael was walking so fast that Wanda had to run to keep up.

Around noon, I passed by Michael's office for the umpteenth time that day. The door was still closed. Wanda's chair was empty. I turned my back, pretending to examine the papers in my hands. The hallway was quiet, and I strained to hear something, anything, through the door.

'Excuse me,' a woman said, pushing past me. It was our head of PR, a woman in a bright green dress and a crisp bob, her bracelets jangling as she knocked hurriedly on Michael's door. Her perfume had a distinctive musky scent, a trail she left whenever she barreled through the hallways to put out a fire. A smell I had come to associate with panic. She opened the door without waiting for a response. A loud conversation erupted through the opening before she slammed it shut again.

I walked back to my side of the floor, scanning faces and computer screens and conversations for clues. The floor was emptier than usual, but the lunch hour would explain that. A muted TV flashed silently in the lobby. Two analysts tossed a Nerf football back and forth from their opposing desks. The wind outside had picked up, and when I stood at the windows at the edge of the building, I could see black umbrellas popping up like mushrooms on the street far below. The last of the lingering snow would be gone by the afternoon.

At my desk, I hit the space bar a few times to wake my computer. I watched Roger nodding his head to the music in his earbuds, typing with emphatic keystrokes, looking perfectly normal, exactly like he looked every day.

But I knew, even if I didn't know what: something was wrong.

That night was supposed to be the Spire holiday party, an extravagant dinner at the Waldorf or the Pierre followed by a long night of drinking. It had been canceled this year. The recession made it impossible, both financially and optically. The secretaries felt bad for us, so they improvised. Tinsel was strung in the hallways, and miniature Christmas trees and menorahs decorated their desks. Around 6:00 p.m., someone went around offering beer and Champagne. There was a scrappy, festive mood that night. The year from hell was nearly over.

But I was restless. That afternoon, like something out of a dream, I found myself back at Michael's door, arm raised and fist clenched, ready to knock. *Stop,* I thought, and I shook my head. Whatever it was, Michael could handle it. I stayed at my desk the rest of the day, willing my mind to focus, trying not to obsess about things I couldn't control.

Roger was drinking a beer. He'd stolen the Nerf football from the other analysts and was tossing it up and down with one hand. He was in the middle of a running monologue about what to order for dinner.

'Hey, Evan,' Roger said, chucking the Nerf at my chest. It bounced to the floor before I had time to catch it. 'Listen. We need to decide. Italian or Chinese?' He burped. 'Let's get more beer, too. We can expense it, right? Anyway . . .'

Roger may have hated me, but he liked an audience more. He sounded out every mundane thought that passed through his head, narrating every part of his life. I was used to it by then. I let it wash over me without really listening.

'Y'know, though, there's a new Vietnamese place I think we should try, too. Shit – what's it called?' He sat down at his computer, his cheeks ruddy from the beer. 'You know, the one on Forty-fifth. Or is it –'

I heard a ping from Roger's computer, the sound of an e-mail arriving. He clicked, his monologue trailing off, then he went silent. His eyes were scanning the screen. I heard the same ping sounding on the computers around me, like a chorus of chirping birds.

'Holy shit,' Roger said. 'Holy shit.'

'What is it?' I tilted back in my chair, tossing the Nerf from one hand to the other.

Roger's face went pale. 'Check your e-mail. Right now.'

The message came with a bright red exclamation point. A news alert. I double-clicked to open it. My stomach plummeted as I read the headline:

SPIRE UNDER SCRUTINY

Evidence of bribery sparks investigation

No, I thought. *No, no, this can't be happening.* But of course it was happening. It was the exact fear I'd been trying to suppress all day. I clicked through and began to read the article:

Federal authorities have initiated an investigation into whether Spire Management, a New York City–based hedge fund, bribed the Chinese government to obtain favorable terms on lumber imports.

The investigation was launched after the *Observer* contacted authorities for comment on Spire's practices in China. The paper learned, through confidential sources within the company, that Spire Management has bribed highly placed Chinese government officials in order to arrange for tax-free imports of lumber to China from several Canadian companies. Spire has taken an aggressive position on these companies, which includes the conglomerate Pacific WestCorp, and stands to profit significantly from their growth.

A review of WestCorp's most recent quarterly statement shows that exports to China have increased substantially over the third quarter, and the company expects continuing significant growth in the next fiscal year . . .

The byline at the top of the story stood out in big, bold letters. Adam McCard.

Roger was staring at me when I finished reading. The floor had gone silent while everyone read the news. The only sound was of the building's joints, creaking in the high wind.

'Did you know about this?' Roger asked, in a charged whisper.

Was I being paranoid again, or were people murmuring as I passed? A numb panic spread through my body: my limbs had gone leaden, but my mind was racing faster and faster. I speedwalked over to Michael's office. All the e-mails and phone calls back and forth with WestCorp. The delivery to Chan in Las Vegas. Security footage from the cameras in the hallways at the Venetian. Chan's cackling demands. The $20,000 in cash, still sitting in my sock drawer. There were a thousand different trip wires suddenly lying in wait.

Wanda was back at her desk. Her fingers flew across

the keyboard; ten different lines blinked red on the phone. A half-eaten salad lay forgotten at her elbow.

'I need to talk to him,' I said.

She looked bewildered for a second, then laughed. 'Are you kidding?'

'But it's about this story. The WestCorp story. Please, Wanda.'

'Evan. This is way above your pay grade, okay? Just go home, get some rest. It's the best thing for now. Trust me, hon. I'd help you if I could.'

When I got back to my desk, Roger stared at me with a mixture of pity and contempt, maybe even a little bit of awe. I turned off my computer, pocketed my phone, put on my coat. The elevator whisked me down to the ground floor. Outside, the night was consumed by a vicious rainstorm, dark and howling and damp. I walked to the subway at Times Square, dodging umbrellas and sprays of water from cars streaking by. One foot in front of the other. Just keep walking. I elbowed my way into the middle of the train for a seat and collapsed, my clothes dripping wet.

I thought of Brad, shouting and seething with anger that night in Las Vegas. It would have been nothing to him to pick up the phone and vent it all to a reporter. Michael had a fat bull's-eye painted on his back. Anyone who resented him, anyone who wanted him gone, any of those people would have happily spilled the news. And who knew how many people Brad could have told? Chuck, or Roger. Roger, his jealousy barely guarded by derision. He wasn't someone used to coming in second. On the roof that day in September, the day of the crash, he had been the one to summon forth Adam McCard's name. *I always read the* Observer. *Just for their finance guy. He's good.* Adam's silky touch might be exactly what Roger's wounded ego needed. Making Roger feel like he was doing the right thing. It explained Adam's pointed questioning when he ran into me at Thanksgiving. He'd been chasing the scent of the story. Roger had acted so surprised when the news broke.

Who would do this? *Why* would he do this? If someone really hated Michael, if he wanted him gone, there were other ways. Roger or Brad could have gone straight to David Kleinman, and Kleinman would have handled it – probably would have rewarded the whistle-blower, to boot. Instead, whoever did it had gone nuclear. Someone was willing to blow up the whole company because of some petty jealousy. I felt my blood rising. It stank of hypocrisy. Everything Spire did, every bet we made and trade we transacted, was dependent on some kind of asymmetry. We had better information, faster networks, a heavier footprint. We got rich to the detriment of some other party. That's how it always worked. For this particular deal to be singled out was completely arbitrary. How many hundreds of morally questionable deals had been made at Spire in years past? Who had the gall to decide that, here, a line had been crossed? Who had the *right?*

I knew how it would go. It would be a fucking

nightmare. The country had just been devastated, and it needed someone to pin the blame on. The SEC would come in with guns blazing. In the papers, on TV screens, broadcast over radio waves: people wanted blood. They bayed for revenge. The complexity of subprime mortgage products meant that the real bad guys might never face punishment. But this story, our story, was easy to understand. Rich guys bribe the Chinese in order to become richer. All while the rest of the country shrivels in a drought of our own creation. I saw it from the outside for the first time, just how bad this looked.

The train pulled into 77th Street. The crowd moved up the stairs in a slow trudge, each person pausing at the top to open an umbrella or pull up a hood. It was earlier than I usually came home, the tail end of rush hour still thick with commuters. My thoughts looped back to Adam. That slimy bastard. Preying on disgruntled employees to get his next story; converting other people's unhappiness into fuel for his ambition. I wondered what Julia ever could have seen in him, even as a friend.

Then it occurred to me, as I waited for the light to change on 3rd Avenue. Julia. Had she seen Adam lately? Had she mentioned his name? I sifted through my memory: no, she had never said anything. But this city wasn't very big. Even I had run into Adam, and what were the odds of that? And Julia kept in touch with everyone, even people she claimed to dislike, even the bitchy girls from prep school. But she hadn't uttered his name once since that rainy March night, sophomore year, when she'd disappeared upstairs with Adam during that party. I wasn't stupid. I could guess what had happened. But after that party, the fights tapered off. Things felt steadier, calmer. She went away to Paris, and, after that, we were happier than ever. We never spoke about it again. It had been left completely, resolutely in the past.

As I turned onto our block, I passed a group crowded under a bar awning, smoking cigarettes in soggy Santa hats and holiday sweaters. 'Rockin' Around the Christmas Tree' blasted out through the bar's open door. A girl wearing an elf costume stumbled into me as I pushed through the crowd. 'Whoa!' she said, sloppy and laughing. I mumbled an apology. She stuck out her tongue, swaying on her feet. 'Merry Christmas, grinch!' she shouted at my back.

The image materialized as I dug my keys out of my pocket. Julia, turning at the sound of her name. At a bar or a party, or some sidewalk in the city. Smiling at an old friend. Softening and bending toward him, like she had all those years before. A little lonely, bored in her job, with so many hours alone in that tiny apartment. So much restless energy. What might have happened between the two of them, reunited after so long? The conversations, hours and hours of conversation, saying everything she had to say. The things she was no longer saying to me. Julia always loved a good listener.

The apartment was dark when I opened the door. The light, when I flipped it on, illuminated a strange scene. The blanket was rumpled around a fresh-looking dent in the futon. A take-out container of soup sat on the coffee table, still steaming with heat. The dread swelled, a tinge in the back of my throat. Where was she? I spun around, surveying the room for clues. But the rest of the furniture was neat and in place. A bowl and mug sat on the drying rack next to the kitchen sink. The tea towels hung square from the oven door. The bed was smoothly made, the pillows plumped. A stupid phrase came to mind: *There was no sign of struggle*. Julia had just up and left moments earlier.

I pulled out my phone and called her. I belatedly realized that the ringing was louder than usual, coming not just from the speaker next to my ear but also from somewhere in the room. I followed the chime and buzz to the coffee table, where her phone was partially obscured by a stack of take-out napkins. I picked up her phone, which was glowing from my missed call.

The wallpaper on her iPhone screen, for a long time, had been a picture of the two of us taken during that summer in Europe. She had handed her phone to another tourist while we leaned against the railing that separated the rocky path from the bright blue sea below. She loved that picture. The two of us smiling and squinting, happy and tired and sunburned from an afternoon trekking through the Cinque Terre. After the digital shutter snapped, we relaxed our smiles, Julia thanked the tourist, and we walked back to our B and B in Monterosso. That night we drank wine on the terrace overlooking the Mediterranean. She pulled her hair loose from its bun and tilted her head back to look at the stars. I took her hand and led her back to our room under the attic rafters. We fell asleep curled together as the waves crashed far below. But that photo, that moment, that life was gone. In its place, on the phone screen, was a generic image of planet earth floating in space. That image wedged in my brain like a shard of glass. Erasure of our happiest memories. Evidence of just how far we had drifted.

But that's not what I was really looking at. I was reading, over and over again, the text message that appeared on the locked screen of the phone. Eight short words, but that was all it took. It became suddenly, painfully clear who was behind the revelations about Spire. Who had been drawing closer and slipping information to the person on the other side of the table.

Adam McCard, *thirty-two minutes ago*.

I'm sorry, babe. I had to do it.

PART III

CHAPTER 14

Julia

Last week I was lying in bed, pretending to take a late afternoon nap but really just staring at the ceiling, when I heard a car pull up in the driveway.

My father wouldn't be back from work until dinner. My mother was busy all day with errands and meetings. I was home alone on that sunny May day. I pulled aside the curtain and saw my sister shutting the trunk of her silver Saab.

It was like Elizabeth had forgotten, for a moment, that I was living at home. A look rippled across her face as I appeared at the top of the stairs. There she was, fresh from her junior year at college, embarking on summer break with all its possibilities – and as I dragged myself down the stairs in ratty old leggings and a T-shirt, I was there to remind her of everything that could go wrong. Failure, heartbreak. A vector for a disease she might catch, too. But the look vanished in a second, and Elizabeth threw her arms around me in a hug.

We had seen each other at Christmas and when she

breezed through over spring break before hopping a flight to Belize. But those had been short, distracted visits, and the depths to which I was sinking weren't yet clear. It was evident enough now: months had passed, my excuses were running out, and I was still hiding inside with unwashed hair and worn-out clothes. After settling at the kitchen table, Elizabeth asked me how I was. The look on her face said she wanted the full answer.

I'm okay. That's what I've been saying all along, hoping that eventually I'll trick myself into making it true. It's been months now. I'm getting over it. I'm okay.

But I'm also, distinctly, not okay. I'm not getting over it. Sometimes I feel like I'm living on two planes: the present in Boston, which I move through physically like a hollow zombie, and that night in New York, where I'm stuck forever mentally, replaying the same disastrous sequence on a loop. The memory persists like a hot cavity. I shut my eyes, and I see Evan. I try to fall asleep, and I see Evan. And I see him as he was at the very end, his face written with disappointment. That's the worst part. It wasn't shock or anger. It was like he'd always known that it would come to this. Four years of my life disappeared into that expression. All the good things that had come before were negated by that pitch-black reminder of what I was capable of – of the person I had been all along.

I called my mother later that December night. I was jobless, single, with nowhere to live. But she was too busy to help, so I moved myself out. I shipped a box of books home. I took a taxi to Penn Station with two bulging suitcases in the trunk. A man in a Santa costume stood on the corner of 34th Street, ringing a bell, collecting for the Salvation Army. Tourists streamed down the sidewalks, eyes shining in the holiday lights, on their way to Radio City or the Rockefeller Center tree. It all receded so quickly. The train pulled out of the station, right on time for once, and a few hours later I was in Boston. As fast as that. My life in New York had ended.

It was like I'd been hit by a truck. My joints felt sore, my skin tender. I hibernated through the winter, confining my movements to the bedroom, the kitchen, the den. I slept too many hours every night – sleep was the only thing I wanted to do, the only way to make the time pass. Lately, though, I'm plagued by a different problem: insomnia. Maybe my body is trying to tell me to move on after the glut of the last several months, but my mind won't let me. So I'm awake late into the night. Nothing works: warm milk, hot baths, prescription pills. I spend hours going for drives through the darkened suburbs, past shuttered windows and empty parking lots, with only the radio for company. My mother hates my middle-of-the-night peregrinations and the way I sleep so late, wasting daylight hours. So now I'm presented with a double serving of guilt: for what I did last year in New York, and for the way I am constantly failing to get over it.

An hour after Elizabeth arrived, my mother got home from her errands, carrying a box from the local bakery.

She beamed when she saw Elizabeth sitting in the kitchen. She was the good daughter, the successful daughter. Elizabeth would never derail her own life, like I did. She was too smart for that. She was only home for a few days before moving to New York for the summer, where she was interning for a famous painter, Donald Gates, in his Tribeca studio.

Elizabeth had just turned twenty-one. We had her favorite meal that night: lasagna and garlic bread, then chocolate cake from the bakery for dessert. Elizabeth leaned forward and blew out the candles, their light pale and flickering in the spring twilight. She looked up at me a few minutes later, while I pushed a swab of frosting around my plate. 'Jules?' she said quietly, but I just shook my head. Evan's birthday had been last week. It was always twinned, in my mind, with Elizabeth's. I was melancholy not because I'd been thinking of him. I was melancholy because, despite my fixation on Evan, I'd forgotten about his birthday until that moment. Time was passing. I was forgetting things, the specific things. Evan was becoming an abstract longing. I was losing him all over again.

Elizabeth's college schedule complemented my insomnia, and we lay awake that night in her bed, the lamp in the corner casting exaggerated shadows across the walls. A cluster of glow-in-the-dark stars floated on the ceiling, a reminder of the lives we had lived in these bedrooms before going away and trying to become grown-ups.

'I wish I could stay longer,' she said. 'It's kind of nice, being home.'

'Me, too. It's so quiet here without you.'

She picked at the dark polish on her thumbnail. 'You could come visit.'

'New York?'

'My roommate is going to be gone most weekends. Her boyfriend lives in DC.'

'I haven't gone back since I moved out.'

'So? You're not banned from the city. It's not like they're going to turn you away at the border.'

'Very funny.'

'You have to meet Donald. He's so great.'

I made some noise of equivocation.

'Come on. What else are you doing up here? It could be good for you, you know – a distraction. Get out of the house.'

'You sound just like Mom.'

'Ugh. Shut up. You know what I mean. It'd be fun. We can go out together.'

'I'll think about it.'

She sighed. 'I'm not tired yet.'

'Welcome to my world.'

Elizabeth lifted a finger and delicately scratched the side of her nose. She was so deliberate, so economical in her gestures. The fidgety tendencies I'd noticed among girls our age – twisting their hair, touching their faces, biting their lips – Elizabeth was completely devoid of. When had she become so mature, so self-possessed? I had been so immersed in my own life the last five years that I had completely ignored hers. I wondered what else I'd missed.

'So Mom's being hard on you?' she said. 'I bet she's going crazy right now, with you hanging around all day. She probably hates it.'

I laughed. 'Yeah, you can tell?'

'Maybe it's good for her. This will teach her a lesson. Not everyone can have perfect children all the perfect time.' She paused. 'But she's always been hard on you. Did you ever notice that? They were both so tough. They set such high standards. I think I had it easier. They didn't pay as much attention to me.'

I propped myself up on my elbows, staring at her. 'Are you kidding me? *You*? You are one hundred percent the favorite.'

'I'm not saying that. It's just – I don't know. With you it's like they had to check every box. You were the first kid. Once you did everything you were supposed to do, they kind of let go of me. Don't get me wrong, it's been great for me. But I always felt kind of bad for you. Everything you did had to be a certain way. Like, do you remember the first time you brought Evan home?'

'Jesus,' I groaned. 'Poor Evan. That was such a disaster.'

It had been terrible. A weekend toward the end of freshman year, we took the train up to Boston for the first parental meet and greet. My dad spent the whole night on the phone with a client. Elizabeth had a friend over for dinner, and they did their best to distract us by chattering about high school gossip. But my mother's mood descended on the table like an unpleasant odor. She decided, instantly, that she didn't like Evan. That he

312

was all wrong for me. That he would never, ever live up to Rob. Evan was sweating through his shirt during dinner.

So your parents own a grocery store, I hear, she said, eyebrow arched as she dragged her knife through her green beans.

That's right, Evan said. *It's doing really well. They've started stocking a lot more organics lately. It's catching on even in our little town.*

Elizabeth laughed at the memory. 'That was great, actually. She didn't have a *clue* what to say to him. I still remember the look on her face when you told her you were dating a Canadian hockey player. It was worth it just for that.'

Her laughter stopped as soon as the words escaped her. 'Oh, God. I'm sorry. I didn't mean – sorry.'

I shook my head. 'It's fine, Lizzie. Tell me more about Donald.'

The night crept by, the house silent around us except for the occasional chime of the hall clock downstairs. Around 3:00 a.m., Elizabeth finally started to yawn. She drifted off while telling me about a new photo series she was working on. I tucked the blanket around her and went back to my own room, to wait for sleep.

And it was the truth. It was, surprisingly, fine. It was the first time I had talked about Evan with anyone since the breakup. My parents pretended it had never happened. Elizabeth, I think, had pieced together most of it, but she had some of our mother in her – she didn't probe when the topic was too delicate. Whenever Abby brought Evan up, I tended to change the subject. She'd snapped at me once. 'Julia. Seriously. Enough of this repressive WASP bullshit. We *have* to talk about this at some point.' There was a long silence, then she sighed. 'I'm sorry. That was unfair.' But where could I begin?

'It's just . . .' I'd said. 'I just need more time.'

And so to finally say his name aloud was a relief. Like ice shattering. Evan. He existed. He still existed.

I thought I had rid myself of any feeling for him, so that when the break came, it would be clean and easy. Just like the switch from Rob to Evan four years earlier. Adam would be waiting, baton extended, and I would simply reach for it and keep going. But this wasn't to be. Adam wasn't there (how could I have ever thought he would be?), and, more important, Evan wasn't someone I could leave behind so painlessly. At this age perhaps we take change for granted: you can adopt and discard different identities as easily as Halloween costumes, and from that comes the arrogance of thinking that you can decide when, and how, you get to change. Evan had been one chapter of my life, I thought, but for the next – for Adam – I was going to become a new kind of person.

But when everything washed away in the ensuing mess, I was left with something not so easily discarded after all: the girl I had been before everything started. The girl who had loved Evan, who had finally understood that the past didn't have to determine what would come in the future; the girl who had learned to be happy. It seemed that I had her back now, but I worried it was too late. She doesn't fit in anymore. But this is me. This is the real me. I so desperately don't want to lose it, that tender flame of being.

I spent that December weekend trying very hard not to think about my outpouring to Adam. Through my pounding hangover that Saturday, I cleaned the apartment. I beat the rugs on the fire escape, washed the windows, scrubbed the bathtub until it shone. That night I went to Abby's holiday party. Her apartment was cheery and cozy, garlanded with lights and tinsel, mulled cider bubbling on the stove. I drank only water, still feeling sick from the night before. Evan had mentioned the party. I'd texted him to ask if he was coming, but he didn't respond. Whenever a wave of noise announced an arrival, I found myself hoping – for the first time in months – that it would be Evan walking through the door. I wanted something beyond our stilted interaction on the stoop that morning. I felt it dangling in the air, like a sharp blade, the danger of what we hadn't said.

By 2:00 a.m., as the party was emptying out, I gave up and left. Evan came home later and slept for a few hours before heading back to work early Sunday morning. I woke up nervous and jittery, needing distraction from my ballooning guilt. (But guilt over what, over which part? I still didn't quite know.) I went to the Met that afternoon, but I couldn't focus on the art. My lack of concentration seemed like a failure, and it gave the museum an oppressive air: another reminder of my inability to engage, to find a passion, to *figure it out*. A tour was wending past, and I clung to it, sheltering myself in the monologue of the leader. It was dark by the time I left the museum, and I went to bed early, falling into a shallow sleep. Evan got home past midnight, and I awoke wondering if I ought to turn on the light and try to talk to him, *actually* talk to him. To offer a real apology. But he lingered in the living room, and I fell asleep again.

Monday morning brought a new sting. Maybe I could pretend things were fine over the weekend, but on a weekday my unemployment was impossible to ignore. I went to the coffee shop down the block and looked online for job openings. I couldn't concentrate. The whirring and banging of the espresso machines, the tinny jazz, the yoga-toned mothers with their lattes. Distractions everywhere. I was waiting for something, but I didn't know what. Adam hadn't called or texted. He hadn't said a thing since Friday night. I reach back and try to remember what I was thinking about Adam at that moment, but I can't quite say. My memory of that time is so infected by what I feel now. Or perhaps it's that I was starting to realize the scope of my mistake. I wasn't fixated on Adam anymore, because Adam wasn't the person I'd have to reckon with. Evan was.

But that can't be entirely true. Later that Monday

night, after I ventured out into the rain to pick up dinner, some thought of Adam had driven me to open my computer. At home, I shook a packet of oyster crackers across my container of too-hot soup while I navigated to the *New York Observer*'s website. Maybe I was curious to see whether Adam had been working all weekend. Maybe I wanted to check the news after ignoring it for a few days. Or maybe an alarm bell was already ringing in my subconscious, finally forcing me to acknowledge the trigger on which I'd been resting my finger for months. I had only lifted one spoonful of soup to my mouth before I saw the headline strung across the top of the website in big, bold black letters for the whole world to see.

———⋄———

Last night I thought about calling Evan. It was near midnight, and I was driving down the empty roads in our neighborhood, killing time, the changing colors of the stoplights cascading and reflecting like a beat on the wet surface of the pavement. I pulled over, the car idling askew in a parking lot while I dialed his number. My pulse skittered. I wanted so badly to hear his voice. My finger was hovering over the button when my mind flashed to him, two hundred miles south in New York, his phone vibrating on the surface of his desk or on some bar. Lifting it to check the caller and grimacing at the sight of my name, silencing it without a second thought.

What could I say? What could I ever say that would

explain what I had done? I switched off my phone and turned back toward home.

I read the article on my computer through blurring vision. What stood out the most was the byline at the top of the story. Adam McCard.

It was so obvious. I was so stupid. *Through confidential sources within the company*. Everything I'd chosen to ignore or dismiss or rationalize through the fall – every sign had been pointing to this outcome. Adam had been playing me all along.

I called Adam over and over. It rang before going to voice mail, then eventually it went straight to voice mail. Why bother answering? He knew exactly why I was calling. And I had served my purpose. I sent him a string of texts, my hands shaking. Call me back. WTF?? What the hell is this? I felt a hot bellow of anger at him, but especially at myself. I had done this. This was *my fault*.

I stared at my phone from across the room, wanting to smash it into a hundred pieces. I couldn't think straight. I needed to go somewhere, out, away. In my rush to leave, grabbing a raincoat and enough money to get myself a drink, I left my phone sitting on the coffee table. I realized my error belatedly, in a bar five blocks from home, halfway through my first drink. But I wonder now if I did it on purpose. Evan would have seen the article, would be searching for an explanation, wondering who the betrayer was. He deserved an answer. Maybe I wanted to give Evan the final pleasure of catching me in the act, and myself the punishment of finally being caught.

Yesterday Elizabeth waved good-bye through the open window of the taxi that was taking her to the station, for her train to New York. She insisted on taking a taxi, saying she was too old for a big scene at the train station. I was walking back up the stairs to the front porch when my phone rang.

I could picture Abby on the other end, taking a break from her usual Sunday run around the reservoir, hair pulled back in a ponytail, dodging strollers and dogs. I sank into the wicker chair that my parents' interior designer had artfully placed in the corner of the porch, where it caught the summer breeze and a view of the blooming hydrangea. The yard was brilliantly green. Abby had only a few weeks of teaching left in the school year, then a summer of freedom. She and Jake, who had finally quit his job, were planning a trip to Spain, maybe Morocco, maybe Greece – a wandering months-long itinerary.

Abby cleared her throat. 'I have to tell you something.'

I wondered for a flash if she and Jake were moving in together. I never would have predicted that she'd wind up with a preppy finance guy, but they just clicked. The rule book, as far as I could tell, had been thrown out the window. She was happy, and I was happy for her. I had decided, some months earlier, to bury the secret of me and Jake somewhere deep and unfindable. It was some-thing I was glad to let go of.

'What's up?' I said.

'Jake's parents are getting a divorce.'

I wasn't surprised. Perhaps a little that I was hearing this from her – surely my parents had known? – but the Fletchers hadn't seemed happy for a long time.

'Oh, Abby, I'm sorry. That sucks. How's Jake doing?'

'He's okay. But that's not really – it's not just the divorce. It's – well. Dot found out Henry has been cheat-ing on her.'

Of course. He and Eleanor weren't exactly subtle.

'What? Really? That's . . . that's horrible.'

'With your old coworker, actually. Eleanor. I guess it had been going on for a while. Apparently Dot always had her suspicions. There's been a whole string of women from the foundation who Henry's slept with.'

'That's awful.'

Abby was silent on her end. I could hear honking and traffic in the background, a barking dog, a faraway siren. The sounds of the city.

'You there?' I said.

'Okay, Jules, this is going to sound really weird. But I feel like I have to tell you.'

'What is it?'

'Promise you'll stay calm, okay? Deep breaths.'

'Abby? You're freaking me out.'

'So all these women Henry slept with, they were always girls who worked at the foundation. And they were usually – ugh – they were usually Laurie's assistants. I guess Laurie often hired friends of the family as a favor to the Fletchers. They were always the young, pretty ones. Henry's type, I guess. He went through them fast. Eleanor was the exception.'

'Creepy.'

'Dot found this out a while ago. Back in November or December, around the gala. Dot confronted him, and she made Laurie clean house. They fired Eleanor around Christmas. And – God, Jules. She made Laurie fire you, too.'

'Abby? What –'

'Dot's going to keep the foundation after the divorce. She'll have plenty of money to keep it running. But she wanted to get rid of anyone she suspected might have slept with Henry. Which included you. So she made Laurie fire you. The story about having financial problems was a cover.'

I barked out a hybrid cough-laugh-sob. 'Oh, my God.'

'I'm so sorry. I thought you should know.'

'Jesus.'

'Jules, for what it's worth, this is only Dot's paranoia. I told Jake that Julia Edwards is not like that. You just wouldn't do that. Never, ever. You're way too good a person. She's a total bitch for thinking that about you.'

I felt a sick pain in my stomach. Maybe at one point I had been a good person, but not anymore. I couldn't pretend to be offended or outraged at the insinuation. For so long I'd been able to cling to this purity, at least: my firing had been unjust. I was justified in my complaints – until now, suddenly, I wasn't. I *was* a liar. I *was* a cheater. Maybe Laurie had seen that about me all along. This explained her cold attitude all those months. The things she must have thought about me. The roses on my birthday. Sucking up to Dot at the gala. Another pliable, too-eager-to-please young woman making a fool of herself.

The whole time, I'd thought I was too good for that place. But at last I knew the truth, and while the suspicion was wrong, the underlying moral lapse wasn't. Abby was going on, trying to convince me it was going to be fine, fuck them, they're terrible for thinking that about me. The knife twisted. That was the worst part, the unearned sympathy. Abby, my best friend, the person who saw only the good in me, who believed I was innocent. I hung up before she could realize how hard I was crying.

The 2nd Avenue bar that rainy Monday night was nearly empty. The bartender saw my wet hair and distraught expression and gave me one on the house. I felt like I was in the last stage of a long race, pushing for the finish line, trying to outrun whatever was chasing me, but I realized – after my second or third vodka soda, I can't remember – that it was pointless. It was done. It was already over.

Evan was sitting on the futon when I opened the door, his head cradled in his hands, a weary cliché. My phone was sitting on the coffee table. He looked up.

'Julia. How could you do this to me?'

I was silent. I had no defense, no excuse. Only pathetic tears, invisible in the slick of rainwater that streamed down my face.

'How long?'

'Two months. Evan, I —'

He shook his head. It was almost like pity. He stood up, put on his coat, and picked up a duffel bag that was sitting by the door.

'I'm going to a hotel for the rest of the week. You can stay here, but you need to be out by Friday. I'm going to call the landlord and get you taken off the lease.'

I should have apologized. I should have at least tried to explain myself, should have thrown myself at his feet, but the expression on his face said he didn't want to hear it. He looked like a person who knew better than to waste any more emotion on something that had been dead for so long.

He paused, one foot propping the door open. A memory flashed — the day we moved in together, Evan turning to me before going down for the boxes that hot June morning. 'Julia,' he said finally. 'It's over. I don't want to see you again.'

———•———

'Mom? Dad?' My voice echoed in the front hall, the screen door slamming behind me. Abby's words were running through my head, loud and clamoring.

'We're in here,' my mom called from the living room.

She and my father were sitting on the couch, the Sunday paper spread out between them. My father looked at me over the top of his glasses. 'What's wrong?' he asked.

'Did you know the Fletchers were getting divorced? Did you know why?'

My mother glanced at my father, panic skipping across her face. 'Sweetie –'

My father interrupted. 'Why don't you sit down, Julia.'

'Do you want to know why I *really* got fired? Or did you know the whole time and you just didn't feel like telling me?'

He took off his glasses, placed them carefully in his pocket. 'Julia. You know I'm bound by attorney-client privilege. You know what that means.'

'I'm your *daughter*. Doesn't *that* mean something?'

'Of course it does,' my mother said. 'Honey, it just didn't seem like it was going to make it any better. You were already going through such a hard time. We didn't think –'

'What? You didn't think I deserved the truth?'

'Watch your tone,' my father said, his voice snapping into firmness.

'James, that isn't necessary.'

'Nina, don't *coddle* her. And Julia, for God's sake, this isn't all about you.' This was the voice I'd overheard through the years, during so many fights and arguments. His end-of-the-rope voice. I'd never before been on the receiving end. I'd never dared. But a new anger was bubbling up in me. My parents, all that time, listening to me complain about my firing, letting me humiliate myself with every retelling of the story, choosing to keep quiet about the truth. The knife twisted again.

'So you were fine with it,' I said. 'You were fine with them thinking I was some stupid slut. I guess that's more important to you, right? I mean, God forbid you *defend* me. You would never want to stir anything up with the beloved *Fletchers*.'

'*Enough.*' He stood up and pointed at the stairs. 'That's enough. Go to your room.'

My mother looked like she was on the verge of tears. She started to open her mouth. My father barked, '*Nina,* don't. She needs to get control of herself.'

I scoffed. I knew he would hate it, this show of insubordination. 'I'm not a kid anymore. You don't get to talk to me like that.'

'You are. You're a child, you're our child, and you'll listen to me.'

'I'm a person,' I shouted. 'I'm a fucking *person,* Dad.'

My mother came upstairs, knocking light as a butterfly on my door. She sat on the edge of my bed. I was curled up, facing the wall. I had stopped crying an hour earlier, but my pillow was still damp with tears.

'I don't want to talk about it,' I mumbled.

She reached over and laid her palm on my forehead, like she was checking for a fever. 'Honey. I'm sorry about your father. He shouldn't have lost his temper like that.'

Why were we always apologizing for the wrong things? My father and his temper, Dot and her paranoia, my betrayal of Spire's secrets. They were all proxies for the real problem. We talked in circles to avoid what we didn't want to admit. My father, the chauvinist. My selfishness, my complete lack of empathy. But I feared my problems were anchored by even deeper roots than that. I didn't know what it was to love. I had never known. All I had to do was look at my parents. My heart had grown a hard shell a long time ago, long before I had ever thought of boyfriends or lovers or careers or a life of my own. Maybe, under other circumstances, that shell would have made me impervious to heartbreak. But it was only a brittle barrier, and with enough pressure it had shattered and left me exposed.

A month later. Spring unfurls into summer with a string of sunny days. I scan job listings and compose halfhearted cover letters, but each attempt sinks like a stone. I hear about other classmates getting laid off, too many to count, classmates who have also moved back home or applied to the shelter of grad school. I ought to find solace in this company, in the collective misery of the country, but it does nothing to mitigate the specific pain – it's like taking painkillers that flood the body when you have a big, throbbing splinter in your thumb.

There is a certain comfort to bottoming out. To knowing what you're capable of enduring. These past months at home, I kept waiting for things to improve, for the upward swing to arrive. There was one more thing left, though. The last piece of the puzzle. A memory, one I had tried so hard to forget, that finally helped me understand why things had gone so wrong last year.

———•———

The night of the day when I found out the truth from Abby, after my mother left me alone in my room, I found I couldn't stop thinking about it. What, really, was wrong with me? Why had I done the terrible things I'd done? The nasty voice that had started dogging me the summer after graduation, the doubts and insecurities: it seemed clear where that came from. I had always been the girl who did everything right, who had followed the rules and checked every box. The problem emerged from my failure to continue that trajectory. I had grown too unsure about everything. I hesitated, I wavered. I needed someone to tell me what to do next.

There was the clink of cutlery downstairs. My parents were going to eat dinner like it was any normal night, pretend that fight hadn't just happened, like we'd been pretending all along. Then I heard a soft tap on the door. 'Julia?' my mother said. 'I made you a sandwich. I'm going to leave it here, okay?' Silence, but I could tell she hadn't walked away. 'Sweetheart. We were only trying to protect you because we love you so much.'

I took a long shower. I meant to leave the sandwich untouched in protest, but I was hungry, and my mother's words had softened me. And while I ate, I started thinking. What if I was wrong? What if I hadn't needed someone to tell me what to do next? Last year, after graduation, I'd had no idea what I was supposed to do with my life, and I wanted an answer. But what if the point was the question, not the answer?

It's so tempting. Being told: this is who you are. This is how your life will go. This is what will make you happy. You will go to the right school, find the right job, marry the right man. You'll do those things, and even if they feel wrong, you'll keep doing them. Even if it breaks your heart, this is the way it's done.

That night sophomore year. The memory I had been trying not to think about for so long. After Adam invited me into his room, upstairs at his party, he stepped close and backed me up against the wall. He leaned in and kissed me. For the first time all night – all year – I stopped thinking. I stopped thinking about everything confusing and difficult and uncertain. Doubts about my relationship, about friendships, about what I should major in. The sickening look of disappointment on Evan's face, downstairs. The feeling of having too much space and not ever knowing what I was supposed to do with it. It vanished. Adam was such a good kisser. My mind was finally at peace, focused on only one thing: the person in front of me.

Then a bang sounded from the party below, a speaker blowing out, the music stopping abruptly. We pulled apart, and Adam looked at the door. A loud chorus of booing filled the void. And then, a second later, the music started again. Adam, satisfied that the problem had been fixed, turned back to me. There was a gleam in his eyes, a hunger for something he knew he was about to consume.

But I was frightened of myself, of what I was doing. I'd been this person before – a cheater, a liar – but I didn't want to be that person again. I wanted to be better. Adam slipped his hands to my waist. The clash between temptation and resistance made me nauseous. I wanted this; I didn't want this; I'd been daydreaming about this for months. He kissed me harder and started sliding his hands under the hem of my dress.

'No,' I said, turning so his lips grazed my cheek. 'No, Adam, I can't do this.'

'Yes, you can,' he muttered, kissing me on the collarbone.

'No,' I said, more forcefully this time. 'No, I can't. Please stop.'

I pushed him away. He looked confused. 'You're joking, right?'

'No, Adam. I have a boyfriend. You know that.'

'You're serious?'

I started for the door, but he grabbed my hand. 'Let me go,' I said.

'What the hell, Julia? This is exactly what you wanted.'

'No, it's not. Adam, *stop*.' I tried to wrest my hand free. He laughed. 'You are such a fucking tease.'

'I'm not – I'm sorry if I led you on. I thought we were just friends.'

'You're *sorry?* Julia, what the fuck do you want? You really want to go back to Evan? Like he's going to make you happy?' He laughed again. 'He's *never* going to make you happy. Anyone can see that.'

I shook my head. 'You're wrong.'

'I'm not wrong, Jules. I mean, you guys are going to break up sooner or later. It's so obvious. So what's the problem here?'

'You don't know him. You don't know anything about it.'

'I know exactly who Evan is. And I know who you are. You're bored. You want more, don't you? You want something better. I know you do.'

He was waiting for me to say something. When I didn't, he stepped closer, his hands against the wall on either side of me. He leaned in so his mouth was next to my ear.

'Let me tell you how this is going to go,' he said in a low voice. I closed my eyes. 'You're going to forget about Evan. Forget about everything else. It's just you and me, right now. Isn't that what you wanted?' I could feel the damp heat of his breath against my neck. 'I know you, Julia. The real you. I know what you want. You're going to stay here with me.' I was thinking: *Is he right?* Does he know the real me? Is that so impossible to imagine? 'You're going to take that dress off. And then you're going to –'

'I'm leaving,' I said, ducking under his arm. He didn't know me. I'd been so stupid, letting my boredom disguise such an obviously bad idea as a good one. I wanted to be better than I had been before. I *was* better. Adam didn't know the real me. He was wrong.

But he grabbed my hand and yanked me back. He pinned me against the wall with his weight and used one hand to pull up my dress, the other to unbutton his jeans.

'What the fuck are you doing?' I squirmed away from his hands.

'Come on, babe,' he said, trying to kiss me. He pressed against me, harder.

'Let me go. Adam, *stop!*'

Finally I got my hands onto his shoulders and used the leverage of the wall behind me to shove him away. He stumbled backwards, tripping.

'Fucking *asshole,*' I said, gasping for air.

He stared at me, his cheeks flaming red, then cooling. Then, after what felt like an eternity, he shrugged. 'You know what, babe? I feel bad for you. I was just trying to help you out.'

I straightened my dress and wiped his spit away from my mouth. 'Your loss,' he called as I slammed the door shut.

He graduated two months later. It took more than two years before he finally acknowledged what had happened that night. And by then – as awful as that night had been – the scar tissue had hardened so much that I couldn't even feel the original wound underneath. I saw Adam again, and I didn't remember what had come before. I didn't want to remember. From the moment

331

Adam came back into my life, I grew restless and unhappy and yearned for something new. I thought he was the answer. I never stopped to think that Adam was the source of my unhappiness. I thought my life was the illness and Adam was the cure. But the more time we spent together, the deeper my dissatisfaction grew. His presence was the only thing that could distract me from it. And so I kept returning to the well, drinking deeper and deeper.

Maybe that's why, even though I've spent so much time thinking about last year, I don't think about Adam that much. In the end, what we had went no deeper than the quick hit of a drug. All those dinners, those bottles of wine, those nights in his bed – they add up to nothing. The lie I told myself collapsed in one shattering moment, and now I can only start from scratch.

———

In the past month, I've carved out a new, careful routine for myself. I wake up early. I've started running again in the mornings, before the heat sets in. I take Pepper on long walks through the woods, throwing sticks for him until my arm is sore. I come home and eat lunch, leftovers or sandwiches, cleaning up after myself like a guest. My father is always at work, and my mother is always at her meetings and committees. Most days it's just me and Jasmine, the housekeeper. We move on our separate tracks, nodding when we pass each other.

I have a stack of books from the local library. I'm

filling the holes in my education, all those English classes I never took because I thought I hated the subject. Austen, Dickens, Brontë. Ovid and Homer, Woolf and Joyce. I have a vague plan to work my way up to the present. Some of the books make me laugh, some make me cry, some bore me to death, some I suspect I am utterly missing the point of. It doesn't really matter. It's the act of concentration that I need to relearn. I am trying to be present. Some afternoons I go to the Boston MFA, where I spend hours sitting in the galleries, losing myself in the artwork, grasping at the feeling I had in Paris.

In the mornings, I scan the news for a mention of Spire. The coverage has lessened as the months have gone by. In the beginning, the story was everywhere: the investigations, the plummeting of WestCorp's shares, the promises of full cooperation with the authorities. Michael Casey ducking and covering his head whenever the cameras chased him. In those early weeks, every ringing phone or approaching car put me on edge. I was certain it had caught up to me. An officer at the door, ready to serve me with a subpoena, ready to haul me off and take my statement.

But that's not what anyone cared about. The leak paled in comparison to the laws that had been broken, and Spire and the feds had bigger fish to fry. What mattered was the crime, not the telling. And I bet no one suspected Evan of being connected to it. Evan was chosen precisely because he would never run his mouth. I studied every picture in the paper and every clip on TV for a glimpse of his face, for evidence of what had happened to him. But there was nothing. The cameras were focused solely on Michael Casey, the one whose head the public demanded. Once or twice I saw Adam on TV, commenting on the latest update in the Spire story, grinning broadly under the hot studio lights. He's finally as famous as I always thought he would be.

My mother, meanwhile, has been watching from a wary distance.

Most days she's out the door before I've even left for my run, on her way to one of her appointments or Pilates classes, but the other morning she lingered at the kitchen table. I looked up from the paper and found she had a rare gaze of contentment.

'Julia.' She reached for my hand. 'Sweetie, I'm proud of you. I'm so glad you're feeling better. I can't tell you how happy it makes me.'

'Thanks, Mom.'

She stood up. Sentiment over. While she fussed for her purse and car keys, she kept talking.

'You know who I ran into at the coffee shop yesterday? Rob's mother. She didn't know you were back.'

'Oh. That's nice.' I hadn't told Rob, or anyone, that I was back. I couldn't find a way to mention it without inciting cloying pity.

'Rob's coming out from Cambridge for dinner on Friday night. His mother's invited you over, too. I think it would be really nice if you went. She seemed a little hurt that you hadn't been by to see them. She's always loved you.'

'I don't know. I'm not –'

'She's not going to take no for an answer. *I'm* not going to take no for an answer. Call her and tell her you'll see her on Friday. It will be good for everyone. Okay?' She kissed the top of my head, rearranging a few rogue strands of hair before she left.

Friday evening, I knocked on Rob's parents' door. In the past, I would have let myself in.

Rob opened the door. He grinned and kissed me on the cheek. 'Come in,' he said, gesturing me into the front hall. 'They can't wait to see you.'

Rob's parents weren't so different from my parents – this was true for all my friends except Evan – and the flow and contour of the conversation made me feel at home. It was instantly comfortable in a way I hadn't quite expected: the same worn wood of their kitchen table, the familiar view of their backyard through the window. Rob's father was a lawyer, and his mother had a successful career as a cookbook ghostwriter. She was an excellent cook. The wine, the chicken Marbella, the fragrant basket of bread and the yellow butter – the flavors were unchanged. His mother had a deep, lusty laugh I had always loved. His father still liked a Cognac after dinner. For a moment, it felt like the last four or five years had been a mere skip of the record.

After we finished dessert, a homemade pear tart, Rob and I stood to help his parents clear the table. His mother shook her head. 'No – you two go on. I'm sure you want to catch up.' I wondered if she was in cahoots with my mother.

Rob held the front door open. 'Let's go for a walk. It's a nice night.'

He filled me in on everything that had happened since Thanksgiving, when I'd seen him last. He had been accepted at Harvard Medical School. He'd also been accepted at Johns Hopkins, Stanford, and Columbia, but he'd decided on Harvard. He wanted to be a neurosurgeon eventually.

'So you're staying here? I mean, in Cambridge?'

'Yup. Hey, you remember Mindy? From biology senior year?'

'Yeah, why?'

'She's going to be in my class at Harvard.'

'The girl who threw up when we dissected the pig? Mindy wants to be a *doctor*?'

He laughed. 'I wonder how she's going to handle anatomy.'

We walked in silence for a stretch. I was tempted to take his hand; it only felt natural to do what we'd done so many times before. I stole a glance at him when we got to the park near his house. His face was illuminated by the far-off floodlights on the tennis court. I was trying to decide if he was different. He looked almost the same as he had in high school. Maybe a fraction taller, more stubble in his beard. But he was still, mostly, the person I'd fallen for when I was sixteen years old. What I was wondering was whether I was mostly the same person, too.

'What about you?' he said after we stopped and sat on a bench. 'Are you going to stay?'

'Here? I don't know.'

'How is it, living at home?'

'You know what my mom's like.'

He held up his hands. 'I plead the Fifth.'

'It's fine, actually. It's not so bad. They pretty much leave me alone. I guess I need to figure out what I actually want to do next. You know. Where I want to go.'

'Why not here? I know one reason for you to stay.'

The trees made a rushing sound when the night breeze blew through them, a sound like rain falling. The park was empty except for the two of us. I pulled my sweater tighter around me. I slid my feet free of my sandals and felt the cold, spongy grass between my toes. I used to play tennis in this park. The past, my past, was everywhere in this town. When I turned back to Rob, he was looking at me. He'd stated it as a fact, and he was right. He *was* one reason for me to stay.

I shrugged. 'I'm not in any hurry. Just taking it one day at a time.'

'Do you want to come back to Cambridge tonight?'

'Not till the third date, buddy,' I said with a laugh.

'No, not like that. My roommates are having people over. A party.'

'It's kind of late.'

'It's, like, ten o'clock, grandma.'

'Well, I told my parents I'd walk the dog before bed.'

He offered a hand to help me up. 'So living at home does have its downside.'

'Free food, though. Unlimited laundry.'

When we got back, his house was dark. I had parked at the bottom of the driveway, borrowing the Volvo for the night, and Rob's old green Jeep was parked in front of it. It was the same junky car he'd driven in high school. On winter weekends in boarding school, we'd sometimes drive out to the beach on the North Shore. I'd dared him to go swimming once, on a frozen and windy January day, and before I could tell him I was kidding he had stripped to his boxers and run into the steel-gray Atlantic. Rob gave me a thumbs-up, his chest chapping red in the wind, then ducked beneath a crashing wave. We were alone, the only people on the beach. A moment passed. Another moment. Rob didn't emerge back up. Five seconds, at least. Ten seconds. That was way too long. Just as I started sprinting for the water, he popped back up, grinning like a jack-in-the-box. 'You're insane!' I shouted over the roar of the wind. He'd done it just to get a rise out of me. To be able to say, later, that I'd been so worried about him I'd almost gone in myself. He was covered in goose bumps, lips turning blue, but he laughed the whole way back. Rob was like that.

I didn't know what we were doing. Rob took my

hands and pulled me toward him. I kept my gaze fixed to his shoulder.

'How about next week?' he was saying.

'What about it?'

'We should hang out again. Lunch?'

'Okay.' Thinking. Lunch was innocuous enough.

'Tuesday work for you?'

'Well, I'll have to check my calendar. I'm a busy woman.'

'Good. Tuesday it is.' He tugged me in and kissed me on the cheek before letting go. As I drove away, he waved good-bye from the bottom of the driveway, and I watched him shrinking into the night in the rearview mirror.

Elizabeth had been calling in her spare moments to tell me about New York, doing her best to distract me. She was always rushing, always late to something.

'What about this weekend?' she said. It was Monday, the day before I was going to meet Rob for lunch. 'My roommate's going to be gone. I already cleared it with her. You can stay in her room.'

'I don't know, Lizzie.'

'You know I live in Chinatown, right? It's really far from the Upper East Side. You won't run into him. You're going to have to set foot in New York at some point.'

'Yeah, it's just that –'

'Donald is throwing a party this weekend. In his loft.

It's going to be amazing. Jules, come on. You need to get out of that house. Shake it up a little.'

Rob was waiting for me when I arrived the next day. The Thai restaurant he'd picked was cool and dark inside, a bamboo fan spinning lazily on the ceiling. The restaurant was empty at the lunch hour, most people coming for takeout.

'It's not fancy,' Rob said, drinking his beer. 'But I like it.'

'So how much longer are you working at the lab?'

'The end of July, I think. It's sort of arbitrary. It's not like I'm really leaving. I'm staying in the same apartment next year.'

'You didn't want to take time off before school?'

'I did. I took this year.' He reached across the table to try my noodles. 'Hey, we're going out to the Cape this weekend. One of my buddies rented a place for the summer. You should come.'

'You and your roommates? A bunch of dudes?'

'The girls are coming, too. It's going to be awesome. It's right on the beach.'

I took a small sip of beer. Elizabeth, urging me to New York. Rob, inviting me to the Cape. I knew this point would come eventually, my hibernation forced to an end. The weekend on the Cape would be fun. I could picture it: the burgers sizzling on the grill, the Frisbee floating back and forth. But I also had the feeling that if I were to do it – to go with Rob for the weekend, to be with him again – the previous four years really would vanish without a trace. Every way in which I thought I'd changed would be wiped out by the easy backslide into his arms. It was tempting, to so cleanly erase the messiness of the past. Adam, Evan, all the mistakes I'd made. The man was going to be a *brain surgeon*. Our life together could be a good one.

But I shrugged. 'I might go stay with Elizabeth in New York this weekend.'

'I need to know by tonight, so I can save you a place in the car.'

'I'm not sure.'

He stared at me, quizzical. 'I'm not going to wait around forever, Jules.'

We emerged from the cool darkness of the restaurant onto the too-bright sidewalk. I was squinting, disoriented, my vision spotty from the sunshine, and when Rob said good-bye he kissed me square on the mouth. His lips were still spicy from the noodles. 'Let me know by tonight, okay?'

CHAPTER 15

Evan

There were thunderstorms over New York that December night, earsplitting booms and low rumbles that would have kept me awake if I hadn't been already. I lay fully dressed on top of the covers in the midtown hotel room, counting down the hours until it was time to go back in.

David Kleinman had been stuck in DC because of the storm. The thwack of helicopter blades overhead greeted me as I hurried into the lobby on Tuesday morning. I arrived on the floor just as he did. Kleinman walked through the silent hallways without meeting anyone's eyes. He went straight to his office, dusty from the previous few months, and slammed the door behind him.

Roger plopped down across from me with a wolfish smile. 'How'd you sleep, my friend?'

I stared at my steaming coffee, willing it to cool so I could start drinking it.

'Listen, you lawyered up yet? Huh? Hey, I'm talking to you here.'

'No, Roger. I haven't.'

'You *haven't*? Shit, Peck, what are you waiting for? You know they're gonna be after your ass.'

'Knock it off.'

'Whoa, whoa. So hostile. I'm just trying to help.'

'It's none of your business.'

He snorted. 'You're kidding, right? You don't think you and Michael made it my business when you decided to fuck everything up for the rest of us? When you broke the *law*?' Roger shook his head. 'You could have said something, you know. Why didn't you go to Kleinman?'

He waited, but I didn't have an answer.

I went past Michael's office that morning, but it was empty and dark. Wanda's desk was vacant, too. Rumors raced like wildfire: Michael had hired a security detail to protect him and his wife. He'd fled to Europe. He'd lawyered up and was refusing to talk. He'd come in at dawn via the freight elevator and cleared out his things. No one knew what was true and what was false. It wasn't like the market crash back in September. We weren't in this thing together. This time, everyone fractured into distinct modes of panic, scrambling for seats on invisible lifeboats. Some claimed they'd seen it coming. Others were already on the phone with headhunters. I came around a corner in the hallway and heard a pair of angry voices, one of them saying he couldn't *believe* what Michael had done. But when the pair saw me, they shut up. That's how it went that day. Conversations halted when I came too close. I was persona non grata.

Kleinman gathered everyone that afternoon in the

same conference room where he'd addressed us on the day he left for Washington. The mood was more somber this time. He once again emphasized that this crisis – a new crisis, one of our own making – would not be the undoing of Spire. This was an aberration, one rogue actor. A man who didn't stand for what Spire was. Spire would be cooperating fully with authorities. The rest of the firm was clean. Kleinman wasn't going to let this destroy us. *Us*. Us. That's what I focused on. I was still there, still part of the team.

A hand touched my elbow as I filed out. David Kleinman's secretary, giving me a sympathetic look. 'Evan? He'd like to see you.'

Kleinman was waiting inside his office. A grandfather clock ticking in the corner marked the silence. He watched me sit, fiddle with my cuffs, shift in my chair, like he was waiting for a truth to reveal itself. Or did he want me to speak first?

At last he said, 'I hear you were the one working with Michael on this deal.'

'Yes, sir.'

'You'll have access to a lawyer, one of ours. From now on you shouldn't say a single thing about this without your lawyer present. Okay? Complete silence unless the lawyer is there. Not to your mom, your friends. Your girlfriend, whatever.' I swallowed; my mouth went dry. 'But right now is the exception. Right now I need you to be totally straight with me. What did you know and when did you know it?'

344

After I told him everything – the beginning of the deal, what I'd overheard in Vegas, the briefcase for Chan, the $20,000 in cash from Michael – he nodded and dismissed me. Kleinman didn't say anything about where Michael was, or what was going to happen to him. Maybe it would have been stating the obvious. On the walk back to my desk, I noticed a team of strange men in dark suits in the conference room. Files and stacks of paper and laptops covered the table. The blinds were lowered on the windows. They looked like they were setting up for war.

The SEC took over one conference room, and our lawyers took over another. The nameplate outside Michael's office had been pried off by the end of the first week.

Kleinman's speech his first day back didn't do much good. The death spiral began immediately. Investors pulled their money. No one bought what Kleinman was selling – that this was a contained crisis, the mistake of one greedy egomaniac. Michael had been the acting CEO. His fingerprints were on everything. Any deal conducted during his tenure was tainted. Every last skeleton was going to be dragged out of every last closet. We were getting hammered.

'Michael *fucking* Casey. I could murder this fucking guy,' one trader said to another in the kitchen. People had stopped bothering with silence around me. They didn't care anymore, or maybe they'd already forgotten who I was.

The other guy laughed bitterly. 'You're gonna have to get in line.'

I felt my throat tighten as I stirred milk into my coffee.

'Fine. I'd settle for just pissing on his corpse if I had to.'

By that point, it was clear to me that Michael was almost certainly going to jail. And the odd thing was, I felt pity for him. If we hadn't been caught, those same guys would have declared him a hero. They would have admired his brilliance and ballsiness for pulling it off. But in this game, you didn't score points with hypotheticals. Execution was the only thing that mattered.

Christmas snuck up on me. It was just another day to get through: reruns, takeout, a quiet apartment. My parents called, and so did Arthur. They had seen the news when it broke a few weeks earlier. They knew the outlines of what had happened, but I let the calls go to voice mail. I didn't feel like talking about it, not yet. There was too much that I hadn't made sense of. How was I supposed to feel? Guilty, contrite, apologetic? What was I supposed to say? I understood, intellectually, how bad it looked to other people. To people like Arthur and my parents. Normal people. But there was some of me that still saw the upside in what Michael had done. I felt guilt over the wrong thing – over the role I'd played in making the news public. The deal had been working. It was going to make Spire an enormous amount of money. I wasn't ready to let go of that yet.

★

After the holidays, I was sitting at my desk when I felt a tap on my shoulder. A man with a crew cut and an ill-fitting suit told me to follow him. We went into the conference room, where another man who looked just like him sat at the table. One was named John, the other Kurt, both of them from the SEC. I immediately forgot who was who.

'Have a seat,' one of them said. 'Help yourself to water or coffee or whatever.'

'Thanks,' I said, although their hospitality seemed pretentious when it was our conference room they were occupying.

'You have a good holiday?' one of them asked.

'Um, yeah. It was fine.'

John looked over at Kurt, or vice versa. 'Did I tell you I had to drive all the way to Short Hills on Christmas Eve? For that new Elmo doll. Jesus.' He rolled his eyes, then said to me, 'Don't ever get married, okay?'

I laughed. At that moment, the door to the conference room opened. A blond woman in a skirt suit came in, brandishing a briefcase in one hand and a large Starbucks in the other. She stopped, froze. 'What did you say to them?' she said, her eyes wide.

'We were just shooting the shit,' John or Kurt said. 'Don't worry.'

'*Never* talk to him without me here. Understood? That goes for you, too,' she said to me. 'You really should know better, Evan.'

But I didn't even know why I needed a lawyer. The

questions that John and Kurt asked were easy, straight-forward. I nodded, confirmed, clarified, helped them establish the particulars of the deal: the timeline, the players. As the week went on, my fear started to dissipate. They were treating me like I had done nothing wrong. Maybe I'd be okay. Maybe all wasn't lost just yet.

'Hold that?'

I pushed the Door Open button. Roger hurried into the elevator. 'Oh,' he said, catching his breath. 'Thanks, Evan.' I think it was the only time he'd ever thanked me for anything. It was definitely the only time he'd ever used my first name.

'Good weekend?' I asked.

He glanced away, staring instead at the ticking floor numbers as we zoomed up the skyscraper. 'Yeah. What about you?'

'Fine,' I lied. The weekends felt endless without the distraction of work. I went through a case of beer without even trying. I had no idea what to do with the time.

We were silent for the rest of the ride up. Both of us were in early. Roger was working on some big new deal with Steve. And I'd been coming in early because I knew that appearances mattered. I needed to prove that I was ready to hit the ground running when this mess was over. I'd been removed from every project, every e-mail distro, but things would be back to normal soon enough.

As Roger and I approached our desks, I saw an

unfamiliar woman standing near my chair. A spark of hope: maybe she was there to give me a new assignment.

'Evan Peck?' she said, and I nodded. 'Could you come with me, please?'

She led me to the other side of the floor and stopped in front of what I'd always assumed was a supply closet, tucked in the building's core, far away from the windows. She balanced a stack of binders in one arm while she shuffled through a ring of keys with the other hand. 'Do you mind?' she said with a smile, handing me the binders. She was kind of cute.

'Here we go,' she said, finally finding the key. She opened the door and flipped the light switch. It was a small, windowless office. A bare desk, a computer, a chair. It smelled like paint. Yes, I realized, I had in fact seen the janitor opening and closing this door just the other week. 'This is nicer, isn't it?' Her voice had gone up an octave. 'Your very own office.'

'I'm supposed to work here?'

'You know, I've never heard of an analyst getting his own office before.'

'But why? Why are you moving me?'

She turned on the computer, swept her hand across the desk, nodded at the whole array. 'It's nice in here, actually. Nice and clean and quiet. Don't you think?'

'So I just . . . are people going to know where to find me?'

'Well, it sounds like you've been spending most days in deposition with the SEC. While you're tied up with that, we figured we'd move you in here so we could free up your old desk.'

'Free it up for who?'

'I'm really just here to help you get settled. Actually, I have to go. I have a nine o'clock on another floor. Here's the key. The door locks automatically.'

There was a forgotten industrial-size bottle of window cleaner in the corner. I used that to prop open the door while I settled in. A minute later, I looked up to see that the door was pushing the heavy bottle across the carpet, gradually trying to close itself against the outside world.

The following week, when I walked into the conference room for our usual 9:30 start time with the SEC, something had changed. I couldn't put my finger on it at first. Then, as I poured myself a cup of coffee from the setup at the side of the room, I realized that John and Kurt were both silent. My heart started beating faster. They were staring purposefully at the papers in front of them instead of engaging in their usual stupid banter.

My lawyer arrived, and John or Kurt turned on the recorder. 'So Evan. We have new testimony from Michael that we need to ask you about.'

'Okay,' I said, glancing over at my lawyer. She nodded.

'You've stated that you were unaware of Michael's relationship with the Chinese officials until the night of' – he looked down at his papers – 'November thirteenth, 2008.'

'Right. The first night in Las Vegas.'

'Now, Michael has testified that you were aware of his relationship with the Chinese officials from the beginning. Since' – he looked down again – 'August eighth, 2008.'

'No. I didn't know anything until Vegas. I wasn't even supposed to hear that. They didn't know I was –'

'Michael stated that you were aware of his trip to China, taken in August, to facilitate the initial meeting with the officials.'

'No. I mean, yes, I knew about the trip, but I didn't know what it was for.'

'Michael stated that you did.'

'I didn't! He didn't say anything about it, except that he was going to China.'

'Michael said, and I'm quoting here, "Evan knew exactly what we were doing."'

'Can we have a minute, please?' my lawyer said.

We stepped out into the hallway. Her high heels brought her up to my eye level. 'Evan. Point-blank, is there anything you haven't told me? I don't like surprises.'

'No. Nothing. Why would Michael say that?' My heart was beating even faster.

'It could be part of his strategy. Make it seem like you had more responsibility than you actually did. So he's not the only one who looks bad.'

'Do you think I look bad?' My voice cracked.

She cocked an eyebrow. 'It doesn't matter how I think you look. It matters that I protect you. Understood?'

We went back into the conference room. I could feel John and Kurt staring as I took a small sip of coffee. The scratching of pen against paper, the buzz of the fluorescent light above. A dull ache throbbing through my temple.

'Are we good?'

'Go ahead,' my lawyer said.

'Evan, you turned over the twenty thousand dollars that Michael gave you on November twenty-fourth, 2008. You had said, in previous testimony, that Michael gave you this money as a – I'm quoting here – a token of his appreciation. Is that correct?'

'Yes. That's what he said.'

'But you didn't deposit or spend any of the money.'

'Right,' I said, relieved. 'It's all there.'

'Why didn't you spend any of it? What were you waiting for?'

'I'm sorry – what?'

'Twenty thousand dollars is a lot of money. Is there a reason you were so hesitant to touch it?'

'Is this really relevant?' my lawyer said.

'Do you think you deserved that money?'

'I – I didn't ask for it. Michael just gave it to me.'

'But you didn't turn it down. You didn't give it back. Clearly you thought you were entitled to that money in some respect. Except that you didn't spend any of it. See,

352

that's what doesn't make sense to me, Evan. You make it seem like you were just a low-level player. But Michael Casey wouldn't be giving you a twenty-thousand-dollar payoff unless you were intimately involved with this deal.'

'It wasn't a payoff!'

'Then what was it?'

'A . . . a bonus. It was a bonus.'

'Spire didn't give out bonuses last year.'

'Can we move on?' my lawyer said. 'I don't see that we're getting anywhere with this.'

'Fine,' John or Kurt said. 'The next thing we'd like to ask you about is Wenjian Chan. Has he been in touch with you since you saw him in Las Vegas?'

'I already told you. No. I never heard from him.'

'Well, it's possible he might have reached out to you since we took your testimony the other week. Has he?'

'Why would he do that? He knows we're being investigated.'

'Maybe he wanted to find out what exactly you were telling us. Maybe he wanted to make you an offer for your cooperation.'

I felt like I was going to throw up. 'Don't you think that I would have told you? That I would have told you if I'd heard anything from him?'

'Come on, Evan,' John or Kurt said. 'You don't exactly have a great track record with that. That's the whole reason we're here.'

'What the fuck does that mean?'

'Evan,' my lawyer said, in a warning tone.

'It means you kept this deal a secret long after you knew the truth. It means you chose to keep silent about Michael's plan even though you knew it was wrong. It means we can't trust you to give us the full picture unless we ask.'

'I didn't keep it a secret!'

'Then who did you tell about it?'

'Okay,' my lawyer said, shutting her briefcase with a firm click. 'I think that's enough. Let's take a break.'

My lawyer and I had lunch together that day at the Indian place on 9th Avenue. Roger and the other analysts were at another table in the restaurant. I hadn't been invited to lunch with them in months.

My lawyer spent most of the meal on her BlackBerry. 'Sorry,' she said. 'My nanny has the flu. We had to use the backup. Now the kids are sick, too. It's a fucking nightmare.' She noticed my untouched food. 'Hey. You okay?'

'No.'

She put her phone down. 'You know it's not personal, right? The things they were saying back there. They really don't give a shit about you.'

'It doesn't feel like that. It feels like they're after me.'

'They're only trying to get as much out of you as they can. So they can nail Michael and the Chinese. You've got the testimony they need. But you're small fish, Evan. I mean that in a good way.'

Roger and the others walked past on the way out.

Roger bumped into my chair. 'Oops. Didn't see you there, Peck,' he said, grinning. 'Hot date, huh?'

After we finished eating, after she paid and we stood up to put on our coats, she asked: 'What did you mean before? When you said that you didn't keep it a secret?'

'Oh.' I was hoping she had forgotten about that. 'I didn't really mean anything. Just that, um, I didn't *consciously* keep it a secret.'

When we returned to the conference room, John and Kurt looked up in unison. 'Actually, we're done,' one of them said. 'For now, at least. We don't need anything else. You can go back to work.'

'That's it?' I said.

'We might need to call you back for a few things as they crop up. But yeah, that's it. You're done. Thanks for your help.'

'You must be relieved,' my lawyer said, walking me back to my office-slash-closet. 'Now you can go back to normal, right?'

'I guess.' I did feel relieved – that weak but good feeling that comes after you've finally thrown up – but I also felt confused. Shortchanged somehow. What would come next? What was going to happen to me?

We stopped outside my door. 'Well,' she said. 'Good luck, Evan.'

———•———

My life went soft at the edges. The same feeling permeated the hours at work, the hours at home: emptiness, futility, like a bucket with a hole in the bottom. The SEC investigation had been my last vestige of purpose. For a few weeks I continued to arrive early, stay late, and keep my closet door propped open so that anyone walking past might imagine me hard at work. Then I left a little earlier. Arrived a little later. Started shutting my door at lunch so I could watch the postgame highlights with the sound on. January became February, then February became March. Eventually I gave in to it. I punched in and out. I ate dinner; I drank. I'd go entire weekends without speaking, so that my voice felt scratchy and strange when I greeted the security guards on Monday mornings. I arrived hungover and shut my door for long stretches to take naps on the coarse industrial carpet, letting time pass like high clouds drifting through the upper atmosphere.

I realized at a certain point that I'd been celibate for nearly three months. It was the longest by far I'd gone without having sex. In high school, it was only ever a few weeks at a time, and in college, too, and after that came Julia. It was like a portal to an earlier time. The texture of this frustration was identical to what I'd felt as a virginal teenager. It was almost as if, by going so long without sex, I had become my younger self again. I felt confused and melancholy in a way I hadn't in a decade. I could have gone out to a bar and ended the celibate streak with a one-night stand easily enough. But in a way, I liked being alone with my former self. I indulged it. I liked recalling how it felt when adulthood was still a distant mystery.

When the concrete details – an apartment in Manhattan, a high-paying job – would have been sufficient by themselves. I hadn't realized, back then, how messy it actually was. I wanted to go back and hide inside that ignorance.

I kept waiting for the SEC to come knocking, to ask the question I'd never answered. *What did you mean, you didn't keep it a secret?* I had blurted it out without thinking, and they treated it like a throwaway. A pathetic, confused, nonsense lie. But it was the truth; I *hadn't* kept it a secret. I was the whole reason the SEC was there, shining a bright light on the dirty deal. No one ever asked about the leak. Maybe they always assumed it was me, the young analyst gone nervous and blabby, or maybe they just didn't care. It was a paltry defense in any case. I *had* told somebody, but not the right somebody.

One day in March I lay down for a nap after lunch, intending to sleep off another hangover. When I woke up, it was late – past 8:00 p.m. I'd slept for almost five hours. On my way to the elevator, I passed the other analysts, gathered near Roger's desk.

'Steve's riding you that hard?' one of them was saying to him.

'Go without me,' Roger said. 'I've got at least six hours left here.'

Roger's face was puffy and pale, exhaustion and caffeine lending a nervous twitch to his features. But when he noticed me approach, he grinned like his old self. 'Look,' he said. 'Peck can take my place. Make him pick up the tab. He's rich.'

Everyone had heard about the $20,000. They knew I had to turn it over, but it was fodder nonetheless. Roger laughed. 'Still can't take a joke, huh, Peck?'

'You can come along if you want,' one of the other analysts mumbled, a residual politeness kicking in. The group walked slow, including but not quite acknowledging my presence. No one knew what to say to me. I glanced back over my shoulder at Roger. He was staring so closely at his screen that it looked like he was going to tip over. Just as I must have looked, so many nights during the previous year. It was like coming across a photograph of myself that I didn't remember being taken.

When had I become so invisible? I thought as the elevator descended and the analysts traded stories I knew nothing about. When had I become an afterthought? Other people made mistakes and were forgiven. I didn't know how much longer I could endure this. I knew it was fucked up, but I missed Michael. Or maybe it was more that I missed the way Michael made me feel. Like I was part of something bigger.

The neon sign for McGuigan's glowed ahead of us in the darkness. It was the same as always – the stale beer smell, the jukebox, the crack of cue against billiard ball, the rattle of ice. But before I could follow my coworkers to the usual booth in the back, my eye caught another familiar sight.

'Evan?' she said. Her eyes wide, uncertain. Almost regretting it.

Then she smiled.

★

358

I nursed my Guinness. It wasn't until late, long after my coworkers had gone, leaving bills stuck to the damp table, that Maria came and sat next to me.

'Do you want another?' she asked, pointing at my empty glass.

'I'm okay.' For the first time in a while, I didn't feel like getting drunk.

'Sorry. I meant to come over earlier. It was a crazy night. How are things?'

'Good, I guess.'

Good? I missed the way things had been between us in the fall, but I didn't know how to go back to that. I doubted it was possible.

'I have to say something,' Maria said at last. 'I should have said this a long time ago. I'm sorry things got kind of weird when I started dating Wyeth. That was bitchy, bringing him in like that. I should have told you.'

'Oh,' I said. 'That. That's fine. You didn't owe me an explanation.'

'That's not true. I really liked you, Evan.' Her voice wavered. 'I just – I kept waiting. You know? I kept waiting for you to make a move or do something or say something. Eventually it seemed like you didn't want anything like that. And Wyeth was cute, and he asked me out. So I said yes.'

She shrugged. 'You seemed pissed afterward. Then you didn't come around for a long time. But you're back now, and – I don't know what I'm trying to say. I don't know what's going on in your life or why you're back, but I want us to be friends again. I'd like that. If you want to.'

I stared down at the bar, blinking, willing the seams to hold together.

'Are you okay?' she asked in a soft voice.

I shook my head. 'God, Maria. I'm sorry. I'm a jerk.'

'No, Evan. I shouldn't have put you in that position. I –'

'No. I'm an asshole. I didn't make a move last year because I had a girlfriend.'

'A girlfriend?'

'I should have said something. I'm sorry.'

'Oh, my God. That makes so much sense. A girlfriend!' She laughed, then stopped. 'Wait. Did you say "had"?'

'Yeah. We broke up a while ago.'

'Oh.'

'It was complicated. It's better that it's over.' Was that true? Was that what I really thought? 'It had been dragging itself out for a long time.'

'What happened?'

'Well,' I said. 'How much time do you have?'

The next morning, as I passed Roger's desk, I noticed that he was wearing the same clothes as the day before. Shirt wrinkled, tie stained with oil, smelling and looking like he hadn't slept in days. It was the first morning in a long time that I had woken without a hangover. I'd picked up breakfast, which I never did, the toasted bagel radiating heat through the white bag. I stopped next to Roger's desk.

'Want breakfast?' I said, extending the bag toward him. He raised an eyebrow. 'They messed up my order,' I lied. 'I asked for sesame but they gave me an everything. So they did it over, but they gave me both.'

'Um. Okay. Thanks,' he said warily, taking the bag.

'You're welcome,' I said. Then, before I lost my nerve: 'Do you need any help?'

He tore off a bite of the bagel. 'Help?'

'With whatever you're working on. It looks like you're slammed.'

He stared for a beat. 'You're joking, right?'

'Nope. Not joking. I've got time to pitch in.'

Then he laughed. 'Well, yeah. Duh. They can't staff you on anything. The investors would freak out.'

My stomach turned at the smell of the warm cream cheese.

'They told us not to talk about any live deals in front of you,' Roger continued. 'It's a liability. You're going to be gone soon, anyway.'

'A liability?'

Roger's expression softened. 'Look,' he said quietly. 'I'm not trying to be a dick. Do you want my advice? Just cash your checks and ride this out. Then you can move on to another firm. Start fresh. Somewhere else, they won't even care.'

Down the hall, the other employees were arriving for the day. Roger rearranged his face back into its usual smug grin. 'Thanks for the bagel, but just get out of here, okay?' he said under his breath. 'I shouldn't be talking to you.'

I went back to McGuigan's that night, and the next, and the next. I drank Coke, and I watched whatever was on the TV – a Yankees game, *Jeopardy!,* the local news – killing time, waiting for the bar to quiet down enough for Maria to take a break. She was the only person I had talked to in months. I couldn't lose her again.

That first night, I told her the whole story: Michael, the bribery, the trip to Las Vegas. The Julia part, too. I figured it was fine. The investigation was nearly finished, and the findings were going to be public soon enough. Maria stared at me, rapt.

'Have you heard from her since you broke up?' she asked at the end.

'Nope.'

'But you haven't called her, either?'

'There's nothing to say.' I jabbed at a melting ice cube with my straw. 'She checked out a long time ago. I don't think she was ever going to come back.'

'Why are you still here, then?'

'What do you mean?'

'Why stay? I mean, you must be miserable at Spire, right? And you always said you weren't that crazy about New York. You could go somewhere totally different. Don't you want to start over? Leave it all behind?'

But where would I go? How could I explain? I couldn't

leave, because for the first time, New York finally felt like home. Last year the city was a backdrop separate from my life, something I was only borrowing. But the shift had happened not long ago, when I realized that I had changed. That the city had been witness to different versions of myself. It gave me a new claim over this place. I had tried, failed, collapsed, but I was still here. The city was still here. The scale of the place had become newly comforting. It had a way of shrinking my pain to a bearable smallness. It was nothing compared to the towering skyscrapers or the teeming crowds. Any given day, in any given subway car, there were people who were happier than I, people who were sadder than I. People who had erred and people who had forgiven. I was mortal, imperfect, just like everyone else. It was good to be reminded of that.

But that mortality also made me old. I felt like I might vanish in a second. I realized – knowledge that arrived all at once – how much the world would continue to change after I was gone. Someday, people would look back on this era in the same way I had looked back on the settlers of the New World or the cowboys of the West in the slippery pages of my schoolbooks, strangers whose lives were distilled down to a few paragraphs and color illustrations. They would shake their heads, not believing that we could have known so little. It was nearly impossible to imagine the continuity. Then they would turn away from the past and continue their lives in a world transformed by technology or disease or war. By rising oceans or collapsing economies or by something that we – we soon-to-be relics – couldn't even imagine.

But I wanted to. I wanted to imagine, and then to see. I clung to the time I'd been given. I didn't want to leave.

On my fourth night in a row at McGuigan's, Maria said, 'I'm off early tonight. You want to get dinner? I can cook.'

A cat was purring atop the refrigerator when she opened the door to her studio apartment, up in the northern reaches of Morningside Heights. 'Make yourself at home,' she said, turning on the stove with the click and hiss of gas igniting. She handed me a beer, and I wandered around. I liked her apartment right away. She had houseplants on the windowsill, a rag rug, a desk covered with textbooks and notes from law school, a refrigerator layered with family pictures and yellowed recipes. I stood at the other side of the room and watched Maria at the stove – apron tied around her waist, humming along to the radio – and I remembered the night I came home to Julia cooking in our tiny kitchen. How she had glowed from a happiness that I thought belonged to both of us. That was the worst part: I'd been misreading it all along. It was why I couldn't bear to think about Julia, not even the good parts, because I couldn't be sure that there ever were good parts.

After dinner, after sex that was surprisingly intimate for a first time, we lay in Maria's bed, which was tucked in the corner next to an open window. I was half asleep when she climbed out of bed, wrapped herself in a robe, and turned on the desk lamp. 'Stay there,' she said. 'I'm going to study for a few hours.' She was taking the bar exam that summer. Her cat had been asleep on top of Maria's stack of textbooks. The cat unfurled and stretched, purring regally as she hopped down to the floor and made way for her owner.

The next morning, Maria kissed me good-bye, and we made plans for dinner the following night. It was while I was shaving in front of the bathroom mirror back at home that I felt it. I'd told someone the truth. The actual, whole truth. And it was okay.

Was it that Maria had finally given me the thing I had craved for so long? Acceptance and forgiveness; grace? I thought so at first, but I realized that wasn't it, because she wasn't the one whose forgiveness I needed. What Maria had given me was simply a reminder that the loneliness didn't have to last forever. I didn't have to know what came next in order to have hope.

One morning in early May, Kleinman summoned me to his office.

'Peck. Have a seat. You're aware that we're approaching a settlement with the SEC in the WestCorp case.'

'I had guessed as much, sir.'

'And you probably know about the compromised state of the firm right now. We've taken a lot of hits in the last few months. We're starting a round of layoffs later today. Someone from HR will be calling you around eleven to go over your package. But I wanted to give you a personal heads-up.'

I had been expecting this for a long time, but it was still strange to hear the words actually spoken. Kleinman smiled at me.

'You know, I can see why Michael liked you so much. You're loyal, and that goes a long way. In another life, you probably would have had a great career ahead of you here. But you understand why we can't keep you on.'

I nodded. 'Yes, sir.'

'You're Michael's guy. He made you his guy. If I kept you around while laying off a bunch of people who had nothing to do with this – you know how bad that would look. People would hate you, to be frank. And then they'd hate me. You'd just remind everyone of what came before. What we need here is a fresh start. We're going to be a lot smaller, but we'll rebuild eventually.'

Kleinman stood up and extended his hand. 'Well. Best of luck, Peck. Thank you for your cooperation these last few months.'

The HR woman fetched me shortly afterward. It was the same woman who had moved me into my windowless closet office. I wondered whether she felt guilty about her earlier deception; she must have known, even then, that she'd have to deliver this news eventually. There was a piece of paper that listed my severance package: several months' salary, a one-time payment in exchange for my signing a nondisparagement agreement. It was a lot of money. She cleared her throat delicately.

'Mr Peck, I should also remind you that your visa will run out eventually, given that you're no longer employed by Spire. You can, of course, obtain sponsorship from your next employer. We have excellent contacts at other firms in the city and in Connecticut. Mr Kleinman has offered to write a glowing reference. We're confident you'll find a good home. Would you like a –'

'No, thank you,' I said loudly. Then I stood up. 'Is that everything?'

She looked startled. 'Yes. That's it. Just turn in your badge at reception.'

I had purposely avoided thinking too much about what came next. But now that the time had arrived, I knew one thing for sure. This wasn't what I was meant to do. Five minutes later, I turned off the computer and shut the door for the last time, leaving the keys dangling in the lock for the janitor.

'So should we celebrate?' she said when I walked into McGuigan's at midday.

'Celebrate me getting fired?'

She grinned. 'I can't think of a better reason.'

Maria got someone to cover the rest of her shift. We bought tallboys of beer in paper bags and picked up Sabrett hot dogs and ate them in Columbus Circle. I thought of Julia, the night we had spent out here, drinking wine and watching the traffic swirl. That moment felt distant and immediate all at once. The city was like that, layered with memories that existed in multiple tenses. Ever since I had started sleeping with Maria, five weeks earlier, I had been thinking about Julia more. Memories of her were creeping back in. But Julia only existed as that, I reminded myself – as a memory, as the past.

'Was it weird? Finally saying good-bye to that place?'

'A little. Mostly it's a relief.' I shook my head. 'It's sort of surreal, you know? I can't believe all that shit actually happened. I can't believe I just went along with it.'

'Well,' she said, crumpling up her ketchup-stained napkin. 'It's amazing what people can rationalize. Humans are a delusional bunch.'

'You're gonna have to tone down that sympathy when you start prosecuting the bad guys instead of serving them their drinks.'

She laughed. 'You criminals are humans, too.'

The previous week, Maria had gotten a job offer at the district attorney's office. The pay was miserly, the hours long, but it was work that actually made a difference. I envied her sense of purpose, her accomplishment, but it was easy to forget the years of hard work that had led her to this point. I put my arm around her and pulled her in for a kiss.

'Actually,' she said. 'That reminds me. I'm getting together with my new coworkers tomorrow night, so I won't be able to do dinner after all.'

'No problem. I can come over afterward?'

'Sure, if you want.'

She leaned back against the stone steps and tilted her head up toward the sun. Already it was slipping away. The bar exam was in a few months. Her start date at work was soon after. Maria had carved out a life for herself in this city long before I arrived. I knew she liked me, liked what we shared, but the need was one-directional. Maria brought me back into the real world, but I was seeing that it stemmed from compassion rather than love. She asked nothing of me; there was nothing I could give her that she didn't already possess. And maybe I didn't need love right then. Being with Maria was the first time I felt remotely like a grown-up. Like a person capable of surviving on my own.

She stood up. 'Do you want to walk home?' Her home, not mine: she never once set foot in my apartment. 'It's a beautiful day.'

There were several guys from the hockey team also living in the city, Sebi and Paul and a few others. Most of them worked in finance. When we got together for drinks a few days after my firing, they were envious of my situation.

'You are fucking lucky, man,' Sebi said. Late on a weeknight at a bar in Murray Hill, which was so similar to McGuigan's that if you squinted you couldn't tell them apart. 'I would quit my job in a second if I got that kind of package.'

'What are you gonna do next?' Paul asked.

'Don't really know. I thought about joining a league, just for fun.'

'You should,' Sebi said. 'Actually, one of my buddies plays up in Westchester, in a midnight league. They're always looking for players. I'll give you his number.'

Which was how I found myself lacing up rental skates one night the following week. The other players were men mostly older than me, fathers going gray and potbellied, but I was rusty from so many months off, and we were evenly matched. The team I was on for the scrimmage lost, but it still felt good. After the game, just as I'd cracked a Coors in the locker room, one of the guys on the team came over to me.

'Evan Peck?' He extended his hand. 'I'm Frank Donovan. Call me Donny. Sebi told me about you. I heard you might be looking for work.'

'Oh,' I said. 'Yeah. Well, yes, sort of.'

'I've got something to offer you for the next few months, if you're interested in hearing about it.'

A few weeks later, I was back on a train to Westchester. I had to call my parents and get them to ship my hockey stuff back to New York. I was going to work as an assistant coach at a summer hockey camp for middle schoolers up in Westchester. Donny needed someone to help with his program, running drills and reffing games. I got to the rink early on the first day, before any of the campers arrived. After the first lap around the glassy ice, I felt dizzy and short of breath. I had to pause and lean against the boards. The sound of my blades against the ice, the smell of the cold air, the mustiness of the rink – it was almost too much to bear. Hockey had always been more than a sport to me. It had been the thing that rescued me from the suffocation of a small town, and when I escaped it, it was the thing that I clung to in a strange new world. But I realized – chest heaving, heart aching, my breath escaping in curls of white fog – that it wouldn't work this time. I couldn't hitch my dreams to it anymore. I couldn't love it the way I used to.

Donny dropped me off at the train station at the end of the first day. We chatted during the drive about the kids and how the day had gone. I had to stifle a yawn when we said good-bye – I hadn't worked so hard in months. Before I closed the car door, he asked, 'You gonna be back tomorrow?'

I laughed. 'Wouldn't miss it.'

The week went fast. That Friday night, I called Maria.

'Hey, stranger.'

'Hey, I know. I'm sorry.' All week I'd been coming home, making dinner, and going straight to bed. My new routine was already digging grooves: apartment, Metro-North station at 125th Street, grocery store. McGuigan's felt like another universe.

'Yeah, I know how it goes. First week on the job and all.'

'Can I see you tonight?'

'I'm off at midnight. Come over then?'

A few hours later we lay in her bed after having sex,

the sounds of the street floating in through the open window. Maria had turned on the fan, which rotated toward us every few seconds. There was something different that night. The way she lay there with her eyes open, when normally by then she'd be drifting off, or back at her desk. Her silence had an alert quality. I could sense her thinking.

'Hey,' I said, running my hand along her arm. 'Is everything okay?'

She turned to face me, resting her chin on my chest. A serious gaze.

'Evan, you know, we don't need to keep pretending for no good reason.'

'Maria.' I swallowed. A lump formed in my throat.

'This has been fun. I'm going to miss you,' she said.

Something within me was finally falling. My fingers were being pried away when I wasn't ready to let go.

'Can't we just . . .' I said. 'We don't have to do this right now, do we?'

She propped herself up on one elbow, rested her hand on my chest. Her palm covered my heart. 'It's time.'

Maria stood up and padded into the bathroom. I heard the sound of the bath running. Her cat was atop the refrigerator, purring loudly in her sleep. I got dressed and hovered outside the bathroom door, my hand almost touching the doorknob. I could smell the candle she liked to burn while she was in the bath. And then I stopped. I withdrew my hand. I let myself out, looking around the apartment one last time to make sure I hadn't forgotten anything.

Arthur was passing through the city the following weekend. He had been accepted to all the top law schools in the country – no surprise there – and was making up his mind about where to go. He was in town to visit NYU and Columbia before swinging up to see Harvard and Yale, and he was staying with me for the night.

'This is weirdly good,' Arthur said. 'I had no idea you knew how to cook.'

'I'm learning.' Enchiladas, nothing special. It was Friday night, a week since I'd last seen Maria. I thought about her, but only occasionally. She had been right. Arthur and I sat on the futon, plates balanced on our knees. 'So you're really up for spending another three years in New Haven?'

'There are worse things. I don't think it would be anything like undergrad. It would probably feel like a totally different place. Different people. You know what I mean?'

'Yeah, I think I do.'

'You going to be ready to go in a minute?' he asked. Arthur's phone kept buzzing. A friend from college was throwing a party that night in her Williamsburg apartment. Really more Arthur's friend than my friend. He had a lot of people to see during his short visit to the city. 'What's the best way to get there?'

'The six to the L, I think.'

When we got to the party, I recognized a few people from school. I asked one guy what he'd been up to since graduation, and he cocked his head. 'Same thing as before, man,' he said, taking a long draw from his beer. His tone was odd, almost offended. And then I fuzzily recalled: it was *this* guy. I'd talked to him at a party not so different from this one, several months earlier. Back when I was still at Spire and still with Julia. 'Sorry,' I said, shaking my head. 'Shit. Sorry. I knew that. I have a bad memory.'

My memory was fine. But memory was beside the point when I wasn't even noticing things in the first place. The thing that kept me going through the months at Spire – it was the same thing that had kept me alive through playoffs and postseason intensity in the past. An adrenalized tunnel vision, everything else dropping away into background noise. And maybe that was okay in short bursts, but there was a danger when it went on for too long. For months at a time. It was like a hole in my brain. There was an entire section missing.

A little later, I felt a hand on my elbow. I turned around and saw Abby.

'Evan,' she said after we hugged. 'Wow. It's so nice to see you.'

'Been a while, huh? How are things?'

I didn't really have to ask. Her happiness was obvious.

'Well, I'm in the home stretch.'

'School's almost done for the year?'

'Praise the Lord.' She laughed.

People came in and out, rearranging our corner of the room. Abby and I didn't get to talk for much longer. I caught her eye a few times and started to move toward her, but then someone else would get in the way. Her gaze said the same thing – we were both thinking about the one thing missing from this night. The hip-hop on the stereo, the keg in the bathtub, the Solo cups scattered across the kitchen counters. It was almost like college. Almost, but not quite.

'Hey,' Arthur said, coming over. 'Ready to go? I've got an early train.'

I glanced back over at Abby, stuck in conversation with some close talker. I took a deep breath. I wanted to interrupt. This merited interruption, didn't it? A chance for news of the person I had spent four years of my life with and hadn't heard from in months? But Arthur was already holding the door open, waiting for me.

We took the subway back to the Upper East Side. 'Pizza?' Arthur pointed at the neon sign of the slice joint on Lexington. It was just like old times. Two pepperoni for me, one cheese for him.

'Was it weird?' he said on the walk back to the apartment. 'Seeing Abby?'

'Kind of.'

'You don't talk about her much, you know.'

'Who? Julia?'

'No, the Mona Lisa. Yes, dummy. Julia. The girl you used to live with?'

I shrugged. 'What is there to say?'

'Well, you don't have to be so stoic. You can admit that you're upset. Or mad or whatever. You don't have to pretend like nothing happened. It's kind of strange.'

'I'm not. I'm just . . .' I shrugged again. 'I've learned to live with it.'

We walked for a while. By silent agreement we sat down on the stoop outside my building, finishing our pizza. I felt a click, the temperature rising a notch. 'Why?' I said. 'Did you want to say something about Julia? Do you have something you need to say?'

'What do you mean?'

'Come on. You're not tempted to say "I told you so"? That you could have seen this coming all along?'

'I'd never say that.'

'Aren't you the one who called her self-centered? Don't you remember?'

'Yes,' he said, picking at his pizza crust. 'But I didn't mean like that.'

'What did you mean, then?'

Arthur was silent for a long time. Finally he cleared his throat. 'Okay. Yeah, maybe I thought you guys shouldn't have lived together. That wasn't a great idea. I'll stand by that. But it doesn't mean I don't *like* her. It doesn't mean I think she's some terrible person, that you should never think about her or talk to her again. I mean, she made some pretty big mistakes. But so did you, right? You guys both screwed up. I just don't think it does anyone any good if you keep hanging on to it. If you don't let your-self move past it.'

'You think I'm hanging on to it?'

'Aren't you?'

It was almost exactly a year earlier that Arthur and I had our big fight. A night just like this: late walk home, pizza, warm air. Part of me was itching for a redo. To shout until my throat was raw. To scream even if no one was listening. But there was a difference, a big one. Last year, I hadn't been able to hear what Arthur was saying. I was so focused on the idea of what came next. On the idea of packing up the last of my boxes and putting them in the U-Haul with Julia's and arriving later that week at our apartment in New York, beginning the next chapter of our life together. That's all that had mattered, the continuation of the present into the future, the unin-terruption of that dream.

'Do you see what I mean?' Arthur said. Arthur knew the whole truth of what had happened by then, but this was the first time he'd voiced the other side. That I'd screwed up. That as much as Julia had betrayed me, I had betrayed her, too.

'I'm just saying,' he continued. 'Don't act like it's noth-ing. But don't be so hard on yourself. And don't be so hard on her. I don't know. Maybe it wouldn't be such a bad idea to give her a call. I can tell you're still thinking about her.'

'How?' I said. Was it that obvious? In the previous few

weeks, she'd come back into my mind, memories growing stronger and stronger. That was the real reason I couldn't leave. I needed to know whether the Julia I had known and loved was the real Julia; whether that Julia would ever come back. I had no idea how long I'd have to wait.

He shrugged. 'I'm your friend, Evan. I just can.'

CHAPTER 16

Julia

The loft was in an old building in Tribeca. There was a freight elevator, which he used sometimes for moving his oversize canvases, but we took the narrow metal staircase. He had the whole second floor – half for his living space, half for his studio.

I started to knock on the unmarked metal door, but Elizabeth said, 'Don't bother. No one can hear you.' She pulled a jangling ring of keys from her purse.

Saturday night, the night of the big party. She'd shown me pictures of Donald Gates, and he looked exactly the same in real life: unkempt gray hair, paint-stained cargo shorts and plastic Crocs, a belly that strained against his T-shirt. But his voice was deep and booming, and even from a distance, I could see the brightness in his eyes. He had a pipe clamped between his teeth. He looked like the king of his small kingdom.

'Donald,' she said. 'This is my sister, Julia.'

'Julia. Lovely. Elizabeth talks about you all the time.'

'Did the frames arrive this afternoon?' she asked.

He sighed. 'They got the order wrong. We have to send them back.'

The apartment was one big undivided space, vast and pleasantly chaotic. A kitchen in one corner, with a metal sink as big as a bathtub. A long wooden table in the middle of the room covered in dripping, flickering candles. A massive living area with mismatched couches and armchairs grouped around rugs and coffee tables. A thick slab of a sliding wooden door, standing partially ajar, opened into the studio.

'I'll show you the studio later,' Elizabeth said, pouring us each a glass of wine at the island in the kitchen. 'It's pretty spectacular.'

'So this is where you work?'

'Most days. He's getting ready to mount a new show at a gallery in Chelsea, so we're over there sometimes, prepping the space. Here. You should meet the others.'

Donald Gates had several assistants working for him. Some, like Elizabeth, were on summer break from college. Others were closer to my age, young artists pursuing their own careers in their spare time. They were sitting at the long wooden table watching a skinny Asian boy roll a joint. 'Hey, guys, this is my sister, Julia. She's visiting for a while,' Elizabeth said as we slid next to them on the bench. The others looked up and said hello in unison.

I'd been skeptical about tagging along. It made me feel so old, the idea of following my younger sister to this downtown loft. Elizabeth is cooler than me, I'd always known that, but I wasn't sure if I was ready to have it rubbed in. She already seemed to know the city better than I ever had. But I was skeptical for another reason, too. Those orbiting the great Donald Gates would surely resort to insufferable pretension when they got together. The thought made me cringe: lofty theories and showy name-dropping, a posture of sophistication, conjuring – for me, at least – the ugly ghost of previous seductions.

But as I sipped my wine and listened to their patter, I found I was wrong. They talked about their work with a weary professionalism, like union members down at the local. The walls in the Chelsea gallery weren't right for the kind of mounting they usually used. Pearl Paint was out of Donald's preferred brush. Donald wanted to finish a big series, and they were all going to have to work late to get it done. The work wasn't about pretension. It was about humble logistics. Theirs was a mild sort of complaint, and I could tell that Elizabeth and her coworkers actually took pleasure in it. It was the breaking down of something big into a series of finely grained tasks, like glass melting into sand, something you could sift through your fingers.

The skinny Asian boy handed me the joint. I took a small toke before passing it. I didn't want to get too high or too drunk. I'd gotten to New York a day earlier, on a sweltering Friday afternoon, and that was overwhelming enough on its own. I tilted my head up. The ceiling of the loft was so high that I could barely see it. Donald had bought the space in the 1970s, when the city was teetering on the edge of bankruptcy. I tried to imagine what it would be like to live in one place for so long. Keeping your head turned to the light, letting the seasons change and the decades pass, doing your work.

A little later, when we stood to get another drink, Elizabeth led me to the wooden door. 'Don't tell anyone,' she said. 'We're not really supposed to bring other people back here.' She made sure no one was watching, then we slipped through the opening.

The noise of the party vanished behind us. The studio was even bigger than the living space. The dim light that filtered through the windows gave just enough illumination to see by. The room had the patina of long use: paint-splattered floor, walls spidered with cracks, empty tubes and crusty brushes. But the artwork hovered above and separate from the ordinary mess of the room. Donald Gates was known for his big, aggressive, abstract canvases, a throwback to an earlier era. 'You can get closer,' Elizabeth said, nudging me forward. I felt drawn to the paintings like a magnet to iron. The thick and tactile smears of paint. The blend and contrast of colors. They were so beautiful, but so ordinary, too. It was just paint, applied by the human hand. They glowed, gently, through the darkness. I couldn't believe that something that revealed itself to be so simple, when seen up close, had the power to move me so much.

'It's amazing, isn't it?' Elizabeth said. 'It's hard to turn away.'

'Exactly.'

'He's just a guy. He sleeps, eats, breathes just like the rest of us. Gets grumpy, makes stupid jokes. But then he does *this,* and I realize I have no idea what's going on inside his head. How he comes up with it.'

'It's so beautiful.'

'I know.' A beat later: 'We should get back to the party.'

The night continued. Guests arrived bearing bottles of wine and gifts of food. Some were young, like us, but many were closer to Donald's age. The gathering felt like an assortment of friendships collected over a long period of time, like a plant shooting off vines in radius. As the hours passed, the room gradually quieted until it was only the lingerers with their empty glasses. Donald was holding forth from a high-backed velvet chair, a shaggy mutt curled at his feet. Elizabeth stood up, stretched, and yawned. 'I'll say good-bye, and then we can go, okay?'

Despite the late hour, in bed back at Elizabeth's apartment, I couldn't sleep. I kept remembering how Elizabeth had looked, when she said good-bye to Donald. The dog awoke, his tail thumping the floor when Elizabeth reached down to scratch his ears. Donald patted Elizabeth on the shoulder. Together they looked like a version of home. Elizabeth had found the tiny nook in the world that was shaped just for her. She possessed a sense of belonging that seemed so rare to me in this city. But I'd encountered it before; a path that I'd been too foolish to pursue. I turned on the bedside lamp. My wallet was sitting on the dresser, and inside it was the business card I'd been hanging on to all these months. I took it out and stared at it for a long time.

In the morning, the card fell loose when I stood from the bed. I double-checked the time – well past noon on a Sunday. A perfectly reasonable time to call. I took a deep breath and dialed.

I hadn't been planning to stay longer than the weekend. My tote bag held a few changes of clothing, my phone charger, a book, and that was it. I took the train down midday on Friday, and I had a return ticket for Monday morning. Rob sounded nonchalant when I called. 'Okay,' he said. 'No worries. I gotta go. See you around, Julia.'

Elizabeth met me at her apartment on Friday afternoon. 'If you want to shower, the shower's weird,' she said, showing me around. 'The faucet is on backwards. Let's see . . . help yourself to whatever's in the fridge. You can use my computer if you want. I have to go back to the studio for a few more hours, but maybe we can get takeout or something for dinner. Oh, and I already changed the sheets on the bed for you. You're welcome.'

I smiled. Despite the grubby Chinatown setting and Elizabeth's budding artistic pursuits, her habits were reflexive – the manners of a good hostess, which our mother had instilled in us. The apartment was small, but it was sunny and clean, the window propped open to let in the breeze. A bouquet of bodega carnations sat on the bookshelf. Her roommate's bed, where I'd be sleeping, was neatly made with hospital corners. I'd taken a nice bottle of wine from my parents' collection and stuck it in my bag as a housewarming gift. We'd drink it later, on the roof, with our cheap dinner.

I had an e-mail on my phone from Abby. She and Jake were in Barcelona. We'd promised each other that we'd Skype at least once a week while she was on her European jaunt. Her e-mail asked if I wanted to talk that afternoon around 4:00 p.m., their nighttime in Spain. It was 3:52. I opened Elizabeth's computer and logged on, and soon the computer chimed with the sound of an incoming call.

'Abby?'

'Buenas noches, amiga!'

'Hey, you're practically fluent!'

She laughed, her voice echoing as it traveled the span of the Atlantic.

'Are you guys having fun?'

She sighed, or I think she sighed. I couldn't tell with the lousy audio connection. 'Holy shit, Jules, it's amazing. I'm quitting my job and never leaving.'

'How long are you there?'

'Barcelona for another two nights. Then Valencia next week, then Málaga, then we're going over to Morocco.'

'Where's Jake? How is he?'

'Too much wine at dinner. He passed out. He's good. We're' – she smiled, glancing down – 'I'm really happy. Things are really good.'

'Oh, my God, you're *blushing*. When's the wedding?'

'Shut up.'

'You know, I'm the reason you guys met. Dibs on maid of honor, right?'

'All right, all right. Hey, what about you? Where are you? I don't recognize it.'

'In New York. I'm staying at Lizzie's.'

'Jules! You had to wait until I was gone, huh?'

'It's just for a few days. I'm going home on Monday.'

'Why such a rush?'

'Well,' I said, looking around the tiny apartment. 'For one, I don't live here anymore. And I'm staying in Lizzie's roommate's bed. She's back on Monday.'

'You should stay longer. You can stay at my place. It's just sitting there.'

'You didn't find a subletter?'

She shrugged. 'Too much of a hassle. My rent is cheap. Jules, I'm serious. You should stay there. What else are you going to do? Aren't you bored to death up in Boston?'

'But your roommate –'

'Cat won't care. You know she practically lives with her boyfriend.'

It seemed too crazy, too all-at-once. 'I don't know. Let me think about it.'

'I'm going to e-mail Cat now. I'm gonna say that you'll call her tomorrow and get the keys, okay? I'll send you her number and stuff. Hey, have you talked to Evan lately?'

'Evan?' His name felt funny when I said it out loud. 'No. Why?'

'Well, are you going to see him? Now that you're back?'

'I doubt it. We haven't talked since December.'

Abby was quiet on the other end. I thought the video had frozen, but I could see the flicker of her eyes. Part of me was tempted to change the subject, avoid the Evan minefield, but I remembered what Abby had said on the phone. *Enough of this repressive WASP bullshit.* She was right. 'Okay, spill. What's up?'

'I saw him. The other week. At a party.'

'You saw Evan? How is he?'

'Are you sure you want to hear?'

My stomach dropped. He was with another girl. Or he'd launched into a tirade against me. Or both. But I needed to know, all of a sudden. Evan. The thought of him filled me with an aching curiosity. 'Yeah. Tell me.'

'He's good, actually. He has a new job. Spire let him go. They let a bunch of people go. It sounded like things were pretty rough for a while.'

'Where's he working?'

'Brace yourself. He's a hockey coach.'

'You're joking.'

'At some summer program up in Westchester. It's sort of temporary while he figures out what he's going to do. I guess he got a bunch of severance from Spire. He seems to like it, though. He said the kids are great.'

'Is he still living in our old place?'

'I think so. Jules, listen. You should call him. Or at least let him know you're back in town. Don't you think that's only fair?'

Fair. I was glad for the shitty video connection,

disguising the hot beginnings of tears. I could only think of that night, Evan making it so clear that he didn't want to see me again. Fair wasn't a factor.

'I don't know,' I said. 'Abby. Did he . . . um, did Evan –'

'Did he ask about you?' She shook her head. 'I think he wanted to. I mean, you know Evan. He's so Canadian. He probably didn't want to be rude and put me on the spot. But so what? Call him. Life is too short. Hey, so I'm sending you Cat's number. Go get the keys from her. Deal?'

'Deal.' I smiled. 'I miss you.'

'I miss you, too. I'm glad you're back.'

That night, on the sticky tar roof of her apartment building, I told Elizabeth about Abby's idea. Part of me was hoping for one last exit ramp, for Elizabeth to raise her eyebrows and say it was crazy. But instead she exclaimed that it was a brilliant idea, and she clinked her plastic cup of wine against mine. I wondered how my parents were going to take the news. I'd have to ask my mother to send down a box of clothes.

'This is great, Jules,' Elizabeth said, crumpling the wrappers from our banh mi into a tight, waxy ball. 'It's going to be a great summer.'

On Sunday, Cat opened the door. We'd met a few times, through Abby.

'That's all you have?' she said.

I shifted my tote bag on my shoulder. 'Yup. For now.'

She showed me around their West Harlem apartment quickly, apologizing for her abruptness, but she was on her way downtown to meet friends for dinner. 'That's the thing about this neighborhood,' she said, responding to a text, slipping on her sandals, tying her hair back in a bun, a flurry of motion. 'I love it, but it's so far from everything. Anyway, I sleep at Paolo's most nights. He's in the East Village. It's just easier.'

I spent a lot of time walking that first week. I had nothing else to do. I woke up in the morning, and it was always the first thing I realized: there was nothing I had to do that day. But this was different from how I'd felt in Boston. Then, the emptiness of the day stretched before me like a punishment. The discipline of my routine was a way of combating the loneliness, the reading and running and walking the dog like beads on a rosary. But at Abby's I woke to an empty apartment, and the emptiness actually felt good. Peaceful. Every morning was different. Sometimes I'd make coffee in the kitchen, drinking from Abby and Cat's mismatched mugs. Other mornings I'd go to the diner on the corner, watching the sidewalk traffic over eggs and bacon. Or I'd set out on a long walk to some unknown destination and pick up things on the way. Coffee from a Cuban restaurant, milky and sweet. A hot, spicy samosa for breakfast at 11:00 a.m., because I could do whatever I wanted.

Was it that the city had changed since I left? Was it such a different place, altered by the events of the previous year – the collapse of the economy, the election of a new president? Maybe it was, in small ways. The quieted construction sites, halted until the money started flowing again. The real estate listings, marked down further and further. The miasma of worry that hovered in the subway cars, nervous and desperate job seekers, commuters distractedly thinking of their 401(k)s. But mostly, life went on. Before long, it would be back to normal. The market would rebound. Apartment prices would pause, catch their breath, then resume their relentless climb.

But my city, my New York, was different. It was empty of the people I had known, of the associations I had clung to before. Abby was gone, on another continent for the summer. Evan was living his own life. Adam had surely moved on to another girl. Elizabeth was busy with work. This, too, was different from what I'd felt the summer before: neglected, and bored, and constantly waiting. Waiting for Evan to get home, waiting for his attention to refocus on me, waiting for him to fill whatever this vacuum was. Waiting, and wanting, for someone else to solve my problems.

I walked down Frederick Douglass Boulevard, near Abby's apartment, or through the twisting blocks of the West Village, or down the Bowery, or along the Battery. One day I walked across the Brooklyn Bridge and along the promenade in Brooklyn Heights, looking at the city from a new angle. The skyscrapers glittered in the late afternoon sun; the harbor was dotted with the white slashes of sailboats; the spray from a Jet Ski refracted the light. I could pick out Jake's apartment building, the balcony where Abby and I had stood during his party the previous summer.

Through it all, I began to see how badly I'd gotten things wrong. I kept looking for salvation in other people. I kept waiting for something else to come along. But that was never going to be the solution. The solution wasn't going to be Rob, either. It wasn't going to be staying at home, listening to my parents. I was lonely because I was alone – because everyone was, and no one could solve that for me. I could only learn to solve it for myself. For once, that knowledge didn't feel oppressive. I walked through the dusk back across the bridge to Manhattan. I didn't know where that realization pointed me. But for the moment, I let myself be content with it, with knowledge divorced from action.

I saw Elizabeth for dinner every couple of days. We'd eat something cheap and easy in her apartment, pasta with butter or scrambled eggs with cheese. I ate a lot of my meals alone, on bar stools or park benches. I liked the way it felt. I was free to observe the city, uninhibited because no one was observing me. I'd been slow to appreciate the invisibility New York grants. No one cares what you do, and that's a good thing. I felt more alive that week than I'd felt since graduation. Or maybe even further back, since that summer in Europe. In the middle of that first week, my mother sent a box of clothes to Abby's apartment. In among the T-shirts and sundresses she had tucked a note, written in her delicate script on a sheet of her monogrammed stationery. *Jasmine was cleaning out the kitchen drawers, and she found this old disposable camera. She got the pictures developed — I thought you might want them. We miss you. It's very quiet here without you. xxx, Mom.*

I walked, and I walked. I walked down the West Side a lot. I could pass Adam's apartment building on Riverside Drive, and it was surprisingly easy — I felt nothing. I finally acknowledged what I'd been carrying around for so long, and I had started to make my peace with it. But the one neighborhood I avoided was the Upper East Side. I didn't even like to cross the invisible midline of Central Park. I worried about what might happen if I ever ran into Evan. What scared me was the possibility that I could inflict more hurt. That there was more damage to be done. That Evan and I might bump into each other, and I would say or do something that only made things worse.

I knew what was on that camera that Jasmine had found. I kept the unopened envelope of pictures on the desk in Abby's room. Over the following few days, it gradually disappeared underneath an accumulation of receipts and spare change. I didn't forget about it. I would open it eventually. But I wanted to take my time.

Sara Yamashita was waiting for me in a booth at the back when I walked into Balthazar at 12:30 on Wednesday. She stood up and kissed me on the cheek, smelling like mint and cigarettes. It had taken her a moment to place my name when I'd called, the Sunday before. A pause, then recognition. 'Julia! Of course. Adam's friend. I always wondered what happened to you.'

The room was buzzing, the mirrored walls reflecting a sea of attractive faces. 'Have you been here before?' she asked, stirring a packet of sugar into her iced tea. 'I'm getting the cheeseburger. You can't go wrong with that.'

'I'll do the same,' I said, closing my menu.

'So you went back to Boston? What happened?'

'It's a long story.'

'Well,' she said, spreading her arms. 'That's why we're here, isn't it?'

I had never really told anyone the full truth. Adam knew, and Evan knew. Abby, my parents, other friends – they knew about the breakup, but they didn't know what had triggered it. No one searched for a precise, time-stamped reason amid the rubble. But Sara was different. She knew about me and Adam. I wouldn't be able to leave him out of the story. It was why I forced myself to stick to the plan, even when gripped with nausea on the walk to lunch. If I didn't take this chance, I wasn't sure I ever would.

'Was it something to do with Adam?' Sara asked. 'You're not still seeing him, are you?'

'Yes. And no. We're not still seeing each other. Adam is part of the reason I left last year.' I took a deep breath and told her the whole story. My relationship with Evan. The things that started going wrong. Adam's reappearance in my life at exactly the right time. Everything Evan confided in me and the way I'd repeated it. And then, eventually, the implosion. By then our food had arrived. Sara listened attentively, nodding and asking a question every now and then. She didn't dispense excessive sympathy or judgment or outrage. She just listened until I was finished.

'Wow,' she said. 'Holy shit. You must be hungry after that.'

I nodded and picked up my burger. I was hungry. Starving, actually.

'You seem like you're doing okay, though. All things considered.'

'I am. I think so, at least.'

'God. I wish I could say I was surprised.'

'You're not? Has he —'

'Has he done stuff like this before? Yes. Unfortunately.'

I swallowed a bite of my burger. 'To you?'

'Maybe never as bad as this. But he's just *shady*, you know? We were dating freshman year, and I applied to an internship in the city for the summer. I asked him to read my cover letter — you know, proofread it, edit it. He took a long time to give it back to me. Like, a week, two weeks. He kept saying he was busy, but he'd get to it. When I finally gave up and went ahead and applied, I found that they'd already filled the position. Another Yale student.'

'Adam?'

'He was like, why are you pissed? He acted like I was totally nuts. Then he broke up with me two days later. But you know what? This shit's going to catch up with him eventually. I've seen him around a few times since the Spire story. He's insufferable. But he knows this was a fluke. His editors are already asking for more. They want their genius reporter boy to keep working his source. Which is you, I guess.'

I pictured Adam squirming in his editor's office. Sara smiled.

'Yeah,' she said. 'Exactly. I'm sure he's spinning the bullshit for them as fast as he can.' She dragged a french fry through a hill of ketchup. 'But you came back, huh? Do you know what you want to do?'

'I'm not sure,' I said. This stretch, as nice as it was, wasn't going to last forever. Within the hour, most people in this restaurant would push back from their tables and return to their offices, where they'd continue carrying out whatever slight rearrangement of the world their jobs demanded of them. But they were doing it. They were in it. They had found a way to fit themselves into the flow of time. I poked at the remains of my burger. 'I'm still figuring it out,' I said. 'I'm staying at a friend's place for a while. I guess I'll start applying to jobs soon.'

Sara cleared her throat. 'Can I give you some advice?'

'Of course.'

'I'm an only child. I never had an older brother or sister or anything like that. You're the oldest?' I nodded. 'Right, so you can understand. I always wished someone had warned me about what it was like after college. How weird things are. And I had it really easy. My parents are connected. I got a job right after I graduated. I had *nothing* to complain about. But I still felt like shit. No one told me how hard it was going to be. It sounds like you went through this last year, too. You can relate.'

She leaned back, letting the waiter clear our plates. 'Dessert? Coffee?' he asked, glancing toward Sara. 'Two coffees?' she said. Then she continued.

'What I mean is there's nothing *wrong* with you. You had a shitty job, a shitty guy who messed things up for you. But that happens. You can't really avoid that stuff. It's not easy, figuring out what you want. It's really hard. And I mean what *you* want, not what your friends want, not what someone else wants.'

I was quiet. She paused. 'Is this making sense?'

'Yeah,' I said. 'I guess I just – I know what you're saying, but I don't know . . . how do you actually do it? I mean, how do you figure that out?'

'Well,' she said, sitting up straight. Then she laughed. 'This is kind of silly. I'm, like, two years older than you. Tell me if I'm being obnoxious.'

'No, not at all.'

'Well, I don't know. It takes a while. It's trial and error. But you just have to start doing it. And you have to trust yourself, to know what matters to you. You're a smart girl. You're going to be fine. Don't let other people think they know better.'

The waiter set the coffees in front of us, two china cups quivering in their saucers. Sara tore open three sugar packets at once and emptied them into her coffee. 'I have such a sweet tooth,' she said, shaking her head. 'It's terrible.'

Time seemed to slow down – the dissolve of the milk

into my coffee, the clink of the spoon against the cup, the breeze from the door opening at the front of the restaurant, the grains of sugar falling from between Sara's fingertips into the black liquid. I thought about what Sara had said. I thought about the canvases, hovering, in Donald Gates's studio. I thought about the unopened envelope of photos back at Abby's apartment. I thought about the loneliness of the spring, which had recently transformed into something else. A purer, simpler feeling. Like the satisfied, heavy-limbed awakening that follows a long night of sleep.

I looked up. Sara wrapped her hands around her coffee cup, waiting for me to speak.

'Thank you for that. It's really good advice.'

'Is it? I'm not sure it would have actually helped if someone told me that after college. Honestly, I probably wouldn't have listened.'

'Can I ask you something?'

'Please.'

'Why did you ask me to lunch? I mean, last year at the party. I'm grateful, really, but why do all this?'

'You seemed smart. You seemed better than the situation you were in.' She shrugged. 'Also, you seemed better than that asshole Adam. I can relate to that. I only wish you had called sooner. We had a job opening a few months ago that would have been great for you.'

My stomach dropped. I had been in Boston, I reminded myself. I hadn't been planning to move back to New York. 'You filled it?'

'I did. I'm sorry, Julia. I wish I had something to offer you now. But things come up. I hear about things through friends. You *are* looking for a job here, right? You're staying in New York?'

'Yes. Yes, I'm staying.'

'Good,' Sara said, smiling.

I saw Cat every few days when she returned to the apartment for a change of clothes or, occasionally, to spend the night. She had tattoos and cool thrift-store outfits, and when I first learned she was a musician, I thought, *That makes sense.* Then she clarified that she was a cellist, studying at Juilliard. Her boyfriend, Paolo, was the lead singer in an indie band. It was a Thursday night. Cat was standing in the kitchen, eating a bowl of cereal before she headed back downtown.

'You sure you don't want to come along?' she asked, rinsing her bowl in the sink, opening the fridge. Cat's visits to the apartment were always crammed with action, a determination to squeeze as much utility as she could from her trip uptown. 'They're playing at the Bowery Electric. It'll be a great crowd. We're going out afterward.'

'I think I'm going to stay in. Thanks, though.'

'Text me if you change your mind.' She paused amid her flurry and looked at me. 'You know, the drummer – he's single, and you are totally his type.'

I laughed. 'Go, I'll be fine.' Cat waved as she walked out the door, and then the apartment was quiet again. Cat had lived in this apartment for four years, since she had started at Juilliard, and the place carried the sediment of permanent life: framed posters, painted walls. I could see why she didn't want to give it up. There was an elaborate sound system in the living room. Cat sometimes plugged in her stereo headphones and listened to recordings of her work, head nodding and eyes scrunched closed, opening only when she paused to scribble down notes.

A towering stack of CDs sat next to the speakers. I don't know what inspired me that night, after Cat left, to crouch down and examine them for the first time. She had gestured at them before, telling me to play them whenever I liked. A familiar title stood out in the stack. *Kind of Blue,* which Adam used to play for me. I slid the CD into the tray. A moment later, the music began, filling the apartment. The twinned initial steps of piano and bass, the soft invocation, the shimmering light of percussion, the eventual pierce of the trumpet. Adam liked to put things before me, novels or albums or movies, and when he told me of their greatness I'd nod along, feigning comprehension, letting his gestures guide my response. I must have heard this album a dozen times at his apartment, but that night was the first time I actually listened to it. I let it fill me, like water rising in a glass.

I'd finally opened the envelope of photos that afternoon. I felt myself on the verge of something. My mother would have opened the photos after Jasmine had them developed; it was the only way for her to have known they were mine. I imagined her pulling the first

399

one from the stack, her hand twitching instinctively toward the trash bin. No one would have been the wiser. But instead she had sent them to me. I felt grateful to her in that moment, when I took out the photos for the first time. At least she was letting me decide this for myself.

My digital camera had broken while we were in Rome, two summers earlier. The battery fritzed, refusing to hold a charge. I bought a disposable camera in the train station on our way to La Spezia. We were spending the last week of the trip in the Cinque Terre. The first photo I'd taken, the photo at the top of the stack, was of Evan in Riomaggiore. He was standing on a stone boat ramp that led to the sea, his back to the water, the afternoon light casting his long shadow before him. The boats around him were painted like wooden candy, bright blues and greens and pinks. Evan had resisted when I told him to go stand for the picture. 'Come on, Jules, let me take one of you,' he said with a laugh. 'You're the good-looking one in this relationship.' But I shook my head. 'This picture is for me,' I said. 'I want this for when we get back.'

The magic had faded so quickly. I must have misplaced the camera when I was back at home, unpacking from the summer and repacking for senior year. That by itself wasn't so remarkable, but I felt a surge of sadness when I sat back onto Abby's bed and looked at the pictures for the first time. Why hadn't I missed these? Why had I never thought of that August afternoon on the edge of the Mediterranean, and let that lingering memory spark the recollection of the camera I'd misplaced? I'd never even bothered to miss it. I'd never bothered to appreciate what we had.

Evan looked so peaceful in that picture. His smile was wide and unselfconscious. He had a backpack slung over one shoulder, a cone of gelato in his other hand. The vividness of that afternoon: raising the camera to look through the plastic viewfinder and pausing for a moment. Evan was backlit by the lowering sun, his sandy hair sprayed with golden light. 'What is it?' he called over the noise of the motorboats puttering out to sea. A family walked between us, parents trying to corral their children, and I paused for a moment, letting the frame clear. He smiled at me – the smile of someone who knew exactly how lucky he was, in this postcard village more than four thousand miles from home. Finally I pressed the button, and the shutter snapped with a satisfying pop, and I returned the camera to my purse.

The music kept playing, filling the apartment with its mellow swells. I took out the photos again and spread them across the carpet in the living room. I was surprised to find that I remembered almost every single one of them: dinner on the terrace of our B and B in Monterosso; our sunburned faces after a hike one blistering afternoon; on the steps of the Duomo on our last night in Florence. It was Evan's first time abroad. He was a boy from the middle of nowhere who had decided he wanted more. Who wasn't satisfied with the path laid before him. I saw, for the first time, the bravery it had taken for him to do all of this.

I had obsessed over it all through the spring, that awful night, the idea of taking back what I had done. But maybe it was time to let that go. Maybe I was seeking an answer to a question that didn't matter, because it had already happened, because the undoing was impossible. Sara was right. It was a messy, difficult, shitty process – growing up, figuring out what you wanted. Some were lucky enough to figure it out on their own. I could see Elizabeth doing it already. Others were lucky enough to find a partner in the process, someone to expand their narrow views of the world. Abby and Jake, as unlikely as it seemed, were doing just that. But maybe there would always be people like me. Those for whom figuring it out came with a steep cost. I could feel it happening, slowly, in the smallest of steps. The future getting brighter. Where I was that day was in fact better than where I had been a year earlier. But the painful part was admitting what had happened to get me there. The implosion of two lives so that I might one day rebuild mine.

I saw it before I felt it, the darkened spots on the carpet, the drops of water on the glossy surface of the photos. I was crying, but this was different. It wasn't like the helpless spasms of guilt that had followed the breakup or the crushing anger I'd felt after learning the truth about the Fletchers. I wasn't crying for Evan or for what I had done to him. I was crying for the person I had been before. That night, the music on the speakers, the night air through the window, the prickle of the carpet against the back of my legs: what washed over me was the realization that I was finally letting go of that girl. The girl who clung desperately to a hope that it would all work out, that everything would make sense if she just waited a little longer, if she just tried a little harder. I let myself cry for a long time. Until, gradually, the spotlight faded to black. The curtain lowered slowly, a silent pooling of fabric against the floor. The hush that followed. The stillness that felt as long as a eulogy.

And then the house lights coming up. The room blinking back to life. And me, alone, surrounded by a sea of empty seats. I stood up and opened the door.

The next morning, I had an e-mail from Sara. We had promised to stay in touch after our lunch.

> Julia – so great to see you on Wednesday. A friend of mine is looking to hire an intern for her gallery. It's part-time, doesn't pay much, but she needs someone to start ASAP. I told her she should hire you. Can you call her today at the number below? I think you will hit it off. Yours, S.

I left a message for her friend, one of the associate directors at an art gallery in Chelsea. She returned my call an hour later, while I was trying to focus on the crossword puzzle and not stare at my phone too obsessively. Sara's friend seemed impressed by the Fletcher Foundation on my résumé – 'They do really important work. I'm a big admirer of their president, Laurie Silver' (who knew?) – and five minutes later, I was hired. 'You can start on Monday?' she asked, and I said yes. 'Great. I have your e-mail from Sara. I'll send you all the details.'

We hung up. I was gratified by how quickly it had happened, but my reaction was more tempered than it had been when Laurie had hired me a year ago. This wasn't going to be the only answer. The internship didn't pay much, and I'd have to find another part-time job, or maybe two, to make a livable wage. The gallery didn't offer health insurance. I'd have to work nights and weekends on occasion. But interns sometimes turned into full-time employees. It was hard work, a fast-paced and demanding job, but if I liked it and could prove myself, there was room to move up. And if I didn't, if it wasn't for me, then I could leave with no hard feelings.

It was another beautiful June day. A blue, cloudless sky. I'd e-mail Sara to thank her. I'd tell Elizabeth the good news, and Abby, and my parents – but later. I wanted to be alone with it for a while. I wanted to let the idea sink in. It was past noon when I left the apartment. I bought an ice cream cone for lunch. Eventually I found myself walking through the western edge of Central Park, looping around the edge of the reservoir, down toward the Great Lawn. I lay down on the grass, pulling out the book I'd brought along. I read for a while, then closed my eyes against the brightness. Friday afternoon sounds. People talking into their cell phones as they walked home. A girl reading aloud a magazine quiz to her friend. A couple debating what to have for dinner. I dozed off, and when I woke up the sun had moved toward the Upper West Side. My watch said it was close to 4:00 p.m. As I brushed the blades of grass from my shorts, I found that I had crossed into the eastern half of the park. Past the invisible midline that I'd always been careful not to violate. When I started walking again, I was walking east. I let my feet lead me without focusing on the destination.

They had taken down the scaffolding at the corner of 3rd Avenue. The approach to our block looked different, bare and vulnerable. But our building was the same – the glass door tattooed with handprints, a FedEx slip taped at eye level. I sat down on a stoop on the other side of the street, facing our old entrance. I didn't really have a plan. I just wanted to look, for a while, at the place I used to call home.

The foot traffic on the street thickened as the hour passed, people coming home from work, their arms laden with dry cleaning or groceries or gym bags. I wondered if Evan was on the train right then, riding back from Westchester. I had talked to Abby on Skype that week. She and Jake had moved on to Morocco, her tan deepening. She asked me whether I had been in touch with Evan. 'No,' I said. 'I will, eventually. I'm just waiting for the right time.'

'What do you mean? Just do it, Jules. It's not going to get any easier. Rip the Band-Aid off.'

'I don't know. I just don't think he wants to hear from me.'

'Do you want to see him? Do you miss him?'

I nodded. 'Yeah. Kind of. I do.'

'Then call him! It's not that complicated. I'm telling you, I saw him, and he's okay. Jules, he's *fine*. Better, in fact. He hated his old job. You know that.'

The afternoon was slipping into evening. Evan was probably going to be home soon. Maybe Abby didn't know the full truth of why I was so nervous about calling him, but I could see she had a point, no matter what. It wasn't going to get easier. If I wanted to see him, if I wanted a chance to stand before him and let him look at me, let myself look at him, I just had to do it. I had to live with whatever the consequences might be.

The light changed on 3rd Avenue. A stream of pedestrians crossed the intersection. Some turned up the avenue, and some turned down. As the crowd thinned, I saw him emerge, like an image sliding into focus. He was wearing jeans and a T-shirt, the old baseball hat he'd often worn in college. He held a bag of groceries in one hand. I remembered the morning he'd returned from Las Vegas, the eeriness of seeing him down the block. How unfamiliar he had seemed, contorted by his situation into a person I didn't recognize. I sat on the stoop, perfectly still, and watched Evan walk down the block toward our old apartment – toward *his* apartment. He still lived there, I reminded myself. I saw what Abby meant. He seemed okay. Happy, even. It was evident, something in the way he slung the grocery bag from one hand to the next with an easy gesture, digging for his keys in his pocket. Evan had a new life, a life he managed to rebuild without me. This was nothing like the morning he'd returned from Las Vegas. The Evan I was watching was the Evan I had always known. The person I had fallen in love with years ago.

He was standing outside the door. He dug deeper into his pocket and wrinkled his brow. Set down his grocery bag and swung his backpack from his shoulders. He unzipped the front pocket, and after a moment of blind groping, he pulled out his keys. He slung his backpack over his shoulder again, and picked up his grocery bag. He must have learned how to cook. I found myself overwhelmed with so much curiosity that I almost shouted his name. There was so much I wanted to know. What he was going to have for dinner that night. What his new job was like. How his day had been. Whether he ever thought about me. Every tiny, mundane detail of his life, every glittering grain of sand that made up the person he had become.

I stood up and started to make my way down the stairs, but Evan had already opened the front door. I had waited too long. He was about to disappear. I was at the curb, about to hurry across, when a cab blasted past, roaring down the block. It slammed on its brakes with a sharp squeal. The driver, stopped, continued to blast his horn at the cars ahead of him. I noticed that Evan, too, had paused because of the noise. One foot propping open the door, the other still outside.

And then he turned, surveying the street. Maybe he

was curious whether this minor rip in the neighborhood fabric had been noticed by anyone else. Whether it would be remarked on, acknowledged by a shared shrug with a neighbor. Or whether it was just another passing mishap of city life, fading into oblivion almost as soon as it happened, a tree falling in a forest with no listeners. That's when he saw me.

'Julia?' he called, raising one hand to shield his eyes from the sun. This was the Evan I had always known, and I could see it on his face already – the recognition of who I was. The understanding of everything that had come before and everything that would come after.

I didn't know what to say. Not yet. It would take a while, I knew. Maybe a long time. But I crossed the street and climbed the steps. What he said next made me realize that we would get there, eventually.

'Julia,' he said. His steady, light-colored eyes, the eyes that had managed to see the parts of me that I hadn't known existed. 'You came back.'

Acknowledgments

Thank you to Allison Hunter for her guidance, fierce wisdom, and unmatched savvy. Thank you to Carina Guiterman, who saw what this book could be and then made it a thousand times better with her deft and brilliant edits. I am lucky to have you both in my corner.

Thank you to Lee Boudreaux for taking a chance on me. Thank you to everyone at Little, Brown for giving me such a good home.

One of the reasons I became interested in the world of finance and hedge funds is Michael Lewis's writing, particularly *Liar's Poker* and *The Big Short*. I will forever be a grateful admirer. I also found invaluable illumination in *More Money Than God* by Sebastian Mallaby, *Too Big to Fail* by Andrew Ross Sorkin, and *Hedge Hogs* by Barbara Dreyfuss. And an enormous thank-you to my friends Cal Leveen and Lee West, who provided sharp-eyed feedback.

Thank you to Kate Medina, who has taught me so much about books, writing, reading, and life.

Thank you to my parents, Ed and Kate. Thank you to my sister, Nellie. Thank you for making me laugh, for laughing at me, for reading and rereading so many drafts of this book, and for always believing in me.

Last but not least, thank you to Andrew, whose love has made me a better person.

thrust should first be driven home, that there was adequate time, and that, in any case, a precipitate retreat without fighting would give Samsonov, who was much nearer the Vistula, the chance to cut off the main German forces. Prittwitz, however, curtly told them that the decision rested with him and not with them. He then left the office, leaving them to continue the argument with Waldersee – and, eventually, to persuade him to take bolder measures. It was decided that, to gain time, and room, an attack should be launched against Samsonov's left or western flank. And for this purpose three divisions should be railed back from the Gumbinnen area to reinforce the XX Corps, while the remainder of the force there (I Reserve and XVII Corps) were to retreat westwards by road. Here was the foundation of the Tannenberg manoeuvre.

On returning to the office Prittwitz agreed to their moves, and spoke no more of retiring behind the Vistula. Next day he grew quite cheerful when word came that his forces had been disengaged safely from Rennenkampf's front, and that Samsonov had almost come to a standstill. But on the 22nd, when the headquarters had been moved north to Mühlhausen, a bombshell was exploded by a telegram which announced that a special train was on its way with a new Commander-in-Chief and a new Chief of Staff on board – the first being General von Hindenburg and the second, General Ludendorff. Half an hour after came the delayed telegram which told Prittwitz and Waldersee that they had been superseded.

Not until later did the astonished staff discover the clue to this dramatic upset. It lay in the fact that while Prittwitz was out of the office, during the discussion on the 20th, he had not only telephoned to Mackensen and to the Lines of Communication authorities, to tell them that he was going to retire behind the Vistula, but had telephoned also to the Supreme Command – then at Coblenz on the Rhine. He had even told Moltke that he could only hold the Vistula line if he received reinforcements. To crown his nerve-broken folly, he forgot to tell his staff of this telephone talk when he came back, and so prevented them informing Moltke of his change of plan. And Moltke, whose own loss of nerve and lapse into pessimism were still to come, though imminent, was remarkably quick to penalize it in a subordinate.

He looked round at once for a man of decision and found him in Ludendorff, who had just wrenched victory from defeat at Liége. Then as an afterthought, he chose a nominal superior for Ludendorff, who was summoned to Coblenz. Arriving there on the 22nd, he had the situation in East Prussia explained to him, dispatched his initial orders direct to the unfortunate Prittwitz's corps commanders, caught the train for his new 'command', and picked up his 'commander', Hindenburg, at Hanover.

Let us pause to contemplate this delightful and amusing picture of the German system of command. The staff officer chosen first and alone consulted, while the figurehead waits unclaimed in the 'lost property office' at Hanover; the staff officer telegraphing *his* orders, and then collecting his 'baggage' on the way; but the supreme jest was that the plan had already been framed and the necessary movements made by a still more junior staff officer, Hoffmann, who was to remain under Ludendorff in his post as head of the Operations branch.

The calculated daring of the plan, moreover, owed much to an earlier experience of Hoffmann's. For Schlieffen, with discerning insight, had picked this impishly brilliant young captain, whom many deemed merely a witty *flâneur*, to go as observer with the Japanese forces in the war against Russia. There he learnt much about the Russian army, and not least a story that two Generals, Rennenkampf and Samsonov, had boxed each other's ears on the railway platform at Mukden. Thus, in his judgement, Rennenkampf would be in no hurry to aid Samsonov by pressing on from Gumbinnen. He had also learnt in Manchuria the incredible carelessness of Russian methods and this knowledge led him in August, 1914, to accept the intercepted Russian wireless orders, sent out 'in clear', as authentic, whereas his seniors were distrustfully inclined to regard them as an artful deception.

Paradoxically, the fulfilment of Hoffmann's plan and its development by Ludendorff - the plan on which Ludendorff was to rise to world fame - were hindered by Ludendorff's initial orders. For, in order to amputate Prittwitz's control, Ludendorff had telephoned from Coblenz to the several army corps, telling them to act independently until he arrived. The I Reserve and XVII Corps on Rennenkampf's front utilized this order to take a day's rest in their retreat westwards. Another check on rapidity was that the whole of the Eighth Army headquarters had to move back to Marienburg to meet the new commanders.

On arrival there on the 23rd, Ludendorff was pleasantly surprised to find that the movements already in progress fitted in with his own half-formed plan, and he confirmed Hoffmann's arrangements. Next day it became clear that Rennenkampf was not moving forward in pursuit, and Ludendorff enlarged the plan by accelerating the retirement of the I Reserve Corps (Below), so that it could strike Samsonov's right flank. Then, on the 25th, intercepted wireless messages showed him the slowness of Rennenkampf's movements, and he began to think that he could use the XVII Corps (Mackensen) also, leaving only the cavalry to watch and hoodwink Rennenkampf. Thereby he might strike hard at not one but both of Samsonov's flanks, and bring off a decisive double envelopment. Unfortunately for his now matured plan, even forced marches could not overtake the lost day of rest.

Samsonov meantime had been staggering forward, driven on by telegraphic lashes from Jilinsky who had jumped to the conclusion that the Germans were doing what Prittwitz had contemplated – retreating to the Vistula. And in driving Samsonov on to cut them off, Jilinsky not only neglected to hasten Rennenkampf, but even diverted his energy by orders to invest Königsberg. Meantime Samsonov's army was spread out over a front of nearly sixty miles, and his right, centre and left were widely separated. If they had been linked by mobility, this width might have been an advantage, but with sluggish troops and bad roads it became a danger. And an attempt to side-step farther west as he advanced led through self-dislocation to self-destruction.

Scholtz's XX Corps had been slowly giving way, and wheeling back westwards, before the advance of the Russian centre (XIII and XV Corps) towards the line Allenstein–Osterode. Fearing both the strain and the effect of a further retirement, Ludendorff ordered François' I Corps to attack on the 26th and break through the Russian left wing (I Corps and two cavalry divisions) near Usdau. François protested that part of his troops, three-quarters of his field guns, all his heavy guns, and his ammunition columns had not yet arrived; he also urged that instead of making a frontal attack he should get round the Russian flank. Ludendorff summarily overrode these objections. His sense of time was perhaps greater than his sense of tactical reality. But François, who had no wish to repeat Mackensen's experience at Gumbinnen, avoided the Russians active resistance by passive resistance to Ludendorff's orders, and contented himself with the capture of an outlying ridge. And any danger to Scholtz's XX Corps was avoided by the inactivity of Samsonov's exhausted troops – one corps, for example, had marched more than 150 miles in twelve days over roads that were merely deep sand.

But the 26th did not pass without hard fighting. For away on the other flank the Russian right wing (VI Corps and cavalry division), separated by two days' march distance from the rest of the army, had encountered near Lautern the two German corps that were marching back from the east front. The Russian right wing was thrown back in confusion, but the attacks of Below and Mackensen were badly coordinated, their troops were tired by the forced marches, and they did not press the pursuit. Thus the Russian right wing, although disorganized, was able to retire safely. Part of one division, however, had been hemmed in with their backs to the Bössau Lake, and in the panic a number were drowned. From this small incident arose the legend that Hindenburg had driven Samsonov's army into the lakes and marshes, drowning thousands.

The real crisis of the battle, as a whole, came on the 27th. For that morning François, now amply supplied with shells, opened a fierce bombardment on the position of the Russian left wing near Usdau. The Russian troops could not stand high explosive on top of an empty stomach, and they broke in flight without waiting for the German infantry. François ordered the pursuit to be made towards Neidenburg, to get across the rear of the Russian centre, but a Russian counterattack against his outer flank caused him to wheel south towards Soldau. At daybreak on the 28th, however, he discovered that the beaten Russian left wing had retired precipitately from Soldau across the frontier, and he once more turned his forces eastwards to Neidenburg.

The time that he had lost on the 27th was compensated for by the fact that the Russians had engulfed themselves still further - to their doom. For although Samsonov knew the night before that his right had been beaten and his left was menaced, he had ordered his centre to strike northward again. As he can be acquitted of undue optimism, there are two possible explanations - that he was too rigidly loyal to his orders in trying to carry out his mission, or that he was unwilling to retreat when Rennenkampf, his old enemy, was advancing. His attack probably saved the Germans a repulse, for Scholtz had been ordered by Ludendorff to chime in after François' attack. As it was, the Russian centre made several cracks in Scholtz's front, although at the price of further exhaustion to itself. These cracks seem to have momentarily cracked Ludendorff's nerve, for he ordered François both to send back assistance and, with the rest of his corps, to march north-east towards Lahna, against the immediate rear of the Russian centre. This direction, which traversed thick forest country, would have given François less time and chance to bar the Russian line of retreat. Fortunately, he again disregarded his orders, and continued towards Neidenburg. Soon after midday Ludendorff discovered that the Russians were not attempting to deepen the cracks, but, rather, were showing signs of retreat. So he sent François fresh orders not only to move on Neidenburg but, through it, eastward on Willenburg. And by the night of the

29th, François' troops held the road from Neidenburg to Willenburg, with a chain of entrenched posts between, forming a barricade across the line of retreat of the Russians who were now flowing back, and becoming inextricably mixed in the forest maze which François had avoided. With its rear closed and its roads congested, the Russian centre (XIII, XV and half the XXIII Corps) dissolved into a mob of hungry and exhausted men, who beat feebly against the ring of fire and then let themselves be rounded up in thousands.

The crowning scene of the tragedy was enacted by Samsonov himself, who had moved up from Neidenburg on the 27th to control the battle, only to find himself caught up in the swirling eddies of the retreat. Unable to do anything he turned and rode south again on the 28th, only to get lost in the depths of the forest. In the darkness he turned aside, and his absence was unnoticed by his staff until a solitary shot rang out – he had taken his own life rather than survive the disaster.

But when he died the disaster was not so complete as his despair, nor so certain. If the Russian centre had only been able to reorganize itself for an aimed attempt to break out, it might well have succeeded. For François' barricade was thin and was itself menaced from the outside. The source of the menace was Artamanov's I Corps which, after its defeat at Usdau and retreat over the frontier, had been reinforced, and now returned to the rescue. Air reports warned François of the danger on the 29th, but he stoutly refused to give up his 'blockade', although he dispatched such force as he could possibly spare to check the advancing Russians at Neidenburg. Even so, the town was lost on the 30th, but Ludendorff was already sending reinforcements, and Artamanov, having made little attempt to press his advantage, retreated south once more on the 31st.

The cause of François' weakness, however, and the escape of part of Samsonov's army, was due to the failure of Mackensen and Below from the east to join up with François. Thus the barricade was neither as firm nor as complete as it might have been. Owing to faulty cooperation between Mackensen and Below, and lack of clear guidance from above, their corps abandoned the pursuit of the Russian right wing and turned northwards towards Allenstein – marching, in good German style, 'to the sound of the guns' instead of weaving a net round the enemy's rear in Hannibalic style. Ludendorff, divided between fear of Rennenkampf's advance and his desire to annihilate Samsonov, issued a contradictory series of orders which did not help to sort out the tangle into which Mackensen and Below had got their forces. In the outcome, he thereby risked more and gained less. For he took longer to close up his battle accounts and left a gap in the south-east through which part of the Russian XIII Corps actually escaped, and most of it might have escaped – if Mackensen, on his own initiative, had not turned south-wards again in an effort to close the gap, and the Russians had not been blinded by panic.

Nevertheless, 92,000 prisoners were taken, two and a half army corps annihilated, and the other half of Samsonov's army severely shaken, especially in morale. The Germans were certainly favoured by the enemy's folly – above all, in dispersing the fog of war at intervals by unciphered wireless messages. Yet if we make due allowance for these flashes of light, we should take due account of the 'blindness' and the difficulties of this wild region. The victory of Tannenberg remains a great achievement, as it was a unique one in the history of the war. But Ludendorff was not the designer of victory, and still less Hindenburg. To Hoffmann is due the chief credit of the design, if Prittwitz and Ludendorff have some share for accepting it in turn, and Ludendorff also for certain additions of detail. Nor was Ludendorff even the agent of victory, for François' share was the most essential. And against Ludendorff's share must be offset the fact that his original telegram from Coblenz was the original and echoing cause of the failure to complete Samsonov's encirclement. For the battle of Tannenberg was not a second Cannae, deliberately planned, as it has so often been acclaimed. The aim was to break the force of the Russian invasion, and not to surround the Russian army, and the idea of the double envelopment only an afterthought, which became possible of fulfilment when Rennenkampf continued to remain passive. As much an afterthought as the very name given to the victory. For Ludendorff's order for the pursuit on the 28th had been headed 'Frögenau', when Hoffmann suggested that he might aptly wipe out a stain on German annals by using instead the name of the town in front of them, Tannenberg, where in 1410 the Teutonic knights had suffered an historic rout.

CHAPTER FOUR

SCENE 3

The Man Who Juggled with Armies, and Broke Them – at Lemberg

No man in Europe had worked harder for war than Conrad von Hötzendorf, the directing head of the Austro-Hungarian armies. None surpassed him in eagerness. Fate determined that he, of all the military chiefs, should come to grief most utterly in the first clash of the armies. Yet he was, perhaps, the ablest strategist among them. Moltke, Joffre, and the Grand Duke Nicholas were conscientious pedestrian soldiers, with marked differences of temperament but not of *tempo*. They were slow-moving and slow-thinking, whereas Conrad had a sense of mobility and an aptitude for bold manoeuvre. His strategy blended the spirit of an artist with the suppleness of an acrobat. If his ideas were bounded by the walls of the nineteenth-century school of war, they represented its best fruits. Also its worst defect – a failure to appreciate the growing part that material factors play in modern war. Lacking a sense of tactical reality, he would attempt feats of strategic virtuosity for which his instrument was inherently unfitted. When it bent under the strain, he merely pressed on it the harder – until it broke in his hands.

The Austrian Army was the most obsolete in equipment among those of the Great Powers; its field guns were fewer in proportion and shorter in range; some two-thirds of the rifles were of old pattern, a quarter of a century old, and its reserve was so inadequate that, even in September, the troops holding the Carpathian passes had to be issued with single-loaders; its transport was so scanty that it had to be supplemented by a cumbersome collection of assorted farm-carts, which congested the roads. Yet with all these hindrances to vigorous action the training of the Austro-Hungarian army had been devoted purely to the offensive. This infatuation with a tactical impossibility seems to have been due to the influence of Conrad von Hötzendorf, who had himself compiled the manuals on which the army had been trained.

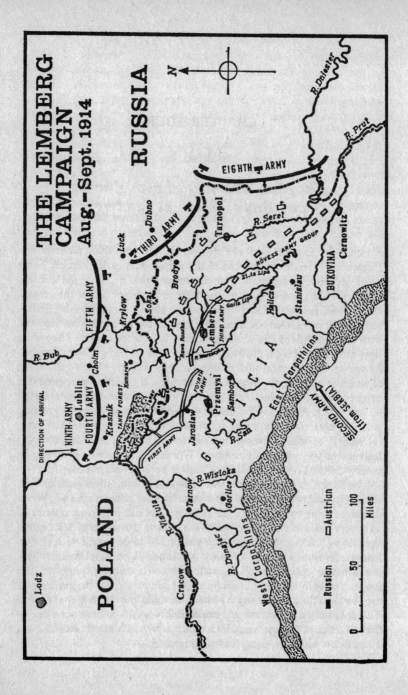

THE LEMBERG CAMPAIGN
Aug.–Sept. 1914

RUSSIA

POLAND

N

Lodz

R. Dniester

R. Prut

EIGHTH ARMY

Dubno

THIRD ARMY

Luck

Tarnopol

R. Seret

Cernowitz

KÖVESS ARMY GROUP

Brody

Zl.ta Lipa

BUKOVINA

FIFTH ARMY

Krylow

Sokal

Gnila Lipa

Stanislau

Halicz

THIRD ARMY

R. Bub

Cholm

Nowa Roszke

Lembery

R. Wereszyca

Komarow

TANEV FOREST

FOURTH ARMY

G   A   L   I   C   I   A

East Carpathians

DIRECTION OF ARRIVAL

NINTH ARMY

Lublin

FOURTH ARMY

Krasnik

Jaroslaw

Przemysl

Sambor

R. San

SECOND ARMY
(from SERBIA)

FIRST ARMY

R. Wisloka

Tarnow

Gorlice

R. Dunajec

R. Vistula

Cracow

West Carpathians

0   50   100

Miles

Russian   Austrian

If the tactical instrument of his plan was brittle, its strategic foundation was hollow. The Polish salient, deep thrust between the jaws of Austrian and German territory, was on the map a morsel so inviting that any amateur strategist would have jumped at the idea of biting it off. It excited Conrad beyond discretion. He pictured to himself a strategic super-Sedan, with his own armies thrusting up from Galicia and the Germans driving down from East Prussia, to cut off the Russian masses in the wide plains of Poland. But this project was not easy to adjust to the practical problem of a double-fronted war conducted by a double-headed alliance.

Germany had long decided to concentrate her initial efforts against France. At a meeting in 1909, Moltke had told Conrad that he hoped to settle with France within six weeks, and then to switch his forces to the Russian front in support of Austria. In view of the German decision, Conrad might wisely have decided to stand on the defensive until the reinforcement came. If he had done so, geography and Russian lethargy would have worked in his favour, to gain time. The rivers and streams that run north from the Carpathians would have provided a series of delaying obstacles; and the Russian armies' slow rate of concentration would have withheld early danger. But, even to gain time, Conrad could only conceive one form of action – the offensive. And, with this obsession, Russia's lengthy process of mobilization served him as a justification. The sooner he struck the less force he would have to meet. It was calculated that the Russians would have thirty-one divisions on the Austrian front by the twentieth day of mobilization (August 18th) rising to fifty-two by the thirtieth day. Conrad counted on having available a force equal to the Russians by the first date, whereas he would be in an inferiority of three to four by the second. To him this was an incentive to prompt action, although to anybody save a military optimist of the 1914 kind bare equality of strength, and strength of such a dubious quality, might have seemed inadequate odds in launching a would-be decisive offensive.

But Conrad also counted on the strength of a vague promise from Moltke, in 1909, that the German forces in East Prussia would take the offensive. Although no direction was mentioned, and even the intention lapsed, Conrad continued to assume that such an offensive would take place.

If the German General Staff bears the responsibility of having failed to undeceive him – instead, Moltke indulged in schoolboyish exhortations to 'thrust the knout-carriers into the marshes of the Pripet and drown them there' – Conrad was certainly eager to deceive himself, rather than forgo the opportunity of displaying his art. His two strongest armies, the First and the Fourth, were assembled on the left of his line in Galicia for a northward thrust, while the Third covered their eastern flank; it was to be joined by the Second when this eventually arrived from its 'circular tour' on the Serbian front. Conrad had admitted the possibility that the Russians, instead of assembling to be cut off in the Polish salient, might concentrate for an offensive against his eastern flank; in that case he proposed to swing his armies round to face them, on a line through Lemberg; but, as such a possibility did not accord with his desires, he was more than ready to discount it. This did not prove difficult, thanks to the defective means of information on which he relied. He had over a hundred thousand cavalry, but a mere forty-two aircraft, and of these only a few were serviceable.

The Austrian advance 'was preceded by a great mass of cavalry' sent forward on August 15th on a hundred-mile excursion to search a front 250 miles wide. Within a few days 'so many of the horses had sore backs that several entire divisions were put out of action'. Only a small proportion came within reach of the enemy, who did not use a cavalry screen; thus these Austrian cavalry bumped into the Russian infantry, who took heavy toll of them. The Austrian Official History candidly remarks that 'the results of the distant cavalry reconnaissance were not worth the cost of casualties'.

But the slight indications that he gleaned sufficed to satisfy Conrad that the Russians were assembling according to plan – his plan. So, on the 20th, he gave the fateful order for the northward offensive into the depths of Poland. Groping in the dark, the Austrian infantry pushed on towards Lublin, while Conrad, in false confidence, expressed his belief that 'there is no sign of any Russian movement from the east against the right flank'.

His delusion was soon to be rudely dispersed, for two whole Russian armies were marching against this flank. In contrast to the Germans, Conrad seems to have discovered too late the possibility of intercepting the enemy's wireless orders, although he learnt the trick in time to escape the closing of the net into which he had blindly walked.

By comparison, the Russian plan was of shrewd and simple design. It offered two essentially different alternatives, but the initial dispositions were made to suit either. In any event, all the Polish salient west of Warsaw and the Vistula was to be evacuated. The Russian forces were divided into two groups, one assembling on the north-western front facing East Prussia, and the other on the south-western front facing East Galicia. Each group comprised three armies, with a fourth guarding its outer flank. If the Germans concentrated for an offensive against Russia, the alternative that would be adopted was Plan G ('Germania') by which the Russian forces would fall back to a north-and-south line through Brest–Litovsk, retiring farther if and when necessary, until the arrival of the troops from Siberia and Turkestan enabled them to take the counter-offensive in strength. If the Germans made their main effort against France, and remained inactive in the east, Plan A ('Austria') came into operation. In this, the south-western group of armies, reinforced by one from the north-western, would take the offensive against the Austrians: the remainder of the north-western group would invade East Prussia.

In the light of orthodox theory, this plan of delivering a double attack on two widely separated points and in divergent directions, may seem unwise – and be too hastily condemned. Its justification lay in the weakness of the German forces in East Prussia and in the importance of a distraction to their effort against France – as the event proved. Also it would shield the flank of the main offensive, and shorten the front if it succeeded, while paving the way for the ultimate advance of the main armies into Silesia. Here were strong arguments. Moreover, it would have been difficult, because of poor communications, for more troops to be used effectively on the Galician side. The defects of the plan were less in the general design than in the conduct of the northern offensive and the crudeness of the instrument. Unfortunately, these defects were aggravated by the pressure which the French applied to the Russian command to accelerate its action.

The Grand Duke Nicholas resisted their suggestion that he should advance direct against Silesia, ignoring the enemy on his flanks; but in loyalty to his allies he began to assemble two fresh armies on the centre with a view to such a move, as soon as possible. Also, he tried to hasten the execution of his present moves, and thereby put a greater strain on the Russian organization than it could safely bear. If the consequences were most harmful on the East Prussian side, where they led to 'Tannenberg', their effects were felt earlier on the Galician side.

Here the Russians, like the Austrians, had a picture of their enemy's plan that was exactly the reverse of the reality. And no more than the Austrians did they have the means of information to correct it. Ivanov, commanding the south-western group of armies, imagined the enemy moving east: they would be met by his strong Third and Eighth Armies, advancing west: and then his Fourth and Fifth Armies would descend from the north across their rear. A delightful picture; and, although it was incorrectly conceived, it came near to being fulfilled – the other way round.   ·

The opening, however, was unpropitious. Under pressure from the Grand Duke Nicholas, and contrary to Ivanov's wish, the Fourth Army on the extreme west began moving down before its mobilization was complete. In this unready state it collided on the 23rd with the Austrian First Army pushing northward. Both were surprised. But in this battle of Krasnik, superiority of force was on the Austrian side, and it enabled General Dankl to turn the flank of the Russians and drive them back.

The news of this reverse was an unpleasant shock to the Grand Duke and Ivanov; but, with eyes still glued on their original picture, they too easily slipped into the deduction that the Austrian stroke came merely from an offensive flank guard. And to punish the audacious intruder Plehve's Fifth Army was ordered to wheel westward against his flank and rear, so as to cut him off. Another picture.

Unfortunately for the Russians, this wheel presented their own flank to the northward-advancing Austrian Fourth Army (Auffenberg). The clash took place on the 26th. In this battle of Komarov, the Russians suffered the worse because their own commander was continuing to urge the westward wheel while the enemy was forcing them to face round to the south. Under this double pressure the Russian Fifth Army became badly bent, especially on the flanks, and by the evening of the 28th it was in grave danger of being encircled by Auffenberg's. It might have crumpled sooner if the Austrian cavalry had not fallen a prey to a panic, due to their own carelessness, which temporarily unhinged Auffenberg's advance. That hitch in drawing close the net had fateful consequences.

For the grey waves of the main Russian advance were now rolling on towards Lemberg, perilously close to Auffenberg's line of supply and retreat. The caution and cumbrousness of the Russian armies, by acting as a brake on their advance, had helped to keep Conrad in ignorance of the impending menace. And his own temperament had contributed to make this worse. Enthused by the opening success of his northward advance, he had drawn three divisions from the weak Third Army near Lemberg to increase Auffenberg's strength. And at the same time he approved a suggestion that what remained should advance east from Lemberg to strike at the supposedly small Russian forces now reported in that direction. His Second Army from the Danube was only just beginning to arrive on the scene – at Stanislau in the south.

The Third Army's rash advance to the Zlota Lipa on the 26th was followed by still rasher attacks, unprepared and disjointed, on the heads of the Russian columns, which had a five-to-two advantage in numbers. The Austrians recoiled in disorder to the Gnila Lipa. Lemberg itself, twenty-five miles behind the battlefield, was filled with panic-stricken fugitives that night. Next morning Conrad ordered the battered Third Army to fall back on Lemberg, and sent word to Auffenberg to return the three divisions loaned to him. Conrad, indeed, was about to halt his two north-bound armies when news came that the Russians were not pursuing their progress. Thereupon he changed his mind, and also his previous orders.

Ivanov, still believing that he was faced by the mass of the Austrian forces, had decided to pause for forty-eight hours, so that his columns might close up and deploy for battle on the Gnila Lipa. Had he pushed on at once it is likely that he would have crashed through the shaken Austrians as through a paper screen. The Grand Duke, when he heard of the halt, sent orders that the advance on Lemberg was to be resumed immediately.

A remote Commander-in-Chief may propose, but his executive subordinates dispose – the troops under their control. The Russian attack did not develop until the 30th, and even then its decisive impulse came, not from Ruzski's army facing Lemberg, but from Brusilov, who had made a side-step northward with the bulk of his army (the Eighth) by night, and then delivered a smashing blow with his right corps against one sector of the Austrian front. Its collapse produced a general reflux. The roads to the rear were congested with fugitives, intermingled with guns and transport. The Austrian Official History candidly relates that a mere cry of 'the Cossacks are coming' often sufficed to cause another panic surge. They were not coming, however, anything like as fast as in the Austrians' fears. Once more the Russians gave their enemy time to recover. They took nearly three days to advance the eighteen miles which their fugitive opponents had covered in less than one. Then, their belated approach produced fresh panics, which opened such gaps on the enemy front that Conrad was constrained to abandon Lemberg, late on September 2nd. But his enemy had given him time that he could not have gained.

He used it, not to hedge, but to plunge more heavily, staking everything on the completion of his success in the north. Here, by the 30th, Auffenberg's wings were well round Plehve's flanks, while Dankl's right was driving a wedge between the two Russian armies. Confident of an early decision, Auffenberg begged for two days' grace to achieve it. It was far easier for the local commander to ask than for Conrad to concede such an interval; he bore the responsibility for the whole, and had to face the alarming fact that only thirty miles and a panicky mob separated Ruzski and Brusilov from the communications of his own northern armies. Notwithstanding this grim situation, Conrad accepted Auffenberg's plea and allowed him to retain the extra divisions.

Like a left-handed swordsman beset by two adversaries, Conrad would guard his right side with a frail wicker shield while thrusting full out at the man in front of him. His will-power commands admiration: it would command unreserved admiration if one was sure that it was not fostered by self-delusion.

Moreover, in the modern war of masses, the will of the commander-in-chief, however strong, cannot dominate those of the men upon whom he depends; his will will not work unless his mind is attuned to theirs. In the events that now followed, the gulf between Conrad's ideas and the capacity of his instrument became manifest.

On the night of the 30th, the commander of the menaced Russian Fifth Army sought to extricate himself by an order for withdrawal. That order might not have availed to save him if fortune had not on this occasion favoured the discreet. Next morning the jaws of the trap, instead of closing, were drawn back. Two Archdukes controlled the jaws, Joseph on the right and Peter on the left. A solitary Austrian aeroplane, reconnoitring, magnified a handful of Russian cavalry into a division marching against Joseph's rear; he pulled back a large part of his force to guard it. On the other wing, the Austrian cavalry reported a similar threat, equally mythical, whereupon Peter drew back his whole force, to cover his rear. Thus the Russians safely withdrew, leaving an empty battlefield. Too late, Auffenberg the next morning ordered a rapid pursuit. Counter-orders came from Conrad.

These new orders were born of hope rather than of anxiety. It was unfortunate that Plehve's army had not been surrounded, but to Conrad's eyes it was routed. It is fair to point out that he could only see the enemy's condition through the magnifying glass provided by subordinates eager to flatter his hopes and enlarge their own achievements.

Encouraged by this view of a Plehve definitely removed from the board, Conrad conceived the picture of a new and greater encirclement. Auffenberg should turn about and descend from the north upon the slowly advancing armies of Ruzski and Brusilov, while the newly arrived Austrian Second Army should strike from the south against their other flank, and lap round their rear. It was a masterly conception, which in breath-taking boldness was worthy of Napoleon. Unfortunately, Conrad's picture did not coincide with the reality of his opponents' situation, and was affected by a change in their plans. Ivanov had ordered Ruzski to incline northward, with Brusilov conforming, so that he might take in flank and rear the forces that were pursuing Plehve. The effect on Conrad's plan was that this movement brought Ruzski round to face the south-bound Austrians instead of presenting them his flank; also, it contracted the space in which Auffenberg could manoeuvre between his late and his new opponent. Even this might not have mattered if Conrad's instrument, the Austrian army, had been fitted for bold and swift manoeuvre. Its palpable unfitness formed Conrad's worst breach with reality.

Moreover, a new danger was arising. There were now two armies instead of one facing his own extreme left. For the newly formed Russian Ninth Army had been brought down the Vistula to support the Fourth. While the latter pinned Dankl's army, the former was to push past his flank and round the Austrian rear. Then the whole of the Austrian armies might be cut off from their natural line of retreat. Thus while Conrad was trying to catch part of Ivanov's forces in a deadly embrace, Ivanov was side-stepping to get round his left and take him in the rear.

The clash of these two plans produced a series of acrobatics such as huge armies have not attempted before or since, and to which these particular armies were most unsuited.

Auffenberg duly turned about and marched south, leaving the Archduke Joseph's divisions as a rearguard; the supposedly beaten Plehve also turned about and followed. On September 6th Auffenberg, expecting to strike Ruzski's flank, found Ruzski knocking against his own at Rava Russka. Fortunately for him, Ruzski was equally surprised, and this gave Auffenberg a chance to face round. Away to the far south, Conrad's other pincer had been no more effective; the Austrian Second Army came fresh, too fresh, to the fighting, but was travel-worn. Its advance soon petered out in a series of disjointed attacks, unsupported by artillery, which culminated in a rippling wave of panic during the night.

When the tangle was straightened out, the Austrian Second, Third and Fourth Armies stood in a line facing east. The one clear fact that emerged was that the Russian armies were inclining northward. This inspired Conrad to the conception of yet another offensive design, regardless of the state of his troops. On the evening of September 8th, Auffenberg was given the task of holding the Russians who faced him, while the other two armies left their prepared defensive positions and wheeled northwards to roll up the Russian line. But the day of the 9th brought disillusionment. Brusilov was also intent on taking the offensive, and the two sides met head on. The condition of the Austrian forces discounted their superiority of numbers, and the battle ended in stalemate, leaving each side with an exaggerated impression of the other's power.

With faith unquenched, Conrad that night sent a fresh order to his armies for a 'concentric attack against the enemy on the Lemberg front'. Next morning he went forward himself with the idea that his presence might be an encouragement. Not unnaturally, his presence at – or rather behind – one point of a fifty-mile line made no appreciable difference. He sent an urgent message to the commander of the Second Army to 'attack without halting, vigorously and regardless of loss'. The commander of the Second Army did not think the order worth passing on to the troops. Such orders were to be repeated so many thousand times on all sides during the World War that it would seem as if to those who uttered them they had the virtue of a magic incantation. An economy of the phrase might have endowed it with more potency. It is rare to trace any effect on those to whom it was addressed – still less on the enemy.

By his persistent pursuit of the tactically impossible, Conrad had engulfed his armies in a pit whence escape was hopeless unless fortune threw them a line. Fortune relented and did so – by a telegram that did not travel along a line.

While Conrad's disordered forces were throwing themselves against the Russians near Lemberg, in fulfilment of his plan, and becoming more entangled in the process, dark masses of the enemy were looming across their rear. Away to the north-west, Dankl's isolated army was struggling to hold up the Russian Fourth and Ninth Armies, double its strength, who were pushing down from the north. On the 9th Dankl warned Conrad that he could hold them no longer, but must fall back behind the San. Worse still there was a thirty-mile gap between Dankl's inner flank and Ruzski's. Into this gap Plehve's army and a whole cavalry corps were marching, unseen and unforeseen by Conrad.

But the ingenuous Russian command came to his rescue in the nick of time. Early on the 11th the Austrians intercepted a wireless order which the Russians, according to their habit, had sent out unciphered. The order showed that Plehve's left wing was expected to reach points well behind Rava Russka by that evening. Still clutching at straws Conrad delayed a few hours in the hope of a miracle on his other flank, and meantime sent an order for the remnant of the Archduke Joseph's divisions to drive back the intruding mass. Auffenberg did not think such an order fit to pass on. So, in the afternoon, as no news of a miracle came, Conrad at last gave the order to disengage the armies and fall back behind the San, as fast as possible.

By cne of history's strangest coincidences, it was at almost the same hour that Moltke accepted the inevitable and gave the order that converted the enforced withdrawal of his right wing into a general retreat of the German armies in France.

The Austrian retreat, however, if less final, was far longer and harder. To quote the moving words of the Austrian Official History – 'Day and night behind a huge train of transport vehicles marched the infantry, with bowed heads, yet undiscouraged (sic); the artillery, sinking in up to their axles in the morass that the roads became ... the cavalry regiments, like horsemen of the Apocalypse, in molten confusion, made their way on, their presence palpable from afar by the penetrating smell of the festering galls of hundreds of led horses.'

The deep-churned mud of the roads luckily served as a brake on the inherently sluggish Russians. And frequent flickers of light from their wireless orders helped to guide the Austrians in evading interception. But Auffenberg's troops could only do so by turning so far south that they became intermingled with the retreating tide of the Third Army. Less than two-thirds of the Austrian troops whom Conrad had confidently pushed forward in August reached the shelter of the San. Even there they did not tarry. They were so obviously unfit to fight that on September 15th, when the first Russians approached, Conrad ordered a fresh retreat to the Dunajec, a farther eighty miles west, leaving behind the great fortress of Przemysl and its garrison as an obstacle to the pursuers. Conrad would, almost surely, have saved himself and his country this additional draught of gall if he had abstained from his last futile assaults near Lemberg. But his rosy imagination had prevented him.

This had certainly revived when, after the war, he wrote in his memoirs: 'The Austro-Hungarian armies were not beaten. They had to be withdrawn to escape a situation that might well have led to a defeat if the battle had continued. From this they were saved!' He saved them from annihilation but not from ruin. He had lost some 350,000 men out of 900,000, and the survivors had retreated over 150 miles, abandoning the province of Galicia. But the ultimate effects were worse than the immediate results. Conrad had juggled with armies – and broken them. If he was able to collect the pieces and stick them together with German glue, they never again had a sound ring.

CHAPTER FOUR

SCENE 4

'First Ypres' – The Real and the Shadow Battle

Within nine months of its beginning, the war produced two Battles of Ypres. And of these 'First Ypres' was itself a twin battle. In its inception and its course it was closely related to the struggle simultaneously in progress along the Yser between Ypres and the sea. But it had also a dual nature. There was the battle fought by the Allied troops who held the shallow trenches in front of Ypres. There was a different battle being fought, in imagination, by the two chief commanders on the Allied side – at their headquarters behind Ypres. The latter were attacking shadows while the former were defending themselves against the sternest realities. Rarely, if ever, have the view at the front and the view behind the front been so widely apart.

The clash at Ypres followed, yet was not truly a continuation of, the outflanking attempts that followed the deadlock on the Aisne. For while Joffre and Foch continued to concentrate their gaze on the immediate western flank of the German line in France, and their thoughts on the next overlapping move, Falkenhayn had shifted his attention to Flanders and was planning a wider manoeuvre – as wide, in fact, as the coastline would allow. A new Sixth Army, composed of troops switched from the eastern flank in Lorraine, was to counter Joffre's next narrow swing. Meantime another fresh army would sweep down the Belgian coast behind the Allies' flank. That army, the Fourth, was made up of the troops set free by the fall of Antwerp together with four newly raised army corps; in these an enthusiastic crowd of young volunteers was blended with a 25 per cent nucleus of trained reservists.

The abandonment of Antwerp, and its possible consequences, did not obtrude into Foch's horizon. On October 10th he sketched out his picture of the future – 'I propose to advance our left (Tenth Army) by Lille to the Scheldt at Tournai or Orchies, the British army ... forming line from Tournai through Courtrai ... In this way all the French, British and Belgian detachments would be united on the left banks of either the Scheldt or the Lys. After that we can see.'

Had this intention been fulfilled the Allied forces would have been moving eastward while the new German forces were marching southward behind their backs.

On the 13th Foch wrote to Joffre concerning Sir John French's intentions: 'The Marshal wishes at all costs to go to Brussels. I shall not hold him back.' Fortunately for the Allied troops, King Albert held them both back by his sagacious reluctance to let go of the coast and embark on an inland excursion. And the Germans soon supplemented his restraining check, besides confirming his wisdom.

When the British II Corps began moving forward to fulfil its part of the wheeling sweep, it found that the French left was falling back. By the 18th it had been brought to a halt itself, before Lille even was reached. The III Corps, and Allenby's Cavalry Corps, coming up on its left, were likewise held up, and on the 20th found themselves resisting an enemy offensive. The day previously the German onslaught on the Yser line, near the sea, had begun.

Until now the six weak Belgian divisions, stiffened by Admiral Ronarc'h's brigade of French marines, had been occupying the line from the sea almost to Ypres. But, just in time, two French Territorial divisions, covered by Mitry's Cavalry Corps, took over the right half of the line, as far as Dixmude, reinforcing Ronarc'h's brigade and linking up with Rawlinson's force at Ypres.

The attack on the Belgian sector was made by Beseler's three divisions from Antwerp. Screened by these until the last moment, a greater force was converging against the Dixmude–Ypres sector.

At this moment of approaching crisis Foch was still intent on carrying out his eastward offensive, and his chief concern seems to have been with the uncertain spirit of the British Commander-in-Chief. Sir John French had moved his forces to Flanders only after prolonged hesitation, anxious lest by taking position on the left flank of the French he might again be exposed as at Mons in August. Once committed to the move, he had quickly become optimistic, with the help of Foch's tactful handling and assiduous flattery. Then, however, he was disquieted by the resistance his II Corps met in the initial advance towards Lille: he spoke of constructing a huge entrenched camp at Boulogne to shelter the whole Expeditionary Force.

Sensitive as a weathercock, his mind had swung round again by the 19th, under Foch's gusts of optimistic encouragement. Although Rawlinson's attempt that day to advance eastward on Menin had been abortive, French ordered Haig's corps to advance north-eastward 'with the object of capturing Bruges', saying that 'the enemy's strength on the front Menin–Ostend is estimated at about a corps and no more'. Yet his own intelligence officers estimated, and underestimated, the enemy's strength as being three and a half corps. As one of the officers later explained: 'The old man only believed what he wished to believe.' Foch's power of 'suggestion' for the moment dominated French's mind. For two more days French persisted in the belief that he was attacking, while, in reality, his troops were barely holding their ground.

The imagined offensive remained imaginary, because it clashed with the opening of the German offensive against Ypres and a simultaneous renewal of the German offensive against the southern part of the British line. Everywhere the British were thrown on the defensive, and in several places lost ground. But French that evening renewed his attack orders to Haig, apparently with the idea that his left wing would still find the enemy's open flank. So on the 21st Haig's corps duly tried to advance past Rawlinson's flank, only to be first held up and then menaced on its left. The troops dug in where they stood, and, as their left had been swung back, the Ypres salient of now immortal memory was formed.

That same day, Joffre, visiting Flanders, had come to see French and, as an encouragement to fresh offensive efforts, had told him that the French detachment was being increased by the dispatch of the IX Corps. The weathercock, however, was now veering – back to a former direction. Until the French reinforcements arrived, the British commander was unwilling to give any more far-reaching order than that 'action against enemy will be continued tomorrow on general line now held.' It was a euphemistic way of recognizing the defensive!

Foch still persisted in the offensive idea. Although the enemy's strength was now unmistakable, he ordered his own troops – now forming the embryo of d'Urbal's Eighth Army – to make a general offensive on the 23rd in the three widely spread directions of Roulers, Thourout, and Ghistelles. At the same time he asked the Belgians and British to take part, the latter again to swing east. If they had done so they would have laid open their flank. Happily the enemy gave them no chance of trying.

Foch's request did not reach British General Headquarters until a few hours before the French attack was supposed to start. It was also complicated by the receipt of a request from d'Urbal that the British would attack in a different direction, and by d'Urbal's instructions to his own right wing to advance on a line which would take it through the British front. The official history remarks, with moderation, that such proposals 'could not be taken seriously'. On hearing of them Haig telegraphed to GHQ that 'there must be some misapprehension of the situation, that there was no time for concerted action, and every chance of confusion'. But his anxiety was needless. The leading French troops did not appear until the afternoon, and the enemy's fire at once stopped their attempt to advance. But they were a welcome reinforcement to the line of defence. Their arrival made the two sides approximately equal in strength, numerically, from Ypres to the sea.

Next day, the 24th, the French IX Corps was ordered 'to continue to advance'. Foch telegraphed direct to the corps commander, Dubois, 'all the units of the IX Corps are detrained' – which was anticipation, not fact. 'Make your dispositions that all these units are employed today, and that the action receives a new impulse. There must be decision and activity.' The result at least gave an air of vindication to Foch's theory, for Dubois' men advanced over half a mile before they were finally held up, while the British, fighting defensively, lost some ground. But the German records suggest that in the proportion of loss inflicted the defensive was the more profitable, and that by the night of the 24th the new German corps had blunted their fighting edge.

Realizing that their effort was spent, the German Fourth Army commander pinned his hopes to a continued effort against the Yser sector, 'where a decision seemed imminent'. This, if achieved, would open the path to Dunkirk and Calais. Under cover of darkness the Germans had gained a footing across the Yser near Tervaete on the night of the 22nd. Counter-attacks failed to dislodge them, all the Belgian reserves were used up, and the French 42nd Division, which would have been invaluable for the purpose, had unfortunately been committed to a vain offensive in the coastal corridor near Nieuport. By the 24th the Germans had brought the infantry of two and a half divisions across the Yser to expand this foothold, and the Belgian centre gave way under the strain. Fortunately it managed to rally on the embankment of the Dixmude–Nieuport railway, whither the 42nd Division was switched in time to stiffen the resistance. And Ronarc'h's marines splendidly withstood a succession of assaults on the key point of Dixmude.

But the situation was still critical, and next day King Albert sanctioned the attempt to create a water barrier by opening the locks at Nieuport so as to flood all the country between the Yser and the railway embankment. These arrangements took time. But, happily, the line of the railway embankment was held, without suffering much pressure, until at high tide on the evening of the 28th the Belgian engineers succeeded in opening one of the locks at Nieuport and letting in the sea. If it crept in slowly, each day brought a fresh reinforcement to the flood, until 'it seemed to the Germans as if the whole country had sunk with them and behind them'. With the impetus of desperation they renewed their attack and breached the embankment line of defence at Ramscapelle. But the rising flood came to the rescue, and during the night the Germans began to retire across the Yser to escape being cut off.

The crisis on the Yser was the prelude to a greater crisis at Ypres. This, again, followed on a fresh attempt by the Allies to take the offensive, which weakened them for the subsequent defensive struggle.

No sooner had the first crisis at Ypres passed than Foch resumed the offensive – in his own mind he had never discontinued it. That he had again infused French with his own assurance is clear from the telegram which French had sent to Kitchener: 'The enemy are vigorously playing their last card.' In the night of the 24th French wired again, suggesting that the battle was 'practically won'.

But on the 25th the Allied offensive made practically no progress against newly wired German defences. On the 26th Dubois and Haig continued the attack, but only advanced a few hundred yards. In contrast, the sharp southern corner of the salient, where Rawlinson's men (the 7th Division) stood, was smashed in by a German attack, and for a time converted into an equally sharp re-entrant. Luckily the assailants did not follow up their success. They were preparing and screening a greater stroke.

A new German army under Fabeck was being brought up, to be inserted like a wedge on the south side of the Ypres salient, between the Fourth and Sixth Armies. This wedge was made up of six divisions, heavily buttressed with artillery. Its entry into the battle on the 29th would give the Germans a two-to-one superiority of numbers. With unforeseeing irony, French had just wired to Kitchener that they were 'quite incapable of making any strong and sustained attack'.

For two days more the Allied offensive was continued without effect, although Dubois had been reinforced by a third division. Faced with a strong line, and themselves provided with little ammunition, the fighting commanders were wise enough to water down the orders received from behind. And although on the night of the 28th these orders again prescribed the offensive, the troops in front suspected the coming storm. It broke, over the British front, at half past five next morning. It was now the Germans' turn to leave the shelter of their trenches and offer themselves as targets. An infantry trained to fire 'fifteen rounds rapid' in the minute with the the the rifle was thus enabled to prove its hitting power, and to produce a leaden counterstorm that obscured its lack of machine guns so well that its German assailants thought it had 'quantities'; they declared that 'over every bush, hedge and fragment of wall floated a thin film of smoke, betraying a machine gun rattling out bullets'. Thus at the end of the day the British front was intact, save at one point – Gheluvelt crossroads. But Haig, under whom all three divisions had now been placed, had no reserve left intact.

During the day French had been to Cassel for another injection of Fochian serum. Foch told French that he was satisfied with 'the advance' of his own troops between Ypres and the sea, but admitted that he was 'far from well informed as to their doings'. French on his return ordered the British advance to be continued! He also wired to Kitchener that 'if the success can be followed up, it will lead to a decisive result'. Haig, with the greater realism that came from a closer view, told his troops to entrench, and added that he would postpone 'orders as to the resumption of the offensive' until he saw what the situation was in the morning.

The enemy command at the same time was issuing an Order of the Day which said: 'The breakthrough will be of decisive importance. We must and therefore will conquer, settle for ever the centuries-long struggle, end the war, and strike the decisive blow against our most detested enemy. We will finish with the British, Indians, Canadians, Moroccans, and other trash, feeble adversaries who surrender in mass if they are attacked with vigour.'

The attack was aimed at the Zandvoorde and Messines ridges – to break through the southern hinge of the salient with the object of reaching the Kemmel heights. Thus the main weight fell on the 7th Division and on the thin chain of three dismounted cavalry divisions which linked Haig's force with the III Corps. A bad break was made in the cavalry line. But the war-experienced assailants did not show the reckless courage of the volunteers who had been repulsed earlier, and their caution in following up their success enabled Haig and Allenby to 'putty up' the gaps. Haig also made an appeal to Dubois, who generously sent his own small reserve to strengthen the line south of Ypres, where it certainly did more good than in supporting an imaginary offensive on the north side.

Foch, back on the hill of Cassel, had little idea of what had happened. Towards the end of the afternoon a first report of these events was brought to him, but, as he says: 'It was impossible for me to estimate their full significance.' About 10 PM one of his staff came back with word that 'there was certainly a gap in the British cavalry front, which they could not fill for want of men. If this breach was not quickly closed, the road to Ypres would be open.' Foch at once telephoned to the British GHQ at Saint-Omer to ask for fuller news, but was told that 'nothing more definite was known'. So, just before midnight, Foch himself set off for St Omer. To counteract French's depression, and to fill the physical gap, he promised that if French would hold on he would send him eight battalions of the 32nd Division, which was just arriving in the French sector. Foch did not get back to Cassel until about 2 AM. Summarizing his action up to this moment, he said, pointing to the map: 'I've stuck a wafer there and there; then, at Hollebeke, the English broken through, the Boches passing through – a wafer here.'

A few hours later, after daybreak, the worst crisis of the whole struggle arose. The main German attack was once more aimed, with odds of five to one, at the sagging line of Allenby's cavalry. But this line, now reinforced by a few battalions of British infantry and Dubois' timely contribution, stood firm until the attacks died away at nightfall. Half, a bare half, of Foch's promised contribution arrived in time to relieve part of the line in the evening.

The crisis of the battle occurred farther north – at Gheluvelt on the Ypres–Menin road. Lying on a forward spur of the low ridge that covers Ypres, Gheluvelt was the last point retained in British hands from which the eyes of ground observers could overlook the enemy's line. Under increasing pressure the front of the 1st Division caved in, and shortly before noon Gheluvelt was lost. The divisional commander, Lomax, on hearing the news, rode back to the headquarters he shared with Monro of the 2nd Division, and laconically remarked: 'My line is broken.' Half an hour later a shell burst into the room where they were holding a conference with their staffs. Lomax and several others were fatally injured. Only one of those present was unhurt. Control was temporarily disorganized.

Haig meantime had left his headquarters at the White Château and ridden forward up the Menin road 'at a slow trot with part of his staff behind him as at an inspection'. If the sight of him brought reassurance to the stragglers and wounded who were trickling down the road, the sight of them and the nearer fall of the enemy shells told its significant tale to him. On his return he heard definite news of the break in the line. It moved him to issue orders for his troops to fall back to a rearward line just covering Ypres, and to hold it to the last, if they could not hold on where they were. But, unknown to him, the immediate danger had already been averted.

Soon after the Germans captured Gheluvelt, a counter-attack by a remnant of the 1st South Wales Borderers had retrieved the position on the flank. But, clearly, it could only be maintained if an adequate re-inforcement arrived. So Brigadier-General FitzClarence, commanding the 1st (Guards) Brigade, sent up the few oddments he still had at hand, and then raced back to find the divisional commander. Lomax's resources were exhausted, but he had arranged with Monro that in case of any break the 2nd Division reserves should aid him by coming down on the enemy's flank from the north. And earlier in the morning, one battalion (the 2nd Worcestershires) had been placed at his disposal. Thus Lomax, barely half an hour before being himself mortally wounded, was able to give FitzClarence the means of saving the situa-tion. Swiftly, FitzClarence studied the map and the ground and gave his orders to Major Hankey, commanding the 2nd Worcestershires; his staff officer, Captain Thorne, went with them as guide. The counter-stroke caught the Germans relaxing after their own success, and, com-ing unexpectedly, tumbled them out of Gheluvelt before they could rally. If the German artillery was quick to exact a toll, the German infantry had shown a remarkable incapacity to exploit their opportuni-ties. The disciplined cohesion of their superior numbers enabled them to break into the thin Allied defences; once inside, and themselves disordered, they failed to produce the initiative that might have guided them through, and became the victims of their own too machine-like discipline. It was a serious reflection on the system and spirit of their pre-war training.

But the enemy's initial success, naturally, made a strong impression behind the defender's front, where impressions perforce operate sooner than facts, and often more decisively. Sir John French himself came up to the White Château about 2 PM. No better news had yet come to relieve the gloom, and French had scarcely need to be told of the critical situation, for he could feel it in the atmosphere. Haig himself was in a mood that recalled the night of Landrecies during the retreat from Mons. Every reserve had been used, and French had none to offer. White with anxiety, he hurried off on foot to regain his car and go in search of aid from Foch. But he had barely departed when, just as Haig was preparing to ride forward himself, Brigadier-General Rice 'came galloping back, as red as a turkeycock and sweating like a pig, with the news that Gheluvelt had been retaken and the line re-established'. Charteris adds: 'It was just as if we had all been under sentence of death and most suddenly received a free pardon.' Haig alone showed no sign of the reaction; pulling at his moustache, he remarked: 'I hope that it's not another false report.' Despite Rice's assurances, he seemed still doubtful, although he sent an aide-de-camp to tell French.

The aide-de-camp caught up French just as he had reached his car. How far the news was convincingly communicated, and how far French understood its significance, is uncertain. He drove off at breakneck pace on the way to Cassel. But as his car slowed down in passing through Vlamertinghe a French staff officer recognized him and told him that Foch was there, conferring with d'Urbal and Dubois in the town hall. French went thither to catch Foch. In making his appeal for aid he painted a black picture of the situation and the state of Haig's corps. The reality was certainly dark, but perhaps the picture seemed blacker because Foch and French had so long persisted in seeing it brightly coloured. French naturally told Foch of Haig's orders for a withdrawal, and it was equally natural for Foch to regard any limited withdrawal as tantamount to disaster. He protested vehemently against any withdrawal, crying: 'If you retreat voluntarily you will be swept up like straws in the gale' – he could not picture the palsy that afflicted the Germans in following up their attacks.

According to Foch, French replied that if his exhausted troops were asked to continue the battle, 'there is nothing left for me to do save to go up and be killed with the I Corps'. It is possible that the dramatic note was heightened in interpretation. Whether or not Foch replied: 'You must not talk of dying, but of winning', he certainly proposed to apply his usual remedy. 'I'll attack to right and left.' He promised that at daybreak six battalions of the 32nd division – actually two less than he had promised at midnight – should counter-attack on the right flank of the I Corps, while part of Dubois' corps counter-attacked on its left.

He then sat down and drafted a note: 'It is absolutely essential that *no retirement is made*, and to that end to dig in wherever you happen to be. This does not prevent you from organizing a rear position which should join up, at Zonnebeke, with our IX Corps. But any movement made to the rear by a considerable body of troops will lead to an enemy push and to certain disorder among the retiring troops. This must absolutely be prevented ...' He handed this epistle to French with the words: 'There, if I were in your shoes, those are the orders I'd send to Haig.'

Of Foch's influence on French there is little question. It is reflected in the note which French now dispatched to Haig along with Foch's memorandum. 'It is of the *utmost importance* to hold the ground you are on now. It is useless for me to say this, because I know you will do it if it is humanly possible. I will see if it is possible to send you any more support myself when I reach headquarters. I will then finally arrange with Foch *what* our future role is to be.'

But of Foch's practical influence on the battle situation at the time there is no evidence. The Worcestershires' counter-attack had saved it before Foch and French had their talk. And before their notes reached Haig he had settled his new line of resistance. For tactical security he had decided to straighten the front of the 1st Division by withdrawing to a line just behind Gheluvelt, while the 2nd Division was to stand on its existing line. And as the enemy pressure had ceased, what Foch said merely confirmed what had already happened. We may admire the spirit that inspired it, but we cannot regard this celebrated note as materially and historically decisive.

For the next ten days Haig's line remained without change and unshaken, save for a minor withdrawal of his right on the 5th to conform to a recoil of the French troops on his right.

On November 1st the main German effort was again made on the flank of the salient, against its southern hinge. This time they tried an assault under cover of darkness, as early as 1 AM, and the experiment was repaid by the capture of the Messines ridge. The inward bulge of Allenby's line was deepened by over a mile. But the arrival of the French 32nd Division soon after daybreak relieved the strain, although its counter-attack could not redeem the lost ground. If the other French 'attack' on Haig's left also made no measurable progress, its appearance likewise tended to discourage the enemy from pressing his own attack.

Foch wrote: 'The battle continues. It seems to me calmer. More troops are constantly arriving. In a few days we shall be able to renew the attack in full force.'

On the 2nd the French attack to reduce the Messines bulge was forestalled by a German attack, causing a French recoil, during which Wytschaete was lost and the bulge somewhat deepened. But most of the French 39th Division and half of Conneau's Cavalry Corps arrived from the south to relieve the strain; and the 43rd Division was just detraining. The French now took over the larger part of Allenby's line. Thus they held henceforth two-thirds of the battle line formed by the Ypres salient and the Messines re-entrant, leaving the weary and inter-mixed units under Haig's command to maintain the central sector. Worst hit of all was the 7th Division, whose infantry were reduced from 12,300 men to 2,400 – a bare fifth of their original strength.

During the next few days Foch pursued his attacks – without progress. While those of November 1st and 2nd by their boldness damped the enemy's will to advance, these later attacks had no such moral effect to compensate their lack of visible progress. For the German command was marking time until, by combing their line elsewhere, they could bring up six more divisions for a renewed effort. In this, the points of their attack were to be successively closed inwards like a pair of calipers. Initially, abandoning the attempt to deepen the Messines bulge, they would place the points against the two hinges of the salient.

Meantime, Foch and d'Urbal were playing into the enemy's hands by a reckless persistence in abortive local attacks. The sequel to this self-exhausting impulse is to be traced in the dangerous recoil which came on November 6th at the southern hinge in face of the Germans' new pressure – itself a preliminary to their final stroke. At St Eloi the grey tide came within two miles of Ypres, lapping round the rear of the British, who were holding the nose of the salient. Haig warned his chief that, to avoid being cut off, he would have to fall back to a line through Ypres itself. Foch, however, sent to assure Haig that he would regain the lost ground by an attack next day. At 9.30 AM on the 7th he sent a message that the French line had been re-established. But in fact nothing had been done. His men were too dead-beat to respond to orders. And when eventually they were spurred to an offensive effort, it naturally failed, thus failing to remove the menacing wedge that lay embedded in the flank of the salient.

On the 8th Haig went with French to see Foch at Cassel, and found him as exuberantly confident as ever. But it was his indefiniteness rather than his assurance that kept them from fulfilling their intention to fall back to a straighter and safer line. So, unable to obtain any satisfaction, and unwilling to leave his allies in the lurch, Haig was fain to hold on as best he could, scraping the human putty off one crack to cement another. Happily, if deceptively, the next two days were comparatively quiet along the British sector. Not so for the French.

For on November 10th the enemy struck heavily against the northern hinge of the salient, and as far as Dixmude. The blow was parried, the French profiting by the natural line of the Yser canal, across which their left retired. Its more significant result was to convince the French command that their own line north of Ypres was the spot selected for the enemy's final effort. And thither were diverted such few reserves as they could spare, at the expense of the already weakened southern hinge.

But this blow against the northern hinge had been intended by the Germans as simultaneous with one against Gheluvelt and the southern hinge (as far south as the Comines canal): a blow for which a new corps under Plettenberg had been brought up – it comprised a division of the Prussian Guard and another picked division. As Plettenberg was not ready, the left-hand blow had been postponed.

On the 11th the attack was launched, in a grey November mist, and prepared by the heaviest bombardment yet experienced. But at all save two points it was repulsed. One was at the actual hinge, where the wedge was driven in as far as the later famous Hill 60. The French detachment there appealed for help to the French and British corps on either side, but neither could spare any reserves. The 'ever-willing' Dubois, however, once more sent his only reserve, and with its help the line was restored. The other and deeper penetration was made in the British line just north of the Menin road. Here the German 1st Guard Brigade broke through the weak front of the British 1st (Guards) Brigade – a strange coincidence of history, even though only the remnants of one Guards' battalion were left in the latter brigade. But the Prussian Guardsmen, bewildered by the woods, failed to exploit their success and were driven back by a flank counter-attack. In this the 52nd Light Infantry played the leading part, as they had done in repelling the final assault of the Imperial Guard at Waterloo.

Although the blow had been heavier than on October 31st, the situation had never been so critical, perhaps largely because it had made less impression on the minds of the commanders in rear. And with the failure of this blow on November 11th – date of prophetic symbolism – the crisis at Ypres finally passed. It is true that the German Higher Command would, in its own mind, still deliver several powerful attacks before it admitted defeat. But the men who were called on to execute its orders were no longer capable of vigorous effort, or inclined to pursue such an unhopeful prospect. Thus the spasmodic attacks that continued during the following week, chiefly against Dubois' front, were but the fading flickers of a storm that is travelling away. The relief of the I Corps, so long demanded by Haig and refused by Foch with the word 'Impossible', was now carried out, and the French took over for a time the whole salient.

'First Ypres' had been essentially a 'soldier's battle' – a greater Inkerman. In a memorable sentence General Edmonds has epitomized the situation: 'The line that stood between the British Empire and ruin was composed of tired, haggard, and unshaven men, unwashed, plastered with mud, many in little more than rags.' Its only divergency from accuracy lies in its one deviation from stark simplicity. The British Empire has shown a capacity for survival, even when its military expeditions have actually been driven back to their ships, and when its enemy has been in possession of the Channel ports. And it is by no means sure that, if the expeditionary force had been defeated at Ypres, the Germans were capable of following so closely on its heels as to bring disaster. In the light of the succeeding years there is, indeed, reason for regret that Haig did not fulfil his idea of withdrawing to the straighter and stronger line along the canal through Ypres. It would have saved cost and simplified defence. And its hindrance to the later attempts at the offensive in Flanders, an impossible country for the offensive, might have been an additional advantage.

The danger at 'First Ypres' was certainly aggravated by the failure of Foch, French, and d'Urbal to realize this impossibility. Herein lay their most material influence on the battle. For the real handling of the battle was left in the hands of Haig and Dubois. Even they, for want of reserves, could do little more than cement the crumbling parts of the defence by judicious thinning of other parts of an ominously thin front. Perhaps to Dubois, for the way he took, not once alone, the calculated risk of parting with his own reserves, is due the highest credit of command earned in the defensive battle.

Foch undoubtedly had a moral influence on the battle, no less by his obstinate refusal to listen to reason than by the unconquerable strength of his will. This never wilted. Detach it from the actual ebb and flow of the battle line, and we can admire it unreservedly. It made an impression on all who came in contact with it. But one is not able to detect any point at which it touched the men in the battle line. And where it touched the fighting commanders the effect seems to have become a source more of exasperation than exaltation. The one sure point where Foch's will fortified another will was at the back of the front – at the allied general headquarters. While some of the claims made for its influence on the Belgian command may be discounted, especially in regard to King Albert, they cannot be disregarded. On Sir John French the influence is more measurable, but here the measure of its effect is inevitably as infinitesimal as Sir John French's influence on the battle.

The German design was foiled, and Ypres saved, in spite of the delusions of the Higher Command – by the troops in the front line. The men who defended Ypres against the German onslaughts were front-line troops in the strictest sense – their defence had length without depth. Its shallowness was the measure of their numerical weakness, but also the supreme tribute to their moral strength. The 'thin red line' of the past was never so thin as the line at Ypres – and never so hardly tried. The 'thin khaki line' withstood a strain that lasted for weeks compared with the hours of the past.

By a patriotic falsification of history, into which military chroniclers easily lapse, too many accounts of 'First Ypres' have represented it as a nearly all-British battle. Ungenerously, and untruly, they have obscured the great part played by our Allies, just as a century earlier they distorted the outline of Waterloo, and the vital share of the Prussians. To correct the proportions does not diminish the credit of the British troops. It is in quality, not in quantity, that military virtue lies. And no battle in Britain's annals has given clearer proof of fighting quality, and of its value, than 'First Ypres'. It was a battle in the natural line of British tradition – a defensive attitude combined with timely ripostes. Thus it suited the nature of the troops who conducted it. If it did not directly fit their pre-war tactical training, predominantly offensive in imitation of the continental fashion, it appealed to their native instincts, which count for more than a fashionable dogma under the test of battle. And because of the extent of their training, compared with the conscript armies of the Continent, they had acquired elements of skill that were of value in any form of action. Above all was this true of their shooting skill – with the rifle. In defence it had greater scope and effect than in attack. Such was the ability of the British infantry to produce 'fifteen rounds rapid' a minute that the Germans credited them with 'quantities of machine guns' whereas, in fact, each battalion had come to France equipped only with two, and in many cases had lost these by the time Ypres was reached. The delusion in the minds of the enemy, which such weapon-skill created, redressed the delusions of the Allied Higher Command, and was a decisive factor in the issue. Indeed, it was the decisive factor when coupled with the morale of the men who handled the weapons.

No praise can be too high for the indomitable spirit which inspired their collective endurance. This was, in a sense, a special product. The enemy had no lack of courage. Their discipline was equally strong – and perhaps too strong for their own tactical effectiveness. But the little British Army had a corporate sense that was unique. To this its very smallness, as well as its conditions of service and traditions, contributed. 'First Ypres', on the British side, was not merely a soldiers' battle but a 'family battle' – against outsiders. The family spirit was its keynote, and the key to the apparent miracle by which, when formations were broken up and regiments reduced to remnants, those remnants still held together. They attained their end – in both senses. Ypres saw the supreme vindication and the final sacrifice of the old Regular Army. After the battle was over, little survived, save the memory of its spirit.

CHAPTER FIVE

1915 – The Deadlock

Before the end of 1914 the state of deadlock on the Western Front was realized, if in varying degree, by the Governments and General Staffs of the warring countries, and each was seeking a solution. The reaction varied in form and in nature, according to the mental power and predisposition of the different authorities. With the Germanic Powers the opinion of Falkenhayn was the decisive factor, and the impression derived not merely from his critics, but from his own account, is that neither the opinion nor the direction was really clear as to its object.

On his appointment after the Marne reverse, he still adhered to the Schlieffen plan of seeking a decision in the west, but he did not follow the Schlieffen method of weakening his left wing in order to mass on the vital right wing. The autumn attack at Ypres was made largely with raw formations, while war-experienced troops lay almost idle between the Aisne and the Vosges. Colonel Gröner, Chief of the Field Railways, even went so far as to submit a detailed plan to Falkenhayn for transferring six army corps to the right wing, but it was rejected. When we remember how close to breaking point the British front came at Ypres, it can only be said that for a second time the German Supreme Command saved the Allies. At this juncture, too, Ludendorff was pleading for reinforcements to make his wedge-blow at the Russian flank near Lodz decisive, but Falkenhayn missed the chance by delaying until the Ypres failure had passed from assurance to fact.

Reluctantly dissuaded from a fresh attempt to break the trench barrier in the west, Falkenhayn seems to have been vague as to any alternative object. His feeling that the war must ultimately be decided in France led him to distrust the value, as he doubted the possibility, of a decision against Russia. Hence while he realized that the Eastern Front was the only practicable theatre for operations in the near future, he withheld the necessary reinforcements until his hands were forced by the threatening situation of the Austro-Hungarian front. And even then he doled out reserves reluctantly and meagrely; enough to secure success, but never in sufficient quantity or in time for decisive victory.

It is to his credit, however, that he realized a long war was now inevitable, and consequently set to work to develop Germany's resources for such a warfare of attrition. The technique of field entrenchment was carried to a higher pitch than with any other army; the military railways were expanded for the lateral movement of reserves; the supply of munitions and of the raw material for their manufacture was tackled so energetically and comprehensively that an ample flow was ensured from the spring of 1915 onwards – a time when the British were only awakening to the problem. Here was laid the foundation of that economic organization and utilization of resources which were to be the secret of Germany's resisting power to the pressure of the British blockade. For the scientific grasp of the economic sphere in war Germany owed much to Dr Walter Rathenau, a great captain of industry. She was also a pioneer in the psychological sphere for, as early as the autumn of 1914, German agents launched a scheme of propaganda in Asia to undermine British prestige and the loyalty of Britain's Mahommedan subjects. The defect of German propaganda, its crudeness, was less apparent when concerned with primitive peoples than when applied to the civilized peoples of Europe and America.

The same period witnessed also the one great success for German diplomacy, the entry of Turkey into the war, although this was fundamentally due to a combination of pre-war causes with military events. Since 1909 the country had been under the control of the Young Turk party, to whom traditions, including that of friendship with Britain, were abhorrent. Germany, filled with her own dream of a Germanic Middle East – of which the Baghdad railway was the symbol – had skilfully exploited the opportunity to gain a dominating influence over the new rulers of Turkey. Their leader, Enver Pasha, had been military attaché in Berlin; German instructors permeated the Turkish army; and a definite understanding existed between Germany and the Young Turk leaders as to common military action – urged by the common bond of necessary safeguard against danger from Russia. The arrival of the *Goeben* and *Breslau* reinforced the moral pressure of Wangenheim, the German Ambassador, and eventually on October 29th the Turks committed definite acts of war – at Odessa against Russia, and in Sinai against Britain.

Falkenhayn has shown 'the decisive importance of Turkey joining in the struggle' – first as a barrier across the channel of munition supply to Russia, and secondly as a distraction to the military strength of Britain and Russia. Under German dictation, Turkey struck as early as mid-

December against the Russians in the Caucasus, but Enver's over-ambitious plan ended in disaster at the battle Sarikamish. Turkey was no more fortunate in her next venture – to cut Britain's Suez Canal artery with the east. The Sinai Desert was a check on an invasion in strength, and the two small detachments which got across were easily repulsed, at Ismailia and Tussum, although allowed to make good their retreat. But if both these offensives were tactical failures, they were of great strategic value to Germany by pinning down large Russian and British forces.

As an offset to Turkey joining the Central Powers, Italy definitely threw over the artificial ties of the Old Triple Alliance and joined the Entente. On May 24th she declared war on Austria – her hereditary enemy – although avoiding an open breach with Germany. If her main object was to seize the chance of redeeming her kinsmen in Trieste and the Trentino from Austrian rule, there was also a spiritual desire to reassert her historic traditions. Militarily, however, her aid could not have an early or far-reaching effect on the situation, for her army was unready to deliver a prompt blow, and the Austrian frontier was a mountainous obstacle of great natural strength.

On the Entente side the reality of the trench deadlock produced different and diverse reactions. If the desire to hold on to territorial gains swayed German strategy, the desire to recover their lost territory dominated the strategy of the French. It is true that their mental and material concentration on the Western Front, where lay the main armed force of the enemy, was justified by military tenets, but without any key to unlock the barrier they were merely knocking themselves to pieces. Winter attacks in Artois, on the Aisne, in Champagne and the Woevre afforded costly proof that against the Germans' skill in trench fighting, Joffre's 'nibbling' was usually attrition on the wrong side of the balance sheet. As for any new key, the French were singularly lacking in fertility of idea.

Britain's trouble was rather an excess of fertility, or rather an absence of decision in choosing and bringing to fruition these mental seeds. Yet in great measure this failing was due to the obscurantism of professional opinion, whose attitude was that of blank opposition rather than expert guidance.

British-inspired solutions to the deadlock crystallized into two main groups, one tactical, the other strategical. The first was to unlock the trench barrier by producing a machine invulnerable to machine guns and capable of crossing trenches, which would restore the tactical balance upset by the new preponderance of defensive over offensive power. The idea of a machine for this definite purpose was conceived by Colonel Swinton in October, 1914, was nourished and tended in infancy by Mr Winston Churchill, then First Lord of the Admiralty, and ultimately, after months of experiment hampered by official opposition, came to maturity in the tank of 1916.

The strategical solution was to go round the trench barrier. Its advocates – who became known as the 'Eastern' in contrast to the 'Western' school – argued that the enemy alliance should be viewed as a whole, and that modern developments had so changed conceptions of distance and powers of mobility, that a blow in some other theatre of war would correspond to the historic attack on an enemy's strategic flank. Further, such an operation would be in accordance with the traditional amphibious strategy of Britain, and would enable it to exploit the advantage of sea power which had hitherto been neglected. In October, 1914, Lord Fisher, recalled to the office of First Sea Lord, had urged a plan for landing on the German coast. In January 1915, Lord Kitchener suggested another, for severing Turkey's main line of eastward communication by a landing in the Gulf of Alexandretta. The post-war comments of Hindenburg and Enver show how this would have paralysed Turkey. It could hardly, however, have exercised a wider influence, and it was anticipated by another project – partly the result of Churchill's strategic insight and partly due to the pressure of circumstances.

This was the Dardanelles expedition, about which controversy has raged so hotly that the term just applied to Churchill may be disputed by some critics. This is answered by the verdict of Falkenhayn himself – 'If the straits between the Mediterranean and the Black Sea were not permanently closed to Entente traffic, all hopes of a successful course of the war would be very considerably diminished. Russia would have been freed from her significant isolation ... which offered a safer guarantee than military successes ... that sooner or later a crippling of the forces of this Titan must take place ... automatically.' The fault was not in the conception, but in the execution. If the British had used at the outset even a fair proportion of the forces they ultimately expended in driblets, it is clear from Turkish accounts that victory would have crowned their undertaking.

The cause of this piecemeal application of force, and dissipation of opportunity, lay in the opposition of Joffre and the French General Staff, supported by Sir John French. Despite the evidence of the sequel to the Marne, of the German failure at Ypres, and of his own ambitious yet utterly ineffectual offensive in December, Joffre remained confident of his power to achieve an early and decisive victory in France. His plan was that of converging blows from Artois and Champagne upon the great salient formed by the entrenched German front, to be followed by an offensive in Lorraine against the rear of the enemy armies. The idea was similar to that of Foch in 1918, but the vital difference lay in the conditions existing and the methods employed. A study of the documents conveys the impression that there has rarely been such a trinity of optimists in whom faith was divorced from reason as Joffre, Foch, his deputy in Flanders, and French – albeit the latter's outlook oscillated violently. In contrast, the British Government considered that the trench front in France was impregnable to frontal attacks, had strong objection to wasting the man power of the new armies in a vain effort, and at the same time felt increasing concern over the danger of a Russian collapse. These views were common alike to Churchill, Lloyd George and Kitchener, who on January 2nd, 1915, wrote to Sir John French – 'The German lines in France may be looked upon as a fortress that cannot be carried by assault and also that cannot be completely invested, with the result that the lines may be held by an investing force while operations proceed elsewhere.'

Lloyd George advocated the transfer of the bulk of the British forces to the Balkans, both to succour Serbia and to develop an attack on the rear of the hostile alliance. In a memorandum on January 1st he suggested Salonika or the Dalmatian coast as bases of operation. That same day, curiously, Galliéni proposed to the French Government a landing at Salonika, as a starting point for a march on Constantinople with an army strong enough to encourage Greece and Bulgaria to combine with the Entente. The capture of Constantinople was to be followed by an advance up the Danube into Austria-Hungary in conjunction with the Rumanians. Franchet d'Esperey expressed similar views. But the commanders on the Western Front, buoyantly confident of an early breakthrough, argued vehemently against any alternative strategy, stressing the difficulties of transport and supply and insisting on the ease with which Germany could switch troops to meet the threat.* If there was force in their contention, it tended to ignore the experience of military history, that 'the longest way round is often the

* The Germans, in contrast, pointed out in their staff calculations that it was far easier for the Allies to move troops by sea to the Balkans than for them to move troops by rail! The facts show that troop shipments from France to Salonika averaged a week, and from England about twelve days; whereas the Germans took nine days to move an army corps even from the French to the Russian frontier. To move any considerable force to the Balkans would have taken over a month. If sufficient shipping had been made available, the Allies could have sent a force far quicker by sea.

shortest way there', and that the acceptance of topographical difficulties has constantly proved preferable to that of a direct attack on an opponent firmly posted and prepared to meet it.

The weight of 'Western' opinion prevailed and the Balkan projects were stifled. But misgivings were not silenced, and at this juncture a situation arose which revived the Near Eastern scheme in a new if attenuated form.

The Dardanelles. On January 2nd, 1915, Kitchener received an appeal from the Grand Duke Nicholas for a diversion which would relieve the Turkish pressure on Russia's army in the Caucasus. Kitchener felt unable to provide troops and suggested a naval demonstration against the Dardanelles, which Churchill, appreciating the wider strategic and economic issues, proposed to convert into an attempt to force the passage. His naval advisers, if not enthusiastic, did not oppose the proposal and, in response to a telegram, the Admiral on the spot, Carden, submitted a plan for a methodical reduction of the forts and clearance of the minefields. A naval force, mainly of obsolete vessels, was got together with French aid and, after a preliminary bombardment, entered the straits on March 18th. Drift mines, however, caused the sinking of several ships, and the attempt was abandoned.

It is a moot point whether a prompt renewal of the advance would not have succeeded, for ammunition in the Turkish forts was exhausted, and in such conditions the mine obstacle might have been overcome. But the new naval commander, Admiral de Robeck, decided against it, unless military aid was forthcoming. Already, a month before, the War Council had determined on a joint attack, and began the dispatch of a military force under Sir Ian Hamilton. But as the authorities had drifted into the new scheme, so were they tardy in releasing the necessary troops, and even when sent, in inadequate numbers, several more weeks' delay had to be incurred – at Alexandria – in order to redistribute the force in its transports suitably for tactical action. Worst of all, this fumbling policy had thrown away the chance of surprise, which was vital for a landing on an almost impregnable shore. When the preliminary bombardment took place in February, only two Turkish divisions were at the straits, this was increased by four by the date of the naval attack, to six when Ian Hamilton was at last able to attempt his landing. For this he had only four British divisions and one French division – actually inferior in strength to the enemy in a situation where the inherent preponderance of defensive over offensive power was multiplied by the natural difficulties of the terrain. His weakness of numbers and his mission of aiding the passage of the fleet compelled him to choose a landing on the Gallipoli peninsula in preference to one on the mainland or on the Asiatic shore; and the rocky coastline limited his possible landing places.

On April 25th he made his spring, at the southern tip of the peninsula near Cape Helles, and – with Australian and New Zealand troops – near Gaba Tepe, some fifteen miles up the Aegean coast; the French, as a diversion, made a temporary landing at Kum Kale on the Asiatic shore. Owing to the Turks' uncertainty the British were able to gain a lodgement on several beaches, strewn with barbed wire and swept by machine guns. But the momentary asset of tactical surprise was forfeited, and the difficulties of supply were immense, while the Turks held the commanding heights and were able to bring up their reserves. The invaders managed to hold on to their two precarious footholds, but they could not expand them appreciably, and the stagnation of trench warfare set in. They could not go on, and national prestige forbade them to go back.

Ultimately, in July, the British Government decided to send a further five divisions to reinforce the seven now on the peninsula. By the time they arrived the Turkish strength in the region had also risen, to fifteen divisions. Ian Hamilton decided on a double stroke – a reinforced blow from Gaba Tepe and a new landing at Suvla Bay, a few miles north – to sever the middle of the peninsula and secure the heights commanding the Narrows. He deceived the Turkish Command and achieved surprise on August 6th, but the first blow failed and the second lost a splendid chance by the inexperience of the troops, and still more by the inertia and fumbling of the local commanders. For over thirty-six hours, before reserves arrived, only one and a half Turkish battalions barred the path. Energetic new commanders, for whom Ian Hamilton had previously asked, were sent out when the opportunity had passed. The British were once more condemned to hang on to tenuous footholds, and, with the autumn rains setting in, their trials were increased. The Government had lost faith and were anxious to withdraw, but fear of the moral effect delayed their decision. Ian Hamilton was asked for his opinion, however, and when he pronounced in favour of continuing – in which course he still had confidence – he was replaced by Sir Charles Monro, who immediately declared for evacuation.

It was a remarkable example of prompt decision. While Monro visited Anzac, Suvla, and Helles during a single morning, without going farther than the beach, his Chief of Staff sat on board ship drafting the recommendation for evacuation. Well may Churchill say – 'He came, he saw, he capitulated.' Kitchener at first refused to sanction the withdrawal and himself hurried out to investigate. The Government was most relieved to see him go because they hoped to utilize his absence to relieve him of his post. Most of the Coalition Cabinet were united in dissatisfaction with his secretiveness and his administration, although disunited over the question of evacuating Gallipoli. Mr Bonar Law, the leader of the Conservative Party, took a strong line on both questions. The Prime Minister, however, feared a public outcry over Kitchener's removal only less than he feared Mr Bonar Law's resignation, and so temporized by giving way to Bonar Law's demand for evacuation, and by excluding Churchill from the War Committee of the Cabinet. Evacuation, therefore, was virtually decided upon before Kitchener reached Gallipoli. The fresh wave of opinion at home undoubtedly had an effect on his mind, and after his revived proposal for a fresh landing near Alexandretta had been vetoed by the War Committee, he reluctantly veered round and consented to evacuation.

Curiously, in the last phase it was the navy that tried to avert this. For de Robeck, who had passively resisted since March all promptings to a further naval attack, was now relieved by Admiral Wemyss, who not only opposed evacuation but, basing himself on a plan devised by Commodore Keyes, offered 'to force the straits and control them for an indefinite period'. The proposal came too late. The forces of opposition at home were now too strong, and in obedience to orders a withdrawal of the troops was carried out from Suvla and Anzac on the night of December 18th, and from Helles on that of January 8th. If the bloodless evacuation was an example of masterly organization and cooperation, it was also a proof of the greater ease of such operations in modern warfare. And as a final touch of irony Monro and his Chief of Staff, who had nothing to do with its skilful execution, received high decorations in reward. Thus the curtain rang down on a sound and far-sighted conception, marred by a chain of errors in execution almost unrivalled even in British history.

The German Campaign. While the British were striving to unlock the back door to Russia, the Germanic Powers were hammering the Russians, whose resistance was collapsing in large measure from a lack of munitions which could only be made good by foreign supplies through that locked entrance, the Dardanelles. This fact and its effect was acutely appreciated by Russia's most formidable opponent. In the autumn of 1915, Hoffmann emphatically declared that the success of Germany's efforts against Russia depended on keeping 'the Dardanelles firmly closed'. For if 'the Russians saw that there was no means of exporting their wheat, or importing war material, there would be a gradual collapse in that country.'

On the Eastern Front, the campaign of 1914 had shown that a German force could count on defeating any larger Russian force, but that when Russians and Austrians met on an equality victory rested with the Russians. Falkenhayn was forced, reluctantly, to dispatch German reinforcements as a stiffening to the Austrians, and thus was dragged into an offensive in the east, rather than adopting it as a clearly defined plan. Ludendorff, in contrast, had his eyes firmly fixed on a particular object, and from now on advocated unceasingly a wholehearted effort to break Russia. Ludendorff's was a rigid strategy of decision; Falkenhayn's an opportunistic strategy of attrition. The one took too little account of political factors, the other too much.

In the conflict of wills between these two men, lies the clue to the resultant strategy of Germany – highly effective, yet not decisive. This tug of wills was marked by the 'offensive' use of the telegraph and by the unceasing pull of wires, with the Kaiser as the chief puppet. While Falkenhayn was constantly trying to nullify a potential supplanter by denuding Hindenburg of the power to strike the enemy effectively, Ludendorff countered by screwing Hindenburg up to threats of resignation. Well might Hoffmann watching the intrigues, note in his diary – 'When one gets a close view of influential people – their bad relations with each other, their conflicting ambitions, one must always bear in mind that it is certainly much worse on the other side among the French, English and Russians, or one might well be nervous'. His intuition was correct. 'The race for power and personal position seems to destroy all men's characters. I believe that the only creature who can keep his honour is a man living on his own estate; he has no need to intrigue and struggle – for it is no use intriguing for fine weather.'

The Russian plan for 1915 embodied some of the lessons of experience and was soundly conceived, but the means were lacking and the instrument defective. The Grand Duke Nicholas aimed to secure both his flanks solidly before attempting a fresh blow towards Silesia. From January until April, under bitter winter conditions, the Russian forces on the southern flank of the Polish salient strove to gain possession of the Carpathians and the gateways into the Hungarian plain. The Austrians, with a German infusion, parried their efforts, and the loss was disproportionate to the small gains. But the long-besieged fortress of Przemysl, with 120,000 men, at last fell into Russian hands on March 22nd. In Northern Poland the Russians were preparing to strike upwards at East Prussia, when they were forestalled by a fresh Ludendorff stroke eastwards towards the frontier of Russia proper. The blow was launched on February 7th, over snow-buried roads and frozen swamps, and was distinguished by the envelopment and capture of four Russian divisions in the Augustovo forests – near the Masurian Lakes. Moreover, it extracted the sting from the Russian attack farther west.

These moves were, however, merely a 'curtain-raiser' to the real drama of 1915. But before turning to this it is necessary to glance at events on the Western Front, the importance of which is partly as a signpost to the future and partly because of their reaction on the Eastern Front.

While a way round the trench barrier was being sought in Gallipoli and experiments with a novel key were being carried out in England, the Allied Commands in France were trying more orthodox solutions. In February and March the French lost 50,000 men in nibbling their way 500 yards into the German defences in Champagne; in his report Joffre claimed that the offensive 'was none the less fecund in results'. In April the French sacrificed 64,000 men in an attack against the St Mihiel salient which proved a complete fiasco. Smaller, yet more significant, was the British attack at Neuve Chapelle on March 10th. Save as a pure experiment the attempt stood self-condemned. For it was an isolated attempt on a small front with inadequate resources. The arrival in France of several new regular divisions – made up from foreign garrisons, of the Indian Corps, and of the 1st Canadian Division, had brought the British strength up to thirteen divisions and five cavalry divisions, besides a number of selected Territorial battalions. This increase enabled French to divide his forces into two armies, and gradually to extend his share of the front. But Joffre was insistent that French should relieve the French of the Ypres salient, which they had taken over in November, and he made the intended French attack contingent on this relief. Sir John French considered that he had not sufficient troops for both purposes, and so decided to carry out the attack single-handed. An additional motive was his resentment of the constant French criticisms that the British were not 'pulling their weight'.

In design, however, the attack, entrusted to Haig's First Army, was both original and well thought out. After an intense bombardment of thirty-five minutes' duration on a 2,000 yards' frontage, the artillery lengthened their range and dropped a curtain of fire to prevent reinforcements reaching the enemy's battered trenches, which were rapidly overrun by the British infantry.

Complete surprise was attained, and most of the first positions captured; but when, in the second phase, the frontage was extended, the artillery support proved inadequate. Further, owing to scanty information and to the two corps commanders waiting upon each other, a long pause occurred which gave the Germans five clear hours to organize fresh resistance. Then, too late and mistakenly, Haig ordered the attack to be pressed 'regardless of loss'. And loss proved the only result. An underlying factor was that the narrowness of the attack sector made the breach more easy for the defenders to close, although this defect was unavoidable owing to the general shortage of munitions, especially heavy guns and high-explosive shell for them.

The British had been slower than the Germans to awaken to the scale of munition supply required for this new warfare. Even so, deliveries fell far behind contract, owing largely to the handicap imposed by trade-union rules on the dilution of skilled labour. These could only be modified after long negotiation, and the shortage of shells became so obvious in the spring of 1915 as to lead to a public outcry initiated by Colonel Repington, the military correspondent of *The Times*, after consultation with Sir John French. Lord Northcliffe, with fearless disregard of the odium, threw the full weight of his newspaper into the campaign which culminated in the establishment of a Ministry of Munitions, under Lloyd George, to coordinate and develop both the supply and the manufacture of raw materials. Although this press campaign failed to recognize some of the major causes of the shortage, as well as the fact that the need was for more heavy guns and not merely for more shells, its general effect was of incalculable value. Nothing else could have so roused the people or cleared away obstructions. Apart from shells, the crudeness and inferiority of all the British trench-warfare weapons, compared with the German, made such a radical reorganization overdue, and its urgency was emphasized by the near approach of the time when Britain's new national armies would take the field. If the task was undertaken late, it was carried out with energy and thoroughness, although improvisation was long in overtaking the evil consequences of earlier neglect. Apart from labour difficulties the immediate fault lay largely with military shortsightedness, which manifested itself in a constant tendency to underestimate needs and underrate novelties.

It is significant that as far back as 1908 the Financial Secretary of the War Office, impressed by an official observer's report of the growing use of machine guns in the German Army, wrote to the Master-General of the Ordnance that 'if the military members of the Council would like to have more machine guns for the Army that at any rate the Finance

Department of the War Office would make no objection'. He received the reply that two machine guns per battalion were enough. And to that scale the War Office authorities stubbornly adhered, although in 1909 the School of Musketry urged an increase to six.

Even when the machine gun had obviously gained a dominance of the battlefield, General Headquarters in France resisted its growth from the puny pre-war scale of two in each battalion. One army commander, Haig, declared that it was 'a much overrated weapon' and that this scale was 'more than sufficient'. Even Kitchener laid down that four were a maximum and any in excess a luxury – until the Ministry of Munitions came to the rescue of the machine-gun advocates and boldly multiplied the scale of provision by sixteen. It was due also to Mr Lloyd George that the Stokes gun, a quick-firing light mortar, had the chance to surmount the official barrier and develop into the outstanding and ubiquitous trench weapon of the war. And later, the Ministry of Munitions succoured the tank when it was repeatedly threatened by the suffocating embrace of the War Office.

Nevertheless the ultimate responsibility for the munition failure lay with the British people, and their representatives in Parliament. Although, before the war came, the new Committee of Imperial Defence had done much preparatory spadework, a strict limit was set to its efforts by the passivity as well as parsimony of Parliament and people in face of the growing danger of war. Preparedness crawled forward to meet the onrushing menace. Most fundamental of all faults was the neglect to organize the industrial resources of the country for conversion and expansion in case of war. While an increase in the fighting forces may, by its air of threat, accelerate the danger of war, readiness for industrial mobilization is unprovocative and, if war comes, a more essential foundation for the power to wage it.

The pre-war neglect is a far graver charge against the Government which declared war on August 4th, 1914, than any failure to increase the army estimates or to introduce conscription. Yet in making that declaration the Government, however conscious of the political and moral issues, appears to have been unconscious that it was dooming the manhood of the nation to a terrible drain of life through want of weapons. It is a moral question how far, in such circumstances, any Government is justified in taking the decision for war and in retaining office. The only excuse lies in the sanction of public indifference to such needs. And unhappily, experience has shown the practical difficulties suffered by a democratic Government which tries to outstrip public opinion. Thus the ultimate responsibility falls on the British people.

Even the military conservatism which obstructed improvements and reorganization during the war may be charged to lack of public concern with the training and selection of officers in peace. In the light of 1914–18 the whole people bear the stigma of infanticide.

No belated wartime spurt could overtake the consequences of pre-war neglect until many thousands of lives had been wasted vainly. Even the Somme offensive was to be hampered by a limited supply of ammunition, while of this much was wasted because of the failure of hastily produced fuses. Not until the end of 1916 did the flow of munitions reach a volume, still expanding, which finally removed any material handicap on the strategy of the British leaders.

The tactical sequel of Neuve Chapelle was less fortunate. It was clear that the small-scale experiment had only missed success by a narrow margin, and that there was scope for its development. But the Entente commands missed the true lesson, which was the surprise attainable by a short bombardment that compensated its brevity by its intensity. And only partially did they appreciate the fact that the sector attacked must be sufficiently wide to prevent the defender's artillery commanding, or his reserves closing, the breach. Instead, they drew the superficial deduction that mere volume of shell-fire was the key to success. Not until 1917 did they revert to the Neuve Chapelle method. It was left to the Germans to profit by the experience against the Russians in May.

But before that occurred, the Western Front was destined to increase the tally of military blunders. In the first, it was the Germans' turn to find and misuse a new key to the trench deadlock. This was the introduction of gas, and, unlike the British introduction of tanks later, the chance, once forfeited, did not return, owing to the relative ease of providing an antidote. On October 27th, 1914, in the Neuve Chapelle sector, the Germans fired 3,000 shrapnel shells containing a nose and eye irritant as well as bullets. This was the first battlefield experiment, but the effect was so weak that the fact was not even known until revealed by the Germans after the war. Then, in a local attack in Poland on January 31st, 1915, the Germans tried the use of improved lachrymatory gas shell, but the experiment was a failure owing to the nullifying effect of the intense cold. At the next attempt the gas was lethal and was discharged from cylinders owing to the failure of the authorities to provide the inventor, Haber, with adequate facilities for the manufacture of shells. Further, the initial disappointment led the German Command to place little trust in its value. In consequence, when gas was discharged against the French trenches at Ypres on April

22nd, there were no reserves at hand to pour through the wide breach it created. A strange green vapour, a surging mass of agonized fugitives, a four-mile gap without a living defender – such was the sequence of events. But the resistance of the Canadians on the flank of the breach and the prompt arrival of English and Indian reinforcements saved the situation in the absence of German reserves.

The chlorine gas originally used was undeniably cruel, but no worse than the frequent effect of shell or bayonet, and when it was succeeded by improved forms of gas both experience and statistics proved it the least inhumane of modern weapons. But it was novel and therefore labelled an atrocity by a world which condones abuses but detests innovations. Thus Germany incurred the moral odium which inevitably accompanies the use of a novel weapon without any compensating advantage.

On the Entente side, wisdom would have counselled a period of waiting until their munition supply had grown and the new British armies were ready, but the desire to regain lost territory and the duty of relieving the pressure on Russia, combined with ill-founded optimism to spur Joffre to premature offensives. The German losses were exaggerated, their skill and power in defence underrated, and a series of diffused and unconnected attacks were made. The chief was by the French between Lens and Arras, under Foch's direction, when the earlier experience of failure to make an effective breach in the trench barrier was repeated. The attack was launched on May 9th by d'Urbal's army (of eighteen divisions) on a four-mile frontage. It was quickly checked with murderous losses except on the front of Pétain's corps which, thanks to meticulous preparation, broke through to a depth of two miles. But the penetration was too narrow, reserves were late and inadequate and the gap closed. Foch, however, persevered with vain attacks which gained a few acres of ground at excessive loss. Meantime Haig's First Army had attacked towards Aubers ridge simultaneously with the larger French attempt. The plan was to penetrate at two points north and south of Neuve Chapelle, four miles apart – the total frontage of the two being two and a quarter miles – and then to converge in exploiting the double penetration. But the Germans, profiting also from the experimental value of Neuve Chapelle, had developed their defences. Thus the attack died away quickly from a surfeit of German machine guns and an insufficiency of British shells. Under pressure from Joffre the attack was renewed on May 15th on the Festubert sector south of Neuve Chapelle, and continued by small bites until May 27th. The larger French offensive between Lens and Arras was not abandoned until June

18th, when the French had lost 102,500 men - nearly double the defenders' loss.

The effect of these attacks was, moreover, to convince even the dubious Falkenhayn of the strength of his western line, and of the remoteness of any real menace from the Franco-British forces. His offensive on the Eastern Front had already opened. Tactically unlimited, its strategic object was at first only the limited one of relieving the pressure on the Austrian front, and, concurrently, of reducing Russia's offensive power. Conrad proposed and Falkenhayn accepted a plan to break through the Russian centre as the best means to this end. In this plan the Gorlice -Tarnow sector between the upper Vistula and the Carpathians was selected as offering the fewest obstacles to an advance and best protection to the flanks of a penetration.

The breakthrough was entrusted to Mackensen, whose Chief of Staff and guiding brain was Seeckt, the man who was to rebuild the German army after the war. Mackensen's force comprised the newly formed German Eleventh Army - made up with eight divisions from the west, and the Fourth Austro-Hungarian Army. The Ypres gas attack and a large cavalry raid from East Prussia were initiated to cloak the concentration on the Dunajec of fourteen divisions and 1,000 guns against a front held by only six Russian divisions. This front was composed of several lines of trenches but not highly fortified. Between the opposing sides there was a wide no-man's-land, as much as two miles across, in which 'the inhabitants were still living in their farms, the cattle pasturing undisturbed' - until the Germans removed these people as a precaution against any leakage of news.

Mackensen's army arrived on the scene and took over its allotted sector during the last week in April, being inserted between two Austrian armies. For his 18-mile front of attack Mackensen had one field gun to every 45 yards, and one heavy gun to every 132 yards. If this was not large by later standards it was ample to solve the problem of breaking *into* a position such as the Russians had organized. The greater problem was that of maintaining the momentum of the advance so as to break *through* the rearward positions before the Russian reserves could arrive and man them. To meet this need Seeckt issued instructions that 'all staffs must strive to keep the advance continuously moving'. No definite daily objectives were to be assigned to corps and divisions 'lest by fixing them the possibility of further progress might be stopped'. 'The quick advance of one part of the front will ease the situation at other parts where there is more resistance ... disposition in depth should enable the success at one place to be extended to a neighbouring front'. This conception of a varying progress coupled with a flexible use of reserves foreshadowed the famous 'infiltration' method of 1918, with its keynote of backing up success instead of trying to redeem local failure. To the further benefit of the Germans Ivanov (the Russian Army Group commander) would not believe reports of the impending attack and was thus caught with his reserves badly placed.

During the night of May 1st the storm troops moved forward across no-man's-land and dug in close to the enemy front line. At 10 AM on the 2nd, after a four hours' intense bombardment had flattened the Russian trenches, the attack was launched and the infantry swept forward through the dust and smoke. 'Here and there loam-grey figures jumped up and ran back, weaponless, in grey fur caps and fluttering, unbuttoned greatcoats. Soon there was not one of them remaining. Like a flock of sheep they fled in wild confusion.' The surprise was complete, the exploitation rapid, and despite a gallant stand on the Wisloka river, the whole Russian line along the Carpathians was rolled up, until on May 14th the Austro-German advance reached the San, eighty miles from its starting point. Russian defeat almost turned into disaster when the San was forced at Jaroslav, but the impetus of the advance had momentarily spent itself and reserves were lacking. A new factor was introduced by Italy's declaration of war against Austria, but Falkenhayn persuaded the Austrian Command, with some difficulty, not to move troops from the Russian front, and to maintain a strict defensive on their Italian frontier, which was secured by the mountain barrier. He realized that he had committed himself too far in Galicia to draw back, and that only by bringing more troops from France could he hope to fulfil his object of transferring troops back there. For this could only be possible when Russia's offensive power was crippled and her menace to Austria removed. Strengthened by these reinforcements, Mackensen attacked again in cooperation with the Austrians, retook Przemysl on June 3rd and captured Lemberg on June 22nd, cutting the Russian front into two separated portions.

But neither Falkenhayn nor Conrad had foreseen such results, and in consequence no arrangements had been made to maintain supplies during so long an advance. Hurried improvisation could not atone for lack of preparation, and the consequent delays allowed the enemy to retire without dissolving, though he left copious drippings.

The Russians, from their vast man-power resources, had almost made good the loss of 400,000 prisoners, so that Falkenhayn's anxiety about the stability of his Austrian Allies led him to yield to Seeckt's insistence and to continue the offensive, although still with limited objects and with one eye on the situation in France. Mackensen's direction was changed, however, from eastwards to northwards, up the wide corridor between the Bug and Vistula, where lay the main Russian forces. In conjunction, Hindenburg was ordered to strike south-east from East Prussia, across the Narew and towards the Bug. Ludendorff disliked the plan as being too much of a frontal attack; the Russians might be squeezed by the closing in of the two wings, but their retreat would not be cut off. He urged once more his spring scheme for a wide enveloping manoeuvre through Kovno on Vilna and Minsk. Conrad took the same view. Falkenhayn opposed this plan, fearing that it would mean more troops and a deeper commitment. And on July 2nd the Kaiser decided in favour of his plan. But the result justified Ludendorff's expectation – the Grand Duke extricated his troops from the Warsaw salient before the German shears could close on him. Falkenhayn, on the other hand, considered that Ludendorff had not put his full weight into the attack. The controversy became bitter. Hindenburg wrote not only to Falkenhayn but to the chief of the Kaiser's Military Cabinet, declaring that his title of Commander-in-Chief on the Eastern Front had become a 'cutting irony'. Falkenhayn unkindly took him at his word, by taking away one of his armies, and forming a fresh group of armies, thus reducing his status.

By the middle of August, 750,000 prisoners had been taken, Poland had been occupied, and Falkenhayn decided to break off large-scale operations on the Eastern Front. Bulgaria's entry into the war was now arranged and he wished to support the combined attack of Austria and Bulgaria against Serbia, as well as to transfer troops back to meet the French offensive expected in September. Yet, in hope of redeeming the lost opportunity and placating his personal opponents, he was led to sanction one more effort to break the Russians. Ludendorff was given belated permission to carry out his Vilna scheme, with such resources as he had, while Conrad planned to strike eastward from Luck in an attempt to repeat 'Gorlice' and cut off the Russian forces south of the Pripet marshes.

Ludendorff's move began on September 9th, Below's army of the Niemen and Eichhorn's Tenth Army forming two great horns which gored their way into the Russian front, the one east towards Dvinsk and the other south-east towards Vilna. The Russians were driven back in divergent directions and the German cavalry, advancing between the horns, far overlapped Vilna and drew near the Minsk railway. But the German strength was slender, and the Russians free to concentrate against this isolated menace. In face of stiffening resistance and shrinking supplies Ludendorff was driven to suspend operations. The crux of the situation was that the Russian armies had been allowed to draw back almost out of the net before the long-delayed Vilna manoeuvre was attempted.

The Austrian offensive did not develop until September 26th, and then failed dismally. Conrad unwisely persisted in renewing it, and, by the middle of October, the Austrians had sacrificed 230,000 men without affecting the general issue. Russia had been badly lamed, but not destroyed, and, although never again a direct menace to Germany, she was able to delay the full concentration of German strength in the west for two years, until 1918. Falkenhayn's cautious strategy was to prove the most hazardous in the long run, and indeed to pave the way for Germany's bankruptcy.

By October, the Russian retreat, after a nerve-racking series of escapes from the salients which the Germans systematically created and then sought to cut off, came to a definite halt on a straightened line, stretching from Riga on the Baltic to Czernowitz on the Rumanian frontier. The Russian armies, however, had gained this respite at a ruinous price, and their Western Allies had effected little in repayment of Russia's sacrifice on their behalf in 1914.

For the Franco-British relief offensive of September 25th had been no more fruitful than its predecessors. The main blow was launched by the French in Champagne, in conjunction with a Franco-British attack in Artois, on either side of Lens. One fault was that the sectors were too far apart to have a reaction on each other, but a worse was that the Command tried to reconcile two irreconcilable factors – they aimed at a breakthrough, but preceded it with a prolonged bombardment which gave away any chance of surprise. Joffre's plan was that the breakthrough in these two sectors was to be followed by a general offensive on the whole Franco-British front which would 'compel the Germans to retreat beyond the Meuse and possibly end the war'. The unquenchable optimist! Both in Champagne and Artois the attacks penetrated the German forward positions without difficulty, but subsequent delay in bringing reserves forward allowed the German reserves to close the gaps, a task simplified by the narrowness of the frontage of attack. The slight gains of ground in no way compensated for the heavy price paid for them – the Allied loss was approximately 242,000 against 141,000 Germans. And if the Allied Commands had gained more experience, so had the Germans, in the art of defence. The British share in this offensive is, however, notable as marking the appearance in strength of the New Armies; at Loos they were 'blooded', and if inexperience detracted from their effectiveness, their courage and driving force were an omen of Britain's power to improvise a national effort comparable with the long-created military machines of the Continent.

The direction of this effort inspired less confidence, and Sir John French gave place to Sir Douglas Haig as Commander-in-Chief, just as already in September the Russian Command had been transferred from the Grand Duke Nicholas, nominally to the Tsar, as a moral symbol, but actually to General Alexeiev, the new Chief of Staff.* Simultaneously, French's Chief of Staff, William Robertson, who had been long slighted by him owing to Henry Wilson's stronger influence, went home to become Chief of the Imperial General Staff, in order to give a stronger direction to the general strategy of Britain – if also to give it a Western Front bias. Somewhat curiously, Haig chose as his own Chief of Staff an old friend, Kiggell, who had not hitherto seen any service in France.

Italy's First Campaign. Italy's military contribution to the Allied balance sheet of 1915 was handicapped not only by her unreadiness, but by the awkward strategic position of her frontier, difficult for initiating an offensive and hardly more favourable for a secure defensive. The Italian frontier province of Venezia formed a salient pointing to Austria and flanked on the north by the Austrian Trentino, on the south by the Adriatic. Bordering on the Adriatic was a stretch of relatively low ground on the Isonzo sector, but the frontier then followed the Julian and Carnic Alps in a wide sweep round to the north-west. Any advance eastwards inevitably suffered the potential menace of an Austrian descent from the Trentino upon its rear.

Nevertheless the easterly sector, though difficult enough, seemed to offer more prospect of success – besides threatening a vital part of Austria – than an advance northward into the Alps. When Italy was preparing to enter the war, General Cadorna, who assumed command, drew up his plan on this basis of an offensive eastwards and a defensive attitude in the north. The overhanging menace of the Trentino was mitigated by the expectation of simultaneous pressure upon Austria from Russia and Serbia. But on the eve of Italy's declaration of war this

---

* General Brusilov, Russia's most successful commander, has described him as 'a fine strategist. His chief fault was indecision and want of moral courage.' 'I consider that had he been the Chief of Staff of a real Commander-in-Chief, he would have been beyond criticism. But with a commander [the Tsar] whose mind he had to make up for him, and whose feeble will he had to strengthen, Alexeiev was not the right man.' Trotsky, more contemptuously, depicts him as a 'grey mediocrity, the oldest military clerk of the Army, worn out through mere perseverance'.

hope faded, the Russian armies falling back under Mackensen's blows, while the Serbs, despite requests from the Allies, failed to make even a demonstration. This lack of pressure enabled the Austrians to dispatch five divisions to the Isonzo from the Serbian front, these being relieved by three newly formed German divisions. Three more divisions were sent from Galicia. Even so there were only some thirteen divisions in all available to oppose the Italians, who had a numerical superiority of more than two to one.

In order to secure good covering positions on the north a limited advance was made into the Trentino, with success, but another into the north-east corner of the frontier salient – towards Tarvis in the Carnic Alps – was forestalled. This local failure was to have unfortunate results later – in 1917, for it left the Austrians with a good strategic sally port into the Tagliamento valley.

Meantime the main Italian advance, by the Second and Third Armies, had begun at the end of May, but out of their total of twenty-four divisions only seven were ready. Bad weather increased the handicap, the Isonzo coming down in flood, and the initial advance soon came to a standstill. The Isonzo front crystallized, like the others, into trench warfare. The Italian mobilization, however, was now complete and Cadorna mounted a deliberate attack, which opened on June 23rd. This first battle of the Isonzo continued until July 7th with little gain to show. A fresh series of efforts after a ten days' pause were hardly more effective, and the front then relapsed into the spasmodic bickering characteristic of trench warfare, while Cadorna made preparations for a new and larger effort in the autumn. When it was launched in October he had a two-to-one superiority in numbers, but was weak in artillery. This defect, coupled with the superior experience of the defender, rendered the new offensive as barren as its predecessors. It was sustained too obstinately and, when finally broken off in December, the Italian loss in the six months' campaign totalled some 280,000 – nearly twice that of the defenders, who had shown on this front a fierce resolution which was often lacking when they faced the Russians.

The Conquest of Serbia. While stalemate, although with marked changes beneath the surface, had once more settled in on both the Russian and French fronts, the later months of 1915 witnessed fluid operations elsewhere which were to have an unforeseen influence on the war.

One of the most remarkable 'blind spots' in the strategy of the Allies was the failure to perceive the importance of Serbia as an irritation, and consequent distraction, to the Austro-German alliance in a most sensitive region. Such a menace to uneasy Austria's rear flank was an invaluable distraction to the forces and plans of the enemy alliance as a whole. It was, indeed, a necessary distraction if Serbia's allies were to concentrate with effective results in the main theatres. Geography made Serbia a potential 'Austrian ulcer', at a politically and militarily tender spot. To maintain the irritation, quality rather than quantity of aid was needed. Not the dispatch of large Allied forces, which could scarcely be supplied until communications were improved; but the provision of technical troops and material. The Serbs themselves were magnificent fighting troops, and naturally suited to the terrain: what they required were the means of fighting effectively. To provide these was a far more urgent, and more economic, step than to equip the newly raised armies of Britain. By neglecting it the Allies allowed their Austro-German opponents to operate on and excise the ulcer: this blindness was the source of wider, and widening, trouble to themselves.

Austria had proved capable of holding the Italians on the Isonzo, and once the Russian danger began to fade under the pressure of the summer offensive, her Command was anxious to deal conclusively with Serbia. Austria's attempted invasions in August and September, and again in November, 1914, had been brusquely repulsed by Serbian counterstrokes, and it was not pleasant for a great power, especially one with so many Slav subjects, to swallow such military rebuffs. Her impatience coincided with Falkenhayn's desire to gain direct railway communication with Turkey, hard pressed at the Dardanelles. Throughout the summer the rival coalitions had been bidding for Bulgaria's support, and in this bargaining the Entente suffered the moral handicap of military 'failure, and the material handicap caused by Serbia's unwillingness to give up any part of Macedonia – of which she had despoiled Bulgaria in 1913. As Austria had no objection to offering territory that belonged to her enemy, Bulgaria accepted her bid. This accession of strength enhanced the chance of a decision against Serbia, and in August Falkenhayn decided to reinforce the Austrian Third Army with Gallwitz's army from the Russian front. In addition two Bulgarian armies were available. Mackensen and Seeckt were sent to direct the operations. To meet this new threat Serbia, apart from her own relatively small forces, had only a treaty guarantee of Greek aid and promises from the Entente Powers. The first disappeared with the fall of Venizelos, the pro-Ally Greek Premier, and the second, as usual, were too late.

On October 6th, 1915, the Austro-German armies attacked southwards across the Danube, with a flanking movement across the Drina on the right. The sturdy resistance of the Serbs in delaying actions and the natural difficulty of the mountainous country checked the advance but before Franco-British reinforcements could arrive the Bulgarian armies struck westwards into southern Serbia, across the rear of the main Serbian armies. This drove a deep wedge between the Serbs and their Allies, moving up from Salonika, and automatically loosened the resistance in the north. With their line bent at both ends until it resembled a vast bow, threatened with a double envelopment, and with their retreat to the south cut off, the Serbian armies decided to retire west through the Albanian mountains. Those who survived the hardships of this mid-winter retreat were conveyed to the island of Corfu, and after being re-equipped and reorganized, joined the Entente force at Salonika in the spring of 1916. The conquest of Serbia – though not, as it proved, of Serbian military power – relieved Austria of danger on her southern frontier, and gave Germany free communication and control over a huge central belt from the North Sea to the Tigris. For the Entente this campaign dug a military sump-pit which for three years was to drain their military resources, there to lie idle and ineffective. Yet ultimately that sump-pit was to overflow and wash away one of the props of the Central Alliance.

The Salonika Expedition. When at the beginning of October the Entente Governments had awakened to Serbia's danger, British and French divisions had been dispatched hurriedly from Gallipoli to Salonika, which was the only channel of aid to Serbia – by the railway to Uskub. The advanced guard of this relieving force – which was under the command of General Sarrail – pressed up the Vardar and over the Serbian frontier, only to find that the Bulgarian wedge had cut it off from the Serbians, and it was forced to fall back on Salonika, pursued by the Bulgarians. On military grounds an evacuation of Salonika was vigorously urged by the British General Staff, but political reasons induced the Allies to remain. The Dardanelles failure had already diminished their prestige, and by convincing the Balkan States of German invincibility had induced Bulgaria to enter the war and Greece to break her treaty with Serbia. To evacuate Salonika would be a further loss of prestige, whereas by holding on the Allies could check German influence over Greece, and maintain a base of operations from which to aid Rumania, if, as expected, she entered the war on their side. To this end the Salonika force was augmented with fresh British and French divisions, as well as contingents from Italy and Russia, and there also the rebuilt Serbian army was brought. But apart from the capture of Monastir in November, 1916, and an abortive attack in

April, 1917, the Entente forces made no serious offensive until the autumn of 1918. Its feeble effect was partly due to the natural difficulties of the country in the form of mountain ridges guarding the approach to the Balkans, partly to the feeling of the Allied Governments that it was a bad debt, and partly to the personality of Sarrail, whose conduct and reputation for political intrigues failed to command the confidence and cooperation essential if such a mixed force was to 'pull its weight'. On their side the Germans were content to leave it in passivity, under guard of the Bulgarians, while they steadily withdrew their own forces for use elsewhere. With gentle sarcasm they termed Salonika their 'largest internment camp', and with half a million Allied troops locked up their gibe had some justification – until 1918.

Mesopotamia. Nor was Salonika the only 'drain' opened in 1915. Mesopotamia was the site of a fresh diversion of force from the centre of military gravity, and one which could only be excused on purely political grounds. It was not, like the Dardanelles and Salonika, undertaken to relieve a hard-pressed ally, nor had it the justification of the Dardanelles expedition of being directed at the vital point of one of the enemy states. The occupation of Mesopotamia might raise British prestige, and it might annoy Turkey, but it could not endanger her power of resistance. Although its origin was sound its development was another example of 'drift' due to the inherent faultiness of Britain's machinery for the conduct of war.

The oilfields near the Persian Gulf were of essential importance to Britain's oil supply, and thus, when war with Turkey was imminent, a small Indian force of one division was dispatched to safeguard them. To fulfil this mission effectively it was necessary to occupy the Basra vilayet at the head of the Persian Gulf, in order to command the possible lines of approach.

On November 21st, 1914, Basra was captured, but the rising stream of Turkish reinforcements compelled the Indian Government to add a second division. The Turkish attacks in the spring of 1915 were repulsed, and the British commander, General Nixon, judged it wise to expand his footing, for greater security. Townshend's division was pushed up the Tigris to Amara, gaining a brilliant little victory, and the other division up the Euphrates to Nasiriya. Southern Mesopotamia was a vast alluvial plain, roadless and railless, in which these two great rivers formed the only channels of communication. Thus a hold on Amara and Nasiriya covered the oilfields; but Nixon and the Indian Government, inspired by these successes, decided to push forward to

Kut-el-Amara. This move led the British 180 miles farther into the interior, but had a partial military justification in the fact that at Kut the Shatt-el-Hai, issuing from the Tigris, formed a link with the Euphrates by which Turkish reserves might be transferred from one river line to the other.

Townshend was sent forward in August; he defeated the Turks near Kut, and his cavalry carried the pursuit to Aziziya, halfway to Baghdad. Enthusiasm spread to the Home Government, anxious for a moral counterpoise to their other failures, and Nixon received permission for Townshend to press on to Baghdad. But after an indecisive battle at Ctesiphon, the growing superiority of the Turkish strength compelled Townshend to retreat to Kut. Here, isolated far from help, he was urged to remain, as several fresh divisions were being sent to Mesopotamia. Kut was invested by the Turks on December 8th, 1915, and the relieving forces battered in vain against the Turkish lines covering the approach on either bank of the Tigris. The conditions were bad, the communications worse, the generalship faulty, and at last on April 29th, 1916, Kut was forced to surrender. However unsound the strategy which dispatched Townshend on this adventure, it is just to emphasize the actual achievements of his small force in face of superior numbers. With inadequate equipment and primitive communications, and utterly isolated in the heart of an enemy country, it wrote a glorious page of military history. When these handicaps are compared with the four-to-one superiority in number, and highly organized supply system of the force which ultimately took Baghdad, the comparison explains the awe in which Townshend and his men were held by the Turks.

The Home Front, 1915. Perhaps one of the most significant landmarks in the transition of the struggle from a 'military' to a 'national' war was the formation of a National Ministry in Britain, which occurred in May, 1915. For the prototype of Parliaments to abandon the deep-rooted party system and pool the direction of the war was proof of the psychological upheaval of traditions. The Liberal Prime Minister, Asquith, remained, but the Conservative element acquired a preponderant voice in the Cabinet, although the dynamic personality of Lloyd George began to gain such a hold on public opinion that the real leadership slipped into his hands. Churchill, whose vision had saved the menace to the Channel ports and made possible the future key to the deadlock, was shelved, as already had been Haldane, the creator of the Expeditionary Force.

Political changes were general in all countries, and were symptomatic of a readjustment of popular outlook. The early fervour had disappeared, and been repulsed by a dogged determination which, if natural to the British, was in strange contradiction to popular, if superficial, conceptions of the French temperament.

Economically, the strain had yet to be felt severely by any country. Finance had shown an unexpected power of accommodation, and neither the blockade nor the submarine campaign had seriously affected food supply. If Germany was beginning to suffer some shortage, her people had more tangible omens of success to fortify their resolution than had their enemies. In 1916, however, the strain on them was to be intensified by the failure of the 1915 harvest – the worst for forty years. Fortunately for Germany's powers of endurance the danger was to be relieved, and the British blockade partly nullified, by the inexpensive capture of a wheat-growing country on the Eastern Front. Ironically, the enemy were to throw Germany this lifebuoy, by encouraging Rumania to enter the war, after Falkenhayn had almost drowned the war-will of the German people in a bath of blood and tears by his renewed offensive on the Western Front.

CHAPTER FIVE

SCENE 1

The Birth of a 'Plan' –
the Dardanelles

A giant, three ships, and the fear of a rape were the main factors in bringing Turkey into the war against her traditional ally, Britain. The giant was Baron Marschall von Bieberstein, who for fifteen years, until 1912, was German Ambassador at Constantinople. To a race whose sole criterion of conduct and admiration was might, whose 'chivalry' was only extended to the mighty, Marschall von Bieberstein's huge frame, scarred face and trampling manner formed a living picture of the growing power of Germany. Perhaps one man alone could have counteracted the impression with that of Britain's more mature and quieter strength. This man was Kitchener, who, curiously, seems to have felt an ungratified desire for the post. Instead, the British Ambassador during the critical years was one from whose personality the requisite prestige and strength were absent – and who, during the critical weeks, was even absent on leave.

The ships were the new German battle cruiser *Goeben*, and the British-built battleships *Sultan Osman* and *Reschadieh*. A shrewd step to enhance German prestige and weaken the one remaining foothold of British influence – that of the naval mission – the *Goeben* was sent out early in 1914 to Constantinople and for long lay anchored near the entrance to the Golden Horn. Then, in the war-charged atmosphere of late July, the ever-present Turkish fear of Russian lust for the Dardanelles developed almost to panic point. It was none the less powerful because mingled with Turkish lust for wider dominion. Certain of war between Germany and Russia, uncertain of Britain's entry, and egged on by the Germanophil Enver Pasha, the Turkish Grand Vizier responded to previous German overtures by asking the German ambassador, on July 27th, for a secret alliance against Russia. Next day the proposal was accepted, and on August 2nd the treaty was signed –

unknown to most of the Turkish Cabinet. On the morrow the first mines were laid in the Dardanelles; and Enver had already mobilized the Turkish forces on his own initiative. But the news of Britain's entry into the war was a shock which nearly burst the new treaty like a paper balloon. Indeed, so much 'hot air' was generated during the next few days that it even sufficed to blow out another *ballon d'essai* – the astonishing offer to Russia of a Turkish Alliance. But this offer did not suit Russia's ambition, even though it promised her the one chance of having a channel through which she could receive munitions from her Western allies. She preferred isolation to the sacrifice of her dream of annexation, and did not even report the offer to her allies.

But Turkey's sudden reversal of attitude, and the predominance of her fear of British power over the fear of Russian ambition, were short-lived. And the revival of confidence was greatly helped by annoyance. Turkey, smarting under her wounds of the Balkan war, had been await-ing the delivery of her first two modern battleships with an eagerness and pride all the more general because the money had been raised by collections among the people. On August 3rd, however, the British government informed Turkey that it was taking over the ships – and the announcement caused an explosion of indignation. Every man who had contributed his mite felt an injury akin to a personal betrayal. This popular outcry was at its height when, on August 10th, the *Goeben*, accompanied by the cruiser *Breslau*, appeared at the entrance to the Dardanelles, having slipped past the British fleet near Sicily.

An officer of the German Military Mission, Lieut-Colonel von Kress, brought the news to the War Minister, Enver Pasha, and told him that the forts were asking instructions as to whether they should allow the warships to enter. Then a vital interchange took place. Enver – 'I can't decide that now. I must first consult the Grand Vizier.' Kress – 'But we must wire immediately.' A moment of inward turmoil. Then – 'They are to allow them to enter.' A further and guileful question from Kress – 'If the English warships follow the Germans, are they to be fired on if they also attempt an entrance?' 'The matter must be left to the decision of the Cabinet.' 'Excellency, we cannot leave our subordinates in such a position without issuing immediately clear and definite instructions. Are the English to be fired on or not?' Another pause. 'Yes.' As General Kannengiesser, a German witness of this eventful discussion, says – 'We heard the clanking of the portcullis descending before the Dardanelles.'

International law was evaded, British objections frustrated, Turkish pride satisfied, and Enver's dubious colleagues calmed by arranging the fictitious sale to Turkey of these warships. Turkey was not yet ready for nor agreed upon war, and Britain had every motive to avoid it.

Thus, during the weeks that followed, the Turks were successively enabled and emboldened to advance along the path to war by the passivity of Britain in face of growing provocation. The German crews were kept, the German Admiral appointed to command the Turkish Navy, the British naval Mission removed from control, and then forced to withdraw; British ships were detained, their wireless dismantled; German soldiers and sailors filtered into Constantinople, and the straits were closed. Meantime Turkish ministers, ever ready with glib assurances, congratulated themselves on the gullibility of the British, whose restraint was rather due to an acute sense of vulnerability, as a power with millions of Moslem subjects. Conciliation was pressed to the point of folly, however, when the British Admiralty's intention to appoint Admiral Limpus, ex-chief of the Naval Mission to Turkey, to command the British Dardanelles Squadron was abandoned for fear of giving offence to the Turks! And when the need for conciliation had passed, a misplaced chivalry seems to have taken its place in preventing the use of the one man who knew the Turks and the Dardanelles intimately.

Even the Germans began to be worried when a series of raids on the Egyptian frontier could not goad Britain to war. So the German Admiral, with Enver's connivance, led the Turkish fleet on a raid into the Black Sea against Britain's more sensitive ally, shelling Odessa and other Russian ports. The story of this provocation, as related to and recorded by Lord D'Abernon after the war, is illuminating. The official sanction came to the German Embassy in a sealed envelope addressed to the Admiral. An official took the initiative and precaution to open it and send on merely a copy. The first report that reached Constantinople was that the *Goeben* had been sunk, and so, thinking that the order had sunk with her, the Grand Vizier conciliatingly replied to Russian protests by denying that any such order had been given. Thereupon the German Embassy sent to him, saying – 'The order of which you deny the existence, because you think it was sunk with the *Goeben*, is in a safe place ... at the German Embassy ... Pray cease to deny that the Turkish government has given the order to attack Russia.' Thus the war-fearing Grand Vizier was compelled to stand aside helplessly while German cunning removed any excuse to the Triple Entente for avoiding war – at the end of October.

The best chance for both Britain and Russia was now in making war, instantly. The defences of the Dardanelles were obsolete and still incomplete. The only two munition factories in Turkey lay on the shore close to Constantinople and open to easy destruction by any warships which penetrated thither. The misuse of the opportunity is a tale of almost incredible haphazardness on the part of Britain, of equal short-sightedness on the part of Russia.

On November 3rd the Allied fleet carried out a short bombardment of the outer forts at the Dardanelles, the only use of which was to help the German authorities in trying to overcome Turkish inertia over the defences. They had sunk back into lethargy again when, six weeks later, a British submarine gave a fresh alarm and gained its commander a VC by diving under the mines and sinking a ship near the Narrows. But the effect of these warnings has been overrated. Turkish lethargy was almost as boundless as British folly. Not until the end of February did the Turks post more than one division on the Gallipoli peninsula, and not until March did the improvements in the defences of the straits approach completion. In part, this state of weakness seems to have been due to a feeling that it was waste of energy to try to prevent a passage, which could not be prevented against any serious attempt. If the few well-informed experts, German or Turk, were dubious of their power to stop a purely naval attack, they were still less confident of resisting a combined attack. And the Turkish staff history frankly says: 'Up to 25th February, it would have been possible to effect a landing successfully at any point on the peninsula, and the capture of the straits by land troops would have been comparatively easy.'

At one time the Entente might have found such troops, in quantity, without touching their own resources. For in mid-August the Greek Prime Minister, Venizelos, had formally and unreservedly placed all his country's forces at the disposal of the Entente. The offer was not accepted, owing mainly to Sir Edward Grey's desire to avoid antagonizing Turkey, whose hatred for Greece was stronger than for any other of her adversaries of 1912. But the hope, if not the desire, soon began to fade and before the end of the month Russia asked Greece whether she would send an expedition to help in forcing the Dardanelles. King Constantine agreed, but made the proviso that Bulgaria's neutrality must be assured, to avoid the danger of a stab in the back. The Greek plan, a thorough one, was that 60,000 men should land near the outer tip of the peninsula to take in rear the forts guarding the straits, while another 30,000 landed near Bulair to seize and hold the isthmus; but, by the time Turkey entered the war, Constantine had withdrawn his reluctant consent, believing that Bulgaria was already pledged to Germany.

In England the only leader who showed a consistent appreciation of the importance of opening the Dardanelles was Churchill. From August onwards he frequently tried to arouse the interest of the War Office – which, for several years, had not even made a perfunctory review of the question. Three weeks after Turkey had entered the war he raised it again at the first meeting of the new War Council, but all eyes were still focused on the French front, and he got no support from Kitchener. The Turks were granted a fresh lease of repose. But during December the blankness of the prospect on the Western Front was realized by many in England, and a few in France. Simultaneously the growth of the new armies evoked a natural question as to their use. The two factors combined to freshen, if not to clear, the atmosphere. Suggestions for a new strategic line of approach came from several quarters.

The most definite and practical was contained in a paper of December 29th, written by the Secretary of the War Council, Lieut-Colonel Maurice Hankey, who emphasized the deadlock in France, and, while urging the development of new mechanical and armoured devices to force a passage through the wire entanglements and trenches, suggested that Germany could be struck most easily through her allies, especially Turkey. He advocated the use of the first three new army corps for an attack on Constantinople, if possible in cooperation with Greece and Bulgaria, as a means not only to overthrow Turkey and bring the weight of the Balkans into the Entente scale, but to open communication with Russia. Further advantages would be to bring down the price of wheat and release 350,000 tons of shipping. The argument revealed a grasp of grand strategy, whereas the horizon of most soldiers, especially the highest, was narrowly bounded by tactics.

Sir John French, of course, objected to any effort outside his own command in France, but at this juncture an appeal came from the Grand Duke Nicholas for a British demonstration to relieve the pressure on his forces in the Caucasus. Ironically, this danger had almost passed before his appeal was received. Still more ironically, the emergency had been due to his own objection to spare troops from the main front.

Kitchener's response was to suggest the Dardanelles as the best place for such a demonstration, and also that 'reports could be spread at the same time that Constantinople was threatened'. Fisher now chimed in, to suggest not a demonstration but a combined attack on a large scale, in conjunction with which old warships should be used to 'force the Dardanelles'. He concluded characteristically and prophetically – 'But as the great Napoleon said, "Celerity – without it Failure".' Churchill knew how little hope there was of obtaining troops for a large-scale attack, but eagerly caught hold of the naval possibility. Later in the day, January 3rd, he telegraphed, with Fisher's agreement, to the Admiral on the spot, Carden - 'Do you consider the forcing of the straits by ships alone a practicable operation?' Back came Carden's answer - 'I do not consider Dardanelles can be rushed. They might be forced by extended operations with large numbers of ships.'

Carden's detailed plan was submitted to the War Council on January 13th. The fatal decision was to be taken in a fateful atmosphere. Strategy instead of being the servant of policy had become the master, a blind and brutal master. From many sides there was an urgent call upon policy. Russia was faltering before she had even got into her stride; Serbia had barely escaped a fall; Greece and Rumania were leaning back the more that Bulgaria seemed to be leaning forward to grasp Germany's outstretched hand; Italy was sitting on the fence. The one front where troops were available was in France: and there ammunition was not - for the scale of ammunition that would suffice in other theatres would not even make a dent in the trench barrier in France. But strategy, as embodied in Sir John French, balked the desires of policy, and as he was loyally rather than logically supported by Kitchener, the rest of the Cabinet was persuaded by a sense of numb, though not dumb, despair, aggravated by their amateur status. Hence they clutched too desperately at a straw of professional opinion which offered the chance of making bricks without men. And the words in which the decision was formulated was an epitome of their confused thought - 'to prepare for a naval expedition in February, to bombard and take the Gallipoli peninsula, with Constantinople as its objective'. The suggestion that ships were to 'take' a part of the land is delightfully naïve.

A few days later Churchill made an attempt to strengthen his plan by suggesting to the Grand Duke Nicholas that the Russians should co-operate by a simultaneous land and sea attack on the Bosphorus. Strategically, his suggestion was the best possible. Paradoxically, it proved void because the political aspect here dominated the mind of the Russian strategists! Strong as was their desire to possess Constantinople, they had no wish to cooperate with their allies in gaining it. The corner-stone of Russian policy was the annexation of both Constantinople and the Dardanelles. Sazonov, the Foreign Minister, had tried to make this claim more palatable to his allies by suggesting the internationalization of Constantinople in return for Russian control of the straits, but the weight of military opinion had overborne this partial concession. Thus it is not surprising that military Russia viewed with jealousy and suspicion any move of her allies towards her own goal, and withheld her assistance. Even Sazonov records – 'I intensely disliked the thought that the straits and Constantinople might be taken by our allies and not by the Russian forces ... when the Gallipoli expedition was finally decided upon by our allies ... I had difficulty in concealing from them how painfully the news had affected me.' Russia would not help even in helping to clear her own windpipe. She preferred to choke rather than disgorge a morsel of her ambition. And in the end she was choked – the verdict should be *felo de se*.

In England, too, fresh complications arose. Churchill's quarrel with the plan was that the scale was too petty; Fisher's, that it might become too large – and so obstruct his Baltic project. And from this divergence a quarrel developed between the two – the political and the professional heads of the Admiralty. At the next War Council meeting Fisher rose to tender his resignation, but Kitchener intervened and, drawing him aside, persuaded him to fall in with the general opinion of the meeting. Thus the compromise plan was a compromise even in its acceptance. Most apt is the verdict of General Aspinall-Oglander in his official history – that operations on the Western Front were a gamble with pounds for a possible gain of pence, whereas in the east 'pence were to be wagered in the none too sanguine hope of winning pounds'.

The naval attack began with the bombardment of the outer forts on February 19th – curiously, the anniversary of Admiral Duckworth's successful attempt to pass through the straits, in 1807. Five days of bad weather then intervened and, when the bombardment was renewed on the 25th, the forts were outranged and the Turks retired from them. Next day the fleet began the second phase, the crushing of the intermediate defences – more difficult because these, being inside the mouth of the straits, were more difficult targets to observe. Although results were disappointing, the chance was taken to land demolition parties, on the tip of the peninsula, which destroyed the guns in the abandoned outer forts. Thereby history, at least, gained a dramatic comparison. For on the same spot where this handful of marines moved about freely on February 26th, thousands of men fell two months later. Further landings were made next day, and again on March 3rd, but on the 4th they met slight opposition, and were re-embarked.

Meantime, the bombardment continued in rather desultory fashion – due in part, but not wholly, to the bad weather – and trawlers made a few rather feeble attempts to sweep the first minefield. Lack of aircraft to observe and correct the shooting was, however, a great handicap, and on the 9th Carden reported that he could do not more until his air service was reinforced, and would meanwhile concentrate on clearing the minefield.

But the weeks were slipping away and the Admiralty could not help feeling that Carden's caution was disproportionate to the importance of his task – and of speed in his task. Hence, on March 11th a telegram was sent to urge him to decisive action, and to free him from any fear of being held responsible if serious loss ensued. Carden responded at once and arranged a general fleet attack, under cover of which the mines were to be cleared. And the principle governing the attack was to be that the battleships should only move in, and fire from, waters clear or already cleared of mines. At this point Carden fell sick and was succeeded by his second-in-command, de Robeck.

The attack was begun on March 18th and was foiled not by resistance but by inadvertence; for, evading the British destroyer patrols, a little Turkish steamer had laid a new line of mines well outside the main minefield, dropping them parallel to the shore in Eren Keui Bay, where the Allied fleet had taken up its position in earlier bombardments. This new line of mines lay undiscovered and unsuspected while the fleet advanced past it to engage the forts. By 1.45 PM the forts had been practically silenced, with little damage to the battleships, and the minesweepers were now sent forward to clear the main minefield, while the French Battle Squadron, in the van, was temporarily withdrawn. As this squadron was retiring through Eren Keui Bay, a tremendous explosion was heard, and a dense cloud of smoke seen, in the *Bouvet*, and in less than two minutes she had heeled over and sunk with nearly all her crew. But the relieving line of battleships continued the attack from closer ranges and the fire from the forts, momentarily renewed, became more and more flickering as guns were buried in rubble and telephone wires cut. Suddenly, however, about 4PM, the *Inflexible* and *Irresistible* were seen almost simultaneously to have a heavy list. Mystery accentuated the moral effect.

No one suspected the presence of the new line of mines, and guesses as to the cause ranged from that of a shoal of floating mines, turned loose to drift down with the current, to that of torpedoes fired from some hidden point on shore. Fear of the unknown prompted Admiral de Robeck's decision to order a general retirement forthwith, and even as this was in progress the *Ocean*, sent to the *Irresistible*'s aid, struck the same line of mines, and both foundered during the night. Although the whole British fleet lost only sixty-one men in casualties, the loss in material was large, for out of the eighteen Allied battleships three had sunk and three more were badly damaged. But a far worse loss was that of nerve and of imagination – to see the enemy's side – among the naval authorities. Actually, the enemy were suffering greater depression, and with more reason. More than half their ammunition had been expended and they had no reserve of mines. Many of the gun crews were demoralized, and the widespread opinion among both Turkish and German officers was that they had little hope of opposing a renewal of the attack.

But that attack, contrary to their expectation, was never renewed. When he came out of action de Robeck had the full intention of renewing it, and so had the Admiralty, which informed him that five more battleships were being sent out to replace his losses, and added that it was 'important not to let the forts be repaired, or to encourage the enemy by an apparent suspension of the operations'. But on the 23rd he sent a telegram which not only revealed his reversal of view but reversed the opinion of the Admiralty – except Churchill, who had to bow to the weight of professional opinion. For de Robeck's new opinion was that the fleet could not get through without the help of the army, and that any further effort must be postponed until this was ready. And, in practice, this opinion meant that the navy was to hand over the whole offensive burden to the army, and to stand by, watching, while the army spent itself in vain assaults unaided by any fresh naval attack. Perhaps the underlying factor was that service tendency of mind which sentimentally values things more than lives, a tendency which may have its foundation in totemism, but is also accentuated by the peacetime shortage of material and the penalties attached to any loss of it. The artilleryman's love of his guns, and readiness to sacrifice his life to avert the disgrace of losing them, is paralleled by the sailor's adoration of his ship, even an old and obsolete ship such as these at the Dardanelles. It hinders him from adopting the common sense view that a ship, like a shell, is merely a weapon to be expended profitably. Perhaps, also, a powerful auxiliary factor in the sailors' decision was now the presence of soldiers and their willingness to assume the burden.

For, coincidently with the preparations for a naval attack, the British government had drifted independently towards a land attack. It had its origin, not in a wider consideration of the Dardanelles problem, but in a separate consideration of where the new armies could be used as an alternative to France. The committee reported in favour of Salonika, as an immediate aid to Serbia and an ultimate stab in the back to the Central Powers – up the Danube. The opinion won favour at the meeting of the War Council on February 9th, being reinforced by the news that Bulgaria had contracted a loan with Germany and by the desire of encouraging Greece to support Serbia. And Kitchener, who had declared that he could find no troops for the Dardanelles plan, now announced that he would send the Regular 29th Division to Salonika, in conjunction with a French division. The promise of two divisions, however, was naturally not enough to allay Greek misgivings; Greece was unwilling to accept the offer unless Rumania was persuaded to join, and Rumania was held back by the sight of Russia's misadventures.

But the fact remained, and could no longer be hidden from the Cabinet by Kitchener's veil of mystery and authority, that the 29th Division was available. Nor did he for the moment seek to withhold it. In consequence the War Council, on February 16th, decided that it should be dispatched to the centrally placed harbour of Mudros in the Aegean 'at the earliest possible moment, together with troops from Egypt', with the idea that 'all the forces [were] to be available in case of necessity to support the naval attack on the Dardanelles'. No one, however, suggested that the naval attack should be postponed to obtain surprise and the greater effect of a combined operation. The troops were merely to mount guard over what the navy gained.

But the 29th Division immediately became the rope in a tug-of-war between the 'Eastern' and 'Western' schools of thought, and on to the western end were pulling not only the British headquarters in France, but Joffre. Joffre's foresight was always, and only, quick when his own preserves were threatened, and he saw in the dispatch east instead of west of the newly assembled 29th Division a disquieting omen of the destination of the new army divisions. Kitchener could easily have hardened his heart against French, but he could not against the French. Just as his loyalty to France was an earlier instinct than his love of the east, so it now proved stronger than his belief in the eastern theatre. At the next meeting of the War Council, only three days later, he turned about face and asserted that the 29th Division could not be spared. In its place he suggested the dispatch of raw Australian and New Zealand troops, two divisions from Egypt. And he even notified the Admiralty behind Churchill's back that the 29th was not to go, thereby interrupting the collection of the transports required to carry it.

That same day the naval attack had opened – and the bombardment echoed throughout the Near East. When the news came, that the outer forts had fallen, the Turkish government made ready to flee into the interior of Asia Minor. The Germans expected not only the appearance of the Allied fleet off Constantinople but that its appearance would be the signal for a revolt against Enver, and the consequent signature of peace by Turkey. For the Turks, in any case, could not have carried on the war once Constantinople, their only munition source, was abandoned. Italy and Greece began to incline more strongly towards war, and Bulgaria away from it. On March 1st Venizelos proposed to land three Greek divisions on the Gallipoli peninsula – but here Russia fatally intervened by notifying Athens that 'in no circumstances can we allow Greek forces to participate in the Allied attack on Constantinople'.

Only the neutral part of these favourable echoes reached the War Council in London, but it was sufficient to encourage the believers and win over the doubters. The original idea that the naval attack was only tentative, to be abandoned if found difficult, now faded and all save one were agreed that the attack must be carried through, if necessary with land forces. The one dissenting voice was that of Lloyd George, who objected to the Army having 'to pull the Navy's chestnuts out of the fire'. Curiously, he alone sounded the warning truth of history that the renewal along the same line of an attack that has failed is rarely justified, and that it is better to switch the effort in a fresh direction. If his just objection was not immediately justified it was because of the Turks' lethargy in profiting by their warning.

In contrast, Kitchener laid down emphatically that 'having entered on the project of forcing the straits there can be no idea of abandoning the scheme'. But not until March 10th did he make up his mind to release the 29th Division and, perhaps worse, not until the 12th did he nominate a commander for the expedition. Yet the French, despite Joffre's refusal to contribute from the field armies, had scraped together a division from the interior and had begun to embark it as early as the 3rd. At the War Office in London not a single preparatory step had been taken. One result was that when Ian Hamilton departed on the 13th none of his administrative staff were available, and he had to leave without them. Further, the sum of his information comprised a 1912 handbook of the Turkish army, a pre-war report on the Dardanelles forts, and an inaccurate map! To compensate for this deficiency some of his staff had scoured the book-sellers for guidebooks to Constantinople.

The one swift action in this halting period was Ian Hamilton's passage out to the Dardanelles. A chain of special trains and fast cruisers whisked him thither faster than he could have travelled in peacetime by the Orient Express, and he reached the fleet on March 17th – the eve of its attack. His first discovery was the unsuitability of Lemnos as a base, owing to lack of water, as well as lack of piers and shelter in Mudros harbour. His second, was that the troops already present were so ill distributed in their transports that they would have to be disembarked and redistributed before they could land on an open and hostile shore. Hence his first step, on the 18th, had to be the unfortunate one of changing his base to Alexandria and directing all transports there. So ill-conceived and chaotic had been the original loading that battalions were separated from their first-line transport, wagons from their horses, guns from their ammunition – and even shells from their fuses. One infantry battalion of the 29th Division had actually been split up among four ships. Even with the ample wharfs and camps of Alexandria, unloading and reloading was a slow business, not accelerated by the delayed arrival of the administrative staff.

On March 22nd, after the naval attack and before sailing for Alexandria, Ian Hamilton with his chief assistants met de Robeck in conference. 'The moment we sat down de Robeck told us he was now clear he could not get through without the help of all my troops.' Soldiers could not argue with a naval verdict, even had they any wish, and so without discussion the Army was committed to the task. And the task was committed to the Army. For although Ian Hamilton politely suggested to the Admiral that he should 'push on systematically' with the attack on the forts, and Churchill made similar representations, the Admirals both at the Admiralty and at the Dardanelles were as rigid as rock in passive resistance, and henceforth the fleet was dedicated to what Churchill has aptly termed the 'No' principle – an 'unsurmountable mental barrier'. Sired by strategic confusion and dammed by naval negation, the landing on Gallipoli was born – and marred in delivery by muddled military midwifery. From this welter only one clear note emerged, in a memorandum drawn up for the Prime Minister by Maurice Hankey on March 16th. In it he emphasized that 'combined operations require more careful preparation than any other class of military enterprise. All through our history such attacks have failed when the preparations have been inadequate, and the successes are in nearly every case due to the most careful preparation beforehand. It would appear to be the business of the War Council to assure themselves, in the present instance, that these preparations have been thoroughly thought out'. He pointed out that surprise had already been forfeited and in consequence the task had become far more formidable. Hence he enumerated a comprehensive list of practical points upon which the War Council should cross-examine the naval and military authorities, saying, in conclusion – 'Unless details such as these ... are fully thought out before the landing takes place ... a serious disaster may occur.' It may occur to the historian that Hankey was the only expert adviser of the British government who had thought out the foundations of strategy. For when the Prime Minister, loth to question Kitchener's omniscience, tentatively asked if any scheme had been worked out, Kitchener replied, that 'that must be left to the commanders on the spot', and thereby shut down all discussion. No heed was given to the wider aspects of the plan – its immediate and potential needs in men, guns, ammunition, and supplies. In consequence, the expedition was to live from hand to mouth, nourishment being always too small and too late, yet in sum far exceeding what would originally have sufficed for success.

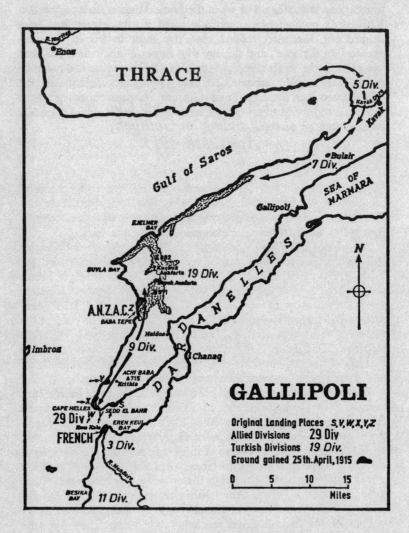

THRACE

5 Div.
Kavak Dgh
Kavak

Gulf of Saros

●Bulair
7 Div.

Gallipoli

SEA OF
MARMARA

R.KILMER
BAY

992
Kuchuk
Anaforta
19 Div.

SUVLA BAY

Buyuk Anaforta

971

A.N.Z.A.C.
GABA TEPE

●Imbros

Maidos
9 Div.

Chanaq

ACHI BABA
▲715
●Krithia

D
A
R
D
A
N
E
L
L
E
S

→Y
→X
CAPE HELLES
29 Div W
  S SEDD EL BAHR
EREN KEUL
BAY
Kum Kale
FRENCH
3 Div.

R.Mendere

BESIKA
BAY
11 Div.

N

GALLIPOLI

Original Landing Places *S,V,W,X,Y,Z*
Allied Divisions   **29 Div**
Turkish Divisions   *19 Div.*
Ground gained 25th. April, 1915

0   5   10   15

Miles

CHAPTER FIVE

SCENE 2

The Slip Twixt Lip and Cup –
The Landing on Gallipoli,
April 25th, 1915

Despite the chain of folly which preceded it, was there still a chance of success when the belated land attack on the Dardanelles was launched? The verdict of history is affirmative. Part, if not all, of the opportunity forfeited by the British was redeemed for them by the Turks.

The panic caused by the opening of the naval attack, and the feeling that the passage of the Dardanelles could not be prevented, led the Turks to order new military dispositions which, in the words of Liman von Sanders, head of the German Military Mission, 'did away with any defence of the exterior coast of the Gallipoli peninsula with its dominating heights; it did away with the defence of the Asiatic coast at the mouth of the Dardanelles. It was the feeblest imaginable defensive measure.' That it was not put into operation may have been due to Liman von Sanders' protests – with which, however, Enver replied that he did not concur – but was more probably due to pure inertia.

The absence of renewed naval attacks after the failure of March 18th was, rightly, taken as a sign that a land attack was being prepared, and this assurance was confirmed by abundant reports from various Mediterranean ports, especially Alexandria and Port Said. This was the less surprising in that public reviews of the troops were held at Alexandria and Cairo, while at least one member of Ian Hamilton's staff received official letters from home through the ordinary post, addressed 'Constantinople Field Force'. Any chance of secrecy had indeed disappeared, with the necessity of disembarking the force in Egypt.

Thus, on March 25th, Enver was led to form a separate army for the defence of the Dardanelles, and to place it under the command of Liman von Sanders. After a hurried survey Liman exclaimed to his subordinate, Hans Kannengiesser – 'If the English will only leave me alone for eight days.' They left him for four weeks. This month of grace, he records, 'was just sufficient to complete the most indispensable arrangements and to bring the 3rd Division under Colonel Nicolai from Constantinople'. Its arrival brought his strength up to six divisions – six times the strength present on Gallipoli before the naval attack began.

But he found them dispersed 'as coastguards', and his first step was to concentrate them. To do this effectively he had to decide where to expect a landing. The Asiatic coast, where movement and an approach to his rear was easy, he deemed the point of greatest danger. And so he placed two divisions near Besika Bay to cover the line of forts on this side. On the European side he most feared a landing at the neck of the peninsula, near Bulair, where the waters of the Gulf of Saros were separated by a mere three-and-a-half-mile strip from the waters of the Sea of Marmara. A landing here would cut off the defenders of the peninsula from Thrace and Constantinople, although if they did not lose their nerve they might be able to maintain themselves by drawing supplies from the Asiatic side, across the Narrows. This, however, was only a possibility. Near Bulair, therefore, Liman von Sanders posted two more divisions. The two other, and lesser danger points were near Gaba Tepe at the six-mile waist – a low waist – of the peninsula, where a wide valley ran across to Maidos at the Narrows; and near Cape Helles, at the southern end, where the gradual ascent up the slopes of Achi Baba might be swept by the fire of the British fleet. Liman von Sanders distributed one division to guard the whole of the southern part of the peninsula while his remaining division, under Lieut-Colonel Mustapha Kemal, was posted near the waist as a general reserve. The scheme of defence was essentially based on mobility, and to obtain the utmost value from his dispositions, as well as to offset the British ease of sea movement, he concentrated his energy on increasing and improving the roads.

Liman von Sanders' dispositions are the best justification for Ian Hamilton's plan. In this the governing factors were the small size of the British force and its mission. The force comprised only five divisions, 75,000 men to the Turks' 84,000. The object was to open a path for the fleet through the Narrows, not to engage independently in a campaign for big strategic prizes. Kitchener's bare instructions 'strongly deprecated', although without explanation, an advance on the Asiatic side; and there the guns of the fleet could give no support beyond the initial landing. The Gulf of Saros was obviously the most vulnerable strategic point but, as Liman von Sanders himself has pointed out, 'it afforded no direct artillery effect against' the defences of the straits. Moreover, the beaches near Bulair were seen to be strongly prepared for defence, while a landing on the west side of the Gulf would be uncomfortably close to the Bulgarian frontier, and with difficult country to traverse. In either case, a small force would be in danger of being itself attacked in flank and rear from the mainland of Thrace, and so being caught between two devils and the deep sea.

Weighing up these conditions, and his handicaps, Ian Hamilton decided on a dual blow in the southern half of the peninsula. The 29th Division was to land on four beaches at the toe and seize Achi Baba, while the French waited in support, meanwhile sending a regiment to land at Kum Kale on the Asiatic side as a feint and distraction. The two divisions of the Australian and New Zealand Army Corps – whose initials were to enrich both dictionary and history with the word 'Anzac' – were to land north of Gaba Tepe, while the Royal Naval Division made a feint near Bulair.

If the idea of security seems to have dictated the landing at the toe, surprise was to be its effect. And surprise was assiduously sought in manifold ways. Commander Unwin was inspired by the proximity of Troy to make the apt suggestion of reproducing the immortal wooden horse – in this case to be a sea-horse. A collier, the *River Clyde*, was to be run ashore at V Beach and to disgorge troops through large openings cut in its sides. Ian Hamilton himself added another stratagem – which had some parallel to Wolfe's at Quebec – whereby a detachment of two battalions was to be landed farther up the coast at a spot apparently inaccessible, and so unlikely to be defended, whence it could menace the rear of the Turks defending the southern beaches. This spot was christened Y Beach. Further, the French transports were to make a pretence of landing troops at Besika Bay. Ian Hamilton also wished to increase the chance of local surprise, and decrease the risk of loss, by landing at night, even though it meant forgoing the support of the guns of the fleet. But Hunter-Weston, commanding the 29th Division, preferred a daylight landing, to avoid the risk of confusion. He gained his way through the support of naval opinion, which was based on the difficulties of the current. For the Anzac landing, the corps commander, Birdwood, wisely preferred any risk to that of the obvious, and if his landing was to suffer in effect through confusion – which was more due to lack of training than to initial loss of direction in the dark – it escaped the heavy losses of the 29th Division.

By April 20th the preparations for the venture were complete and the troops assembled at Mudros on their transports. The weather, almost continuously unfavourable for several weeks, was both the determining and the most uncertain factor. Not until the 23rd did it allow the scheme to be set in motion. For the mechanism, like an alarm clock, required, and was timed to strike, thirty-six hours from the start of the movement.

On the evening of the 24th eleven transports of the Royal Naval Division sailed for the Gulf of Saros, escorted by warships which opened a slow bombardment at daybreak on the Bulair lines. Towards evening boats were ostentatiously swung out, filled with troops, and began pulling for the shore – to return to the ships as soon as darkness cloaked them. During the night an officer, Lieut-Commander B. C. Freyberg, swam ashore from a boat two miles out and lit flares along the beach. His feat, and its effect, was an outstanding proof that in war it is the man, and not men, who count – that one man can be more useful than a thousand.

For the Gaba Tepe landing, 1,500 men of the covering force were carried in three battleships to the rendezvous five miles offshore. They clambered down into the boats at 1.30 AM just as the moon was sinking. Then, towed by the battleships and followed by seven destroyers with the rest of the covering force, they moved silently inshore until the distance was halved. Here the twelve 'tows', each with a steam picket boat at the head, cast loose and continued the approach. But darkness and the strong current caused the tows to arrive off the beach a mile north of the intended point, and so on a more rugged part of the coast, skirted by precipitous cliffs, seamed with steep gullies and covered with scrub. Day was just breaking when at 4.25 AM, under a scattered and erratic fire from a few small and stupefied posts, the forty-eight boats were rowed across the last fifty yards until they touched bottom. Then, in a headlong rush and scramble, the Australians swept inland. Hardly a man had fallen, but units were badly mixed, and soon became worse. The next contingent landed from the destroyers, suffered rather more, at least on the left, but carried the advance over a mile inland. One small party even penetrated far enough to see the glistening straits beyond and beneath.

The Helles landing was less fortunate, although the opponents were little more numerous. Only two Turkish battalions were present in the whole area south of Achi Baba, and only two of the five selected landing places were covered by wire entanglements and machine guns. These were the central beaches W and V on either side of Cape Helles itself. The British covering force comprised the four battalions of Hare's 86th Brigade, which with an extra half battalion were to land at V, W, and X Beaches; one battalion at S Beach; and two battalions at Y Beach for the threat to the enemy's rear. Thus seven and a half battalions were to be thrown ashore initially, followed by five more of the main body, and ultimately by the French division. At 5 AM, under cover of a heavy fleet bombardment, the tows crept towards the shore. The first mischance was the slow progress, against the current, of the tows making for S Beach, on the east flank, which caused those destined for the three main beaches to be held back until nearly 6 AM. Nevertheless, the tows for X Beach, round the western tip of the peninsula, landed without a casualty beneath a low cliff, where their arrival was unexpected by the Turks and opposed only by a picket of twelve men. But at W, the next beach eastwards, the landing parties ran into a well-prepared death trap. Not a shot was fired as the boats rowed in but, as they grounded, they were swept by bullets and the men, jumping overboard, were entangled in submerged wire. Despite heavy loss they struggled forward, drove off the defenders, and gained a lodgement on the cliffs. But Hare, too gallantly exposing himself, was wounded, and the effort subsided.

The landing at V Beach, beside the old fort of Sedd el Bahr, fared still worse. Here the invaders ran, like gladiators, into a gently sloping arena designed by nature and arranged by the Turks – themselves ensconced in surrounding seats – for a butchery. The tows, checked by the current, were caught up by the *River Clyde*, and as it grounded hell yawned. In the incoming boats oars dropped like the wings of scorched moths, while the boats drifted helplessly with their load of dead and wounded. Many men jumped overboard only to be drowned in water stained with their own blood. A few gained the beach and found shelter beneath a low bank – which was to mark the limit of the day's advance. Those who tried to emerge from the *River Clyde*, and reach the shore across a bridge of lighters, were no more fortunate, and fell in heaps. The few survivors on the beach and the thousand left in the *River Clyde* could only wait for nightfall to release them. Two companies of Turks, distributed between V and W Beaches, had checked the main British landing.

But S Beach, at the other side of Morto Bay, was, like X, an unlikely spot and so guarded by only a platoon of Turks. The landing battalion got safely ashore and then, having had preliminary instructions to await the advance from the other beaches, fulfilled them to the letter. Its inertness, however, was approved by Hunter-Weston, owing apparently to an exaggerated estimate of the Turkish strength. Actually the two intact battalions ashore at the two flank beaches, S and X, totalled four times the strength of the Turkish defenders of V and W Beaches, and by an advance inwards could have taken them in rear.

Soon, also, that superiority was increased – but not the pressure. Two battalions of the 87th Brigade (the other two had been used for the original landings at S and Y) were put ashore safely on X Beach by 9 AM, but they had been earmarked as divisional reserve, and the Brigadier did not feel justified in using them, except to dig in, unless and until he received instructions from Hunter-Weston. These never came, so the force at Beach X remained passive.

Meantime, after another vain attempt to land at V Beach – in which the commander of the 88th Brigade was killed – the remaining two and a half battalions of the main body were disembarked at W Beach. 'But,' as the official history gently says, 'in contrast to the gallant exploits of the morning a certain inertia seems to have overtaken the troops on this part of the front, who now amounted to at least 2,000 men ... Faced with a definite task – the capture of the beaches – the 29th Division had put an indelible mark on history. But once that task was done, platoon, company and even battalion commanders, each in their own sphere, were awaiting fresh and definite orders, and on their own initiative did little to exploit the morning's success or to keep in touch with the enemy.' Instead, they allowed themselves to be paralysed by an enemy 'whom they had already driven from his trenches and whom, though unaware of the fact, they outnumbered by at least six to one'.

But a still greater opportunity was missed at Y Beach, three miles up the coast, where '2,000 men were safely disembarked without a hitch and without any opposition. For eleven hours they were left undisturbed by the enemy, and throughout that period they alone were equal in numbers to all the Turkish forces south of Achi Baba. Yet throughout the 25th the initial success remained unexploited. During the ensuing night the troops gallantly repulsed a succession of fierce attacks on their line. But the whole enterprise was suddenly abandoned next morning, and the men re-embarked, at the very moment when the enemy himself was in full retreat'.

The one man who realized the opportunity was Ian Hamilton himself, out at sea; but he had delegated the execution of the landing to the commander of the 29th Division, and had kept no reserve. Somewhat naturally, he was loth to interfere except by suggestion, though he was far quicker than the man on the spot to appreciate the check in the south, and as early as 9.21 AM he signalled to Hunter-Weston – 'Would you like to get some more men ashore at Y Beach? If so, trawlers are available.' But Hunter-Weston's attention was glued to the bloody beaches where the enemy was better prepared, and there he preferred to concentrate his efforts.

At Y Beach itself the landing had been made without a shot being fired or a Turk being discovered. But the commander, Colonel Matthews, was content to await further orders. 'Crowds of troops were ... sitting about the edge of the cliff', and not until late in the afternoon did they even attempt to entrench. Towards dark one Turkish battalion was brought up and launched a series of counter-attacks against the two British battalions. Repeatedly beaten off, the Turks finally fled in disorder soon after 7 AM; but their night assaults caused such loss and confusion among the defenders that panic spread. A string of alarmist messages were signalled to the ships and many stragglers poured down to the beach, swarming into the boats sent for the wounded. This state continued even after the disappearance of the Turks, and Matthews, who saw no response to his urgent appeal for reinforcements, reluctantly decided to follow the example set by his stragglers. By 11.30 AM the whole force had re-embarked. Some hours later a naval party under Lieut-Commander Keyes went ashore and made a prolonged search for wounded without being fired on.

But if anything can justify Matthews' action, and previous inaction, it is his utter neglect by his superior, Hunter-Weston. Throughout the twenty-nine hours on land 'no word of any kind reached him from divisional headquarters'. No officer was sent to visit him, no reply was sent to his urgent appeals. And when, early in the morning of the 26th Ian Hamilton once more intervened with the offer of a French brigade (six battalions), Hunter-Weston had no thought but to land them on W Beach – in the enemy's face. The measured verdict of the official history upon Y Beach is that – 'In deciding to throw a force ashore at that point Sir Ian Hamilton would seem to have hit upon the key of the whole situation ... it is as certain as anything can be in war that a bold advance from Y, on the morning of the April 25th, must have freed the southern beaches that morning, and ensured a decisive victory for the 29th Division.'

At Anzac, too, a great opportunity went begging, although here the initiative of one opponent, the then unknown Mustapha Kemal, contributed to its unfulfilment. The surprise landing had placed 4,000 men before 5 AM, and another 4,000 before 8 AM, on a shore guarded by only one Turkish company. The next company was more than a mile to the south, two battalions and a battery in local reserve were four miles inland, and still farther away lay the general reserve of eight battalions and three batteries, commanded by Mustapha Kemal. He was out watching a regiment at training, when suddenly a number of gendarmes, bareheaded and weaponless, came running frantically towards

him, crying – 'They come, they come.' 'Who comes?' 'Inglis, Inglis.'
He turned to ask, 'Have we ball cartridges?' 'Yes.' 'All right. Forward.'
Leading a company himself, and leaving the rest of the regiment to
follow, he raced to the great dividing ridge of Chunuk Bair in time
(about 10 AM) to cross the crest and check the leading Australians as
they were climbing up the steeper slopes on the west. Until now barely
500 Turks had been available to hold up 8,000 Australians, but henceforth the defenders were to be augmented steadily until by nightfall six
battalions (perhaps 5,000 men) had been brought up, and from 4 PM
onwards launched in a series of counter-attacks which forced back but
failed to break the ragged Australian line. Both sides had suffered about
2,000 casualties, the Turks far more heavily in proportion, but the raw
Australians were in unknown country, under fire for the first time, and
the moral effect of the shrapnel from the enemy's handful of guns was
made worse by the absence of their own. Although 15,000 men were
ashore by 6 PM, the front was but a thin and much-intermixed line, and
the beach was crowded with leaderless men who had drifted back –
many because they had lost themselves rather than lost their nerve. But
the sight naturally confirmed the fears of the commanders, themselves
in rear, and so gloomy was their report to Birdwood, when he landed at
10 PM, that he sent a message to Ian Hamilton saying – 'Both my
divisional commanders and brigadiers have represented to me that they
fear their men are thoroughly demoralized by shrapnel fire ... If troops
are to be subjected to shell fire again tomorrow morning there is likely
to be a fiasco ... if we are to re-embark it must be at once.' All available boats were ordered to be sent to the beach.

Only by a fluke did the message ever reach the Commander-in-
Chief, for in the hurry it was not addressed to anyone; but, being thrust
into the hands of the beach-master, who was going out to the flagship,
he handed it when there to Admiral Thursby. After reading it, Thursby
decided to go ashore to discuss the re-embarkation with Birdwood, but
at that moment the *Queen Elizabeth*, with Ian Hamilton on board,
unexpectedly arrived from Helles, so that Thursby went instead to report to him. Thus by a chain of happy mishaps Birdwood's grave message reached Ian Hamilton in time.

Insight must have guided him in an extraordinarily difficult decision,
for no other guidance, or comfort, was available, and no time to obtain
it. The reply which he wrote was epitomized in its postscript – 'You
have got through the difficult business. Now you have only to dig, dig,
dig, until you are safe.'

Like a fresh breeze this definite and confident order dispersed the rumour-laden and gloomy atmosphere on the beach. The rear ceased to talk about evacuation and the front did not know that the rear had been talking about it. When morning broke there was also a respite from the real enemy, for Mustapha Kemal had no further reserves with which to renew his counter-attack, and the shrapnel from his few guns was no longer a terror to troops now safely dug in. Indeed, it was the Turk who suffered demoralization – from the guns of the fleet, and especially the huge 15-inch shells of the *Queen Elizabeth*.

Could the lost opportunity still have been regained? History answers, 'Yes.' And the reason lies in the profound impression made, by Ian Hamilton's original plan, on the mind of the enemy Commander-in-Chief. Liman von Sanders records of the first day, April 25th, that – 'From the many pale faces among the officers reporting in the early morning, it was apparent that, although a hostile landing had been expected with certainty, a landing at so many points surprised and disquieted them.' 'We could not discern at the time where the enemy was actually seeking a decision.' The last sentence is an euphemism, for Liman von Sanders actually thought that the place where the British were merely making a bluff was the place where they were seeking a decision. If he kept his head he lost his sense of direction.

His first act was to order his 7th Division to march from the town of Gallipoli to Bulair. His next, to gallop thither himself. And there he stayed while the critical struggle was in progress at the other end of the peninsula. Not until evening would he even spare five battalions, out of his two divisions around Bulair, to go to the real battle zone, and not until over forty-eight hours after the British landing did he release the remainder.

But the extension of the opportunity was of no avail to the British. Partly for want of fresh troops – when so many, in comparison, were locked up in the Western Front safe-deposit. But partly, also, for want of effort from those who had landed. Ian Hamilton's optimism, although justified, was not shared by his subordinate commanders on the morning of the 26th. It was not merely the Anzac force which remained passive. At Helles, Hunter-Weston, appreciating the tiredness of his troops but not the weakness of the enemy, gave up any idea of advancing until French reinforcements arrived. Expecting a Turkish onslaught, and fearing the result, he issued the order, 'Every man will die at his post rather than retire.' So far from attacking, the Turks went back to a new line in front of Krithia. Well they might, for their total strength here up to the 27th was only five battalions, and casualties had reduced them to a real strength scarcely more than the original two.

Not until the 28th was a new attack attempted, and by then the Franco-British force had almost lost its advantage of numbers and suffered the disadvantages of ignorance of the ground, thirst, increased tiredness, besides complicating its task by combining the attack with a right wheel. The small gains were lost to Turkish counter-attacks, and near the coast the line wavered and broke. The danger here was averted by a single shell from the *Queen Elizabeth*. It burst its 24,000 shrapnel bullets right in the midst of the onrushing mass of Turks, and when the dust cleared not a Turk was to be seen. But by nightfall the whole 29th Division was back at its starting point. Meantime the troops at Anzac were reorganizing and making their front secure. But so also were the Turks, and thus the Anzac force was locked in a tiny cell only one and a half miles long and half a mile deep, while the Turk looked down from the 'roof' upon the arrested trespassers.

The almost blank credit side of the Allied balance sheet was now relieved by a Turkish contribution. Urged on by Enver's peremptory order 'to drive the invaders into the sea', Liman von Sanders launched massed bayonet attacks on the nights of May 1st and 3rd. Several thousand dead were heaped as a sacrifice before the Allied front, which was only, and momentarily, endangered in the French sector.

The Turks' forfeit was soon redeemed – by the British. Two brigades were brought from Anzac and a new brigade, of Territorials, came from Egypt. Even so, the Allied force at Helles could only bring a fighting strength of 25,000 against a Turkish strength now raised to nearly 20,000. And, in the issue, it did not even test their strength. The Allied attack arranged for May 6th suffered every possible disadvantage. It was purely frontal, on a narrow three-mile front, against un-located positions, with an extreme shortage of shells, and a shortage of aircraft to observe the fire, at the shortest notice – Hunter-Weston's orders were not issued to brigades until 4 AM for an attack to begin at 11 AM. Once more the control of the battle and the last remaining reserves were handed over to Hunter-Weston by Ian Hamilton – 'All that was left to him', as the official history says, 'of the high office of Commander-in-Chief was its load of responsibility'.

Fatigue rather than resistance foiled the attack. The troops, worn out by strain and lack of sleep, had not even the energy to press on to the slaughter, and they did not even push back the Turks' advanced posts. As the best remedy for lack of rest Hunter-Weston ordered a fresh effort next morning. This was no more effective, except in draining the ammunition almost to zero. So a third attack was ordered for the third morning. In this the loss at least was confined to a smaller circle, by launching four weak battalions of New Zealanders, in daylight, against a position held by nine Turkish battalions. Then Ian Hamilton, finding that three brigades were still in reserve, himself intervened. The whole Allied line was to 'fix bayonets, slope arms, and move on Krithia precisely at 5.30 PM'. This produced heavy casualties, if nothing else. The attacking force had lost a third of its strength in the three days. Thereafter the front of the two small footholds gained by the Allies inevitably relapsed into stagnation, which soon froze solidly as the Turks converted their hasty defences into an organized trench system.

Now, at last, Ian Hamilton was driven to ask for reinforcements, and to awake the Government to his serious need and situation. Hitherto, although conscious of the inadequacy of his force, he had been too loyal to Kitchener, and perhaps too aware of his old chief's arbitrary methods, to worry him by importunate demands. Before leaving England he had been told that 75,000 men would and must suffice, that even the 29th Division was but a temporary loan, and the fact that Kitchener had warned Maxwell, the commander in Egypt, to help him with additional troops, was not communicated to him by Maxwell despite Kitchener's explicit instructions. Lack of ammunition was another handicap, and when he called attention to it the War Office reply merely told him that it was 'important to push on'. Yet, almost simultaneously with his vain three days' attack, May 6th to 8th, in which he could only use 18,500 shells, Haig was expending 80,000 on Aubers ridge in one day – for less result, a far less object, and twice the loss of life. Up to a point, the astonishing feature of Gallipoli was how near Ian Hamilton came to success with his inferior forces and resources.

His oft-criticized choice of landing place could hardly have been improved on if, by supernatural power, he had been able to know the enemy's mind and dispositions. By avoiding the natural line of expectation, the pitfall of commonplace generalship, and by distracting the enemy's attention to that line, he ensured his own troops an immense superiority of force at the actual landing places – although his total force was less than that of the Turks. The enemy commander let his attention be so fixed on Bulair that for forty-eight hours after the British were ashore their immediate opponents were denied adequate reinforcements. This fact is the best answer to the common criticism that Ian Hamilton should have struck at Bulair, a point so obvious to everyone at home that, curiously, it was also obvious to the enemy. Another popular criticism is that Ian Hamilton dispersed his force at too many points and should have concentrated his effort on one small sector. This is answered not only by the 'pale faces' of which Liman von Sanders tells, but by the next three years' experience of this abortive method on the Western Front – experience which was purchased at an infinitely greater cost.

Perhaps, as an alternative landing place, also in the least-defended area, Suvla Bay might have offered the advantages of Ian Hamilton's choice with less disadvantages. But in April accurate information was lacking and exaggerated faith placed in the effect of the naval guns at Helles.

Another reasonable criticism is that the British power of rapid sea movement might have been utilized more fully – to withdraw troops where checked before they were deeply committed and switch them to reinforce the unopposed landings or to fresh points. Thereby the lack of reserves might have been partly compensated through the power to create fresh ones by 'switching'. This, indeed, had been suggested to Braithwaite, the Chief of Staff, on the day before the landing by Captain Aspinall, an officer of the General Staff. He urged that the plan should be adapted to meet the contingency that either or both the landings at Anzac and Helles might fail. An equal or greater fault in the plan was that it failed to provide for partial success, the most probable case in war, and left no 'floating' reserve in the hands of the Commander-in-Chief ready for prompt application at the most promising point ashore. Unhappily, both the plan and the execution suffered from lack of the elasticity which is an essential axiom in war. And the partial success of both landings in the first phase tended to harden the design – until it became hard and stuck fast.

For years controversy has centred round the incubation period of the Dardanelles project, and the plan which was evolved. More depressing is the later revelation of the opportunities thrown away after the force had landed – lost opportunities hitherto obscured by a halo of romance.

CHAPTER FIVE

SCENE 3

The Gas Cloud at Ypres –
April 22nd, 1915

The sun was sinking behind Ypres. Its spring radiance had breathed life that day into the dead town and the mouldering trench lines which guarded it. A month hence the town would be a shell with all the eerie moonlit grandeur of a greater Colosseum. Three years hence it would be merely a vast ant-heap of tumbled ruins. But on that 22nd day of April, 1915, it had merely the dreariness of incomplete abandonment, momentarily relieved by the fragrance of a spring day's sunshine.

As that fragrance faded with the waning sun, even the guns became silent, and an evening hush spread over the scene as if in awed awaiting of a benediction. The hush was false; purely a prelude to the devil's malediction, with organ pealing, censers swinging. At five o'clock a fearful din of guns broke out and heavy shells struck with reverberating crash on Ypres and many villages rarely or never touched before; and to the nostrils of men nearer the front came the smell of a devilish incense. Those nearer still to the trenches north of Ypres saw two curious wraiths of greenish-yellow fog creep forward, spread until they became one and then, moving forward, change to a blue-white mist. It hung, as it had come, over the front of the two French divisions, one Algerian, one Territorial, which joined up with the British, and held the left of the salient. Soon, officers behind the British front and near the canal bridges, were startled to see a torrent of terrified humanity pouring backward. The Africans, nearest the British, were coughing and pointing to their throats as they fled; mingled with them soon came horse-teams and wagons. The French guns were still firing, but at 7 PM these suddenly and ominously became silent.

The fugitives left behind them a gap in the front over four miles wide, filled only by the dead and by those who lay suffocating in agony from chlorine gas-poisoning. Otherwise the two French divisions had

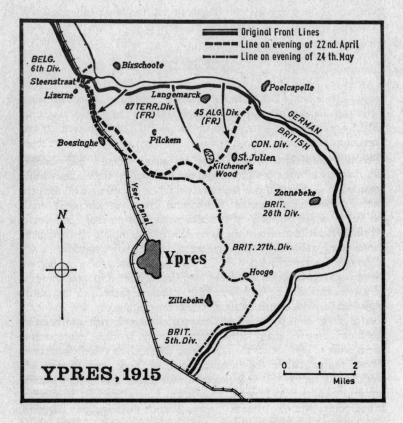

Original Front Lines
Line on evening of 22nd. April
Line on evening of 24th. May

BELG.
6th Div.

Steenstraat
Lizerne

Bixschoote

Poelcapelle

Langemarck

87 TERR.Div.
(FR)

45 ALG. Div.
(FR)

GERMAN

BRITISH

Boesinghe

Pilckem

CDN. Div.

St. Julien

Kitchener's
Wood

Zonnebeke

BRIT.
28th. Div.

N

Yser Canal

BRIT. 27th. Div.

Ypres

Hooge

Zillebeke

BRIT.
5th. Div.

YPRES, 1915

0   1   2
Miles

almost completely disappeared. With the aid of gas the Germans had removed the defenders on the north flank of the salient as deftly as if extracting the back teeth from one side of a jaw. The remaining teeth in front and on the south flank of the salient were formed by the Canadian Division (Alderson), nearest the gap, the 28th Division (Bulfin), and the 27th Division (Snow), which together comprised Plumer's 5th Corps. The Germans had only to push south for four miles to reach Ypres, and loosen all these teeth by pressure from the rear. That evening they walked forward two miles and then, curiously, stopped. The space of four and a half miles between the raw edge of the Canadian front and the canal which formed the chord of the salient, was only filled by a few small posts, taken up hastily by packets of French and Canadians hitherto in reserve, and between these posts there were three untenanted gaps of 2,000 yards, 1,000 yards, and 3,000 yards, respectively. Yet on May 1st the Germans had only advanced a few hundred yards farther. And when the fighting at last died down, at the end of May, the only outward change was that the nose of the salient had been flattened – mainly by a voluntary British withdrawal. But, in curious contrast to normal experience, it was the defenders who had lost most heavily. The British loss was 59,000, nearly double that suffered by the Germans who attacked them.

Why did the gas come as so complete a surprise? Why did the Germans fail to exploit such a surprise? Why did the British escape disaster when taken unawares by the French collapse and yet suffer so disproportionately when the Germans had forfeited their advantage? These are the three crucial questions of 'Second Ypres'.

Towards the end of March, prisoners taken on the south of the salient, then held by the French, gave full details of the way that gas cylinders had been stored in the trenches, and of its method of discharge. Perhaps because they were about to be relieved, the French commanders took no action in regard to this warning, although, curiously, the details appear in the Bulletin of the French Tenth Army, away down in Picardy, for March 30th.

An even more complete and localized warning came on April 13th, when a German deserter gave himself up near Langemarck to the French 11th Division, then holding the sector, and related that 'cylinders with asphyxiating gas [had been] placed in batteries of twenty cylinders for every forty metres along the front'. 'At a given signal – three red rockets fired by the artillery – the cylinders will be opened and the escaping gas will be carried by a favourable wind towards the French trenches ... In order to guard against being poisoned by the gas, each German soldier is in possession of a packet of tow soaked in oxygen' – the deserter handed over one of these embryo gas masks in proof of his statement. The French divisional commander, General Ferry, gravely impressed, warned the French division on his left, the British 28th Division on his right, and the Canadian division – which took over part of his front two days later while the Algerian divison took over the rest. More significant still, Ferry warned his corps commander, Balfourier, and the liaison officer from Joffre's headquarters, who came to visit him.

How did these two key men react? Balfourier deemed Ferry a credulous fool and ignored his suggestions that the German trenches should be shelled in order to destroy the cylinders, and that the number of men in the front line, exposed to the gas danger, should be reduced. The liaison officer not only dismissed the story as a myth, but reproved Ferry, first, for warning the British direct, and, second, for taking steps to reduce the garrison of the front line contrary to Joffre's doctrine. And, following the usual happy custom of the French Army, Ferry was thereafter punished by removal for being right.

General Putz, who, with his two divisions, took over the left of the salient from Balfourier, was no more inclined to believe the story than Balfourier, although a fresh warning came from Belgian sources on April 16th. Putz mentioned the story scoffingly to the British liaison officer from Smith-Dorrien's Second Army, but apparently did not think it worth repeating to his own troops. So they waited in ignorance until suffocation overtook them.

The only measures taken were by the British. Aircraft reconnaissances were made, but failed to observe anything unusual, and Plumer passed the warning to his divisional commanders 'for what it was worth'. No precautions against gas were suggested or ordered, and in the next few days even the fact of the warning was forgotten – perhaps all the easier because it sounded such an 'ungentlemanly' novelty. Yet acquaintance with the German practice of getting in the first verbal blow might well have made the British Command suspect the sinister significance of the German wireless *communiqué* of April 17th – 'Yesterday, east of Ypres, the British employed shells and bombs with asphyxiating gas.'

But one factor which undoubtedly lulled suspicion of an attack was the lack of any sign that the Germans were concentrating reserves for it. This lack of signs was due, not to special precautions, but to the lack of such reserves. And thereby the Germans lost the opportunity created by the most complete surprise of the war.

As scientifically hidebound as its opponents, the German Supreme Command had little faith in the new weapon. So little, that for want of facilities the inventor, Haber, had to use cylinders mainly for projection instead of shells. A discharge of gas from cylinders must be dependent on a favourable wind and, as a westerly or south-westerly wind was the most frequent in Flanders, the Germans thus offered a hostage to fortune. Disclosing their new weapon prematurely and for a paltry prize, they gave their opponents the advantage in retaliation until sufficient gas shell was produced to replace gas cylinders.

However weak their faith, it is incredible, but for the result, that the Germans should have neglected to be ready for a possible success. Yet, actually, Falkenhayn allotted no fresh reserves for the attack, and even refused the request for extra ammunition. Falkenhayn's idea was merely to try the gas as an experimental aid to an attack which itself was merely a cloak to his projected blow against the Russians. If the Ypres salient could be erased, so much the better, but he did not take any longer view.

Originally the attack was to be launched by the XV Corps against the southern side of the salient, and the gas cylinders were in position by March 10th. But the attack had to be postponed repeatedly for want of a favourable wind, and towards the end of March an alternative attack was prepared on the north side of the salient. Intended for April 15th, this in turn was delayed a week. It was then launched by the two divisions of the XXVI Reserve Corps, with one division of the XXIII Reserve Corps attacking on their right. As an aid to the main thrust the other division of the XXIII Reserve Corps was to strike at Steenstraat which was both the hinge of the salient and the junction between the French and the Belgians. Unaided by gas this subsidiary attack made little progress. Only one division was available in army reserve, and this was not released until next day, and was then given to the XXIII Reserve Corps, not to the XXVI, which had an open gap before it.

But if lack of reserves was the fundamental cause of the Germans' failure, the immediate cause was the troops' fear of their own gas. They had only been issued with the crudest form of respirator, which many of them did not even wear; no special tactics had been thought out; and, after passing through the gasping and agonized men who littered the French trenches, they were only too willing to comply with the letter of their limited orders, and dig in as soon as they reached the short-distance objective that had been assigned. The failing light, too, prevented them discovering the extent of their success and the weakness of the few stout-hearted knots of Canadians who were strung across their path. And during the succeeding days they were equally content to act as camp-followers to their artillery, merely taking a short step forward to occupy and consolidate such fresh patches of ground as the guns and gas had swept practically clear of defenders. However shortsighted during the first days, when opportunity lay open to their embrace, this pure siege warfare method was good sense later. It foreshadowed the Verdun method of a year later, and, thanks to Foch, the Allies helped to make it most profitable to the Germans.

Foch was then, as Joffre's deputy, in higher control of the French troops in Flanders, and charged with the duty of coordinating the efforts of the French, British and Belgians. On hearing the news of the German breakthrough, he ordered Putz to make sure of holding his ground, now the line of the canal, and to organize a counter-attack to regain the ground he had lost. But the French had lost their artillery and all they could do was to fulfil the first point. Fortunately, the Belgians baffled the German efforts to break the hinge. Putz, however, told the British that he would be counter-attacking, and to aid him two Canadian battalions made a midnight counter-attack. They penetrated the new German line, and captured Kitchener's Wood, but as no French attack developed they had to withdraw from it later. Next day, the British, scraping together a few handfuls of reserves, attempted further petty counter-attacks which naturally failed at heavy cost, as they were delivered in daylight and with negligible support from the French and from artillery. By evening on the 23rd, however, the broad way to Ypres and the British rear was almost filled, although by only twenty-one and a half sorely weakened British battalions (twelve of them Canadian), who faced forty-two German battalions – and a five-to-one superiority in guns.

Sir John French ordered a continuation of these vain efforts on the 24th – but the Germans anticipated him. At 3 AM they attacked the Belgian 'hinge' and were badly discomfited; henceforth they were unable either to widen or deepen their small foothold across the canal. At 4 AM they launched a heavy blow, with gas, against the jagged corner of the Canadians' front. No respirators were yet available and the only protection were handkerchiefs, towels and cotton bandoliers, wetted with the liquid most readily available in the trenches and placed over the mouth. Many men were overcome and, although there was only a small break in the line at the first onset, this gradually spread. For a time good artillery shooting prevented the Germans probing the breach, but in the afternoon they surged forward to and beyond St Julien. The situation looked critical, but a counter-attack by two Yorkshire Territorial battalions, helped by Canadian batteries firing over open sights, rolled the leading Germans back to St Julien. This slight taste of repulse sufficed to quench the Germans' thirst for further advance that day. But their irresolution was hidden from the eyes of the British commanders by the general confusion. In the patchwork line across the Germans' path, Canadians, British Regulars, Territorials, even Zouaves, of various divisions and brigades, were intermingled, clinging on wherever they had been pushed, like dabs of cement into a crumbling wall. The salient had now been compressed by German pressure into a narrow tongue of land, barely three miles across, although nearly six miles deep. Thus, in attempting to hold it, the defenders were now so crowded that they provided an easy harvest for the German guns.

Yet Sir John French, beguiled by the optimism of Foch and Putz, and the assurance that two fresh French divisions were coming up to retake the lost ground, was unwilling to sanction any withdrawal. Early on the 25th, the day of the Gallipoli landing, a fresh Regular brigade was brought up and thrown blindly into an attack near St Julien, there to be 'mown down like corn, by machine guns in enfilade'. With appalling swiftness 2,400 men were scythed – more loss than Ian Hamilton's army paid for the capture of the Gallipoli beaches. And that evening the bulk of the Canadian division was withdrawn into reserve, having lost some 5,000 men in its gallant efforts to battle against gas and heavy guns with their rifles, supplemented meagrely by guns that the official history terms 'the ancient and obsolete weapons of the South African War'. Nor did the burden of this hopeless struggle cease with the relief of the Canadians; it was merely shifted more fully to other shoulders. For another month operations were to continue, methodical German attacks answered by unmethodical British attacks. Lest I be thought to emphasize the futility unduly, let me quote the sober and sombre words of the official history:

The governing idea was that the French should restore the line lost by them, and that the British should assist ... General Foch ordered immediate counter-attacks which General Putz was not in a position to execute; whilst the British wholehearted attempts to carry out their share by means of offensive action, which was as a rule neither a true counter-attack nor a deliberately prepared attack, led to heavy losses without restoring the situation ... It seemed to the British officers at the front that they were being sacrificed to gain time until the French were ready for a big spectacular effort; but this, even if ever intended, did not materialize.

To study the cause of the tragedy we must shift our gaze from the front to the rear. After expending the Indian Lahore Division and the Northumberland Territorial Brigade in another vain attack on the 26th, with a loss of another 4,000 men, Smith-Dorrien realized the futility of such efforts and the improbability of French cooperation. Hence on the 27th he wrote to Robertson, the Chief of the General Staff, asking him to put the real situation before French, and saying – 'I am doubtful if it is worth losing any more men to regain this French ground, unless the French do something really big.' He further suggested that it would be wise to prepare for a withdrawal to a less acutely bent line nearer to Ypres. All that he got in reply was a telephone message from Robertson – 'Chief does not regard situation nearly so unfavourable as your letter represents.' In fact, however, Smith-Dorrien's letter was far more optimistic than the grim conditions justified. Yet this 'comforting' message from the comfortable and peacefully remote General Headquarters was followed by a still worse rebuff – a telegram, sent through unciphered, telling Smith-Dorrien to hand over command of all the troops engaged at Ypres to General Plumer, and also to send the latter his Chief of Staff, General Milne. Relations between French and Smith-Dorrien had become very strained ever since Smith-Dorrien had saved French's situation against his own orders at Le Cateau in August, 1914. Now, French, true to a habit of his namesakes, seized the chance to punish Smith-Dorrien for making a true diagnosis, and administered a public rebuff which left Smith-Dorrien no option but to send a hint that he would resign if desired. French instantly embraced it and ordered him to hand over his shrunken command and go home.

Nevertheless, Plumer's first instructions from French were to prepare the very withdrawal that Smith-Dorrien had tentatively proposed. Then French went off to see Foch at Cassel and came back with a different outlook. Foch argued vehemently against a withdrawal, said that the lost ground could be retaken by the troops already available, urged that a retirement 'should be forbidden', and begged French 'to support the French *offensive to retake the Langemarck region at all costs*, beginning at noon on the 29th'. The days that followed were a comedy behind the front, a tragedy for the troops in front. Day after day, French heard from his fighting subordinates of the sufferings of the men and of the continued absence of the ever-promised French offensive. Thereupon he would incline towards a withdrawal, only to be swung the other way by Foch's buoyant assurances and flattering entreaties.

Once more let us quote the official history:

For ill now, although for weal in the last year of the war, General Foch was the very spirit of the offensive ... Sir John French, though at first he had wholeheartedly complied with General Foch's wishes, appreciated the small result of the French efforts – or, rather, the smallness of the first efforts – and the heavy losses of his own troops crowded together in the small *place d'armes* of the narrowed salient ... Sir John French then became convinced that he must withdraw his troops, and passed from optimism to pessimism. It was naturally most difficult for his subordinates to follow his moods, particularly when his mind was on the border line between one phase of thought and the next, and when, at the entreaty of General Foch, he more than once agreed to wait a little longer before withdrawing his men – and to order one more counter-attack.

However, he clutched at a straw in the wind when, late on May 1st, Foch confessed that Joffre, so far from sending reinforcements, was calling for troops to be sent from Ypres to strengthen his forthcoming offensive near Arras. French forthwith sanctioned the long-planned withdrawal, by nightly stages, although only to a line some three miles short of Ypres, so that the front still formed a salient, if a flatter one. This was more inconvenient for defence and control than the original salient, the head being exposed to pounding from all sides while Ypres itself formed a dangerously narrow throat of supply and communication. The political and sentimental objection to yielding ground, especially Belgian ground, and the military desire to facilitate the task of any belated French effort, led Sir John French to overrule the fighting commanders' wish to withdraw to the natural straight line of defence formed by the ramparts of Ypres and the canal. So they stayed in the reduced salient, 'one huge artillery target', there to be pounded and gassed incessantly, with their scanty ammunition running out, until relief at last came, in the fourth week of May, through the Germans exhausting their own comparative superfluity of shells. For the Germans had at least the good sense to cease attacks when they came to the choice between economizing infantry lives and economizing artillery ammunition. All that the French had done in the interval was to clear the west bank of the canal, on May 15th, while the continued British bayonet attacks east of Ypres did not even succeed in preventing the Germans switching troops from the British sector to check the eventual small French attack – truly a mountain that was long in labour and brought forth a mouse. And having forfeited 60,000 men for the privilege of acting as midwife, the British were then left to hold the most uncomfortably cramped new salient, or target, at continued expense for over two years.

To throw good money after bad is foolish. But to throw away men's lives where there is no reasonable chance of advantage, is criminal. In the heat of battle mistakes in the command are inevitable and amply excusable. But the real indictment of leadership arises when attacks that are inherently vain are ordered merely because if they could succeed they would be useful. For such 'manslaughter', whether it springs from ignorance, a false conception of war or a want of moral courage, commanders should be held accountable to the nation.

CHAPTER FIVE

SCENE 4

The Unwanted Battle – Loos
(September 15th, 1915)

In early September the 'back of the front' in France was seething with rumours of a great Franco-British offensive which was to shatter the German front; and, if the atmosphere among the fighting troops was tense, it had also an exhilarating breath of confidence in the result. For the first time the New Armies and Territorials were to take a prominent part, and few seemed to expect that the joint hammer blows of British and French together could fail, at least, to dissolve the static trench warfare that had persisted for nearly a year. But there was one extreme contrast to this air of confidence – and that was in the headquarters of the British higher commanders.

For the ill-fated Loos offensive was undertaken directly against the opinion of Haig, the man who, as commander of the First Army, had to carry it out. Haig argued that the supply of heavy artillery and of shells was still inadequate, that its adequacy was the governing factor of the situation, and that until this weakness was remedied, it was little use to make plans for offensives. For in June the British Army still had only seventy-one heavy guns to 1,406 field guns, and the factories in England were turning out no more than 22,000 shells a day, compared to 100,000 by the French, and 250,000 by the Germans and Austrians – according to report.

Haig's view was by no means an isolated one. Robertson, Chief of the General Staff of the British Expeditionary Force, fully endorsed it, but his influence with his own Chief had been undermined by Sir Henry Wilson, who was a devout believer in the infallibility of French military judgement, and Robertson had even been excluded from Sir John French's personal mess. Meantime, Wilson, the friend and confidant of French, was proposing to Kitchener that the British Army should be divided into two groups, one to be located away in Lorraine, so as to

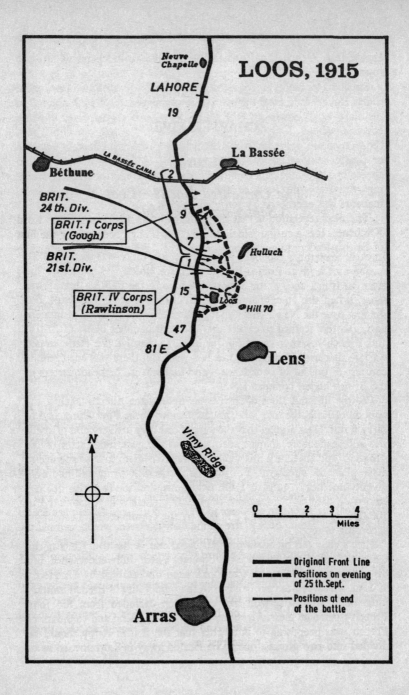

LOOS, 1915

Neuve Chapelle

LAHORE

19

La Bassée

LA BASSÉE CANAL

Béthune

2

BRIT. 24th. Div.

9

BRIT. I Corps (Gough)

7

Hulluch

BRIT. 21st. Div.

1

BRIT. IV Corps (Rawlinson)

15

Loos

Hill 70

47

81 E

Lens

N

Vimy Ridge

0 1 2 3 4
Miles

Original Front Line

Positions on evening of 25th. Sept.

Positions at end of the battle

Arras

ensure that French should be unable to take an independent attitude towards the French!

Equally emphatic, and pessimistic, was Sir Henry Rawlinson, who, under Haig, would have the main task with his army corps. He noted in his diary – 'My new front is as flat as the palm of my hand. Hardly any cover anywhere ... D.H. tells me that we are to attack "*au fond*", that the French are doing likewise and making a supreme effort. It will cost us dearly, and we shall not get very far.' He, however, was left no choice but to do that his men might die. For, in face of all these warnings, only too truly founded, the better judgement of the British commanders was overborne by Joffre's pressure.

The next revelation is that the instrument of this pressure was Lord Kitchener. It is a curious sidelight on one who had been among the first of British leaders to appreciate the state of deadlock in the west and to exclaim against the stubborn folly of seeking to pass the impassable. Kitchener had seen his January doubts fulfilled, and in June had bitterly remarked, as Poincaré has recorded – 'Joffre and Sir John [French] told me in November they were going to push the Germans back over the frontier; they gave me the same assurances in December, March, and May. What have they done? The attacks are very costly and end in nothing.' Yet he was now the determining factor in adding nought to nought.

How was this strange chain of causation forged? Joffre, spiritual twin of his subordinate Foch, in the sense of being an unquenchable optimist, was undeterred by his hard experiences of the spring from the repetition of them in the autumn. In his plan, two great convergent blows were to be delivered from the widely separated sectors of Artois (Arras–Lens) and Champagne (Reims–the Argonne), the former being originally intended as the main blow. Note this point, for it had a vital influence and suffered a vital alteration.

A successful breakthrough both in Champagne and Artois was to be the signal for a general offensive of all the French and British armies on the Western Front. This, Joffre confidently declared, would 'compel the Germans to retreat beyond the Meuse and possibly end the war'.

Yet, in the event, one and a third German divisions sufficed to break the back of the attack of the six British divisions north of Lens, and south of Lens the French attack by fourteen divisions was hardly even developed in face of five German divisions. What a majestic conception was this plan of Joffre's, and how utterly unrelated to the material conditions of modern warfare! And what painful evidence that professional strategy may be the sheerest 'amateur strategy'.

When Joffre's draft plan was sent on June 4th to Sir John French, the British Commander-in-Chief expressed his general agreement. Then a strong gust of common-sense came from his subordinate, Haig, and the military weathervane swung the other way.

Haig had made a personal reconnaissance of the area south of the La Bassée canal (La Bassée–Lens) and as a result declared definitely that it was 'not a favourable one for an attack'. His verdict was to prove most accurate. In his view the German defences were so strong that, until a great increase of heavy artillery was provided, they could only be taken by siege methods. 'The ground, for the most part bare and open, would be so swept by machine-gun and rifle fire both from the German front trenches and from the numerous fortified villages immediately behind them, that a rapid advance would be impossible.' He suggested that, if an offensive on the left of the French was imperative, subsidiary attacks only should be made south of the canal, and the main one delivered astride and north of it. But he concluded with the cold douche already mentioned.

Joffre, however, would not accept arguments for a postponement of the offensive or a change of site. He even remarked with that magisterial infallibility which is so delightful in retrospect, but in retrospect only, that 'your attack will find particularly favourable ground between Loos and La Bassée!' It was certainly both a simple and a magisterial way of brushing aside the adverse evidence of Haig, who had seen the ground.

Meanwhile the Germans, if not yet expecting an attack, were working with feverish energy to strengthen their defences and to create a second system in rear of the front. This was nearing completion by the end of July and knowledge of it accentuated Sir John French's doubts – under Haig's reiteration of his opinion. Hence a conference was arranged at Frévent on July 27th with Foch who, however, maintained that it was essential that, regardless of the ground and the strength of the enemy's defences, Haig's army should make its main attack just north of Lens in close connexion with the French Tenth Army south of Lens, pinching out this maze-like mining town.

The tug-of-war between Haig and French, and Joffre and Foch continued, with Sir John French seeking a way out through a project of cooperating with artillery fire alone. This was quashed and the tug-of-war decided by the intervention of Kitchener. Visiting Sir John French in August, he told him that 'we must act with all energy and do our utmost to help France in this offensive, even though by so doing we may suffer very heavy losses'.

In this reversal of his own previous attitude, he was apparently influenced by the disasters then occurring on the Russian front, and his feeling of the urgent need to succour our Russian Allies, as well, perhaps, by his reaction from the disappointment at the Dardanelles. But two blacks do not make a white and, as he had long since declared his view that the Western Front was impassable, it is difficult to see how he could feel that a hopeless offensive there could bring fresh hope to the Russians.

He may have felt, however, that it would show the need and pave the way for the appointment of a supreme commander of the Entente forces. The official history has discreetly lifted a corner of the veil of history with the statement – 'It is believed that Lord Kitchener himself had anticipated a call to this post.' In that case a timely concession to the French over Loos was likely to make them more receptive towards the other suggestion later.

But the immediate result, to quote the official history, was that:

Under pressure from Lord Kitchener at home, due to the general position of the Allies, and from Generals Joffre and Foch in France, due to the local situation in France, the British Commander-in-Chief was therefore compelled to undertake operations before he was ready, over ground that was most unfavourable, against the better judgement of himself and of General Haig, and, with no more than a quarter of the troops, nine divisions, instead of thirty-six, that he considered necessary for a successful attack.

French was himself, as we shall see, to extinguish its last hope of success. The last but one had been extinguished by a final alteration of the French plan. This was Joffre's decision to make the Champagne attack, and not the Artois, his main attack, for the reason that the ground in Champagne had fewer obstacles or villages in the way of the attackers. The sudden preference for tactical over strategical considerations is in curious contrast to his view where the British attack was concerned.

This change, again, had a damaging influence on the British attack, for both the British and French official accounts make it clear that the French Artois attack south of Lens by seventeen divisions on a twelve-mile frontage – supported by 420 heavy guns – was not seriously pressed once the strength of the defence was realized. Yet the French had nearly twice as many heavy guns to the mile as the British (117 in all). In Champagne twenty-seven French divisions, with 850 heavy guns, were assembled for the attack – on an eighteen-mile frontage. Thus the proportionate artillery support here was still higher.

When the decision to attack at Loos was definitely taken, Haig's first intention, to curtail his commitment and probable loss, was to attack at first with only two divisions. But a too successful demonstration of the possibilities of chlorine gas projected in a 'wave' from cylinders led him to modify his views, and to believe that if the wind was favourable the gas discharge might even procure 'decisive results' and justify him in attacking on the wider frontage of six divisions – Rawlinson's IV Corps (47th, 15th and 1st Divisions) on the right, or south, and Gough's I Corps (7th, 9th, and 2nd Divisions) on the left.

With sound judgement of the chances, Haig urged that 'under no circumstances should our forthcoming attack be launched without the aid of gas', but he was overruled by French and Foch. He then obtained permission to reserve his decision until the last possible moment and to let the choice – between the large or limited attack – depend on the weather conditions. By the irony of fortune, the wind was most favourable for the use of gas on September 15th, the day originally fixed by Foch for the attack, and this fact encouraged Haig's hopes. But the retention of a dual plan led to a distribution of the artillery on the whole army front instead of a concentration on one-third.

Over 5,000 cylinders of gas, containing nearly 150 tons, were carried up to the front trenches and safely installed in special recesses, without one being hit by enemy fire. Even so, there was barely half the volume of gas necessary to maintain a continuous flow for the forty minutes that, in turn, were considered necessary to outlast the protective power of the oxygen apparatus used by the enemy machine-gunners. Hence the cylinders had to be turned on and off intermittently. Smoke candles were used in the intervals to simulate gas, and, at the end, to form the first smoke screen of the war.

The artillery bombardment began on September 21st, the ammunition being eked out by limiting each heavy gun to ninety rounds, and each field gun to 150 in the twenty-four hours. The results were not encouraging, so far as effect could be discovered, and led the commanders to study the wind all the more attentively.

The last night was a time of tense anxiety. Repeatedly Haig studied fresh charts sent in by a chain of meteorological observers. At 6 PM the forecast was that the wind would be 'on the border line between favourable and unfavourable, with a slight bias towards favourable'. At 9 PM the forecast was better, indicating a probable change to a south-westerly or even westerly wind, which would carry the gas over the German trenches. Thereupon Haig unhesitatingly ordered the full-scale offensive with gas, although as a precaution staff officers of each corps had been ordered to stand by their telephones. At 3 AM, after a further report not quite so encouraging, he fixed sunrise (5.50 AM) as the hour for releasing the gas. During the hours of darkness the wind changed as predicted, but only as far as south-west, and, worse still, was so slight as to be almost a calm.

About 5 AM, as soon as it was light, Haig went out. He could feel only the faintest breath of air, and he asked his senior ADC to light a cigarette. The smoke drifted in puffs to the north-east.

Did it justify the venture? Would the gas merely hang in the British trenches? A slight increase of wind was felt and at 5.15 AM Haig gave the decisive order to 'carry on' and climbed his wooden look-out tower. But the improvement was delusive, and a few minutes later one of his staff telephoned to the I Corps, to ask whether it was possible to stop the discharge and the attack. For this emergency the gas officers had made ample arrangements. But Gough replied that it was too late. If it would certainly have been a close shave, one may suspect, especially in view of Gough's record, that with this ardent fighter the wish was at least the midwife, if not the father, of the thought.

When the gas was actually turned on at 5.50 AM it carried fairly well over the German trenches on the right, if too slow and slight for full effect, but on the left was a failure, in some places drifting back and upsetting the attack. In Horne's 2nd Division, the officer in charge of the gas on the 6th Brigade front declined to assume the responsibility of turning on the cylinders. But when this was reported to divisional headquarters, Horne replied with an order that 'the programme must be carried out whatever the conditions...' As a result of this obstinacy many of the infantry were poisoned by their own gas. Those who were able to advance were soon stopped, and slaughtered by the ungassed German machine-gunners. Nevertheless, Horne ordered a fresh assault, which was only abandoned after his brigade commanders had protested against the 'useless sacrifice of life'.

The general infantry assault had been launched at 6.30 AM, and into it was thrown the entire strength of the First Army, except for local reserves. Neither Haig nor the commanders of his two attacking corps kept any reserve, as they understood that the Commander-in-Chief expected a breakthrough and would use his general reserve to back them up promptly.

On the extreme right the 47th Division nearly carried out its task of throwing forward a defensive flank, but the 'not quite' had an important bearing on the surprisingly successful initial rush of its neighbour, the 15th Division, contributing towards the loss of direction which nullified its near approach to a breakthrough, beyond Hill 70. So swift and deep was the advance of these Scotsmen of 'K's' Army that the German Command made hurried preparations to evacuate the whole area, and as far back as Douai 'there were endless convoys of wagons formed up in double lines ready to march away'.

Another ill-effect was due to the long delay in the 1st Division's advance, only partially retrieved. Its left brigade had suffered similarly to Horne's division and, instead of the divisional reserve being sent through the gap made on the flanks, the morning was wasted in futile attempts to renew the frontal assault. This stoppage in the British centre tended to check the whole momentum of the British advance. Further to the left the 7th and 9th Divisions obtained promising results, although the 9th had suffered, both in opportunity and life, from the misguided insistence of the corps commander, Gough, on renewing the vain frontal assault of the left brigade. In wise contrast Capper, commanding the 7th Division, when confronted with a check on his left, had quickly passed his reserve through the gap made by the successful advance of his right.

The fulfilment of any promise, however, depended on the prompt infusion of reserves. This was the crux of the situation and the sealing cause of failure. Even Joffre had said that if French kept his reserve divisions too far back they would 'run the risk of arriving too late to exploit the success of the leading ones. It is indispensable that these divisions are put, before the attack, at the absolute disposal of General Haig'. Haig repeatedly urged that they should at least be brought up close behind him. French's assurances were so vague as to be simultaneously unsatisfying and misleading. As usual his outlook seems to have been governed by contradictory impulses of undue optimism and pessimism.

French's general reserves comprised the Cavalry Corps – which, under modern conditions, did not count except in the minds of cavalry-trained commanders – and the XI Corps. The last included the Guards Division, newly formed, and the 21st and 24th Divisions, newly arrived in France. With curious judgement French left seasoned divisions lying idle on the quiet Somme front, and chose to use these two raw divisions for the critical phase of the battle. Moreover, he had given Haig to understand that they would be immediately at hand for Haig's use, whereas he placed them sixteen miles in rear. And in his subsequent dispatch he untruthfully stated that they were put at Haig's disposal at

9.30 AM on the 25th. Actually, Haig did not hear until 1.20 PM, and then indirectly. Haig bitterly remarked, soon after – 'If there had been even one division in reserve close up we could have walked right through. General headquarters refuses to recognize the teaching of the war as regards the control of reserves.' His confidence was probably exaggerated, at least as to the effect of such a narrow breach, and he was himself to err somewhat similarly in the following July. But his natural disgust, accentuated by French's untruthful dispatch, led first to an acrimonious interchange of letters and then to an irreconcilable quarrel. He seems, also, to have been galled, and not for the first time, at the way his own sound advice had been overruled by Foch's influence with French. French in retort charged Haig with the folly of trying to push reserves through a far too narrow gap. The sequel was that Haig wrote personally to Kitchener and spoke to Haldane about French's failure and incompetence, and thereby helped to precipitate French's downfall and his own succession.

As for the long and slow march up of those divisions, bad traffic arrangements were more responsible than their own inexperience for accentuating the evil caused by the Commander-in-Chief's dispositions. As General Edmonds caustically says – 'It was like trying to push the Lord Mayor's procession through the streets of London, without clearing the route and holding up the traffic.' Folly was capped by farce when, on the outskirts of Béthune, a military policeman stopped the 72nd Brigade because the brigade commander had no pass to enter the area.

Never, surely, were 'novice' divisions thrown into a vital stroke in a more difficult or absurd manner, and in an atmosphere of greater misconception of the situation in all quarters. This amply explains their subsequent failure when their belated attack was at last launched at 11 AM on the 26th, and redresses the hasty judgements which were spread at the time – a stigma that was slow to fade. That in courage they were not lacking is clear, and equally that its fruits were reduced by their rawness, by that of their staff still more.

The handicap of inexperience in these and the other New Army divisions engaged can be over-emphasized. It does not appear that, as a whole, apart from certain battalions in them, the regular divisions were more effective or even as effective in the battle. 'Battlecraft' is a rare quality, the product of gifted and original leadership, and in its absence mere dash is often more effective than so-called experience.

The ineffectiveness of the larger French attack south of the Lens also affected the British opportunity. For the French did not advance until six and a quarter hours after their Allies, and even then made little progress where they did not make merely a demonstration. The bitter experiences of the spring and summer seem to have led the fighting commanders to discount Foch's faith in a breakthrough, and to annul his vehement order by gentle evasion in places. Joffre also put a brake on him from above, for on the second morning he telephoned him to 'go cautiously', and followed this by the warning – 'Stop the attacks of the Tenth Army, taking care to avoid giving the British the impression that we are leaving them to attack alone.' His reason was apparently that he now pinned his hopes to the attack in Champagne, which on the first day gave a delusive promise of a real breakthrough.

It is worthwhile to note that the partial opening success of the attack in Champagne, and also in Artois, was largely due to the obstinate self-delusion of Falkenhayn, who had disregarded ample warnings from many sources, and requests for reserves. Only two hours before the attack began he assured the Kaiser that the local army commanders 'see things too black', and that the French were not in a condition to attack.

Early reports on the 25th had also led Haig to overestimate his initial success, and as early as 10.30 AM he ordered the 3rd Cavalry Division forward. The commander soon discovered Haig's mistake, but Haig, believing that the cavalry had gone on, hurried the 21st and 24th Divisions forward as soon as he could get hold of them. But before they came up the known situation had changed, and the two leading brigades were taken to strengthen the line gained by the original attack. Haig still hoped to break the intact German second line of defences, and to this end the rest (four brigades) of these divisions continued their march across country, and unknown country, in the dark and rain. Tired, hungry, and as confused as their commanders, they were launched to the attack next morning without effective artillery support, and against defences now stronger and more strongly manned than the original first line. For the Germans had not only been reinforced, but had covered themselves with a thick wire entanglement during the night. The attack broke down at or before this uncut obstacle, and the survivors turned and flowed backwards. Their disappearance left a hole in the ragged British front between Loos and Hulluch, which the Guards Division came up to fill. Meantime German counter-attacks were multiplying dangerously, especially on the flanks. At last, on the 28th, Foch came to the relief not only by taking over the British flank sector near Loos, but with a local success on Vimy ridge, which drew off most of the newly arrived German Guard Corps to check it. And in concert with Sir John French he arranged to make a renewed general offensive on October

2nd. The same course was adopted in Champagne, where the French for three days had vainly hurled themselves at the German second position, suffering fearful loss, which would have been worse if Pétain (Second Army) had not stopped his attack in disregard of higher orders.

But as the pause was to be followed by a renewal at the same point, it merely gave the Germans time to strengthen it and accumulate resources in the rear. Local upsets due to German counter-attacks, and the exhaustion of the troops, caused further delay, and the renewed offensive was repeatedly postponed. Eventually all three attacks were delivered on different dates, the British last on October 13th. And, in the words of the official history, it 'had not improved the general situation in any way and had brought nothing but useless slaughter of infantry'. Curiously, Haig's sense of realism waned in this last phase, or, perhaps more truly, it was subdued by his bulldog tenacity; for although Joffre had abandoned the effort, Haig was working up a new general attack for November 7th, an operation whose inevitable cost does not seem to have had any adequate excuse. Happily, Generals Winter and Weather intervened. But the British casualties already amounted to 50,380 – or 60,392 if the subsidiary attacks by Haig's army be included – whereas the German loss was barely 20,000, despite their costly counter-attacks. The French in Champagne and Artois had lost 191,797 officers and men, and inflicted 120,000 casualties – a proportion which suggests that the actual handling of these attacks was better than that of the British, if helped by more powerful artillery. Both Allies had gained in experience, if not in wisdom, but they had afforded the Germans still better experience in the way to frustrate such attacks. And in 1916 it was the Germans who profited heavily both by the offensive and the defensive lesson.

CHAPTER SIX

1916 – The 'Dog-Fall'

In 1914 the centre of gravity of the World War had been on the Western Front; in 1915 it shifted to the Eastern Front; in 1916 it once more moved back to France. Although the Entente had dissipated some of their strength in Salonika and Mesopotamia, the rising tide of England's new armies and of her munition supplies promised the power for an effort far larger in scale than before to break the trench deadlock. Measures had also been taken to keep these new divisions up to strength. By the end of 1915 the British force in France had risen to thirty-eight divisions through the entry into the field of 'Kitchener's Army', as well as of the Territorial divisions. Although the principle of voluntary enlistment had not yet been abandoned, the method was systematized and based on a national register. This scheme, launched in October, 1915, under the aegis of Lord Derby, aimed to reconcile the demands of the Army with the needs of industry, calling up men by groups as they were wanted, and taking single men first. But the response among the latter was not adequate to preserve this graduated principle, and in January, 1916, by the Military Service Act, the voluntary system – system is hardly the correct term – was replaced by conscription.

At the close of 1915, the first serious effort to obtain unity of action between the Allies was made, and a conference of the leaders of the French, British, Belgian and Italian armies, with representatives present from the Russian and Japanese, was held at Joffre's headquarters on December 5th. As a result they adopted the principle of a simultaneous general offensive in 1916 by France, Britain, Russia and Italy. In view of the rawness of the British troops, it was recognized that time must be allowed for training, and Russia also needed time for re-equipment, so that the offensive could not begin before the summer of 1916, although it was hoped to carry out preliminary attacks to wear down the enemy's strength. But in January both Joffre and Foch gave Haig a clear intimation that it was for him to carry out this preparatory task, and that they did not intend to take the offensive until he had done so.

German action was to dislocate this scheme, and only the British share came fully into operation, and not even that into full effect. By a grim jest, however, it forced the French to carry out the wearing-down process – in an indirect form. For Falkenhayn was about to fulfil his long-cherished plan for a western offensive, but with characteristic limitations. Always a believer in the strategy of attrition, he now carried this ruling idea into tactics, and produced the new form of attack by methodical stages, each with a limited objective. In an appreciation made at Christmas, 1915, he argued that England was the staple of the enemy alliance. 'The history of the English wars against the Netherlands, Spain, France and Napoleon is being repeated. Germany can expect no mercy from this enemy, so long as he still retains the slightest hope of achieving his object.' Save by submarine warfare, however, England and her army were out of reach, for their sector of the front did not lend itself to offensive operations. 'In view of our feelings for our arch-enemy in the war that is certainly distressing, but it can be endured if we realize that for England the campaign on the Continent . . . is at bottom a side-show. Her real weapons here are the French, Russian and Italian armies.' He regarded Russia as already paralysed, and Italy's military achievements as unlikely to affect the situation. 'Only France remains.' 'France has almost arrived at the end of her military effort. If her people can be made to understand clearly that in a military sense they have nothing more to hope for, breaking point would be reached, and England's best sword knocked out of her hand.' He added that a breakthrough in mass was unnecessary, and that instead the Germans should aim to bleed France to death by choosing a point of attack 'for the retention of which the French command would be compelled to throw in every man they have'. Such an objective was either Belfort, or Verdun, and Verdun was chosen, because it was a menace to the main German communications, because it offered a salient and so cramped the defender, and because of the moral effect if so renowned a place were lost to France. It has also been suggested that the choice was influenced by a peculiarly German moral, or unmoral, consideration. For Verdun was the ancient gate of the west through which the German hordes had passed to attack the Gauls. Similarly the Germans were fond of christening their trench positions after the heroes of the Nibelungen – Siegfried, Brünhilde and so on. The vein of super-stition is still more clearly suggested in the Kaiser's choice of a second Moltke to guide his armies, and in the original location of their headquarters in the same hotel and same town, Coblenz, as they had occupied in 1870.

The keynote of the tactical plan at Verdun was a continuous series of limited advances, which by their menace should draw the French reserves into the mincing machine of the German artillery. And each of these advances was itself to be secured from loss by a short but intense artillery bombardment. By this means the objective would be taken and consolidated before the enemy could move up his reserves for counter-attack. Although the Intelligence branch at French General Headquarters gave early warning of the German preparations, the Operations branch were so full of their own offensive schemes that the warning fell on deaf ears. Further, the easy fall of the Belgian and Russian fortresses had led to a commonly held view that fortresses were obsolete, and Joffre, persuading the French government to 'declass' Verdun as a fortress, had denuded it of guns and troops. The forts were only used as shelters and the trench lines which took their place were inadequate and in poor repair.

At 7.15 AM on February 21st, the German bombardment began, on a front of fifteen miles, and at 4.45 PM the infantry advanced, although the first day only on a four and a half miles' front. From then until February 24th the defenders' line east of the Meuse was crumbled away as by the erosion of the tide.

Joffre was now aroused so far as to entrust the defence to Pétain, for whose use reserves were assembled. On March 6th the Germans extended the attack to the west bank of the Meuse; but the defence was now stiffening, the numbers balanced, and the immediate threat to Verdun was checked.

A slight lull followed, and during it the Allies of France made efforts to relieve the pressure on her. The British took over the Arras front from the French Tenth Army, their front becoming now continuous from the Yser to the Somme; the Italians made their fifth attack, though in vain, on the Isonzo front; and the Russians hurled untrained masses on the German front at Lake Narocz, near Vilna, where the slight gains were soon lost through a counterstroke. These efforts did not prevent Falkenhayn pursuing his attrition offensive at Verdun. The advances were slight but they were cumulative in effect, and the balance of loss turned definitely against the defenders. On June 7th Fort Vaux fell, and the German tide crept ever closer to Verdun. And in the Asiago region, Conrad had launched his offensive against Italy's Trentino flank.

Again Russia came to the rescue. In the spring of 1916 she had 130 divisions, but still woefully short of equipment, facing forty-six German and forty Austrian divisions. The preparation and reorganization for her intended share in the year's Allied offensive were cut short by the emergency at Verdun, and in relief of her French Allies she had launched the costly and obstinately prolonged attack at Lake Narocz in March. When at last it was broken off, the preparations for the main offensive were resumed. This was to begin in July, coincidently with the Somme offensive; meantime Brusilov, commanding the south-western front, prepared such attacks as he could stage from his own resources as a distraction of the enemy's attention from the main offensive. But the distraction was released prematurely, on June 4th, in response to Italy's appeal to Russia to prevent the Austrians reinforcing their Trentino attack. Without warning, because without any special concentration of troops, Brusilov's troops advanced against the Austrian Fourth Army near Luck, and the Austrian Seventh Army in the Bukovina, whose resistance collapsed at the first shock.

This last vital effort of the Russian Army in the war had important consequences. It stopped the Austrian attack on Italy, already impaired by an Italian riposte. It compelled Falkenhayn to withdraw troops from the Western Front, and so abandon his plan for a counterstroke against the British offensive preparing on the Somme, as well as the hope of nourishing his Verdun attrition process. It led Rumania to take her fateful decision to enter the war on the Entente side, and caused the supersession of Falkenhayn in the supreme command, and his replacement by Hindenburg – with Ludendorff, officially styled First Quartermaster-General, as the directing brain. Although Rumania's entry was the immediate reason, the underlying one was the fact that Falkenhayn's indefinite strategy in 1915 had made possible the Russian recovery which stultified his strategy of 1916. Falkenhayn was history's latest example of the folly of half-measures; the ablest and most scientific General – 'penny wise, pound foolish' – who ever ruined his country by a refusal to take calculated risks. In 1916 he had turned back westwards to pursue his long-cherished goal, and his strategy had faithfully fulfilled the canons of military orthodoxy by taking for its objective the enemy's strongest army and the strongest point of that army's position. It certainly achieved the object of compelling the French to pour their reserves into the Verdun 'blood-bath', but did not achieve any decisive strategic result.

Falkenhayn had rejected Conrad's proposal for a concentration against Italy such as had previously overthrown Serbia. Conrad's reasons had been that such a blow against the 'hereditary enemy' would act as a tonic to the Austro-Hungarian forces, and that the theatre of war lent itself to decisive results by a thrust southwards from the Trentino against the rear of the Italian armies engaged on the Isonzo. The success attained by the relatively light blow of 1917 – Caporetto – lends historical support to his contention. But Falkenhayn was dubious both of the feasibility and value of the plan, and was unwilling even to lend the nine German divisions which Conrad asked for to relieve Austrian divisions in Galicia. In default of this aid Conrad persisted in attempting his design single-handed, taking some of his best divisions from Galicia, and thereby exposing their front to Brusilov's advance without obtaining adequate force to achieve his Italian plan. Falkenhayn's smouldering resentment at this disregard of his views was fanned into flame by the Galician disaster, and he intervened in Vienna to procure the deposition of Conrad. With retributive irony his own fall followed close on that of Conrad.

Brusilov's offensive continued for three months with fair success, but reserves were not at hand for immediate exploitation, and before they could be moved down from the north the Germans were patching up the holes. His later efforts were never so dangerous, but they absorbed all the available Russian reserves, and the huge losses then incurred went far to complete the ruin of Russia's military power.

Great as was the influence of Brusilov's offensive on German strategy, its effect on the Verdun situation was less immediate. But the long-planned offensive on the Somme came to the rescue, and for want of nourishment the Verdun offensive faded away. Nevertheless, although the Germans at Verdun had fallen short of their object, moral and material, they had so drained the French army that it could play but a slender part in the Allied plan for 1916. The British had now to take up the main burden of the struggle, and the consequence was to limit both the scope and effect of the Entente strategy.

On July 1st, after a week's prolonged bombardment, the British Fourth Army (recently created and placed under Rawlinson) attacked with thirteen divisions on a front of fifteen miles, north of the Somme, and the French with five divisions on a front of eight miles, mainly south of the river, where the German defence system was less highly developed. The unconcealed preparations and the long bombardment had given away any chance of surprise, and in face of the German resistance, weak in numbers but strong in organization, the attack failed along most of the British front. Owing to the dense and rigid 'wave' formations that were adopted the losses were appallingly heavy. Only on the south of the British front, near Fricourt and Montauban, did the attack gain a real footing in the German defences. The French, with slighter opposition, and being less expected, made larger gains.

This setback negatived the original idea of a 'breakthrough' to Bapaume and Cambrai, and Haig for a time fell back on the attrition method – of limited advances aimed to wear down the German strength. Rejecting Joffre's desire that he should again throw his troops frontally on the Thiepval defences, Haig at first resumed the attack with his right wing alone, and on July 14th the penetration of the Germans' second position offered a chance of exploitation, which was not taken. From now onward a methodical but costly advance continued, and although little ground was gained the German resistance was seriously strained when the early onset of winter rains suspended operations in November. The effect, however, can be exaggerated, for it did not prevent the Germans withdrawing troops from the west for the attack on Rumania.

But in one respect the Somme shed a significant light on the future, for on September 15th the first tanks appeared. Their early employment before large numbers were ready was a mistake; losing the chance of a great strategic surprise, and owing also to tactical mishandling, and minor technical defects, they had only a limited success. Although the higher military authorities lost faith in them, and some urged their abandonment, more discerning eyes realized that here was a key which, when properly used, might unlock the trench barrier.

The Somme offensive had a further indirect effect, for its relief to the Verdun pressure enabled the French to prepare counterstrokes, carried out by Mangin's corps on October 24th and December 15th, which regained most of the lost ground with small casualties. These economical successes were due to a partial revival of surprise, to a more elastic use of the limited objective method, and to a high concentration of artillery, with a minimum of infantry to occupy the defences crushed by the guns. But the French success was greatly helped by Hindenburg's misguided insistence, for the sake of prestige, on maintaining the earlier gains instead of withdrawing the tired troops to a more secure line somewhat in rear. He at least profited by the lesson, to the Allies' detriment, in the spring of 1917.

Rumania, sympathetic to the Entente cause, had been waiting a favourable opportunity to enter the war on their side, and Brusilov's success encouraged her to take the plunge. Her command hoped that this, combined with the Allied pressure on the Somme and at Salonika, would fix the German reserves. But Rumania's situation had many inherent defects. The strategical position of her territory was bad, the main section, Wallachia, being sandwiched between Austro-Hungary and Bulgaria. Her army, though externally of a modern pattern, had grave weaknesses beneath the surface. Of her Allies, only Russia could give her direct aid, and they failed her. And, with all these handicaps, she launched an offensive into Transylvania, which bared her flank to Bulgaria.

While the Entente fumbled the Germans acted. The plan was initiated by Falkenhayn and developed by Hindenburg-Ludendorff when they took over the Supreme Command on August 28th. While one force concentrated in Transylvania for a counterstroke, a Bulgarian army with German stiffening – under Mackensen – was to strike through Rumania's 'back door' and invade the Dobruja. This automatically halted the Rumanian offensive in Transylvania, and drew away its reserves; at the end of September the Rumanians were thrown back by the Austro-German counter-offensive, of which Falkenhayn was given executive command. They succeeded in holding the passes of Rumania's mountain border in the west until mid-November, but Falkenhayn just broke through before the snows blocked the passes. Mackensen switched his main forces westwards, and crossed the Danube close to Bucharest, on which both armies now converged. It fell on December 6th, and, despite belated Russian aid, the Rumanian forces were driven north into Moldavia. The brilliantly coordinated German strategy had crippled their new foe, gained possession of the bulk of Rumania, with its oil and wheat, and gave the Russians another 300 miles of front to hold. Sarrail, at Salonika, had not succeeded in fixing the Bulgarian reserves.

The Austrian offensive in the Trentino had interrupted Cadorna's plans for a renewed effort on the Isonzo, but when the former was halted Cadorna switched his reserves back to the Isonzo. In preparation for this offensive the whole sector from Monte Sabotino to the sea was entrusted to the Duke of Aosta's Third Army, under which sixteen divisions were concentrated against six Austrian divisions. Following a preliminary feint near the sea on August 4th, the attack opened well two days later. North of Gorizia Capello's corps swept over the long-impregnable Monte Sabotino, which guarded the approach to the river, and, crossing the river on the night of August 8th, occupied the town. This compelled an Austrian retreat in the Carso sector to the south, but attempts to exploit the success eastward failed against fresh positions of resistance. Three more efforts were made in the autumn, and if they imposed a wearing strain on the Austrians, they caused greater loss to the attackers. During the year Italians had suffered some 483,000 casualties, and inflicted 260,000.

The only territorial success that the Entente could show for their year's campaign – and, even so, it did not reveal itself fully until the New Year – was away in Mesopotamia – the capture of Baghdad. This moral token was seized on with an enthusiasm which, militarily, it hardly warranted. The bitter experience of the past had damped the ardour of the British Government, and Sir William Robertson, the new Chief of the Imperial General Staff, was opposed to any further commitments which drained the strength available for the Western Front. But Maude, the new commander on the spot, by subtle if unconscious steps succeeded in changing this defensive policy into one of a fresh offensive. After thorough reorganization of the Mesopotamian force and its communications, he began on December 12th, 1916, a progressive right wheel and extension of his front on the west bank of the Tigris above and below Kut. These methodical trench-warfare operations had placed him ready for a spring across the Tigris at the Turks' line of retreat, which was thus parallel to his front. But despite his four-to-one superiority of force, the failure of his right to pin down the enemy, and of his cavalry to cut off their retreat, prevented a decisive success. But it led to permission for an advance on Baghdad, and he entered the Mesopotamian capital on March 11th, 1917. A series of skilfully conducted operations then drove the Turks into divergent lines of retreat and secured the British hold on the province.

Ever since the abortive Turkish attempt to invade Egypt early in 1915, the British had kept a fairly large force there, even when the Dardanelles expedition was crying out for troops. When Gallipoli was evacuated, the release of the Turkish forces threatened a fresh move on Egypt. To forestall this danger the authorities in Cairo had gained Kitchener's approval for a landing in Ayas Bay near Alexandretta, but the proposal had been opposed by the General Staff at home and then nullified by the political objections of the French to any British intervention in Syria, which they already counted as part of their share of the spoils of war. Thus throughout 1916 the large British garrison of Egypt (at one time over a quarter of a million strong) remained passive while the Turks, by using a few thousand men in Sinai and by stirring up the Senussi in the Western Desert, created trouble on both flanks which reacted on the unrest within the frontiers of Egypt.

But the British, also, contrived to secure an Arab ally, on the eastern side of the Red Sea. This was the Sherif of Mecca, who had already rendered them valuable service by refusing to proclaim the *Jihad* from the Holy Cities at the Turks' behest, and had thus extinguished the prospect of rallying the Moslem peoples for a Holy War against the

British. Then, in June 1916, the Sherif raised a revolt in the Hejaz against Turkish rule, and thereby created a distraction to the Turks which the British had hitherto failed to provide with their own forces. Its first effect was on the British, who now decided to undertake an advance to El Arish, which would give them command of the Sinai Desert and restore their possession of the frontier. But although another Turkish incursion was punished at Romani in July, Sir Archibald Murray's advance was slow to develop, being governed by the time taken in laying a railway and pipeline (for water) across the desert. It was not until Christmastide that the British occupied El Arish, and pounced on the outlying Turkish posts at Magdhaba and Rafah.

This new 'Exodus inspired' the British Government to carry out an invasion of Palestine, at as cheap a cost in troops as possible. The towns of Gaza, on the coast, and Beersheba, twenty-five miles inland, guarded the approach to Palestine. Murray attacked Gaza on March 26th, 1917, but the attempt fell short when on the brink of success. By nightfall Gaza was practically surrounded, but the victorious position was given up bit by bit, not under enemy pressure, but on the orders of the executive British commanders, through faulty information, misunderstandings, and over-anxiety. Nor did the harm end there, for Murray reported the action to the Government in terms of a victory, and without hint of the subsequent withdrawal, so that he was encouraged to attempt, without adequate reconnaissance or fire support, a further attack on April 17th–19th, which proved a costlier failure against defences now strengthened.

Britain's new Arab allies, however, provided a valuable distraction which counteracted these Turkish successes, with no drain on the British forces beyond a handful of technical advisers. After its opening success the revolt had been in danger of collapse; but the situation was saved and the scales changed by Feisal's sudden flank move up the Red Sea coast to Wejh, whence the Arabs harassed the Hejaz railway. This move was prompted by a young archaeologist turned temporary soldier, Captain T. E. Lawrence. Steeped in the history and theory of warfare, he had the elasticity of mind to adapt his knowledge to irregular conditions and the magnetic personality to combine the Arabs' 'loose shower of sparks into a firm flame' which consumed the Turkish resources. In May 1917, he set off with a party of Arabs on a lone-hand expedition which, after sowing fresh seeds of revolt in Syria, culminated in a descent upon Aqaba. The capture of this sea base on the northern arm of the Red Sea removed all danger to the British communications in Sinai and opened the way for the Arabs to become a lever on the flank of the Turkish forces opposing the British. Already more Turks were occupied in guarding the long line of the Hejaz railway and the territory south of it than were facing the British in Palestine.

The War at Sea, 1915–16. Germany's first submarine campaign – associated by Allied opinion with the name of Admiral von Tirpitz, the exponent of ruthlessness – had been a signal failure, both in its meagre results and the disproportionate ethical damage it did to Germany's cause. A series of notes, exchanged between the American and German Governments, culminated in April, 1916, in a virtual ultimatum from President Wilson, and Germany abandoned her unrestricted campaign. The deprivation of this weapon spurred the German navy to its first, and last, attempt to carry out the initial plan on which it had begun the war. Late on May 30th, 1916, the British Grand Fleet left its bases on one of its periodical sweeps through the North Sea, but with reason to expect a possible encounter. On May 31st, early in the morning, the German High Sea Fleet also put to sea, in the hope of destroying some isolated portion of the British fleet.

For such an encounter the British Admiral, Jellicoe, had formulated an outline plan in the early months of the war. Its basis was the cardinal necessity of maintaining the unimpaired supremacy of the Grand Fleet, which he viewed as an instrument, not merely of battle, but of grand strategy, the pivot of the Allies' action in all spheres, economic, moral and military. Hence, while desirous of bringing the German fleet to battle under his own conditions, he was determined not to be lured into mine and submarine-infested waters.

Early in the afternoon of May 31st, Beatty, with his battle cruisers and a squadron of battleships, after a sweep to the south was turning north to rejoin Jellicoe, when he sighted the German battle cruisers, five in number. In the initial engagement two of Beatty's six battle cruisers were hit in vital parts and sunk; when thus weakened he came upon the main German fleet under Admiral Scheer. He turned north to lure them into reach of Jellicoe, fifty miles distant, who raced to support him. Mist and failing light put an end to an indecisive action, which, however, left the British fleet between the German and its bases. During the night Scheer broke through the destroyer guard, and although sighted was not reported. Thus he slipped safely through a net which Jellicoe dared not draw too close in view of his guiding principle, and of the danger of torpedo attack.

If the battle of Jutland could be counted a tactical advantage to the Germans, it had no effect on their strategic position. The grip of Britain's blockade was unrelaxed. Once more Germany fell back on submarine warfare, and the first development was an extension of range. In July one of her large submarine cruisers appeared off the American coast and sank several neutral ships.

In the narrow seas the Mediterranean was the scene of active operations, but the immediate pressure on Britain was relaxed during the summer. For Scheer, in a fit of pique at the German Government's surrender to President Wilson's threat, refused to let his submarines operate under the code of visit and search. Hence the burden of the restricted campaign fell on the Flanders flotillas, and, fortunately for Britain, the German naval chiefs had been obtusely slow to realize and exploit the advantages of the Belgian coast as a base. The six months lost originally through neglect to organize a base were never fully redeemed, and the scale of the forces here was never in proportion to the possibilities of menacing Britain from this close-range post. On October 6th, Scheer was overruled by an order to reinforce the effort with his flotillas. This veiled renewal of the general submarine campaign was inspired mainly by Admiral von Holtzendorf, the Chief of the Naval Staff, and Captain von Bartenbach, the Chief of the Flanders flotillas. The indirect result was to deprive Scheer automatically of the submarines which he required to safeguard his own sorties and lay traps for the British fleet.

Thus the paralysis of the German fleet henceforth was the result of the Germans' own alternative plan, and not of Jutland. And it did not even leave the British Grand Fleet in possession of the North Sea. For the moral effect of a submarine ambush which marked the German sortie of August 19th was so great, even though it miscarried, that henceforth the Grand Fleet was almost as confined as an old-time debtor in the Fleet Prison, and was definitely debarred from the southern half of the North Sea. Jellicoe and the Admiralty were agreed upon the necessity for this self-imprisonment. The 'command of the sea' became almost a burlesque when the danger of a German invasion of Denmark loomed up that autumn and, after examination by the Admiralty and War Office, the verdict was that – 'For naval reasons it would be almost impossible to support the Danes at all.' The shadow of the submarine was longer than the shadow of Nelson's column. With illuminating candour the British official naval history says – 'The Grand Fleet could only put to sea with an escort of nearly one hundred destroyers, no capital ship could leave its base without an escort of small craft, and the German U-boats had hampered our squadrons to an extent which the most expert and far-sighted naval officer had never foreseen.' Yet, with curious inconsistency, the voices of naval officers have been heard ever since the war proclaiming the sovereignty of the battleship, the ineffectiveness of the submarine.

The Grand Fleet in the autumn of 1916 was all the more heavily fettered because its warders were reduced, owing to the call for light craft to combat the new 'veiled' submarine campaign against commerce. Despite all counter-measures this was so successful that the monthly loss of shipping rose steadily from 109,000 tons during June, to 368,000 tons in January, 1917 – approximately half being British. During the 'veiled' campaign the Mediterranean was both an ill-favoured and, by the Germans, too well-favoured area, for besides simplifying the submarine's task of finding targets it simplified the problem of evading the undertakings given to America – in the Mediterranean there was little risk of injuring American ships or interests by mischance. One U-boat alone in five weeks' cruise sank 65,000 tons of shipping.

Counter-measures proved utterly unable to stem the rising tide of sinking ships, even when more destroyers and other small craft became available. During one week of September, 1916, thirty ships were sunk by two, or at the most, three submarines in an area patrolled by ninety-seven destroyers and sixty-eight auxiliary craft. Among the remedies tried were those of secret routes, of hoisting false colours, and of decoy ships. This last ruse was carried out by what were known as Q-ships, equipped with torpedo-tubes, depth charges, and guns concealed behind collapsible bulwarks, while disguised as merchant ships. The disguise was enhanced by the acting of the crews who coolly simulated panic under conditions where most men would not have needed to do so, and thereby lured the molesting submarine to the surface within close range. Although these Q-ships provided the most romantic phase of the naval war, and sank eleven U-boats, their effect was almost exhausted by the end of 1916, save that it made the enemy more wary – and naturally less inclined to merciful discrimination between armed and apparently unarmed ships. This Q-ship risk to the U-boat was accentuated by the British arming of ordinary merchant ships, which placed the slow, fragile and half-blind U-boat in a perilous dilemma. The more merciful the U-boat the greater danger it ran; the less heed it paid to the nature of its target and the rescue of those on board the more its safety and success were assured. Hence the outcry in Germany for a policy of sinking at sight was naturally strengthened.

Moreover, if Britain was feeling the strain of economic pressure, so also was Germany, and her leaders feared that the race between decisive success on land and economic collapse would end against her. The naval authorities declared that a renewal of the 'unlimited' submarine campaign, which with her increased numbers could now be far more intense, would bring the Entente to their knees. Accepting this opinion, Ludendorff agreed to a step which he had hitherto opposed; the combined weight of naval and military opinion overbore the protests of the Imperial Chancellor. A proposal of peace discussions, and its foreseen rejection by the Entente powers, was made the moral justification for openly abandoning the restrictions of visit and search, and for withdrawing the promise given to President Wilson. On February 1st, 1917, the 'unrestricted' policy – of sinking all ships, passenger or cargo, without warning – was proclaimed – with the full realization that it involved the weight of America being thrown into the scales against Germany. Doubts of its wisdom in Germany were stifled by the plea of necessity, the promise of certain victory, and the argument of inevitability – that America was bound to come to the help of the Allies in order to ensure their ability to pay their debts to her. But the Germans reckoned on victory before America's weight could count in the scales.

CHAPTER SIX

SCENE 1

The Mincing Machine – Verdun

It is a truism that the war of 1914–18 revolutionized all ideas of time, in a military sense, and especially in the duration of its battles. For several thousand years of warfare a battle, however great the scale, had been a matter of hours. This remained the general case down to the beginning of this century, though a few battles from the Napoleonic Wars onwards increased the span to days – for example, Leipzig, Gettysburg. The real change was inaugurated with the Russo-Japanese campaign, when battles at last had to be reckoned in weeks. With the World War the standard became months – because the battles had usually become sieges, without being recognized or scientifically treated as such. The change, it is to be hoped, is a transitory one, for quantity does not imply quality, and duration does imply immobility and indecisiveness – which are perforce the negation of generalship. So that whether from the standpoint of military science or from that of the drain of human life, long battles are bad battles.

The prolongation, too, has complicated the task of the military historian, for unless he desires to fill massive tomes with profuse detail, it is difficult to pick out salient features where there are either none, or else so many that they tend to merge into a formless mass. And of all the so-called 'battles' of the war, Verdun holds the duration record, extending from February 21st to December 15th, 1916. Even if the suspension of the German offensive be taken as the last date, and the French counter-offensive considered as distinct, the duration is seven months.

This difficulty of singling out any one date is unfortunate, for no battle of the whole war was more heroic or more dramatic in its course, or made so vivid an appeal to the sympathies of the watching nations. It was France's supreme sacrifice and her supreme triumph, and to the splendour of her achievement all the world paid homage.

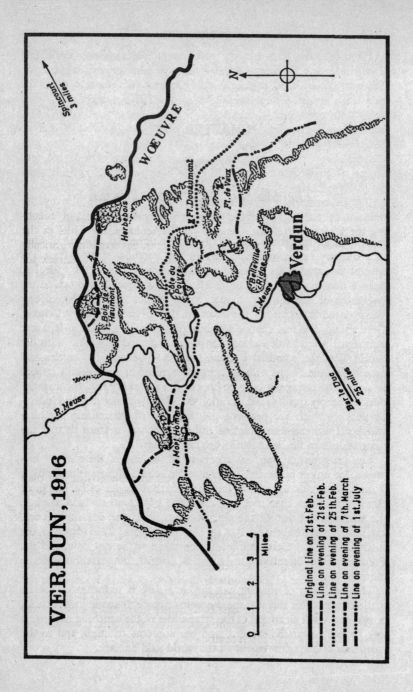

VERDUN, 1916

Spincourt
3 miles

WOEUVRE

Herbebois

Bois de
Haumont

Côte du
Poivre

R. Meuse

le Mort Homme

× Ft. Douaumont

Ft. de Vaux

Belleville
Ridge

R. Meuse

Verdun

Bar le Duc
25 miles

Miles
0 1 2 3 4

———— Original Line on 21st. Feb.
——·—— Line on evening of 21st. Feb.
·········· Line on evening of 25th. Feb.
—··—··— Line on evening of 7th. March
—·—·— Line on evening of 1st. July

From February 25th onwards, there was a series of crises until June 23rd, and many French authorities select the former date as the chief. Yet who should know better than the Germans the moment when the tide really turned against them? So distinguished a critic as General von Zwehl considered that the real turning point was on March 9th, when the Germans failed to capture the Côte de Poivre. It was on March 4th that the Crown Prince called on his army group for a supreme effort to take Verdun, 'the heart of France'. On March 6th, after a two days' bombardment, the new blow fell, and by the 9th was definitely frustrated.

The determination of such a datum point is affected also by the question as to the object of the German Supreme Command in launching the attack on Verdun. General von Falkenhayn, the Chief of the Great General Staff and the responsible officer, has stated categorically that it was to bleed France white by choosing a point of attack for which, sooner than let go, the French Command would have to fight to the last man. He has also quoted from a paper prepared at Christmas, 1915, to show that he argued that a breakthrough in mass was not necessary for this purpose.

Yet, despite his post-war statements, there is still a just doubt as to the initial object. A prominent German critic, Colonel Foerster, pointed out how difficult it was to reconcile Falkenhayn's statement with the manner in which the attack was carried out, and declared that the initial operation was obviously an accelerated attack for the purpose of breaking through. He based himself on extracts from Falkenhayn's own order of January 27th, 1916, and the latter's vehement marginal criticisms on the explanation of failure rendered by the Crown Prince's headquarters on March 31st. These show Falkenhayn calling for an unchecked and continuous advance.

Others, including Pétain, believe the real idea underlying the plan was that of a revival of the 'Sedan' double envelopment which had been attempted in September 1914. In 1916 such a plan had more favour-able chances, for the salient was more acute than at the time of the Marne battle, owing to the St Mihiel wedge that had been driven into its eastern flank. And the fact that the salient lay astride a river, the Meuse, would hamper the defenders in holding back the German pincers. Moreover, this hypothesis provides a logical explanation for what outwardly seems the unaccountable German mistake in launching their first attack only on the east bank of the river. But if a Sedan was the Germans' object, they might expect that their attack on the east bank would draw the French reserves thither so that the later attack on the west bank, when released, would be able to sweep across the rear of the French, using the river as their prison wall. Thereby, not only would part of the French army be cut off, but the rest be cut in two, while the vast breach would ensure the collapse of the whole trench front in France.

Fresh light on this enigmatic battle has, however, come from the German archives and from important witnesses; the evidence collated in a book by Hermann Wendt is particularly illuminating. From this new material it would appear that the explanation of Falkenhayn's purpose lies in his opportunism; and the explanation of the curious course of the German operations, in one more of the internal conflicts that wrecked so many plans.

Falkenhayn, whose course was apparently none too clear in his own mind, seems to have rested on the hope that something might happen – that 'something' might be a moral collapse behind the French front, produced by the combination of natural depression and subsidized propaganda. But if he was wiser than other strategists in realizing the importance of political effects, he does not seem to have had clear ideas as to how to produce them. And, unfortunately for him, his executive subordinates had a purely military outlook. The scheme drawn up by the Crown Prince's Chief of Staff, Schmidt von Knobelsdorf, diverged widely from Falkenhayn's line of thought. It proposed an attempt to pinch off Verdun, by a vigorous attack on both flanks, 'so as to avoid a long-drawn-out battle of material, with its incalculable expenditure of force'.

This big gamble did not suit Falkenhayn's book, so he reduced the plan to an attack on the east bank only, apparently hoping to control the executive commander's impetuosity by keeping a tight hand on the reserves. In this purpose, as in his greater one, he was to fail. It is not easy to determine whether that failure was due more to his own mis-judgement in adjusting the means to the end, or to his inability to adjust his subordinate's views to his own. Princely subordinates were difficult to control, and Falkenhayn's position was too unstable for him safely to exert strong pressure. Also, whatever his failings, he at least has the credit of affirming a new principle in tactics.

The German offensive was to be based on fire power rather than on man power, and its main agent was to be an intense artillery bombardment, making up for its relatively short duration by the number of batteries and their rapidity of fire, and so seeking to regain the supreme advantage of surprise which was inevitably lost by an artillery preparation of several days, or even a week – as the Allied method had been at

Loos, in Champagne, and was still to be on the Somme. To increase their chance of surprise the Germans constructed none of the customary 'jumping off' trenches close to the enemy lines, confident that their tremendous artillery bombardment would enable their infantry to cross the wide no-man's-land, in places half a mile across, without meeting effective resistance. With their rear preparations they were less successful. But although the Intelligence branch at French General Headquarters was thus able to deduce the German intentions, the Operations branch disregarded the warning. On February 1st a driblet of two Territorial divisions was sent, but only at the last moment were adequate reinforcements – two army corps – ordered there. Even when the first of these arrived there were only three divisions on the right bank of the Meuse, two on the left, and three south of the fortress facing east – with no reserves at hand. It is not difficult to guess what would have happened if the German attack had come on the 13th, as intended, before this first corps arrived. Bad weather saved the defenders in a double sense, for it also hampered the moving forward of the Germans' heavy guns.

There is, however, another important aspect of this preliminary phase which is comparatively little known. A hasty generalization from the easy fall of the Belgian and Russian fortresses may have caused much of the subsequent critical position at Verdun. Originally the French fortresses were not under the control of the field army, but Joffre used the examples of Liége and Namur as an excuse to persuade the French Government to 'declass' Verdun as a fortress, and, having got control in August, 1915, from then on he drained it of its men and armament. This removal of guns continued even until January 30th, 1916, and the casemates were simply used as shelters for troops. Instead of an all-round defence a single trench position was taken up beyond the forts, and in rear only one subsidiary trench line was usable.

For this continuous front, the commander, General Herr, had not enough men or material – to garrison it or keep it in an efficient state of defence. Its wire was incomplete, and it had scarcely any shell-proof cover. Little wonder that when the blow fell the trench position was blotted out. In contrast was the extraordinary imperviousness of the forts. Forts Douaumont and Vaux fell into German hands, and when they were recaptured in October the French found that months of tremendous bombardment had made scarcely an impression. The underground cover remained intact, not one field-gun turret was destroyed, and hardly any of the casemates rendered unoccupiable. It was a grim jest of fate that the French should have thrown away their shield for a target, through a hasty assumption that fortresses were valueless.

The original Governor, General Coutanceau, had not shared this view, but when, before a Parliamentary delegation, he dared to express his opinion, in contradiction to the Army Group commander, General Dubail, he was not only rebuked but dismissed. For some time, rumours had percolated through to Paris about the inadequate state of the Verdun defences, and in December Galliéni, as Minister of War, had written to Joffre asking for information and an assurance that they should be developed. Joffre's reply might well be framed and hung up in all the bureaux of officialdom the world over – to serve as the mummy at the feast. Rebutting the suggestions, he added – 'But since these apprehensions are founded on reports which allege defects in the state of the defences, I request you to ... specify their authors. I cannot be a party to soldiers under my command bringing before the Government, by channels other than the hierarchic channel, complaints or protests concerning the execution of my orders ... It is calculated to disturb profoundly the spirit of discipline in the Army.' The enemy was soon to dispel his doctrine of infallibility, as the mutinies of 1917 were to show that the incapacity of generals and their waste of human life are the most potent factors in disturbing the spirit of discipline. But retribution is slow. Colonel Driant, Deputy for Nancy and a well-known military writer, who had given the warning, was one of the first victims of its neglect, while Joffre for a time gained fresh popular laurels from the heroic sacrifice of Driant and his fellows.

At a quarter past seven on the morning of February 21st, a cold, dry day, the German bombardment began on both banks of the Meuse and on a front of fifteen miles. Steadily the trenches and wire were flattened out or upheaved in a chaos of tumbled earth. 'The craters made by the huge shells gave to all the countryside an appearance like the surface of the moon.' Familiar as it was to be later, in February, 1916, so violent a bombardment was new, and therefore the more appalling. So it went on – until at 4 PM the fury of the shell-storm reached its height. Another three-quarters of an hour and a thin skirmish line of German infantry began to advance almost unnoticed, followed by bombing parties and flame-throwers, to feel the French position before the rest of the infantry was launched. This method economized life, and it also disclosed the unequal effect of the German bombardment, which in parts suffered from the deadly counter-battery fire of the French artillery. Moreover, the initial German attack was made by only six divisions and only along a four-and-a-half-mile front between Bois de Haumont and Herbebois on the east bank. On so narrow a front the few scattered packets of surviving Frenchmen caused more delay than should have been the case on a reasonable frontage, and the early onset of darkness halted the attack after the foremost trenches had been occupied. But next day the attack developed more widely, and from then until the 24th the defenders' line was progressively crumbled away.

The French commanders on the spot asked permission to evacuate the Woevre plain and draw back the line on to the Meuse heights on the right bank. Even this they felt must be only a preliminary to the evacuation of the whole right, or eastern, bank of the Meuse. But behind the front the full gravity of the situation was hardly realized. 'Operations' still asserted that the Verdun offensive was a feint to cover the real blow, in Champagne. Even when the news of the crumbling front came through, Joffre was not moved, much less disturbed. At last, on the evening of the 24th, General de Castelnau – who, since his appointment as Chief of the French General Staff, had been adroitly side-tracked by Joffre's ever-zealous, and jealous, *entourage* – took the initiative and, going direct to Joffre, gained his permission to send Pétain's army to take over the defence of Verdun. Still more alarming reports came in later, and at 11 PM de Castelnau, with unique daring, insisted that the orderly officer should rap on Joffre's locked door and wake him up. Before the great man returned to resume his unvarying ration of sleep, he had given de Castelnau authority to go to Verdun with 'full powers'.

Leaving Chantilly during the night, de Castelnau motored post haste to the headquarters of the Army Group commander, de Langle de Cary. Joffre meanwhile had telegraphed that the front north of Verdun must be held at all costs: 'Every commander who . . . gives an order for retreat will be tried by court martial.' He left it to de Langle de Cary to decide whether to swing back his right on to the Meuse heights, and the latter acted on this permission.

De Castelnau's first day at Verdun was not auspicious; for on the 25th occurred the strange incident of Fort Douaumont, and with it the first crisis of the long battle. Like most of the other forts it had no garrison, except for a crew of twenty-three gunners who manned one turret. When, however, the German tide approached the fort, General Chrétien, commanding the right sector, dictated an order that the line of the forts was to be made the principal line of resistance. This was shortly before midnight on the 24th. Unfortunately his staff waited for the preparation of some sketches to attach to the order, and so delayed its issue until 9.45 AM on the 25th. Meantime a patrol of Branden-burgers, finding the drawbridge down and no sign of any defenders –

the gunners had fallen asleep dead-beat – walked in and took possession without firing a shot. A triumphal German *communiqué* announced the capture of Douaumont 'by assault' in the presence of the Kaiser. This piece of official bombast, however, was to be outclassed and out-farced when, owing to a misunderstood telephone message, the *communiqué* of March 9th announced the capture of Fort Vaux – three months too early. But the cream of the jest was that both the divisional commander who made the report and the officer who had *not* taken the fort, received from the Kaiser the highest Prussian order, *Pour le Mérite*! A bad telephone is not without compensations.

On February 25th Pétain took over command at Verdun, and the nucleus of a reserve army was assembling in rear. His first problem was not so much defence as supply. The German heavy guns had closed all avenues except one light railway and the Bar-le-Duc to Verdun road – which later became immortal as 'the Sacred Way'. To push up troops was no use unless they could be fed and supplied with ammunition. The road was already cracking under the strain of the incessant transport, and so gangs of Territorial troops were brought up to keep it in repair and to double it by parallel tracks. Henceforward the flow of traffic rose to as many as 6,000 lorries in the twenty-four hours. Up in front Pétain was organizing the front into sectors, each with its own heavy artillery, and throwing in repeated counter-attacks. If these gained little ground, they disconcerted and checked the attacking Germans. Another assisting factor was that the farther they advanced on the east bank the more did they expose themselves to flanking fire from the French artillery across the river. The advance lost its momentum, slowed down, and already on the German side 'a grievous pessimism had set in', so Zwehl tells us.

Falkenhayn was now led to widen the front of attack, although he doled out only four divisions. On March 6th, after two days' bombardment, the Crown Prince attacked on the west bank of the Meuse, and on the 8th the troops on the east bank joined in this supreme effort. The gains did not repay the losses, and against Mort Homme on the west and the Poivre height on the east the attack beat in vain. Any hope of a breakthrough faded, for the defence was now consolidated and the numbers had been balanced. Whatever we think of his foresight, there can be no question that Joffre's imperturbable temperament was a great asset in calming the anxiety of those days, and in Pétain he made the right choice for the emergency. It is proverbial that fortune favours the brave, and two great pieces of luck befell the French – the fortunate destruction of all the German 17-inch howitzers by the French long-range guns, and the blowing up of the great German artillery park near Spincourt, which held 450,000 heavy shell, unwisely kept fused. One authority, indeed, General Palat, gives it as his opinion that these two factors saved Verdun.

From March 9th onwards, there can be no question that the German policy was primarily attrition, and that so far as Verdun was aimed at it was as a moral objective. Publicity had given it a symbolical value definitely superior to its military value. It must be confessed that the strategy nearly succeeded – but only, after a long interval, through the introduction of a new agent. In the meantime the Germans paid an exorbitant price for little gain. Nevertheless, they put a heavy tax on the French. Pétain did his best to mitigate the strain by a rapid rotation of reliefs, which kept each division under fire for the shortest possible time. But, as a result, a great part of the French Army was drawn through the 'mincing machine', and the drain on the French reserves almost bankrupted their share in the forthcoming Somme offensive.

On the German side, the disappointing results produced an earlier reaction. At the end of March Falkenhayn enquired whether there was 'any chance of progress within a reasonable time'; and he contemplated an alternative attack at Ypres. But the Crown Prince confidently declared that the greater part of the French reserves had been used up, and that he was 'unreservedly of the opinion that the fate of the French Army would be decided at Verdun'. Moreover, the fatally old-fashioned idea of the executive command was betrayed in the remark that 'the destruction of the French reserves ... should be completed by the employment of men, as well as of apparatus and munitions'. Falkenhayn gave way to this plea.

So the Crown Prince, egged on by Schmidt von Knobelsdorf, continued to pour out his men's blood, while Falkenhayn spent the time in study of possible alternatives. But at the end of April the barren result of constant nibbling attacks led to a decision to revert to wider ones.

These proved equally futile, so that even Schmidt von Knobelsdorf was led to admit the hopelessness of further attack. Yet when he visited Falkenhayn in this mood of repentance, he found the latter had also changed his mind – to the opposite view. So Schmidt von Knobelsdorf was reconverted, and the offensive continued. But the wastage of life was now balanced by Joffre's misguided instructions that Fort Douaumont must be recovered; he also removed Pétain's restraining hand by promoting him to command of the Army Group and placing Nivelle in direct charge at Verdun. By launching repeated attacks, Nivelle now played into Falkenhayn's hands, and lost on the rebound.

On June 7th, after a heroic resistance, Fort Vaux really fell − by another German telephone mistake the wrong officer again received the credit − and with it a large stretch of ground was submerged by the German tide, that now seemed to the anxious watchers to resemble the forces of nature rather than of men. On June 11th Pétain was forced to ask Joffre to hasten the relief offensive on the Somme. Then on June 20th, the Germans introduced a new kind of diphosgene gas shell with startling effect. It paralysed the French artillery support, and on the 23rd came a deep advance that brought the Germans almost to the Belleville height, the last outwork of Verdun. Mangin's incessant counter-attacks could do no more than put a brake on the advance, and Pétain made all ready for the evacuation of the east bank, though to his troops he showed no signs of anxiety and ever repeated the now immortal phrase, 'On les aura!' Four divisions were hurriedly dispatched to him by Joffre, thus further weakening the Somme reserve.

But the Germans had used their new lever too late. Strategically, the defenders were now made secure, indirectly, as Falkenhayn stopped the flow of ammunition to Verdun on the 24th − when the British bombardment began on the Somme, preparatory to the long-arranged attack which was delivered on July 1st. From that day on the Germans at Verdun received no fresh divisions, and their advance died out from pure inanition. The way was thus paved for the brilliant French counter-offensives of the autumn, which retook by bites what had been lost by nibbles. It is no disparagement of the sterling defence to recognize, as we must, that the Somme saved Verdun, and, second, that the Germans after throwing away their best chance by too narrow an attack frontage, came desperately close to their goal four months later.

CHAPTER SIX

SCENE 2

The Brusilov Offensive

On June 5th, 1916, began an offensive on the Eastern Front which was to prove the last really effective military effort of Russia. Popularly known as Brusilov's offensive, it had such an astonishing initial success as to revive enthusiastic dreams of the irresistible Russian 'steamroller', that was perhaps the greatest and most dangerous myth of the war. Instead, its ultimate achievement was to sound Russia's death knell. Paradoxical in its consequences, it was still more so in its course – an epitome of the delusive objectives, of the blunders leading to success, and the successes leading to downfall, which marked perhaps the most erratic war in history. In 1915 the Entente had pinned their hopes on Russia, only for the year's campaign to close with the Russian armies, battered and exhausted, barely escaping complete disaster by a seemingly endless retreat. When Falkenhayn turned in 1916 to inaugurate the Verdun attack he left Russia lamed but not crippled, and her surprisingly rapid, if perhaps superficial recovery, enabled her to dislocate the German plans for 1916. As early as March she attacked at Lake Narocz, on the Baltic flank, in a gallant sacrificial attempt to relieve the pressure on France. Her command then prepared, for July, a main offensive, also in the north. But before this was ready the needs of her Allies once more led her into a premature move. While the strain at Verdun was growing ever more serious, the Austrians took the opportunity to launch an attack in the Trentino, against the Italians, who appealed to their Russian ally to prevent the Austrians releasing further forces from the Eastern Front to reinforce the Trentino menace.

Meantime the Tsar had held a council of war of his Army Group commanders on April 14th. It was here arranged that the main Russian offensive should be made by Evert's centre group of armies, while Kuropatkin's northern group wheeled inwards to assist it; and it was proposed that Brusilov's southern group should stay strictly on the defensive as his front was unsuited to the offensive. But Brusilov regarded this as a reason for taking the offensive – because helpful to surprise – and argued that past lack of success was due to the way the Russian armies had allowed the enemy to utilize his central position by not attacking simultaneously. As a result of the discussion Brusilov was given permission to act as he wished, and, with such resources as he had, to stage an offensive that would draw the enemy's attention away from the main blow planned in the north, near Molodeczno. Realizing that his best chance of success lay in surprise, he began preparations at over twenty places, so that even deserters could not give away the real point of attack. And, instead of concentrating his reserves, he divided them.

The appeal of Russia's ally hastened his action. On May 24th Alexeiev telegraphed to ask how soon he could attack. Brusilov replied that he would be ready to do so on June 1st, provided that Evert also attacked. Evert, however, was not ready; it was finally agreed that Brusilov should strike on the 4th, and Evert ten days later. On the night of the 3rd Alexeiev rang up Brusilov and expressed doubts of the wisdom of a plan so unconventional, suggesting that he should concentrate his troops for an attack on a narrow front, instead of distributing them on a wide front. Brusilov demurred and Alexeiev eventually gave way, saying, 'God be with you. Do as you like.'

The troops were moved up during the night for an apparent gamble, in which every factor save the possibility of surprise weighed against success. Brusilov's strength was no more than equal to that of the opposing force – thirty-eight against thirty-seven divisions – and it was widely distributed. But the absence of any concentration gave the Austrians no warning of the impending move, and when, on June 4th, the Russian Eighth Army, under Kaledin, advanced near Luck for what was little more than a reconnaissance in force, they took the Austrians by surprise. The front broke like a crust of pastry at the first touch, and almost unresisted the Russians pushed between the Austrian Fourth and Second Armies. By the following day 40,000 prisoners had been taken, and the number swelled rapidly as Brusilov widened his offensive. Although the Russian Eleventh Army (Sakharov) failed near Tarnopol, the other two armies farther south gained as rapid success as that at Luck. The Seventh Army (Shcherbachev) drove the Austrians back across the Strypa, and the Ninth Army (Lechitski), breaking through in the Bukovina, captured Czernowitz – the southernmost position of the Austrian front. By the 20th, Brusilov had captured 200,000 men.

Never has a mere demonstration had so amazing a success since the walls of Jericho fell at Joshua's trumpet blasts. With both flanks collapsed, the Austro-German armies in the south were in danger of a greater Tannenberg, if only the Russians could exploit their chance. But all the reserves were massed in the north for the intended main offensive, and this was not developed. First, Evert said that on account of bad weather he could not begin until the 18th, and, even so, did not expect to be successful. The Tsar and Alexeiev lacked the resolution either to coerce or to replace Evert, and instead authorized him to prepare an attack at a different place – which meant further delay. But neither Evert nor Kuropatkin showed any inclination to take the offensive; and, as Alexeiev could not move them, he tried instead to move their reserves. Poor lateral communications, however, prevented these reaching Brusilov before the Germans could hurry reinforcements to stem the tide. The German Command showed its usual cleverness, using the first reinforcements for a counterstroke by Linsingen against the northern edge of the Luck breakthrough, and this at least checked the Russian progress at the most critical point. To the south, in the Bukovina, the Russian advance continued until it came to a natural halt against the barrier of the Carpathian Mountains.

Late in July the Russian attack was renewed, first in the centre towards Brody and Lemberg by Sakharov, then farther north towards the Stokhod river and Kovel, by the Russian Guard Army, long prepared for a supreme effort. But the opportunity had passed, and although the attacks still dragged on throughout August, the gains in no way compensated for their heavy cost, and an effort which opened in a blaze of sunshine faded out in autumn gloom.

Its indirect were, however, greater than its direct effects, although not unmixed in benefit. It had compelled Falkenhayn to withdraw seven divisions from the west, and so abandon his plan for a riposte against the British Somme offensive, as well as the hope of nourishing his attrition process at Verdun. It led Rumania to take her fateful decision to enter the war on the Entente side – to her undoing. And it wrought the downfall of Falkenhayn, who had 'spoiled the ship for a ha'porth of tar.'

But these indirect effects were purchased at a heavy price. Brusilov had captured the Bukovina and much of Eastern Galicia; he had captured 350,000 prisoners – but, through prolonging the offensive when opportunity had passed, over 1,000,000 men had been lost. This loss undermined morally, even more than materially, the fighting power of Russia. The imminent sequel was to be revolution and collapse. For the last time Russia had sacrificed herself for her allies, and it is not just that subsequent events should obscure the debt.

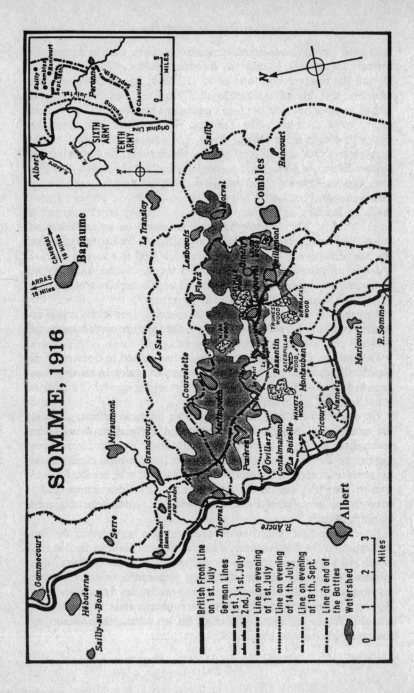

SOMME, 1916

British Front Line on 1st. July
German Lines { 1st. } 1st. July
{ 2nd. }
Line on evening of 1st. July
Line on evening of 14th. July
Line on evening of 18th. Sept.
Line at end of the Battles
Watershed

Miles
0   1   2   3

CHAPTER SIX

SCENE 3

The Somme Offensive

The 'battle' – or, to be strategically accurate, the series of partial actions – in Picardy which opened on July 1st, constituted the offensive campaign of the Franco-British armies in 1916. Into it was thrown the entire British effort of the year on the Western Front, and such part of the French effort as was available after the exhausting strain of the long defensive 'battle' of Verdun. And it proved both the glory and the graveyard of 'Kitchener's Army' – those citizen volunteers who, instantly answering the call in 1914, had formed the first national army of Britain.

The Somme offensive had its genesis at the Chantilly Conference of the Allied commanders on December 5th, 1915. Joffre, in his appreciation of the situation, claimed that the autumn offensives in Champagne and Artois (including Loos) had brought 'brilliant tactical results', and ascribed the failure to develop these into a strategical success, partly to bad weather and partly to a temporary shortage of ammunition. The essential for the next effort was that 'the Higher Command must have no anxiety as regards ammunition', and for this reason it could not be undertaken in less than three months. By early February he had realized that the date must be later still, if, as was essential, the Russians were to attack simultaneously and the British were to take an adequate share with their newly raised armies. At a meeting with Haig he emphasized the view that a broad frontage of attack was the method of success, and to this end desired a combined offensive by the French and British *'bras dessus bras dessous'*, with the attacking line of one Ally prolonging that of the other Ally. Joffre envisaged the French attacking with forty divisions on a twenty-five miles' front from Lassigny to the Somme, and the British attacking thence to Hébuterne, fourteen miles, with twenty-five divisions, or as near that number as possible.

The British Official History remarks that Joffre's decision to make the offensive in a sector which 'might be considered the strongest' for defence, on the Western Front, 'seems to have been arrived at solely because the British would be bound to take part in it. The reasons advanced by General Joffre will hardly bear examination'. Even Foch, if it was not his habit to weigh tactical difficulties, disliked the choice of sector as being a strategic dead-end. Haig would have preferred to make his attack in Flanders, on the lines of the offensive which he carried out in 1917, assisted by a landing on the Belgian coast.

Joffre also pressed the British to make a preparatory attack north of the Somme in April, and another in May – to draw in the enemy's reserves, so easing the way for the Franco-British main blow. Haig preferred to trust in one great stroke, with all the forces available and when they were fully prepared. Although Haig's attitude was justified by the incompleteness of his resources and by the barrenness of such preparatory attacks the previous autumn, the critic is compelled to recognize that Joffre had the experience of history on his side, and that the experience of the war was to show that decisive offensives were vain until the enemy's reserves had been attracted elsewhere. But Haig was unquestionably right in maintaining that any such preparatory attacks, to fulfil their object, should only precede the general offensive by ten days or a fortnight.

He suggested that the British might deliver one such attack if the French made others. This idea did not appeal to Joffre who, according to Poincaré, had now 'in mind a war of attrition which must be chiefly carried out by our Allies, England, Russia, and even Italy'. So discussions continued. It is amusing to note that the British staff took refuge in the explanation – 'The British Army is ready to do its full share, but we cannot cope with the politicians, who, after the Germans, are our worst enemies.'

Eventually, at a conference on February 14th, an agreement was reached by which Haig accepted Joffre's plan for the Somme offensive – dated for July 1st – while Joffre gave up his demand for preparatory offensives.

The result of the postponement of the Allied offensive, whether inevitable or not, was to yield the initiative to the Germans, and their attack at Verdun, from February 21st onwards, impaired the whole of the Allied plan and campaign in 1916. Yet such a possibility had not even been mentioned at the conference on the 14th.

On February 22nd Joffre asked the British to aid him by relieving part of his troops in the north. Haig accordingly hastened the relief of the French Tenth Army, round Arras, which was sandwiched between his own First and Third Armies. Allenby's Third Army sideslipped northwards, and the newly formed Fourth Army, under Rawlinson, took over its front between Maricourt and Hébuterne. The British now held a continuous eighty-mile front from Ypres almost to the Somme.

As the French were drained of their strength at Verdun, so did their share of the Somme plan evaporate. Ultimately their front of attack shrank from twenty-five miles to eight, and their force from forty divisions to sixteen, of which only five attacked on July 1st. From now onwards the British were to take up the main burden of the Western Front campaign and, because of this fact alone, July 1st, 1916, is a landmark in the history of the war.

Nevertheless, Haig did not adjust his aims to the shrinkage of resources. It is true that he continued preparations for an attack at Messines, and formed an alternative plan, to switch his reserves thither in case of complete failure. But he does not seem to have foreseen the case of mixed success and failure -- always the greater probability in war. And for this want of elasticity his plan suffered in execution. Realism was equally lacking. The hopeful intention of the British Command was, in the first stage, to break the German front between Maricourt and Serre; in the second stage to secure the high ground between Bapaume and Ginchy, while the French seized that round Sailly and Rancourt; in the third stage to wheel to the left and roll up the German flank as far as Arras, so enlarging the breach. With this object all available troops, including cavalry, would work northwards, from the line Bapaume–Miraumont, while a cooperating attack was launched against the German front south-west of Arras. Fourthly, was to come a general advance towards Cambrai–Douai. What a contrast between intention and achievement! In outline, the plan was shrewdly designed, and Haig was wise to take such long views. But he does not seem to have looked clearly enough at the ground beneath his feet. The very belief in such far-reaching possibilities suggests a failure to diagnose the actual conditions. There was a fundamental unrealism in a plan which, while discarding the old and ever-new master key of surprise, made no pretence to provide a substitute.

The main attack, on a fourteen-mile front between Maricourt and Serre, was entrusted to Rawlinson's Fourth Army of eighteen divisions, of which eleven were to lead the attack, with five in close reserve. Only two, together with a cavalry division, were in army reserve. But Haig also placed at Rawlinson's disposal, for exploiting success, a force of two cavalry divisions under Gough, with a corps of two divisions to follow. Two divisions of the Third Army were to make a subsidiary attack round Gommecourt. The artillery concentration totalled 1,537 guns, 467 being heavy. This meant one gun to every twenty yards of front, a record at that time, although far eclipsed by later concentrations. It was double that of the Germans for their great Dunajec breakthrough, but the defences on the Russian front a year before could not be compared with the network of wire and trenches on the Somme front. Another significant contrast was that whereas the French had 900 heavy guns, the British had less than half this number for a far wider front – one to every fifty-seven yards.

The British Official History remarks that 'The problem facing the Allies was, in fact, that of storming a fortress, in which, according to history and precedent, there should be a main assault on the largest breach (or weakest spot), several subsidiary ones on minor breaches – which must be strong enough to be converted into main assaults and carried through – and false attacks.' Instead, the distribution of force was as uniform as the methods of attacks were stereotyped. The artillery, in any case deficient, was spread evenly along the whole frontage. 'It must be confessed that the problem was not appreciated at GHQ.' What were the causes of this blindness? They had a pre-war base. 'It must be admitted that the problems of semi-siege warfare and the large concentration of guns necessary for the attack of great field defences had never been studied in practice by the General Staff. Under the influence of General H. H. Wilson (the late Sir Henry Wilson) it had been content to follow French ideas as to the nature of the next war, and ignored and almost resented hearing of the information obtained by its Intelligence branch as to the preparations being made and methods practised at manoeuvres by the Germans.'

To understand both the problem and the course of the battle a brief description of the ground is necessary, for in few battles on the Western Front did topography have so important an influence or make so deep an impression on the minds of the combatants. From Péronne, where the Somme makes a right-angled turn south, a range of hills runs northwest, forming the watershed between the Somme and the basins of the Scarpe and the Scheldt. This ridge, intersected by the narrow valley of the little river Ancre, had been in German possession since the 'Race to the Sea' of October, 1914, and it gave the enemy command and observation over the Allied lines and the land behind them. For the first year this disadvantage mattered little, for when British troops relieved the French here in July, 1915, the front had an air and a condition of peacefulness astonishing to men accustomed to the incessant 'bickering'

of Ypres or La Bassée. Report said that in some places the troops of our
Ally went back for *déjeuner* to villages hardly touched, close to the line,
leaving only sentries in the trenches; that in another hamlet which stood
in no-man's-land the sleeping accommodation was nightly shared
between the opposing sides by tacit consent. I can vouch for the fact that
in the first months after the British had taken over this front it was
possible for battalions to drill undisturbed on fields in full view of the
German lines – whereas six months later billets several miles farther
back were harassed by gunfire. The campaign policy of the French,
except when engaged in active operations, was 'live and let live', and in
retrospect there seems little doubt that it was wiser than the British
policy of continual 'strafing'. For when the Germans held the dominating positions as well as a superiority in ammunition and equipment
these worrying tactics wore down the British troops more than the
enemy – attrition on the wrong side of the balance sheet. Further, they
stirred the Germans to strengthen their trench defences, to develop by
art the advantages of nature, so that the offensive came against an
almost impregnable fortress instead of against the relatively weak
defence system which existed in the autumn of 1915. Masefield, in his
book, *The Old Front Line*, expressed the situation aptly – 'Almost in
every part of this old front our men had to go up hill to attack ... The
enemy had the look-out posts, with the fine views over France, and the
sense of domination. Our men were down below, with no view of anything but of stronghold after stronghold, just up above, being made
stronger daily.' Today the tumbled desolation that was the Somme
battlefield has passed. Though he underestimated the time, Masefield's
instinct was correct that 'when the trenches are filled in and the plough
has gone over them the ground will not keep the look of war. One
summer with its flowers will cover most of the ruin that man can make,
and then these places, from which the driving back of the enemy began,
will be hard indeed to trace, even with maps'. 'Centre Way, Peel
Trench, Munster Alley, and these other paths to glory will be deep
under the corn, and gleaners will sing at Dead Mule Corner.' Yet, while
even memory finds it difficult to recapture the wartime aspect, a tranquil visit impresses the mind with the steepness of the ascent and the
command from the ridge, even more than in days when progress was
reckoned in yards and the contour was seen from the eye-level of
trenches and shell-holes. From an artillery point of view there were
advantages in attacking uphill, because the German trenches were more
clearly displayed, but in other ways it was a physical and psychological
handicap – not only to the attacking infantry.

Surprise, difficult in face of such commanding positions, was the more difficult because the art of concealing preparations, and of camouflage, had yet to be relearnt. The construction of new hutments on both sides of the Ancre provided the Germans with the first clue, in February, and thenceforward signs continually multiplied. Falkenhayn contemplated an attempt to dislocate the British offensive, but found that he could not spare the necessary troops. If the vast preparations had not given it away, a bombardment of a week's duration would in any case have announced the coming assault. Even earlier, a censorship error in allowing publication of a speech to munition workers by the Minister of Labour, Mr Arthur Henderson, on June 2nd, had given the German Command a hint of its early delivery. The one redeeming factor was that despite accurate predictions and warnings of the attack both from the immediate army command (the Second) and from agents abroad, Falkenhayn continued to believe that it was only a preliminary to the real blow farther north, apparently feeling that British preparations were too blatant to be true. In consequence he withheld reinforcements, and not until July 5th was he convinced that the Somme was Haig's chosen battleground. In the meantime he dismissed the Chief of Staff of the Second Army for having been right and 'asking for more'.

This divergence of views in the German Command left the British a chance which was to be forfeited by a divergence of views in their own command. The extent of this difference, and its effects, has only come to light in recent years. For the offensive was only a few weeks old when the story was spread by officially inspired apologists that Haig was throughout aiming at a campaign of attrition and had not dreamt of a 'breakthrough'. This denial was vehemently maintained for years, long after the war; it forms one of the most elaborate perversions of historical truth that has come to light. The 'smoke screen', composed of particles of truth dishonestly mixed, was finally dissipated by the publication of the Official History in 1932.

This revealed that Joffre was only contemplating an attrition battle, and that Rawlinson inclined to the same view, while Haig, the middle man, both sought and believed in a breakthrough. His judgement dictated the British aim. But Rawlinson's doubts led to the British plan being a compromise of method, which made it largely unsuitable to either aim. In view of his 'comparatively small resources' in artillery, and the depth of the German position, Rawlinson favoured a prolonged bombardment and an advance by limited stages. The first inevitably diminished the chances of surprise – the most potent compensation for small resources – while the second was a check on exploiting any success that was gained, giving the enemy time to recover and to bring up reserves. Haig justly realized the latter defect and also inclined to a short bombardment; but, perhaps, being an untechnically minded cavalryman, he skimmed over the problem of cutting the wire entanglements that covered the approach to the enemy's position. After discussion Rawlinson was allowed his long bombardment, but was ordered to swallow part of the German second position, as well as the first, at one gulp.

The Official History, while showing that a breakthrough could hardly have had decisive results, and even suggesting that it would merely have created a dangerous salient, implies that a breakthrough was possible. But not in the way it was attempted. For his breakthrough aim, Haig actually relied on the one means in which he was, by all advice, too limited. His artillery adviser told him that he was 'stretching' his artillery too much. Rawlinson 'expressed the fear' that he was 'asking too much' of the force available, that its gun power would be spread too thinly for effect, and that an attempt to bite off part of the second position would be 'a gamble'. Nevertheless, it was to that gamble that Haig decided to commit his subordinates and their men.

'Increasing optimism' was shown by Haig as the day of battle drew nearer, though French resources, and consequently their share, were steadily shrinking owing to the drain of Verdun. What is perhaps more remarkable is the way his chief subordinates joined in the chorus of optimism, singing so loudly as apparently to drown the doubts they had felt during cool consideration of the problem. They not merely deferred to his judgement; they made it their own. Loyalty could go no further.

'Privately' Rawlinson 'was convinced that they (Haig's instructions) were based on false premises and on too great optimism'. Yet he 'impressed on all at conferences and other times ... "that nothing could exist at the conclusion of the bombardment in the area covered by it", and the infantry would only have to walk over and take possession'. This current of optimism was passed downwards with the result that even when the bombardment was proving ineffective, battalions 'which reported that the enemy machine guns had not been silenced were told by the divisional staffs that they were scared'. Terrible words for an official history to record as being said to men who were about to pay with their lives for this disregard of their words!

Because of its disastrous effects, the causes of this fantastic optimism demand analysis. With some officers in large degree, and perhaps most officers in some degree, care for their personal interests may have had an influence. Viewed fairly, that is no particular reproach to soldiers;

for in any profession where life-careers are concerned it is human nature to follow the cue given from above.* But a wider cause would seem to have been genuine self-delusion. In some cases this may have been induced by the confused idea of loyalty – 'blind loyalty' – that the nineteenth-century military system had fostered; even here, the Fourth Army instructions, which omitted so many tactical points of vital importance, took pains to lay down with heavy emphasis that 'all criticism by subordinates ... of orders received from superior authority will in the end recoil on the heads of the critics...' But in other cases optimism was so buoyant as to need no inspiration from on high. Thus when Haig, anxious over the inadequate preparedness of one army corps, sent General Charteris thither with power to countermand its attack, 'for it had little chance of complete success', his envoy found the commander 'more than satisfied', and saying exuberantly that he felt 'like Napoleon before the battle of Austerlitz'. So Charteris yielded to his desire, although he 'came back feeling very miserable'.

The Official History suggests that the root of this fatal optimism among the higher command may be traced to an astounding failure to grasp the main lesson of previous experience – a lesson that most regimental soldiers had long since learnt. 'The failures of the past were put down to reasons other than the stout use of the machine gun by the enemy and his scientifically planned defences.' Such expert 'reasoning' is certainly one of the most remarkable recorded cases in all history of missing the wood for the trees.

Rationally it seems inexplicable that the bombardment should have been counted on to leave nobody alive in the opposing trenches. For, beyond Rawlinson's original doubts, there is the fact that he himself spread his limited artillery evenly along the front 'without regard to the strength and importance of any particular part', with the result that 'their fire was necessarily so dispersed that many strong points and machine-gun posts were never touched'. Moreover, a large proportion of the heavy guns available were of obsolete pattern and poor range, while much of the ammunition was defective. Thus the shells could not penetrate the dug-outs in which the German machine-gunners were

* Perhaps its ill-effects could only be curtailed if war was conducted by amateurs, or at least by soldiers who had become civilians after being trained: the point is illustrated in General Charteris' remark on one such appointment late in the war. 'He has one very strong asset ... a very big job in civil life to go back to whenever he may wish ... It is difficult for any regular professional soldier not to be influenced by consideration of his own future prospects. — has the independence of a civilian and the training of a soldier.'

sheltering – in waiting. Yet it is only on the assumption of a potentially overwhelming bombardment that we can understand at all the tactics adopted by the British command. One can hardly believe that anyone with a grain of common-sense or any grasp of past experience would have launched troops to the attack by such a method unless intoxicated with confidence in the effect of the bombardment. The method is certainly an object-lesson in supreme negation.

The Official History continues – 'In the early discussions Haig had said that corps were not to attack until their commanders were satisfied that the enemy's defences had been sufficiently destroyed; but this condition seems to have been dropped as time passed.' This carelessness to maintain an essential condition of all warfare, especially siege warfare, is another extraordinary fact. It would have been culpable in the commander of a company.

Let us, in justice, record a redeeming point of precaution – or what might have been one. Haig had suggested tentatively that, before the mass of the infantry were launched, the result of the bombardment and the state of the defences might be tested by sending ahead patrols or small parties, such as the Germans had used at Verdun. But this suggestion was 'rejected by his army commanders'.

Was there anything that might have rescued success, or at least mitigated the sacrifice? Yes – if the British infantry could have reached the enemy trenches before the defenders were able to open fire. There were two ways in which this might have been achieved. By crossing either before the enemy could see to fire or before they were ready to fire. Without fog, natural or artificial, the only chance of the first lay in an assault during the darkness or in the dim light before dawn. We learn that 'a few commanders ... desired that at least the assault should be made at the first streak of light, before the enemy machine-gunners could see their prey'. We are told that 'Rawlinson himself accepted' the suggestion 'and pressed his French neighbours to agree'. But they had double his quantity of heavy guns and wanted good observation for them. So he agreed to the later hour, apparently with little misgiving.

The question that remained was whether the British infantry could cross no-man's-land before the barrage lifted. It was a race with death – the greatest of such races – run by nearly 60,000 men in the first heat. They were hopelessly handicapped. The whole mass, made up of closely packed waves of men, was to be launched together, without discovering whether the bombardment had really paralysed the resistance. Under the Fourth Army's instructions, those waves were to advance at 'a steady pace', symmetrically aligned like rows of ninepins ready to be knocked over. 'The necessity of crossing no-man's-land at a good pace, so as to reach the parapet before the enemy could reach it, was not mentioned.' But to do so would have been physically impossible, for the heaviest handicap of all was that 'the infantryman was so heavily laden that he could not move faster than a walk'. Each man carried about 66 lb, over half his own body weight, 'which made it difficult to get out of a trench, impossible to move much quicker than a slow walk, or to rise and lie down quickly'. Even an army mule, the proverbial and natural beast of burden, is only expected to carry a third of his own weight!

The 'race' was lost before it started, and the battle soon after. The barrage went on, the infantry could not go on, the barrage could not be brought back, and infantry reinforcements were pushed in just where infantry could not go on – a compound tragedy of errors.

The bombardment began on June 24th; the attack was intended for June 29th, but was later postponed until July 1st, owing to a momentary break in the weather. This postponement, made at French request, involved not only the spreading out of the ammunition over a longer period, and a consequent loss of intensity, but a greater strain on part of the assaulting troops, who, after being keyed up for the effort, had to remain another forty-eight hours in cramped trenches under the exhausting noise of their own gunfire and the enemy's retaliation – conditions made worse by torrential rain which flooded the trenches.

July 1st dawned a day of broiling heat, and at 7 AM, the bombardment rose to its height. Half an hour later the infantry advanced from their trenches – and thousands fell, strewing no-man's-land with their bodies, before the German front trench was even reached. For their opponents were the Germans of 1916, most stubborn and skilful fighters; while the shells flattened their trenches, they sheltered in dugouts or shell-holes, and then as the barrage lifted dragged out their machine guns, to pour an unslackening hail of lead into the unduly dense waves of the attackers – for 1916 marked the nadir of infantry attacks, the revival of formations that were akin to the eighteenth century in their formalism and lack of manoeuvring power. Battalions attacked in four or eight waves, not more than a hundred yards apart, the men in each almost shoulder to shoulder, in a symmetrical well-dressed alignment, and taught to advance steadily upright at a slow walk with their rifles held aslant in front of them, bayonets upwards – so as to catch the eye of the observant enemy. An excellent imitation of Frederick's infantry *automata*, with the difference that they were no longer advancing against muskets of an effective range of barely a hundred yards. It is hardly remarkable that by nightfall many battalions were barely a hundred strong. Only as the upstanding waves were broken up by the fire did advance become possible. For then human nature and primitive cunning reasserted themselves against authorized tactics; the more enterprising and still uncowed survivors formed little groups, usually under some natural leader, and worked their way by short rushes, and crawling from shell-hole to shell-hole, stalking the opposing machine guns, and often progressing to a considerable depth with little further loss. But in many places packets of the enemy and nests of machine guns were left in their wake, to take heavy toll of the supports, in similarly dense formations.

Thus, save in the south, the force of the tide slackened and later ebbed. Fricourt, on the right centre, formed a turning point both in the front and in the fortune of the day. The French, south of the Somme and north of it as far as Maricourt, gained all their objectives with slight loss. This success they owed partly to their more flexible tactics and heavier artillery concentration, partly to the lesser strength of the German defences, and to the fact that the attack here came as a tactical surprise to the Germans who had expected an attack only on the British front. Between Maricourt and Fricourt the British XIII Corps (30th and 18th Divisions) reached its objectives, though with greater loss, capturing Montauban. On its left the XV Corps partially achieved its task of pinching out the bastion of Fricourt village and wood. The 7th Division turned one flank by capturing Mametz, and on the other flank the 21st Division penetrated some half a mile into the German lines, holding on to a narrow tongue of captured land with both its own flanks in the air until Fricourt fell next day.

But the 21st Division marked the boundary of success, and all to the north was failure – with the heaviest British loss of any day's fighting in the war. One significant factor was the greater width of 'no-man's-land'. In the III Corps, fractions of the 34th Division pushed past La Boisselle to Contalmaison, but were forced to fall back. Against Ovillers the waves of the 8th Division beat practically in vain. A renewed attack was ordered for the afternoon – 'wiser counsels, however, prevailed'. Northward, again, in the X Corps the assault of the 32nd Division was broken again the defences of Thiepval – 'only bullet-proof soldiers could have taken Thiepval this day'. The 36th Ulster Division, however, celebrated the anniversary of the Boyne by penetrating deep into the German front past Thiepval towards Grandcourt. Unhappily, the corps commander used his reserve to reinforce the division that was hopelessly held up and refused it to the Ulstermen who had made a hopeful opening. Thus their advanced parties were cut off, and at nightfall only small fractions of the German front trenches remained in British hands. The attack of the VIII Corps (29th, 4th and 31st Divisions) on the left flank was shattered more abruptly, though here again a few isolated parties pressed through to Beaumont Hamel and Serre. A muddled argument over a question of one mine explosion led to the heavy artillery 'lifting' ten minutes before the infantry assault – with fatal result. As for the subsidiary attack by the VII Corps at Gommecourt, the failure of the 46th Division nullified the opening success of the 56th, while the value of the heavy sacrifice made by the corps as a whole was nullified by the failure of the main offensive.

The tally of prisoners who passed through the corps cages that day is in some degree an index of the comparative initial success – XIII Corps (Congreve), 934; XV Corps (Horne), 517; III Corps (Pulteney), 32; X Corps (Morland), 478; VIII Corps (Hunter-Weston), 22. In contrast, the French had taken over 4,000 prisoners at little cost. The assault of their XX Corps next to the British was cloaked by a river mist in crossing no-man's-land, and quickly overran the German first position. The French then proposed to push on, but gave up the idea on hearing that their British neighbours were held back by orders from the higher command. The French attack south of the Somme, by two divisions of the Colonial Corps and one of the XXXV, enjoyed a surprise effect through being delivered two hours later than elsewhere. It not only gained all its objectives, but was pushed beyond, and by nightfall was within reach of the German second position.

For the French, in view of these results, July 1st may be counted a victory. But the major attack was that of the British, and here the Germans could justly claim success, for with only six divisions available, and roughly a regiment holding each British division's sector of attack, they had only yielded 1,983 prisoners and a small tract of ground to the assault of thirteen British divisions. The high hopes built up beforehand had fallen to the ground, and the months of preparation and sowing had only garnered a bitter fruit. Yet although a military failure, July 1st was an epic of heroism, and, better still, the proof of the moral quality of the new armies of Britain, who, in making their supreme sacrifice of the war, passed through the most fiery and bloody of ordeals with their courage unshaken and their fortitude established.

All along the attacking line these quondam civilians bore a percentage of losses such as no professional army of past wars had ever been deemed capable of suffering – without being broken as an effective instrument. And they carried on the struggle, equally bitter, for another five months. Experience would improve their tactical action, still more their handling by the Higher Command, but no subsequent feats could surpass the moral standard of July 1st, 'a day of an intense blue summer beauty, full of roaring violence, and confusion of death, agony, and triumph, and from dawn till dark. All through that day little rushes of the men of our race went towards that no-man's-land from the bloody shelter of our trenches. Some hardly left our trenches, many never crossed the green space, many died in the enemy wire, many had to fall back. Others won across, and went farther and drove the enemy back from line to line till the Battle of the Somme ended in the falling back of the enemy.' That falling back, however, was long postponed, and when it came was so timed as to discomfit the attackers far more than it advantaged them.

Why did Haig persevere on the Somme after so disastrous a start, and discard the alternative he had prepared in the north? The Official History has 'little doubt that the Messines attack, carried out so successfully in 1917, would have had in 1916 a far better chance of decisive result, especially if combined with a coastal attack, than had an offensive astride the Somme'. As late as June 5th Haig had warned Rawlinson that if the Fourth Army attack 'met with considerable opposition he might decide to stop it and proceed with the Messines operation'. The experience of July 1st certainly fulfilled his condition. Perhaps his continuance is best explained by the very marked 'bulldog' element in his make-up. He hated to accept a rebuff, to loosen his grip once he had got his teeth into the resistance. If repulsed everywhere he might have found it easier to switch his reserves north to Messines. But, having bitten into a slice of the German front, Haig wanted to go on and bite deeper. Why, then, did he not bite quicker on the one soft part? In part, because of a fog of war that was thickened by human frailty in facing facts.

Behind the front the higher commanders had been rendering reports more rosy than the dim facts warranted, and also apparently than their own belief. 'Capture of prisoners, but not the heavy casualties, were regularly reported.' Ignorance in such conditions was natural, but deception less excusable. Meantime the opportunity of developing the success in the south went begging.

Late on July 2nd, Haig, confronted with a difficult situation, decided to press the attack where success had been gained, instead of making a fresh frontal assault on the intact defences from Ovillers northwards. The tactical experience of the later years – and earlier history – confirms his wisdom, and the only question is why the exploitation of the success in the south was not more prompt. Part of the dense infantry strength which had been used to strew no-man's-land with dead might better have been kept to swell the reserve for such a purpose. Even as it was, the Germans were badly shaken, and if British reserve divisions were few, theirs were less, as their delay in counter-attacking showed. But the Fourth Army made no attempt to push reserves through at the sectors of least resistance and at 10 PM on the 1st merely ordered its corps to 'continue to attack', evenly along the whole front. At Rawlinson's suggestion, Gough was put in charge of the two left corps (X and VIII) which had most obviously failed – 'an unenviable task' for a man who had been intended, and was best fitted for the role of exploitation. The corps commanders pointed out the hopelessness of a fresh attack without adequate preparation. Gough wisely concurred, and the orders were cancelled. As these corps were not in a state to attack unbroken defences again, nothing happened on the 2nd. Meantime the XIII Corps, which had made a real penetration on the extreme right, was held back. This passivity was the more regrettable because, in conjunction with the French, it had already shattered a ragged and fumbling night counter-attack by a German division hurried up from Cambrai – the one enemy reserve immediately available.

Opportunity receded further when, for the 3rd, Rawlinson merely ordered a renewed attack by the left wing in conjunction with his centre. This plan, Haig approved but modified – with not altogether happy results. He was now turning his eyes to the right, and he reduced the morrow's attack to thrusts by small packets against Thiepval and Ovillers. The rearrangement accentuated the defects due to divided control, so that the attacks became not only petty in scale but disjointed in delivery – and proved void of any effect except further casualties. Meantime, troops of the XIII Corps on the right walked into Bernafay Wood almost without opposition, but were restrained from going farther. The French XX Corps next to it was, as a corollary, also constrained to inactivity, but south of the Somme the French captured the German second line and the high ground overlooking Péronne.

Haig was now convinced of the advisability of concentrating his effort on the right. But he met a French stumbling block. Both Joffre and Foch – who was in direct charge of the French share of the offensive – insisted that Haig should capture the ridge from Pozières to Thiepval in the centre as a preliminary to any attack on the right, or Longueval, sector. Haig's contention that he had not enough ammunition to cover effectively a renewed attack on the whole front, and that the Longueval ridge defences were weaker than at Thiepval, made no impression, and Joffre declared that if the British attacked Longueval they would be beaten. Indeed, he went so far as to give Haig a direct order to attack in the centre, whereupon Haig retorted that he was responsible to the British Government, and that, although he was ready to follow Joffre's strategy, in matters of tactics he would take his own line. This settled the question.

A long interval followed, however, before the Fourth Army was ready for the attack on the enemy's second line. The interval was the longer because Haig considered it necessary to clear away all the enemy's outlying footholds before attempting the main stroke, and sought to seize these by a series of nibbling attacks. At the same time the X and VIII Corps on the left were definitely transferred from Rawlinson's Fourth Army to Gough's reserve army, later to become the Fifth, and the available reserves and guns were concentrated on the reduced Fourth Army front.

Thus, during the days immediately following July 1st, when the German defence was seriously shaken in the southern sector – Montauban – La Boisselle – the renewed attacks were slight in strength and spasmodic. The resistance had breathing space to reorganize and harden, to strengthen its hold on the commanding ridge, Ginchy-Pozières, where ran the German second line. The British progress became very slow, and a special obstacle was offered by Mametz Wood. The three days' abortive attacks – by the 38th (Welsh) Division – and consequent delay here were to prejudice the main stroke. But as great a handicap was imposed from above.

If the British Higher Command had been over-ambitious and unduly optimistic before July 1st, it perhaps now tended to the other extreme. Rawlinson, however, had been brought to realize that bold and rapid measures were essential if he was to forestall the German reinforcements and labour which were rebuilding, in rear, the fortified front faster than the British could force a way through it. If the British waited until their front line had been carried near enough to the German second line (Braune Stellung) for a close assault, they might well be confronted with a barrier as firm as the original of July 1st. Rawlinson framed a plan to attack and break the German defences on a four-mile front between Delville Wood on the right, and Bazentin-le-Petit Wood on the left. His right was fully three-quarters of a mile distant from this second line, with the vital tactical feature of Trônes Wood between still in German hands. Thence towards his left no-man's-land gradually narrowed, until in front of Mametz Wood it was only about 300 yards wide; but Trônes Wood enfiladed a large part of the line of advance. If the obvious course was adopted, and an attack delivered only on the left, the prospects were barren; for the experience of 1915 had shown that an attack on a narrow frontage against an enemy with ample guns might gain an initial success, only to be blown out of the captured fragment by the concentration of hostile gunfire thus facilitated.

Instead of the obvious, Rawlinson took a course which for all its risks – calculated risks – was more truly secure and economical of force. The troops were to cross the exposed area by an advance under cover of darkness, followed by a dawn attack, preceded by a hurricane bombardment of only a few minutes' duration. This plan revived the use of surprise, which lay rusting throughout the greater part of the war, until in fact the last year from Cambrai onwards.

In 1916 the ideas of a night advance and of such a brief bombardment were alike so fresh in revival as to be a shock and appear a gamble to orthodox opinion. That he should attempt the manoeuvre with New Army troops, men who had been civilians less than two years before, made his plan seem yet more rash. The Commander-in-Chief was strongly opposed to it, preferring a more limited alternative, but Rawlinson persevered, his own confidence reinforced by the confidence of the actual troop leaders in their ability to carry out the night operation. For once, Horne, who was usually as apt to agree with Haig's views as he was dependable in other ways, agreed instead with his immediate superior, and this fact may have helped to tilt the scales. Rawlinson gained his way, but instead of the already delayed attack being launched on July 13th, as he intended, the reluctance of the Higher Command caused it to be postponed until July 14th – a day's delay that was to have grave consequences. Another drawback was the lack of French cooperation, owing to lack of faith in the prospects of the attack.

The attacking troops were composed of the 9th and 3rd Divisions of the XIII Corps on the right (W. T. Furse and J. A. L. Haldane), and the 7th and 21st Divisions of the XV Corps on the left (H. E. Watts and D. G. M. Campbell), while on the extreme right flank Maxse's 18th Division had the task of clearing Trônes Wood. On the extreme left the III Corps formed a defensive flank between Bazentin-le-Petit Wood and Contalmaison. Cavalry divisions were brought up close and placed under the orders of the two attacking corps.

The German front was held by only six battalions of mixed divisions in General Stein's group, with the 7th Division in reserve south of Bapaume. The trenches of the Braune Stellung ran just in front of

Delville Wood, Longueval, Bazentin-le-Grand and Bazentin-le-Petit Woods, with High Wood, 'like a dark cloud on the skyline' behind, dominating the whole area of approach. From it the Germans could see several miles behind the old British front line of July 1st.

On the right, markers went out some hours after darkness had fallen on July 13th and placed white tapes to guide the troops along their 1,000 yards' approach; then further tapes at right angles to mark the forward line on which the troops were to form up, so that they should start parallel with their objective. The hazardous and difficult task was carried through successfully, and soon after midnight the battalions assembled in the shelter of Caterpillar Valley, moving up in long worm-like lines of companies or platoons in single file. At 3.20 AM the barrage fell on the German trenches, and five minutes later the whole line moved forward to the assault. The vision which had dared to attempt such a surprise stroke, and had supported imagination with good staff work, was justified. The whole of the German second line was rapidly overrun, and the attacking troops passed beyond. From left to right, the 21st Division pressed through Bazentin-le-Petit Wood to the village, the 7th Division cleared Bazentin-le-Grand Wood and pushed up the slopes towards High Wood, the 3rd Division captured Bazentin-le-Grand, and the 9th Division fought their way, albeit with difficulty, through Longueval to the outskirts of Delville Wood.

On this right flank every yard of advance was bitterly opposed, and in the depths of Delville Wood, during the ensuing days, the South Africans made their supreme sacrifice of the war – where today a white stone colonnade of peaceful beauty commemorates, and contrasts with, the bloodiest battle-hell of 1916.

But on the left flank opportunity – and open country – stretched out its arms. Soon after midday the German resistance was clearly disintegrating on the front of the 7th Division, and an effort was made to exploit the chance, although some hours were lost. The 7th Division moved forward soon after 6 PM with two squadrons of cavalry working on their flank – the first mounted cavalry seen on a British battlefield since 1914. Roseate expectations pictured open warfare on the skyline, but once more it proved a mirage in the military desert. The troops of the illustrious 7th Division were a shade battle-weary; their depleted ranks had been filled with many untried drafts. Whatever the cause, the advance tended to lack vigour, and although most of High Wood was cleared that evening, the northern corner of the flanking trenches remained in the Germans' grip. Worst of all, twenty-four hours' postponement had enabled fresh reserves to come up, and as their strength

steadily swelled the German hold tightened, the British relaxed. Late
on July 15th the wood was evacuated under pressure of counter-attacks,
and two months were to pass before possession was regained. The surprise storm of the Somme 'Bastille' on July 14th brought the British to
the verge of a strategic decision; thereafter their effort degenerated into
a battle of attrition.

After the disappointing end of the July 14th stroke, Haig played for
smaller stakes. His overdrawn supplies of ammunition were causing
concern, and he had in mind no effective substitute for gun-pounding as
an 'opener' for the enemy's sealed front. Early in June he had contemplated the step of transferring his main offensive to the Messines sector
in Flanders if the German reserves held him up on the Somme. And the
Anzac Corps began to move thither in readiness. But by July 7th he had
decided instead to pour his own reserves down to the Somme – now, for
the enemy, the line of expectation – and to throw all his weight into the
direct offensive there.

He ordered, however, a number of local attacks in the north as a
means to fix the enemy's attention and keep his reserves there, and
away from the Somme. The method reveals a most curious military
delusion, for while simulated preparations for a large-scale offensive
would cause the enemy natural apprehension, the actual delivery of a
narrow-fronted local attack would merely disclose the bluff. One consequence was the shattering of the 5th Australian Division in an
absurdly advertised attack at Fromelles, an attack which was the final
link of an almost incredibly muddled chain of causation.

The rest of the Anzac Corps had been moved to the Somme, where
Haig's aim was now to enlarge his lodgement on the main ridge. He had
favoured the idea of trying to carry out his original third phase – of
rolling up the German front northwards – although the original conditions had not been fulfilled. But he had not sufficient elbow-room to
deploy an adequate force for it. And it would have diverged from the
line of cooperation with the French. Hence he decided to continue his
main pressure with his right, eastward towards the French line of convergence, while on his left Gough sought to gain the Pozières–Thiepval
end of the ridge, and so widen the British holding upon it.

To this end Gough was given the Anzac Corps (Birdwood), and on
July 23rd he launched part of it against Pozières in conjunction with a
renewed assault by the three corps of the Fourth Army along the whole
of its narrow front, from Guillemont to Bazentin-le-Petit. This failed
completely; on the left the 1st Australian Division gained a footing in
Pozières. Haig reverted to the method of nibbling, now to be exalted as

a definite and masterly strategy of attrition, and to be defended by optimistic miscalculations of the German losses.

Nearly two months of bitter fighting followed, during which the British made little progress at much cost, and the infantry of both sides served as compressed cannon-fodder for artillery consumption. On the left flank the Anzac Corps was the main agent of the new plan of 'methodical progress'. The effect is best described in the measured words of the Australian official history:

Doubtless to the Commander-in-Chief, and possibly to the Cabinet, the use of terms implying leisurely progress brought some comfortable assurance of economy of life as well as of munitions; but to the front line the method merely appeared to be that of applying a battering-ram ten or fifteen times against the same part of the enemy's battlefront with the intention of penetrating for a mile, or possibly two, into the midst of his organized defences...

'Even if the need for maintaining pressure be granted, the student will have difficulty in reconciling his intelligence to the actual tactics. To throw the several parts of an army corps, brigade after brigade ... twenty times in succession against one of the strongest points in the enemy's defence, may certainly be described as 'methodical', but the claim that it was economic is entirely unjustified.

Twenty-three thousand men were expended in these efforts for the ultimate gain, after six weeks, of a tiny tongue of ground just over a mile deep. And what of the moral effect?

Although most Australian soldiers were optimists, and many were opposed on principle to voicing – or even harbouring grievances, it is not surprising if the effect on some intelligent men was a bitter conviction that they were being uselessly sacrificed. 'For Christ's sake, write a book on the life of an infantryman (said one of them...), and by doing so you will quickly prevent these shocking tragedies.' That an officer who had fought so nobly as Lieutenant J. A. Raws, should, in the last letter before his death, speak of the 'murder' of many of his friends 'through the incompetence, callousness, and personal vanity of those high in authority', is evidence not indeed of the literal truth of his words, but of something much amiss in the higher leadership ...' We have just come out of a place so terrible (wrote —, one of the most level-headed officers in the force) that ... a raving lunatic could never imagine the horror of the last thirteen days.'

The history indicates that Birdwood lost much of his Gallipoli popularity through his failure to interpose against Gough's impetuous desire for quick results and his lack of thought. This may have been a factor in leading the Australian troops to reject Birdwood's personal appeal when they voted against the conscription of other men to share the horrors that they had experienced.

But Pozières was matched on the other flank by Guillemont – now a peaceful hamlet amid cornfields, then a shambles of blended horror and mystery. From Trônes Wood it is down one slope, up another, only a few hundred yards of farm road now, yet in July and August, 1916, an infinite distance. Division after division essayed to cross it, felt the petty prize within their fingers, and then slipped back unable to maintain their hold. And when it was at last secured on September 3rd, Ginchy, a few hundred yards farther up the slope, was a similar obstruction until September 9th. Save Thiepval, still defiant, no hamlets have exacted a heavier price for their possession.

Now at last the British line was straightened on a seven-mile front running north-west from Leuze Wood, overlooking Combles, where it joined up with the French. They had just extended farther south the attack south of the Somme, storming three miles of the old German front line near Chaulnes and taking 7,000 prisoners. On August 30th Rawlinson had recorded in his diary – 'The Chief is anxious to have a gamble with all the available troops about September 15th, with the object of breaking down German resistance and getting through to Bapaume.' And he added, somewhat illogically – 'We shall have no reserves in hand, save tired troops, but success at this time ... might bring the Boches to terms.' Despite his professed faith in attrition, Haig was now reduced to gambling on a breakthrough.

The attack was to pivot on the left wing – Gough's army. The primary object of the main blow, by Rawlinson, was to break through what had originally been the Germans' last line between Morval and Le Sars, in cooperation with a French thrust to the south between Combles and the Somme – thus pinching out Combles. If the opening success warranted the attempt the British attack was to be extended northward to seize Courcelette and Martinpuich. Eight divisions were deployed for the original attack, and two detailed for the 'extension'. A special feature was the employment for the first time of tanks, the armoured cross-country machines which had been invented as an antidote to the defensive obstacle of machine guns and barbed wire. In disregard of the opinions of the tank's progenitors, and of their own expressed agreement with these opinions, the British Higher Command had decided to utilize such machines as were available, as a stake to redeem the fading prospects of the Somme offensive. When this decision was taken only sixty of the initial 150 machines had been transported to France. Forty-nine were actually employed, to work in tiny detachments of two or three machines – another breach with the principles laid down by Colonel Swinton. The scant and hasty preparation combined with the mechanical defects of this early model to reduce the total, so that only thirty-two reached the starting point. Of these, nine pushed ahead with the infantry, nine failed to catch the infantry, but helped in clearing the captured ground, nine broke down and five were 'ditched' in the craters of the battlefield. The first nine rendered useful aid, especially in capturing Flers, but the greater prize – of a great surprise stroke – was a heavy forfeit to pay for redeeming in a limited degree the failure of the Somme offensive.

After three days' bombardment, the attack was launched at dawn on the 15th in a slight mist. The mist, together with the clouds of smoke, prevented the German gunners in many places from seeing the light-signals fired by their infantry, and the consequent lack of artillery support on the German side eased the path of the British infantry. Thus the XV Corps in the centre made early and good progress; by 10 AM its left division was beyond Flers. Its progress was greatly helped by the tanks, of which the German regimental histories give a vivid impression – 'The arrival of the tanks on the scene had the most shattering effect on the men. They felt quite powerless against these monsters which crawled along the top of the trench enfilading it with continous machine-gun fire, and closely followed by small parties of infantry who threw hand grenades on the survivors.' But on the right the XIV Corps lost heavily and was held up long before it could reach Morval and Lesboeufs. The III Corps, on the left, also fell short of its objectives, although its 47th Division finally cleared the long-sought High Wood. On the extreme left the projected extension of the attack was carried out, and both Martinpuich and Courcelette were taken. As a result of the day the crest of the ridge had been gained, except on the right, and with it the commanding observation which the Germans had so long enjoyed.

The failure on the right was redressed on September 25th, by another big attack which, in conjunction with the French, compelled the Germans to evacuate Combles. Next day Thiepval at last fell to an attack by four divisions of Gough's army. German accounts make it clear that the decisive break in their front was 'caused by the appearance of three British tanks ... on the outskirts of Thiepval village'.

Haig still called for pressure 'without intermission' and, as a result of further small gains, by the first week of October the Germans were back in their last completed line of defences, which ran from Sailly-Saillisel, on the right, past Le Transloy and in front of Bapaume; they were busily constructing fresh lines in rear, but these were not yet complete. On the other hand these days had proved the continued strength of the German resistance, and the limited success held but little hope of a real breakthrough or its exploitation. The early onset of the autumn rains made this hope more slender daily. The rains combined with the bombardments to make the ground a morass in which guns and transport were bogged, while even lightly equipped infantry could barely and slowly struggle forward. Attacks under such conditions were terribly handicapped; that most of them failed was inevitable, and if a trench was taken the difficulties of consolidating it liquidated the gain.

By October 12th Haig seems to have been at last convinced that he could not pierce the German defences that year. But Joffre and Foch continued to urge him on, and in partial response Haig continued to call for fresh attacks through the mud towards Le Transloy, until a strong protest was made by Lord Cavan, commanding the XIV Corps, who desired to know whether it was deliberately intended to sacrifice the British right in order to help the French left, and pointedly added – 'No one who has not visited the front can really know the state of exhaustion to which the men are reduced.' But other corps commanders had less moral courage, and Rawlinson, although sympathetic, seems to have yielded against his better judgement to his Chief's determination. Hence the III and Anzac Corps continued a hopeless series of petty attacks until November 16th. Their ineffectiveness was redeemed, as their ineptitude was obscured, by a welcome, last-hour success of Gough's army.

The wedge that had been slowly driven eastward between the Ancre and the Somme had turned the original German defences north of the Ancre into a pronounced salient. For some time Gough's army had been preparing an attack against this and a temporary improvement in the weather allowed it to be launched on November 13th, by seven divisions. Beaumont-Hamel and Beaucourt-sur-Ancre were captured, with 7,000 prisoners, but on the left Serre once more proved impregnable. Haig was pleased – because it would 'strengthen the hands of the British representatives' at the forthcoming Allied Military Conference at Chantilly. So the Somme offensive could at last be suspended with honour satisfied.

The folly of the last phase, from September 25th onwards, was that having at last won the crest of the ridge, and its commanding observation, the advantage was thrown away by fighting a way down into the valley beyond. Thereby the troops were doomed to spend the winter in flooded trenches. 'Somme mud' was soon to be notorious.

Thus the miscalled Battle of the Somme closed in an atmosphere of disappointment, and with such a drain on the British forces that the coincident strain on the enemy was obscured. This strain was largely due to the rigidity of the German higher commanders, especially General von Below of the First Army, who issued an order that any officer who gave up an inch of trench would be court-martialled, and that every yard of lost trench must be retaken by counter-attack. If German mistakes do not condone British mistakes they at least caused a vain loss of life, and still more of morale, which helped to balance the British loss – until on August 23rd Below was compelled to swallow his own orders and modify his method of resistance, in accord with that of the new Hindenburg-Ludendorff régime.

CHAPTER SIX

SCENE 4

The Growing Pains of the Tank

On September 15th, 1916, a new instrument of war received its baptism of fire, and helped to make the British attack on that day one of the landmarks of the Somme offensive. It was one of the few attacks which did not require the use of a large-scale map and a magnifying glass to detect its progress. But, far more significant, it cast its shadow over the whole future of the war. And as it thus becomes a greater landmark in the history of the war than in the history of the Somme, so it is likely to become a still greater landmark in the history of war.

For this new instrument – the tank – changed the face of war by substituting motor-power for a man's legs as a means of movement on the battlefield and by reviving the use of armour as a substitute for his skin or for earth-scrapings as a means of protection. Hitherto he could not fire if he wished to move, and could not move if he wished for cover. But September 15th, 1916, saw the simultaneous combination in one agent of fire power, movement, and protection – an advantage until then enjoyed in modern warfare only by those who fought on the sea.

But although sea warfare on land may be the ultimate consequence of the tank, and was foreshadowed in its first name of 'landship', the original intention was more limited and more immediately practical – to provide an antidote to the machine gun which, in alliance with barbed wire, had reduced warfare to stagnation and generalship to attrition.

The cure was a British production, the most significant achievement of British brains during the World War. Yet it has an essential transatlantic link, symbolical in view of the association on the battlefield that was soon to follow. For the source of both the evil and the antidote was American. The trench deadlock was due above all to the invention of an American, Hiram Maxim. His name is more deeply engraved on the real history of the World War than that of any other man. Emperors, statesmen, and generals had the power to make war, but not to end it. Having created it, they found themselves helpless puppets in the grip of Hiram Maxim, who, by his machine gun, had paralysed the power of attack. All efforts to break the defensive grip of the machine gun were vain; they could only raise tombstones and not triumphal arches. When at last a key to the deadlock was produced, it was forged from the invention of another American, Benjamin Holt. From his agricultural tractor was evolved the tank – an ironic reversal of the proverbial custom of 'beating swords into ploughshares'.

The eventual effect of the tank is best appreciated by studying the evidence of those who had to face it. Was it not Ludendorff himself who spoke of the great tank surprise of August 8th, 1918, as the 'black day of the German army in the history of the war', and added, 'mass attacks by tanks ... remained hereafter our most dangerous enemies'. More emphatic still is the comment of General von Zwehl – 'It was not the genius of Marshal Foch that beat us, but "General Tank".' Nor can it be suggested that these were afterthoughts put forward in mitigation of defeat, for the most striking evidence of all, red-hot from the forge of battle, is to be found in the momentous report submitted, on October 2nd, 1918, by the representatives of the German Military Headquarters to the leaders of the Reichstag – 'The Chief Army Command has been compelled to take a terribly grave decision and declare that according to human possibilities there is no longer any prospect of forcing peace on the enemy. Above all, two facts have been decisive for this issue; first, the tanks...' The confession thus made gains force from comparison with the earlier disparagement of the tanks by the German Command.

For history the first question is how the tank came to be introduced, and the second, why its decisive effect was delayed until 1918. The first question is befogged rather than guided by the popular question, so widely raised during and after the war – 'who invented the tank?' So many claimed the honour, many with some show of reason, and still more without, that the public became confused. And the Government did not help to establish the actual chain of causation, perhaps influenced by the instinct of the Treasury to avoid the recognition of financial obligations. Thus it did not become clear until the evidence in an action brought against the Crown in 1925 was available to supplement that given in 1919 before the Royal Commission on Awards to Inventors. In order to defeat this unjustified claim to reward the Treasury had to provide an opportunity for evaluating the genuine claims to honour.

The historical evolution of the tank has been confused also by the lack of any clear definition of the tank and its purpose, and this vagueness owes something to the fact that prior to the time when the camouflage name 'tank' was invented, the machine was known as a 'landship' or 'land cruiser'. Such a title, due to its being mothered in infancy by the Admiralty, however prophetic of its still distant future, is far from applicable to its past, in the war. Regarded as a landship, or even as an armoured battle-car, the origin of the tank is lost in the mists of antiquity. Among its forbears might be included the ancient war-chariot, the Hussite war-carts which formed their famous *'wagenburg'*, even, with some show of reason, the battle elephants of Pyrrhus, or the mediaeval knight in armour.

If the search be limited to self-moving, as distinct form men- or animal-moved machines, its origin might be traced to Valturio's wind-propelled war-chariot of 1472, or to the proposals made by that many-sided genius, Leonardo da Vinci, to his patron Ludovico Sforza. In 1599 Simon Stevin constructed for the Prince of Orange two actual landships, wheel-borne and sail-propelled. As far back as 1634, David Ramsey took out the earliest patent for a self-moving car capable of use in war. So through an endless chain of experiments the origin might be traced. The caterpillar track itself – perhaps, in general opinion the distinctive feature of the tank – goes back to the early nineteenth century, or even to Richard Edgeworth's device of 1770.

If the definition be drawn still closer to mean a petrol-driven tracked machine for military use, the Hornsby tractor, used at Aldershot in 1908, takes precedence of the American Holt tractor in the ancestry of the tank. If the use of 'tank-like' machines as weapons be the test, then Mr H. G. Wells deserves the credit popularly accorded him for priority of conception, although his prophetic story of 1903 in the *Strand Magazine* was itself twenty years behind the writings and drawings of M. Albert Robeida in *La Caricature*; if similarity of design, then one recalls Mr L. E. de Mole's model, superior to the 1916 tank, which was pigeon-holed in the War Office in 1912. To these add also the story of the Nottingham plumber whose hobby it was to make toy machines of this nature, and whose design, submitted to the War Office in 1911, and duly pigeon-holed, was unearthed after the war, the file bearing the terse official comment, 'the man's mad'.

The chief result of this historical survey, however, is to show the futility of trying to determine the credit for the origination of this decisive weapon of the World War without a clear understanding and definition of its particular purpose. Leonardo da Vinci and the Nottingham plumber alike may claim to be among the fathers of mechanical warfare, but for the parentage of the actual tank of the World War we must look closer. The test of its origin it tactical rather than technical. It was a specific antidote for a specific disease which first broke out virulently in the World War. This disease was the complete paralysis of the offensive brought about by the defensive power of serried machine guns, and aggravated by wire entanglements. This disease doomed the manhood of the nation to a slow and lingering end, prolonged only by the capacity to produce fresh victims for the futile sacrifice. Wycherley's phrase, 'necessity, mother of invention', has never had a truer example, and it provides the real test to determine the immediate origin of the World War tank.

The first military physician who diagnosed the disease and conceived the antidote was Colonel Ernest Swinton, whose pen-name of 'Ole-Luk-Oie' had become well known through *The Green Curve* and *Duffer's Drift* – studies of war in fiction form, wherein the pill of knowledge was delightfully coated with jam. A term of hard labour on the British official history of the Russo-Japanese War gave him the opportunity to analyse its tendencies and to deduce the potential domination of the machine gun. Later, he took an interest in the Holt tractor experiments. These two impressions soon fitted together like the two segments of a circle. For when, soon after the outbreak of war, he was sent to France as official 'Eyewitness' at General Headquarters, he was both well placed and well prepared to recognize the first symptoms of stalemate, and to suggest a remedy. On October 20th, visiting London, he saw Colonel Maurice Hankey, the Secretary of the Committee of Imperial Defence, and after describing the situation – domination of defence based on the machine gun – outlined his proposals for an antidote. These were, in brief, to develop such a machine as the Holt tractor into a bullet-proof trench-crossing machine-gun destroyer, armed with one or more small quick-firing guns. In Hankey he found an acute and receptive mind, and a further discussion the next day led to an understanding that Hankey would take up the matter at home and Swinton in France. On October 23rd, Swinton took up the question at General Headquarters, but the suggestion came up against a blank wall.

Meanwhile Hankey put the idea before Lord Kitchener, with equally barren result. But he also submitted to the Prime Minister (Mr Asquith), a memorandum on various ways, strategic and technical, of overcoming the deadlock, which embodied, among others, Swinton's suggestion. This reached Mr Churchill. His mind was already active with the problem of enabling armoured cars to cross broken ground and trenches, because of his concern with the armoured-car detachments of the Royal Naval Air Service operating on the Belgian coast. On January 5th, 1915, Churchill wrote a letter to the Prime Minister supporting and amplifying the suggestion in Hankey's memorandum for the use of armoured caterpillar tractors to overrun trenches. This letter was sent by Asquith to Kitchener. By a coincidence Swinton had called at the War Office on January 4th to press anew his proposals, now extended owing to the continued experience of conditions in France.

The seed thus planted at the War Office by two sowers fell on stony soil, and after some attention finally withered, owing largely to the freezing verdict of Sir Capel Holden, Director of Mechanical Transport. Fortunately, the general idea was kept alive on other soil, for Churchill, in February, formed a committee at the Admiralty, which later became known as the Landships Committee. But this committee, though investigating many lines of thought and experiment, did not make much practical headway, its energies being diverted for a time in the direction of a landship with giant wheels. A worse blow was the removal of Churchill's vision and driving force, though even when he left the Admiralty it was his influence which kept the experiments alive. By this time also, fortunately, the committee - under the guidance of Mr Tennyson d'Eyncourt, the Director of Naval Construction - had got on to the right line, that of the caterpillar. Even so, concrete results seem to have been hindered, and energy leaking, through lack of any exact specification of the military requirements of such a machine, for in the scheme of scientific war the tactical takes precedence of the technical.

This essential, but hitherto missing, link came in a memorandum forwarded from General Headquarters, and once this was available progress became rapid and practical. The memorandum was compiled by Swinton, who had surmounted the barrier of unbelief and convention by an appeal direct to the Commander-in-Chief. It formulated the performance required of the machine, and on this specification the newly framed joint committee of War Office and Admiralty went to work.

On July 19th, Swinton returned to England as acting Secretary to the War Committee of the Cabinet, and got in touch with the Joint Committee later, on the Prime Minister's authorization, calling an Inter-Departmental Conference to coordinate the work on the new machines. On September 19th, an inspection was held at Lincoln of a provisional machine, 'Little Willie', but this was rejected by Swinton as failing to conform to requirements. He was then shown a full-size wooden model, or mock-up, of a larger machine, which had been specially designed by Mr Tritton and Lieutenant Wilson to meet the latest army specification. This was accepted, as it looked capable of complying with the two main conditions – to climb a vertical face of five feet and cross a ditch eight feet wide – and it was decided to concentrate on the production of a sample machine of this type.

Finally, on February 2nd, 1916, at Hatfield was held the official trial of this machine – christened 'Mother' or 'Big Willie', and as a result forty of these machines were ordered, a number subsequently increased to 150. The French, now, had independently begun similar experiments through the initiative of Colonel Estienne, whose project was sanctioned by Joffre on December 12th. Although both idea and machine were later in maturing than the British, it is a significant contrast that the first French order was for 400; and that order was soon doubled.

During the summer of 1916 the crews for the new machines were being trained in a vast secret enclosure, surrounded by armed guards, near Thetford in Norfolk. They formed a unit that was christened the Heavy Section, Machine Gun Corps. For secrecy sake also a new name had been chosen for the machines. The need was to find a name sufficiently mystifying and yet plausible to any outside observer who might see the tarpaulined machines in transit on the railway, and after discussing the merits of 'tank', 'cistern', and 'reservoir', the choice fell on the first.

Through the secrecy so well maintained, surprise was obtained when the 'tanks' made their début on the battlefield. Unhappily the fruits of the surprise were forfeited. Herein lay the tragedy of September 15th, 1916; for the official guardians disregarded the entreaties of the parents and insisted on putting the tank to work before it was mechanically mature and before its numbers were adequate. Thus they not only endangered its future usefulness but threw away the chance of surprising the enemy while he was unprepared with any countermeasures. The consequence was to prolong the hardships and toll of the war.

The reply normally made to this charge is to point out the mechanical defects which the early tanks developed, the numbers that were 'ditched', and to argue that a weapon must be tested under battlefield conditions before mass production is begun. The contention is plausible, but unconvincing in view of the facts. The tank first used in the shell-mangled chaos of the Somme, and against the deep and intricate trench systems of 1916, was built to a specification laid down in the summer of 1915, when trench lines were far less developed and artillery bombardments were not so heavy as to turn the ground into a morass – as in 1916 and 1917.

Moreover, the apologists gloss over the fact that in September, 1916, the tanks were hurried out to France and rushed into battle before their crews were fully trained and before the commanders in France had time to think, or had been given instructions, how to use them. Again, the very likelihood that the proportion of mechanical failures in this early model would be high was surely a logical reason for the production of a large number, so that sufficient might survive to reap the harvest of surprise. As the British nation was paying over several million pounds a day for the pleasure of watching and occasionally tapping on the locked gates of the German front, it would surely have been worth risking an extra day's expenditure in the purchase of a possible means of breaking the lock.

Let us probe a little further the mystery of the premature use of this immature instrument. In December, 1915, Churchill drafted a paper on the use of the tank. Printed for the Committee of Imperial Defence, copies were given to the Commander-in-Chief in France. In February, 1916, as soon as the design and armament of the machine had been settled sufficiently for accurate calculations, Swinton produced a more comprehensive and detailed memorandum. This emphasized that the vital factor was the secret production of tanks until masses could be launched in a great surprise stroke, and that on no account should they be used in driblets as they were manufactured. Haig expressed his full agreement with this memorandum in the spring. Yet in August he suddenly decided to use the mere sixty then available. At that time the offensive on the Somme had practically come to a standstill, and the reports of petty gain at heavy loss grated unpleasantly on the ear of the public.

Haig's decision came as a shock to the Cabinet at home, and Lloyd George, now War Minister, energetically protested, while Montagu, his successor at the Ministry of Munitions, went out to General Head-quarters in a vain attempt to avert the premature use of the tanks. Haig was immovable and the powerless parents had to submit to the sacrifice of their offspring's future.

Thus history is left to surmise that the tanks were 'pawned for a song' – of the Somme. Pawned to pay for a resounding local success which might draw an encore from the public – and, incidentally, drown the growing volume of criticism. But the greater prize thus lost beyond recall was a heavy forfeit to pay for redeeming in a limited degree the ill success of the Somme offensive. With Haig this act may have been prompted by a laudable if unwise desire to economize the lives of his infantry without giving up his offensive. He had certainly shown his eagerness to clutch at any new aid. But the attitude of some of his staff cannot be similarly excused.

For the breach of principle does not complete the tally of General Headquarters. Swinton's memorandum laid down a number of conditions which were disregarded in September, 1916, only to be adopted after bitter experience had shown their necessity. The sector for tank attack was to be carefully chosen to comply with the powers and limitations of the tanks – this condition was neither considered nor fulfilled until the Cambrai offensive in November, 1917. Their routes of approach were to be specially prepared, as well as suitable railway trucks or barges to bring them up – despite six months' warning these preparations were not begun until the tanks arrived in August. The need for reserves of tanks was stressed – but the lesson was not even learnt by the time of Cambrai, nor indeed, until August, 1918. The combined tactics of tanks and infantry were expounded – also to be overlooked until Cambrai. In addition to shell, the tank guns were to fire case shot. It was designed but its manufacture was debarred until the commanders in France clamoured for it after the Somme. Some of the tanks were to be equipped with wireless sets; these were designed and operators trained – but General Headquarters would not allow the equipment to be sent out, and it was dispersed. The attitude and mentality prevailing at General Headquarters is illustrated by a story current at the time. A general on Haig's staff gave instructions that the tanks were to be brought to the front by a certain railway route. The technical expert in charge of the movement pointed out that this was impossible because of the loading gauge. The General retorted – 'What the hell is a loading gauge?' The officer explained, and pointed out that by another route they could avoid the two tunnels that made this route impossible. But the General, still refusing to recognize the impossible, curtly said – 'Then, have the tunnels widened.'

The trial of the tank on the Somme did not complete its trials. A thousand of a new model had just been ordered by the Ministry of Munitions in England. But their opponents – by which one means not the Germans but the General Staff in France – made haste to report so adversely that the War Office cancelled the order. Unfortunately for their intention, if fortunately for England, the officer in charge of the construction of tanks was a temporary soldier, Major Albert Stern, whose permanent position in the City enabled him to bear with equanimity the frowns of his temporary superiors. Disregarding the order he went straight to the War Minister, to find that the cancellation had been sent without Lloyd George's knowledge. And having satisfied himself of Lloyd George's opposition to any such foolish measure, Stern called on the Chief of the Imperial General Staff, Sir William Robertson, to intimate that he was not going to carry out the cancellation order.

Nevertheless, let it be said to the credit of those who, on the General Staff, opposed the tank, that if they had not the ingenuity to devise means of beating the Germans they were fertile in devices to beat the sponsors of the tank. Swinton, as merely a soldier, was not a difficult adversary and almost at once was ousted from his position in command of the whole tank unit in England. In July, 1917, d'Eyncourt and Stern were neatly excluded from the meetings of the committee, which now at the War Office controlled tank design and production; a committee whose three military members had not even seen a tank until a few weeks previously. The programme of building 4,000 tanks for the next year's campaign was then cut down by two-thirds. And in October, under pressure from the Generals, Stern was removed from his post at the Ministry of Munitions and replaced by an Admiral who had not seen a tank at all. The General Staff would seem to have profited from contact with their French colleagues, and to have learnt that the most important point when proved wrong is to get rid of the uncomfortable prophet who has proved right. Just as Swinton was sacrificed to balance for the General Staff's folly in launching the first model into the Somme battle, so Stern seems to have been chosen to expiate the folly of throwing the next model into the swamps of Passchendaele. Instead of losing faith in their own judgement the General Staff again lost faith in the tank.

Happily, the younger regular soldiers who had taken charge of the tanks at the front had overcome their first doubts and, realizing the stupidity of Passchendaele, fought for the chance to give the tanks a fair trial. They obtained it at Cambrai in November, a battle which at last fulfilled the pattern designed in February, 1916. Although, for want of the resources wasted at Passchendaele, the victory itself was but a tinsel crown, it yielded the tanks a solid crown which none could any longer dispute. As 1917 was the year of vindication, so 1918 proved the year of triumph. Yet it is a sobering reflection that the price in lives might have been cheaper if tanks had been available in thousands instead of hundreds. The numbers manufactured under the reduced programme of 1917 sufficed to bring victory; but they could not bring back the dead. May the tank's hard childhood be an object lesson for future generations, so that if war engulfs them they may learn by the experience of others and not at their own cost.

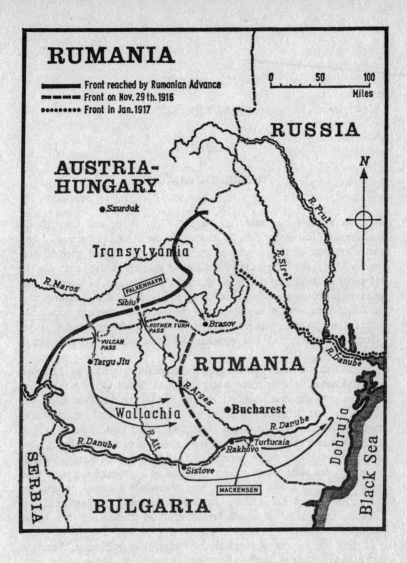

RUMANIA

———— Front reached by Rumanian Advance
— — — Front on Nov. 29 th. 1916
•••••••• Front in Jan. 1917

0   50   100
Miles

RUSSIA

N

**AUSTRIA-
HUNGARY**

● *Szurduk*

Transylvania

R. Maros

R. Prut

R. Siret

FALKENHAYN

Sibiu

ROTHER TURM
PASS

● *Brasov*

VULCAN
PASS

● *Targu Jiu*

RUMANIA

R. Arges

● *Bucharest*

Wallachia

R. Alt

R. Danube

R. Danube

R. Danube

Rakhovo   *Turtucaia*

Sistove

MACKENSEN

Dobruja

Black Sea

SERBIA

BULGARIA

CHAPTER SIX

SCENE 5

Rumania Swallowed

Rumania entered the war on August 27th, 1916, and the fall of Bucharest on December 6th, 1916, marked the virtual extinction of her war effort and of the misplaced exhilaration which had greeted her entry on the side of the Allies. Less known and less studied than almost any other campaign of the world struggle, it has a special interest, and deserves far more attention than it has received, because it epitomized the Allies' fundamental weakness and the Germans' strength – the evils inherent in a co-partnership system of conducting war as opposed to the concentration of effort and economy of force which springs from a single control.

Nor is this the sum of its lessons; there are others which have a more practical value, because more easily remedied. It revealed the fallacy of numbers, and the much-abused Napoleonic saying that God is on the side of the big battalions received yet another historical contradiction from the Alexandrine principle of quality rather than quantity. Once again the blend of superior hitting power with superior mobility played havoc with an army which pinned its faith to weight of human bodies. Moreover, the swift three months' conquest of Rumania has a particular value for British study, because it was essentially a war of movement, carried out under the difficult natural conditions, topographical and climatic, for which the small British army is trained and has to be prepared.

During the preceding years of the war, public opinion in Rumania had gradually consolidated in favour of intervention on the Allies' side, and the friendly sentiments of Jonescu and Filipescu found a powerful lever in the people's desire to rescue their kinsmen in Transylvania from a foreign rule far more drastic than Alsace-Lorraine had suffered. At last, in the summer of 1916, the spectacular, but, as we now know, superficial successes of the Russian advance under Brusilov encouraged

Rumania to take the decisive step – into the abyss. She might have fared better if she had declared war earlier, when Serbia was still an active force and Russia a real one. The two years of preparation had doubled the numbers of the Rumanian army, but in reality reduced its relative efficiency, for while her foes, under the pressure of hard experience, had developed their means of fire power and equipment, Rumania's isolation and the incapacity of her military leadership had combined to prevent the transformation of her army from a militia of bayonetmen into a modern force.

Her infantry had no automatic rifles, gas equipment, trench mortars, and few machine guns – in the ten active divisions only the usual pre-war proportion of two per battalion, and of the thirteen new divisions eight had none at all. Her artillery was inadequate, and her air force negligible. She had only six weeks' supply of ammunition at the start – an explosion in the Bucharest arsenal had destroyed 9,000,000 rounds of small-arm ammunition – and her Allies failed to maintain the daily supply of 300 tons which they had promised. And the unwieldy size of her divisions, added to the indifferent quality of her corps of officers, was in itself a brake on mobile operations.

Her strategical situation was another source of weakness – her territory forming an 'L' reversed, with the bottom section, Wallachia, sandwiched between Transylvania and Bulgaria. Moreover, the length of her frontier was out of all proportion to the depth of the country, she suffered a shortage of lateral railways, and the capital was within thirty miles of the Bulgarian frontier. Further, she had in the Dobruja – on the other side of the Danube – a 'backyard' strip which offered an easy way of access.

These internal and geographical handicaps were accentuated by the divergent counsels of her Allies as to her action. While the British General Staff favoured a southward advance against Bulgaria which might have crushed the latter between the Rumanians and the Salonika army, the Russians urged a westward advance which would, in theory, be in closer cooperation with their Bukovina advance. The political and moral advantages of a move into Transylvania led the Rumanians to adopt the second course, and bitter as the upshot was, their folly is not so certain as their critics have suggested. The Bulgarian territory offered many obstacles to an effective invasion by such a defective instrument as the Rumanian army proved, and they had ample ground to doubt the energy of Sarrail in pushing forward to meet them.

On the other hand, we now know that a more rapid invasion of Transylvania by the Rumanians would have put the Austro-Germans in a grave position, and that even with the breathing space they were unluckily given they were almost at their wits' end to scrape together forces for this new front. Rumania's fault was less in her choice of objective than in her incapacity to strike for it rapidly and forcefully.

The Rumanian advance began, on the night of August 27th–28th, with three main columns, each of about four divisions, moving in a general north-westerly direction through the Carpathian passes, the conception being to pivot on the left and wheel the right up into line facing west when the Hungarian plain was gained. Three divisions were left to guard the Danube, and three more in the Dobruja 'backyard', whither also the Russians had promised to send one cavalry and two infantry divisions – the Rumanians' stipulation originally had been for a force of 150,000 Russians.

The slow and cautious advance of the Rumanian columns, hampered by the bad mountain roads and the Austrian destruction of bridges, but not by resistance, withheld danger from the five weak Austrian divisions which covered the frontier and enabled the Supreme Command to bring up five German and two Austrian divisions and concentrate them on the line of the River Maros ready for a counter-offensive. In fulfilment of the other half of Falkenhayn's plan, a Bulgarian force of two divisions, and two more to follow, with a German detachment and an Austrian bridging train, was placed under Mackensen to invade the Dobruja. Falkenhayn adds that preparations were made for 'the abundant equipment of Mackensen's army with such weapons, not yet known to the Rumanians, as heavy artillery, mine-throwers, gas'.

Thus, at the outset, Rumania had twenty-three divisions against seven, but within a week she would have sixteen against her, so that her chances of success turned on the rapidity of her action. While her columns were creeping westward into Transylvania, Mackensen stormed the Turtucaia bridgehead on September 5th, destroyed the three Rumanian divisions which covered the Danube front, and then, with his flank secure, pressed eastwards into the Dobruja. It was a shrewd moral blow, for the automatic strategic effect was to draw away the Rumanian reserves intended to support the Transylvanian offensive, and so check its progress for want of nourishment. And the dispersion left them weak everywhere. Thus on September 18th, when Falkenhayn arrived to conduct the Austro-German offensive in Transylvania, he found the Rumanian advance almost at a standstill, and their columns widely separated over a 200-mile front. One must mention that Falkenhayn had now been replaced in the Supreme Command by Hindenburg (and Ludendorff), and given this executive command as a consolation.

Falkenhayn's decision was first to concentrate against the Rumanian southern column, which had crossed the Rother Turm Pass, while using smaller forces to hold off the other columns. Even allowing for his superior information, he took bold risks and suffered anxious moments before success, as so often in war, favoured the brave. The Alpine Corps, by a fifty-mile march in three days over the mountains, turned the Rumanians' southern flank, and combined with the skilful manoeuvre of the reserves in the direct attack to throw back the Rumanians from Sibiu (Hermannstadt), and force them to retreat through the mountains.

His next move was facilitated by the fact that the Rumanian Higher Command, like Napoleon's opponents, 'saw too many things at once'. They kept their Transylvanian armies inactive while diverting their reserves for an abortive attempt to force a crossing of the Danube at Rakhovo and take Mackensen in rear. This enabled Falkenhayn to concentrate against the Rumanian centre column at Brasov (Kronstadt) and by October 9th he had driven this back in turn, but he missed his greater goal of encircling and destroying it, which would have opened a clear passage into Rumania.

The mischance jeopardized the whole German plan and almost saved Rumania, for with all the passes through the mountain barrier still in their hands, her troops sturdily repulsed the Austro-German efforts to press through on their heels, and compelled them to wait for reinforcements. A prompt attempt by Falkenhayn to swing farther south and force a way by the Vulkan and Szurduk passes was also stopped, and the beginning of the winter snows was on the point of blocking operations when a concentrated last-minute effort at the same point, November 11th–17th, broke through to Targu Jiu. A rapid pursuit through the Wallachian plain hustled the Rumanians back to the line of the Alt.

It was the signal for the next move in the ably coordinated plan. Mackensen, leaving only a fraction to hold the northerly part of the Dobruja, withdrew the bulk of his forces westwards to Sistovo, where, on November 23rd, he forced the crossing of the Danube and automatically turned the flank of the Rumanian line on the Alt. A prompt and well-planned Rumanian counterstroke, inspired by General Presan, their new Chief of the General Staff, for a brief time threatened danger to Mackensen's force and almost enveloped its flank. But once the counterstroke was parried the converging pressure of Mackensen and Falkenhayn proved too great for the Rumanians' last desperate resistance on the line of the Argesu, and on December 6th the Austro-Germans entered Bucharest. The pursuit pressed the Rumanians and the Russians, whose action in the Dobruja had been ineffectual, rapidly back to the Sereth–Black Sea line. The greater part of Rumania, with its wheat and oil, lay under the heel of the invader, and the Rumanian Army was crippled, while her Allies had suffered a moral setback greater than any material advantage for which they might have hoped from her intervention.

For military history this brief campaign furnished an object lesson that men do not count more than machines, but instead, that the better machine controlled by a better man – the commander – can discount the value of 'big battalions'. Weapons and training count far more than mere numbers.

PERSIA

N

R. Diyala

Baghdad
•Diyala
•Ctesiphon
•*Aziziya*

SHUMRAH BEND
•*Sanniyat*

Kut al Imara
Sheik Sa'ad

•*Al Hillah*

SHATT AL HAI

•*'Amara*

R. Tigris

•*As Samawah*

R. Euphrates

•*Al Qurnah*

R. Karun

MESOPOTAMIA

Basra
•*Mohammerah*
SHATT AL ARAB

PERSIAN GULF

0   40   80
Miles

CHAPTER SIX

SCENE 6

The Capture of Baghdad

The entry of the British into Baghdad on March 11th, 1917, was an event which impressed the imagination of the whole world, both because of the romantic appeal of the famed city of the Arabian Nights, and because it symbolized the first streaks of dawn coming to illumine the darkness which had lain like a pall over the Allied cause throughout 1916. If the historical data that are now available dim the radiance of popular impressions, revealing that the military achievement was less striking than it appeared at the time, the moral significance and value cannot be minimized. But in justice to those who earlier fought and failed, it is well to realize the fallacy underlying this contemporary public view that the operations which led to the fall of Baghdad were as white as those which culminated in the surrender of Kut were black.

The strategy and organization of the campaign were infinitely more sound and more sure, but on the lower scale of tactical execution the record of the advance is spotted with missed opportunities, despite an overwhelming preponderance of force. While recognizing the difficulties of the country, the historian cannot but feel that a sledge-hammer was used to crush a flea – and the flea escaped being crushed. And if quality rather than quantity be the test of a feat of arms, comparison suggests that the advance and retreat of Townshend's original 6th Division, in face of superior numbers, with inadequate equipment, primitive communications, and utterly isolated in the heart of an enemy country, forged an intrinsically finer link in the chain of British military history.

Credit for the 1917 success is due, above all, to the strategical direction, and to the ability and energy of those who put the organization of supplies and transport on a sound and efficient basis. These assets, moreover, sufficed to attain the military goal, without any further uneconomic drain on the forces in the more vital theatres of war. The general direction was now transferred to Whitehall. After the surrender of Townshend at Kut – despite the gallant but costly efforts to relieve him – the Chief of the Imperial General Staff, Sir William Robertson, was emphatically in favour of a defensive strategy in Mesopotamia. He inclined to adopt a withdrawal to Amara as the simplest and cheapest way of safeguarding the oilfields, and of commanding the two river arteries – the Tigris and Euphrates. But the new commander, Maude, who had been Robertson's own choice, maintained, after examination, that the advanced position at Kut was both militarily secure and politically wise. He was supported by Duff and Monro, the successive Commanders-in-Chief in India, and Robertson gave way, accepting the judgement of the man on the spot. There is profound psychological interest in studying how the strong personality of Maude and the military results which, step by step, he obtained, combined to change this defensive policy, almost imperceptibly, into a fresh offensive policy. The mirage of Russian cooperation had also an influence, for, beginning as a mere supplementary aid to a Russian offensive, the advance became an all-British achievement.

The whole summer and autumn of 1916 were devoted to thorough reorganization and preparation, initiated by Lake, but greatly expanded and intensified by his successor, Maude. He strove to ameliorate the condition of the troops, to improve both their health and training, to develop the precarious lines of communication, and to amass a large reserve of supplies and ammunition. Thus Maude ably established a secure base for his subsequent and sustained offensive, fulfilling Napoleon's maxim. The design of his plan of operations was equally admirable, blending boldness and circumspection. A study of his orders, both initial and during operations, shows that the lack of decisiveness cannot be charged to his want of energy. Where he tended to err was in excessive centralization and secrecy. If the latter is usually a fault on the right side, it seems here to have been partly responsible for the pause at Aziziyah, on the advance to Baghdad. For his Inspector-General of communications had to complain that even he had not been given warning that such a move was intended, and thus he had made no special preparations in readiness.

This 'imperceptible' offensive began on December 12th, 1916, the first step in a series of well-thought-out trench 'nibbles', methodical and deliberate, on the west bank of the Tigris. When it began, Maude faced the Turkish trenches at a right angle to the Tigris, and gradually brought his left shoulder up, pivoting on the river, and at the same time extending his front farther and farther upstream. At last by February

22nd, 1917, he had cleared the west bank, his extended line facing the main Turkish forces on the other bank, from Sannaiyat to the Shumran bend above Kut. Thus the Turks had not merely to guard against a direct attack from the south upon their fortified position at Sannaiyat, but against a cross-river blow from the west, which might cut their communications. The length of this patient siege-warfare process was not merely due to the intricacy of the defences or the stubborn resistance of the weak Turkish detachments on the west bank. Robertson had no taste for further adventures, and his instructions from home were framed to prevent them. The historian who studies the orders and operations gains the impression that Maude's operations were contrived, consciously or unconsciously, to undermine the stability, not merely of the Turkish position, but of Robertson's instructions.

The outcome of these deliberate and economical operations was that by the third week in February Maude was able, and admirably placed, to play for a bigger stake. His plan was to pin the Turks' left at Sannaiyat while he sprang at their communications, by forcing the river crossing at the Shumran bend – where the right flank ended and their line of retreat prolonged their line of battle. Wisely he realized that a mere feint at Sannaiyat was useless and that a real simultaneous menace to both extremities was essential if the Turkish force was to be held while it was being cut off. Unhappily his purpose was not fulfilled. Splendid as was the gallantry of the troops at the Shumran crossing, the difficulty of the task made progress slow, and the Sannaiyat attack could not pin the defenders long enough.

Even so, the Turks were placed in such peril that, as they confess, 'only the slowness of the enemy' saved them from disaster. The main cause was the tardy and feeble action of the cavalry in pursuit – partly due to Maude's too strict control, partly to the cavalry commander's want of energy and initiative, and partly to the inherent vulnerability of cavalry under modern conditions. On February 24th, when there was a splendid opportunity of turning retreat into rout, the cavalry division broke off to go back to bivouac at 7 PM, after a mere twenty-three casualties. And on subsequent days they were no more effective. The excuses offered are the need to water and the obstacle of modern fire-arms, and their admission rather accentuates than impairs the lesson as to the restricted modern value of cavalry – even in Asia. Only the daring pursuit of the naval flotilla disturbed the Turks' orderly retreat – acting on the river as a few cross-country armoured cars might have done on land.

The strategic victory had at least won Maude sanction for an attempt to gain Baghdad, and on March 5th his advance from Aziziyah began. When a check came at the line of the Diyala, Maude switched the cavalry division and 7th Corps to the west bank, for an outflanking move direct on Baghdad. More mistakes enabled the Turks to hold up this menace, but realizing their hopeless inferiority of strength and the inevitable end, against two powerful converging advances, they gave up Baghdad on the night of March 10th, and retired northward up the river. Next afternoon Maude entered the city, and another name was added to the roll of Baghdad's innumerable conquerors. For the prestige of Britain and the morale of all the Allies the capture was an invaluable stimulant worth the immediate effort, if not the sum of the efforts which had gone to fill the debit side of the victors' balance sheet.

CHAPTER SIX

SCENE 7

The Battle of Blind Man's Buff –
Jutland

Only once during over four years of war did the Grand Fleet of Britain and the High Seas Fleet of Germany meet. It would be more exact to say that they 'hailed each other in passing' – with a hail that was awe-inspiring but leaving an impression that was merely pen-inspiring. No battle in all history has spilt so much – ink. On the afternoon of May 31st, 1916, the fleet that had been built to dispute the mastery of the sea stumbled into the fleet that had held it for centuries. In the early evening these two fleets, the greatest the world had seen, groped towards each other, touched, broke away, touched again and broke away again. Then darkness fell between them. And when the 'glorious First of June' dawned a sorely puzzled Grand Fleet paraded on an empty sea.

A fundamental difference between the higher naval and military leadership in the World War was that the Admirals would not give battle unless sure of an initial advantage, and perhaps not then, whereas the Generals were usually ready to take the offensive whatever the disadvantages. In this attitude the Admirals were true to their art, the Generals were not. The sole reason for employing men who have made war their profession is the presumption that by training they have acquired a mastery of their art. Anyone with sufficient authority or inspiration can lead or push men to battle, especially if he is furnished with technically trained assistants who can help him to regulate the marshalling of the forces in movement and fire. For this shepherding of sheep to the slaughter, perhaps artful but essentially inartistic, a practised demagogue would have a definite superiority over the tongue-tied professional warrior. But the custom of employing a professional is based on the idea that through art he will be able to obtain more profit at less cost.

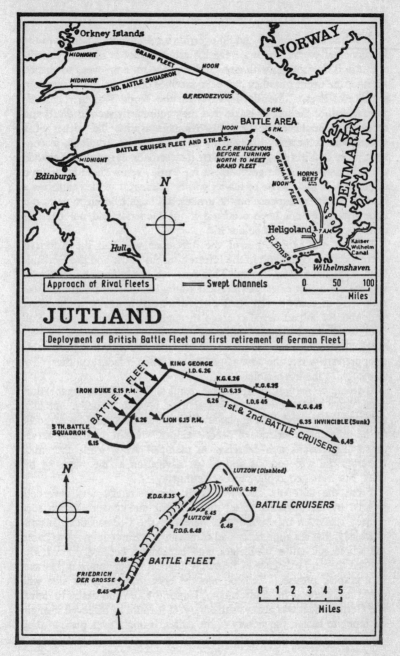

JUTLAND

Only one consideration should override a commander's fidelity to the fundamental truths which govern his art, and that is national expediency. It is for the government, and not for its employee, to decide whether the needs of policy compel a sacrifice of art and the consequent sacrifice of lives. Curiously, however, in the World War the Generals were so full of the lust of battle that they voluntarily sacrificed art, and repeatedly sought battle at a disadvantage against the wishes of a government reluctantly dragged in their wake. The Admirals, in contrast, were so faithful to their art that they sometimes ignored or evaded the express wish of the government for battle even without an assured advantage. If their sense of reality was refreshing, it tended to throw a heavier burden of expense on the armies, although it is fair to point out that this might not have occurred if the Generals had not been so extravagantly eager to shoulder it.

Perhaps one explanation of the difference was that the Admirals exercised their command in the forefront of the battle and the Generals from headquarters far in rear. This does not imply that the difference was merely a matter of the physical courage required, for some Generals were as ready to risk their own lives as their men's, while others undoubtedly gained moral courage through physical remoteness. But, undoubtedly, imagination and sense of reality are quickened by personal contact with the situation; a commander so placed is better able to appreciate where the advantage lies and when it fades; quicker, also, to recognize the impossible.

It would be natural to expect as a result of this difference that sailors would have a bias towards tactics, soldiers towards strategy. Actually, the reverse occurred. The explanation of the paradox would seem to lie in the different experience of peace training, wherein the soldier serves in small garrisons and exercises in cramped areas, while the sailor traverses the wide oceans and learns navigation as the staple of his craft. For him, geography precedes gunnery.

From the outbreak of war British naval strategy was governed, rightly, by the appreciation of the fact that maintenance of sea supremacy was even more vital than defeat of the German fleet. Instantaneously, that sea supremacy had come into force and upon it was based the whole war effort of Britain, and her Allies, because upon it depended the very existence of Britain. Churchill has epitomized the issue in a graphic phrase – 'Jellicoe was the only man on either side who could lose the war in an afternoon.' Hence the aim and desire to defeat the German fleet was always subsidiary. If it could be achieved it might do much to hasten the victory of the Allies. It might even prevent their defeat. The collapse of Russia as well as the near starvation of Britain by the U-boats may well be traced to the inability of the British navy to crush the German fleet. But if, in trying to defeat the German fleet, the British lost so heavily as to lose its strategic superiority national defeat would be certain.

The aim of German naval strategy since August, 1914, had been to avoid the risk of a decisive action until the British fleet was so weakened that the prospect of success veered from gloomy to fair. Mines and torpedoes were the means on which the Germans relied to achieve this preliminary weakening. And it was the fear of such underwater weapons, the possibility that by trap or chance they might dramatically alter the balance of strength, which infused an extra degree of caution into the British strategy of precaution. In a letter of prophetic foresight on October 14th, 1914, Jellicoe had warned the Admiralty that if a chance of battle came he would regard the turning away of the German battlefleet as a sign that it was trying to lure him into such a trap, where mines and submarines lay in wait; that he would refuse to be drawn into it and, instead, would move quickly to a flank. In other words, he would side-step to avoid the chance of being surprised, and so not only disarm the enemy of his best potential weapon, but possibly throw him off his balance. The calculation is an indication of how thoroughly Jellicoe had thought out his theory of war, up to a point.

Both the German and the British strategic keynotes were well attuned to the reality of their respective conditions; the question remains whether more energy and subtlety could have been shown in executing them. The situation in May 1916, after nearly two years of war, was that the British fleet was still waiting for a favourable chance of battle and the German fleet was further away from the attainment of its preliminary aim of weakening the British. Despite a few losses due to mines and torpedoes, the British fleet was proportionately much stronger than at the beginning. In the coming clash it was to bring thirty-seven capital ships (battleships and battle cruisers) of the Dreadnought type against the German twenty-three, and in gun power the margin was still greater, 168 guns of 13.5-15 inch calibre and 104 of 12 inch could be brought against 176 German guns of only 12 inch calibre. It is true that the German fleet also included six pre-Dreadnought battleships, but in a fleet action these would be little better than a target for the heavier guns of the British. Moreover, by their presence they reduced the already slower German fleet to a still more marked inferiority in speed. The British had also a comfortable superiority in cruisers and destroyers - eight armoured and twenty-six light cruisers, against eleven of the last; eighty destroyers against sixty-three.

Another advantage gained since the outbreak of war was in the sphere of knowledge. For the British had not only gained from occasional contacts a clearer idea of the capacity of the enemy's weapons, but had discovered his signal-code. In August, 1914, the German light cruiser *Magdeburg* had been sunk in the Baltic, and clasped in the arms of a drowned under-officer the Russians had found the cipher and signal books of the German navy, as well as their squared maps of the North Sea. These were sent to London and thereafter, by intercepting the enemy's enciphered wireless messages, the British Intelligence was able to obtain advance information of many of the enemy's movements. Although suspicion led the enemy to make variations in their codes and maps, their efforts to seal up the leakage of information were offset by the development of directional wireless as a means of locating the position of ships. And this was the source of the one naval battle of the war - Jutland.

In January, 1916, a new commander was appointed to the German High Seas Fleet. This was Admiral Scheer, the nominee of Admiral von Tirpitz, and an advocate of a more aggressive war policy. The pressure of the British blockade and the relaxation of the German submarine blockade - under pressure from President Wilson - combined to provide an urge to action. And a rumoured division of the British fleet, to protect the coast from raids, came as an encouragement to action. In mid-May Scheer crystallized his plan. A cruiser raid on Sunderland was intended to draw out part of the British fleet to counter it, and lying in wait for this detachment would be the German submarines with the High Seas Fleet behind, ready to pounce. The submarines were duly dispatched, but bad weather prevented reconnaissance by the German airships. Without this safeguard Scheer would not move, and thus the submarines exhausted their sea-going endurance. On May 30th, Scheer decided to abandon his plan, and the use of his submarines, for an alternative. This was to send the Scouting Force, of battle and light cruisers, under Admiral Hipper, to demonstrate off the Norwegian coast, while he followed, out of sight. He calculated that the danger to the British cruiser patrol and shipping might draw part of the British fleet to the spot and give him a chance to destroy it. Hipper steamed north early in the morning of the 31st, with Scheer fifty miles astern.

Already, the previous evening, the impending departure of the Germans, although not their purpose, was known to the British Admiralty, and the Grand Fleet was ordered to sea. Jellicoe with the main section of the fleet sailed eastward by 10.30 PM for a rendezvous some fifty miles off the Norwegian coast, being joined on the way by Jerram's squadron from Invergordon. Beatty with the battle cruisers, reinforced by four of the latest *Queen Elizabeth* type battleships, sailed simultaneously from Rosyth (near Edinburgh) with orders from Jellicoe to reach by 2 PM on the 31st a spot sixty-nine miles south-south-east of the main rendezvous. From this, if no enemy had yet been sighted, Jellicoe would sweep southwards toward Heligoland Bight, while Beatty was ordered to close to within sight of him.

Beatty reached his own rendezvous at the assigned hour and was just turning north towards Jellicoe when the *Galatea*, one of his screen of light cruisers, sighted a stray merchant steamer and, instead of turning with the rest, continued east-south-east to examine her. This was the first of many jests of fate. For simultaneously a German light cruiser, screening Hipper's western flank, also sighted the steamer and decided to investigate. Within a few moments the two unsuspecting rivals had sighted each other – and warned their respective superiors. Thereby the strange steamer not only brought on the battle of Jutland, but probably cost the British a decisive victory. For if this chance meeting had not occurred, the two forces might not have met until they were farther north – when the Germans would have been farther from shelter and nearer the jaws of Jellicoe.

Minutes were now to be momentous. Controversy as to their use has been acrid, but much of the criticism on both sides seems pedantic – more apt for the proverbial armchairs, although here occupied by professional sailors, than for the vague conditions in the North Sea on the afternoon of May 31st, 1916.

At 2.20 PM the *Galatea* signalled 'Enemy in sight. Two cruisers probably hostile bearing south-east, course unknown'. The sound of guns from the distant *Galatea* had just been heard when at 2.32 PM Beatty turned again south-eastwards to cut off the retreat of the enemy cruisers. Unfortunately, his signal to turn, made by flags, was not read owing to smoke and want of wind by Evan-Thomas' squadron of battleships which had been following five miles astern. In consequence Evan-Thomas did not turn until 2.40 PM and thereby found himself ten miles behind Beatty's battle cruisers.

It has been argued that the signal should have been made, more simply and effectively, by searchlight flashes – an argument that seems irrefutable. It has been argued that Evan-Thomas should have turned on his own initiative, as he must have seen Beatty turning – an argument which seems highly disputable in view of his general orders and his ignorance of Beatty's tactical intentions. On the other side, it has been contended, first, that Beatty himself should have acted earlier; second, that he should also have given Evan-Thomas the chance to close up to him – either by continuing on his northward course while Evan-Thomas was turning or, still better, by swinging towards him before turning. But this ideal perhaps unduly discounts the conditions – physical and psychological. Both Jellicoe and Beatty had been steaming leisurely, with hope of an encounter waning as the hours passed, and all the more because the Admiralty had signalled that, by directional wireless, the enemy fleet had been located still at its anchorage. Yet another unlucky mishap.

If fair account be taken of the hazy situation, Beatty would seem to have taken his decision with all reasonable promptness. As for the decision itself he had every reason, from past experience, to fear that the German cruisers would give him the slip, and little reason to suspect that they masked a greater force. At the most he might meet the German battle cruisers, and they were only five in all, while he had six. If his temperament was impetuous rather than calculating, both past experience and the general strategic situation would here seem to justify his action in forfeiting extra strength to gain extra minutes.

Finding that the enemy cruisers were apparently following the Galatea north-westwards, Beatty himself gradually changed his course until he was steaming north-east. Thereby he and Hipper were converging towards each other and about 3.30 PM they came in sight of each other. Hipper promptly turned to fall back towards his own battle-fleet and Beatty duly turned on a parallel course. At 3.45 PM both sides opened fire at a range of about nine miles. Owing to bad light the British miscalculated the range, and so not only lost the advantage that their guns outranged the Germans, but made poor shooting. In contrast, the British were silhouetted against the western sky. Just after 4 PM catastrophe burst upon the British. A shell from the Lutzow, Hipper's flagship, plunged into the midship turret of the Lion, Beatty's flagship. With both legs shattered, Major Harvey of the marines managed before he died to call down the voice tube the order to flood the magazines – and thereby saved the ship from being blown up. But the Indefatigable, hit by a salvo of three shells from the Von der Tann, dropped out of the line and, hit again, turned over and sank with 1,000 men. Fortunately, at this critical moment, Evan-Thomas, by cutting the corners, had come within range, and his accurate fire disturbed the accuracy of the Germans' – although the poor quality of the British shells, which burst without penetrating their armour, saved the Germans from vital injury. And at 4.26 PM they scored afresh, when the battle cruiser *Queen Mary*, hit by a salvo, blew up and sank with her crew of 1,200 – her grave and their grave marked by a gigantic pall of smoke 800 feet high. Thus Beatty was reduced from six ships to four, against five. About this time also, the *Princess Royal* vanished momentarily in an ominous cloud of smoke and spray, and a signalman on the *Lion* laconically reported, '*Princess Royal* blown up, sir.' Whereupon Beatty as curtly said to his flag captain – 'Chatfield, there seems to be something wrong with our damned ships today. Turn two points to port' – nearer the enemy.

It was a tribute to his cool nerve, although the crisis had really passed with the entry of Evan-Thomas into the fight. That entry marred the trap which Scheer was planning for Beatty. For instead of steering to catch Beatty between the two jaws formed by Hipper and his own main fleet, Scheer was forced to steam direct to Hipper's aid.

At 4.33 PM Goodenough's light-cruiser squadron, two miles ahead of the *Lion*, sighted battleships to the south-east, and signalled the news to Beatty. Goodenough boldly held to his course until he could definitely identify the High Seas Fleet and then sent a wireless message direct to Jellicoe – who had already quickened his pace towards Beatty.

Beatty also held his course until he had sighted Scheer's battleships and then, at 4.40 PM, turned about to run north towards Jellicoe. The turn was well timed to let Beatty's force, now the bait, be seen by Scheer without letting it come within range of Scheer's guns. But the signal to turn, again made by flags, was again missed by Evan-Thomas, who held to his southward course until he had passed Beatty running north. Thereby he came under fire from Scheer's leading battleships, and became both the bait to Scheer and the shield to Beatty during the run north.

Danger during Beatty's turn, which was made in succession round a fixed point, was partly averted by the disconcerting and gallant attacks of the British destroyers. Two had been crippled and, drifting helplessly between the oncoming lines of battleships, with glorious impudence fired their last torpedoes before they were riven by shells. German destroyers chivalrously stopped to pick up the survivors.

Meantime the two great fleets were rushing towards each other, Scheer in ignorance, Jellicoe in knowledge of his enemy's approach – but not of his exact course. But upon such detailed knowledge Jellicoe's own dispositions must depend. Unfortunately the haze over the North Sea was mental as well as physical. Beatty, leading the run north, had lost touch with Scheer's fleet and even with Hipper's, which was steaming roughly parallel to him in the mist. And although Evan-Thomas was still in touch with Scheer he sent no reports. The only messages Jellicoe received came at the very start of the retirement, four from Goodenough and one from Beatty, whose wireless had been shot away – so that he had to transmit the message through a third ship. But the importance of this lack of information of the enemy can be, and has been, exaggerated. For the German fleet did not vary its course and the real trouble came from British error in reckoning their own position – on the part of both Jellicoe's and Beatty's flagships. The result was that when the two came in sight of each other the *Lion* was found to be some seven miles farther west than Jellicoe had anticipated. And, as a corollary, the enemy also were sighted on the starboard bow, ie, on Jellicoe's right front instead of straight ahead. More frequent reports of the position of Beatty's fleet might have provided, through averaging, a more accurate reckoning.

Jellicoe was advancing south in a compact mass of six parallel columns, like a six-pronged comb, four miles wide from flank to flank. This is not a fighting formation, for only a minimum of the total guns would be able to fire, forward, if an enemy was met. To deliver the maximum fire the ships must bring their broadsides to bear, and must form into line of battle. If the enemy were found directly ahead each column had only to wheel to the right or left for the whole fleet to be in line, firing their broadsides at the enemy. The Grand Fleet only required four minutes to make this deployment, but it required that the enemy should be in exactly the right position. An alternative method, if the enemy lay to a flank, was for one of the columns – normally a wing column – to steam on while the remainder wheeled to follow in its wake. In this case the fleet would still be able to form a single chain within four minutes, but would take much longer to straighten their line.

Let us now see what actually happened. Jellicoe had dispatched the 3rd Battle Cruiser Squadron (Hood) to support Beatty, but owing to the error in reckoning already mentioned it moved too far eastward. Thereby it became unintentionally the upper jaw of a trap into which the unconscious Hipper was putting his head. Hipper meantime was still running parallel to, but out of sight of, Beatty. At 5.40 PM Hipper suddenly sighted Beatty afresh – to the westward – and coming under fire, swerved more to the eastward. Then he heard Hood's guns opening fire on his light cruisers. Alarmed, he turned away to the south-east at 6.34 PM, only to see his light cruisers attacked by four of Hood's destroyers, which he imagined to be the forerunners of Jellicoe's main fleet. So he swerved again, to the south-west.

Meantime, Jellicoe and Beatty had not sighted each other until just before 6 PM, although their advanced cruisers had made visual contact at 5.30 PM, when about five miles apart. At 6.1 PM Jellicoe flashed the question – 'Where is the enemy's battlefleet?' No answer came. Beatty was busily intent on his own 'disappearing' opponent, Hipper – following him on a long outer curve which, incidentally, was carrying Beatty across Jellicoe's front. At 6.10 PM Jellicoe repeated his question and four minutes later Beatty, almost simultaneously with Evan-Thomas, reported the enemy's bearing. The two reports enabled Jellicoe to judge Scheer's rough position, although not the course he was steering – which, actually, was north-westward in Hipper's wake.

Within a minute of Beatty's report Jellicoe had made his decision and given the order to deploy – on his left wing. Two minutes later his right wing opened fire, as it was wheeling to the left. It has been argued that he should have deployed earlier; but this would have meant acting on uncertain information, and the risk of putting himself in an unfavourable position. It has been argued that he should have deployed on his right; but this would have meant the risk that the enemy crossed the head of his line before he could cross theirs, and the certainty that until the line was straightened out – twenty-two minutes later – only a part, if a growing part, of his fleet could fire. It has been argued, by Churchill, that he might have deployed on one of the centre divisions and thereby have saved seven minutes, besides gaining the advantage of deploying within closer, yet not too close, reach to the oncoming foe. This, however, was a manoeuvre rather more complex and less practised, and would at least have meant that the fire of the left fork of the tail was temporarily masked.

Jellicoe's actual deployment ensured that he would have time to cross the head of the enemy's line – the historic and deadly manoeuvre of 'crossing the T' – and also that none of his battleships would have their fire masked by others while the chain was straightening. Nor does there seem much actual substance in the criticism that a chance was lost by deploying farther away from the enemy. Rather was it gained. For Scheer had no intention of fighting the Grand Fleet unless at an advantage.

Thus he no sooner saw that Jellicoe's line – obscured for a time by the smoke of the cruiser action in the intervening space – was likely to 'cross the T' than he made, at 6.30 PM, an instant turn about. This was a deft emergency manoeuvre whereby each ship, beginning from the rear, began to turn in almost simultaneous succession; it enabled the whole line to slip out of range in the minimum time. His precipitancy was due to the fact that he mistook Hood's battle cruisers for Jellicoe's leading battleships, and so thought the British manoeuvre was further advanced than in reality. His mistake was to his opponent's disadvantage. For Jellicoe had signalled at 6.29 PM for his line to turn south-south-east by sub-divisions, in order to get closer to the enemy, but had cancelled the order on finding that his tail had not yet straightened out. Nor had it done so when Scheer made his 'somersault' turn, under cover of a torpedo attack and a smoke screen. This hid Scheer's retirement for the few minutes before he was swallowed up in the mist. Although several of his leading battleships had suffered heavy hits, the only complete loss had been one of Hipper's light cruisers, the *Wiesbaden.* And, before disappearing, Hipper had destroyed another British battle cruiser, the *Invincible*, and one armoured cruiser, and had left a second sinking.

But the potentially vital fact in Scheer's retirement was that he had turned westward – away from his own harbours. If he had sighted the British battlefleet on his flank, as would have happened if Jellicoe had deployed in any other way, the natural course for Scheer would have been, not to turn about, but to turn right – and so retire towards his own harbours. Thus the best justification for Jellicoe's choice is that it gave him the opportunity to cut off Scheer's path of retreat. It also placed Scheer against the western sky.

This opportunity Jellicoe promptly exploited. To give direct chase to Scheer, when his own line was already six miles astern of Scheer, and only two hours' daylight remained, was a move that promised little. It would also have exposed the battlefleet to the very risk of running into mines dropped and torpedoes fired by the enemy, which Jellicoe was intent to avoid.

Instead, at 6.44 PM he ordered each division to turn south-east – so that they were once more in six columns echeloned back like a staircase from left to right. In the next quarter of an hour he made two more partial turns. The effect was to bring him round in a gradual curve between the unseen Germans and their line of retreat, while edging closer to them. Only the coming darkness and the increasing mist threatened the advantage gained by his skilful manoeuvre. One criticism, however, appears reasonable – that, either on Beatty's initiative or Jellicoe's orders, the Battle Cruiser Fleet, whose essential role was that of 'feelers' for the battlefleet, might have swung round more sharply and sought to keep touch with the enemy. Actually, the battle cruisers were farther away than the battlefleet from the enemy.

The enemy, however, was about to make touch himself – to his own danger. Having slipped out of one trap he almost slipped into another, created mainly by his own miscalculation. For, after steaming west for about twenty minutes, Scheer suddenly reversed his direction and steamed east again – to appear out of the mist at about the same point as before. He claimed in his subsequent dispatch that his idea was to strike a second blow so as to keep the initiative, and maintain German prestige. The claim is at his own expense, for no good tactician would steam into the middle of the superior British fleet for such a purpose. The logical hypothesis is that he expected to cross the tail of the British fleet, thereby gaining the chance to punish part of it and regaining his path home. For, as already mentioned, he had mistaken Hood's squadron for the van of the battlefleet and so he overestimated the distance that the battlefleet had moved. Hence, when Scheer appeared out of the mist at 7.10 PM he was opposite the centre of the 'stepped' British line.

Its rear squadron, being nearest, opened fire first – at a range of only about five miles. Within the next few minutes the greater part of the British fleet joined in. But with a perhaps excessive fear of partial exposure, Jellicoe ordered his rear squadrons to form astern of him – in non-technical language, to wheel eastward and follow in his wake. Thereby he drew them farther away from the enemy. And at this moment Scheer had also decided to go away. Indeed, he was in such a hurry to get out of Jellicoe's jaws that he not only performed a fresh 'somersault' manoeuvre, less neat than before, under cover of smoke screens and destroyer attacks, but also launched his battle cruisers in a 'death ride'.

The destroyers proved the most effective of these agents of his salvation, for seeing their torpedoes loosed, at long range, Jellicoe swung his ships away by two quick turns of two points each (22.5 degrees in all). This turn away was a long-practised method which the majority opinion in the navy approved as the best expedient, and only a minority opposed on the score that the torpedo danger was overrated, and that its adoption tended to abnegate the offensive value of the battleship. A decision between these opinions is difficult. One can only draw the logical conclusion that if the precaution was essential, it was a confession of the weakness of the battleship, and of the ease with which its offensive movements could be paralysed by an infinitely less expensive instrument of war. At Jutland the justification for the precaution is that only one British battleship was hit by a torpedo, and the justification for the minority opinion is that this battleship was so little affected that it kept its place in the line.

As a means of freeing the German fleet the destroyer attack was not only the most effective but the cheapest, for only one destroyer was sunk – by a counterstroke of the British light cruisers – while the German battle cruisers suffered heavily. The *Lutzow* was disabled before the 'death ride' began, and the other four were hit repeatedly in the few minutes before a signal of recall from Scheer reprieved them.

The tactical effect of the destroyer attack was that while the German fleet was going west the British fleet was going the opposite way. A quarter of an hour later, satisfied that the torpedo attack had spent itself, Jellicoe corrected his turn away, but continued on a course almost due south. Not until 8 PM did he turn west. In this delay there seems to be ground for criticism. For to maintain his tactical advantage of being across the enemy's line of retreat, it was desirable both to shepherd him away from his own coast and to keep in touch with him so that he had less chance of slipping past the British mobile barrier in the dark.

By one school of criticism much emphasis has been given to the fact that after sighting the enemy again at 7.40 Beatty sent a further wireless signal to Jellicoe ten minutes later – 'Submit van of battleships follow battle cruisers. We can then cut off whole of enemy's battlefleet.' But excellent as this sounds, and was its meaning, its historical value is rather diminished by the fact that, before it was decoded and handed to him, Jellicoe had already turned the battlefleet west, while Beatty was merely going south-west according to his last message. Moreover, the German fleet was already cut off from its base. Perhaps Beatty meant 'head off' – his own next order to his light cruisers, to locate the head of the enemy's line, which was now steaming south, suggests this explanation. Moreover, he succeeded in heading off the enemy on his own, for when they came under his fire about 8.23 PM, they promptly sheered off to the westward again. And by checking their course south this encounter helped them in slipping past the British tail later.

The best, indeed the only, chance of closing with the Germans had passed in the half-hour following their 7.20 PM turn away. The great question that remained was whether Jellicoe could continue to bar their way during the night so that he could re-engage at dawn with a whole day's light before him, and thereby profit from his strategic advantage – now added to superior strength.

When the blanket of darkness spread across the sea about 9 PM it not merely accelerated the haziness of the day, but changed it to blindness. The battleships lost their advantage of range, the torpedo craft gained the advantage of coming to close range with minimum risk. And all ships would have difficulty in distinguishing friend from foe.

Jellicoe wisely rejected the hazard of a night battle, for it would have meant staking his double advantage on a pure gamble. Thus his problem was to prevent the enemy finding an open way home during the five and a half hours before daylight. There were three likely routes, each leading to a swept channel through the minefields which covered the approaches to the Heligoland Bight and the German harbours. One, on the east, was past Horn Reefs and down the Frisian coast; a second, more central, eventually led past Heligoland; the third, in the extreme south-west, was entered near the German coast and led eastward past the mouth of the Ems. The distance to this was 180 miles, and being the farthest it was the least obvious choice. Hence Jellicoe might justly fear that an astute enemy might take it – but for one factor. This was the inferior speed of the German fleet compared with his own. If the Germans had enjoyed equal or greater speed the Ems route would have offered them more chance and scope for evading an uncertain guard during the hours of darkness. Lacking it, they were wise to take the greater immediate risk of the shorter route.

Jellicoe, however, was unwilling to uncover one completely in order to cover the others more closely. And he chose a 'beat' which certainly reconciled as far as was possible the difficulties of covering all. Indeed, it left the Germans only one good chance – that of slipping behind Jellicoe and taking the Horn Reefs passage. Hence, one would anticipate that Jellicoe would be specially sensitive to any signs of an attempt to pass astern of him.

At 9.17 PM Jellicoe ordered the fleet to take up night cruising stations – the battleships being closed up in three parallel columns. The course of the fleet was to be due south, and the speed seventeen knots. The destroyers were massed five miles astern, a disposition which prolonged the moving barrier, protected the rear of the battlefleet against torpedo attacks, and, above all, prevented the risks of mistaken identity in the darkness. If the battleships sighted destroyers, or the destroyers battleships, each would know that the dim shapes were those of an enemy. Beatty had already taken station with the battle cruisers ahead of and on the western, or enemy, flank of the battlefleet. The historical significance of his night position is that it made impossible any attempt of the Germans to outstrip or pass south of the British, and so might have provided a further cause for sensitive suspicion of an attempt to pass astern. The formation of the Grand Fleet might be likened metaphorically and symbolically to that of the traditional British lion,

Beatty's battle cruisers and light cruisers being the nose and ears, and the destroyers – the lion's tail. The nose was to smell nothing, the ears to hear something, the tail to be twisted, but the lion as an entity to remain as majestically unmoved as those which surround Nelson's column.

One preliminary remains to be mentioned – Scheer's intention. It was simple, not subtle, and to that extent simplified the problem of parrying it. Desperation, at the morning's dire prospect, seems to have inspired it. For he took the shortest route home – by Horn Reefs – prepared to lose heavily but determined to break through. Unlike Jellicoe, he could at least feel that the luck lurking in a night encounter was more likely to be a friend than otherwise to his bold course. To enhance his prospects and safety he posted his lame battle cruisers and old battleships in rear and covered his van with destroyer and light-cruiser tentacles.

The scene was set. Would the monarchs of the seas, taking the call, clash in blind battle? Thus the anticipation. But only the tinkle of the jester's bell was heard from the darkened stage. And when light came, the stage was empty.

The first tinkle came at 9.32 PM when the *Lion*, Beatty's flagship, inquired by flashing-lamp of the *Princess Royal* – 'Please give me challenge and reply now in force as they have been lost.' The reply seems to have been seen, in part, by an enemy ship. For, about half an hour later, several cruisers were sighted by the *Castor*, which was leading one of the British destroyer flotillas. They took the initiative and challenged her by making part of the British secret challenge for the day. As, however, they next switched on their searchlights and opened fire, the *Castor* replied in a similar unfriendly fashion, but several of her attendant destroyers withheld their torpedoes from a natural doubt as to the true identity of the cruisers. But the effect of this mischance, and missed chance, can be exaggerated. For, from 10.20 PM to 11.30 PM, the British tail was repeatedly in action with the enemy, who were trying to elbow their way through. At 10.20 PM they 'elbowed' Goodenough's light cruisers, but sheered off after the light cruiser *Frauenlob* had been sunk by a torpedo from the badly battered *Southampton*. In the next hour the British destroyers suffered the contusion and caused confusion. The light cruiser *Elbing* was rammed by the battleship *Posen* and left sinking, while the British destroyer *Spitfire* acted up to her name by ramming the battleship *Nassau*. She not only 'got away with' this act of impertinence, but with a long strip of *Nassau*'s plating as proof of her prowess. Once more the German fleet sheered off, but veered in afresh about 11.30 PM and this time broke through, although harassed by the British hornets for more than an hour at the cost of four of their number.

They had contributed much gallantry, but little intelligence. The only report of these encounters that came to Jellicoe was one from Goodenough at 10.15 PM, and, owing to the *Southampton*'s wireless being shot away this did not reach Jellicoe until 11.38 PM. For the light craft, hotly engaged, there was some excuse for failure to send information, although even those which were not engaged sent no word of what they saw. But Evan-Thomas' 5th Battle Squadron was also astern of the main fleet, forming an intermediate link; it was well aware of the constant attacks and its two rear battleships actually saw the leading German battleships in their wake. The *Valiant*, at 11.35 PM, noted 'two German cruisers with at least two funnels and a crane amidships, apparently steering eastward at a high speed'. The crane identified them so unmistakably as battleships of the *Westfalen* class, that the mistake of assuming them to be cruisers would be incredible were it not fact. The *Malaya*, five minutes later, noted 'enemy big ships, three points abaft the starboard beam, steering the same way as ours'. It had evidently sighted the enemy battleships as they were making a momentary swerve in face of the destroyer attack. It noted the 'conspicuous crane' of the leading ship, and drew the correct deduction that it was 'apparently *Westfalen* class'. Neither the *Valiant* nor the *Malaya* reported what they had seen, apparently assuming that the *Barham*, their flagship ahead, had seen it likewise. How the *Barham* failed to see it has never been explained. The one clear fact is that no word from the squadron was sent to the Commander-in-Chief.

Was there, then, no information which might have quickened Jellicoe's suspicion or upon which he might have acted? Two reports reached him from the Admiralty, which had been intercepting German wireless messages. The first, giving the German location at 9 PM, was valueless because, owing to an error, the position indicated was obviously inaccurate. This did not encourage him to accept the second – which was only too accurate. It stated that the German fleet had been ordered home at 9.14 PM and gave the dispositions, course and speed. But, by another fateful slip, it omitted the most significant fact contained in the several enemy messages which it summarized – that Scheer had asked for an airship reconnaissance near Horn Reefs at daylight. Here was the unmistakable scent to his bolt-hole.

This message was received at 11.5 PM and read, after deciphering, about 11.30 PM. One other message reached Jellicoe, being received at

11.30 PM – and so read later than the Admiralty message. It came from the light cruiser *Birmingham*, and reported that 'battle cruisers probably hostile' were in sight, steering south and well to the westward. Unfortunately, the *Birmingham* had sighted them at a moment when they had sheered away from the British torpedo attacks. If Jellicoe already distrusted the Admiralty message, upon which he took no action, it was natural that he should regard the two later reports from the *Southampton* and *Birmingham* as support to his doubts.

Yet, it is curious, and not easy to explain, that he should have been so insensitive to the definite indication of fighting astern. For, apart from these two reports, the recurrent firing was heard and the flashes seen both by his flagship and the other battleships. That this fire was obviously from light guns did not, it is true, reveal the presence of enemy battleships, but it was no proof that they were not there, for at night battleships would naturally be using their secondary armament if engaged with British light craft. More curious still is the fact that Jellicoe made only one attempt, at 10.46 PM to inquire the source of the firing, and the wording of his signal suggests a preconceived idea that it was merely an enemy destroyer attack. Thus, in sum, the conclusion is that while Jellicoe's lack of certain knowledge was due to the neglect of his subordinates, his lack of suspicion is the measure of his own responsibility – and the salvation of Scheer.

One more serious contact occurred before the German fleet was at last safely free. In the dim light before dawn it was sighted by Captain Stirling's 12th Destroyer Flotilla. The exception, when he should have been the rule, Stirling sent a wireless report to Jellicoe at 1.52 AM, before he engaged the enemy and another during the action. His attack torpedoed and sank the German battleship *Pommern*, and thereby achieved more than the whole Grand Fleet had done. But his reports did not reach Jellicoe, presumably owing to a wireless failure. Thus the British battlefleet continued serenely on its course southward, and the German, on its course homeward.

When daylight came Jellicoe turned about, at 2.39 AM, and steamed northward, expecting to see the German fleet and seeing only an empty sea. Then came another Admiralty message to say that the German fleet was close to Horn Reefs, and this time its evidence was accepted. After searching for enemy stragglers, and finding none, the Grand Fleet in turn steamed homeward. Its total loss had been three battle cruisers, three armoured cruisers and eight destroyers to the German one battleship, one battle cruiser, four light cruisers and five destroyers. In officers and men, the British had lost 6,097 killed to the German 2,545, and 177 prisoners to none.

Thus the one naval 'battle' of the World War was but a casual item in the long butcher's bill. Its value as a battle was in every sense negligible. To trace to it the ultimate and bloodless surrender of the German fleet two and a half years later is absurd, confounding mere sequence with causation. If Jutland did little to encourage the Germans to provoke a decisive clash at sea it did little to discourage them. They had won the first game, against the battle cruisers, and superior gunnery had yielded them honours 'above the line'; they had been out-manoeuvred in the second game, with honours easy, and had scored several tricks in the third before the game had been broken off. As they could not hope to gain the rubber because of their opponent's stronger hand, the interruption left them at least a flattering sense of their own skill. As a new and untried creation the German navy inevitably suffered an inferiority complex in face of a navy which enjoyed a matchless roll of victories and the 'Nelson tradition'. Jutland had dissipated this fear of the untried in face of the known unknown.

Within twelve weeks the German fleet was to make a bolder bid to take the British at a disadvantage. Covered by airship patrols it advanced close to the English coast on August 19th with the idea of bombarding Sunderland as a bait to draw the Grand Fleet south on to a waiting ambush of submarines. Battle was again balked by caution and an accident. One of Beatty's advanced cruisers was torpedoed and Jellicoe, suspecting instead a new-laid minefield, turned back and steamed north for two hours. When he again came south the German fleet had gone. For Scheer had received a report of a strong British force – actually the light force from Harwich – coming up from the south, and hastily assumed that this was the Grand Fleet. If so, it had not only evaded his trap but, turning the tables, threatened to cut him off. Hence he turned for home.

For the British Navy, Jutland would better not have been fought at all. However unpalatable the admission, it undoubtedly depreciated British naval prestige in the eyes of Allies and the home public more than the inspiring feats of individual gallantry and the fact of Britain's continued supremacy at sea could redeem. That supremacy was to ensure the ultimate downfall of German power to continue the war. But no victorious battle helped, as such a battle might, to shorten the gloomy and costly process of exhaustive slaughter on land. Jutland merely ensured what was already ensured without a battle, so long as the British navy maintained its passive superiority of strength.

Here was the general aspect. On the technical side, Jutland was more significant if not more productive of enthusiasm. It showed that the German standard of gunnery was far higher than complacent or patronizing opinion in England had recognized, and it tended, less fairly, to reflect unfavourably on British gunnery owing to the lapse of some, and the lack of opportunity of other, elements of the fleet. In material, Jutland showed also that the Admiralty and its technical advisers had failed to foresee or profit by experience as well as the Germans. Against the inferior armour-piercing qualities of the British shells must be set – but not offset – the fact of insufficient protection of the British ships against plunging fire, and especially against the flash from an explosion in a gun turret passing down into the magazine. This was the probable cause of the mysteriously sudden end of the *Queen Mary* and *Indefatigable*. More debatable perhaps were the results of the policy of building huge battle cruisers in which a large degree of protection was sacrificed for a small increase in speed. Speed in itself confers indirectly a high degree of protection, but essentially through diminishing the target, in the sense of making it more difficult for the enemy to hit. For effective protection in this way a diminution of size is required, not merely a diminution of armour for the sake of a few extra knots.

The tactical side of Jutland has aroused still more criticism and controversy than the technical side. Criticism of its foundation is less easy to counter than criticism of the actual direction. The naval neglect of tactical study, the absence of tactical textbooks, and the secrecy which by custom had enshrouded the meagre instructions, have ever been a source of wonder to soldiers, who know from history and experience that good and flexible tactics in an army are essentially the product of ceaseless reflection and discussion by many minds. '*La critique est la vie de la science.*' Students of military history know that the attempt to keep tactics secret defeats its own end – and its own employer. There was no mystery in the tactics by which Alexander's Macedonians, the Romans, the Mongols, Gustavus' Swedes, Frederick's Prussians, Wellington's Peninsular infantry, won their repeated triumphs. Only a matchless harmony of execution through practice and understanding which gave them the advantage no rival and imitator could overtake. Secrecy leads to rigidity of tactics; open discussion and criticism, to flexibility and the well-attuned initiative of subordinates when confronted with the unexpected. The basic criticism of naval tactics during the World War period is that they undermined the basis of tactics – elasticity. Moreover, the fleet fought at Jutland as a single body, as did armies in the days before Napoleon developed the system

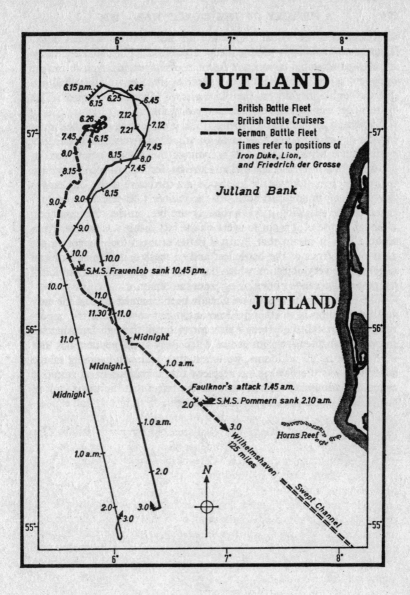

JUTLAND

British Battle Fleet ————————
British Battle Cruisers ————————
German Battle Fleet – – – – – – –

Times refer to positions of
Iron Duke, Lion,
and Friedrich der Grosse

Jutland Bank

JUTLAND

6.15 p.m.
6.45
6.15
6.25
6.45
6.26
7.12
7.21
7.12
7.45
6.15
7.45
8.0
8.15
8.15
8.0
7.45
8.15
9.0
9.0
9.0
10.0
10.0
S.M.S. Frauenlob sank 10.45 p.m.
10.0
11.0
11.30 11.0
11.0
Midnight
11.0
Midnight
1.0 a.m.
Midnight
Faulknor's attack 1.45 a.m.
2.0
S.M.S. Pommern sank 2.10 a.m.
1.0 a.m.
3.0
Horns Reef
1.0 a.m.
2.0
Wilhelmshaven 125 miles
2.0
3.0
Swept Channel

N

of independent divisions. Tactically, the fleet was an armless body. Thus however skilfully Jellicoe manoeuvred his fleet he could not justly hope to paralyse his opponent's freedom of movement. And to pin an opponent is the vital prelude to a decisive manoeuvre; this dual act gives a double meaning to the old maxim – 'divide to conquer'. The British fleet was all too truly 'one and indivisible'.

Subject to this dominant proviso, Jellicoe's handling of the fleet during the day of May 31st may fairly be adjudged a very able if cautious performance when we take full account of the obscure conditions. In 1916 this obscurity had reached an extreme, for aircraft reconnaissance had not yet been adequately developed as a corrective to the long ranges developed by progress in guns. As for Jellicoe's oft-criticized deployment on the left wing it was probably the best in the circumstances, although praise of it is apt to overlook the fact that it was not free from trouble. For it meant that Beatty's battle cruisers took longer to get clear of the front of the battlefleet and so masked its fire and caused checks – the very objection which has been brought against Churchill's suggested alternative of deploying from the centre.

The lessons of the night have already been summed up, and the only further question is whether Jellicoe might not have seized the opportunity to forestall the enemy's attempt to break through by using his torpedo craft offensively instead of defensively as his pendent tail. But if, discounting all criticisms, we admit that Jellicoe's handling of the battlefleet was the flawless masterpiece that numerous naval admirers argue, the admission only strengthens the belief that the worst fault of the Jutland battle was that it was ever fought.

CHAPTER SEVEN

1917 – The Strain

Despite incessant provocation for two years, since the *Lusitania* incident, President Wilson held to his neutral policy, and if his excess of patience angered many of his own people it was at least the means of consolidating American opinion and reconciling it as a whole to intervention in the war. Meantime he strove by speech and by the agency of Colonel House – his unofficial ambassador – to find a basis of peace on which the belligerents could agree. This effort was doomed to failure by his misunderstanding of the psychology of the warring peoples and of people at war. He was still thinking in terms of traditional warfare, between governmental policies, while the conflict had long since passed into the wider sphere of the struggle of peoples dominated by primitive instincts and chained by their own catch-phrases to the chariot wheels of Mars-mechanized.

The declaration of the unlimited submarine campaign brought convincing proof of the futility of these peace hopes and of the reality of the German intentions, and when followed by the deliberate sinking of American ships and an attempt to instigate Mexico to action against the United States, President Wilson hesitated no longer and, on April 6th, 1917, America entered the war against Germany.

Her potential force in man power and material was illimitable. But, even more unready than Britain in 1914, it must be long in exerting more than a moral influence, and Germany confidently anticipated that the submarine campaign would take decisive effect within a few months. How near her calculation came to fulfilment the record of 1917 and 1918 bears witness.

The year 1916 had closed in gloom for the Entente. The simultaneous offensive on all fronts, planned a year before, had misfired, the French Army was at a low ebb, the Russian still lower, the Somme had failed to produce visible results in any way proportionate to its cost, and another fresh Ally had been overrun. At sea the negativeness of Jutland was a disappointment, and although Germany's first submarine campaign had been abandoned a stronger one was threatened. To offset these debits, the Entente could only show the capture of distant Baghdad and the limited Italian success at Gorizia in August, whose value, however, was mainly that of a moral fillip to Italy herself.

Among the Allied peoples and their political representatives there was a growing sense of depression. On the one hand it took the form of dissatisfaction with the conduct of the war, and, on the other, of discouragement over the prospects of a victorious conclusion to the war, and a tendency to discuss the possibilities of a peace by negotiation. The first-named tendency was the first to come to a head and was signalized in London, the political mainspring of the Allies, by the replacement of Asquith's Government on December 11th by one with Lloyd George as its chief. The order of precedence in events had a significant effect. For Lloyd George had come into power as the spokesman of a widespread demand for a more vigorous as well as more efficient prosecution of the war.

The second tendency received an impulse from the German peace move of December 12th, after the fall of Bucharest, which proposed an opening of peace discussions. This suggestion was rejected as insincere by the Allied Governments, but it afforded the opportunity for President Wilson, on whose behalf Colonel House had long been sounding the belligerent Governments as to the prospects of mediation, to invite these to define their war aims as a preliminary to practical negotiation. The German reply was evasive, the Allied replies were considered by their opponents unacceptable as a basis of discussion, and the tentative peace moves subsided. But while this wave of depression was surging on the 'home front', the Allied commanders continued optimistic. In November Joffre assembled, at Chantilly, a further conference of the commanders at which it was agreed that the Germans were in great difficulties on the Western Front, and that the situation of the Allies was more favourable than it had ever been.

The fighting strength of the British Army in France had grown to be about 1,200,000 men, and was still growing. The fighting strength of the French Army had been increased by the incorporation of native troops to some 2,600,000, so that, including the Belgians, it was estimated that the Allies disposed of about 3,900,000 men against about 2,500,000 Germans.

Joffre, however, declared that the French Army could maintain its strength for one more great battle, and that thereafter it must progressively decline, as France had no longer a sufficient number of men of military age to replace losses. He therefore warned Haig that during the coming year the burden must fall more and more upon the British Army. It was also agreed that in view of these factors the relative superiority of the Allies on the Western Front would be greater in the spring of 1917 than at any time which could be foreseen with certainty. In consequence it was decided to take the earliest opportunity of pressing the advantage gained on the Somme, and to continue the process of exhausting the enemy's reserves as preparation for an effort which should be decisive. An alternative proposal was made by General Cadorna that the French and British should cooperate in a combined thrust from the Italian front against Austria with the object of knocking this weaker partner out of the war. But it was rejected by the French and British commanders, despite Lloyd George's espousal of it at the Allied conference held in Rome in January. Their objection was that it involved a fresh diversion of strength away from the main front, where alone, they held, success could have decisive results.

An offensive towards Vienna would have had formidable difficulties to overcome, especially from the mountainous country; but in judging the objections to it the historian is compelled to note that the Franco-British strategists showed no signs of recognizing a fundamental truth of strategy – that a concentration at one place is unlikely to succeed unless an adequate distraction to the enemy's counter-concentration is provided elsewhere. In their justifiable conviction that the main effort of France and Britain must be made on the Western Front, they seem to have dismissed too lightly the possibility of helping Italy to create a distraction to their own benefit. Yet, with Russia palpably flagging, the need to develop some fresh channel of pressure had become more urgent. When Robertson dogmatically asserted that the first lesson of history was to concentrate all available force in the main theatre, and that 'any departure from this rule has invariably proved to be disastrous', he exposed his own ignorance of history. Lloyd George might well have reminded him of the effective way in which the Italian theatre had been used by Eugene, with Marlborough's support, as a lever against France in the War of the Spanish Succession; and by Napoleon Bonaparte, as a lever against Austria in the War of the First Coalition. It was a reflection on modern strategists that, with superior facilities, they treated as insuperable the obstacles of nature which their ancestors had repeatedly overcome. To turn the Italian theatre into an effective distraction in favour of the Western Allies, quality rather than quantity of aid from them was needed. The initial task of breaching the Isonzo front would have demanded the concentration there of heavy artillery from the Western Front – but with a promise of much-increased effect in proportion to their number. The subsequent advance would have depended less on weight of numbers than on providing the forces with an adequate spearhead of troops suitable for mountain fighting. In the organization of their respective forces as in the organization of their total resources, a cardinal defect of the Allies in their strategy was that they concentrated by count of numbers instead of concentrating on the most effective utilization of suitable tools.

Poverty of thought, not poverty of resources, produced the bankruptcy of the scheme drawn up at the Chantilly Conference. The military cupboard was abundantly stocked with men and munitions, but its shelves were bare of constructive ideas. The proceedings reveal only too clearly the want of any deep understanding of war and knowledge of its history. The Allied peoples were clamouring for something fresh. This instinct was true if their motives mixed. But all that the combined brains of Chantilly offered them was a skeleton swathed in a few mouldering platitudes.

The Entente plan for 1917 was soon to be complicated by changes in the command. French opinion had tired of the meagre results of Joffre's attrition strategy, and the method of the limited objective had fallen into disfavour because of the unlimited losses on the wrong side, which accompanied it without apparent gain. They contrasted the dull course of Joffre's strategy with the brilliant results gained by Mangin at Verdun, in the autumn, under Nivelle's direction, and as a result Joffre gave place to Nivelle, who promised a real breakthrough. His confidence so inspired Lloyd George, the new British Prime Minister, that Haig was subordinated to him for the forthcoming operations – an arrangement which violated the axiom that a general cannot direct one force while exercising executive command of another. For carrying out a plan essentially audacious, Nivelle had two further handicaps; he failed to convert several of his subordinates to the idea, and he was given less rein by the Government than his predecessor. Again, while Joffre had intimated that the British must take the chief part, Nivelle changed this policy, and in his desire to conserve the glory for France overlooked how severely the French fighting power had been strained.

Joffre's plan had been for a renewal of the Somme offensive on a widened front – the British to attack north of the Somme, including but extending beyond the old battleground, and the French south of it to the Oise. This attack was to open early in February and to be followed a fortnight later by a smaller French attack in Champagne, between Reims and Craonne.

The French had in mind comparatively short-distance objectives;

hence, unless German resistance unexpectedly collapsed, the bulk of the British forces would subsequently be transferred to Flanders for a fresh offensive there. Analysis of the facts does not tend to support the idea that the chance of early victory for the Allies was forfeited through the abandonment of Joffre's plan. The hard frosts that came in late January would have aided its early development; but it would have been too early for any prospect of a simultaneous offensive in the other theatres; and although it might have disturbed the Germans' execution of their plan, they were better prepared to rally in rear than were the Allies to press home the advantage.

Nivelle's plan was more far-reaching than Joffre's. He intended to deliver a convergent attack on both flanks of the great salient Lens–Noyon–Reims, with the French striking the main blow in Champagne immediately after the British and French attacks north and south of the Somme had attracted the enemy's attention and resources. In this 'preparatory' offensive, Nivelle's design was to avoid the old Somme battlefield and, instead, to strike on each side of it. Haig's frontage of attack would thus be reduced, and in return Nivelle wished him to take over the French front south of the Somme, as far as Roye, so as to release additional French forces for the main attack in Champagne, where Nivelle hoped to achieve a decisive breakthrough.

Haig was rather sceptical of such a possibility, and in favour of a later date for the offensive, but he recognized certain advantages in the new plan – especially the fact that it implied a greater effort by the French. On the other hand, he objected strongly to an extension of his front which would reduce the British forces available for his cherished idea of an offensive in Flanders. This objection produced the first crack in the Nivelle plan. To Nivelle's pressing letter of December 21st, Haig made indefinite reply, saying that he could only relieve the French if he himself obtained six additional divisions; and Nivelle, feeling that there was no time to lose, appealed through his own Government to the British. In mid-January, as a result, a conference was held in London: here Haig's appeal that they should wait for the Russian and Italian attacks in May was overruled, and the date fixed for not later than April 1st. It was also settled that Haig should relieve the French south of the Somme, and he was promised two additional divisions for the purpose – after further argument he eventually received eight. Haig was instructed to carry out this agreement 'both in the letter and in the spirit'.

But the difficulties, especially those of personal feeling, had not been smoothed out. Tension between the French and British headquarters increased, the former complaining of obstruction and the latter of attempted domination. This tension was magnified by British dissatisfaction with the French railway service, and on this point Haig now made an appeal to his own Government which led to a fresh conference at Calais on February 26th. But here, to his surprise, the French seized the opportunity to raise the wider issue of a unified control of operations, and produced a scheme by which, for this purpose, the British armies would be placed under Nivelle, whose orders to them would be issued through a British chief of staff at his headquarters. To this proposal, Haig and Robertson naturally took exception, and after heated discussion a compromise was reached by which Haig agreed to act under Nivelle's direction during the forthcoming offensive, subject to the right of appeal. But the chance of a smooth-working arrangement was vitiated by the deep-rooted suspicions of the British Higher Command, and these in turn were accentuated by the way that some of Nivelle's satellites agitated for Haig's removal.

A few days later, Haig, nettled by a rather peremptory letter of instructions from Nivelle, found cause for exercising his right of appeal in the signs of a German withdrawal on the Somme front; laying a perhaps excessive emphasis on the possibility that the Germans might switch troops north and attack him in Flanders, he notified the British Government and Nivelle that he might have to reduce his share in Nivelle's offensive and postpone its execution. Nivelle not unnaturally felt that Haig was evading his obligations, so one more conference was called, in London on March 12th. Here some further safeguards were inserted in the agreement, but the discussion mainly turned on the form rather than on the substance of Nivelle's instructions, and after a personal talk between the two commanders the trouble over these niceties of phrasing was settled. Nivelle was at last free to concentrate his mind on the plan for the forthcoming offensive.

Before it could begin the Germans had dislocated it. Ludendorff's first step had been to set on foot a complete programme for the reorganization of German man power, munitions and supplies. While this was developing, he intended to stand on the defensive, hoping that the new submarine campaign would either decide the issue or pave the way for a decisive blow on land when his reserves of men and material were ready. As a 'coefficient of safety' in face of the Somme offensive, he had previously ordered a new line of defence, of great artificial strength, to be built across the chord of the arc Lens–Noyon–Reims. Early in the new year, anticipating the renewal of the Entente advance on the Somme, Ludendorff hurried on the completion of this rear line and arranged for the utter devastation of the whole area inside the arc. There was a satirical, or satyrical, aptness in the code word for this programme of destruction – 'Alberich', the name of the malicious dwarf in the Nibelung Saga! The Crown Prince Rupprecht thought of resigning rather than carry out these extreme measures, but satisfied his conscience by refusing to sign the order for them. Houses were demolished, trees cut down, and even wells contaminated, while the wreckage was littered with a multitude of explosive booby-traps.

The rearward move was preceded on February 23rd by a local retirement from the awkward salient in front of Bapaume. This timely step relieved the Germans of British pressure and from the risk of interference. Although it gave the Allies a clear hint of what was in prospect they were not able to take advantage of the warning. Nivelle did not believe that the retirement would extend to his front, while Haig, who did, believed also in caution – that only a carefully mounted attack was feasible under modern conditions. The Germans evaded one such attack by another local retirement in the early hours of March 12th. Then on the 16th the main withdrawal began, the German forces marching back unhurried to the new line called by them the 'Siegfried' and by the Allies the 'Hindenburg' line. A consummate manoeuvre, if unnecessarily brutal in application, it showed that Ludendorff had the moral courage to give up territory if circumstances advised it. The British, confronted with a desert, were cautiously slow in pursuit, and their preparations for an attack on this front were thrown out of gear, limiting them to the sector around Arras, where the front was unchanged.

On April 9th Allenby's Third Army opened the spring offensive at this point, taking the long-sought Vimy ridge, but failed to develop its initial success, and continued the attack too long after the resistance had hardened. This costly action was ostensibly prolonged in order to take the pressure off the French. For the French thrust between the Somme and the Oise had also been stultified by the German retirement, and the main attack on April 16th east and west of Reims was a worse fiasco with a dangerous sequel. If it was scarcely Nivelle's fault that the foundations of his strategic plan had been upset, he betrayed *la folie de grandeur* in the way he persisted in it when the conditions had vitally changed. And his tactical plan, over-elaborate and inelastic, had no compensating elements of success against an enemy who was fully forewarned. With a prolonged bombardment giving away any chance of surprise and without first drawing away the German reserves, the idea of a rapid breakthrough was doomed to fail. The high hopes that had been raised caused the greater reaction, and the troops were weary of being thrown against barbed wire and machine guns to no apparent effect.

Accentuated by service grievances, mutinies occurred in the French armies, and no less than sixteen corps were affected. The flame of revolt broke out in a regiment of the 2nd Colonial Division on May 3rd, and although momentarily extinguished soon spread, to the tune of such cries as 'We will defend the trenches, but we won't attack!' 'We are not so stupid as to march against undamaged machine guns!' The fact that the mutinies always occurred when the troops were ordered into the line is clear proof that disgust with their leadership rather than seditious propaganda was the real cause of revolt. A significant sidelight is that cases of desertion in the French Army rose from 509 in 1914 to 21,174 in 1917. So general was the rot that, according to the Minister of War, only two divisions in the Champagne sector could be relied on fully, and in places the trenches were scarcely even guarded.

The saviour of the situation was General Pétain; and his instrument, a change of policy based on psychology. On April 28th the Government had made him Chief of the General Staff as a brake on Nivelle's reckless offensive, and on May 15th they took the wiser and more honest step of appointing him to replace Nivelle. For a month he travelled along the front by car, visiting nearly every division, summoning both officers and men to voice their complaints. Essentially patriarchal and not familiar, he inspired confidence both in his firmness and in his promises. Tours of duty in the trenches were equalized, regularity of leave ensured, rest camps improved. Within a month calm was restored – at the price of only twenty-three executions, although more than a hundred of the ringleaders were deported to the colonies.

But if the French Army was convalescent, Pétain had still to revive its fighting confidence and power. To this end he first reorganized its training and tactics on the basis that fire power should economize man power, and then aimed to try his newly sharpened blade in easy tests that should not risk blunting it again. Thus, for the rest of the year the British bore the brunt of the campaign. Their strength in France was now at its highest – sixty-four divisions, supplied with an abundance of artillery and ammunition. The strain on them, however, was increased by the failure of Russia to make any effective contribution to the pressure on Germany owing to the revolution which broke out in March. Haig decided to keep the Germans occupied by carrying out the original plan for an offensive in Belgium, but even if the principle was right the method and choice of site were opposed to all the experience of history.

The initial move was an attack on the Messines ridge in order to straighten out the Ypres salient and attract the enemy's reserves. Carried out on June 7th by the Second Army under Plumer (with Harington as Chief of Staff) it proved a model example of the 'limited' attack, in which the surprise effect of nineteen huge mines, simultaneously exploded, and supplemented by an overwhelming artillery concentration, was exploited just as far as, and no further than, the point where the German 'numbness' began to wear off.

This coup was tardily followed on July 31st by the main attack at Ypres which, hampered in execution by the heavy rain, was foredoomed by its own destruction of the intricate drainage system of the area. The British Command had persevered for two and half years with the method of a prolonged preparatory bombardment, believing that quantity of shells was the key to success, and that, unlike all the great captains of history, they could forgo the aid of surprise. The offensive at Ypres, which was finally submerged in the swamps of Passchendaele in early November, threw into stronger relief than ever before the fact that such a bombardment blocked the advance for which it was intended to pave the way – because it made the ground impassable. The discomfiture was increased by the new German defensive method of thinning the front defences and using the men so saved for prompt local counterattacks. The defence was built up of a framework of machine guns distributed in concrete 'pillboxes' and disposed in great depth. On the British side the profitless toll of this struggle in the mud was to some extent mitigated by better staff work when the direction of the attack was progressively handed over to Plumer's Second Army.

Three months of dreadful struggle came to an end with the British no appreciably nearer their immediate object of driving the Germans from their submarine bases in the Belgian ports, and if they had worn down the German strength they had worn down their own still more.

The 1917 campaign in the west closed, however, on a note brighter in promise if not in accomplishment. Appreciating from the first days the futility of using tanks in these Flanders swamps, the Tank Corps headquarters looked around for an area where they could try out a new and different method. They drew up a project for a large-scale raid to scour a canal-enclosed 'pocket' near Cambrai, where the rolling downland lent itself to tank movement. The basic idea was the release of a swarm of tanks without any preparatory bombardment to give warning of the attack. When their hopes at Ypres waned, the British Command adopted the scheme, but transformed it into a definite offensive with far-reaching aims, for which they had not the resources because of the drain of Ypres. It was to be carried out by Byng's Third Army with six divisions, and the date was fixed for November 20th. Led by nearly 400 tanks, the attack came as a complete surprise, and despite minor checks achieved a penetration far deeper and at less cost than any past British offensive. But all the available troops and tanks were thrown into the first blow, and no reserves were at hand to exploit the success. The cavalry, as always on the Western Front, proved unable to carry out this role.

Thus the advance died away, and on November 30th the Germans launched a counterstroke against the flanks of the salient created by the British advance. In the north it was parried but in the south broke through, and a disaster was narrowly averted. But if Cambrai closed in disappointment it revealed that surprise and the tank were the combination by which the trench barrier could be unlocked. Meanwhile Pétain, after overhauling his instrument, the French Army, sought to test its readiness for 1918. In August a stroke by Guillaumat's army at Verdun recovered all the remainder of the ground lost in 1916, and in October Maistre's army flattened the south-west corner of the German front, seizing the Chemin des Dames ridge.

The Collapse of Russia. The temporary breakdown of the French fighting power was not the worst of the troubles which together crippled the Entente offensive in 1917. The collapse, first partial and then complete, of Russia was a loss which even the entry of America into the war could not possibly compensate for many months, and before the balance was restored the Western Allies were to be perilously near the brink of defeat. Russia's enormous losses, due to her defective machine but incurred in sacrifice for her Allies, had undermined the moral even more than the material endurance of her forces. Revolution broke out in March, superficially against the corrupt *entourage* of the Tsar, but with more deep-seated moral causes beneath. The Tsar was forced to abdicate and a moderate Provisional Government climbed into the saddle, but without reins. This was only a makeshift, and in May another succeeded it, more Socialist in tendency and outwardly led by Kerensky. While clamouring for a general peace and undermining discipline by a system of committee control suitable to a trade union but not to the field of battle, Kerensky imagined he could send troops against the enemy by platform appeals. Brusilov succeeded Alexeiev in the Supreme Command, and on July 1st the army gained some initial success against the Austrians, especially in the region of Stanislau, only to stop as soon as real resistance was met, and to crumble directly the Germans counter-attacked. By early August the Russians had been driven out of

Galicia and the Bukovina, and only policy halted the Austro-German forces on the frontiers of Russia itself. Since the departure of Hindenburg and Ludendorff in 1916, Hoffmann had been in real control of the Eastern Front; his clever combination of strategy and policy did much to complete the paralysis of Russia, and thus release German troops for use in the west. In September the Germans took the opportunity to practise their new artillery methods, for future use in France; their surprise attack, under Hutier's command, achieved the capture of Riga with scarcely a show of opposition. Next month the Bolsheviks under Lenin overthrew the wordy Kerensky, imposed their self-constituted rule on the Russian people and sought an armistice with Germany, which was concluded in December.

The Breakthrough in Italy. The defection of Russia did not end the Entente tale of woe. Each autumn, with demoralizing regularity, Germany had seized an opportunity to eat up one of the weaker Allies. In 1915 it had been Serbia's fate, in 1916 Rumania's, and now it was to be Italy's turn – or so the Germans intended. Ludendorff's decision, taken in September, was determined by the appeals of the Austrian authorities, who felt that their troops could not endure the strain of another defensive battle on the Italian frontier. In May, Cadorna had attacked once more on the Isonzo front but an Austrian counter-attack in the Carso sector had retaken part of the small gains. Losses, however, were more nearly balanced than formerly. The question of Allied cooperation on the Italian front was raised afresh without result, Haig protesting strongly. Cadorna, nevertheless, initiated in August an 'eleventh battle of the Isonzo'. Capello's Second Army captured a large part of the Bainsizza plateau, north of Gorizia, but a long-sustained effort brought no further success and Cadorna was forced to break off the offensive after four weeks' struggle. But it had so strained the resistance of the debilitated Austrians that, in Ludendorff's words, 'it became necessary to decide for the attack on Italy in order to prevent the collapse of Austria-Hungary'.

Ludendorff had a difficult problem to solve, Russia had not yet capitulated, the front there was already weakly held for its extent, and the British offensive in Flanders made impossible a large withdrawal of troops from France. As he could only scrape together six German divisions, and the Austrians' quality was lower than ever, he came to the conclusion that the only chance of decisive results was to pick out a particularly weak sector which coincidently offered scope for a strategic exploitation of the breakthrough. This was found in the Tolmino–Caporetto sector. On October 24th, after a short bombardment, the blow was launched and pushed deep down the western slopes of the mountains, imperilling the Italian forces to both south and north. On October 28th the advance reached Udine, the former Italian general headquarters, and on October 31st the Tagliamento.

Not the least significant feature of this offensive was the way it was prepared, by a moral bombardment. Propaganda had been exploited for months as a means of sapping the Italian discipline and will to resist. But its effect can be exaggerated – the most formidable propaganda, as with the French in April, was that supplied by the attrition strategy of the Italian Command, which had sickened the troops by its limited results at unlimited cost.

But the result also surprised Ludendorff, who with his slender forces had not calculated on such distant objectives as were now possible of attainment. As the direct pursuit was slowing down he belatedly tried to switch troops from the left wing to Conrad's army which flanked the north of the Venetian salient, but was foiled by the inadequacy of the railways. Even so, Cadorna, with his centre broken through, only saved his wings by a precipitate retreat to the line of the Piave, covering Venice, leaving 250,000 prisoners in the enemy's hands. The same day Cadorna was superseded in supreme command by Diaz. Italy's Allies had begun to rush reinforcements, two army corps, one British and one French, to her aid, and on November 5th their political and military chiefs arrived at Rapallo for a conference, out of which sprang the Allied Council at Versailles, and ultimately a unified command.

The invaders had outrun their transport, and the resistance of the Italians, morally braced by the emergency, succeeded in holding the Piave in face of direct assaults and strenuous efforts by Conrad to turn their left flank from the Trentino. At the beginning of December, the British and French, who had been waiting in reserve in case of a fresh breakthrough, moved forward to take over vulnerable sectors, but the attack was only renewed in the north, and on December 19th it came to an end with the coming of the snows. If Caporetto seriously damaged Italy, it also purged her, and after an interval of recuperation she was to vindicate herself at Vittorio Veneto.

The Capture of Jerusalem. Once more a distant theatre of war provided the sole triumph of the Entente cause during the year – this time in Palestine. The second reverse at Gaza, in April 1917, had led to a change of command, Murray being succeeded by Allenby, who was strong enough and fortunate enough to obtain the adequate force for which Murray had asked in vain. The British Government was anxious for a spectacular success to offset the moral depression of the Nivelle failure and the decline of Russia, and the British General Staff desired to dislocate the Turk's attempt to recapture Baghdad by drawing away their reserves.

Allenby took over in July and devoted the first three months to intensive preparations for an autumn offensive, when the season would be suitable. The command was reorganized, the communications developed, and his own headquarters moved forward from Cairo to the front. By complete secrecy and ruses he deceived the Turks as to the point of attack. The defences of Gaza were bombarded from October 20th onwards, and an attack followed on November 1st to pin the enemy and draw in his reserves. Meanwhile, as a necessary preliminary to the real blow, the inland bastion of Beersheba was seized by a convergent manoeuvre on October 31st, a prelude to the decisive attack on November 6th, which broke through the enemy's weakened centre and into the plain of Philistia. Falkenhayn, now in command at Aleppo, had also been planning an offensive, but the better communications of the British decided the race, and although Falkenhayn tried to stem the tide by a counterstroke against Beersheba, the breaking of his centre compelled a general retreat. The pursuit was hampered by lack of water and of initiative. Even so, by the 14th, the Turkish forces were driven apart in two divergent groups, the port of Jaffa was taken, and Allenby wheeled his main force to the right for an advance inland on Jerusalem. He gained the narrow hill passes before the Turks could block them and, after a necessary pause to improve his communications, brought up reserves for a fresh advance, which secured Jerusalem on December 9th. By the time the winter rains set in the British had expanded and consolidated their hold on the region. As a moral success the feat was valuable, yet viewed strategically it seemed a long way round to the goal. If Turkey be pictured as a bent old man, the British, after missing their blow at his head – Constantinople – and omitting to strike at his heart – Alexandretta – had now resigned themselves to swallowing him from the feet upwards, like a python dragging its endless length across the desert. The difficult process of assimiliation, however, was assisted by the spreading paralysis of the Turkish strength under the needle-pricks of Lawrence and the Arabs.

The Clearing of East Africa. The year 1917 witnessed another overseas success, the clearing of German East Africa, although not the close of the campaign. More than a year elapsed after the rebuff at Tanga before a serious attempt was made to subdue the last German stronghold on the African continent. To spare troops from the main theatres was difficult, and the solution was only made possible by the loyal cooperation of the South African Government. In February 1916, General Smuts was appointed to command the expedition and formed the plan of a drive from north to south through the difficult interior, in order to avoid the fever-rampant plain on the coast. In conjunction with this central wedge, a Belgian force under Tombeur was to advance eastwards from Lake Tanganyika, and a small British force under Northey was to strike in from Nyasaland in the south-west. The Germans under Lettow-Vorbeck were weak in numbers but handled with masterly skill, and with all the advantages of an equatorial climate, a vast and trackless region – mountainous in parts and covered with dense bush and forest – to assist them in impeding the invader. From Dar-es-Salaam on the coast to Ujiji on Lake Tanganyika ran the one real line of rail communication, across the centre of the colony. After driving the Germans back across the frontier and seizing the Kilimanjaro gap, Smuts moved direct on this railway at Morogoro, over 300 miles distant, while he dispatched a force under Van Deventer in a wide sweep to the west to cut the railway farther inland, and then converge on Morogoro. Lettow-Vorbeck delayed this manoeuvre by a concentration against Van Deventer, but Smuts' direct advance compelled him to hurry his force back, and thus enabled Van Deventer to get astride the railway.

However, Lettow-Vorbeck evaded the attempt to cut him off and fell back in September on the Uluguru mountains to the south. The Belgians and Northey had cleared the west and the net had been drawn steadily closer, confining Lettow-Vorbeck to the south-east quarter of the colony. Early in 1917 Smuts returned to England, and Van Deventer conducted the final operations which ended with Lettow-Vorbeck avoiding envelopment to the end, slipping across the frontier into Portuguese Africa. Here he maintained a guerrilla campaign throughout 1918 until the general Armistice. With an original force of only 5,000, five per cent being Europeans, he had caused the employment of 130,000 enemy troops and the expenditure of £72,000,000.

The Mastering of the Submarine. The military side of 1917 is thrown into shadow by the naval, or more strictly the economic, side. The vital issue turned on the balance between Germany's submarine pressure and Britain's resistance. April was the worst month. One ship out of every four which left the British Isles never came home. The Allies lost nearly a million tons of shipping, sixty per cent of it British, and although the German navy's promise of victory by the end of the month was proved a miscalculation, it was clear that, ultimately, the continuance of such a ratio of loss must starve the civilian population and automatically prevent the maintenance of the armies. Britain, indeed, had only food enough to sustain her people for another six weeks.

The Government sought to counter the menace by the indirect means of rationing, increasing home production, and the expansion of ship-building; by the direct means of the system of convoys with naval escorts, and a counter-offensive against the submarine, aided by new devices to detect the presence of submarines and the use of thousands of patrol craft. The most effective countermeasure, that of penning the Germans in their bases by close-in minefields, was hindered by the British failure to obtain a real command of the North Sea, through a decisive victory. The British destroyer flotillas daringly laid thousands of mines in the channels left by the Germans through the Heligoland Bight, but their ceaseless efforts were largely foiled by the German minesweepers, which were able to work freely under the protection of the German fleet. Nevertheless these mines hindered and delayed the passage of the U-boats and increased that demoralizing nerve-strain on the U-boat crews which was, above all, the cause of the decline of the submarine campaign. Too few submarines and trained crews in propor-tion to the task – and too great a strain upon them – spelt ultimate collapse.

But the British crisis of the spring of 1917 was averted less by an offensive than by a defensive method. For the convoy system was the main agent of salvation. The method of patrolled areas had been con-tinued, despite its proven futility of 1916, during the early months of 1917. As Churchill says – 'In April the great approach route to the south-west of Ireland was becoming a veritable cemetery of British shipping.' And other cemeteries were only small by comparison. Be-sides 516,000 tons of British shipping, 336,000 tons of Allied and neutral were buried beneath the waves during April, and the direct loss of food and raw materials to the island kingdom was augmented by the growing unwillingness of neutral shipping to take the risk of supplying such a customer. Only the 'guts' of her merchant seamen in going to sea after being several times torpedoed lay between Britain's stomach and starvation. And the blindest blunder of the British Admiralty was in opposing the introduction of the convoy system in face of the futility of their other methods to avert the close-looming disaster. At last the advocacy of younger officers was decisively reinforced by Mr Lloyd George's intervention, and in April voyages under convoy were sanc-tioned as an experiment on the Gibraltar and North Sea routes. The first left Gibraltar homeward bound on May 10th. Crowned by unmistakable success, the convoys were extended to the transatlantic routes when the arrival of American flotillas under Admiral Sims increased the number of destroyers available for escorts. The loss of shipping in such convoys was reduced to a bare one per cent and when, in August, the convoys were extended to outward-bound shipping the British loss fell next month below the 200,000-ton level. Meantime the offensive campaign – now reinforced by special submarine chasers, aircraft, and the new horned mines – exacted an ever-rising toll of submarines, and by the end of 1917, the menace, if not broken, was at least subdued. If the British people had to tighten their belts, and their food rationing, they were now secure against starvation.

During the early months of 1918 the number of German submarines declined as steadily as their losses rose, until in May fourteen were lost out of 125 on service, while the effect of those that were operating declined disproportionately to their number. In all, the German war loss totalled 199 submarines, of which 175 fell victims to the British navy. And of the various weapons the mine claimed forty-two and the depth charge thirty-one submarines. Hunted from the narrow seas, the U-boats were even shut out from the ocean during the last phase by a vast mine barrage, laid mainly by the American navy, across the 180-mile-wide passage between Norway and the Orkney Islands. It consisted of no less than 70,000 mines, of which the British laid 13,000. This was a direct counter to the main submarine operations against the ocean-brought supplies of Great Britain.

The shorter-range operations of the small submarines from the Belgian coast were crippled by the perfected barrage across the straits of Dover, by the daring attack of Admiral Keyes' force on the night of April 22nd, 1918 – which for a time blocked up the exit from Zeebrugge – and by the progressive demoralization of the U-boat crews. Yet the removal of the menace should not lead to an underestimate of its powers for the future. The 1917 campaign was launched with only 148 submarines and from the most unfavourable strategic position. Great Britain lay like a huge breakwater across the sea approaches to northern Europe, and the submarines had to get outside through narrow and closely watched outlets before they could operate against the arteries of supply. And despite these handicaps they almost stopped the beat of England's heart.

The Economic Reinforcement. In restoring circulation America's first-aid became a potent factor long before her military assistance. It embraced her provision of light craft to reinforce the British anti-submarine fleet, her rapidly developed construction of new mercantile ships and still more her financial aid. By July, 1917, Britain had spent over £5,000,000,000, her daily expenditure had risen to £7,000,000 and the burden of financing her Allies as well as her own efforts was straining even her resources, when America's aid came to ease the pressure. In the first months after her entry into the war the appeals for loans came as a shock to Congress. Unable from remoteness and inexperience to realize the inevitable costs of the war, a large section of the American public felt that its new associates were trying to dip their hands too freely into the capacious pockets of Uncle Sam. Thus Mr McAdoo, the Secretary of the Treasury, could satisfy neither the Allies nor the American public, the former feeling that he was stinting them and the latter crying that he was spending the nation's money like a drunken sailor. Hence further loans were vigorously opposed in Congress. Northcliffe graphically, if perhaps hyperbolically, summed up the situation when he cabled – 'If loan stops, war stops.'

Actually, up to mid-July the USA had advanced £229,000,000 to the several Allies, with the restriction that this was to pay for supplies bought in the United States, while Britain in the same period had added £193,000,000 to the £900,000,000 already lent to her Allies – without such restriction. On the top of this fresh strain came the fear of having to sell securities in order to liquidate the earlier 'Morgan loan' – with consequent damage to British credit. Mr Balfour, then Secretary for Foreign Affairs, was so alarmed that he cabled to Colonel House – 'We seem on the verge of a financial disaster which would be worse than defeat in the field. If we cannot keep up exchange neither we nor our Allies can pay our dollar debts. We should be driven off the gold basis, and purchases from the USA would immediately cease and the Allies' credit would be shattered.' The danger was met by the action of the United States Treasury in continuing monthly advances, despite opposition, until a coordinated inter-Allied finance council could be created; by the formation of an official purchasing commission to take over the unofficial functions formerly fulfilled by J. P. Morgan and Company on behalf of the British Government; and by sending Lord Reading to Washington as a combined political and financial representative to oil, by frankness and sympathy, the creaking machinery of demand and supply. The overwhelming success of the Liberty Loan campaign was at least an equal asset. Advances to the Allies were authorized at a maximum average monthly rate of $500,000,000. By the end of the year the problem itself was shifting its basis; for, owing to the vast needs and purchases of the American Government for its own forces, the supply of credit to the Allies began to exceed that of the supply of goods. The difficulty of the Allies was now that of obtaining the material they needed for munitions rather than of obtaining the money to pay for it.

While America's entry into the war thus secured the position of the Allies, it also conferred one great offensive benefit even before America's armies threw their weight into the scale. No longer was the grip of the naval blockade hampered by neutral quibbles, but instead America's cooperation converted it into a stranglehold under which the enemy must soon grow limp, since military power is based on economic endurance. As a party to the war, the United States, indeed, wielded the economic weapon with a determination, regardless of the remaining neutrals, far exceeding Britain's boldest claims in the past years of controversy over neutral rights. Thus the surface blockade of Germany began to tighten coincidently with the flagging of the submarine blockade of Britain.

The Air. Another new form of action reached its crest at the same time as the submarine campaign. As the submarine was primarily an economic weapon, so was the aeroplane primarily a psychological weapon. The explosive bullet had virtually ended the Zeppelin raids in 1916, but from early in 1917 aeroplane raids on London grew in intensity until by May 1918 the air defences were so thoroughly organized that the raiders thereafter abandoned London, as a target, for Paris. If the stoicism of the civil population took much of the sting from a weapon then in its infancy, the indirect effect was serious, interrupting business and checking output in industrial centres, as well as drawing off, for defence, many aircraft from the front. In reply the British belatedly formed a small Independent Air Force, which carried out extensive raids into Germany during the closing months of the war, with marked effect on the declining morale of the 'home front'.

Propaganda. The beginning of 1918 witnessed the development and thorough organization of another psychological weapon, when Lord Northcliffe, who had been the head of the British War Mission in the United States was appointed 'Director of Propaganda in Enemy Countries', and for the first time the full scope of such a weapon was understood and exploited. Northcliffe found his best blade in President Wilson's speeches, which with idealism if not with entire realism unvaryingly distinguished between Germany's policy and the German people, and emphasized that the Allied policy was to liberate all people, including the Germans, from militarism. This blade, sharpened by the armourer, Colonel House, was trenchantly wielded by Northcliffe with the aim of severing the common ties which held together the enemy nations and their rulers. But these ties were stout enough to turn any blade until they had been frayed by military pressure. In July 1917 the effect of President Wilson's speeches, acting upon war-weariness and anti-militarism in Germany, produced a parliamentary revolt and under Erzberger's management the Reichstag passed a peace resolution, which forswore territorial annexations. But the only effect was to break Bethmann-Hollweg, the unhappy rope in the tug-of-war between the military and the political parties. The parliamentary representatives of the German people were as helpless to withstand the iron will of the General Staff as was Imperial Austria, now utterly sick of, and only anxious to abandon, the war which she had provoked. These peace movements received small practical response from the enemy democracies; for President Wilson as their spokesman reiterated the declaration that they would negotiate no peace with military autocracy. His encouragement to the enemy peoples to throw off this control was excellent in precept but vain in fact when addressed to those who were so firmly manacled. They were not Houdinis.

In January 1918 there was, indeed, a significant attempt at popular revolt, when over a million German workers joined in a general strike, but this was soon quenched and even forgotten in the fresh exhilaration of the great offensive. Only when the military machine itself began to crumble could the slaves of the machines free themselves from the grip, or propaganda help them in loosening it. Perhaps only then did an active will to peace reinforce their mere passive weariness of war. The inner strength of militant patriotism lies in the fact that it is not merely a gag but a drug.

CHAPTER SEVEN

SCENE 1

The Halt and Lame Offensive – Arras, April, 1917

On April 9th, 1917, the British armies in France entered upon what they had hoped was to be the final and decisive campaign of the World War. To the ordinary observer the day was a brilliant contrast to all previous offensives, but it proved yet another mirage in the military desert. This was perhaps inevitable before zero hour.

The Arras offensive had its roots deeply embedded in the battles of the Somme, 1916. Its strategic conception sprang from the Somme, for, in conjunction with the other attacks – still-born or prematurely deceased – planned for the spring of 1917, it was an effort to complete the overthrow of German power and man power which it was believed that only the onset of winter had prevented on the Somme. Its strategic failure was the outcome partly of the situation produced by the Somme and partly of the inability of the higher command to forget the barren methods employed on the Somme. And the germ of the Arras plan dated from the time of the Somme.

For as early as June, 1916, a plan known as the Blaireville project had been drawn up for a blow near Arras to take place as a supplement to the Somme offensive. Postponed because of the immense casualties on the Somme, which drew off all available forces to that human sump-pit, it was revived and extended in October as part of the spring plan. The gradual British advance eastwards on the Somme had left a German-held bulge between it and Arras – a bulge of which Gomme-court formed the westernmost point. This bulge seemed to offer the opportunity for a right- and left-hand blow on the respective sides, converging towards Cambrai. If successful this might not only cut off the German forces holding the bulge, but create a gap too wide for the German reserves to block, and so pave the way for an advance towards Valenciennes and against the enemy's line of communications and retreat through the Belgian 'trough'.

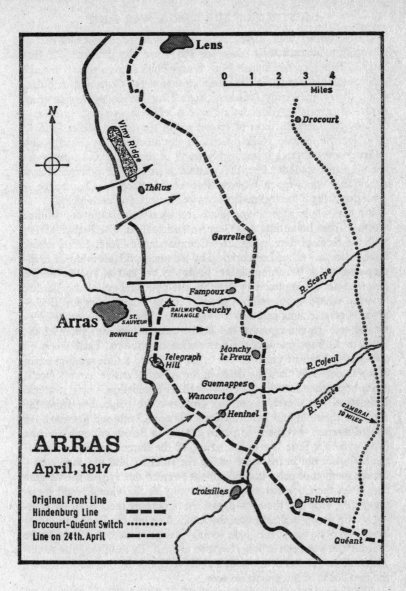

ARRAS
April, 1917

Original Front Line	━━━━━
Hindenburg Line	━ ━ ━
Drocourt-Quéant Switch	··········
Line on 24th. April	━ ▪ ━ ▪ ━

N

Lens

0 1 2 3 4
Miles

Drocourt

Vimy Ridge

Thélus

Gavrelle

R. Scarpe

Fampoux

Arras

ST. SAUVEUR
RONVILLE

RAILWAY TRIANGLE
Feuchy

Telegraph Hill

Monchy le Preux

R. Cojeul

Guemappes

Wancourt

R. Sensée

Heninel

CAMBRAI 10 MILES

Croisilles

Bullecourt

Quéant

On November 18th, 1916, the Allied Commanders-in-Chief met at Chantilly to discuss their plans for 1917, and the outcome was that early in February the British Fourth and Fifth Armies should resume their Somme offensive on the southern side of the Gommecourt bulge, while the Third Army (Allenby) struck on the northern side from Arras. After gaining Monchy-le-Preux Allenby was to push south-east to close the German lines of retreat along the Cojeul Valley, and, if possible, the Sensée Valley also. In conjunction, the First Army (Horne) was to attack immediately north of the Third and form a defensive flank, and the French to attack south of the Somme. Three weeks later the French blow was to be launched in Champagne – an undue delay if the two main blows were to react on each other.

But the whole scheme was dissolved by a combination of French action, British hesitation, and German anticipation. The French action took the form of dismissing their Commander-in-Chief, Joffre, whose bubble reputation had been pricked by the unconcealable evidence of ill-preparedness at Verdun and, less justly, by the lack of success on the Somme. He was replaced by Nivelle, the popular hero of the Verdun *ripostes*, whose appointment caused a change in the plan for 1917 – towards greater aims and also towards giving the French a more spectacular role. In consequence the British had to take over more of the front, to the impairment of their own offensive projects. Tactlessness on one side and sensitiveness on the other produced a time-wasting series of arguments that caused a delay in the Allied offensive. And before it could begin the Germans had disrupted its foundation – by a strategic withdrawal not merely from the Gommecourt bulge, but from the whole of their old and indented front between Arras and Soissons. An absurd attempt was made to picture this as a British triumph and the fruit, even if a little late in garnering, of the Somme offensive. It was the fruit, but not in the sense which the British command suggested – for the method of petty limited attacks pursued throughout the autumn had given the Germans ample opportunity to dig, literally and metaphorically, a pit for their assailants. Straightening their front by retiring to the newly built Hindenburg Line, they left the British to follow laboriously through the intervening desert which, with immense thoroughness of destruction, they had created. By nullifying the Allies' preparations for attack this withdrawal restricted them to the sectors on the two flanks of the evacuated area.

The main role in the British attack thus fell to the Third Army under Allenby. If he could break through the old defences just to the north of where the Hindenburg Line ended, he would automatically take this line in flank and rear. But in anticipation of such a move the Germans had dug a switch line from Quéant, near the northern end of the Hindenburg Line, through Drocourt – covering the rear of the old defences north of Arras. Thus Allenby's whole chance of strategic success depended on whether he could reach and break through this partially completed switch line – some five miles behind the front system – before the German reserves could arrive in strength. Surprise was the only key which could open this gate. Because of this the real drama of the Arras offensive lies in the preliminary discussions and preparations even more than in the battle itself.

Surprise had been discarded in the Somme offensive, except on July 14th – indeed, this master key of all the great captains of history had been rusting since the spring of 1915. The two means by which surprise could be obtained, and the Drocourt–Quéant switch reached in time, were by launching a mass of tanks or by a hurricane bombardment, brief but intense. The first means became impossible owing to the slowness in delivering new tanks after the discouraging reports made upon them in 1916, so that sixty old machines were all that could be scraped together. Allenby and his artillery adviser, Holland, were anxious to have the shortest possible bombardment, and originally proposed that it should last only forty-eight hours. If this, according to later standards, was more than forty hours too long, it was a tentative step in the direction of surprise. But the Higher Command was faithful to the theory of prolonged bombardment, and had a deep-rooted distrust of such an innovation. Nevertheless Allenby stood firm until General Headquarters hit upon the deft device of promoting his artillery adviser to another sphere and replacing him by one who shared their view. Then the plan of a five days' bombardment, preceded by three weeks of 'wire-cutting', was adopted. This, together with the too visible preparations, spelt the doom of surprise. In the bombardment 2,879 guns (989 heavy) took part – a gun to every nine yards.

The most vivid impression of the British disregard for surprise at Arras is perhaps to be found in the German account of the counter-preparations which they were able to make during the three weeks' 'notice' they were so clearly given – 'Field and heavy artillery in long columns awoke the approach roads of the *Hinterland*; flying-corps formations and machine-gun units ... responded to the call. Innumerable crowds of working parties laboured day and night ... at the repair and deepening of the defence system. Night and day in unbroken sequence trains from the Homeland laden with material and munitions reached the main depots ... Mountains of shell were piled up in the ammunition dumps ... The construction of the defences and the organization of the troops was completed ... The enemy could come, the troops had now the word.'

Ludendorff himself visited the sector and was satisfied that although the British might break into the forward positions, if they liked to pay the price, they would then be held up by his new system of defence in depth.

The difficulties, however, were not all of German manufacture. General Charteris, the head of Haig's intelligence service, has provided a significant sidelight in his diary notes at the time: 'Allenby shares one peculiarity with Douglas Haig: he cannot explain verbally, with any lucidity at all, what his plans are. In a conference between the two of them it is rather amusing. D.H. hardly ever finishes a sentence, and Allenby's sentences, although finished, do not really convey exactly what he means.' 'They understand one another perfectly' – other evidence throws a doubt on this point – 'but as each of their particular staffs only understands their immediate superior a good deal of explanation of details has to be gone into afterwards ... At these army conferences no one dares to interfere ...'

In smaller points Allenby still sought for surprise, notably in linking up the underground sewers and quarries of Arras, St Sauveur, and Ronville, in order to shelter two divisions which were to pass underground and leapfrog through the leading divisions. Another feature of the plan was that after the three assaulting corps of the Third Army had broken the enemy's first system of defence, the Cavalry Corps (Kavanagh) and XVIII Corps (Maxse) were to pass through in the centre between the human buttresses, and drive forward towards the switch line. Partly for concealment, the daring risk was taken of moving this pursuit force through the city of Arras, whose houses extended almost up to the front line. This plan, refreshingly ingenious, was vitiated, however, not only by the absence of initial surprise, but by the comparatively narrow front of the opening attack – about twelve miles. Thus the central bottle-neck was, in turn, so narrow that its end could be easily stopped. Ludendorff in his Vilna offensive in the autumn of 1915 had revealed a better method – a dual penetration by two horns goring their way into the enemy's front, while through the wide gap between the horns the pursuit force unexpectedly issued.

A fundamental defect of the Arras plan, moreover, was the width of its base compared with its fighting front – the routes of supply and reinforcement all converging on Arras, with the result that the narrow mouth of this bottle-neck became utterly congested. When the initial attack failed to make the progress anticipated, this congestion was increased by the arrival of the cavalry in the forward area – although the experience of 1915 and 1916 had shown that such advance was futile unless and until a wide path had been swept clear of the enemy.

Yet if the strategic object was practically forfeited before zero hour on April 9th, the tactical success was at first a vivid and enheartening contrast to all previous British offensives. The new British gas shell was most effective in paralysing the defending artillery, for it not only compelled the gun crews to keep on their gas masks for hours at a time, but by killing off the horses like flies prevented ammunition being brought up. The attack was delivered by the VII, VI and XVII Corps of the Third Army and the Canadian Corps of the First Army. On the extreme right, or south, lay Snow's VII Corps, with the 21st Division near Croisilles forming a pivot on which the rest of the corps – the 14th, 30th and 56th (1st London) Divisions – advanced. To their left lay Haldane's VI Corps, with the 3rd, 12th and 15th Divisions attacking and the 37th Division waiting to leapfrog through and seize the key position of Monchy-le-Preux. The marshy valley of the Scarpe, the boundary between the VI Corps and its neighbours, separated the British right and left wings. North of the Scarpe the attack was entrusted to Fergusson's XVII Corps, composed of the 9th, 34th and 51st Divisions, with the 4th to leapfrog through the 9th on the Corp' right. Farthest north of all, Byng's Canadian Corps was to assault the ill-omened Vimy ridge, which had so long proved an impregnable barrier to the Allied forces. The capture of a large part of the ridge on April 9th gained all the greater *éclat* from the fame – or, to the Allies, ill-fame – which this ridge had acquired. The Canadians' feat was as finely prepared as it was executed. Yet it is but just to recognize that in one important condition the task was easier than farther south, for the very fact of attacking uphill gave the attackers here better artillery observation and drier ground than those who had to traverse the sodden or marshy area near the Scarpe.

At 5.30 AM the assaulting infantry moved forward on the whole front, covered by a superbly timed creeping barrage, and in less than an hour almost the whole German first-line system was captured. North of the Scarpe the success continued, and after the leading divisions had gained their three successive objectives, the 4th Division passed through on the corps' right, and by seizing Fampoux breached the last German line in front of the Drocourt–Quéant switch. But south of the Scarpe the German resistance, first at the Railway Triangle and Telegraph Hill, then on the Wancourt–Feuchy line – helped by machine guns from Monchy-le-Preux Hill – was so strong that it badly delayed, although it could not stop, the advance of the 12th and 15th Divisions. Thus the reserve 37th Division could not pass through that day, and behind them the cavalry had moved up not only in vain but to add to the congestion.

The results of the opening day had been greater and quicker, both in prisoners and progress, than in any previous offensive – yet they had extinguished the dim hope of a strategic breakthrough. A contributory factor was the misuse of the tanks. With only sixty machines available it would have been wiser to have concentrated them in aid of the vital effort to gain Monchy-le-Preux instead of spreading them over the front. The error was repeated in the next phase, whereas, if all available tanks had been concentrated on the south side of the salient formed by the first day's attack, they could have taken the German resistance in enfilade, and might have rolled it up.

So on April 10th the Third Army butted direct at a stiffening resistance, with its guns too far back to support the infantry. Not until the morning of April 11th did the arrival of four tanks help a battalion of the 37th Division to seize Monchy-le-Preux – driving in a wedge which was, however, too narrow and too late.

That same morning part of Gough's Fifth Army launched a converging assault from the south against the Hindenburg Line, in an attempt to relieve the pressure of German opposition to the Third Army. It was a desperate remedy for a despairing situation. For this army, after painfully toiling over the evacuated area, had neither been able to make the preparations nor to bring up the artillery necessary for a normal trench attack, far less an assault on the massive defences of the Hindenburg Line. The difficulty led to a novel expedient, which contained the germ of the method which was triumphantly successful later at Cambrai. But instead of 381 tanks as at Cambrai, only eleven could be gathered. As artillery support was deficient, this handful of tanks was to act as a mobile barrage and wire destroyer, leading the 4th Australian Division against the Hindenburg Line near Bullecourt.

The gamble failed – the preparations were too hasty, the resources inadequate, and the front too narrow. For a few hours there was an illusion of success. If the tanks arrived too late for their intended role, they at least helped to distract the enemy's attention, and caused a panic which 'sent part of the German garrison fleeing across the countryside'. The Australians broke into the Hindenburg Line, but then became the target of counter-attack from all sides, while the illusion of a sweeping advance prevented the artillery from protecting them.

With better security the gain might have been held, but the British could hardly have done more, as the obstinate German resistance at Heninel and Wancourt, to the right of the Third Army, prevented any chance of the two armies joining hands. Next morning a gallant assault by the 21st and 56th (1st London) Divisions conquered these two bastions, but the increasing intensity of German counter-attacks brought the first and main phase of the offensive to a close on April 14th. If strategic success had been missed, 13,000 prisoners and 200 guns had been taken.

The next phase had little result to put in relief against the depressing total of British casualties. The French offensive of April 16th on the Aisne, to which Arras had been the prelude, proved a worse downfall, shattering Nivelle's extravagant hopes and predictions, and burying his career in its ruins. The British were not ready to resume their offensive until a week later, and although Haig decided to continue 'the full pressure of the British offensive ... in order to assist our Allies', there was by then no French advance to assist. On April 23rd and 24th Allenby pushed forward his line, at heavy cost and against heavy pressure, to include Guemappe and Gavrelle. At a conference of the army commanders on April 30th, Haig showed that he placed little faith in the possibility of a further French offensive, but decided to continue his own attacks, 'to move steadily forward up to a good defensive line'.

Despite fruitless assaults and sacrifices on May 3rd and 5th, 'bald-headed' assaults which showed more obstinacy than imagination or care, this line was not reached, and the offensive which had been prolonged to so bitter a conclusion was at last broken off. The British offensive centre of gravity was then transferred to the north – to open as brilliantly at Messines on June 7th, and to fade out still more miserably in the swamps of Passchendaele in October.

CHAPTER SEVEN

SCENE 2

The Siege-war Masterpiece – Messines

On June 7th, 1917, took place a battle which on the morrow was hailed as a brilliant military achievement, and which today, unlike so many historically tarnished 'masterpieces' of 1914–18, stands out in even higher relief. For we appreciate now that the capture of the Messines ridge by General Plumer's Second Army was almost the only true siege-warfare attack made throughout a siege war. It was also one of the few attacks until late in 1918 in which the methods employed by the command completely fitted the facts of the situation.

But if today its abiding historic interest lies in its perfect suitability of method, at the time this was overshadowed, and rightly, by its value as a moral tonic. Perhaps this was almost too strong a stimulant to those not in direct charge of the operation, leading them to place too high hopes in the subsequent operations at Ypres, where the conditions were different and the methods also. But such a reflection does not dim the value of Messines, which came as a tonic badly needed after the depressing end of the spring offensive at Arras and on the Aisne.

While Pétain was striving to rally and rejuvenate the French Army, Haig decided to transfer the weight of his attack to Flanders, and, as a preliminary step to his main action at Ypres, to fulfil his long-formed plan of securing the high ground about Messines and Wytschaete as a flank bastion to the Ypres advance. For while in German possession it gave the enemy complete observation of the British trenches and forward battery positions, enabled them to command the communications up to the Ypres salient, and to take in enfilade, or even reverse, the trench positions therein.

Preparations had been begun nearly a year before, although their real development dated from the winter. Thus, when Haig asked Plumer, on May 7th, when he would be ready to deliver the Messines attack, Plumer was able to say, 'A month from today' – and keep his promise exactly. The calm confidence of this businesslike statement betrays no sign of the anxiety suffered, nor does it do justice to the will-power demanded of Plumer in carrying through his purpose.

The key factor in the success was the simultaneous explosion of nineteen great mines, containing 600 tons of explosives and involving the tunnelling of 8,000 yards of gallery since January, in the face of active countermining by the enemy. A couple of months before the attack it was reported to Plumer that the Germans were within eighteen inches of the mine at Hill 60, and that the only thing to do was to blow it. Plumer was firm in his refusal, and equally staunch under the wearing strain of ominous rumours and reports throughout the following weeks. His justification came at 3.10 AM on June 7th, when this mine went up along with eighteen others – only one out of twenty had been blown up by the Germans.

Another example of his will-power was in withstanding strong and insidious pressure from General Headquarters to change his artillery adviser. Before the Arras offensive the same thing had happened with the Third Army, and Allenby's artillery plan had been radically modified – to the loss of all hope of surprise – by the removal of his artillery adviser to another sphere and his replacement by one who gave a different opinion. But before Messines, Plumer resisted all attempts at a change, and finally quelled them by saying flatly that as long as he was responsible he intended to have his own men. If Plumer could be strong in resisting expert advice at need, no commander was more keen to secure it from all sources, and none weighed it more carefully – as a foundation for his own decision. In Harington, he had a Chief of his General Staff of blended intelligence and sympathy. And their happy combination was a symbol of the cooperation which was diffused throughout the Second Army staff, and through them to the fighting troops.

Trust and receptiveness to ideas and criticisms were the keynotes of the Second Army. They were instanced in the schools and courses behind the front, where free questioning and criticism were encouraged, while an answer and a reason to any point raised was always forthcoming. They were also marked in the preparation of an attack. Where other high commanders were apt to lay down a series of objectives which their troops must gain, Plumer's method was to suggest certain provisional lines, and then to discuss them, and each fraction of them, with the corps and divisional commanders concerned, adjusting the several objectives to the local conditions and opinions until a final series was pieced together like a mosaic, on which all were agreed.

Further, the impartial common-sense of his judgement was shown by the fact that, although he could oppose technical advice from General Headquarters when it conflicted with reality, he welcomed it when it coincided. The Western Front in 1914-18 was pre-eminently an engineers' war, yet historians will be perplexed at the small part played by engineers in its direction, and the overweening influence of cavalry and infantry doctrine in the attempt to solve its problems. Messines, however, was in sharp contrast, for here the methods and the training were largely based on a manual, S.S. 155, compiled by the engineers from their special knowledge and experience of siege warfare.

For Messines was to be a strict siege operation, the capture of a fortified salient at the minimum cost of lives by the maximum substitution of mind – in preparation – and material – in execution – for human bodies. Mines, artillery, tanks,. and gas all played their part. But a contrary wind curtailed most of the scheme of gas projection, and the effect of the mines and artillery was so overwhelming that the tanks were hardly needed. On a front of just over nine miles a total of 2,338 guns – of which 828 were heavy – were concentrated. There were also 304 large trench mortars. Thus the artillery strength here was approximately one gun to every seven yards of front, or 240 to the mile; five and a half tons of ammunition were thrown on each yard of front.

The fact that the attack would converge against a salient increased its chances, but it complicated the staff, troop and artillery organization of the attack. For the sectors of each attacking corps were of varying depths, and contracted more and more in width up to the final objective which was the chord of the arc forming the salient. As, however, it was a siege operation, without any attempt at exploitation or a breakthrough, it was easier to avoid the congestion which had occurred at Arras. And the problem was further simplified by the plan of so allotting sectors that five of the divisions had sectors of equal breadth from front to rear, while the four which filled the interstices had smaller tasks. Further, when the main ridge was captured, fresh troops were to 'leapfrog' through to gain the final Oosttaverne line across the base of the salient.

Meticulous organization and forethought marked every stage of the preparation, but this was based on personal touch – staff officers continually visiting the units and trenches – not on paper reports and instructions. Another feature was the special intelligence scheme, whereby the information obtained from prisoners, ground and air observation and reconnaissance, photography, wireless interception, and sound ranging, was swiftly conveyed to an army centre, established for a fortnight at Locre Château, and then sifted and disseminated by summaries and maps.

The bombardment and 'wire-cutting' began on May 21st, were developed on May 28th, and culminated in a seven days' intense bombardment, mingled with practice barrages to test the arrangements. The consequent forfeiture of surprise did not matter in the Messines stroke, a purely limited attack, in contrast to that at Arras, where it had been fatal to the hope of a breakthrough. For although there was no surprise there was surprise effect – produced by the mines and the overwhelming fire – and this lasted long enough to gain the short-distanced objectives that had been set. The point, and the distinction between actual surprise and surprise effect, are of significance to the theory of warfare.

It was fortunate, however, for the British that the Germans played into their hands. When the attack preparations were suspected, Rupprecht's chief of staff, Kuhl, had made the suggestion to 'evacuate the salient and withdraw behind the Lys'. But the corps commanders maintained the traditional belief in the value of 'commanding' positions; and their opinion prevailed. Obsessed by the soldierly conviction that ground should never be given voluntarily, they even insisted on holding the forward positions in strength. Thus German stupidity made possible the success of the British plan, preventing the short step to the rear that would have nullified the British mines and wasted the labour devoted to them.

In the British plan nine infantry divisions, with three more close up in reserve, were to advance to the assault. On the right (or south flank) was the II Anzac Corps (Godley) composed of the 3rd Australian, New Zealand, and 25th Divisions, with the 4th Australian Division behind. In the centre came the IX Corps (Hamilton-Gordon), the attack here being led by the 36th, 16th, and 19th Divisions, with the 11th in reserve. On the left was the X Corps (Morland), composed of the 41st, 47th, and 23rd Divisions, backed up by the 24th.

At 3.10 AM on June 7th the nineteen mines were blown, wrecking large portions of the Germans' front trenches. Simultaneously the barrage fell. When the débris and shock of the mines subsided, the infantry advanced and within a few minutes the whole of the enemy's front-line system was overrun, almost without opposition. Resistance stiffened as the penetration was deepened, but the training of the infantry and the efficiency of the barrage, based on the finest shades of calculation, enabled continuous progress to be made, and within three hours the whole crest of the ridge was secured.

The New Zealand Division had cleared the intricate fortifications of Messines itself – here the pace of the barrage was regulated to 100 yards in fifteen minutes instead of the general pace of 100 yards in three minutes. The garrisons of Wytschaete and the White Château held out for some time, but the first village was captured after a fierce struggle by troops of the 36th (Ulster) and 16th (Irish) Divisions in a combined effort – a feat of symbolical significance. Perhaps the most difficult sector was that of the 47th (2nd London) Division, which had not only to overcome the highly fortified position of the White Château, but had the Ypres–Comines canal as an oblique interruption across its line of advance. The Londoners, however, overcame both and by 10 AM the objective of the first phase was reached along the whole attacking line. While it was being consolidated, over forty batteries were moved forward to support the next pounce.

At 3.10 PM the reserve divisions and tanks 'leapfrogged' through, and within an hour almost the whole of the final objective was captured. Some 7,000 prisoners had been taken, apart from dead and wounded, at a cost to the attacker of only 16,000 casualties. The success had been so complete that only feeble counter-attacks were attempted that day. When the expected general counter-attack was launched on the whole front on the morrow, it failed everywhere against defences that had been rapidly and firmly organized, and in the recoil yielded the British still more ground.

The peculiar glory of the Messines attack is that, whereas in 1918 the decline in the German power of resistance brought the conditions to meet the methods almost as much as the methods were developed to meet the conditions, on June 7th, 1917, the methods were perfectly attuned to a resisting power then at its height.

CHAPTER SEVEN

SCENE 3

The 'Road' to Passchendaele

On July 31st, 1917, began what is termed the Third Battle of Ypres. And it is symbolical of its course and its issue that it is commonly spoken of by the title of 'Passchendaele', which in reality was merely the last scene of the gloomiest drama in British military history. Although called the Third Battle, it was not a battle, but rather a campaign, with the fighting more defined than the purpose – of the nature so familiar in the military annals of Flanders, and the Low Countries generally. And, like its German forerunners of 1914 and 1915, it achieved little except loss – in which, again, it repeated the earlier history of this theatre of war. So fruitless in its results, so depressing in its direction was this 1917 offensive, that 'Passchendaele' has come to be, like Walcheren a century before, a synonym for military failure – a name black-bordered in the records of the British Army. Even the inexhaustible powers of endurance and sacrifice shown by the combatants, or the improved executive leadership which did much in the later stages to minimize their sufferings, tend to be not merely overshadowed, but eclipsed in memory by the futility of the purpose and result.

What was the origin and what the object of 'Third Ypres'? An offensive in this sector had formed part of Haig's original contribution to the Allied plan for 1917. Its actual inauguration had been postponed by the unfortunate turn of events elsewhere. When the ill-success of the opening offensive in the spring at Arras and in Champagne was followed by the threatened collapse of the French Army as a fighting force, Haig's 'first-aid' treatment was to allow the British offensive at Arras, by the Third Army, to continue for some weeks longer with the general object of keeping the Germans occupied, and with the local object of reaching a good defensive line. When successive thrusts, against an enemy now fully warned and strengthened, failed to reach this line, Haig decided to

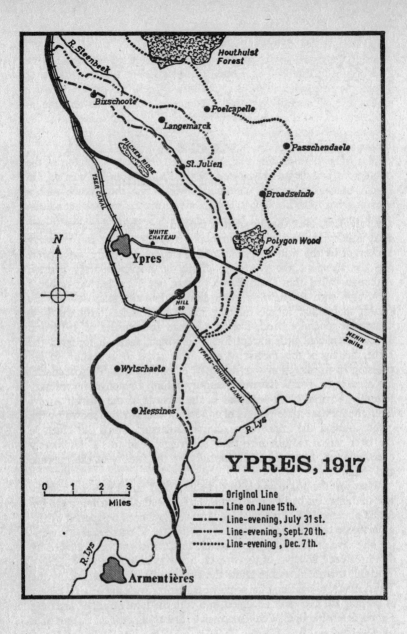

YPRES, 1917

———	Original Line
—·—·	Line on June 15 th.
—··—··	Line-evening, July 31 st.
·····—	Line-evening, Sept. 20 th.
········	Line-evening, Dec. 7 th.

transfer the main weight of this effort northward to Flanders, as he had originally intended. An intense conviction of the importance of giving the enemy no respite inspired him to press on with an offensive policy, even though French cooperation was lacking. His remarks, at the conference of the army commanders on April 30th, show that in his own mind he had practically written off the French share as a bad debt on the balance sheet of 1917.

It is right to emphasize that, at this moment, Haig's opinion of the strategy to pursue was supported by the Prime Minister, who was in favour of continuing the offensive provided that the French took a vigorous part in it. But it soon became clear that this essential condition would not be fulfilled, and thenceforward he tried in vain to restrain Haig. If the need to distract the enemy's attention from the French, the crisis at sea caused by the submarine campaign, and the need to second the still possible Russian offensive, combined to justify Haig's decision in May, the situation had radically changed before the main offensive was actually launched on July 31st. In war all turns on the time factor. By July the French army, under Pétain's treatment, was recuperating, if still convalescent, the height of the submarine crisis was past, and the revolutionary paralysis of the Russian army was clear. Nevertheless, the plans of the British High Command were unchanged. The historian may consider that insufficient attention was given to the lessons of history, of recent experience, and of material facts in deciding both upon the principle of a major offensive and upon its site. The axis of the attack diverged from, instead of converging on, the German main communications, so that an advance could not vitally endanger the security of the enemy's position in France. Haig curiously was to adopt here the same *eccentric* direction of advance which a year later his advice prevented Foch and Pershing from taking on the other flank of the Western Front. Thus an advance on the Belgian coast offered no wide strategic results, and for the same reason it was hardly the best direction even as a means of pinning and wearing down the enemy's strength on a profitable basis. Moreover, the idea that Britain's salvation from starvation depended on the capture of the submarine bases on this coast has long since been exploded, for the main submarine campaign was conducted from German ports. The story of how this delusion was fostered is a curious one.

In the middle of June, Haig was called home to see a Cabinet which had grown uneasy over his offensive schemes. Its members were agreed in wishing to postpone serious operations until the French had recovered and the Americans had arrived on the scene, and to save up their strength for 1918. Haig marshalled his arguments, and committed himself to 'the definite opinion that if the fighting was kept up at its present intensity for six months Germany would be at the end of her available man power'. Here he went beyond even the estimate of his optimistic intelligence service, which had at least made its forecast dependent on Russia's continued efforts. As the Cabinet were growing sceptical of military arithmetic, Haig's arguments failed to make the impression he had hoped. Suddenly, the Admiralty came to the rescue of his plans – by telling the Cabinet that 'the Navy could not keep going unless the Germans were turned out of the Belgian coast'. Even in high military quarters, as the chief of Haig's intelligence staff has admitted, 'no one really believed this rather amazing view'. But it served as a welcome lever to make the Cabinet give way – as was the result.

The real source of the offensive, more potent than any of the arguments with which he buttressed his case, seems to have been Haig's optimistic belief that he could defeat the German armies single-handed – in Flanders. In large measure it was to be a battle fought for British prestige. If such a single-handed design had little support in the history of war, the geography of Flanders offered still less. A plan that was founded on faith rather than on reason, both plan and faith were to be sunk in the mud of Flanders. Foch, himself the past exponent of 'faith-healing' strategy, forecast the verdict when he deprecated the British offensive as a 'duck's march' and expressively remarked '*Boche* is bad and *boue* is bad; but *Boche* and *boue* together—!'

Haig adopted the plan in face of formidable facts. His meteorological advisers had collated weather statistics, based on the 'records of eighty years', which showed that he could not hope for more than a fortnight, or at the best three weeks, of fine weather.

Worse still, the Ypres offensive was doomed before it began – by its own destruction of the intricate drainage system in this part of Flanders. The legend has been fostered that these ill-famed 'swamps of Passchendaele' were a piece of ill luck due to the heavy rain, a natural and therefore unavoidable hindrance that could not be foreseen. In reality, before the battle began, a memorandum was sent by Tank Corps Headquarters to General Headquarters pointing out that if the Ypres area and its drainage were destroyed by bombardment, the battlefield would become a swamp. This memorandum was the result of information from the Belgian 'Ponts et Chaussées' and local investigation – the facts had, indeed, been brought to light by the engineers in 1915, but apparently forgotten. The area had been reclaimed from marshland by centuries of labour and in consequence the farmers of the district were under penalty to keep their dykes clear. Land used for pasture was such because it was subject to flooding and too wet for cultivation. In the disregard of this warning is epitomized the main and inevitable cause of the barren results of the 'Passchendaele offensive'.

Perhaps the very brilliance of the preliminary stroke at Messines on June 7th had helped to raise unfounded expectations over what was in conception and purpose a totally different operation. Nearly two months passed before the preparations for the main advance were completed, and during that interval the Germans had ample warning to prepare countermeasures. These comprised a new method of defence, as suited to the waterlogged ground as the British offensive methods were unsuited. Instead of the old linear systems of trenches they developed a system of disconnected strong points and concrete pillboxes, distributed in great depth, whereby the ground was held as much as possible by machine guns and as little as possible by men. While the forward positions were lightly occupied, the reserves thus saved were concentrated in rear for prompt counter-attack, to eject the British troops from the positions they had arduously gained. And the farther the British advanced the more highly developed, naturally, did they find the system. Moreover, by the introduction of mustard gas the Germans scored a further trick, interfering seriously with the British artillery and concentration areas.

Thus, when the fully expected blow fell, the Crown Prince Rupprecht was so far freed from his usual pessimism as to record in his diary – 'My mind is quite at rest about the attack, as we have never disposed of such strong reserves, so well trained for their part, as on the front attacked.' This actual front was held by the troops of the German Fourth Army (Sixt von Arnim).

The certainty that the Germans were aware of the coming offensive, and would be moving up reserves, led the chief of Haig's intelligence staff to urge that the attack should be advanced by three days 'in spite of the fact that our preparations were not fully completed; it was a choice of evils'. But 'the army commanders pressed for delay', and Haig reluctantly accepted their view. There was also a difference of view over the extent of the initial aim. Here Gough, like Rawlinson on the Somme, wished to make a series of limited advances, but Plumer urged that after so long a preparation they should go 'all out' – and Haig once again inclined to a breakthrough aim.

The main role in the attack was given to Gough's Fifth Army, with one corps of the Second Army playing a subsidiary part on the right flank, and a French corps on the left. The British artillery strength totalled 3,091 guns, of which 999 were heavy – an average of one gun to every six yards. During the bombardment, four and a quarter million shells were fired (£22,000,000 worth). It meant that four and three-quarter tons were thrown for every yard of the front.

The bombardment proper opened on July 22nd, and continued for ten days until at 3.50 AM on July 31st the infantry of twelve divisions advanced on an eleven-mile front to the accompaniment of torrential rain. On the left substantial progress was made, Bixschoote, St Julien, and the Pilckem ridge being gained, and the line of the Steenbeek reached. The 'green line' (third objective) was attained in most places, an advance of nearly two miles. But on the right, in the more vital sector round the Menin road, the attack was held up, short of the second objective. And the rain continued day after day, postponing the next major attempt, and hastening the conversion of the undrainable ground into a swamp in which first the tanks and ere long even the infantry were bogged.

Even the ardent Gough 'informed the Commander-in-Chief that tactical success was not possible, or would be too costly, under such conditions, and advised that the attack should be abandoned'. But Haig was too determined, and still too optimistic, to be thus dissuaded. And it would seem that none of the army commanders ventured to press contrary views with the strength that the facts demanded. One of the lessons of the war, exemplified at Passchendaele, is certainly the need of allowing more latitude in the military system for intellectual honesty and moral courage. As it was, Haig continued to send home to the War Office confident reports that the enemy were 'fast approaching' the exhaustion of their forces: actually, Ludendorff was making preparations not only to attack the Russians at Riga but to crush the Italians by sending eight or ten divisions to reinforce the Austrians. Haig's reports, indeed, had 'gone much further' than those his intelligence furnished.

The second blow, on August 16th, was a diminished replica of the first in its results. The left wing was again advanced across the shallow depression formed by the little valley of the Steenbeek and past the ruins of what had been Langemarck. But on the right, where alone an advance might have a strategic effect, a heavy price was paid for nought. The tally of prisoners shrank from six to a mere two thousand. Nor did men feel that the enemy's skilful resistance and the mud were the sole explanation of their fruitless sacrifice. Complaints against the direction and staff work in Gough's army were general and bitter, and their justness seemed to receive recognition when Haig extended the Second Army's front northward to include the Menin road sector, and thereby entrusted to Plumer the direction of the main advance towards the ridge east of Ypres. It was a thankless task at the best, for the experience of war attested the futility of pressing on in places where failure had already become established, and it seemed heavy odds that the laurels earned by Messines must become submerged in the swamps beyond Ypres.

Yet, in the outcome, the reputation of Plumer and the Second Army staff, headed by Harington, was enhanced – less because of what was achieved in scale than because more was achieved than could reasonably have been expected in so hopeless a venture. Applying, as at Messines, siege-warfare methods to a task that was more a siege than a battle, their plan was that of a series of shallow advances, not pressed beyond the point where the artillery support was outrun, and leaving both the infantry fresh enough and the artillery close enough to deal with the inevitable counter-attacks.

Bad weather and the need for preparation delayed the resumption of the offensive until September 20th, but that morning the Second Army attack, on a four-mile front, achieved success in the area of previous failure – on either side of the Menin road. Six divisions (two being Australian) were used; but infantry were kept down to the minimum with artillery at the maximum. Plumer had 1,295 guns – a gun to every five yards. Of these 575 were heavy, which meant one to every twelve yards compared with one to eighteen on July 31st. The infantry advanced at 5.40 AM; by 6.15 AM the first objective was gained almost unopposed, and, with the exception of one or two strong points, the third and last objective was gained soon after midday, and the counter-attacks were repulsed by fire. A fresh spring on September 26th, and another on October 4th – the last a larger one on an eight-mile front, by troops of eight divisions (four Anzac) in the Second Army, and of four in the Fifth Army on the left flank – gave the British possession of the main ridge east of Ypres, with Gheluvelt, Polygon Wood, and Brood-seinde, despite torrents of rain, which made the battlefield a worse morass than ever. And on each occasion the majority of the counter-attacks had broken down under fire, a result which owed much to the good observation work of the Royal Flying Corps and the quick response of the artillery. Some 10,000 prisoners were swallowed in the three bites, and this widening maw frightened the enemy into modifying his elastic tactics and strengthening his forward troops – to their increased loss under the British artillery fire.

These attacks had at least done something to restore prestige, if they could have little strategic effect on a campaign which was foredoomed, and in which both the time and the scope for extensive penetration had long since vanished. Unhappily, the Higher Command decided to continue the pointless offensive during the few remaining weeks before the winter, and thereby used up reserves which might have saved the belated experiment of Cambrai from bankruptcy. For having wasted the summer and his strength in the mud, where tanks foundered and infantry floundered, Haig turned in November to dry ground – where a decisive success went begging for lack of reserves.

At Ypres the comparative success of the late September attacks produced an unfortunate intoxication. On the evening of October 4th the chief of the intelligence staff expressed the opinion that there were no fresh enemy reserves 'within immediate reach of the battlefront'. (Actually, fresh German divisions began to take over the line next day; before the next attack on October 9th, 'the whole of the battered front was held by fresh troops, and an extra division had been inserted'.) Even the sober Second Army staff seem to have been momentarily carried away, and at a conference with the war correspondents Harington said that the crest of the ridge was 'as dry as a bone'. The Australian Official History records the impression of one who was present: 'I believe the official attitude is that Passchendaele ridge is so important that tomorrow's attack is worth making whether it succeeds or fails ... I suspect that they are making a great, bloody experiment – a huge gamble ... I feel, and most of the correspondents feel, terribly anxious ... I thought the principle was to be "hit, hit, hit, *whenever the weather is suitable*!" If so, it is thrown over at the first temptation.'

The anxiety of the correspondents was to prove more justifiable than the hopes of the military chiefs. There had been rain each day since October 4th, and on the afternoon of the 8th it became torrential; the meteorological experts said that no improvement could be expected. Yet Haig decided to press on, and his army commanders, although dubious, did not care to protest. So next morning the attack was launched, again on an eight-mile front – and proved a tragic fiasco, except in the low ground on the left. The curious nature of military judgement is illustrated in the diary of Haig's chief intelligence officer (October 8th): 'With a great success tomorrow, and good weather for a few more weeks, we may still clear the coast and win the war before Christmas.' (October 10th) 'D.H. sent for me ... He was still trying to find some grounds for hope that we might still win through here this year, but there is none.'

Nevertheless, a fresh attack was ordered for the 12th – with still deeper objectives. Gough doubted its wisdom, but Plumer 'had decided that an attack was practicable', and Haig gave the order on the 10th. At this moment 'little was known of the true experiences and results of the recent fight' (Australian Official History). There was still time to find out, but this duty seems to have been neglected. After renewed rain on the 11th, Gough, to his credit, telephoned to Plumer to suggest a postponement. But after consulting Godley, the corps commander mainly concerned, Plumer preferred to continue. Next day the would-be dash for Passchendaele ended with the attacking troops, save those who perished in the mud, back almost on their starting line.

Haig now seems to have realized there was no foundation for anticipating a great strategic success. But he was determined to reach Passchendaele, and for this purpose brought up the Canadian Corps. Meantime a combined attack by the Fifth Army and the French was tried, with small result, on October 22nd. On the 26th the Second Army made its fresh effort with the Canadians and suffered a fresh disappointment. They tried again on the 30th, while the Fifth Army loyally yet sceptically struggled to advance alongside – '300 yards or so being the limit'.

Progress so trifling, save in its cost, was largely explained by the exhaustion caused in pushing forward over a morass and to the fact that the mud not only got into and jammed rifles and machine guns, but nullified the effect of the shell bursts. The attackers' troubles were augmented by the enemy's increasing use of mustard gas, and by his renewed adoption of his tactics of holding the bulk of his troops well back for a counter-attack. Thus, when on November 4th, a sudden advance by the 1st Division and 2nd Canadian Division gained the empty satisfaction of occupying the site of Passchendaele village, the official curtain was at last rung down on the pitiful tragedy of 'Third Ypres'. It was the long-overdue close of a campaign which had brought the British armies to the verge of exhaustion, one in which had been enacted the most dolorous scenes in British military history, and for which the only justification evoked the reply that, in order to absorb the enemy's attention and forces, Haig chose the spot most difficult for himself and least vital to his enemy. Intending to absorb the enemy's reserves, his own were absorbed.

He was lured on by a lofty optimism that extended even to the cost. After the disappointing attack of July 31st, he advised the Government that the enemy casualties exceeded the British 'not improbably by a hundred per cent'; and in his final dispatch he still declared that it was 'certain that the enemy's loss considerably exceeded ours'. That optimism was nourished by ignorance of the situation, due in part to the failure – a moral failure – of his subordinates to enlighten him.

Perhaps the most damning comment on the plan which plunged the British Army in this bath of mud and blood is contained in an incidental revelation of the remorse of one who was largely responsible for it. This highly placed officer from General Headquarters was on his first visit to the battle front – at the end of the four months' battle. Growing increasingly uneasy as the car approached the swamplike edges of the battle area, he eventually burst into tears, crying, 'Good God, did we really send men to fight in that?' To which his companion replied that the ground was far worse ahead. If the exclamation was a credit to his heart it revealed on what a foundation of delusion and inexcusable ignorance his indomitable 'offensiveness' had been based.

The only relief to this sombre review is that a bare fortnight later was enacted, on a different stage, and with a technique suggested in early August, a 'curtain-raiser' which was to be developed into the glorious drama of autumn, 1918.

CHAPTER SEVEN

SCENE 4

The Tank Surprise at Cambrai

On November 19th, 1917, the German troops in front of Cambrai were contemplating with undisturbed minds the apparent normality and comparative tranquillity of the British lines opposite them; contrasting their own security in the massively fortified and comfortable trenches of the Hindenburg Line with the unsavoury lot of their comrades struggling in the shell-churned mudholes of the Ypres salient; indulging in self-congratulation not only on the impregnability of their famous line, but on the pertinacity of the unteachable English who had so engulfed themselves at Ypres that there could surely be no danger of any other assault elsewhere before winter came.

On November 20th, 381 tanks, followed by a relatively small proportion of infantry rolled forward in the half-light upon the astonished Germans without even the courtesy of a preliminary bombardment to announce their coming. Always good hosts, the Germans might well feel aggrieved at the omission of a warning which had customarily given them four or five days' notice to prepare a suitable reception.

On November 21st the bells of London rang out in joyous acclaim of a triumphant success that seemed a foretaste of victory, perhaps at no distant date. And Ludendorff, back at the German Supreme Command, was hurriedly preparing emergency instructions for a general retreat. Both the bells and Ludendorff were premature – although prophetic – by some nine months.

For on November 30th came a German retort so full of menace that the public thereafter showed a strong distaste for premature celebrations. Applause changed to reproaches; the cause of the disasters was the subject of inquiry; and in public opinion the name of Cambrai came to be associated more with the ultimate reverse than with the initial success. Actually, however, the fuller knowledge now available suggests that the black date in the national calendar should be the 20th,

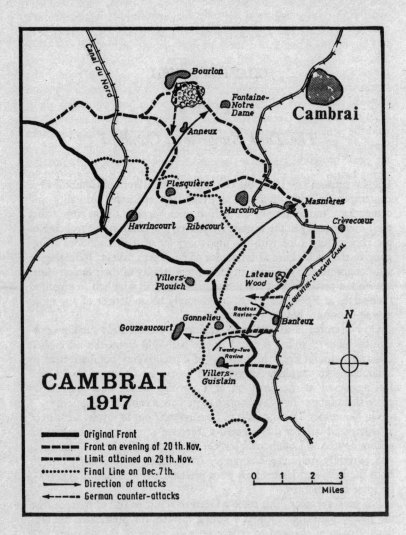

Canal du Nord

Bourlon

Fontaine-
Notre
Dame

Cambrai

Anneux

Plesquières

Masnières

Marcoing

Crèvecœur

Havrincourt   Ribecourt

Villers-
Plouich

Lateau
Wood

ST. QUENTIN—L'ESCAUT CANAL

Gonnelieu

Banteux
Ravine

Banteux

Gouzeaucourt

N

Twenty-Two
Ravine

Villers-
Guislain

CAMBRAI
1917

━━━━ Original Front
╌╌╌ Front on evening of 20th. Nov.
▬·▬·▬ Limit attained on 29th. Nov.
·········· Final Line on Dec. 7th.
——▶ Direction of attacks
◀╌╌╌ German counter-attacks

0   1   2   3
Miles

and not the 30th, of November. Yet gloomy as is this page of World War history, it forms one of the most striking examples of the proverb that 'every cloud has a silver lining'. If November 20th, 1917, is in itself a tragedy of errors, its eventual effect on the fortunes of the Allies was beneficent – pointing and paving the way to the victorious method of 1918, and, to take a still longer view, it is seen to be one of the landmarks in the history of warfare, the dawn of a new epoch. Thus we may say that the joy-bells, if immediately wrong, were ultimately right.

In contrast, the Germans failed to profit by the warning and later paid the penalty – as their official historians recognize. While the more far-sighted German officers urged the necessity of replying in kind to the new British method others argued that 'the further mechanization of the battle' would impair the moral qualities of the troops. And their fervent traditionalism fathered the thought that 'the tank terror was more of a phantom than a real danger'. The success of the counter-offensive was a support to men who did not care to face an unconventional reality, and the weight of conservative opinion prevailed – as so often in the history of armies. Thus it was left for the post-war historians of the German Army to record, in bitterness of soul, that 'the outwardly brilliant German offensive battle held within a deep tragedy'.

These eleven days form perhaps the most dramatic of all episodes in the World War. Yet, sensational as was their course in its abrupt change of fortune, the real story of 'Cambrai' lies beneath the surface. First is the question of its origins, of paramount importance because it ushered in a new cycle of warfare. Its initial source is to be found nearly two years, and its immediate source nearly four months, earlier.

The guiding idea of those who sponsored the tank in infancy had been to release it unexpectedly in a large concentration, and this idea had, as we have seen not only been formulated but worked out in detail as early as February, 1916 – seven months before a driblet of tanks were launched on the Somme under conditions which violated all the essentials therein laid down. Fortunately, in 1917, the headquarters of the Tank Corps in France, although unlike General Headquarters they had not seen this memorandum, had come by experience to similar ideas. Further, the eternal yet too often underrated principle of surprise was deeply rooted in their minds, and thus when insight apprised them in the very first days of Third Ypres – the Passchendaele offensive – that the 'mudlark' was futile, an alternative project was quick to blossom.

The chief general staff officer, Colonel Fuller, on August 3rd, 1917, drew up a plan for a great tank raid in a more suitable sector. In the preface to it this significant example of prevision may be read: 'From a tank point of view the Third Battle of Ypres may be considered dead. To go on using tanks in the present conditions will not only lead to good machines and better personnel being thrown away, but also to a loss of morale in the infantry and tank crews, through constant failure. From an infantry point of view, the Third Battle of Ypres may be considered comatose. It can only be continued at colossal loss and little gain.'

Then came the alternative proposal: 'In order to restore British prestige and strike a theatrical blow against Germany before the winter, it is suggested that preparations be at once set on foot to take St Quentin.' It was further pointed out that the operation was strategically a sound one as a preparatory step to an advance towards Le Cateau, and then Valenciennes, the following year. Discussion of this project brought out the objection that it required a combined British and French operation, which might lack the simplicity and smooth working essential for the novel method to succeed. Therefore, on August 4th, a second project was framed, for a tank raid south of Cambrai. The word 'raid' should be stressed, for, as originally conceived, the object was 'to destroy the enemy's personnel and guns, to demoralize and disorganize him, and not to capture ground'. As the preliminary notes stated: 'The duration of the raid must be short – eight to twelve hours – so that little or no concentration of the enemy may be effected for counter-attack.' Had this been followed there would have been no need to lament the 30th November. 'The whole operation may be summed up as "advance, hit, retire". Big raids of this description will not only reduce the enemy's fighting power, but will reduce his initiative with reference to any big battle which at the time may be in progress.' For this raid a force of three tank brigades of two battalions each, and 'one, or better, two, divisions of infantry or cavalry', with extra artillery, was suggested, operating on an 8,000-yard front. The object, as proposed, was 'to raid the re-entrant formed by the L'Escaut–St Quentin Canal between Ribecourt–Crèvecoeur–Banteux'. The raiding force was to be divided into three groups, the main one to scour the country in this canal-enclosed pocket, while smaller groups formed offensive flanks on each side to protect the main operation. 'The essence of the entire operation is surprise and rapidity of movement. Three hours after zero the retirement might well begin, the tanks and aeroplanes operating as a rearguard to the dismounted cavalry retiring with their prisoners.'

The proposed sector lay in the area of the Third Army, under General Sir Julian Byng, and on August 5th the detailed project was taken informally to him by one of the Tank Corps brigadiers. Byng was receptive to the idea, although inclined to expand it from a raid into a breakthrough attack to gain Cambrai. Next day he went to General Headquarters, saw Haig, and suggested a surprise attack with tanks at Cambrai in September. The Commander-in-Chief was favourable, but his Chief of Staff, General Kiggell, offered strong objections on the ground that the army could not win a decisive battle in two places at once, and should rather concentrate every possible man in the Ypres sector – which, incidentally, he never visited until the campaign was over. Thus the enlarged idea helped to postpone the raid, as the refusal to recognize reality at Ypres postponed the attack at Cambrai until too late for decisive results to be possible.

The historian, while respecting Kiggell's emphasis on the principle of concentration, may doubt whether Ypres was a suitable site for the fulfilment of this principle, and may also hold that distraction of the enemy's force has ever been an essential complement to concentration – of one's own effort.

Kiggell's objections sufficed to dissuade Haig, who still valued the tank as only 'a minor factor'. Thus the Cambrai project was postponed indefinitely, while the High Command persevered with their hopeless efforts in the Passchendaele swamps. But neither Byng nor the Tank Corps were willing to let the idea drop, and certain opinions at General Headquarters were in accord, so that as the Ypres offensive became a more palpable failure, a readier ear was lent to an alternative which promised to redeem British prestige. Finally, in mid-October, the Cambrai plan was sanctioned, and fixed for November 20th. But now the situation had changed for the worse, for, if the plan were crowned with success, that success must be barren for want of reserves to reap the harvest. The reapers were engulfed at Passchendaele.

It is just to recognize that if General Headquarters had missed the opportunity, General Headquarters had now perhaps a surer appreciation than the Third Army Command of the limitations imposed by their lack of means. Kiggell urged that Bourlon Hill merely should be the first objective, followed by a lateral exploitation northward, and Haig put a time limit on the operation. But the Third Army orders were more ambitious in scope and objectives, despite the fact that all their available infantry divisions and tanks were being thrown into the initial 'breakthrough' effort.

Byng's plan was (1) to break the German defensive system, the famous Hindenburg Line, in the neck between the Canal de L'Escaut and the Canal du Nord, (2) to seize Cambrai, Bourlon Wood and the

passage over the River Sensée; (3) to cut off the Germans in the area
south of the Sensée and west of the Canal du Nord; and (4) to exploit
the success towards Valenciennes. The force allotted for this ambitious
plan comprised the III (Pulteney) and IV (Woollcombe) Corps, each of
three infantry divisions, the Cavalry Corps (Kavanagh) of three divisions (plus one under IV Corps), a total of 381 fighting tanks, and
roughly 1,000 guns. Thus of the original project only the fundamental
idea, the tank method, and the locality remained. Otherwise there were
marked alterations, and in these lay the germ of disaster. The raid had
been transformed into a large-scale offensive, with far-reaching aims.
Instead of securing a 'pocket' and withdrawing, an organized advance
was to be made up a narrow 'lane', bounded by two canals. A protection
to a raid, these became a danger to such an attack, circumscribing the
action of the tanks and preventing the formation of tank-offensive
flanks. Otherwise the ground was good, mostly rolling downland, excellent for tank movement; it was marked by two features, the Flesquières–Havrincourt ridge and Bourlon Hill.

The fundamental weakness of the general plan, however, was not
topographical, but the complete lack of reserves, unless the four cavalry
divisions can be considered such – and the futility of so regarding them
was amply shown in their fresh inability, in face of modern weapons, to
influence the action. The six divisions employed in the initial attack
were all that the Third Army commander had at his disposal – for a
plan that visualized a penetration beyond Cambrai to Valenciennes! It is
extremely difficult to understand what was in mind as to the future, for
without reserves complete success could only mean the creation of an
excessively deep and narrow salient, requiring scores of divisions to
hold it. It is true that the Guards and one or two other divisions could
be made available, and were ultimately brought to the scene, but they
were too far away for a prompt intervention. The situation, indeed, had
some reminder of Loos. The French also moved a corps to the Senlis–
Péronne area just before the attack, but after the first day were told
that they were no longer required!

The best comment on this lack of reserves is contained in a story of
General Franchet d'Esperey, which one has on the authority of the
officer to whom the words were spoken. A long motor ride, in search of
information, brought him to a British headquarters at Albert. Entering,
he interrogated a senior General Staff officer, flinging at him a string of
crisp questions as to the progress of the attack, its frontage, depth.
Then came the final, the vital question: 'And where were your reserves?' 'Mon Général, we had none.' The French commander ex-

claimed, 'Mon Dieu!' turned on his heel and fled.

Turning now to the tank plan, the problems were to gain surprise, to cross the wide and deep obstacle of the Hindenburg Line and to ensure cooperation between the infantry and tanks for their common security. Careful organization and the absence of a preliminary bombardment contributed to the accomplishment of the first object. The difficulty presented by the Hindenburg Line was overcome by devising super-fascines, huge bundles of brushwood, which were carried on the nose of each tank and released on reaching the edge of the Hindenburg trenches; the tanks, working in sections of three, had thus the power to cross three successive obstacles. Thirdly, a strictly drill attack was worked out and practised by which in each section an advanced-guard tank moved about 100 yards ahead of the two main-body tanks, keeping down the enemy's fire and protecting the main body as they led the infantry forward. The infantry, moving in flexible file formations, followed immediately behind the main-body tanks. While the tanks cleared a way for them through the deep belts of enemy wire and sub-dued the hostile machine-gun fire, the infantry acted as 'moppers-up' to the tanks and were also ready to protect them from the enemy's guns at close quarters. The one fault of the tank plan was that, against expert advice, the tanks attacked on the whole frontage instead of against selected tactical points, with the result that no tank reserves were kept for use in the later stages.

The preparations for the battle were made with great skill and secrecy, while to mislead the enemy as to the scale and frontage of the attack, gas and smoke attacks, dummy attacks with dummy tanks, raids and feints, were carried out on a wide front both north and south of the real sector of attack.

Nevertheless, one man nearly undid the secrecy of a multitude. A prisoner from an Irish regiment gave information of the coming attack, and of the concentration of tanks, but fortunately he was not believed and the German army commander, General von der Marwitz, reported on the 16th that there was no likelihood of an attack. But on the 19th a British telephone message, 'Tuesday Flanders', was overheard near Bullecourt, and, as it sounded like a combined date and codeword, quickened German suspicions. That night the troops were ordered to be specially alert, and Marwitz hastily utilized a division, just detraining from Russia, to strengthen his defences. But if the Germans now antici-pated an attack they also expected the usual preliminary bombardment*

* An attack without heavy bombardment was considered out of the ques-tion, as the position was so strong. Thus the orders for Moser's group, shortly

– and its absence assured the British attack the essential surprise effect. That effect was accentuated by an early morning mist, as in almost all the successful thrusts of the war.

At 6.20 AM on November 20th the tanks and infantry moved forward to the attack on roughly a six-mile front, and gained a demoralizing initial success at all points save in the left centre in front of Flesquières. The main cause of this one serious check was that the commander of the 51st Division, Harper, preferred a method of his own instead of conforming to the formations devised by the Tank Corps, and adopted in all the other divisions. His advance tanks were called 'rovers', and went much farther ahead, and the infantry formations were not as well fitted for close cooperation with tanks as those laid down. The separation seems to have been inspired by his expressed feeling that the whole Cambrai plan was 'a fantastic and most unmilitary scheme' – when on the staff of General Headquarters he had resisted the development of machine guns, and now was equally sceptical of tanks. The result was that the infantry were too far behind the tanks, lost the gaps in the wire, and were stopped by machine-gun fire. An officer who examined the battlefield afterwards could only find three small heaps of machine-gun cartridge cases, from which it would appear that a handful of machine guns held up a whole division – a fact which sheds a striking light on the future of infantry action in open country. The loss of touch between the infantry and tanks lay also at the root of the losses which befell the tanks when they came over the ridge and under the close fire of several German batteries, for infantry accompanying them could have picked off the gunners. Here occurred the famous incident of the solitary German artillery officer who was reputed to have 'knocked out' sixteen tanks single-handed. It must go into the catalogue of historic legends, for only five derelict tanks were to be seen at this point after the attack had moved on, and an intelligence officer who examined the ground found marks which showed clearly that three batteries had been in position there to engage the tanks. It is possible that all save one gun, and one gunner, had been silenced, as was claimed, but impressions in the heat of battle are sometimes misleading. The feat has, however, an ironical significance in the fact that it was blazoned to the world by the British General Headquarters. The incentive of a mention in dispatches was not accorded to enemy feats performed at the expense of the infantry or cavalry.

---

before midnight on the 19th, said – 'Tanks may take part. The four or five hours' artillery bombardment will probably begin between 3 and 4 AM.' This is a suggestive example of how habit may contribute to surprise.

The effect of this battlefield incident has also been magnified. On the right the 12th, 20th and 6th Divisions secured their objectives rapidly, though the 12th had severe fighting at Lateau wood. The 20th Division passed through and captured Masnières and Marcoing, securing the passage of the canal at both and even the bridge intact at the latter. On the left of the 51st the 62nd Division made a brilliant advance, advancing by nightfall as far as Anneux, over two miles in the rear of Flesquières. The Flesquières resistance was thus only an islet, cut off and overlapped by the waves which swept round its flanks and on to Marcoing, Anneux and even to the edge of Bourlon Wood. A penetration of five miles had been made – the equivalent of months of heavy fighting and heavier losses on the Somme and at the Third Battle of Ypres. Decisive success was within the grasp of the British forces, the enemy's three main lines of defences had been overrun, only a half-finished line and the open country lay beyond. But the tank crews were exhausted, the infantry showed little capacity to make progress on their own, and apart from one squadron of the Canadian Fort Garry Horse the two cavalry divisions could contribute nothing towards fulfilling their role of exploitation.

The German official monograph emphasizes the fact that a wide gap remained open for 'many hours, completely unoccupied', between Masnières and Crèvecoeur: 'It was great luck, as no reinforcements could be expected to reach there before evening.' The Germans also had luck in that a relief division from Russia had just arrived when the attack came; by midday on the 20th part of it was in position to cover the direct path to Cambrai. With notable promptness the German Command began moving five reserve divisions to the scene from other parts of the front, and six more were warned to follow. It was thus a race with time; and to the joy of the anxious Germans, their assailants seemed astoundingly dilatory. 'The British failed to utilize the afternoon and evening; they might at least have surrounded the German forces still holding out in Flesquières. The defence ... seems to have deprived the 51st Division of all initiative.' As for the British cavalry, it is remarked that they appeared late and were easily stopped by enfilade fire.

On November 21st local reserves made some further progress. Flesquières was evacuated by its surviving defenders in the early hours, and after dawn the 51st and 62nd Divisions pressed on, clearing the German salient formed by this resistance on the first day and carrying the tide of the British advance as far as Fontaine-Notre Dame, one and a half miles beyond the high-water mark of November 20th. Owing to the British penetration into Bourlon Wood and Fontaine there was a three-mile-wide breach between Walter's and Moser's corps. But, by German witness, the British lapsed into inactivity at the moment of supreme opportunity. On the right, little ground was gained during the day, and, by evening, three of the enemy's reinforcing divisions were on the scene. The opportunity had been forfeited.

Haig's time limit of forty-eight hours had now expired, but owing to the menace of the uncaptured Bourlon Hill to the new British position, as well as the hope of an enemy withdrawal and the desire to relieve the enemy pressure on Italy, he decided to continue the offensive and, somewhat belatedly, placed a few fresh divisions at the disposal of the Third Army. But the Tank Corps, the essential cause of the early success that had apparently surprised the British as much as the German Command, was tired out, men and machines – all had been staked on the first throw.

The fresh attacks met with more failure than success against an enemy now braced to meet the danger. On November 22nd the Germans recaptured Fontaine-Notre Dame; on the 23rd, the 40th Division with tanks captured the whole of Bourlon Wood, but the attempts on Bourlon village and Fontaine-Notre Dame failed. Bitter and fluctuating fighting followed; both villages were won, and lost again. And meanwhile the Germans, with prompt initiative and consummate skill, were preparing a deadly counterblast. Unfortunately there seems to have been a disposition in the superior command, with certain exceptions, to discredit the numerous warning signs of the gathering storm, and even to find amusement in the anxiety displayed by those whose clearer vision was soon to be attested. This attitude was apparently due to over-confidence – partly induced by the easy success of November 20th, and partly due to a belief that the Passchendaele offensive had absorbed all the enemy's reserves. The effect of Passchendaele, indeed, was always overrated.

In contrast, General Snow, commanding the VII Corps on the southern flank of the wedge driven into the German front, had forecast both the place and date of the counterstroke nearly a week before. His subordinate commanders, particularly in the 55th Division (Jeudwine), which adjoined the III Corps, had reported a host of corroborative evidence – that the enemy artillery were registering on spots never bombarded before, that German aircraft were flying over the lines in large numbers, and that the British reconnaissance machines were 'shelled off' certain areas where the enemy could concentrate under cover. Late on November 29th the 55th Division was so convinced of the imminent menace that Jeudwine asked that the neighbouring III Corps might put down a counter-preparation with 'heavies' on the Banteux Ravine just before daylight next morning, but his request was refused. The gathering enemy themselves were surprised that 'nothing was done to disturb the German preparations'.

And next morning they repaid the tank surprise by one which was similar in principle if different in method. Unheralded by any long artillery preparation, a short, hurricane bombardment with gas and smoke shell paved the way for the infiltrating advance of the German infantry – the prototype of the German offensive method of spring, 1918, as the British attack had been the prototype of the Allied offensive method of summer and autumn, 1918. Emerging from the sheltered assembly position of Banteux and Twenty-two Ravines at the very moment when the unfulfilled counter-preparation would have opened, the German stream trickled through the weak points in the British line; then, expanding into a broad torrent which submerged the villages of Gonnelieu and Villers Guislain, swept over gun positions and headquarters, and surged forward to Gouzeaucourt. The menace of disaster was immeasurable, but, fortunately, the complementary attacks on the north of the salient, round Bourlon Wood, were brought to a standstill, and the emergency declined with the recapture of Gouzeaucourt by the superb counter-attack of the Guards' Division and a later effort of the 2nd Tank Brigade. For a time, indeed, there was a chance to 'redouble' and score heavily off the Germans, disordered by this success and hampered by their narrow penetration. But rejecting Snow's plea for a flank riposte by the cavalry, the army commander directed his cavalry head-on against the Germans, and they were soon held up. Thus the invaders were able to consolidate their hold and even to resume their erosion of the British position. During the next few days continued German progress, especially towards Villers Plouich, and British lack of reserves rendered the British position in the Masnières–Bourlon salient so precarious that the greater part of the original gains had to be evacuated. A sombre sunset after a brilliant sunrise.

One shadow which still lingers is that undeservedly thrown on the regimental officers and men by superior officers anxious to exculpate themselves. The official court of inquiry pinned the blame on the troops, ascribing the surprise to their negligence and also asserting, contrary to facts, that they had failed to send up 'SOS' flares. Even Byng declared – 'I attribute the reason for the local success on the part of the enemy to one cause and one alone, namely – lack of training on the part of junior officers and NCOs and men.' Haig, however, who had

been kept in the dark as to the warnings, was an exception to the
'general' rule. In sending his report home, he generously assumed the
whole responsibility – although he also sent home several of the subordinate commanders.

It is thus due for history to record, from the records, that many of the
junior leaders were acutely alive to the danger and gave vain warnings
to their superiors. And as for their resistance, it was more than anyone
had a right to expect of troops who had been kept in action continuously since their attack on November 20th. For military history,
indeed, the lesson of Cambrai is that the welcome renaissance of the
essential principle of surprise was offset by a fundamental breach of the
principle of economy of force – both in adjusting the end to the means
and in appreciating the capacity and limits of human endurance.

CHAPTER SEVEN

SCENE 5

Caporetto

In the chill and sodden gloom of an autumn morning amid the mist-wreathed peaks of the Julian Alps came a rumbling. Before its echoes finally subsided, the Allied cause had been shaken to its foundations. The first rumours of disaster, which were far from exaggerating the reality, came like a thunderclap to the Allied peoples, if not to all their leaders, for 1917 hitherto had seen the Allies on the offensive in all theatres.

The year had begun with the expectation of a sure progress towards victory, of a vast combined offensive culminating in the overthrow of the Central Powers, and if the mirage of early victory had been slowly fading before the evidence of stubborn resistance and heavy losses, the public were still unprepared for a definite change of role from attack to defence. More especially was this unexpected in Italy, for while there was obvious ground for qualms over Russia, the Italians had been attacking during August and September, and the cables had given the impression that the tide of battle was flowing strongly in their favour. And for once, in a war when the output of fiction was greater than that of fact, these reports were correct.

If the gain in ground was small the moral and material effect on the already war-rotted Austrians was large, and, as Ludendorff records, 'the responsible military and political authorities of the dual monarchy were convinced that they would not be able to stand a continuation of the battle and a twelfth attack on the Isonzo'. Thus 'in the middle of September it became necessary to decide for the attack on Italy in order to prevent the collapse of Austria-Hungary'. So urgent was the need that Ludendorff was forced to abandon his preparations for the offensive in Moldavia, which he had intended as the *coup de grâce* to Russia's crumbling resistance. Even so, where could he raise sufficient troops for converting the Austrian defensive into an effective offensive? The

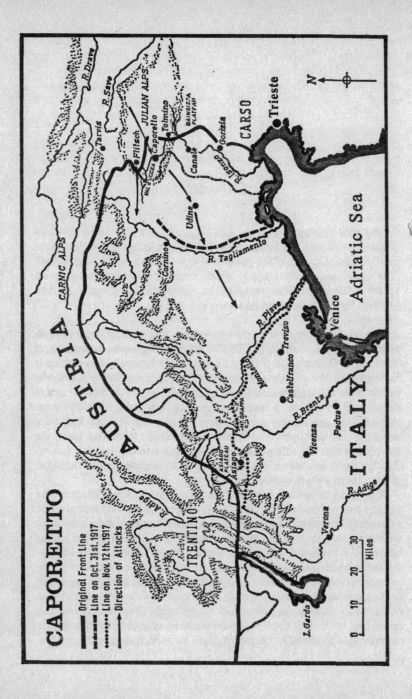

British pressure at Passchendale and the mere length of his immense fronts in France and Russia absorbed his resources until he could force peace on Russia. All he could spare was his slender general reserve of six divisions, which had already been his instrument in countering the Kerensky offensive – Russia's final flicker – and in the coup which captured Riga. His adviser in the strategic design of operations, Major Wetzell, was however of the opinion that the application of even this small force at a 'soft' spot, such as the sector between Flitsch and Canale, would suffice to lame if not to break the Italian menace.

The result proved him right – the trouble was that it unduly exceeded the most sanguine expectations. And it was due to the fact that it was expanded to a more ambitious plan – without increase of means – than was originally intended in the 'germ' scheme, which Waldstätten, of the Austrian General Staff, had brought to the German Command on August 29th. This original scheme was for a breakthrough at Tolmino, followed merely by rolling up the Isonzo front. Caporetto and Cambrai were to have a curious kinship.

Ludendorff sent General Krafft von Delmensingen on a special mission to reconnoitre the ground and report on the scheme. Krafft had led the Alpine Corps in the Rumanian campaign, and was thus an expert in mountain warfare. He found that the Austrians had managed to retain a small bridgehead on the west bank of the Isonzo at Tolmino, and this afforded a jumping-off point for the projected attack. Guns were got up mostly by hand and at night; the infantry came up by seven night marches, taking no vehicles, but carrying their ammunition, equipment, and supplies on the men or on pack animals. Thus the twelve assault divisions and 300 batteries concentrated undiscovered by the Italians, owing partly to able precautions, partly to the country, and partly to the inadequate air reconnaissances of the enemy.

What of the Italians? The Commander-in-Chief, Cadorna, was undoubtedly a man of more than ordinary ability, but, like certain other famous commanders, his intellectual power was offset by his lack of touch with and understanding of the fighting troops. With such men, also, their mental remoteness is often accentuated by the natural isolation in which those in high military position are placed. Considering the comparatively slender weight of the attack, he had enough men and guns to withstand it successfully, but his distribution of them was unsuited to the conditions of the various sectors. Troops already too highly tried were kept too long in the positions of greatest strain. Thus, the combination of faulty distribution with the enemy's unerring eye for the vulnerable spot produced, with other factors, an Austro-German success out of all proportion to the means.

Capello, commanding the Second Army, dissatisfied with the defensive suitability of the positions on which the Italian offensive had stopped, had wished to forestall the attack by a flank thrust northwards from the Bainsizza Plateau, but was overruled by Cadorna, who was not only conscious of his shortage of reserves but had belatedly come to doubt the value of offensive methods. In this he was at least wiser than his subordinate who, alike in offensive spirit, in his manner as a commander, and as the victim of the Germans' new offensive method, was the Gough of the Italian Army. Cadorna had full warning of the enemy's intention from his Intelligence and from deserters – Czech and Transylvanian officers, but he did not feel sufficiently sure of the real direction of the enemy's attack to justify him in committing his reserves beforehand.

Yet it is at least curious that, as information specifically pointed to the Caporetto sector, on its fifteen-mile frontage there were only posted two battalions to the mile compared with eight to the mile farther south. The very fact that this had long been a quiet sector, where both sides sent troops to rest, might have aroused the suspicions of the Italian command. But Capello actually refused the appeal of his left wing here for reinforcements. Perhaps he was the less patient towards arguments because he should have been a patient in hospital. Instead, with misguided pertinacity he stayed in bed at his headquarters, and only yielded the reins of command the day after his front collapsed.

The Italian frontier province of Venezia formed a tongue pointing towards Austria. It was flanked on the south by the Adriatic and on the east and north by the Julian and Carnic Alps – beyond which lay the Austrian Trentino. The six German divisions, with nine Austrian, formed the attacking Fourteenth German Army, under General Otto von Below, with whom was Krafft as Chief of Staff and guiding brain. These troops were to climb the mountain barrier at the tip of the tongue, while two Austrian armies, under Boroevic, were to advance along the stretch of lower ground near the Adriatic shore.

The difficulties of organizing and deploying an attack in the mountains were ably overcome, and after four hours' gas shell and one hour's general bombardment, the attackers moved forward in the drizzle of snow and rain, and in many places rapidly overcame the resistance of infantry who, owing partly to the breakdown of telephone communication, were but fitfully supported by their own artillery. But the misty conditions were the greater factor in the success, as next March in

France; they provided the element of surprise which proved the only and indispensable key to open a way through the enemy's front. Although the right and left wings of the attacking army were delayed by sturdy resistance in the rear positions, the centre group (four divisions) under Stein penetrated completely at Caporetto, and through this breach reserves were pouring by evening. The effect was to make the whole defensive position untenable and to ease the task of the attacking right wing (three and a half Austrian divisions) under Krauss, which now pushed forward almost unchecked down the Val d'Uccea, the shortest line to turn the river barrier of the Tagliamento. This enveloping advance nullified Cadorna's efforts to dam the breach, efforts which also broke down owing to the difficulty of pushing reserves up the narrow mountain roads already congested by troops which had no stomach left for fighting. This convinced Cadorna of the necessity of ordering a general retreat to the Tagliamento, as Capello had earlier urged, and it was successfully achieved after two critical days – October 30th and 31st.

Fortunately the pursuing enemy had suffered from hitches in movements and supply, as well as an increasing friction between the German and Austrian commanders. Their attempt to achieve a surprise capture of the crossings was foiled, and although in a deliberate attack one of Krauss' Austrian divisions got across at Cornino on November 2nd, Cadorna had had breathing space to make preparations for a further retreat to the Piave. Although large bodies of troops were cut off by the enemy's pincer-like advance, the main armies succeeded in reaching the Piave by November 10th, thus reforging their line. Yet its links were very thin. Nearly 600,000 men had been lost, and the Second Army, which had suffered the direct blow, was practically out of action as a force. At this juncture Cadorna gave place to Diaz, whose supreme value was that he understood the mind of the soldiers, and knew how to reinvigorate their morale, playing, in fact, the same role as Pétain in France earlier that year.

Three days later a fresh menace developed, on November 12th when Conrad's troops (Austrian Tenth and Eleventh Armies) sought to move down from the Trentino on the Italian rear. But here Cadorna's preparations for defence had been long initiated and were well matured, so that the threat was frustrated. Ludendorff, too late, tried to switch reinforcements round to Conrad, but was foiled by the inadequate rail communications and deficiency of motor transport – if, fundamentally, by the limited horizon of the original plan.

Meanwhile, French and British divisions had been hurriedly railed to

Italy, their coming preceded by the arrival of Foch and Sir Henry Wilson, but they took some time to concentrate – and were then at first held back in reserve – so that the interval before they relieved divisions of their severely strained Ally was a time of grave stress. The most serious attack came in the sector between the Piave and the Brenta, but here, after five days of struggle, Laderchi's Italian IX Corps brought the attack to halt, and at the beginning of December was relieved by the French, while the British, under Lord Plumer, took over the Montello sector. Contrary to expectation, both were left in peace, and during the remaining months of the campaign the enemy's attack was confined to renewed efforts by Conrad and Krauss farther to the north-west, in the Asiago and Grappa sectors. If these imposed a fresh tax on the weary Italians, it was psychologically worthwhile, for this successful and stalwart resistance by its vindication of their fighting power laid the moral foundations for the Italian 'revanche' of 1918.

Reviewing the drama of Caporetto in the clearer light of history, there is reason to think that excessive emphasis was placed on the effect of enemy and seditious propaganda, and that the major reason of the crumbling resistance early was the same as in France that spring – that the troops were morally tired, and that the result of being hurled endlessly against machine-gun defences had worn down their fighting spirit. The presence of imminent disaster to their country set a new light upon the position, and gave a sacrificial impulse to a duty which on the Piave line, fighting 'with their backs to the wall', they honourably and gallantly fulfilled.

Strategically, however, the most critical stage was past with the passing of Tagliamento, for henceforth what Clausewitz called the 'friction of war' so upset the attackers' communications that their power and speed fell off badly. Some of the causes have been mentioned. But one, which was to operate again next spring in France, deserves emphasis. The well-filled supply depots of the Italian army were too great a temptation to the under-nourished enemy, the desire to eat quenched the desire to pursue, and sudden congestion of the stomach accelerated the congestion of the advance. It is significant that even a German divisional commander, General Lecquis, could exult more at the capture of two or three chickens apiece by his men than of many prisoners, and regarded the possession of a few pigs 'as the height of human felicity'.

CHAPTER SEVEN

PANORAMA

The War in the Air

To relate the action of aircraft in the military sphere is not possible, for it formed a thread running through and vitally influencing the whole course of operations, rather than a separate strategic feature. But a brief outline of the evolution of aircraft action in the field may help to complete the strategic picture. Military appreciation of air values was a slow growth, and the advocates of aircraft had an uphill struggle for recognition. Until the Italians used aircraft extensively against the Turks in Tripoli, 1911–12, general military opinion was aptly represented by General Foch's comment when watching the *Circuit de l'Est* – 'That is good sport but for the Army the aeroplane is worthless.' Even in 1914 the proportion of military aircraft was puny, and their application more limited than with the Italians two years earlier.

In the first month of the war visual reconnaissance was the only role allotted and no provision was made for air combat or bombing. For the inadequacy of its air service and lack of information the German Army paid a heavy price during the invasion of France. But the Royal Flying Corps, although bringing only sixty-three machines across the Channel, twice rendered invaluable service. One reconnaissance unmasked the initial attempt to outflank the British Army at Mons, and another discovered Kluck's historic swerve towards the Marne.

In September the sphere of air cooperation was enlarged to embrace observation of targets for the artillery, communication being at first by coloured lights and eventually by wireless telegraphy. In September also, photography from the air was tried, but its potential value was not recognized by General Headquarters until 1915. By March a special aeroplane camera was supplied, and air photography henceforth developed continuously, although long handicapped by dependence on captured German lenses for the large-scale cameras. A fresh form of cooperation was tried in 1915, although not fully applied until 1916. This was the contact patrol, whereby commanders were informed of the situation of their own infantry during battle, and of threatened counter-attacks by the enemy.

The pursuit of this air cooperation by both sides simultaneously, as well as the desire to baffle the enemy's observation, had naturally led to air fighting, and this, in turn, to a struggle for supremacy in the air. Rifles and pistols were the only weapons available at the outset, so that air combat bore the appearance of an exhilarating and uncertain new form of game-shooting. Soon, however, light machine guns were fitted, although the fighting role was mainly restricted to 'pusher' type aeroplanes, as, on a tractor type, the propeller hindered fire in a forward direction. In May, 1915, the Germans produced a new and fast Fokker fighting machine equipped with an interruptor gear which enabled the gun to fire through the orbit of the revolving propeller without risk of hitting the blades. The Fokkers inflicted heavy losses amongst the British machines, and, for a time, gained air superiority for the Germans.

The Allies replied to this menace not only by new machines but by new methods, settled in joint conference. The 'fighters' were concentrated in special squadrons, instead of being distributed among all, and these squadrons were to seek out their opponents behind the opposing front, thus enabling their own reconnaissance and artillery machines to work undisturbed. This method of offensive patrols was successfully tried by the French at Verdun in February, 1916, and developed by the British on the Somme, where for some weeks the Germans were almost driven out of the air. The offensive was also extended to the enemy's aerodromes – an extension which recalled the historic naval maxim that the enemy's coasts were the frontiers of Britain. Already, in October, 1914, British naval aircraft operating on the Belgian coast had raided the Zeppelin sheds at Dusseldorf and Cologne, destroying one airship; another was destroyed next month in a raid from Belfort on Friedrichshafen.

Although the raids on aerodromes from 1916 onwards did not often succeed in inflicting serious material damage, they had a marked moral effect, for once pilots were safely back in their own aerodrome they were apt to feel that their share of risk was complete. An unforeseen addition was all the worse to bear when the nerve-tension had been relaxed, and when they were taken at a disadvantage on the ground.

The Allied air supremacy of 1916 was not long maintained. The Germans challenged it with improved types of single-seater fighting machines and with the so-called 'circus' system whereby special fighting squadrons were formed – under a picked leader who picked his own pilots – and were successively switched to any part of the front where the higher command desired air superiority to be gained. The most famous of these 'circuses' were those of Boelcke and Baron von Richthofen.

By their superior strategy the Germans regained the upper hand early in 1917, although the total British fighting machines outnumbered theirs by three to one. And the British tragically helped to swell the enemy's 'bag' by sending out swarms of partially trained young pilots from England, under pressure from GHQ. But the Allies soon retorted with fresh machines and gradually, if expensively, won back a superiority in the air which was never lost again – although never so marked as in the summer of 1916. Because of the three-dimensional conditions of air warfare, a command of the air could never be attained in the sense that a command of the sea was possible, and the object became a superiority, which should ensure a local and temporary command of the air over a static front when needed.

The year 1917 was marked also by an increasing development of the method of fighting and flying in formation, which tended to replace the Homeric combats of individual champions – whose mounting score of victims had been followed with the excitement that formerly awaited the return of a Red Indian scalping expedition or the news of a Test Match. Henceforth, knight-errantry yielded to tactics and air fighting gradually assumed the more developed forms of warfare, although carried out on a different plane. By the end of the war an attack was often delivered by formations of fifty or sixty machines which manoeuvred – the actual squadrons compact – with the aim of breaking up the enemy's formation.

Thus they became cavalry of the air, and the resemblance was heightened by another new form of air action, used with great effect in the later stages of the war. This was the attack on ground troops. So long as the rival armies were firmly embedded in trenches, air attack had small scope, although occasionally it came to the relief of hard-pressed packets of infantry. But when the British front broke in March, 1918, all the available fighter squadrons, French as well as British, were concentrated to strike at the advancing enemy. Their overhead counter-attacks during this crisis were an important factor in stemming the German onrush, and one that has been inadequately recognized by military historians. Still greater opportunities came when the enemy tide ebbed in the autumn. After the breaking of the Bulgarian, Turkish, and Austrian fronts alike, air attacks on the retreating columns both hastened and completed the break-up of the enemy armies.

Air attacks on the communications, supply depots, ammunition dumps, and billets of the armies, had been developed much earlier. The battle of Neuve Chapelle in March, 1915, marked the first organized attempt to prevent the arrival of enemy reinforcements, and at Loos in September, a more extended bombing plan was applied against the German railways. Results were small, however, owing to lack of experience, deficiency of equipment, and the want of machines to maintain the intensive bombardment essential for causing an effective stoppage. If a railway was damaged before the battle it could be repaired in time for the passage of reinforcements; and, unless repairs were hindered by continuous bombing, supplies and ammunition would reach the enemy troops before they began to run short. The first lesson was learnt and applied in the later battles of the war, when the bombing of communications played a regular part, but the second lesson was never fully applied owing to lack of bombing aircraft. The very eagerness with which the armies had eventually embraced aircraft as immediately auxiliaries – for reconnaissance, artillery observation, and the protection of these duties – limited the supply of aircraft for roles of indirect cooperation, and curtailed their exploitation of the bombing weapon.

Moreover, their very concentration on these auxiliaries blinded the armies to the greater possibilities of crippling their opponents by hunger. The Germans, especially, neglected opportunities of inflicting decisive injury – as a senior staff officer of the British Second Army revealed a few years ago. This army received the bulk of its supplies from Calais and Boulogne, and in front of these bases was held only three days' reserves of food and ammunition, apart from three days' supplies with the fighting troops. To serve the front there were two double lines and one single; to meet the normal needs of the troops seventy-one trains a day were needed – three-quarters of the total capacity of the three lines. With this narrow margin of safety, the blocking of one line would have sufficed to dislocate the whole system, while the blocking of more than one line would have brought a catastrophe. To cause such a block would have been the easier because outside Calais there was a junction of two of the lines, and near St Omer two converged. Moreover, a block at Arques, near St Omer, would even have cut off the troops from the three days' reserves, which lay in depots farther back along the two lines which converged at this point. It is not difficult to picture the situation which would have arisen if an effective and sustained bombing attack had been launched in April,

1918, to coincide with the German Army's attack, when this area was congested with British and French troops who were trying to dam the breach in the front.

The Allied commanders, also, on the Western Front, were unwilling to spare sufficient aircraft for a real test of the effect of bombing communications. Yet, there was a significant hint of its potency, when on July 16, 1918, the bombing of an ammunition train at Thionville station stopped all traffic along this important section of the German communications for forty-eight hours – the forty-eight hours before the Allied counterstroke on the Marne which turned the tide of the war.

At sea, the Germans, relying on their submarines, fortunately failed to explore the possibilities of air attacks on merchant shipping, or on the ports where that shipping had to unload its freight. And the Allies could not, as their enemy had no shipping in use. There was one fleeting glimpse of such action; as early as August 12th, 1915, a British seaplane, launched from a seaplane carrier near the Dardanelles, gained the distinction of being the first to torpedo a ship. The most valuable service rendered by naval aircraft during the war was in anti-submarine patrolling and escorting convoys – a purely protective role.

Yet seven months before the battle of Jutland, Commodore Sueter of the Naval Air Service had begged the Admiralty to sanction the construction of 200 torpedo-carrying aircraft. His persistence merely led to his removal – to the Adriatic. The year after Jutland, the new Commander-in-Chief of the Grand Fleet asked for that very number to be produced as early as possible. It was too late. The unwanted offspring of Sueter's vision might conceivably have made that one ineffective naval battle decisive. Moreover, a further chance had been forfeited through the oversight by which the *Campania*, a large aircraft carrier, was left behind when the Grand Fleet sailed from Scapa Flow.

It was the Naval Air Service, however, which first proposed, and attempted, to strike at the sources of the enemy's power to make war – his industrial centres. The way was blocked by the narrow view of the Army Command. The idea nevertheless made headway, and in October 1916 was reinforced by the arguments of Colonel Barès, of the French air service, on a visit to London. The Admiralty representative on the Air Board then suggested that the Navy should keep a force of 200 bombers in France for this purpose. But, according to the Official History, the proposal 'drew a strong letter of protest from Sir Douglas Haig ... He stated that the views attributed to Colonel Barès were unsound in theory and should not be accepted in practice'. Haig's opposition killed the scheme – which might have checked the stream of shells that were being hurled at his troops. In 1917, out of fifty air squadrons in France, only two were for bombing, and those were confined to local targets.

Not until late in the war was there any attempt on the Allied side to attack the enemy's 'home' front save for spasmodic raids by a handful of British naval aircraft, as well as by the French. Nor, in the light of human nature, was independent air action likely to be developed so long as this new weapon was handled by and divided between the land and sea forces. The essential fusion between the two parts was delayed until April, 1918, when the Royal Air Force was created. As a sequel, the Independent Air Force was formed in June, and placed under Trenchard, who had been the dynamic leader of the military air arm in France, if also, ironically, a determined opponent of independent air action. In the few months that remained, the repeated and expanding raids of the new force accelerated the moral disintegration of Germany, and, by their moral effect at least hampered the production of munitions in the Rhineland. Even so, the significance of this force was more in promise than fulfilment, for it was barely a quarter of its intended strength when the Armistice came. Similarly, the effect of the German air raids on England should be assessed in the light of the fact that the largest raid was carried out by less than forty bombers.

What might have been achieved is suggested by the fact that the seven principal munition centres in the Ruhr, as well as those in the Rhineland, were all within air range of the British front. Essen (173 miles), Germany's main arsenal, was only as far as the German machines flew in bombing London from their base near Ghent. Again, one factory at Hagen (175 miles) produced two-thirds of the German submarine accumulators. Two of the largest chemical factories were less than 100 miles from the Allied front. Yet this immense opportunity of crippling the munition supply of the German armies was sacrificed in favour of air fighting over the trench front – sacrificed, in fact, on the 'battle' altar of Clausewitz-in-the-air. Even when the Independent Air Force was at last formed, in face of vehement opposition from GHQ, its strength was curtailed to a mere hundred machines (about 2 per cent of Britain's total Air Force) and more than half its raids were directed against tactical, instead of industrial targets. Apart from what was then achieved, a sidelight on its wider indirect effect is shed by the fact that, in the month of August alone, one shell factory, which was never even bombed, received fifty-three false alarms and suffered an output deficit of 3,000 tons. There is also a paradoxical reflection on the GHQ doctrine of concentration on the battlefront in the fact that the menace of these raids drew off no less than twenty German squadrons from the front – three or four times as many machines as were engaged in them!

CHAPTER EIGHT

1918 – The Break

The middle years of the World War had been, in a military sense, a tussle between a lean Hercules and a bulky Cerberus. The Germanic Alliance was weaker in numbers but directed by a single head, the Entente stronger in numbers but with too many heads. Owing to their own excessive losses, diffusion of effort and the collapse of Russia, the Entente at the end of 1917 were faced with the grim fact that the numerical balance had been reversed, and months must elapse before the prospective stream of America's new divisions should tilt the scales once more in their favour. The emergency paved the way for the creation of a unified command but it still needed disaster to bring it into being.

At the conference at Rapallo in November, the formation of a Supreme War Council was decided upon, to be composed of the principal ministers of the Allies, with military representatives, and to sit permanently at Versailles. If a fundamental defect was that it merely substituted a formal for an informal committee, a further flaw was that the military representatives had no executive status. In the economic sphere, where deliberation rather than instant action was necessary, it led to a real improvement in the combination of shipping, food and munition resources. Militarily, it was futile, for it set up a dual advisership – the Versailles representatives on the one hand and the chiefs of the national General Staffs on the other. Yet it is fair to add that this 'dead end' was due to a British obstruction.

Both the Americans and the French desired to give this committee executive power and an executive head, and Pétain logically supported the proposal, which came from Colonel House and General Bliss. But the fundamental offset to its wisdom was that it eliminated the essential control of strategy by the statesman, while the suggested composition of the council repeated the error of the Nivelle era. For it was to consist of the national Commanders-in-Chief and Chiefs of Staff, and thus whichever member was chosen as President would have his freedom of judgement and execution hampered by his responsibility to and for his own national army. Moreover, in fulfilment, the proposal would mean that the council would have a French chief – as the French realized when they supported, and the British when they opposed, the proposal. In rejecting it Lloyd George was guided not only by a wise objection to a purely military council but by his feeling that British opinion was not ripe for it, and that Haig's resistance to another Nivelle solution would be supported by the public at home. Moreover, the suggested inclusion of the Chiefs of Staff introduced a personal complication, for the last thing that Lloyd George desired was to strengthen the influence of Sir William Robertson upon the conduct of the war. Rather was he hoping to sidetrack Robertson, whom he held responsible for the futile and costly strategy of 1917, in favour of Sir Henry Wilson, his nominee for the Versailles committee. And while he sought to make Versailles independent of the narrow purview of the British General Staff, Clemenceau was equally intent to make it merely a microphone for the French General Staff, to amplify its 'voice'.

In default of agreement the military representatives – now Generals Weygand, Wilson, Bliss, and Cadorna – were merely technical advisers. But as the menace of the German attack grew closer, and with it the need for common action, this advisory body was converted into a military executive committee to handle an inter-Allied general reserve, a fresh compromise which set up a dual control – the Commanders-in-Chief and the Versailles committee. Only an enlargement of mind and goodwill could make it workable.

Time was too short. Since early in November the stream of German troop trains from the Eastern to the Western Front had been steadily swelling. When the 1917 campaign opened, there had been a proportion of nearly three Allies to two Germans – actually in March 178 British, French and Belgian divisions against 129 German divisions. Now the Germans had a slight advantage, with the likelihood of augmenting it. But the Allied statesmen, recalling how often their own offensive had failed with equal or greater superiority of force, were naturally slow to appreciate the gravity of the menace or to respond to the sudden fall in the temperature of military opinion. Nor could they agree to draw reinforcements from the other fronts.

The Italians strove against any withdrawal of the Allied contingents from their front, and the French opposed any reduction of the Salonika force. Lloyd George urged an effort to complete the success in Palestine; this was sanctioned on the understanding that no reinforcements went there from France, though it also meant that none came from there to France. Meantime, the German strength had increased to 177 divisions by the end of January, and fifteen more in March. The Allied strength, by the dispatch of divisions to Italy and the breaking up of others owing to the French shortage of drafts had fallen to the equivalent of 173 – counting as double the four and a half large-size American divisions which had arrived. For the French and British had been constrained to follow the Germans in reducing their divisions from twelve to nine battalions each.

Internal friction among the Allies increased their handicap. In part it was due to the difficulties of a fair settlement as to the length of front which each should hold. In the 1917 campaign the British, bearing the burden of the offensive, had been in charge of barely 100 miles of line, while the French, on the defensive, had held 325 miles. At the close of the campaign Haig had come to an agreement with Pétain that he would extend his line to Barisis, just south of the Oise, which made a total of 125 miles. In view of his change to a defensive attitude, the extension can hardly be considered exacting, although his heavy losses made it a greater strain than it would have been on the 1917 basis of strength. But before this extension was complete, Clemenceau, the new French Premier, intervened with a demand that the British should take over an additional thirty miles, as far as Berry-au-Bac. Clemenceau threatened to resign if this demand were not met, but eventually agreed to submit the case to the Versailles committee, which proposed a compromise whereby the British should take over approximately half the distance in dispute. Thereupon Haig threatened to resign; this threat threw the Supreme War Council and its advisory committee into the melting-pot from which the executive committee emerged. Meantime Haig went direct to Pétain and reached a settlement by which he was merely to complete his extension to Barisis, according to the original agreement. This was a noteworthy concession on Pétain's part, which did honour to his spirit of helpfulness. And the Supreme War Council on February 2nd accepted this private settlement between the two Commanders-in-Chief, wisely swallowing the affront to its own dignity. It is astonishing, in view of this fact, that the legend should still persist that Haig was forced by the 'politicians' to extend his line against his will, and likewise the argument that such extension was the cause of the subsequent breakthrough.

The just proportion between the respective fronts is hardly less difficult to determine now, in retrospect, than it was to agree upon them. With ninety-nine divisions the French had to hold 300 miles, while the British with fifty-eight divisions, of somewhat greater rifle strength, took charge of 125 miles – after the extension to Barisis. Of the French line, however, the half from St Mihiel eastwards was of secondary importance. If, even so, the French had cause for complaint on any mileage basis, the British could fairly claim that they had more vital objectives to cover, less room to fall back, and a higher proportion of the enemy already on their front. But the French, in turn, could point to the fact that the main mass of the German reserves was so placed that it might intervene on either front. To weigh a question compounded of such diverse elements required a strategic mind of the purest scientific detachment, whereas it had to be resolved by men whose determined character and strong sense of nationality made it difficult for them to see the other man's point of view. Lloyd George was an exception, but to his endowment with a wider outlook was linked a tendency to be impatient with the point of view of his own men, especially when this seemed to him parochial or obstructive.

Disagreement between him and Sir William Robertson, his official military adviser, had increased throughout 1917, Robertson being suspicious of political interference with military plans and of Lloyd George's unorthodox ideas, while Lloyd George felt that Robertson's sole idea in strategy was to support Haig blindly and frustrate any alternative schemes. The results of this blank-cheque policy at Passchendaele made the Prime Minister more anxious to provide himself with alternative advice, a desire that had influenced him in setting up the Supreme Council with its military committee, and in appointing to it Sir Henry Wilson, whom he regarded as a soldier of more sympathetic and larger outlook. But when the new organ was converted into an executive committee, Robertson insisted that he, as Chief of the Imperial General Staff, should be the British military member. The Prime Minister objected that the combination of the two posts in one man would vitiate the whole principle, maintaining the sectional instead of the detached view. Robertson's stand brought the long-growing dissension to a climax. The Prime Minister went part of the way to meet him by appointing him the Versailles representative, while Wilson was to become Chief of the Imperial General Staff at home with reduced functions. Sprung on Robertson as a surprise, this proposal provoked his refusal. After several days of discussion and domestic crisis, Robertson was offered his former post on the new terms. His refusal to accept them produced his enforced resignation, and relegation to a home command. Wilson succeeded him, and Rawlinson was appointed to Versailles. Such conflicts of view, if unavoidable in human nature and in an alliance, weakened the common front. And as soon as one difficulty was overcome, other sources of dissension came to the fore.

The prolonged waste of soldiers' lives in the swamps beyond Ypres had led Lloyd George and his Cabinet to withhold reinforcements for fear of encouraging fresh squandering. This undoubtedly weakened Haig's initial power of resistance to the German onslaught, yet it is just to point out that it was weakened more – in quality as well as quantity – by the 400,000 British casualties suffered in the offensive of the later part of 1917. Moreover, we should not forget that the Government had the heavy responsibility of being the trustee for the lives of the nation. The real ground of criticism is that it was not strong enough to make a change in, or place a check upon, a command which it did not trust, while supplying the reinforcements necessary for defence. And for this lack of moral strength the public must share the blame, for they had already shown themselves too easily swayed by clamour against political interference with the generals, and too prone to believe that the politician is invariably wrong on such occasions. The civilian public, indeed, is apt to trust soldiers too little in peace, and sometimes too much in war.

These political handicaps, and the accompanying tendency of politicians to work deviously towards what they dare not demand openly, were also seen in the project for a unified command. The Prime Minister, indeed, had gone so far in November as to disclaim faith in his own long-sought cure. Instead he sought a palliative in the inter-Allied executive committee, under Foch's chairmanship, which should control a common reserve of thirty divisions – one-seventh of the total forces. This scheme was decisively annulled by Haig, who, when called on by Foch for his contribution of nine divisions, replied that he could spare none. He preferred to make an arrangement with Pétain for mutual support.

When the test came, a week later, this broke down, and Haig then took a foremost part in hastening and facilitating the appointment of a generalissimo, which he had formerly opposed. His change of attitude had simply an immediate purpose – 'The whole and sole object is to override Pétain and get the French to send reinforcements to prevent the British and French armies being separated.' (Charteris.)

For the actual breakdown the blame has been commonly thrown upon the French, and there is no question that Haig understood from Pétain on March 24th that if the Germans continued their rapid progress the French reserves would have to be used to cover Paris. But in fairness it is essential to add that, whereas the original compact had only pledged the aid of some six French divisions, Pétain actually sent nine by March 24th, and twenty-one (including four of cavalry) by March 26th. If these reinforcements were perhaps slower coming into action than in dispatch, it does not affect the fact that the original pledge was amply exceeded. Thus the fundamental fault would seem to lie in trusting to an arrangement for such slender support by either Ally.

The German Plan. On the German side the submarine panacea for victory had been replaced by a military panacea, and hopes were perhaps exaggerated by the unexpected collapse of Russia. But although Ludendorff promised victory in the field, he did not disguise the fact that a western offensive would be a far harder task than the conquests in the east. He realized also that it would be a race between the effect of Germany's blow and the arrival of American reinforcements, although he hoped to win the race. To secure the rear of his offensive, a definite peace was wrung from the Bolshevik Government of Russia by a military demonstration, and also forced on Rumania. And to secure, if possible, the economic base of his offensive the Ukraine was occupied for its wheat supplies, with little resistance except from Czechoslovak troops who had formerly been taken prisoners from the Austrian Army.

Ludendorff's next problem was to decide his first point of attack. The sector between Arras and St Quentin was chosen, on the western face of the great salient formed by the German front in France. The choice was governed by tactical reasons – this sector was the enemy's weakest point and the ground offered fewer difficulties than elsewhere – although Ludendorff had in mind the possibility of separating the Allied armies and driving the British back against the Channel coast, where they would be too closely penned in to evade his blows. From the experience of the vain Allied attacks Ludendorff had drawn the deduction that 'tactics had to be considered before purely strategical objects which it is futile to pursue unless tactical success is possible'. Hence he formulated a strategical plan based on the new, or resurrected, principle of taking the tactical line of least resistance. Presumably he hoped by firm control to guide these tactical movements to a strategic destination. If so, he failed.

Where did the fault lie? The general view at the end of the war was that the tactical bias had led Ludendorff to change direction and dissipate his strength. That if the Franco-British Command had previously erred by aiming at the strategically correct target without enough attention to the tactical difficulties the German Command had followed it with an equal if opposite error by concentrating on tactical success at the expense of the strategical goal. But a closer examination of the German documents since available, and of Ludendorff's own orders and instructions, throws a different light on the question. It would seem, indeed, that the real fault was that Ludendorff failed to carry out in practice the new principle he had adopted in theory; that he either did not grasp, or shrank from, the full implication of this new theory of strategy. For in fact he dissipated too large a part of his reserves in trying to redeem tactical failures and hesitated too long over the decision to exploit his tactical successes. Ludendorff's strategy in the east had been so forceful and so far-sighted that his indecision and shortsight in the west is difficult to explain. Perhaps he himself was feeling the strain of directing so many vast operations; perhaps it was that he missed the strategical insight and balanced view of Hoffmann who, after being at his side throughout the 1914–16 campaigns, had stayed in the east when Ludendorff went to the Supreme Command. The modern vice of seniority prevented Germany making the fullest use of the man who perhaps approached nearer to military genius than any other general of the war.

In any case the campaign leaves the impression that Ludendorff had neither his former clearness as to the goal, nor the same grip on the changing situations. But in the organization of the attacks his powers were at their highest level. Surprise was to be the key which should open a gate in the long-locked front. The most thorough arrangements were made for concealing and for exploiting the attacks, and the surprise effect of the short but intense bombardment was increased by lavish use of gas and smoke shell. Further, while Ludendorff had settled to strike first on the Somme sector, to which blow the code name 'Michael' was given, he also began preparations for successive attacks at other points, which besides being in readiness for the future helped to mystify the enemy. Two were on the British front and one on the French – 'St George I' against the Lys sector, 'St George II' against the Ypres sector, and 'Blücher' in Champagne.

The 'Michael' attack was to be made by the German Seventeenth, Second, and Eighteenth Armies (sixty-three divisions in all) on the forty-three-mile front Arras–St Quentin–La Fère, but its main force was intended to be exerted north of the Somme, and, after breaking through, the Seventeenth and Second Armies were to wheel north-west and press the British army against the coast, while the river and the Eighteenth Army guarded their flank.

The assault was launched on March 21st, and the surprise was greatly helped by an early morning mist. But while the thrust broke through completely south of the Somme, where the defence – but also the attacking force – was thinnest, it was held up near Arras, a check which reacted on all the attack north of the river. Ludendorff, violating his new principle, spent the following days in trying to revive his attack against the strong, and strongly held bastion of Arras, maintaining this direction as his principal line of effort. Meantime he kept a tight rein on the Eighteenth Army which was advancing in the south without serious check from its opponents. As late as March 26th he issued orders which restrained it from crossing the Avre and tied it to the pace of its neighbour, the Second, which in turn was held back by the very limited success of the Seventeenth Army near Arras. Thus we see that in reality Ludendorff was bent on breaking the British army by breaking down its strongest sector of resistance in a direct assault. And because of this obsession he failed, until too late, to throw the weight of his reserves along the line of least resistance south of the Somme. The intended wheel to the north-west might have come to pass if it had been made after passing the flank, and thus being directed against the rear, of the Arras bastion. On March 26th the attack north of the Somme (by the left wing of the Seventeenth Army and the right of the Second Army) was visibly weakening as the price of its hard-earned gains. South of the Somme the left of the Second Army reached, and was now to be embarrassed by, the desert of the old Somme battlefields – a brake on progress and supply. The Eighteenth Army alone was advancing with unslackened impetus.

This situation led Ludendorff to adopt a new plan, but without relinquishing his old. He ordered for March 28th a fresh and direct attack on the high ground near Arras – by the right of the Seventeenth Army, to be followed by a Sixth Army attack just to the north between Vimy and La Bassée. But the promising situation south of the Somme led him to indicate Amiens as an additional main objective. Even so, he restrained the Eighteenth Army from pushing on to turn the flank of the Amiens defences without further orders! On March 28th the fresh Arras attack was launched, unshielded by mist or surprise, and failed completely in face of the well-prepared resistance of Byng's Third Army. Only then did Ludendorff abandon his original idea and direct his main effort, and some of his remaining reserves, towards Amiens. But meantime he ordered the Eighteenth Army to mark time for two days. When the attack was renewed it made little progress in face of a resistance that had been afforded time to harden, and Ludendorff, rather than be drawn into an attrition struggle, suspended the attempt to reach Amiens.

He had, however, missed vital arteries and decisive results by the narrowest of margins. By March 27th the advance had penetrated nearly forty miles and reached Montdidier, cutting one railway to Paris; by March 30th the German flood was almost lapping the outworks of Amiens. Eighty thousand prisoners and 975 guns had been taken. Once the crust was broken, the very elaboration of the methods of communication built up during three years of static warfare caused the greater flux behind the front. The extent of the retreat was primarily the measure of the loss of control by the British commanders.

Disaster had driven the Allies to an overdue step, and on Haig's appeal and Lord Milner's intervention Foch had been appointed on March 26th to 'coordinate' the operations of the Allied armies. In this hour of crisis, Foch's decisive manner and exuberant promises created confidence. Yet, in actual fact, his appointment made little difference to the flow of reinforcements. And although on April 14th he secured the title of Commander-in-Chief of the Allied armies, it gave him no real power of command. By this time a fresh German menace had developed – though not intended as such.

With a large part of his reserves holding the vast bulge south of the Somme, Ludendorff turned, if without much confidence and merely as a diversion, to release, on April 9th, his 'St George I' attack. Its astonishing early success against a weakened front led him to convert it bit by bit into a major effort. The British were desperately close to the sea, but their resistance stopped the German tide, after a ten-mile invasion, just short of the important railway junction of Hazebrouck, and an attempt to widen the front towards Ypres was nullified by Haig swinging his line back just before and by the gradual arrival of French reinforcements. Haig complained strongly that Foch was too slow in sending French reserves northwards, but the event justified Foch's reluctance to commit himself thither and his seeming excess of optimism in declaring that the danger was past. Ludendorff had doled out reserves sparingly, usually too late and too few for real success; so apprehensive that his new bulge would become another sack, that after the capture of Kemmel Hill, when opportunity opened its arms, he stopped the exploitation for fear of a counterstroke.

Thus Ludendorff had fallen short of strategic results; on the other hand he could claim huge tactical successes – the British casualties were over 300,000. The British Army had been badly mauled; and although fresh drafts to the number of 140,000 were hurried out from England and divisions brought back from Italy, Salonika and Palestine, months must elapse before it could recover its offensive power. Ten British divisions had to be broken up temporarily, while the German strength had now mounted to 208, of which eighty were back in reserve. A restoration of the balance, however, was now in sight. A dozen American divisions had arrived in France and, responding to the call, great efforts were being made to swell the stream. At the crisis in March, Pershing, the American Commander-in-Chief, even relaxed his inflexible opposition to partial or premature use of the American troops so far as to declare that they were at Foch's disposal for use wherever required. It was an inspiring gesture – although in practice he continued to keep a tight hold on his troops and, with rare exceptions, only allowed them to take over parts of the front as complete divisions.

For Germany the sands were running out. Realizing this, Ludendorff launched his 'Blücher' attack between Soissons and Reims, on May 27th. Falling by surprise with twenty-two divisions against eleven, it swept over the Aisne and reached the Marne on May 30th, where its impetus died away. This time the German superiority of force had not been so pronounced as before nor so well aided by nature's atmospheric cloak. It would seem that the extent of the opening success was due in part to the strategic surprise – the greater unexpectedness of the time and place of the blow – and in part to the folly of the local army command in insisting on the long-exploded and obsolete method of massing the defenders in the forward positions – there to be compressed cannon-fodder for the Germans' massed artillery.

But once again Ludendorff had obtained a measure of success for which he was neither prepared nor desirous. The surpriser was himself surprised. The attack had been conceived merely as a diversion, to attract the Allied reserves thither preparatory to a final and decisive blow at the British front in Flanders. But its opening success attracted thither too large, yet not large enough, a proportion of the German reserves. Blocked frontally by the river, an attempt was made to push west, but it failed in face of Allied resistance – notable for the appearance of American divisions at Château-Thierry, where they gallantly counter-attacked.

Ludendorff had now created two huge bulges, and another smaller one, in the Allied front. His next attempt was to pinch out the Compiègne 'tongue' which lay between the Amiens and Marne bulges. But this time there was no surprise, and the blow on the west side of the 'tongue', June 9th, was too late to coincide with the pressure on the east. A month's pause followed.

Ludendorff, though anxious to strike his long-cherished decisive blow against the British in Belgium, considered that their reserves here were still too strong, and so again decided to choose the line of least tactical resistance, hoping that a heavy blow in the south would draw off the British reserves. He had failed to pinch out the Compiègne 'tongue' on the west of his Marne salient; he was now about to attempt the same method on the east, by attacking on either side of Reims. But he needed an interval for rest and preparation, and the delay was fatal, giving the British and French time to recuperate, and the Americans to gather strength. The British divisions previously broken up had now been reconstituted, and as a result of an urgent appeal made to President Wilson in the crisis of March, and the provision of extra shipping, American troops had been arriving at the rate of 300,000 a month since the end of April. By mid-July seven American divisions were ready to help in resisting the next, and final, German stroke. Five more were being acclimatized to front-line conditions away on the Alsace-Lorraine sector, and five with the British, while another four were assembled in the American training area.

The tactical success of his own blows had been Ludendorff's undoing. Yielding too late to their influence, he had then pressed each too far and too long, so using up his own reserves and causing an undue interval between each blow. He had driven in three great wedges, but none had penetrated far enough to sever a vital artery, and this strategic failure left the Germans with an indented front which invited flanking counterstrokes.

The Turning of the Tide. On July 15th Ludendorff launched his new attack, but its coming was no secret. East of Reims it was foiled by an elastic defence, and west of Reims the German penetration across the Marne merely enmeshed them more deeply to their downfall – for on July 18th Foch launched a long-prepared stroke against the other flank of the Marne salient. Here Pétain, who directed the operation, turned the key which Ludendorff lacked, using masses of light tanks to lead a surprise attack on the Cambrai method. The Germans managed to hold the gates of the salient open long enough to draw back their forces into safety and straighten their line; but their reserves were depleted, Ludendorff was forced (on the 20th) to postpone, if not yet to abandon, the offensive in Flanders, and the initiative definitely and finally passed to the Allies.

Foch's first concern was to keep it, by giving the enemy no rest while his own reserves were accumulating. To this end he arranged with Haig, Pétain and Pershing for a series of local offensives, aimed to free the lateral railway communications and to improve the position of the front ready for further operations. To Haig he proposed an attack in the Lys sector, but Haig suggested instead the Somme area as more suitable. Rawlinson, commanding the British Fourth Army in front of Amiens, had already submitted to Haig a plan for a large surprise attack there, and Foch agreed to this in place of his own proposal. He also placed under Haig the French First Army (Debeney) to extend the attack to the south. Rawlinson's army was doubled, and by skilful precautions the enemy were kept in the dark until, on August 8th, the attack was delivered – with 456 tanks. The blow had the maximum shock of surprise, and south of the Somme the troops of the Australian and Canadian Corps rapidly overran and overwhelmed the German forward divisions. By August 12th when the advance came to a halt through reaching the tangled wilderness of the old 1916 battlefields, if also through lack of reserves, the Fourth Army had taken 21,000 prisoners at a cost of only 20,000 casualties. Great, if not fully exploited, as a material, it was far greater as a moral success.

Ludendorff has said: 'August 8th was the black day of the German army in the history of the war ... It put the decline of our fighting power beyond all doubt ... The war must be ended.' He informed the Emperor and the political chiefs that peace negotiations ought to be opened before the situation became worse, as it must. The conclusions reached at a Crown Council held at Spa were that 'we can no longer hope to break the war-will of our enemies by military operations', and 'the object of our strategy must be to paralyse the enemy's war-will gradually by a strategic defensive'. In other words the German Command had abandoned hope of victory or even holding their gains, and hoped only to avoid surrender – an insecure moral foundation.

On August 10th Foch issued fresh *directives* for the preparation of an 'advance' by the British Third Army 'in the general direction of Bapaume and Péronne'. Meantime he wished Haig to continue the Fourth Army's frontal pressure, but Haig demurred to it as a vain waste of life and gained his point. Economy of force was henceforth to be added to the advantages of the new strategy now evolved. Thus the momentum of the Fourth Army had hardly waned before the Third Army moved. From then on Foch beat a tattoo on the German front, a series of rapid blows at different points, each broken off as soon as its initial impetus waned, each so aimed as to pave the way for the next, and all close enough in time and space to react on each other. Thus Ludendorff's power of switching reserves to threatened spots was restricted, as his balance of reserves was drained.

On August 10th the French Third Army had struck to the south; then on August 17th the French Tenth Army still farther south; next on August 21st the British Third Army, followed by the British First

Army on August 26th. Ludendorff's order to the troops holding the Lys salient to retire was hastened in execution by the attacks of the re-formed British Fifth Army, and by the first week in September the Germans were back on their original starting line – the strong defences of the Hindenburg Line. And on September 12th Pershing completed the series of preliminary operations by erasing the St Mihiel salient – the first feat of the Americans as an independent army. Pershing had originally intended to make this a stepping stone to an advance towards the Briey coalfields and the eastern end of the Germans' main lateral railway near Metz, but the project was abandoned for reasons that will be referred to later. Thus no exploitation of the success was attempted.

The clear evidence of the Germans' decline and Haig's assurance that he would break the Hindenburg Line where the German reserves were thickest, persuaded Foch to seek victory that autumn instead of postponing the attempt until 1919. All the Allied armies in the west were to combine in a simultaneous offensive.

The Collapse of Bulgaria. Before this attack developed, an event occurred in the Balkans which, in the words of Ludendorff, 'sealed the fate of the Quadruple Alliance'. He had still hoped to hold fast in his strong lines in the west, falling back gradually to fresh lines if necessary, and with his strategic flanks in Macedonia and Italy covered, while the German Government was negotiating for a favourable peace. At the same time there was alarm as to the moral effect of the Western Front defeats on the German people, their will-power already undermined by shortage of food, and perhaps also by propaganda.

But on September 15th the Allied armies in Salonika attacked the Bulgarian front, which crumbled in a few days. Guillaumat, who had succeeded Sarrail in December 1917, had prepared the plan for an offensive; when recalled to France in the crisis of June as Governor of Paris (and potential successor to Pétain) he won over the Allied Governments to consent to the attempt. His successor in Salonika, Franchet d'Esperey, concentrated a Franco-Serb striking force, under Michich, on the Sokol–Dobropolye sector, west of the Vardar, where the Bulgarians trusted to the strength of the mountain ridges and were weak in numbers. On September 15th Michich attacked and by the night of the 17th the Serbs had penetrated twenty miles deep, while the breach had been expanded to a width of twenty-five miles. On the 18th the British attack on the Doiran front was a tactical failure, but it at least helped to pin the enemy's reserves. Meantime the whole of the enemy's front west of the Vardar had collapsed under the converging pressure of the Serbs and French, whose pursuit drove on towards

Uskub. And on the 21st the Bulgarian forces east of the Vardar began to fall back in turn. This gave the British aircraft an opportunity, and by bombing the narrow Kosturino Pass they 'largely contributed, on that side, to turn the Bulgarian retreat into a disorderly flight'. With their army split into two parts the Bulgarians, already tired of the war, sought an armistice, which was signed on September 29th. Franchet d'Esperey's achievement not only severed the first root of the Central Alliance, but opened the way to an advance on Austria's rear.

The First Peace Note. The capitulation of Bulgaria convinced Ludendorff that it was necessary to take a decisive step towards securing peace. While he was scraping together a paltry half-dozen divisions to form a new front in Serbia, and arranging a meeting with the political chiefs, Foch's grand assaults fell on the western defences, September 26th–28th, and the line threatened to crack.

The German Supreme Command lost its nerve – only for a matter of days, but that was sufficient, and recovery too late. On the afternoon of September 29th Ludendorff was studying the problem in his room at the Hotel Britannique at Spa – an ominously named choice of headquarters! Examination only seemed to make it more insoluble, and in a rising outburst of fear and passion he bemoaned his troubles – especially his lack of tanks – and berated all those whom he considered as having thwarted his efforts – the jealous staffs, the defeatist Reichstag, the too humanitarian Kaiser, and the submarine-obsessed navy. Gradually he worked himself into a frenzy, until suddenly, with foam on his lips, he fell to the floor in a fit. And that evening it was a physically as well as mentally shaken man who took the precipitate decision to appeal for an armistice, saying that the collapse of the Bulgarian front had upset all his dispositions – 'troops destined for the Western Front had had to be dispatched there'. This had 'fundamentally changed the situation in view of the attacks then being launched on the Western Front', for though these 'had so far been beaten off their continuance must be reckoned with'.

This remark refers to Foch's general offensive. The American attack in the Meuse–Argonne had begun on September 26th, but had come practically to a standstill by the 28th. A Franco-Belgo-British attack had opened in Flanders on the 28th, but if unpleasant did not look really menacing. On the morning of the 29th, however, Haig's main blow was falling on the Hindenburg Line, and the early news was disquieting.

In this emergency, Prince Max was called to be Chancellor to negotiate a peace move, with his international reputation for moderation and honour as its covering pledge. To bargain effectively and without confession of defeat he needed, and asked, a breathing space 'of ten, eight, even four days, before I have to appeal to the enemy'. But Hindenburg merely reiterated that 'the gravity of the military situation admits of no delay', and insisted that 'a peace offer to our enemies be issued at once', while Ludendorff plaintively chanted the refrain 'I want to save my army'.

Hence on October 3rd, the appeal for an immediate armistice went out to President Wilson. It was an open confession of defeat to the world, and even before this – on October 1st – the Supreme Command had undermined their own home front by communicating the same impression to a meeting of the leaders of all political parties. Men who had so long been kept in the dark were blinded by the sudden light. All the forces of discord and pacifism received an immense impulse.

While the German Government was debating the conditions for an armistice and questioning Ludendorff as to the situation of the army for further resistance if the terms were unacceptable, Foch continued his military pressure.

The Breach of the Hindenburg Line. The plan of the general offensive embraced a series of convergent and practically simultaneous attacks:

1 and 2. By the Americans between the Meuse and the Argonne Forest, and by the French west of the Argonne, both in the direction of Mézières – beginning on September 26th.

3. By the British on the St Quentin–Cambrai front in the general direction of Maubeuge – beginning on September 27th.

4. By the Belgian and Allied forces in the direction of Ghent – beginning on September 28th.

The general aspect was that of a pincer-like pressure against the vast salient jutting south between Ypres and Verdun. The attack towards Mézières would shepherd that part of the German armies towards the rather difficult country of the Ardennes and away from their natural line of retreat through Lorraine; it was also dangerously close to the hinge of the Antwerp–Meuse line which the Germans were preparing in rear. The attack towards Maubeuge would threaten the other main line of communication and retreat through the Liége gap, but it had farther to go. In these attacks, the Americans had the hardest natural obstacle; the British had to face the strongest defences and the heaviest weight of enemy troops.

Pershing's attack opened well, adding surprise to its superiority in numbers – approximately eight to one – but soon lost impetus owing to the difficulties of supply and exploitation in such country. When it was eventually suspended on October 14th, after bitter fighting and severe losses, the American Army was still far distant from the vital railway. A new force, it was suffering the growing pains which the British had passed through in 1915–16. Pershing's difficulties were enhanced by the fact that he had waived his own proposal for an exploitation of the St Mihiel success towards Metz in view of Haig's objection to a move which, however promising in its ultimate aim, would diverge from the general direction of the other Allied attacks. Foch's original plan for the general offensive had accordingly been readjusted, and in consequence Pershing had not only a more difficult sector, but a bare week in which to prepare his blow. The shortness of time led him to use untried divisions instead of switching the more experienced divisions used at St Mihiel. But in the outcome, Haig's insistence was proved unnecessary, for the British attack broke through the Hindenburg Line before the Meuse–Argonne attack had drawn away any German division from his front.

Haig, by pushing forward his left wing first, facilitated the attack on his right on the strongest section of the Hindenburg Line – the Canal du Nord, and by October 5th the British were through the German defence system, with open country beyond. But on this front the attackers had actually fewer divisions than the defenders,* their tanks were used up, and they could not press forward fast enough to endanger the German retreat.

Within a few days the Supreme Command became more cheerful, even optimistic, when it saw that breaking into the Hindenburg Line had not been followed by an actual breakthrough of the fighting front. More encouragement came from reports of a slackening in the force of the Allies' attacks, particularly in the exploitation of opportunities. Ludendorff still wanted an armistice, but only to give his troops a rest as a prelude to further resistance and to ensure a secure withdrawal to a shortened defensive line on the frontier. By October 17th he even felt he could do it without a rest. It was less that the situation had changed than that his impression of it had been revised. It had never been quite

---

* On September 25th, the eve of Foch's general offensive, there were fifty-seven German divisions facing forty British and two American divisions along the Hindenburg Line between, roughly, St Quentin and Lens. In the Meuse–Argonne sector twenty enemy divisions opposed thirty-one French and thirteen large-strength American divisions – a total equivalent to at least sixty normal-size Allied divisions. The German divisions had shrunk to an abnormally small size, but this fact does not affect the historical comparison of odds met by the right and left pincers respectively of the Allied offensive.

so bad as he had pictured it on September 29th. But his first impression, and depression, had now spread throughout the political circles and public of Germany, as the ripples spread when a pebble has been dropped in a pool.

The combined pressure of the Allied armies, and their steady advance, were loosening the will-power of the German Government and people. The conviction of ultimate defeat, slower to appeal to them than to the army chiefs, was the more forcible when it was realized. And the indirect moral effect of military and economic pressure was accentuated by the direct effect of peace propaganda, skilfully directed and intensively waged by Northcliffe. The 'home front' began to crumble later, but it crumbled quicker than the battlefront.

The Collapse of Turkey. The offensive planned for the spring in Palestine had been interrupted by the crisis in France and the consequent withdrawal of most of Allenby's British troops. The depletion was made up by reinforcements from India and Mesopotamia, and by September Allenby was again ready to take the offensive. He secretly concentrated, on the Mediterranean flank, the mass of his infantry, and behind them the cavalry. Meantime Lawrence and his Arabs, appearing out of the desert like unseen mosquitoes, menaced the enemy's communications and distracted their attention. At dawn on September 19th the western mass attacked, rolling the Turks back north-east towards the hilly interior – like a door on its hinges. Through the open doorway the cavalry passed, riding straight up the coastal corridor for thirty miles, before swinging east to bestride the Turkish rear. The only remaining way of retreat was eastwards across the Jordan and this was closed with shattering effect by the British air bombers. Completely trapped, the main Turkish armies were rounded up, while Allenby's cavalry exploited the victory of Megiddo by a swift and sustained pursuit which gained first Damascus and finally Aleppo. Defenceless and threatened with a direct advance of Milne from Macedonia on Constantinople, Turkey capitulated on October 30th.

The Collapse of Austria. The last Austrian attempt at an offensive on the Italian front, in conjunction with the German assaults in France, had been repulsed on the Piave in June. Diaz waited until conditions were ripe for an offensive in return, until Austria's internal decay had spread and she was without hope from Germany. On October 24th Cavan's army moved to seize the crossings of the Piave, and on October 27th the main attack opened, driving towards Vittorio Veneto to divide the Austrians in the Adriatic plain from those in the mountains. By October 30th the Austrian Army was split in two, the retreat became a rout, and the same day Austria asked for an armistice, which was signed on November 4th.

The Curtain Falls on the Western Front. Already on October 23rd President Wilson had replied to the German request by a note which virtually required an unconditional surrender. Ludendorff wished to carry on the struggle in hopes that a successful defence of the German frontier might damp the determination of the Allies. But the situation had passed beyond his control, the nation's will-power was broken, and his advice was in discredit. On October 26th he was forced to resign.

Then, for thirty-six hours, the Chancellor lay in coma from an overdose of sleeping draught after influenza. When he returned to his office on the evening of November 3rd, not only Turkey, but Austria, had capitulated. If the situation on the Western Front was felt to be rather easier, Austrian territory and railways were now available as a base of operations against Germany. Several weeks before, General von Gallwitz had told the German Chancellor that such a contingency, then unrealized, would be 'decisive'. Next day revolution broke out in Germany, and swept rapidly over the country. And in these last days of tremendous and diverse psychological strain the 'reddening' glare behind was accentuated by a looming cloud on the Lorraine front – Where the renewed American pressure, since November 1st, was on a point more sensitive than other parts, a point where 'they must not be allowed to advance if the Antwerp–Meuse line was to be held any longer'. If this continued the Rhine and not the frontier would have to be the next line of resistance.

But hourly the revolution was spreading, fanned, as peace negotiations were delayed, by the Kaiser's reluctance to abdicate. Compromise with the revolutionaries was the only chance, and on November 9th Prince Max handed over to the socialist Ebert. Germany had become a republic in outward response to President Wilson's demand and in inward response to the uprising of the German people against the leaders who had led them into disaster. The German fleet had already mutinied when their commanders sought to send them out on a forlorn hope against the British. And on November 6th the German delegates had left Berlin to treat for an armistice.

In the days previous to their arrival the Allies had been anxiously debating the terms, but here the voice of Foch was clear, and decisive, for President Wilson suggested that the terms should be left to the decision of the military chiefs. Haig, supported by Milner, urged moderation – 'Germany is not broken in the military sense. During the last weeks her armies have withdrawn fighting very bravely and in excellent order. Therefore … it is necessary to grant Germany conditions which she can accept … the evacuation of all invaded territories and of Alsace-Lorraine is sufficient to seal the victory.' The British also feared the danger of guerrilla warfare and considered that the German Army should be kept undemobilized as a safeguard against the spread of Bolshevism.

Foch agreed that 'the German army could undoubtedly take up a new position, and that we could not prevent it'. But he disagreed with Haig's conditions and insisted not only that the Germans must hand over a third of their artillery and half their machine guns but that the Allies must occupy the Rhineland, with bridgeheads on the east bank of the Rhine. Only by holding the Rhine would the Allies have a guarantee that Germany could not subsequently break off the peace negotiations, whereas Haig's proposals would facilitate the German withdrawal to and consolidation of a new position of resistance. Foch also intimated privately to Clemenceau that the occupation would 'serve as a pledge for security as well as for reparations'.

Pershing went even further than Foch and protested against granting any armistice. Foch, however, answered such objections logically – 'War is only a means to results. If the Germans now sign an armistice under our conditions those results are in our possession. This being achieved, no man has the right to cause another drop of blood to be shed.' The real results he sought by his terms went, however, beyond the armistice. Once the German army was out of the way France might then be able to frame the peace on her terms and not on those of President Wilson. Thus the ironical result of the President's action in allowing the soldiers to settle the armistice conditions was that he nullified the peace conditions set out in his Fourteen Points – and gave the Germans a just complaint, if not a realistic objection, that they had been entrapped to their doom by his promises.

The next point of difference was whether reparations should be mentioned in the armistice. The British objected, but the French insisted. Clemenceau cleverly and disarmingly argued – 'I wish only to make mention of the principle', and advocated the vague but comprehensive formula 'reparations for damages', while the French Finance Minister strengthened its potential effect by inserting the innocent-looking reservation that 'any future claims or demands on the part of the Allies remain unaffected'. With greater innocence Colonel House swallowed this clause and through his support it was added to the terms.

The next question was that of the naval terms, and here the national positions were reversed. Foch, having made his own terms so severe, was anxious to lighten the naval terms and to demand merely the surrender of submarines. He asked somewhat scoffingly – 'As for the German surface fleet, what do you fear from it? During the whole war only a few of its units have ventured from its ports. The surrender of these units will be merely a manifestation, which will please the public but nothing more.' But Sir Eric Geddes, the First Lord of the Admiralty, reminded Foch that it was the British fleet which 'held in check' the German fleet, and pointed out that if the latter was left intact the war strain on the former would continue until peace was settled. Lloyd George suggested that as an effective but less humiliating compromise the naval terms should demand the internment and not the surrender of the German surface ships. This solution was agreed upon, although the Admiralty only gave way under protest, and the final demand, apart from the surrender of 150 submarines, was for the internment 'in neutral ports, or failing them, Allied ports' of ten battleships and six battlecruisers, besides light craft. Owing to the difficulty of finding an adequate neutral port, their ultimate destination became the British base of Scapa Flow. One important effect of this prolonged discussion was that the terms to Germany were not settled until Austria had capitulated – an effect which, as Lloyd George shrewdly foresaw, enabled the Allies to 'put stiffer terms to Germany' with less chance of refusal.

The Germans' acceptance of these severe terms was hastened less by the existing situation on the Western Front than by the collapse of the 'home front', coupled with exposure to a new thrust in rear through Austria. The Allied advance in the west was still continuing, in some parts seeming to gather pace in the last days, but the main German forces had escaped from the perilous salient, and their complete destruction of roads and railways made it impossible for supplies to keep pace with the advancing troops. A pause must come while these communications were being repaired, and thus the Germans would have breathing space to rally their resistance. The advance reached the line Pont à Mousson–Sedan–Mézières–Mons–Ghent by November 11th – the line of the opening battles in 1914 – but strategically it had come to a standstill.

It is true that, to meet this situation, Foch had concentrated a large Franco-American force to strike below Metz directly east into Lorraine. As the general Allied advance had almost absorbed the enemy's reserves, this stroke, if driven in deeply and rapidly, promised the chance of turning the whole of this new line of defence along the Meuse to Antwerp and might even upset his orderly retreat to the Rhine. But

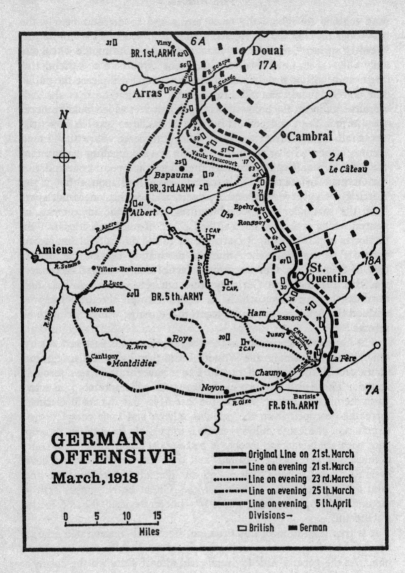

GERMAN OFFENSIVE

March, 1918

——————	Original Line on 21st. March
– – – – –	Line on evening 21st. March
··········	Line on evening 23rd. March
·–·–·–·–	Line on evening 25th. March
■–■–■–■	Line on evening 5th. April

Divisions →
□ British   ■ German

0   5   10   15
Miles

it is unlikely that this Lorraine thrust, prepared for November 14th, would have solved the hitherto insoluble problem of maintaining the initial momentum of advance after an initial breakthrough. Foch did not think so. For when asked how long it would take to drive the Germans back across the Rhine if they refused the armistice terms, he replied – 'Maybe three, maybe four or five months. Who knows?' And his post-war comment on this Lorraine offensive was – 'Its importance has always been exaggerated. It is regarded as the irresistible blow that was to fell and administer the knock out to the Boche. That's nonsense. The Lorraine offensive was *not* in itself any more important than the attack then being prepared in Belgium, on the Lys.'

More truly significant was the decision on November 4th, after Austria's surrender, to prepare a concentric advance on Munich by three Allied armies, which would be assembled on the Austro-German frontier within five weeks. In addition Trenchard's Independent Air Force was about to bomb Berlin on a scale hitherto unattempted in air warfare. And the number of American troops in Europe had now risen to 2,085,000, and the number of divisions to forty-two, of which thirty-two were ready for battle. The internal situation and the obvious external developments which could be calculated were the factors which produced Germany's decision to capitulate – not any single and hypothetical blow on the strongest part of her front. With revolution at home, the gathering menace on their southern frontier and the continued strain on their western, the German delegates had no option but to accept the drastic terms of the armistice, which was signed in Foch's railway carriage in the Forest of Compiègne at 5 AM on November 11th. And at 11 o'clock that morning the World War came to an end.

CHAPTER EIGHT

SCENE 1

The First Breakthrough

At 4.30 AM, on March 21st, 1918, the sudden crash of some 4,000 German guns heralded the breaking of a storm which, in grandeur of scale, of awe, and of destruction, surpassed any other in the World War. By nightfall a German flood had inundated forty miles of the British front; a week later it had reached a depth of nearly forty miles, and was almost lapping the outskirts of Amiens; and in the ensuing weeks the Allied cause itself was almost submerged.

These weeks rank with those of the Marne in 1914 as the two gravest military crises of the World War. In them Germany came desperately near to regaining that lost chance, and best chance, of victory, which she had forfeited in early September, 1914. And to the people of Britain at least the risk seemed even worse, because more fully realized and because their stake was greater.

No episode of the war is so studded with question marks as that on which the curtain rose, March 21st, 1918. Why, when the Allies had been attacking with superior force for two years, were they suddenly fighting 'with their backs to the wall'? Why, after the public had been assured that inter-Allied cooperation was assured and a generalissimo unnecessary, was one urgently demanded and appointed? Why, when the Allies had made so little visible impression on the German front in two years of constant offensive, were the Germans able to tear a huge hole in the Allied front within a few days? Why, as this breach so far exceeded in size the dream-aims of its Allied forerunners, did it fail to obtain any decisive results? In seeking the answers to these several 'whys' lies the main interest of March 21st for history.

The primary cause of the sudden British change from the offensive to the defensive lay in the fact that the German fighting strength on the Western Front was increased by 30 per cent between November, 1917, and March 21st, 1918, while the British strength fell by 25 per cent, .

compared with the previous summer. The bulk of these fresh German troops were transferred from the Russian front, where Ludendorff, as a preliminary to his great bid for victory in the west, had wrung a definite peace from the Bolshevik Government, and also from Rumania. But if these facts explain the change, the causes of its abruptness and extent lie beneath the surface. Chief among them was that the British Command had dissipated its credit, both in balance of man power and with the Government. This doubly unfortunate result was due to the strategy which can be summarized adequately in a single word, manifold in its ill-omened significance – 'Passchendaele'.

Conscious of his responsibility to the nation, and personally distrustful of Haig's judgement, Mr Lloyd George placed a firm check on the flow of reinforcements to France lest they should be poured down another offensive drainpipe. Friction between the two was almost inevitable, because of their extreme contrast of temperament and training. The one a volatile Welshman, and the other a stubborn and taciturn Scot. The one with a magnetic power of drawing even the unwilling to him; the other with an impregnable capacity for holding even the most willing at a distance. The one infinitely adaptable, the other inflexibly consistent, and persistent. In the one, speech and thought so closely coincided that they became fused, while with the other the opening of the mouth automatically cut out the action of the brain. Anecdotes of Haig's inarticulateness, to the point of unintelligibility, are many. One of the best is of the occasion when, presenting the prizes to an Aldershot cross-country team, all that he could get out was – 'I congratulate you on your running. You have run well. I hope you will run as well in the presence of the enemy.'

Again, Lloyd George was as receptive to ideas as he was critical of the pretensions of hierarchical wisdom, and he constantly sought to gather a variety and diversity of opinions as a broad basis for judgement. Haig, as his own admiring biographer, General Charteris, confesses, 'had not a critical mind', and neither knowledge of, nor interest in, affairs outside his own military work. And he took over the command 'genuinely convinced that the position to which he had now been called was one which he, and he alone in the British Army, could fill'. When to his rigidly disciplined outlook was added this feeling of divine right, it raised an almost impassable barrier of character between him and the Prime Minister. Neither made much effort to surmount it, and growing distrust on both sides – a distrust of Haig's military and Lloyd George's personal methods – steadily heightened it.

Throughout the months following Passchendaele and preceding the

German offensive, Lloyd George was assiduously seeking to create a power above Haig, as dismissal would have raised a political storm. His solution was the Supreme War Council in control of a general inter-Allied reserve. But the scheme was thwarted by Haig's action. For, having no belief in the method of battle control by committee, he shattered it by his refusal to contribute his small quota of nine divisions. Whatever the just strength of his objection to the method on principle, his action is not easy either to understand or to justify. For, convinced as he was that the German attack was coming on his front, and conscious of his shortage of reserves, it seems curious that he should not risk a contribution of nine divisions in order to draw from a pool of thirty. He chose, instead, to rely on an arrangement with Pétain for mutual support, whereby in case of need he might be reinforced by six to eight French divisions. This was far less than Haig could hope for from the general reserve, if formed. Moreover, Haig's distrust of French fulfilment of such promises had for years been so marked, his tongue so caustic about them, that it is astonishing that he should have pinned his faith to a small and purely French promise when he could have had a much larger promise from a board on which there was a British representative.

This excessive trust on the part of the British Command, like the Government's withholding of reinforcements, may well have been due to an apparently well-grounded belief in the power of their defence to stop a German attack. Why should the Germans succeed where the British had so often failed? The only close approach to a breakthrough by the British had been at Cambrai, with the tanks – and Haig knew the it was almost impossible for the Germans to have built tanks in quantity.

But in his defensive calculations, as in his offensive actions throughout the past two years, he seems to have underrated the infinite value of surprise, which for 3,000 years of recorded warfare has proved the master key to victory. The real significance of the Cambrai attack on November 20th previous had been that it had revived the use of such a key, forging it from an amalgam of armour and the caterpillar track. Unhappily, the effect of this tank key was largely lost because when inserted in the lock Haig had not the power to turn it fully, through exhausting his strength in the Passchendaele mud.

In the counter-attack of November 30th the Germans had used a key similar in principle if different in design – a short sharp bombardment with gas and smoke shell, followed up by an inrush of infantry, specially trained in the new infiltration tactics. It would seem that by the following March the British had not sufficiently taken this lesson to heart. For, though the Fifth Army's subsequent excuses of weak numbers and a long line had some justification, Gough had expressed confidence beforehand in his power to resist the onslaught.

But when Gough's original front was forced, an inadequate preparation and coordination of the measures to block the enemy's path farther back was revealed. He had failed to arrange for the blowing up of certain causeways and General Headquarters had not given him a definite order. Worse still was the confusion caused by the fact that in the case of the more important railway bridges, this duty was entrusted to the French railway authorities instead of the Fifth Army, and in this way the vital railway bridge at Péronne was allowed to fall undestroyed into German hands.

A similar haziness appeared in the GHQ instructions for the conduct of the defensive battle, for in one place Gough was told 'we should make our preparations to fight east of the Somme', and in another 'it may well be desirable to fall back to the rearward defences of Péronne and the Somme'. To reconcile these alternatives was not easy. It would have been simpler to have forestalled the Germans' attack by a withdrawal similar to their own in 1917, accepting the necessary sacrifice of ground: although political considerations and military sentiments tended to hinder such a course. Adaptation of plan to circumstance may be necessary, and often more advantageous, but it is the hardest test of generalship, and thus demands the clearest thought among those who attempt it. The fog of war is bad enough without being thickened by obscure phrasing: battles may be lost by lack of lucidity as well as by lack of tenacity. The effect of these instructions to the Fifth Army was that labour had to be divided between the alternative defence lines, without time for the satisfactory organization of either. Moreover, a withdrawal to the line of the Somme while the battle was actually in progress demanded a high capacity for rearguard action, and for this the officers and men of the Fifth Army as a whole were neither prepared nor practised. To quote from among many witnesses – Colonel Rowland Feilding has recorded: 'A retreat was the one possibility that had never occurred to us, and, unfortunately, it involves a kind of manoeuvring in which we are unversed, in spite of all our experience.' There is indirect proof of this statement in the fact that no less than 500 guns were abandoned to the enemy in the first two days.

The chance of avoiding a retreat was diminished, as its execution was endangered, because of the scarcity of reserves behind Gough's front and of the way that General Headquarters refused his request to move these nearer the front before the battle. And when it opened he was told that he would have to wait for one extra division until the first four available had been sent to the Third Army. These facts give point to his remark – 'It is impossible for me to say that GHQ showed a full understanding of the circumstances and progress of the battle.' And a chance of improving it was lost because – 'During the whole eight days' battle, the only member of GHQ who came to see and hear things for himself was Haig. He came and saw me once – on Saturday, 23rd. We did not go at all into details of the situation, nor of the action of the Third Army.'

On the eve of the German onslaught, only three out of the eighteen British divisions in reserve were disposed behind the Fifth Army front. Six were behind the Third Army, and the rest were still farther north, where no attack came or was by then expected. Haig's justification for keeping his reserves in the north until he was absolutely certain of the German aim lay in the narrowness of the space that there intervened between the front and the Channel ports. But it is not a complete explanation of his attitude. That was influenced to some extent by his prolonged doubt of the German intentions: at a conference of his army commanders on February 16th he expressed the view that the main blow, if the Germans attacked early, would probably be made against the French. 'Indications from the British front are that no attack in strength in Flanders is possible at the moment, and that there are at present no signs of any big offensive being imminent on the rest of the British front.' A small attack on the First Army front near Lens was a 'possibility'. GHQ was certainly slow to react to the warnings furnished by air reports and by the Fifth Army. At a further conference on March 2nd the likelihood of early attack was recognized but with no greater object than that of 'cutting off the Cambrai salient and drawing in our reserves'. And even on March 8th it was stated that there were no indications of an enemy attack south of St Quentin.

Haig's sense of the key importance of the Arras bastion was justified by the event. But, in keeping the bulk of his reserves in the north, he risked the security of the already thin Fifth Army in order to have ample insurance against a less probable risk to the Channel ports. One reason was that he felt he could better afford to yield ground in front of Amiens than elsewhere. Another was a confidence, which the event unhappily refuted, that the German advance would not go far enough to become a menace to the general situation. Calculated risks are inherent in generalship; the questions that linger in the mind are whether Haig's miscalculation was avoidable and whether he did all that was possible to cover the risks that his dispositions involved. It is at least clear that he preferred to risk his junction with the French rather than his hold on the Channel ports; and that his dispositions eased the task of the enemy more than they could have expected.

If this was good luck for the Germans, their thorough and skilful preparations for the initial assault had earned them success – although here again fortune favoured them.

For the effect of the gas-gained surprise was immensely increased by nature, which in the early hours of March 21st provided a thick mist that cloaked the infiltrating assailants as much as it masked the defending machine guns. Without this aid it is questionable how far the German tactical surprise would have succeeded, and in this lay the essential inferiority of the German means of surprise, compared with that at Cambrai, and later, on August 8th, 1918, which was achieved by armoured machines.

These not only formed the main material from which the key was manufactured but provided the power to press it home and turn it. In contrast, Ludendorff had to depend on unarmoured infantry to exploit the opening created by the brief but intense bombardment with gas shell. For he had failed to grasp the significance of the tank and neglected to develop it in time; only in August, 1918, when it was used to strike him a mortal blow did he put it in the 'urgent' class of war material.

But the German plan was distinguished by a research for tactical surprise more thorough and far-reaching than in any of the earlier operations of the war. The Germans significantly record that 'Haig's dispatches dealing with the attacks of 1917 were found most valuable, because they showed how not to do it'. To Ludendorff's credit he realized that the obvious is an obstacle that superior weight cannot compensate, and, once created, can rarely overcome. And he sought to effect and develop surprise by a compound of many deceptive elements. It is to his credit also that, unlike Falkenhayn, who merely wanted officer clerks, he surrounded himself with able assistants. Captain Geyer compiled the new training handbooks, while Colonel Bruchmüller had emerged from retirement to become the famous artillery 'battle-piece' producer. With a prophetic play upon his name he was known as 'Durchbruchmüller' – Breakthrough Müller. Under his superintendence the masses of artillery were brought up close to the front line in concealment, and opened fire without previous 'registration' through the method he had introduced. The infantry were trained in new infiltrating tactics, of which the guiding idea was that the leading troops should probe and penetrate the weak points of the defence while the reserves were directed to back up success, not to redeem failure. Special reconnaissance parties were assigned simply for the task of sending back early news of progress. The ordinary lines of attacking infantry were preceded by a dispersed chain of 'storm' groups, with automatic rifles, machine guns and light mortars. These groups were to push straight through wherever they could find an opening and leave the defenders' 'strong points' to be dealt with by the succeeding lines. The fastest, not the slowest, must set the pace, and no effort was made to keep a uniform alignment. Further 'the inclination of leaders to assemble their troops and get them in hand after a certain objective has been reached must be suppressed'. 'If the troops know the instructions of the commanders they can go on of themselves.' The assaulting divisions were brought up overnight, those of the second line to a position only about a mile behind the first, and the third only ten miles back. All reserves started moving forward at zero, so as to be at hand when wanted. And when a second-line division was so used it came under the control, not of a higher commander sitting in rear, but of the first-line division commander, who had his finger on the pulse of the battle.

On November 11th at Mons – prophetic date and place – the German 'leaders' had met in conclave to decide on the date and place of the forthcoming offensive. Naturally, according to German custom, the issue was thrashed out, not between the nominal commanders, but between their chiefs of staff – Ludendorff, Kuhl (Crown Prince Rupprecht's), Schulenberg (German Crown Prince's), together with Ludendorff's own strategical adviser, Major Wetzell. Kuhl and Schulenberg each wanted the attack to be made on the front of their own army groups – Kuhl indicating Flanders and Schulenberg the Verdun sector. Wetzell was inclined to support Schulenberg, arguing that an attack on the flanks of Verdun, a salient, would forestall any future Franco-American offensive at that delicate point, and, after defeating the French, the whole German strength could be turned against the British. Ludendorff, however, rejected this scheme on the score that the ground was unfavourable, that a breakthrough at Verdun would lead nowhere decisive, and that the French army had recuperated too well after nearly a year's undisturbed convalescence. He laid down as a first principle that 'the British must be defeated', and thought that the drain of Passchendaele would make them an easy prey. But he disagreed with Kuhl's proposal to strike, between Ypres and Lens, towards Hazebrouck as it would meet the main mass of the British, and this low ground would be long in drying. He favoured instead an attack around

St Quentin, although Wetzell contended that it would be slowed down in crossing the old devastated area on the Somme, and was within easy reach of French reinforcements. A final decision was put off and Rupprecht noted in his diary 'Ludendorff underestimates the toughness of the British'.

In December, Wetzell tried to reconcile, and sagely combine, the two projects, by dividing the offensive into two acts – first, a wide-front attack on both sides of St Quentin, and, second, a fortnight later, a breakthrough in Flanders towards Hazebrouck. The first act was only to be carried far enough to draw the British reserves southward. Wetzell summed up:

> We shall not, in my opinion, succeed in obtaining our object by *one* great attack at *one* place, however carefully it is prepared ... we can only shatter their front by a clever combination of successive, definitely related, mutually reacting attacks on different parts of the front, finally in the direction of Hazebrouck.

It was to be left to Foch to adopt his method without acknowledgement. For, after further conferences, Ludendorff decided on January 27th in favour of the St Quentin attack (known by the code name 'Michael') and against the Hazebrouck attack 'St George' which was only kept in mind and not in immediate readiness.

A further complication arose. The front from the Belgian coast to St Quentin was under Rupprecht, and for political as well as personal reasons it was considered necessary to give the German Crown Prince a chance of redeeming the credit he had lost in the struggle at Verdun in 1916. Hence he was given a share in the offensive by employing the Eighteenth Army (Hutier), which belonged to his army group, on the southern flank of the main offensive. It is a moot question whether he could not have helped better, if less gloriously, by using it for a diversion at Verdun, in order to draw the French reserves away from, instead of towards, the intended breach in the British front.

In a broad sense, Ludendorff's chosen sector, which extended from Arras to La Fère, fulfilled his new principle of taking the line of least resistance, for it was the weakest in defences, defenders, and reserves. Moreover, it was close to the joint between the French and British armies, and so lent itself to a separation. But although it was true, as a generalization, that this sector was comparatively weak, the classification was loose and inaccurate. The northerly third of it was strong and strongly held, by Byng's Third Army, with fourteen divisions (six in reserve), while the bulk of the British reserves were on this flank, which also could and did receive support more quickly from the other British armies which lay to the north. The remaining two-thirds of the sector upon which the German blow fell was held by Gough's Fifth Army. The central part facing Marwitz's army was held by seven divisions (two in reserve). The southern part facing Hutier's army was also held by seven divisions (one in reserve).

But Ludendorff gave Below's army near Arras nineteen divisions for the initial attack, by its left wing only, on a nine and a half miles' frontage. South of it came Marwitz's army. As the British salient towards Cambrai was not to be attacked directly, but pinched out, this four-mile stretch was adequately occupied by two German divisions, and Marwitz had eighteen divisions for his nine-and-a-half-mile attack frontage. On the extreme south, either side of St Quentin, came Hutier's army. Ludendorff gave it only twenty-four divisions to attack on a twenty-mile frontage. Hence we see that it had only half the proportionate strength of the other armies. Despite his principle, he was distributing his strength according to the enemy's strength and not concentrating against the weakest resistance. The direction given in his orders emphasized this still more. The main effort was to be exerted north of the Somme for, after breaking through, Below and Marwitz were to wheel north-west, rolling up the British front, while the river and Hutier formed a screen to cover their flank. Hutier's army was merely an offensive flank guard. This plan was to be radically changed in execution, and to have the appearance of following the line of least resistance, because Ludendorff gained rapid success where he desired it little and failed to gain success where he wanted it most.

What of the British meantime? As the result of a war game played at Versailles Sir Henry Wilson had forecasted that the enemy attack would come on the Cambrai–Lens sector, but that the Germans would wait to deliver it until about July 1st, when their training and accumulation of forces would be complete. Wilson was somewhat outside the mark in place and still more out in time. Haig's intelligence was more accurate, although it did not foresee the full southward extension of the attack. As the time drew near signs multiplied sufficiently to enable Haig to calculate the date. On March 18th German prisoners captured near St Quentin gave the date as the 21st, and on the evening of the 20th Maxse's XVIII Corps was able through raiding to establish the certainty of the morrow's attack.

Thus it is true to say that no strategic surprise was obtained. Nor was it even obtainable under the conditions of 1918 in France. But with the opposing armies spread out in contact along the far-flung line of entrenchments, a quick breakthrough followed by a rapid exploitation along the line of least resistance might promise such a decisive upset as normally is only attainable by choosing the line of least expectation. The hurricane bombardment opened at 4.30 AM on the 21st, concentrating for two hours on the British artillery and then, reinforced by mortars, turning on the trenches. Almost all telephone cables were severed and wireless sets destroyed, while the fog made visual signalling impossible. Thus the troops were made dumb and the commanders blind. At 9.40 AM, or in some parts earlier, the German infantry advanced under cover of a creeping barrage, supplemented by low-flying aircraft.

The British outpost zone was overrun almost everywhere by midday, but this was inevitable and had been foreseen. But the northern attack met such stubborn resistance against the right of Byng's army that it had not seriously penetrated the main battle zone even by the night of the 22nd, and, despite putting in successive reinforcements, the capture of Vaulx-Vraucourt was then the high-water mark of its progress. On most parts of Gough's army front the battle-zone resistance was just as firm, but the flood found a way through on the 21st near La Fère, on the extreme right, at Essigny and at Ronssoy. The resistance of the 21st Division at Epéhy for a time checked this last breach from spreading northward, but it began to crumble so deeply that the neighbouring sectors were affected. Southward, again near St Quentin, the line sagged still more deeply, and on the night of the 22nd Gough was driven to order a general retirement to the line of the Somme. He was hurried into this precipitate decision by a mistaken report that the enemy was already across the Crozat Canal at Jussy and so behind his right flank. Early next morning the Péronne bridgehead was abandoned. Several of Gough's subordinate commanders were even more vague or misled as to the situation, control lapsed, and gaps occurred. The worst was at the joint between Byng's and Gough's armies and this the Germans speedily accentuated. And a new danger arose farther south at the joint between the British and French.

But Ludendorff, continuing to ignore his new principle, was only intent to nourish the attack near Arras, where progress was disappointing. Meantime Hutier, once across the Crozat Canal, was pressing swiftly forward, almost without check save from his own limited role. On the 23rd Ludendorff again emphasizes in his orders that Below's is the principal effort, reinforces it by three divisions, and indicates that the Sixth and Fourth Armies, still more to the north, will chime in to help it. Two days later, when the check to Below has become still clearer, Ludendorff arranges that Below's hitherto passive right wing shall strike direct at Arras on the 28th, in order to overcome this strong place which is hampering and enfilading Below's attacking left wing. And on the 29th the Sixth Army, reinforced by six or seven divisions, is to extend the attack northwards between Arras and Lens – with Boulogne as its goal! Meanwhile Hutier is actually told not to pass the line Noyon–Roye for the time being.

On the 26th Ludendorff begins to doubt Below's chances and to turn his eyes south. But, instead of throwing his weight thither, he merely makes it a second principal effort. And, even so, it is to be towards Amiens by Marwitz's army, while Hutier is told not to cross the Avre without fresh orders. This means that the army which has all the difficult ground of the old 1916 Somme battlefields to cross is pushed on while the army that has a smoother path is held back. The apparent explanation, and the extraordinary flux of Ludendorff's thought, is revealed in a later sentence of the order which shows that he is contemplating a vast fanlike movement in which three armies are to wheel south towards Paris while Below and his neighbours wheel north to crush the British against the sea coast. The grandiose conception was far beyond Ludendorff's resources in reserves. It would seem that for the moment he was intoxicated with success, and, like Moltke in August, 1914, was counting his chickens before they were hatched. Another parallel with 1914 was that the army commanders' reports of progress outstripped their actual stages of advance. Even they, however, were less futuristic than the Kaiser who, according to Rupprecht, 'announced a complete victory' on March 21st.

On the 27th Hutier reached Montdidier, a penetration of nearly forty miles, but next day Ludendorff had a cold douche of reality when Below's Arras attack with nine divisions collapsed under a storm of fire from the expectant defence. No mist came to the aid of the attackers.

Ludendorff then put a belated stop to Below's vain efforts, and countermanded the Sixth Army's attack intended for the morrow. Amiens was made the main objective, and Marwitz was given all the reserves at hand – nine divisions. But Hutier had to pause for two days until four fresh divisions reached him. By this time the surge towards Amiens was almost stagnant, its impetus having slackened far less because of the resistance than because of the exhaustion of the troops and the difficulties of supply. Roads were blocked, transport scuppered, and reserves harassed by the British air attacks, which here played a vital part. When the attack was renewed on March 30th it had little force and made little progress in face of a resistance that had been afforded time to harden, helped by the cement of French reserves which were now being poured into the sagging wall. That day was the first on which their artillery, arriving later than the infantry, had come into action in force. Even so, there was a moment of crisis when the Germans captured the Moreuil Wood ridge, which was not only at the joint between the French and British but commanded the crossings of the Avre and Luce where they joined. And these covered the main Amiens–Paris railway. But the menace was warded off by a swift counterstroke of the Canadian Cavalry Brigade, made on the initiative of and led by General Seely, ex-War Minister turned Murat. The ridge was regained, and although lost again next day, by other troops, the coup seems to have extinguished the now flickering flame of German energy. Nearly a week passed before, on April 4th, a further German effort was made by fifteen divisions, of which only four were fresh. Meeting a reinforced defence, this had still less success.

Seeing that his new effort was too late, Ludendorff then suspended the attack towards Amiens. At no time had he thrown his weight along the line of fracture between the British and French armies. Yet on March 24th Pétain had intimated to Haig that if the Germans' progress continued along this line he would have to draw back the French reserves south-westwards to cover Paris. How little more German pressure would have been needed to turn the crack into a yawning chasm! The knowledge is one more testimony to the historical truth that a joint is the most sensitive and profitable point of attack.

The supreme features of this great offensive are, first, the immensity of its outward results compared with those of any previous offensive in the west; second, its ineffectiveness to attain decisive results. For the first it would be both unjust and untrue to blame the British troops. They achieved miracles of heroic endurance, and the prolonged resistance in most of the battle zone is the proof. The main cause of the subsequently rapid flow-back lay in the frequent breakdown of control and communication. During three years of trench warfare an elaborate and complex system, largely dependent on the telephone, had been built up, and when the static suddenly became fluid the British paid the inevitable penalty of violating that fundamental axiom of war – elasticity.

On the German side, Arras was the actual rock on which their plan broke. It is probable that military conservatism cost them dear. For Bruchmüller has revealed that while Hutier's army carried out his surprise bombardment designs, Below's in the north clung to their old-fashioned methods, refusing to dispense with preliminary ranging. Once again, and near the Somme again, Below's conventional military mind had proved the best asset to the British army.

But a more fundamental cause of the German failure was Ludendorff's own limitations. He had sufficient receptiveness to see a new truth but not sufficient elasticity or conviction to carry it out fully in practice. The principle of following the line of least resistance was too novel for one who from his youth had been saturated in the Clausewitzian doctrine of striking at the enemy's main force. 'The British must be defeated' was his catchword, his vision was bloodshot, and he could not realize that in strategy the longest way round is often the shortest way there – that a direct approach to the object exhausts the attacker and hardens the resistance by compression, whereas an indirect approach loosens the defender's hold by upsetting his balance.

In the actual execution of the offensive by the German troops there is another cause of failure that has been commonly overlooked and yet is of great significance. It is the physical effect on ill-nourished troops of breaking into an area full of well-filled supply depots, and the psychological effect of discovering that the enemy is so much better fed and equipped than themselves – that they have been nourished only with lies, about the result of the U-boat campaign and the enemy's economic condition. This dual effect is to be traced in many sources of evidence. One of the most illuminating and trustworthy is the war diary of the German poet and novelist, Rudolf Binding.

On March 27th he records:

Now we are already in the English back areas ... a land flowing with milk and honey. Marvellous people these, who will only equip themselves with the very best that the earth produces. Our men are hardly to be distinguished from English soldiers. Everyone wears at least a leather jerkin, a waterproof ... English boots or some other beautiful thing. The horses are feeding on masses of oats and gorgeous food-cake ... and there is no doubt the army is looting with some zest.

On the next day follows a highly significant entry:

Today the advance of our infantry suddenly stopped near Albert. Nobody could understand why. Our armies had reported no enemy between Albert and Amiens ... Our way seemed entirely clear. I jumped into a car with orders to find out what was causing the stoppage in front. Our division was right in front of the advance and could not possibly be tired out. It was quite fresh . . .

As soon as I got near the town I began to see curious sights. Strange figures, which looked very little like soldiers, and certainly showed no sign of advancing, were making their way back out of the town. There were men driving cows . . . others who carried a hen under one arm and a box of notepaper under the other. Men carrying a bottle of wine under their arm and another one open in their hand . . . Men staggering. Men who could hardly walk. When I got into the town the streets were running with wine . . .

I drove back to Divisional Headquarters with a fearful impression of the situation. The advance was held up, and there was no means of setting it going again for hours.

It proved hopeless, and the officers were powerless, to collect the troops that day, while the sequel he records was that 'the troops which moved out of Albert next day cheered with wine and in victorious spirits were mown down straight away on the railway embankment by a few English machine guns'.

But the intoxication due to loot was even greater and more general than that due to wine, and the fundamental cause of both was 'the general sense of years of privation'. A staff officer even stops a car, when on an urgent mission, to pick up an English waterproof from the ditch. And in this intoxication the Germans not only lose their chance of reaching Amiens, but ruin sources of supply invaluable to the maintenance of their own advance – wrecking waterworks for the sake of the brass taps. The cause of this senseless craving is revealed in their impression that 'the English made everything either out of rubber or brass, because these were the two materials which we had not seen for the longest time'. 'The madness, stupidity and indiscipline of the German troops is shown in other things as well. Any useless toy or trifle they seize and load onto their packs, anything useful which they cannot carry away they destroy.'

Once this plunder was exhausted the reaction was all the greater and the contrast of their own paucity with the enemy's plenty the more depressing. As hopes of military success fade, and with them the hope of again nourishing their stomachs, and souls, on the enemy's supplies, a moral rot sets in rapidly.

Anyone with personal experience of war knows how the thought of food and of civilized comfort fills the soldier's horizon. How far was the German army's sudden moral decline from July onward, when the last attack proved abortive, due not only to increasing hunger but to the eye-opening conviction of the enemy's greater material power of endurance?

Propaganda and censorship could hide the difference so long as the front was an inviolable wall of partition. But when the Germans broke through the British lines and into the back areas the truth was revealed to the German troops. Is the historical verdict, penetrating beneath the surface of military statistics and acreage to the psychological foundation, then to be that the British disaster of March, 1918, was a stroke of fortune for those who suffered it? If so, it seems a pity that the solution was not tried earlier. Instead of conducting unwilling 'frocks' round the front, the British Command might have arranged visits for Germans to its back areas – that 'land flowing with milk and honey'. Or at least it might have designedly released a proportion of its prisoners after they had been suitably entertained! Such a strategy would certainly have supplied the imagination which many found so lacking in the military leadership.

CHAPTER EIGHT

SCENE 2

The Breakthrough in Flanders

On April 9th, 1918, the first anniversary of the abortive British attempt to break through the deadlocked trench front in Artois, the Germans made a more successful attempt – in the reverse direction. This was the second move in Ludendorff's gigantic offensive campaign which had begun on March 21st. Springing from around Neuve Chapelle, where, three years before, the first British attempt to break the deadlock had penetrated half a mile deep in all, a narrow German jet of attack swept away the opposing Portuguese and before noon on the 9th had penetrated to a depth of over three miles. To the north, but happily not to the south, the flanks of the breach crumbled, and with fresh jets playing upon the British front more sectors gave way.

By the next day twenty-four miles of frontage had been engulfed and, on the 12th, Sir Douglas Haig issued his historic order of the day: 'There is no other course open to us but to fight it out. Every position must be held to the last man ... With our backs to the wall and believing in the justice of our cause, each one of us must fight on to the end.' To the British public, and even perhaps to the British forces, this message came like a thunderclap, awakening them to the graveness of the danger and seeming almost to convey a warning that hope had gone and only honour remained – to go down fighting with their faces to the foe.

Yet at that moment, and still more during the following days, it is probable that the least sanguine and most depressed man was not in the British ranks, but behind the advancing enemy – Ludendorff himself. On March 21st and the next days Ludendorff had seen his carefully contrived strategical plan – for his great bid for victory – going astray. The rapidity with which progress was made where he did not want it, and its slowness where he did want it, had driven him unwillingly to press on towards Amiens across the desert of the old Somme battle-

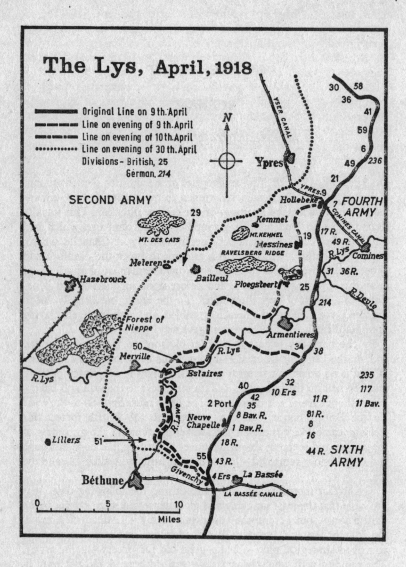

The Lys, April, 1918

Original Line on 9th April
Line on evening of 9th April
Line on evening of 10th April
Line on evening of 30th April
Divisions – British, 25
German, 214

SECOND ARMY

N

Ypres

YSER CANAL

30 58
36
41
59
6
49 236
21

YPRES 9
Hollebeke 7 **FOURTH ARMY**
COMINES CANAL
17 R.
49 R.
Comines
R. Lys
31 36 R.
R. Devle

29
MT. DES CATS
Kemmel
MT. KEMMEL
19
Messines
RAVELSBERG RIDGE
25
Meteren
Bailleul
Ploegsteert
214
Hazebrouck

Forest of Nieppe
Armentieres
34 38
50
Merville
R. Lys
Estaires
235
117
40
32
10 Ers
R. Lys
R. Lawe
42
35
2 Port.
11 R
11 Bav.
Neuve Chapelle
8 Bav. R.
81 R.
1 Bav. R.
8
16
Lillers
51
18 R.
44 R. **SIXTH ARMY**
55
43 R.
Béthune
Givenchy
4 Ers
La Bassée
LA BASSÉE CANALE

0   5   10
Miles

fields, instead of wheeling northwards from the Somme. With the repulse of his delayed assault on the Arras bastion on March 28th he had been forced to relinquish definitely his plan of rolling up the flank of the British armies and penning them back against the coast, isolated from their Allies.

But his thrust towards Amiens failed, however narrowly, to reach its destination – through its belatedness and difficulties of supply. In desperation, rather than in reflection, Ludendorff clutched at Wetzell's rejected scheme, and decided to launch the 'St George' attack against the Ypres–Lens sector. But he had pressed 'Michael' too long and too far. Not only was he short of reserves, but he had to accumulate fresh supplies and ammunition, and switch his heavy artillery northwards. Conferences on April 1st and 2nd showed that the offensive could not be ready until the 9th; and, instead of thirty-five additional divisions, only eleven could be sent in time. With a sense of ironic humour the attack was rechristened 'Georgette'. Ludendorff was in luck at the start, but it was an elusive and delusive form of luck. The luck was that his opening blow fell on the front of the 2nd Portuguese Division, which was just about to be relieved by two British divisions, and had in the meanwhile been stretched to hold the whole corps sector.

The less agreeable aspect – for Ludendorff – of this piece of luck was somewhat unkindly epitomized in the comment that the Portuguese ruined Ludendorff and saved their Allies by running away. For although the extension and development of this attack was 'according to plan', Ludendorff never seems to have been wholehearted in pursuing it. From the point of view of his strategy, and its interests, he either pressed the attack too hard or did not press enough.

The clearest evidence of this irresolution – and depression – is to be found in the captured archives of the Fourth German Army, which attacked in this sector. And their evidence is a better guide than any carefully prepared post-war apologia. They have the further advantage that they fell into enemy hands before any judicious adulterations could be made in the interests of high commanders' reputations. These German records show the General Staff officers, Lossberg for the Fourth Army, Kuhl for the Army Group, and Ludendorff at the Supreme Command, settling all affairs without even the pretence of consulting their respective superiors, Sixt von Arnim, Rupprecht and Hindenburg. They also show Ludendorff doling out divisions with a parsimonious hand, usually too late and inadequate in number for real success; so apprehensive that his new bulge would become another sack that at the moment of supreme opportunity he stops the German advance for fear of a counter-attack.

But all this was hidden from the British commanders and men. They only knew the enemy's blows, not his doubts and disquietude. And if he felt himself in a sack, they felt themselves in a mincing machine – with an unpleasant likelihood of their minced remains being ejected into the sea. That is the sort of wall that an army does not relish having at its back. Whereas on the Somme there had at least been ample room to withdraw, in the north the British troops, bases, and communications were all crowded into and passed through a narrow 'throat' of land sensitive to the least pressure and all too easy to strangle. Apart from the coast railway, the only lateral line of communication ran through St Pol–Lillers–Hazebrouck, barely fifteen miles behind the front trenches. Thus it was that a ten-mile German penetration, reached on April 12th and, happily, never deepened appreciably, was as menacing, if not more so, than forty miles had been on the Somme.

The strain was all the more severe because it fell on troops already strained. Besides the Portuguese, all except one – the 55th – of the six British divisions between the La Bassée and the Ypres–Comines Canals were battle-worn, having come to this front on relief from the battle in the south. Strained, they were also stretched. The drain on Haig's reserves and the greater importance of the vital bastion of high ground, Arras Givenchy, had caused a distribution of strength by which this handful of divisions had to hold a front of twenty-four miles. Worst of all, the greatest stretching of all fell on those who could least bear it. The Portuguese Corps had been holding a six-mile front, on both sides of Neuve Chapelle. It had been in the line for a long time, and increasing cases of insubordination had been a warning of declining morale. General Horne, the First Army commander, reshuffling his dispositions, withdrew the 1st Portuguese Division from the line on April 5th. The 2nd also was to be relieved by British divisions on the night of April 9th, but meanwhile it was given the whole corps sector to hold, although one brigade of the 1st Portuguese was left in reserve near Lestrem, five miles behind the line. The 51st Division had been on the scene for several days and might have been used; indeed, its commander had proposed that he should take over the second line, a strongly concreted position easy to hold. But his request had not been granted. Yet Horne had been warned by his 'Q' staff that the convergence of German railways made the Lys sector the most probable point of attack; indeed, the only point where an attack could be mounted. They had, further, sought permission to prepare special supply dumps fifteen miles in rear to meet the danger of a breakthrough here, but had been rebuffed. Happily, they began preparations – without his knowledge. And the existence of these dumps helped to ease the emergency that followed.

If the state of the local preparations was Horne's responsibility, it is right to point out that he saw eye to eye with Haig in failing to read the writing on the wall-map. Rarely, if ever was this so clear: or surprise less warranted by the signs. For the Germans sacrificed concealment to speed in developing their new offensive. From March 31st onwards the British aircraft reported a general northward movement of the German reserves and artillery, by road and rail. On April 1st, as the Official Air History has revealed, one observer alone in a couple of hours 'counted fifty-five trains on the move along the lines feeding the La Bassée–Armentières front ... The air reports of the next few days, supplemented by air photographs, made it clear that the German concentration was of the most formidable kind'. The reason that GHQ failed to profit by the warning lay in its belief that the enemy would adhere to his original plan, and that the next step in furtherance of his Somme offensive would be a renewal of his attempt to break down the Arras bastion. It would seem that Haig credited Ludendorff with a persistency similar to his own at Passchendaele. Convinced that Ludendorff's correct course was to gain the key position of the Vimy ridge, even though it was the strongest part of his own front, Haig held fast to the idea that Ludendorff, despite his hard lesson on March 28th, was bound to try again.

As late as April 7th, in an appreciation of the situation, GHQ pinned its expectations to 'a converging attack on the Vimy ridge'. Yet, to quote the Air History again: 'There was nothing in the air reports and air photographs up to the 9th of April to support the view, held by General Headquarters, that a converging attack on the Vimy ridge was likely. On the contrary the air information showed that the German troops opposite Arras were being drawn upon to supply reinforcements for the north and should have left little doubt that the immediate enemy concentration was northwards from the La Bassée Canal.'

The air information has also a bearing on Horne's delayed action over the relief of the Portuguese. 'That the relief might come too late was indicated from the air. Throughout the morning of the 7th air observers reported the main roads immediately opposite the Portuguese to be full of moving transport, and ground observers told of men carrying ammunition into the German support lines. The impression conveyed by the combined air and ground reports was that the tactical concentration was nearing completion.' It did not, however, impress the men at the top – or they were slow in reaction.

For at 4.5 AM on the 9th an intense bombardment was opened on the eleven-mile front between the La Bassée Canal and Armentières; the flanks of this sector were deluged with mustard gas – an indication that they were to be paralysed but not immediately attacked. At 7.30 AM, after a slackening in the fire, small groups of German infantry began to move forward, and about 8.45 AM, after the bombardment had swelled again for an hour, the assault was launched by a mass of nine divisions of the German Sixth Army – against three. Once more, as on March 21st, nature afforded it a cloak in the form of a thick mist. At the southern extremity the 55th (a Lancashire Territorial division) held on to Givenchy firmly, opposing so unshakable a resistance as not only to break the attack, but to dissuade the German command from sub-sequent attempts to extend it southwards.

But in the centre the Germans swiftly overran the Portuguese positions. The Portuguese were temporarily holding a front more than double that of the 55th on their flank; although their strength per yard was not much less, comparison of quality made such a distribution risky – and the risk had matured. But the sturdy resistance of King Edward's Horse and the 11th Cyclist Battalion checked the German onrush, and helped, with that of the reserve brigade of the 55th Division, to prevent the Germans crumbling away the southern flank. This resistance, indeed, tended to shepherd the German advance into the north-westerly direction, which it took more and more.

But on the northern flank of the breakthrough, the 40th Division, its own flank laid bare, was partly overwhelmed by the combined pressure. The 51st and 50th Divisions, coming up to dam the breach, were delayed on roads encumbered with Portuguese and shattered vehicles, and, caught by the tide of battle before they reached their positions, could not prevent the Germans, now reinforced by seven divisions, attaining, and even crossing the line of the Lys and Lawe rivers. But next day their resistance so far stemmed the German tide that little more ground was lost except on the north of the original bulge.

That morning, however, the German attack had been extended northwards to the Ypres–Comines Canal, against the southern sector of the British Second Army (Plumer). It was akin to a left-fist followed by a right-fist punch, although this new punch was much lighter – by only four divisions of the German Fourth Army. This lightness was counter-balanced by the enforced diversion of part of the three British defend-ing divisions to the breach made the previous day. The Germans broke through, and between the punches Armentières itself was pinched out, the 34th Division barely escaping from the bag. That night the breach was thirty miles in width, and by the 12th its depth was doubled.

This was the crisis. Less than five miles separated the Germans from Hazebrouck junction. On the 13th British and Australian reserves began to arrive from the south, and the German pressure to show signs of slackening – one self-confessed reason being their 'difficulties of supply under the increasing attacks from the air'. The approach to Hazebrouck, barred just in time by the 4th Guards Brigade, was now finally bolted by the 1st Australian Division, and the remaining German pressure was exerted almost entirely on the northern half of the breach.

Plumer now took over charge of all except the southern fringe of the battle area and, to shorten his line as well as to forestall a fresh extension of the German attack, he began an unhurried withdrawal from the Ypres salient to a line just in front of the immortal town. This was a wise and clear-sighted move, even though it abandoned the few square miles of mud which had been purchased at so terrible a price the previous autumn.

Although the enemy gained Bailleul and the Ravelsberg ridge on the 15th, he was then stopped at Meteren and in front of Kemmel Hill, and by the 18th the storm subsided. Meantime storms of another type had been raging behind the front. Foch's appointment as generalissimo did not seem to Haig to have brought him the prompt support he had expected. Ever since the 10th, and, indeed, before, he had been pressing Foch for French aid and active share in the battle. On the 14th an acrimonious conference took place at Abbeville, and next day Haig made the stricture 'that the arrangements made by the generalissimo were insufficient to meet the military situation'.

Foch, on the other hand, was, perhaps to the point of hazard, intent on husbanding his reserves for an offensive. In his opinion, on April 14th, '*la bataille du nord est finie*' – where to many observers it looked rather as if the British Army was '*finie*'. As usual he illustrated his opinion by a parable – of the rings made by dropping a stone into water, the successive rings growing less marked until the water became still. To hard-pressed Allies these parables were apt to be irritating. But his prediction proved right, even though, as at Ypres in 1914 and 1915, the British troops suffered a terrible strain in proving him right.

Contrary to what has been alleged, five French divisions arrived behind the British front as early as the 14th. But their intended counterattacks, as at Ypres in 1915, did not at first materialize. Let it be said, however, in justice and as a matter of tactical interest, that British counter-attacks throughout this battle achieved consistently little gain, at heavy loss. On the 18th a French division took over Kemmel Hill, and next day the remainder entered the line. On the 25th the Germans resumed their offensive, but only on a limited front. The famous Kemmel Hill was captured from the French, and the British to the north were also forced back. For a few hours a last opportunity was vouchsafed to the Germans, but through Ludendorff's intervention they refrained from exploiting it. After a final, costly and more abortive assault on the 29th, the German offensive was abandoned.

As General Edmonds, the official historian, has penetratingly remarked, 'It is easy to see why Ludendorff collapsed after the 8th of August, 1918 – on the 29th of April he was already well on the way to despair.'

CHAPTER EIGHT

SCENE 3

The Breakthrough to the Marne

Four battle-worn British divisions were 'resting' in a quiet sector north of the Aisne, between Reims and Soissons, far detached from the rest of the army. They had been sent to the French front, after strenuous exertions in the battles of the Lys, in return for French reinforcements which had gone north to aid the British in the later stages of that 'backs to the wall' struggle. On the tranquil Aisne they could recuperate while still serving a useful purpose as guardians of the trench line.

It was too quiet to be true. But the uneasiness of the local British commanders – shared by certain of their French neighbours – was lightly discounted by their French superiors. On May 25th they received from French headquarters the message that 'in our opinion there are no indications that the enemy has made preparations which would enable him to attack tomorrow'. Next morning the French captured two prisoners who told of the impending attack, but the higher command had no plan to meet it, and, even so, did not warn the troops until late in the day. Too late!

For at 1 AM on May 27th, 1918, a terrific storm of fire burst on the Franco-British front between Reims and north of Soissons, along the famous Chemin-des-Dames; at 4.30 AM an overwhelming torrent of Germans swept over the front trenches; by midday it was pouring over the many unblown bridges of the Aisne, and by May 30th it had reached the Marne – site and symbol of the great ebb of 1914. After nearly four years a menace deemed for ever past had returned to a point that endowed it with demoralizing symbolism.

Happily, it proved to be 'thus far and no farther'. Like the two great preceding offensives of March 21st and April 9th, that of May 27th achieved astonishing captures of ground and prisoners, but it brought the Germans little nearer to their strategical object. And, even more than its predecessors, its very success paved the way for their downfall.

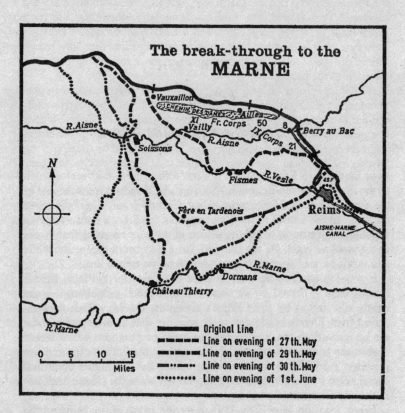

The break-through to the
MARNE

Vauxaillon

CHEMIN DES DAMES Ailles

R.Aisne XI Fr. Corps 50

Vailly IX Corps 8 Berry au Bac

R.Aisne 21

Soissons

N

Fismes R.Vesle

45F

Fère en Tardenois Reims

AISNE-MARNE
CANAL

R.Marne

Dormans

Château Thierry

R.Marne

▬▬▬▬	Original Line	
▬ ▬ ▬ ▬	Line on evening of 27 th. May	
▬ ▬ ▬	Line on evening of 29 th. May	
▬··▬··▬	Line on evening of 30 th. May	
••••••••	Line on evening of 1 st. June	

0   5   10   15
Miles

To the reasons for this we shall come. But why, a month after the last onslaught, in the north, had come to an end; why, when there had been this long interval for preparation and for examination of the situation by a new unified command, should a surprise greater than any before have been possible? This is perhaps the most interesting historical question of the battle.

It has long been known, of course, that the French higher command, the one directly concerned with the safety of the Aisne sector, did not believe in the likelihood of an attack. Nor did the British higher command, which, however, was concerned with the front in the north, and expected a further onslaught there. If not justified by the event, the British had some cause for expecting it, as German disclosures have since attested.

But the Intelligence Service of another of the Allies, better placed to take a wide survey, did give the warning – only to be disregarded until too late. On May 13th, a fortnight after the fighting in Flanders had died away, the British Intelligence came to the conclusion that 'an attack on a broad front between Arras and Albert is intended'. Next day this was discussed at a conference of the Intelligence section of the American Expeditionary Force, and the head of the Battle-Order section, Major S. T. Hubbard, gave a contrary opinion, holding that the next attack would be against the Chemin-des-Dames sector, between May 25th and 30th. Among the reasons given were that, as surprise was the keynote of the German method, this sector was one of the few where it was now possible; that it was all the more likely to be chosen because regarded by the Allies as secure and as a resting ground for tired divisions; that its feasible frontage corresponded well with the limited German resources available at the moment, and that this hypothesis was confirmed by the ascertained location of the German troops, particularly of certain picked divisions.

The warning in detail was conveyed to the French General Headquarters, but fell on deaf ears. Why should credence be given to an opinion coming from such an amateur army, not yet tested in battle, over the verdict of war-tried and highly developed intelligence services? The warning was reiterated, however, and Colonel de Cointet, Chief of the French Intelligence, was won over to its acceptance. But now, as at Verdun two years before, the Operations branch opposed until too late the view of its own Intelligence. This time, however, it was less blameworthy, for it was tugged the other way by the comforting assurances of General Duchêne, commander of the Sixth French Army, in charge of the Chemin-des-Dames sector.

This General, indeed, bears a still heavier responsibility, for he insisted on the adoption of the long-exploded and wasteful system of massing the infantry of the defence in the forward positions. Besides giving the enemy guns a crowded and helpless target, this method ensured that once the German guns had made a bloated meal of this luckless cannon-fodder, the German infantry would find practically no local reserves to oppose their progress through the rear zones. In similar manner all the headquarters, communication centres, ammunition depots, and railheads were pushed close up, ready to be dislocated promptly by the enemy bombardment.

Pétain's instructions for a deep and elastic system of defence had evidently made no impression on General Duchêne, so that it was still less a matter for wonder that the protests of junior British commanders met with a rebuff – and the conclusive '*J'ai dit.*' It was unfortunate also, if perhaps less avoidable, that when the four British divisions forming the IX Corps (Hamilton-Gordon) arrived from the north at the end of April, their depleted ranks filled up with raw drafts from home, they were hurried straight into the line, as the best place to complete their training.

The central backbone of the Aisne defences was formed by the historic Chemin-des-Dames ridge north of the river. The eastern half of this 'hog's back' was to be held by the British, with the 50th Division (H. C. Jackson) on the left, next the 8th Division (Heneker), and beyond the end of the ridge, in the low ground from Berry-au-Bac along the Aisne and Marne canal, the 21st Division (D. G. M. Campbell), joining up with the French troops covering Reims. The infantry of the 25th Division (Bainbridge) was in reserve.

Altogether the French Sixth Army front was held by three French and three British divisions, with four and one respectively in reserve. Against these tired or raw troops, in the main attack from Berry-au-Bac westwards, fifteen German divisions, all but one brought up fresh, were to fall upon five, with two more for the subsidiary attack between Berry-au-Bac and Reims, while seven German divisions lay close up in support.

Even so, the Germans' superiority of numbers was not so pronounced as in the March and April offensives, whereas both the rapidity and the extent of their progress were greater. Once again the tactical surprise of the assault was aided by a thick ground mist, which wrapped the Germans' initial advance in a cloak of invisibility. But they had a series of extraordinarily difficult obstacles to cross – first, the Ailette stream in no-man's-land itself. The conclusion is, therefore, that the advantage was due in part to the strategic surprise – the greater unexpectedness of the time and place – and in part to the folly of exposing the defenders so completely to the demoralizing and paralysing effect of the German bombardment – by 3,719 guns on a front of thirty-eight miles. This last, indeed, was a form of surprise, for the object of all surprise is the dislocation of the enemy's morale and mind, and the effect is the same whether the enemy be caught napping by deception or allows himself to be trapped with his eyes open. Further, the German's success on May 27th, 1918, deserves study and comparison with their other offensives, whose success was almost in mathematical ratio to their degree of surprise. This final year, indeed, read in the light of previous years, affords fresh proof that surprise – or, more scientifically, the dislocation of the enemy's mental balance – is essential to true success in every operation of war. A lesson oft repeated, oft ignored. At the bar of history any commander who risks the lives of his men without seeking this preliminary guarantee is condemned.

Let us pass to the events of May 27th. For three and a half hours the unfortunate troops had to endure a bombardment unparalleled, according to the verdict of the more experienced sufferers, in its intensity. And the ordeal of those hours of helpless endurance, amid the ever-swelling litter of shattered dead and untended wounded, was made more trying by crouching, semi-suffocated in gas masks. Then the grey waves advanced – a relief, if only of action, at last. Three-quarters of an hour later they had reached the crest of the ridge in the centre, near Ailles. This uncovered the flank of the left British division, the 50th, forcing its survivors to fall back down the other slope. Next to it the 8th Division was being forced to give way, although two of its brigades held stubbornly for a time on the north bank of the Aisne.

Here the 2nd Devons earned imperishable glory and a citation in the French Orders of the Day – by sacrificing themselves almost to a man in a stand which gained breathing space for fresh resistance to take form in rear. On the British right, the attack on the 21st Division developed later; this division was awkwardly placed with the swampy Aisne and Marne canal running through the centre of its battle zone, but most of it was successfully extricated and withdrawn west of the canal. By midday the situation was that the Germans had reached and crossed at most points the Aisne from Berry-au-Bac to Vailly – helped by the fact that General Duchêne had been belated in giving the order to blow up the bridges. Hitherto the German progress had been evenly distributed, but in the afternoon a heavy sagging occurred in the centre, at the junction of the French and British wings, and the Germans pushed through as far as Fismes on the Vesle – twelve miles penetration in a single day. This central collapse was natural, both because it is an habitual tendency, and because the heaviest weight – more than four to one – of the assault had fallen on the two French divisions in the centre and the left of the 50th Division adjoining them.

This sagging, together with the renewed German pressure, compelled a drawing back of the flanks. On the east, or British flank, this operation was distinguished by a remarkable manoeuvre of the 21st Division, which wheeled back during the night through hilly wooded country, while pivotting on and keeping touch with the Algerian division, which formed the right of the army.

After forcing the passage of the Vesle and capturing the heights south of it, the Germans paused until fresh reinforcements reached them from Ludendorff. But on the 29th they made a vast bound, reaching Fère-en-Tardenois in the centre and capturing Soissons on the west, both important nodal points, which yielded them quantities of material. The German troops had even outstripped in their swift onrush the objectives assigned to them, and had done this despite the counter-attacks which Pétain was now shrewdly directing against their sensitive right flank. On the 30th the German flood swept on to the Marne, fifteen miles beyond the Vesle. But it was now flowing in a narrowing central channel; and this day little ground was yielded by the Allied right flank, where the four British divisions – the 8th and 50th now merely remnants – had been reinforced by the 19th (Jeffreys), as well as by French divisions. Next day what remained of the original four was relieved by the French, who now took over command from the IX Corps, although fractions of them still remained in the fighting line for another three weeks as part of the 19th Division.

But from May 31st onwards the Germans, checked on the side of Reims and in front by the Marne, turned their efforts to a westward expansion of the great bulge – down the corridor between the Ourcq and the Marne towards Paris. Hitherto the French reserves had been thrown into the battle as they arrived, in an attempt to stem the flood, which usually resulted in their being caught up and carried back by it. On June 1st, however, Pétain issued orders for the further reserves coming up to form, instead, a ring in rear, digging themselves in and thus having ready before the German flood reached them a vast semi-circular dam which would stop and confine its now slackening flow. When it beat against this in the first days of June its momentum was too diminished to make much impression, whereas the appearance and fierce counterattack of the 2nd American Division at the vital joint of

Château-Thierry was not only a material cement, but an inestimable moral tonic to their weary Allies.

Yet it would seem that the most valuable allies of all were the cellars of Champagne, reinforced by the vast stacks of supplies that the French abandoned to their destitute pursuers. At Soissons the desire for such loot brought the forfeit of opportunity. At Fismes there were 'drunken soldiers lying all over the road'. At Jonchery 'battalions stopped in the face of the slightest opposition and it was difficult to get them together again. Progress was very slow although there was no actual fighting. At the villages lamentable disorders took place. The officers could no longer keep control ... a sorry picture of much drunkenness'.

In their victorious onrush, the Germans had taken some 65,000 prisoners, but whereas this human loss was soon to be more than made up by American reinforcements, strategically the Germans' success had merely placed themselves in a huge sack which was to prove their undoing less than two months later. As in each of the two previous offensives, the tactical success of the Germans on May 27th proved a strategical reverse, because the extent to which they surprised their enemy surprised, and so upset the balance of, their own command.

For, as the disclosures of General von Kuhl have revealed, the offensive of May 27th was intended merely as a diversion, to attract the Allied reserves thither preparatory to a final and decisive blow at the British front covering Hazebrouck. But its astonishing opening success tempted the German command to carry it too far and too long, the attraction of success attracting thither their own reserves as well as the enemy's. Nevertheless, we may justly speculate as to what might have resulted if the attack had begun on April 17th, as ordered, instead of being delayed until May 27th, before the preparations were complete. The Germans would have worn out fewer of their reserves in ineffectual prolongations of the Somme and Lys offensives, while the Allies would have still been waiting for the stiffening, moral and physical, of America's man power. Time and surprise are the two supreme factors in war. The Germans lost the first and forfeited the second by allowing their own surprise to surprise themselves.

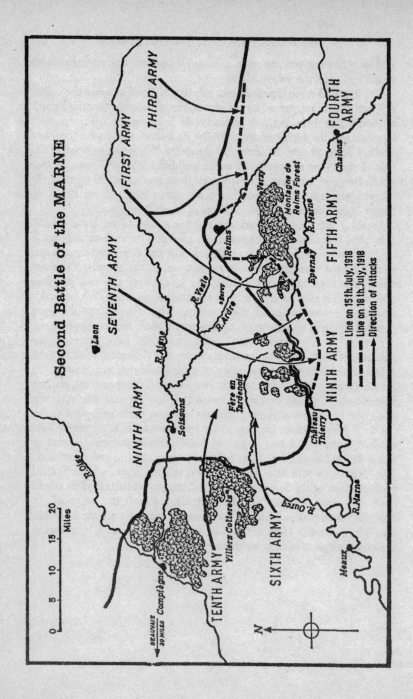

Second Battle of the MARNE

Line on 15th July, 1918
Line on 18th July, 1918
Direction of Attacks

Miles
0   5   10   15   20

N

BEAUVAIS 30 MILES

R. Oise
Compiègne
Soissons
Laon
R. Aisne
R. Vesle
NINTH ARMY
Villers Cotterets
Fère en Tardenois
TENTH ARMY
SIXTH ARMY
Château Thierry
R. Ourcq
R. Marne
Meaux
R. Ardre
Savigny
Reims
Montagne de Reims Forest
Verzy
R. Marne
Epernay
FIFTH ARMY
NINTH ARMY
Châlons
FOURTH ARMY
SEVENTH ARMY
FIRST ARMY
THIRD ARMY

CHAPTER EIGHT

SCENE 4

The Second Battle of the Marne,
July, 1918

How apt, if how strange, the historical coincidence by which, as the Marne had been the first high-water mark and witnessed the first ebb of the tide of invasion in 1914, so four years later it was destined to be the final high-water mark from which the decisive ebb began. For on July 15th, 1918, the shell-churned wastes around Reims were the scene of the last German offensive on the Western Front. The tide of German success was definitely stemmed and three days later the ebb began under pressure of the great Allied counterstroke.

But although the first day marked the last German bid for victory, the actual attack was by no means the Germans' supreme effort, nor had it the decisive aims popularly ascribed to it at the time. For Ludendorff still adhered to his guiding idea that the British, severely shaken in the great battles of March and April, should be the target for his decisive blow and that their front in Flanders should be the stage on which he would produce this final drama of victory.

Thus, as has already been told, the spectacular May 27th attack when the Germans, pouring over the Chemin-des-Dames, across the Aisne and to the Marne, seemed to menace Paris itself, was conceived merely as a diversion to draw the Allied reserves away from Flanders. And its rapid success, surprising Ludendorff as much as his attack surprised Foch, dug a pitfall for the Germans by luring their own reserves thither to exploit and retain this apparent windfall.

So also with the June 9th attack, less bountiful in its fruits, that had been launched near Compiègne to break down the buttress of Allied territory that lay between the huge salients created by the German 'pushes' of March and May. When, instead, this German attack was broken off by Ludendorff, with little gained but his own reserves still further drained, he considered 'the enemy in Flanders still so strong that the German army could not attack there yet'. So he planned a further diversion - to be made by forty-nine divisions attacking on either side of Reims. Another reason for this choice was that the German forces in the Marne salient depended on a single railway, the Laon–Soissons line, which was dangerously exposed both to air and artillery attack. The Chief of the Field Railway insisted that Reims must be captured in order to improve the communications. Otherwise the salient would become untenable - the Germans must get on or get out. Ludendorff chose to attack rather than to withdraw.

The plan was finally settled at a conference on June 18th. The principal blow was to be delivered by the First (Mudra) and Third (Einem) Armies, driving towards Châlons, while the Seventh Army (Boehm) sought to cross the Marne near Dormans and to converge with the main advance in the direction of Epernay.

Outwardly, Boehm's army seemed to have the most difficult problem to solve, having to cross a river eighty yards wide in face of the enemy. The designers relied for success on 'the unexampled boldness of the plan', aided by the methods of concealment which had triumphed on May 27th.

But the sands of time were slipping out for the Germans, and American reinforcements, like the sands of the shore in potential number, were slipping into the Allied line of battle, there to become a cement for this grievously strained rampart. Appreciating this, Ludendorff intended his Flanders attack, once more towards the nodal point of Hazebrouck, to follow on the 20th day, only five days after the Reims diversion. On July 16th actually, as soon as the Reims attack was under way, artillery and aircraft were sent off by train to the Flanders front, and Ludendorff himself moved to Tournai to supervise the staging and production of his decisive drama.

But the curtain was never to rise upon it. The Reims diversion had not even the brilliant opening success of its predecessors, and on July 18th the Allied counterstroke so jeopardized the Germans' situation that Ludendorff felt compelled to postpone, if not yet to abandon, the fulfilment of his dream. The reason why the German offensive 'fell flat' on July 15th was that east of Reims it was played to an empty 'first night' house. One of the great stories of the war which everybody knows is that of the 'elastic defence', in face of which the German onslaught lost its momentum, before it reached the real position of the French resistance. Statesmen and generals have vied with each other in acclaiming the brilliance of 'Gouraud's manoeuvre'. Alas! the story must be consigned to its place with many others in the museum of war legends.

The manoeuvre was entirely due to Pétain, that cool, unemotional company director of modern war, and shrewd economist of human lives, who, called to be Commander-in-Chief after the Nivelle fiasco of 1917, had systematically worked to rebuild the French Army and to restore the stability of its man power and morale that had been so undermined by the extravagant offensive policy of Joffre and Nivelle from 1914 to 1917.

Not content merely to reorganize, Pétain had set himself to insure against a recurrence of the trouble by tactics that should be both an economy of force and of the nervous force of the combatant. To this end, one method was an elastic defence in depth, allowing the initial shock and impetus of the enemy's attack to be absorbed by a thinly held forward position, and then to await him on a strong position in rear, when the enemy's troops would be beyond the range of the bulk of their supporting artillery.

This method Pétain had sought to apply against the German attack of June 9th, but, although partially successful, its full effect was lost through the reluctance of the local commanders, still clinging to their old offensive dogmas, to reconcile themselves to a voluntary yielding up of a few square miles of worthless ground. And before July 15th, when the coming German attack was definitely expected, a week's argument was required before Pétain could persuade the lion-hearted Gouraud, who commanded the French Fourth Army east of Reims, to adopt this elastic manoeuvre.

But even when we have ascribed it to the right source, the accumulation of historical error is not fully corrected. For the method was not the revolutionary innovation that it has been termed. The Germans, in fact, had used it on September 25th, 1915 – nearly three years before – to discomfit the great French autumn offensive in Champagne. And the underlying idea can be traced back 2,000 years – to Cannae, where Hannibal applied it against the Romans in a distinctly more subtle and decisive way.

But it sufficed, even in the mild way of 1918, to thwart the German attack east of Reims, where its effort was immeasurably strengthened by the German failure to achieve a surprise such as had marked their earlier offensives of 1918. Full warning of the coming blow was obtained by the French; the statements of prisoners taken from July 5th onwards being confirmed by air photographs of camouflaged ammunition dumps. And an evening raid on July 14th brought in a prisoner from whom, by withholding his gas mask, the French discovered the exact hour of the bombardment (1.10 AM). The French guns accord-

ingly opened fire ten minutes earlier, and thus before the German
infantry advanced from their trenches they had been trapped and riven
by the French artillery counter-preparation. They withered away before
the machine guns of the French outpost line, and the shrunken remnants that passed beyond failed to make even a crack in the main
position.

But the dramatic nature of this repulse east of Reims has obscured
the fact that it was not the whole battle. West of Reims the front had
only been stabilized for a month since the last German thrust, and the
newly improvised position was a handicap to the execution of the elastic
method by commanders who were slow to grasp it. They chose to hold
the forward position on the river line strongly, and their troops paid
the penalty when the enemy's sudden deluge of gas shells caught
them unawares. The Germans, in contrast, proved the value of
taking the most obviously difficult, and hence most unlikely, course.
Their infantry were ferried over the river under cover of darkness
and a smoke screen, and then pushed forward to the attack, while
a number of bridges were swiftly built under fire – an astonishing
feat.

Thus here the German attack deepened the corner of the great bulge
made in May, and not only·pushed across the Marne but behind Reims,
so that it threatened to undercut this pivot of the Allied resistance. If
the threat had an important influence on the French plan for the
counterstroke, its physical progress was stopped on July 16th. The German attack, unaided by pressure elsewhere, had degenerated into local
actions, disconnected and therefore useless, while the French artillery
and aircraft, by bombarding the Marne crossings, made it difficult for
the Germans to obtain supplies. Next day a queer hush of expectation
spread over the far-flung battlefield. The stage was set for the great
'revanche'.

In an event so significant for the history of the world, the main
historical interest is to determine its causes. The chief among them is to
be found not by any analysis of military art, but by a process far more
true to the character of the World War – that of drawing up a balance
sheet of the previous six months' transactions. When Ludendorff
opened his campaign he had a credit balance of 207 divisions, 82 in
reserve. Now he had only 66 'fit' divisions in reserve, most of them
really so 'watered down' that they could hardly be counted as sound
assets.

If these operations had made serious inroads into the Franco-British
balance of man power, the Allies had at least averted liquidation, and

now, in July, ample and increasing American drafts were being paid
into their account. Like a promissory note, this American aid was of
incalculable value in restoring their credit – their morale and confidence
– even before it made good their material losses. Pétain, the military
economist, had appreciated this primary factor long before, when he
had said – 'If we can hold on until the end of June our situation will be
excellent. In July we can resume the offensive; after that victory will be
ours.'

If this simple calculation of time and numbers has the effect of
attenuating the popular image of an inspired 'Foch counterstroke',
wresting victory from the jaws of defeat, it is regrettable, but it is
reality. Unfortunately, even what remains suffers in examination and,
in the outcome, a further reduction. War is a masculine activity, and so
it is perhaps natural that the feminine maxim, *'il faut souffrir pour être
belle'*, should be inverted. For in military history it is both easy and
pleasant for all concerned to make an image of beauty, whereas it is not
only hard for the seeker to reach the truth but the subject usually suffers
in consequence.

The riddle of July 18th, 1918, might aptly be put in terms of
the old conundrum – 'When is a counterstroke not a counterstroke?'
Foch's mystical faith in the almighty power of the offensive 'will to
conquer' had long since been shown at the Marne in 1914 – where day
after day he had ordered attacks, apparently oblivious of the reality that
his exhausted troops could do and did nothing more than cling pre-
cariously to their ground.

Then at Ypres the same year he had spurred on Sir John French to
order ambitious attacks, while actually the British troops were barely
resisting superior numbers. On these occasions the result justified the
spirit, if not the letter, of his instructions. But when the German gas
attack made a hole in the Allied line at Ypres in April 1915, Foch's
refrain of *'attaquez'*, and his unredeemed promises of a French attack,
caused Sir John French to waver almost nightly from the resolve to
withdraw and straighten out the line, as Smith-Dorrien, to his cost,
urged from the outset. Thus, when this common-sense course was
ultimately followed, the British had merely lost not only Smith-
Dorrien's services but many lives to no purpose.

When Foch was rehabilitated in 1917 this 'offensive' instinct still
dominated him, and when the crisis of March, 1918, called him to the
Supreme Command he had hardly set about his unenviable task of
restoring the battered front of the Allies before he was dreaming of
fresh offensives. Even before the new collapse of the Aisne front in May

he had issued *directives* to Haig and Pétain for attacks to free the lateral railway near Amiens and Hazebrouck.

If this project showed his practical belief in his theory of freedom of action, it is also evidence that he had no idea of luring the Germans into vast salients which he could cut off in flank – which was the conception subsequently extolled by popular propagandists. Similarly, the truth of the great counterstroke of July 18th is that it was not conceived, by Foch at least, as a counterstroke at all. But the refrain *'attaquez'* was chanted so continually that sooner or later it was bound to coincide with a 'psychological moment' – as on July 18th.

In the meantime Ludendorff's keenness in pursuing a similar policy, and the wariness of Pétain and Haig helped to prevent the Allied forces becoming seriously involved in a premature offensive before the balance of numbers changed. In contrast, it was the oft-derided economist, Pétain, the 'cautious', who had conceived the plan of the defensive-offensive battle as it was actually waged – first a parry to the enemy's thrust and then a riposte when he was off his balance. On June 4th he had asked Foch to assemble two groups of reserves at Beauvais and Epernay respectively with a view to a counterstroke against the flank of any fresh German advance. The first group, under Mangin, had been used to break the German attack of June 9th, and was then switched a little farther east to a position on the west flank of the German salient between Soissons and Reims which bulged towards the Marne.

Foch, however, planned to use it for the strictly offensive purpose of a push against the rail centre of Soissons. While this was being prepared, the Intelligence Service made it clear that the Germans were about to launch a fresh attack near Reims. Foch thereupon determined to anticipate it, not retort to it, by launching his offensive on July 12th. Pétain, however, had the contrary idea of first stopping and then smiting the enemy when the latter had entangled himself. And, perchance curiously, the French troops were not ready on July 12th, so that the battle was fought rather according to Pétain's than to Foch's conception. But not altogether. For Pétain's plan had comprised three phases – first, to hold up the German attack; second, to launch counterstrokes against the flanks of the fresh pockets it was likely to make on either side of Reims; third, and only third, when the German reserves had been fully drawn towards those pockets, to unleash Mangin's army in a big counter-offensive eastward along the baseline of the main bulge – the enemy's rear – and so close the neck of the vast sack in which the German forces south of the Aisne would be enclosed.

Events and Foch combined to modify this conception. As already narrated the German attack west of Reims had made an unpleasantly deep pocket, penetrating well over the Marne and threatening to take in rear the natural buttress formed by the Montagne de Reims. To avert the danger Pétain was driven to use most of the reserves he had intended for the second phase of the counterstroke; and to replace them he decided to draw from Mangin's army, and to postpone the latter's counter-offensive – already ordered by Foch for July 18th.

When Foch – full of eagerness and with his spirit still more fortified, if that was possible, by Haig's promise to send British reserves – heard of Pétain's action he promptly countermanded it. Hence on July 18th the French left wing* was launched to its counter-offensive while the defensive battle was still in progress in the centre and on the right wing. This meant that the second phase of Pétain's plan had to be dropped out, and instead of the right wing attracting the Germans' reserves in order to enable the left wing to fall on their naked back, the left wing's offensive eased the pressure on the right wing.

To compensate as far as possible the initial passivity of the right wing,† the British reserves (51st and 62nd Divisions) which were sent thither, were used to relieve the defending troops 'on the move', passing direct to an attack. In the centre,‡ American reserves were similarly used, and thus a general pressure began along the whole face of the great salient.

But this convergent pressure did not begin until July 20th, and by that time the opening surprise – due to the sudden release of a mass of tanks – was over and the left wing had lost its impetus. After advancing

* The spearhead of this consisted of Mangin's Tenth Army, which had ten divisions in the first line (including the American 1st and 2nd Divisions), six divisions and Robillot's Cavalry Corps in the second line, and the British 15th and 34th Divisions in reserve. At 4.35 AM on the dark and foggy morning of the 18th Mangin struck, using his massed tanks on the Cambrai method without any artillery preparation. The left of Degoutte's Sixth Army, on Mangin's inner flank, chimed in one and a half hours later, after a preliminary bombardment. Degoutte's subsidiary role was marked by the fact that he had only seven divisions (among them the American 4th and 26th) in the first line and one in the second; he was later reinforced by the American 42nd, 32nd and 28th divisions, which bore the main burden in the final stage of the advance to the Vesle. Five German divisions faced Mangin and six faced Degoutte; with six and two respectively in reserve. But all were weak and more than half had been reported as of little or no value.

† Berthelot's Fifth Army, comprising nine divisions. It was opposed by eleven German divisions, with one in reserve.

‡ De Mitry's Ninth Army, comprising six divisions (including the 3rd American), with the 28th American and a French one in reserve. It was opposed by six weak German divisions, with three in reserve.

about four miles on the 18th, and a little farther on the 19th, Mangin's army was brought to a standstill on the Soissons flank – near the jugular vein of the salient. Thus the Germans, fighting hard for breathing space, gained the time they required to draw the bulk of their forces out of the sack, even though they left 25,000 prisoners and much material behind. And once they were safely back on a straight and much-shortened line along the Vesle, Ludendorff felt able, on August 2nd, to order preparations to be resumed for fresh attacks in Flanders and east of Montdidier.

Six days later his offensive dreams were finally dissipated; but it is historically important to realize that it was not the second Battle of the Marne, 'Foch's great counterstroke', which dissipated them. This July 18th counterstroke, conceived as such by Pétain and amended by Foch, was by no means decisive in its results. It may be that Foch's impetuosity robbed him of such results; that Pétain's oft-criticized caution would have been more fruitful and collected a larger 'bag'.

Nevertheless, if the battle had no clearly decisive effect, the first taste of victory after such deep and bitter draughts of defeat was an incalculable moral stimulant to the Allies, and perchance its depressing effect on the German morale was more insidiously damaging than was at first visible. So that Foch, who was ever concerned only with moral factors, which cannot be mathematically calculated, may well have been content. He had gained the initiative, and he kept it – that was enough, results mattered little. For his strategy was simple, not the complex masterpiece of art which legend has ascribed to him. It was best expressed in his own vivid illustration – 'War is like this. Here is an inclined plane. An attack is like the ball rolling down it. It goes on gaining momentum and getting faster and faster on condition that you do not stop it. If you check it artificially you lose your momentum and have to begin all over again.'

CHAPTER EIGHT

SCENE 5

The 'Black Day' of the German Army – August 8th

August 8th, 1918, is a date which grows ever larger on the horizon of the historian. So far as any one event of the campaign in the west can be regarded as decisive, it is the great surprise east of Amiens that occurred on this day. And that decisiveness is above all a proof that the moral element dominates warfare.

For although August 8th was 'a famous victory', the most brilliant ever gained by British arms in the World War, and, better still, the most economical, neither its tactical nor its visible strategic results were sufficient to explain its moral effect. Its 16,000 prisoners on the first day, and 21,000 all told, were a handsome prize compared with that of any previous British offensive, but a trifle in proportion to the vast forces then deployed on the Western Front, and in relation to such triumphs of the past as Worcester, Blenheim, Rossbach, Austerlitz, or Sedan. Its initial penetration of six to eight miles, and ultimate twelve miles, were, again, excellent by 1915–17 standards, but in March the Germans had penetrated thirty-eight miles in the reverse direction without achieving any decisive result. Studied on the map, the advance of August 8th–21st merely flattened out the nose and indented one cheek of the shallow German salient Arras–Montdidier–Noyon. It was far from reaching any vital link of the enemy's communications, or even cutting off the troops in that salient.

Yet it unhinged the mind and morale of the German Supreme Command. It led the Kaiser to say – 'I see that we must strike a balance. We are at the end of our resources. The war must be ended.' It made Ludendorff take a similarly despondent view – 'The war would have to be ended.'

In comparing the impression made upon him by the dramatic counterstroke of July 18th on the Marne and that of August 8th, there

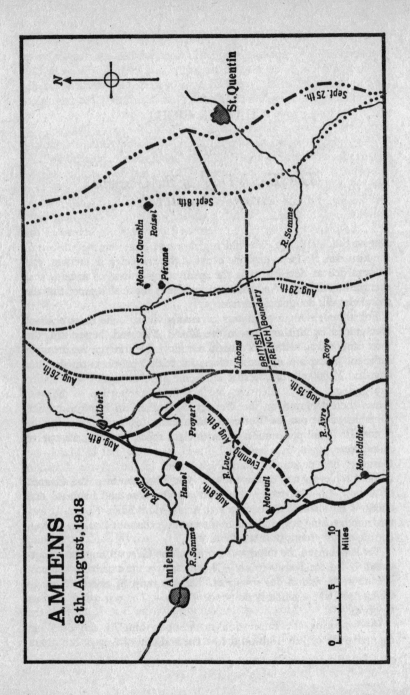

AMIENS
8th. August, 1918

is a remarkable contrast. And in this contrast lies the answer as to which was the more decisive of the two. For after July 18th he had by no means lost hope. He seems to have treated this reverse as hardly more than an unfortunate incident, and as late as August 2nd was ordering preparations for four fresh attacks, including his cherished Flanders blow, if on a reduced scale in comparison with his original intention.

But after August 8th these dreams vanish. There is an abandonment of any idea of returning to the offensive, and, more significant still, no adoption of an alternative strategy. Mere passive resistance to the enemy's kicks cannot be called a strategical plan. Only when it was too late did he formulate the design of a purposeful evacuation of France as a preliminary to a fresh campaign beyond the frontier. By then, however, the moral collapse of the German Command had spread to the German people.

After the war Ludendorff delivered his considered opinion that 'August 8th was the black day of the German Army in the history of the war'. The adjective 'black' is peculiarly apt, for when faintness follows a sudden shock the blackening of the vista is the symptom which precedes the loss of consciousness and the consequent paralysis of the faculties. Thus the primary interest in the story of August 8th is to trace how this shock came about. On July 12th Foch, irrepressibly eager to begin his cherished but oft-postponed idea of returning to the offensive, proposed to Haig that –

> The first offensive to be launched on the British front should be one starting from the front Festubert–Rebecq, with a view to freeing the Bruay mines and forbidding the communication centre of Estaires...

Five days later Haig replied that he saw 'no advantage in an advance over the flat and marshy region between Rebecq and Festubert', and suggested, instead, that —

> The operation, in my opinion, which is of the highest importance and which I proposed to you, as before, should be executed as soon as possible, is to push forward the Allied front to the east and south-east of Amiens so as to free that town and the railway. The best way to carry out this object is to make a combined Franco-British operation, the French attacking south of Moreuil and the British north of the Luce.
> To realize this project I am preparing plans secretly for an

offensive north of the Luce, direction east ... In liaison with this
project the French forces should, in my opinion, carry out an
operation between Moreuil and Montdidier ...

This letter, from the archives, sheds light on several momentous
points of post-war controversy. First, as to the origin of the offensive, it
shows not only that it was purely of British conception, but also that it
was a 'limited' conception – a narrower-fronted 'shove' to secure for
Amiens and the railway a rather wider margin of safety. The question
is often mooted whether the idea sprang from the Commander-in-
Chief, Haig, or from the Fourth Army commander, Rawlinson. Here
the words 'as before' suggest that Haig had priority, for it was the
brilliant little surprise operation at Hamel on July 4th and its revelation of the decline of German morale which inspired Rawlinson with
the idea of a wider offensive.

However, there is little in the question of priority, for the defensive
advantage of freeing Amiens was obvious. Indeed, the fact that Rawlinson's inspiration should not have come until after Hamel suggests his
deeper appreciation of the moral element. The exploitation of an
enemy's moral disintegration is fundamentally an offensive purpose.

Second, as to the plan of the offensive, the letter seems to contradict
the claim, made in *Sir Douglas Haig's Command* and elsewhere, that
the British were forced by Foch, against their will, to let the French
share in the operation – thereby increasing what Clausewitz termed the
inevitable 'friction' of war. Rawlinson certainly, and rightly, argued
against it as inimical to the surprise he sought.

But the letter shows that it was Haig's proposal. It is true that he
proposed leaving a gap a few miles between the French and British
attacks. But both were purely frontal and strategically shoulder to
shoulder. A richer offensive prospect was perhaps offered by a convergent attack on the two flanks of the salient, north of Albert and well
south of Montdidier respectively. But, for the former, a trench-filled
belt of the old Somme battlefields was a difficulty, and subsequent
events do not support the view that another army would have brought
off such a surprise as the Fourth did south of the Somme.

The enlargement of the original project was due to Foch, who, on
August 5th, directed that if the initial attack was successful, it was to be
continued by pushing south-east towards Ham. If the attacks against
the southern flank of the salient which Humbert's and Mangin's armies
began on August 10th and 17th respectively could have coincided with
that of the British, greater material profits might have been yielded. As

it was, the close cooperation of Debeney's army immediately adjoining the British did little to compensate its inevitable hindrance to the plan of surprise. For, lacking tanks, it could not dispense with a preliminary bombardment, and this could not begin, without forfeiting the general surprise, until the British advance started.

Greater material profits, however, could hardly have increased the moral effect of August 8th on the German Command. And this effect came from the shock of perhaps the most complete surprise of the war. How it was achieved is an object lesson for future soldiers, for, like all the masterpieces of moral dislocation in military history, it was a subtle compound of many deceptive factors. Too often surprise is treated as an incidental, to be gained by a simple choice of date or place.

Its foundation was the sudden loosing of a swarm of tanks – 456 in all – in place of any preliminary artillery bombardment.* This method, inaugurated at Cambrai the previous November, had been repeated by the French on July 18th. Before Amiens it was enhanced by manifold devices. Secrecy was sought by holding the preliminary conferences always at different places, by concealing reconnaissances, and by informing the executants at the latest moment compatible with readiness – divisional commanders did not know that an attack was intended until July 31st, and the fighting troops not until thirty-six hours before the start. Even the War Cabinet in London was kept in the dark, and in that august assembly the Australian Prime Minister, Mr Hughes, was in course of a vehement demand that the Australians should be taken out of the line, when a telegram brought the undreamt of news that the Australians were far on the other side of the line. On that same morning also, a general from the neighbouring army made a casual call at Rawlinson's headquarters on his way home for leave, and incidentally inquired why there was such a heavy sound of gunfire from the front.

Deception was sought by making all movements at night – with aeroplanes patrolling the area to check any exposure; by continuing work on the British rear defences until the last evening, by regulating the times and rates of fire of the artillery so that as more and more guns were slipped into concealed positions they registered without any apparent increase in the normal daily quantity of fire. By such means the strength

* In his analytical study of the war, General von Kuhl, the directing brain of the opposing Army Group, attributes the overwhelming effect of the attack to the fact that the British had 'learnt' how to achieve surprise; he adds that in this surprise 'the most important and decisive factor was the tanks'. This statement has the significance that belongs to a verdict in cool reflection, ten years after the event.

of the Fourth Army was roughly doubled – six fresh divisions, two cavalry divisions, nine tank battalions, and another 1,000 guns being concentrated in the area unsuspected by the enemy between August 1st and 8th. This involved the use of 290 special trains (sixty for ammunition and the rest for troops) – and only two lines of railway were available.

Thus by zero hour (4.20 AM) on August 8th, the Fourth Army strength had been raised to thirteen divisions, three cavalry divisions, seventeen air squadrons, ten heavy and two whippet tank battalions (totalling 360 heavy and 96 whippet tanks), and over 2,000 guns and howitzers, including 672 'heavies'. Two-thirds of the heavy artillery was allotted for counter-battery work, and effectively paralysed the hostile artillery.

Distraction also is an essential component of surprise, and in this case it centred round the introduction of the Canadians. Regarding them as storm troops, the enemy tended to greet their appearance as an omen of a coming attack. At the moment the Canadian Corps was near Arras and an aptly chosen fraction of it – two battalions, two casualty clearing stations, and its wireless section – was dispatched northwards to Kemmel in Flanders. There, also, other 'suggestions' of attack were conveyed by erecting extra aerodromes and cavalry wireless. Meanwhile the bulk of the Canadian Corps was filtered down to the Somme, where various ingenious rumours were circulated among the British troops to account for its appearance.

The Fourth Army dispositions were that the main punch was to be delivered south of the Somme, by the Canadian Corps (Currie) on the right and the Australian Corps (Monash) on the left, next the river whilst the III Corps (R. H. K. Butler) advanced north of the river to safeguard the flank of the main punch. But the Canadians did not move into the front line until a few hours before the assault, and meantime the Australians extended their front as far south as the Amiens–Roye road, relieving the French, and thereby lulling the Germans into a false sense of security. For what enemy would expect attack from a force which was spreading itself out defensively?

The whole front of attack was about fourteen miles long, and on the German side was held by six skeleton divisions (averaging barely 3,000 effectives apiece) of General von der Marwitz's Second Army. Their weakness of numbers was accentuated by weakness of defences, and in their rough forward line there were none of the usual deep dug-outs to safeguard morale until the hour of trial.

Five days before the attack an enemy raid captured an Australian post, and three days later a local attack fractured the III Corps front and took 200 prisoners. But such information as the enemy gained only deluded him further. Moreover, the German aircraft were so incessantly harried by the British that for several weeks they could not reconnoitre behind the British front. The only suspicious sign was a certain amount of noise at night. On several occasions the German troops reported that they heard the movement of tanks, but 'the army staff ridiculed the constantly recurring nervousness of the trench troops about tanks'. Actually, there were no tanks near the scene on the dates they were thus reported, and these cries of 'Wolf, Wolf,' hardened the German higher command in its attitude of disbelief and 'indifference'.

Thus when, an hour before sunrise on August 8th, the British tanks swept forward, with the barrage and infantry advance simultaneous, the blow had the maximum shock of surprise. Shrouded by a thick ground mist, it fell on an enemy who had done nothing to strengthen his position by entrenchments, and the Canadians and Australians – matchless attacking troops – surged irresistibly over the enemy's forward divisions. Only north of the Somme, where tanks were few, was there a partial check. To accelerate the momentum all reserves were set in motion at zero hour – copying the Germans' example of March 21st. Soon, too, armoured cars were racing down the roads, to spread confusion behind the German front, even shooting up an army corps staff at breakfast in Proyart.

The day's final objective (six to eight miles distant) was gained over most of the front except the extreme right and left. But the next day saw slight progress and rather spasmodic pressure, and thereafter the attack flickered out as rapidly as it had blazed up. Why this strange contrast? Why was not so complete a breakthrough completed by a dramatic finale? Partly, it would seem, because the advance had now reached the edge of the old Somme battlefields of 1916, a tangled waste of rusty wire and derelict trenches which was a brake on movement, reinforcement, and supply. It is well to remember that the problem of maintaining continuity of advance was never solved in the World War. Again, the original front of attack had not been wide, and it is significant that almost all successful advances in the World War seem to have been governed by a law of ratio, the depth of the penetration being roughly half of the frontage of attack.

Another reason was, as at Cambrai, the lack of reserves. The introduction of the local reserves of the Fourth Army was well timed but, when its thirteen divisions had been engaged, all that were available were three divisions assembled by Haig in the area. Moreover, the Germans, in contrast, succeeded in reinforcing their original six divisions with eighteen reserve divisions by August 11th – ten more than had been estimated.

A fourth cause of the stoppage was inherent in the form of the attack. For being strictly frontal the more it pushed back the enemy the more it consolidated their resistance. This is always the defect of a frontal attack unless an organized force can be rushed through and placed on the enemy's rear. The cavalry as usual were allotted the role of exploitation. This time they rendered serviceable help in gaining and holding certain localities until the infantry came up, but such help was but a slender thing compared with the true role of cavalry in past history. Greater results might have been attained if the ninety-six whippet tanks, instead of being tied to the cavalry, had been used independently to pass through the gap and make a concentrated thrust south-eastwards against the rear of the German army facing the French – as was suggested by the Tank Corps.

But from the broad strategic point of view there was, or was evolved, this time a method behind the lack of reserves. On August 10th Haig had visited this front and studied the situation at close quarters. In consequence, when Foch urged a continuance of the Fourth Army's frontal pressure, Haig demurred to it as a vain waste of life. In a letter of August 14th he told Foch that he had stopped the further attack prepared for next day, and that he was preparing an attack by the Third Army north of Albert.

Foch objected to the delay involved by this alternative step, but at a conference at Sarcus next day Haig stubbornly held to and gained his point. As a result the Third Army struck on August 21st, the First Army farther north on the 28th, while the Fourth Army seized the opportunity of this distraction of the enemy to resume their advance, the Australians gaining Mont St Quentin and Péronne on the 31st, and thereby turning the barrier of the upper Somme. These operations marked the new strategy of successive attacks at different but closely related points, each attack broken off and succeeded by a fresh as soon as its initial impetus was spent.

It would be unjust, as many British writers have done, to claim that Haig initiated this strategy. For it is to be clearly traced in the successive attacks already begun by the French to the south – Debeney's left wing on the 8th, his right on the 9th, Humbert's army on the 10th, and Mangin's on the 21st. But Haig appears to have appreciated first its potentialities for economy of force. While Foch was filled with the idea of maintaining the pressure, Haig was seized with the idea of pressure at the most economical expenditure of life. The Fourth Army's bag of 21,000 prisoners from August 8th–12th had cost only 20,000 casualties.

To the success of this strategy the surprise of August 8th and its effect on the German Command had contributed greatly. Their instinctive response to the shock was to hurry to the spot all possible reinforcements, and thereby they drained their reserve funds to bankruptcy point. The reserve divisions of the army group of Prince Rupprecht, which held the front from the sea to the Somme district, fell from thirty-six to nine by August 16th. Rupprecht's own resolution had done much to bring the British advance to a halt by preventing the local army commanders from carrying out their first panic decision to fall back behind the upper Somme. But this very resolution, perhaps, cost the Germans more in the end.

Thus, in sum, the decisiveness of August 8th came from its dislocation of thought or will, or both, throughout the whole hierarchy of the German Command. The history of 1914–18 repeated the experience of all history that, except against an exhausted or already demoralized foe, decisive success in war is only possible through surprise. And that surprise must be a compound of many subtle ingredients.

CHAPTER EIGHT

SCENE 6

Megiddo – The Annihilation of the Turkish Armies

On September 19th, 1918, began an operation which was both one of the most quickly decisive campaigns and the most completely decisive battles in all history. Within a few days the Turkish armies in Palestine had practically ceased to exist. Whether it should be regarded primarily as a campaign or as a battle completed by a pursuit is a moot question. For it opened with the forces in contact and hence would seem to fall into the category of a battle; but it was achieved mainly by strategic means, with fighting playing a minor part. This fact has tended to its disparagement in the sight of those who are obsessed with the Clausewitzian dogma that blood is the price of victory – and hold, as a corollary, that no victory is worthy of recognition which is not sanctified by a lavish oblation of blood. But Caesar's triumph at Ilerda, Scipio's near Utica, Cromwell's at Preston, and Moltke's, though opportunist rather than sought for, at Sedan, each had the same 'pale pink' complexion. In each, strategy was so effective that fighting was but incidental. Yet no one can deny their decisiveness both as victories and on the course of history. A more serious 'depreciation' of this final campaign-battle in Palestine lies in the fact that Allenby had a superiority of over two to one in numbers, and more in terms of weapon-values.* In addition the morale of the Turks had so declined that it is often argued that Allenby had merely to stretch out his hand for the Turkish army, like an overripe plum, to fall into it. There is force in these contentions; but most of the 'crowning mercies' of modern history, from Worcester to Sedan, have seen almost as great a disparity of

* Allenby's fighting strength was 12,000 sabres, 57,000 rifles and 540 guns. He estimated the Turkish strength at 3,000 sabres, 32,000 rifles and 402 guns. This figure is about double Liman von Sanders' estimate, which, however, seems to be a broad calculation, excluding machine-gun personnel.

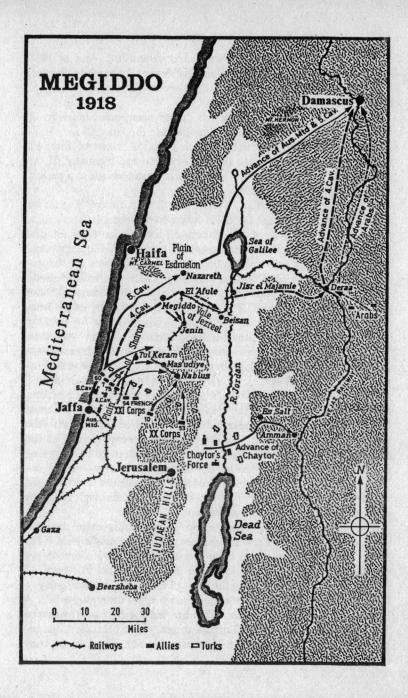

MEGIDDO
1918

Damascus

MT. HERMON

Advance of Aus Mtd & 5 Cav.

O Advance of 4 Cav.

Advance of 4 Cav.

Advance of Arabs

Mediterranean Sea

Sea of Galilee

Haifa
MT. CARMEL
Plain of Esdraelon

Nazareth

Deraa

Arabs

5. Cav.
El 'Afule
Jisr el Majamie

4. Cav.
Megiddo Vale of Jezreel
Beisan

Sharon
Jenin

Tul Keram
Mas'udiye

Plain of
Nablus

60
5.Cav.
75
4.Cav.
54 FRENCH
XXI Corps

R. Jordan

Es Salt

HEJAZ RAILWAY

Jaffa
Aus.
Mtd.

10
53
Amman

XX Corps

Chaytor's Force
Advance of Chaytor

Jerusalem

N

JUDEAN HILLS

Dead Sea

Gaza

Beersheba

0   10   20   30
Miles

⊢⊢⊢ Railways   ■ Allies   ▭ Turks

strength and morale between victors and vanquished. And in 1918 Allenby had to outwit such able commanders as Liman von Sanders and Mustapha Kemal, not such men as those who thrust their heads into the sack at Sedan.

When full deduction is made for the advantageous conditions of September, 1918, the conclusion remains that the triumph immortalized by the already immortal name of Megiddo is one of history's masterpieces by reason of the breadth of vision and treatment. If the subject was not a difficult one, the picture is almost unique as a perfect conception perfectly executed.

The question is often asked, – whose was the conception? Was it that of the titular commander? Or, did it spring from some gifted subordinate? When the victories of Hindenburg on the Russian front are discussed, even the man in the street speaks of Ludendorff's strategy – and the student of war goes still deeper, or lower, and muses on the unassessable influence of Hoffmann's military genius. But with Megiddo it is possible to dispel doubt, through the unanimous evidence of those most intimately concerned. The broad conception sprang entire from Allenby's mind, whatever the credit due to his assistants for working out its executive details. 'Grew', indeed, would be a better word than 'sprang', for the original conception was of more modest dimensions – to break through the Turkish front near the coast and, wheeling inwards, turn the flank of their forces in the Judaean Hills. But, returning one day from a ride during which he had been studying the problem, Allenby suddenly unfolded the plan as it was executed, in all its almost breath-taking scope. It abundantly fulfilled Napoleon's maxim that 'the whole secret of the art of war lies in making oneself master of the communications'. If Allenby had a superiority of strength he was going to use it to make himself master not of one, but of every one, of the Turkish communications. And the success of his attempt to do so owed much to the complementary fact that he had taken thorough measures to be master of his own communications

The three so-called Turkish 'armies', each hardly more than the strength of a division, drew nourishment through a single stem – the Hejaz railway running south from Damascus. At Deraa a branch ran out westwards; crossing the Jordan at Jisr el Mejamie, just north of Beisan, it forked at El Afule in the Plain of Esdraelon, one line going to the sea at Haifa and the other turning south again through the hills of Samaria to Messudieh Junction. This line fed the Seventh (Mustapha Kemal) and Eighth (Jevad) Turkish armies which held the front between the river Jordan and the Mediterranean Sea. The Fourth Army

(Jemal) east of the Jordan was fed by the main Hejaz railway.

Now, to cut an army's lines of communication is to dislocate it: physical organization. To close its lines of retreat is to dislocate it: morale. And to destroy its lines of 'inter-communication' – by which orders and reports pass – is to dislocate it mentally, by breaking the essential connexion between the brain and the body of an army. Allenby planned to achieve not a single but the triple dislocation, and the third element was not the least important to the success of his plan.

The convergence of both roads and railways made Deraa, El Afule, and, to a less extent, Beisan the vital points in the Turks' rear. To get a grip on El Afule and Beisan would sever the communications of the Seventh and Eighth Armies and also close their lines of retreat, except for the extremely difficult outlet to the desolate region across the Jordan eastwards. To get a grip on Deraa would sever the communications of all three armies and the best line of retreat of the Fourth. But it was considerably farther from the British front.

El Afule and Beisan, however, lay within a sixty-mile radius, and hence were within the range of a strategic cavalry 'bound', provided that these vital points could be reached without interruption or delay. The problem was, first, to find a line of approach unobstructed by nature, and, second, to ensure that the enemy could not block it by force. How was it solved? The flat coastal Plain of Sharon afforded a corridor to the Plain of Esdraelon and Vale of Jezreel, in which El Afule and Beisan respectively lay. This corridor was interrupted by only a single door, so far back that it was not guarded by the Turks, formed by the narrow mountain belt which separates the coastal Plain of Sharon from the inland Plain of Esdraelon. But the entrance to the corridor was firmly bolted and barred by the trenches of the Turkish front. Allenby planned to use his infantry to force this locked gate and swing it back, as on a hinge, north-eastwards, so leaving a clear path for his cavalry. But having passed through the front gate they would still have to get through the back door. This the Turks could easily close if they had time and warning. Speed on the part of the cavalry was essential. But not sufficient. The attention and reserves of the Turks must be distracted. Even so, there was still a risk. War experience had shown how easily cavalry could be stopped, and a handful of men and machine guns would suffice to block the two passes through the intermediate mountain belt. To avert this risk the Turkish Command must be made deaf and dumb as well as blind. In this complete paralysis of the Turkish Higher Command lies the main significance and the historical value of the victory of Megiddo.

Let us watch how it was achieved. For it, Allenby had two comparatively novel tools – aircraft and Arabs. Feisal's Arabs, under the guiding brain of Colonel Lawrence, had long been harassing, immobilizing and demoralizing the Turks along the main Hejaz railway. Now they were to contribute more directly to the final stroke by the British forces. On September 16th and 17th, emerging like phantoms from the desert, they blew up the railway north, south, and west of Deraa. This had the physical effect of shutting off the flow of Turkish supplies temporarily – and 'temporarily' was all that mattered here. It had the mental effect of persuading the Turkish Command to send part of its scanty reserves towards Deraa.

The Air Force contribution was in two parts. First, by a sustained campaign it drove the enemy's machines out of the air. This campaign was carried so far that ultimately the fighters 'sat' above the Turkish aerodrome at Jenin to prevent their machines even taking off. Thus it closed the enemy's air eye during the period of preparation. Secondly, when the moment came for the execution of Allenby's plan, the Air Force made the enemy's command deaf and dumb – by decisively bombing their main telegraph and telephone exchange at El Afule, a stroke in which Ross-Smith, who later made history by his flight to Australia, helped England to make history. In addition, the enemy's two army headquarters at Nablus and Tul Keram were bombed, and at the second, the more vital, the wires were so effectively destroyed that it was cut off throughout the day both from Nazareth and from its divisions in the coastal sector. Another and earlier form of air activity was, if less military, perhaps of even wider strategic effect. This was the dropping not of bombs but of an equal weight of illustrated pamphlets showing the physical comforts which the Turkish soldier enjoyed as a prisoner of war. Its appeal to half-starved and ragged men was none the less for being imponderable.

While the Arabs and the Air Force were perhaps the two most vital factors in 'unhinging' the enemy preparatory to the actual push, the plan had also the wide and purposeful variety of ruses which marks the masterpieces of military history. By these Allenby sought to divert the enemy's attention away from the coast to the Jordan flank. In this aim he was helped by the very failure of two attempted advances east of the Jordan, towards Amman and Es Salt, during the spring. Then, throughout the summer he kept a cavalry force, periodically relieved, in the stifling heat of the Jordan Valley to hold the enemy's attention. When the cavalry were ultimately moved surreptitiously across to the other flank, their camps were not only left standing but new ones added, while 15,000 dummy horses of canvas filled the vacated horse-lines. Mule-drawn sleighs created dust clouds; battalions marched by day towards the valley – and returned by night in lorries to repeat this march of a stage army; a hotel was taken over in Jerusalem and elaborately prepared for the mythical reception of General Head-quarters; new bridging and wireless activity fostered the illusion; Lawrence sent agents to bargain for vast quantities of forage in the Amman district.

And all the time more and more troops were filtering down by night marches to the other flank near the sea, there to be concealed in orange groves or in camps already standing. By these means Allenby increased his two-to-one superiority, on the front as a whole, to a five-to-one superiority on the vital sector – unsuspected by the enemy. For some time Liman von Sanders had certainly anticipated a big attack, and indeed, had thought of frustrating it by a voluntary retirement to a rear line near the Sea of Galilee. 'I gave up the idea, because we would have had to relinquish the Hejaz railway . . . and because we no longer could have stopped the progress of the Arab insurrection in rear of our army. On account of the limited marching capacity of the Turkish soldiers and of the very low mobility of all draft animals, I considered that the holding of our positions to the last gave us more favourable prospects than a long retirement with Turkish troops of impaired morale.'

Although he feared an attack near the coast, he feared still more the effect of one east of the Jordan, and even at the last hour the warning of the first given by an Indian deserter on September 17th was offset by the more positive news of the Arab attacks on the vital railway at Deraa. Deceived by his own preconceived idea, Liman von Sanders was, indeed, too ready to believe that this deserter was a tool of the British Intelligence, and his story a blind to cover Allenby's real purpose. Further, Liman von Sanders rejected the plea of Refet Bey, command-ing the coastal sector, who wished to withdraw his troops a mile so that the British bombardment might waste itself on empty trenches. For-bidding Refet to withdraw an inch, he ensured that he should go back 100 miles, to Tyre, leaving his army behind – dead or prisoners.

On the night of September 18th began what was both the last move of the 'distracting' preparation and the first move of the real action. The 53rd Division, which formed Allenby's extreme right, made a spring forward in the hills on the edge of the Jordan Valley. Thereby they would be a step on their way towards closing the only way of retreat – across the Jordan eastwards – left open to the Turks when the main move had fulfilled its encircling purpose.

Far away to the west by the sea all was quiet. But at 4.30 AM 385 guns opened fire on the selected frontage. For a quarter of an hour, only, they maintained an intense bombardment, and then the infantry advanced, under cover of a rapid lifting barrage. They swept, almost unchecked, over the stupefied defenders and broke through the two trench systems, shallow and slightly wired – by Western Front standards. Then they wheeled inland, like a huge door swinging on its hinges. On this door, a French contingent and the 54th Division formed the hinged end; then, with a five-mile interval, the 3rd Indian, 75th and 7th Indian Divisions, formed the middle panel; and the 60th Division, by the sea, the outside panel. The latter reached Tul Keram by nightfall. But what survived of the Turkish Eighth Army had long before been pouring back through the defile to Messudieh in a confused crowd of troops and transport. And upon this hapless mob the British aircraft had swept down with bombs and bullets.

Meantime, through the opened door had ridden the three cavalry divisions of the Desert Mounted Corps (Chauvel). By evening they had reached the Carmel Range, the 'intermediate door', sending detachments with their armoured cars to secure the two passes. By morning they were across. One brigade descended on Nazareth where the enemy's General Headquarters lay, ignorant of the events of the past twenty-four hours because cut off from all communication with its fighting body. Liman von Sanders, however, escaped through a failure to block the northern exit of the town, and after a vigorous street fight the cavalry were forced to retire.

The real strategic key, however, was now not at Nazareth but at El Afule and Beisan. These were reached at 8 AM and 4.30 PM respectively – to Beisan the 4th Cavalry Division had covered seventy miles in thirty-four hours. Passing through the Carmel Range in its wake, the Australian Mounted Division turned south to Jenin to place a closer barrier across the Turks' line of retreat. The enemy's only remaining bolt-hole was east over the Jordan – which flows swiftly, with few fords, through a deep and winding trough, 1,300 feet below sea level at the Dead Sea end. He might have reached this but for the Air Force, as the infantry advance was making slow progress through the hills in face of the stubborn Turkish rearguards. Early in the morning of September 21st, the British aircraft spotted a large column – practically all that survived of the two Turkish armies – winding down the steep gorge from Nablus to the Jordan. Four hours' continuous bombing and machine-gunning reduced this procession to stagnation, an inanimate chaos of guns and transport. Those who survived were merely scattered fugitives. From this moment may be timed the extinction of the Seventh and Eighth Turkish Armies. What followed was but a rounding up of 'cattle' by the cavalry.

Only the Fourth Army, east of the Jordan, remained. This, delaying too long, did not begin to retire until September 22nd. A broken railway and the Arabs lay across its line of retreat to Damascus. And four days later the 4th Cavalry Division moved east from Beisan to intercept it, while the other two converged directly on Damascus, its goal. Escape was impossible, but its fate was different from that of the other armies, a rapid attrition under constant pinpricks rather than a neat dispatch. In this pursuit the Desert Mounted Corps cooperated with, and for the first time met, their real desert allies, hitherto an invisible and intangible factor. Their presence, and identity, was disclosed when a messenger reported – 'There's an Arab on the top of the hill over there in a Rolls-Royce; talks English perfectly and in the hell of a rage!' For no pursuit could be fast enough to satisfy Lawrence's ardent spirit as he urged his Arabs on towards the city of desire. To a British cavalry officer with an apt gift of phrase their march looked 'like some strange oriental version of an old-time Epsom road on Derby Day', but they outpaced the 4th Cavalry Division.

The fragments of the Turkish Fourth Army were finally headed off and captured near Damascus, which was occupied on October 1st. On the previous day the garrison had been intercepted by the Australian Mounted Division as it was trying to escape through the Barada gorge (the Biblical 'Abana'). Sweeping the head of the fugitive stream with machine guns from the overhanging cliffs the Australian Light Horse rolled it back to Damascus, there to swell the 'bag' of prisoners to 20,000.

The next move was a fitting conclusion to this chapter of history. The 5th Cavalry Division was dispatched to advance on Aleppo, 200 miles distant, in conjunction with an Arab force. Its armoured cars led the way and dispersed such slight opposition as was met, reaching the outskirts of Aleppo on October 23rd. Two days later the leading cavalry brigade came up. A combined attack was arranged for next morning, but during the night the Arabs slipped into and captured the town on their own. The British force, too weak to press the retreat of the garrison, was awaiting reinforcements from Damascus when the capitulation of Turkey on October 31st wrote 'finis' to the campaign. During a brief span of thirty-eight days the British had advanced 350 miles and captured 75,000 prisoners – at a cost of less than 5,000 casualties.

In a war singularly barren of surprise and mobility, those keynotes of the art of war, their value had been signally vindicated at the last, and in one theatre at least. Surprise and mobility had virtually won the victory without a battle. And it is worth noting that the Turks were still capable of holding up the infantry attack until the 'strategic barrage' across their rear became known and produced its inevitable, and invariable, moral effect.

Because a preliminary condition of trench warfare existed the infantry and heavy artillery were necessary to break the lock. But, once the normal conditions of warfare were thus restored, the victory was achieved by the mobile elements – cavalry, aircraft, armoured cars and Arabs – which formed but a fraction of Allenby's total force. And it was achieved, not by physical force, but by the demoralizing application of mobility. A new light on Napoleon's dictum that the moral is to the physical as three to one.

CHAPTER EIGHT

SCENE 7

The Battle of a Dream – St Mihiel

For four years a wedge sixteen miles deep lay embedded in the flank of the main French armies. It was the most marked, and most 'ugly', feature of the whole irregular front between the Swiss border and the Belgian coast. Along this long irregular line of trenches salients were numerous, and of all sizes, but none was so acute as that which came down from the heights of the Woevre to the Meuse at St Mihiel – and even protruded beyond the river. All that time it galled France bodily and mentally, for although it was not in itself a convenient springboard for a fresh German offensive it might easily become a menace if a new wedge were driven in on the other side of Verdun; worse still, it crippled the prospects of any French offensive into Lorraine. For such an offensive, whether launched from the Verdun or from the Nancy sector, would not only suffer the menace of St Mihiel in its rear but would be difficult to nourish – because the St Mihiel salient interrupted the railways from Paris to Nancy and from Verdun to Nancy. This handicap was all too clearly manifest in 1916, when the army defending Verdun fought half choked and always in danger of being suddenly strangled.

For two more trying years the defenders of Verdun had to bear the semi-suffocation of their windpipe. And then, at the end of the first hour of September 12th, 1918, 3,000 guns pealed a message of deliverance. Four hours later, deafened yet exhilarated by the thunder of their guns, the infantry of the First American Army advanced from their own trenches across the pulverized earth that had held the enemy trenches. Twenty-four hours later the two sharp points of the American forceps, cutting into each side, met midway, and the ugly fang was removed.

America's First Army had fought its first battle and won its first victory, as an army. The achievement was not merely a good augury

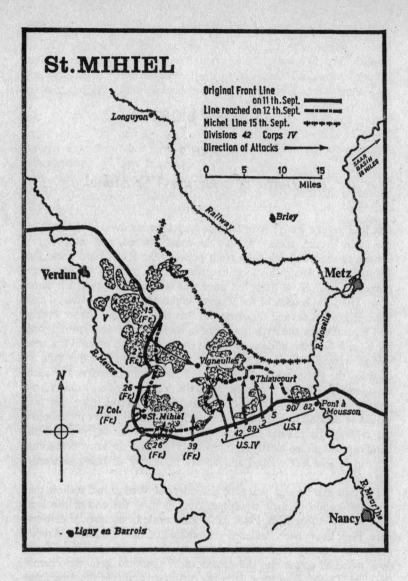

St. MIHIEL

Original Front Line
on 11 th. Sept. ▬▬▬▬
Line reached on 12 th. Sept. ▬ ▬ ▬ ▬
Michel Line 15 th. Sept. +▬+▬+▬+
Divisions *42* Corps *IV*
Direction of Attacks ▬▬▬▬▶

0   5   10   15
Miles

SAAR BASIN 16 MILES

Longuyon

Railway

●*Briey*

Verdun

Metz

R. Moselle

8
15 (Fr.)
V
26
2 (Fr.)

R. Meuse

Vigneulles

●*Thiaucourt*

26 (Fr.)

II Col. (Fr.)

St. Mihiel

90 82
Pont à Mousson

5
1 42 89, 2
U.S. IV

U.S. I

26 (Fr.)

39 (Fr.)

N

R. Meurthe

●*Ligny en Barrois*

Nancy

but a vindication – especially of Pershing. And it was an invaluable tonic both to the army which fought and to the nation behind it, while a proportionate disillusionment to the Germans, who had questioned, even more strongly than her Allies, America's power to produce an effective army.

Apparently, the extraction of the St Mihiel fang was also one of the most perfectly complete pieces of strategic dentistry in the war. Actually, the operation was less satisfactory, and roots were left to cause trouble later. In part, the incompleteness was due to the faulty action of the forceps; in part to the dentist; but still more to the long-concealed fact that the dentist's arm was jogged. Yet there is still a question – whether the operation could have been more effective even if the dentist had not suffered interference.

To answer it, we must examine the cause and course of the operation. It was the fulfilment of a dream and a scheme which almost coincided with the entry of the United States into the war. Indeed, Pershing and his staff had come to Europe in June, 1917, with their eyes fixed on St Mihiel and their minds on Metz, behind it. The British, they knew, were committed to operations in Flanders and northern France, an area which, despite its drawbacks – mud especially – was nearest to their home base and gave them the shortest lines of communication with the Channel ports. The offensive operations of the French had all been carried out in the sector north of Paris and it was natural that they should concentrate to cover their capital.

The choice of the easterly sector facing and flanking Metz was the natural one for the Americans, because it clashed least with their Allies' lines of supply and was easiest of access from their own base ports in the Bay of Biscay. Moreover, this sector was obviously the Germans' most sensitive point, because a thrust there needed to penetrate only a short distance before it would imperil the stability of the whole German position in France – which formed a vast salient jutting southwards between Verdun and Ypres. For to sever the eastern end of the great lateral railway Metz–Maubeuge would at least restrict the free movement of reserves and supplies, and, more significant still, would 'turn' the flank of all the successive lines to which the German armies could withdraw short of their own frontier. Further, such a thrust promised the vital economic result of releasing the Briey iron region and threatening the Saar basin – upon which the Germans largely depended for their munitions. To pinch off the St Mihiel salient was not only a necessary preliminary to a secure offensive, but was a local operation well suited to the first test of a new force.

But the American Expeditionary Force was more intent to conserve its strength until maturity than had been the British. A year passed before it was ready, and before that the Germans had intervened elsewhere to compel a further postponement. Not until August, 1918, when the German tide had begun to ebb, was Pershing able to collect his scattered divisions – which had just helped in stemming it – and to form them into the first all-American army. And even so it had to depend on the French for most of its artillery and on the French and British for part of its aircraft.

On July 24th the commanders of the Allied armies met at Bombon to discuss their future action. The outcome was very modest. Foch did not choose to look far ahead and merely called for a series of local attacks to free his lateral railways. The first was delivered on August 8th in front of Amiens, and its dramatic evidence of the moral rot that had set in among the German troops changed the whole picture. On August 11th the newly formed staff of the First American Army moved to the St Mihiel area, and there developed their plan to a far more ambitious one than had been suggested at Bombon – from that of freeing the French lateral railways to that of threatening the German. Not merely to pinch off the salient but to break through its baseline, where ran the 'Michel' line as an inner barrier against any sudden rupture of the front. The plan framed by General Hugh Drum, the Chief of Staff, visualized the use of fifteen American divisions – each more than twice the strength of a French or British division – and four French divisions. Pershing approved the plan on August 15th and Foch two days later. Indeed, Foch added to it not only six more French divisions, but an extension of the frontage and the direction 'to strike the heaviest blow possible and secure the maximum results'.

But on August 30th Foch came to the American Headquarters at Ligny-en-Barrois with a radically different plan. The change was due to Haig's intervention. August 8th and its sequel had given him a clear perception of the German decline and, disregarding the cautious counsels of his government, he was now willing to test his judgement and risk his reputation by assaulting the ill-famed Hindenburg Line – the strongest defences on the whole German front. But he was anxious to reduce the risk of failure and increase the profit of success, and therefore urged Foch to change the main American attack from a divergent to a convergent direction. It would thus, he calculated, have a quicker and stronger reaction upon the German armies facing him, and by loosening their grip would ease his task – as he would similarly ease the Americans'.

Foch lent his ear the more readily to Haig's argument because his own horizon had enlarged. He now felt that the war might be finished in 1918, instead of 1919. And his enthusiastic assurance led him to transform his new method of alternating attacks at different points into a simultaneous general offensive – '*Tout le monde à la bataille.*' By it he seems to have hoped not merely to stretch and crack the German resistance, but even to cut off and surround the German armies between his converging pincers – British on one side and American on the other. Pétain, when consulted, was quite agreeable to the change of plan, which promised to draw the German reserves to either flank and leave the French a clearer path in the centre.

Thus when Foch came to Ligny-en-Barrois he proposed that the St Mihiel plan should be modified to a mere excision of the salient. This operation was to be a preliminary, and safeguard, to the rear of the American main attack – now to be launched north-west towards Mézières instead of north-east towards Metz. Foch further proposed that, while Pershing's army operated on the easier ground west of the Argonne, a Franco-American army under a French commander should attack the more difficult sector between the Argonne Forest and the Meuse. He also proposed to send General Degoutte to hold Pershing's hand and guide his tactical decisions.

The change of plan came as a shock to Pershing, and the other proposals as an affront. The interview was lively and the atmosphere grew heated. Foch hinted that he would appeal to President Wilson – and the threat had as little effect on Pershing as when previously used. Foch implied that Pershing was trying to shirk his share of the battle, and Pershing retorted that he was fully ready to fight 'as an American army'. Foch ironically suggested that even for St Mihiel Pershing could not raise an all-American army, but had to depend on his allies for guns, tanks and aircraft. Pershing retaliated with the reminder that by Allied request the Americans had shipped only infantry and machine guns during the spring crisis.

Foch wisely dropped the argument and left Pershing to 'chew the cud'. Next day Pershing, after reflection, wrote to Foch. He recognized the potential value of the convergent attack, but dwelt upon the difficulties of American participation. 'Since our arrival in France our plans ... have been based on the organization of the American army on the front St Mihiel–Belfort. All our depots, hospitals, training areas and other installations are located with reference to this front and a change of plans cannot be easily made.' Then he dealt with Foch's second proposal, contending that 'it is far more appropriate at the present moment for the Allies temporarily to furnish the American army with the services and auxiliaries it needs than for the Allies to expect further delay in the formation of the American army'.

Pershing did not attempt to hide his dislike of limiting the St Mihiel attack, and suggested that instead of switching at once to the Meuse–Argonne he should exploit the St Mihiel attack to the full and later, if necessary, mount a fresh attack 'either in the region of Belfort or Lunéville'. Not yet vouchsafed an intuition of victory that autumn, he suggested that these attacks would fit in with the ultimate American aim of taking charge 'during January and February' of 'the sector from St Mihiel to Switzerland'. 'However,' he said, 'it is your province to decide as to the strategy of operations, and I abide by your decision.'

On one question he was unshakable. 'I can no longer agree to any plan which involves the dispersion of our units.' 'Briefly, our officers and soldiers alike are, after one experience, no longer willing to be incorporated in other armies... The danger of destroying by such dispersion the fine morale of the American soldiers is too great.' 'If you decide to utilize the American forces in attacking in the direction of Mézières I accept that decision, even though it complicates my supply system and the care of my sick and wounded, but I do insist that this American Army be employed as a whole.'

The result of this letter was a conference between Foch, Pétain and Pershing on September 2nd, whereat Pershing gave up his own plan for a share in Foch's and Foch conceded Pershing's claim to American unity. The concession was wrung from him by his own realization that without the Americans his right pincer would have a weak and worn point. And as Pershing preferred to attack east of Argonne, where supply would be easier although the ground was more difficult, he obtained his preference.

The one outstanding question was that of St Mihiel. Foch wanted the general offensive to open by September 20th at the latest, and suggested that the St Mihiel attack should be abandoned. Pershing and his staff decided that they must first cut off the St Mihiel wedge to safeguard the rear of their Meuse–Argonne attack. Again, their claim was conceded. But it meant that they would not switch divisions from one battle to the other in time, and that a number of raw divisions had to be used for the Meuse–Argonne attack. In addition, the St Mihiel attack was two days, and the Meuse–Argonne six days, behind timetable.

Each attack interfered with the other. And the consequences were compound, not simple. The first effect was upon the American dispositions. Instead of fifteen double-sized American divisions, which were available, only seven were used in the attack. Although this was a more than ample provision for the task, ensuring a numerical superiority of about eight to one over the Germans, the actual distribution was curious. For while six divisions (including two of Regulars) formed the right pincer, only one National Guard division formed the left. What had happened was that instead of reshuffling the entire dispositions the left pincer had been severely fined down, and the objectives rigorously limited. Foch, indeed, suggested that the left-wing attack should be abandoned.

The plan in detail was that Liggett's I Corps, on the extreme right nearest the hinge, and Dickman's IV Corps should attack the eastern face of the salient at 5 AM. Liggett would demonstrate with the 82nd Division against the hinge, while on its left his 90th, 5th, and 2nd Divisions thrust towards the baseline of the salient. Attacking next to them on the left were Dickman's 89th, 42nd and 1st Divisions. At 8 AM the 26th Division of Cameron's IV Corps would thrust into the western face of the salient, aiming to join hands with the 1st Division. Meantime the French would exert a gentle pressure on the nose of the salient to keep the defenders busy until their retreat was cut off.

But the Germans had for weeks been meditating and preparing to forestall the attack by a retreat. And when the Americans advanced to the assault on September 12th, the Germans had actually begun this withdrawal during the night. This fact has led to a satirical description of St Mihiel as 'the sector where the Americans relieved the Germans'. If there is some truth in the description, it is not the whole truth. Unlike the bigger strategic retreat to the Hindenburg Line in 1917, this withdrawal worked out to the disadvantage of those who planned it. Although the German command were as well aware of the impending blow as most of the population of France, and were not deceived by feints elsewhere, they hesitated too long over their decision and made their preparations too leisurely. Thus they were caught at a moment when part of their artillery had been withdrawn, and although a large part of the American bombardment – from 2,971 guns, mostly French – was wasted on empty trenches, the longer-range fire trapped some of the retiring Germans on the roads. Moreover, the comparative shortness of the bombardment, due largely to Liggett's insistence on the need for surprise, prevented the Germans gaining a comfortable start in their withdrawal. And the swift onrush of the American 2nd and 42nd Divisions, especially, upset their methodical arrangements.

But Pershing's plan was also too inelastic. Before midday Liggett's divisions had reached their final objectives and, soon after, their second day's objectives on the high ground north of Thaiucourt! The rapidity of their advance was accelerated by Liggett's instructions that units should press on as long as possible, without checking to keep alignment with their neighbours. Dazed and unsupported by their own artillery the Germans made practically no resistance. But Pershing felt himself tied by Foch's instructions and refused Liggett's plea for a further bound – which might have ruptured the Michel line. Dickman's and Cameron's converging corps reached their day's objectives with almost equal ease. But there, tied too closely to Pershing's apron strings, they came to a halt and awaited further orders.

Too late, Pershing tried to exploit his opportunity. If the German roads out of the salient were jammed, so also were his own roads into it. His orders for Dickman and Cameron to resume their advance did not reach the troops until after dark. And thus all but some four thousand of the forty or fifty thousand Germans in the bag slipped out before the neck was drawn tight by the junction of the two American corps at Vigneulles next morning. Nevertheless, Liggett had taken over 5,000 prisoners, and the other two corps, together with the French, had taken as many in their original advance. The total came to 15,000, and, more remarkable, 443 guns, for a cost of less than 8,000 casualties. If the result did not entirely satisfy the Americans, they could console themselves with the thought that this first attempt was no different from the past offensives of their Allies in failing to reap the harvest of an initial success.

During the 13th and 14th, Dickman and Cameron wheeled up, with the French 2nd Colonial Corps between, into alignment with Liggett facing the Michel line. Then, and there, the battle was broken off. The only serious fighting had been borne by Liggett's corps, which had met with counter-attacks owing to the menacing direction of its advance – the enemy was willing to evacuate the salient, but had no intention of allowing his baseline to be crossed.

What might have happened if Pershing had not been prevented from trying his original plan? There is no doubt that the Germans were immensely relieved that Pershing did not follow up his success; or that in their view a further advance in this direction would have been a greater menace than the Mézières direction of the Argonne offensive. Pershing's own view was emphatic – 'Without doubt, an immediate continuation of the advance would have carried us well beyond the Hindenburg line [the Michel line was an extension of the main Hindenburg line] and possibly into Metz.' Dickman was still more pungent – 'The failure to push north from St Mihiel with our overwhelming superiority in numbers will always be regarded by me as a strategical blunder for which Marshal Foch and his staff are responsible. It is a glaring example of the fallacy of the policy of limited objectives...'

On the other hand, Liggett, who proved himself perhaps the soundest reasoner and strongest realist in the American Army, has declared – 'The possibility of taking Metz and the rest of it, had the battle been fought on the original plan, existed, in my opinion, only on the supposition that our army was a well-oiled, fully coordinated machine – which it was not as yet.' He has also pointed out that although the attack between the Meuse and Argonne came as a greater surprise to the Germans they were able to throw in reserves so rapidly as to block the original breach by the third day. And even if the Michel line had been broken an advance from St Mihiel would then have met a fresh obstacle, especially on its right, in the defences of Metz. Significant also is the matured verdict of General von Gallwitz, the opposing German Army Group commander – 'An overrunning of the Michel position I consider out of the question. In order to capture this position a further ... operation on a very large scale would have been required.' It is well to remember that for decisive results Pershing would at least have had to reach the Longuyon–Thionville stretch of the lateral railway, a further twenty miles beyond the Michel line, and to have gone far enough beyond it to interrupt the line running back from Longuyon through Luxembourg. It would have demanded a penetration deeper and quicker than any yet achieved by the Allies on the Western Front. With an untried army this was surely a remote hope.

Yet there is one factor of which criticism has taken no account; a factor which endowed Pershing's original plan with a peculiar advantage. Almost every attempted breakthrough in the war had been based on the idea of a single penetration. Among the few exceptions had been the simultaneous Artois and Champagne attacks on September 25th, 1915. But although in form a dual penetration, the effect was that of two single ones, for they were too far apart to cause any prompt sagging and collapse of the sector between. The convergent Argonne and Cambrai thrusts of Foch's new plan had also the same appearance of duality but an even wider interval between them.

Now duality is the very essence of war, although curiously overlooked. Everyone recognizes the advantage which even a light-weight boxer has in using two fists against a one-armed opponent. So in war the power to use two fists is an inestimable asset. To feint with one fist and strike with the other yields an advantage, but a still greater advantage lies in being able to interchange them – to convert the feint into the real blow if the opponent uncovers himself. Nor should duality be limited to the force. Duality of objective, of which Sherman was the supreme exponent, enables the attacker to get his opponent on the horns of a dilemma, and, by mystifying him, to obtain the chance of surprising him, so that if the opponent concentrates in defence of one objective the attacker can seize the other. Only by this elasticity of aim can we truly attune ourselves to the uncertainty of war.

Returning from the general to the particular, we can recognize that the St Mihiel salient offered the chance of attempting the yet untried method of dual penetration under almost ideal conditions. If two powerful attacks had broken through the flanks of the salient – and better still, beyond them to right and left – the defenders in the centre would have dissolved into chaos – and been securely 'caged'. Through this collapsed centre a fresh force might then have driven, with a clear path between the two protecting wings. What we know of the incompleteness of the baseline defences and the time taken before they were completely garrisoned suggests that, on September 12th and 13th at least, they could have been ruptured on a wide front. On a smaller scale, the actual attack fulfilled this process as far as it went, but the wings were then held back and there was no fresh force to pass through the centre.

But it is still a question how far the Americans could have advanced beyond the breach. And here the main factor would not have been defences or defenders, but supplies. The road blocks and transport difficulties actually experienced in the limited advance do not encourage an optimistic answer. It is more likely that the eventual result would have justified Liggett's opinion – and Napoleon's axiom; 'With a new army it is possible to carry a formidable position, but not to carry out a plan or design.' And the last weeks of the war were to show that even experienced armies could not solve the problem of maintaining supplies during a sustained advance, even though almost unopposed. For bulk cancels out experience.

CHAPTER EIGHT

SCENE 8

The Battle of a Nightmare – The Meuse-Argonne

Although a far greater battle in scale the Meuse-Argonne is less significant, except to the combatants, than St Mihiel. Strategically and historically it may even be viewed as an appendix to the unfinished and partly unwritten story of St Mihiel.

In the first place, the ultimate aim was more idealistic than realistic. It was based on the idea that the Ardennes formed an impenetrable back wall to the great German salient in France, and that if the Allies could reach and close the exits east and west they would cut off the German armies in the salient. But the impossibility of the Ardennes had been much exaggerated, especially in Haig's reports. Actually, the Ardennes were traversed by numerous roads and several railways, so that though the severance of the routes east and west might complicate the German withdrawal this would be imperilled only if the objective was attained very rapidly. As always in war, everything turned on the time factor.

To reach the lateral railway from the Meuse-Argonne sector the Americans would have to advance thirty miles. And to be effective they would have to advance more rapidly than from the St Mihiel sector, because their thrust would be aimed close to the main German armies instead of, like the projected St Mihiel thrust, close to the German frontier. The attempt, and hope, was fundamentally unreal. To cross these thirty miles of difficult country, they would first have to break through the German front and then, some eight miles behind it, would meet the untouched defences of the Kriemhilde section of the Hindenburg Line. Pershing might have confidence in the capacity of his untried army, but his faith, like that of the French in 1914 and 1915, was to founder on the rock of machine guns. Pétain, if he underestimated the effect of other factors, was closer to reality when he predicted that the Americans might cover a third of the distance before the winter.

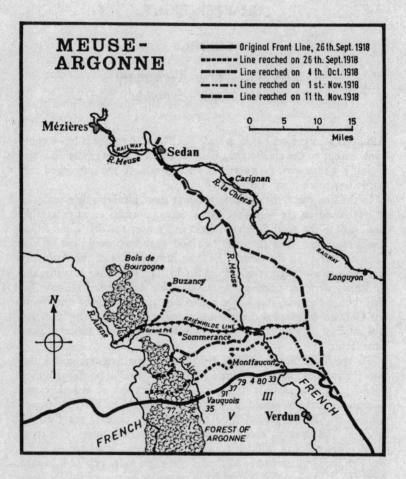

MEUSE-ARGONNE

Original Front Line, 26 th. Sept. 1918
Line reached on 26 th. Sept. 1918
Line reached on 4 th. Oct. 1918
Line reached on 1 st. Nov. 1918
Line reached on 11 th. Nov. 1918

0   5   10   15
Miles

Mézières

RAILWAY

Sedan

R. Meuse

Carignan

R. la Chiers

Bois de
Bourgogne

Buzancy

R. Meuse

RAILWAY

Longuyon

N

R. Aisne

KRIÉMHILDE LINE

Grand Pré

Sommerance

R. Aire

FRENCH

Montfaucon

79 4 80 33
37
91

Vauquois
35

III

V

Verdun

77   28

I

FOREST OF
ARGONNE

FRENCH

That roughly was as far as their original attack reached, and there they stuck, until other factors, unforeseen by Pétain, intervened to relieve them.

In the second place, the Meuse-Argonne attack did not fulfil its immediate aim, the Haig-inspired aim for which Pershing had sacrificed his own plan. For the left-wing attack broke through the Cambrai–St Quentin section of the Hindenburg Line, the strongest artificially, before the Meuse-Argonne attack had drawn off any German divisions from the British front. Thus the result justified Haig's confidence but not his precaution, proving that his troops could break through without indirect help to ease their path. The strength of the defences was nullified by the weakening morale of the defenders.

The irony of the result was increased by the fact that while fifty-seven German divisions faced the left-wing attack by forty British and two American divisions, only twenty German divisions were present to oppose the right-wing attack by thirteen American and thirty-one French divisions – the equivalent of at least sixty ordinary-strength divisions. The difference of result may be explained, in part, by the differing degree of experience, and in part by the difference of conditions. The left-wing attack opened with the British close on the edge of the Hindenburg Line, while on the right wing the Americans had to conquer a deep series of defences before they could assault their section of the Hindenburg Line. And before they reached it their attack had lost its momentum.

Thereafter although stubborn American assaults at heavy cost caused the Germans to draw off, on balance, a further sixteen divisions from the French front, the strategic effect was small. For with shrewd strategic sense the French in the centre appreciated that decisive results depended on the rapid penetration and closing of the pincers, and so did not unduly hasten the retreat of the Germans facing them. In their skilful advance they usually kept a step in rear of their Allies on either flank, moving forward by successive bounds when the enemy had been shouldered back. For the first two years they had borne the main burden of the fighting. If their commanders had been slow to learn how to economize life, they, and still more their men, had learnt it now. Perhaps a shade too well. But it is not for those who were fresh in the evening of the war to complain of excess of caution in those who had suffered the full heat of the day, since dawn.

On the other hand, criticism of the disappointingly early check of the Meuse-Argonne attack has been too apt to overlook the handicap of excessive freshness. The trouble was not merely that the troops were fresh – perhaps it was mostly that the arrangements were fresh. The Americans had scarcely a week of real preparation – an astonishing contrast with the months which preceded the French and British offensives of 1915, 1916, and even 1917. Even though the German fighting power and morale were now in decline, such haste would have put an almost superhuman strain on any troops. Yet it was demanded of new troops with a new organization. Popular opinion might complain of the frequency with which the machine jammed; the miracle is that it did not collapse and, instead, was rapidly repaired to move forward anew.

It is equally creditable to the higher command that the opening attack achieved so high a degree of surprise. This preparatory success owed much to the ingenuity of the Intelligence section in creating the most artistic mirage of an offensive farther east, near the Vosges.

Thus when the real offensive was launched, the twenty-mile front of attack was held by only five German divisions, all emaciated, and all but one composed of low-grade troops. Against them were thrown nine American divisions, with three more in close reserve – a superiority in fighting strength of about eight to one. There were three more divisions in army reserve. But, owing to the difficulty of withdrawing and switching troops from St Mihiel, only one Regular division could be used at the outset, and only three had previous battle experience.

The attack was preceded by a three hours' intense bombardment from 2,700 guns and accompanied by 189 small tanks. It is significant to note that the proportion of tanks was much lower than in the Allied offensives of July 15th and August 8th. It is also noteworthy, in view of Pershing's pre-St Mihiel hint to Foch, that all the artillery was French-made, and half of it manned by the French, as also were forty-seven of the tanks.

Pershing's plan was far-reaching. It certainly cannot be criticized as circumscribed or shortsighted, for the attacking troops were expected to reach and break through the Kriemhilde line on the first day, an advance of over eight miles, and were to exploit the success during the night so that the second morning would find them in open country and almost halfway to Sedan and the lateral railway. Unfortunately, Pershing's orders were by no means clearly worded.

Foch in a personal note had intimated that the American Army must not let itself be tied by the pace of its neighbour, Gouraud's French Fourth Army, and added – 'There is no question of fixing ... fronts not to be passed without a new order – such a restrictive indication tending to prevent exploitation of opportunities ...'

Unfortunately, Pershing's orders to his corps had this very tendency, however far-reaching his aim. Bullard's III Corps on the right and Liggett's I Corps on the left, were to drive in wedges on either flank of the commanding height of Montfaucon, thus helping Cameron's V Corps in the centre, which was to sweep over Montfaucon and on to the Kriemhilde line 'without waiting for advance of the III and I Corps'. This provision was wise, but less happily their advance was to be 'based upon the V Corps'. Here lay the germ of paralysis.

For when the assault was launched, at 5.30 AM on September 26th, the V Corps, which had its flanks protected, made far less progress than its neighbours – although its left division, the 91st, was a happy exception. On the right of the V Corps the 4th (Regular) Division of Bullard's corps penetrated deeply past the flank of Montfaucon, while the 80th and 33rd near the Meuse made good progress. On the left wing of the army, which had the most difficult task and ground, Liggett's orders paved the way for a good start. Thus the 35th Division neatly circumvented the formidable obstacle of Vauquois by an encircling advance, and then, with the 28th Division on their left, drove a wedge nearly four miles deep up the Aire Valley just east of the Argonne Forest. Through the forest itself moved the 77th Division, which had the difficult task of linking up with the French on the west side.

Then, however, Pershing's orders for a halt, on reaching the corps' objective, were construed as putting a brake on the advance, and it was difficult to get up momentum again after the six hours' delay. A method that was sound in siege warfare was, as Liggett's insight told him, a mistake when faced with a weak and temporarily demoralized enemy. The Americans had, as yet, neither the training nor organization for methodical siege warfare, and the best chance of decisive success lay in swamping the defence by a human torrent in the first flush of surprise before the enemy could bring up reinforcements. With the brake put on prematurely, the advance thereafter slowed down and became spasmodic along the whole front. Guns could not get forward to support the infantry, control lapsed, and supplies frequently failed, through inexperience accentuating the natural difficulties of the ground.

All these factors helped the success of the Germans' own tactics in drawing the sting from the attack. For the Germans had repeated the method of elastic defence – with the real resistance some miles in rear. The unexpectant Americans ran into this cunningly woven belt of fire when their initial spurt was exhausted and their formation disordered. Although Montfaucon was taken – by the 79th Division – on the second day, the V Corps only came up level with the two flank corps, and they had made little further progress that day. The great offensive had practically shot its bolt and, in the days that followed, the arrival of fresh German divisions enabled the enemy to counter-attack and force back the disjointed attackers in places. A renewed general attack on October 4th made little progress, except on the left, and revealed once more the folly of trying to overthrow machine guns by sheer weight of human bodies without adequate fire support or surprise. But the value of training was also shown by the regular 1st Division in Liggett's corps which drove in a deep if narrow wedge on the east bank of the Aire. This enabled Liggett, on October 7th, to try a manoeuvre both original and daring; bringing the 82nd Division up in the wake of the 1st, he swung it against the enemy's flank west of the Aire and then northward. If the execution fell below the conception – only a tithe of the division came into action – so that the chance of cutting off the enemy troops in the Argonne was lost, the threat at least persuaded the enemy to retire from the forest while there was time, and by October 10th the American line had passed and was clear of this hampering obstacle.

Meantime, the all too obvious failure to fulfil the original plan had provoked widespread reactions behind the front. Clemenceau visited Foch and bitterly remarked – 'Those Americans will lose us our chance of a big victory before winter. They are all tangled up with themselves. You have tried to make Pershing see. Now let's put it up to President Wilson.' The complaint was rather unfair in view of the fact that the advance of Gouraud's army was well behind that of the American, if by design. But Foch was more generous – or more fully aware of the firmness of Pershing's position – and replied – 'The Americans have got to learn some time. They are learning now, rapidly.' Pétain, indeed, had made the strategically sound suggestion of giving charge of the Argonne Forest sector to a separate army, half French and half American, under General Hirschauer – but Pershing had seen in it only a fresh political manoeuvre, and had rejected it firmly.

Pershing, however, overhauled his own army – and its commanders. The inactive forces east of the Meuse were formed into the Second American Army, to be commanded by Bullard, while Liggett was given charge of the First and of the Meuse-Argonne attack. Pershing himself retained the superior direction of both and left Hugh Drum to continue as Chief of Staff to Liggett. Dickman succeeded Liggett in the I Corps, and Hines succeeded Bullard, while Cameron was replaced by Summerall. Other commanders of all grades fell beneath Pershing's sickle almost as fast as their men beneath the scythe of the German machine guns.

But for a time these changes made little impression on the Germans. The next general attack on October.14th achieved little at large cost – both of men's lives and generals' reputations – and with its failure even the higher command realized that the offensive had reached stalemate. An attempt to press on, with exhausted troops and disordered communications, could exercise no pressure adequate to be any appreciably greater relief to the other Allied armies. Moreover, the British left wing of the Allied offensive, in which the 27th and 30th American Divisions shared, had already broken through the last defences of the Hindenburg Line and by October 5th had emerged into open country, with only natural obstacles, mileage and a devastated area to hinder its advance.

Liggett, who now took charge, was wise to realize that in the circumstances it was far better to rest and reorganize his forces, for a sure bound as soon as possible, than to sacrifice lives in attempting the impossible. While utilizing the breathing space not only to replenish his ranks and supplies but to improve his communications and overhaul his organization, he carried out local operations to obtain a good jumping-off line for the fresh bound. Further, he recast not only the tactics but the plan. Pershing had proposed that the American left should strike first, followed in turn by the remaining corps to the right. This meant battering first at the naturally strong and heavily wooded Bois de Bourgogne area due north of the Argonne, where also the enemy were in strongest force. Liggett preferred to drive a broad wedge in the centre and so outflank the Bois de Bourgogne, threatening its encirclement in conjunction with the advance of the French Fourth Army to the west.

It was well conceived, for when Liggett unleashed his forces on November 1st, this area was the only one which showed resisting power, and by next day the enemy rearguards there had disappeared and were falling back as fast as on the rest of the American front. If the Germans were offering little resistance, the very rapidity of the pursuit – out-stripping the French on the flank – imposed almost as great a strain, and it was a tribute to the overhaul that the First Army machine functioned much more smoothly than in the earlier phase. And this despite the execution of a most difficult manoeuvre by which the whole army wheeled progressively to the right during the course of the pursuit, ready for an attack north-eastwards – against the strong position between the Meuse and Chiers rivers to which the enemy had retired. This wheel was a preliminary to an advance towards Metz, but the

Armistice now rang down the curtain.

Strategically this move was more important, because the Germans here were more sensitive, than the now incidental arrival of the left wing on the Carignan–Sedan section of the lateral railway. This railway had been brought under artillery fire as early as November 3rd, and had been reached by the infantry four days later, but the Germans had already slipped out of the bag. Indeed, the advance to this point, although an exhilarating finish, was chiefly significant in showing the 'liberties' that could be and were taken at the finish. With a somewhat brusque disregard of French feelings Pershing issued a message that he wished the American Army to have 'the honour of entering Sedan' – although it was now in the French sector of advance. Pershing added the encouragement or incitement – 'Boundaries will not be considered as binding.' The message was passed to the corps without being shown to Liggett, and as a result the 42nd Division on the left of the army raced for Sedan. But the vague wording produced a still more unmilitary – indeed, a burlesque– result. For the 1st Division – Pershing's favourite – from the centre corps had also started to race thither by night, crossing the divisions of the I Corps and throwing them into confusion as it impetuously swept through them. It capped the farce by taking prisoner the commander of the 42nd Division. Liggett, however, intervened with prompt action and vigorous language – to restrain both divisions and allow the French the courtesy of entering Sedan, thus to wipe out the bitter memory of 1870.

The historian who scans the whole horizon of the war must recognize that this last offensive, beginning on November 1st, had only a supplementary influence, for Ludendorff had fallen from power – his plea for a renewed stand on the German frontier rejected – and the enemy were already suing for peace before Liggett struck. Nevertheless it was well that the Armistice had tarried long enough to allow the offensive of November 1st to take place. For it provided a counterpoise to the bitter memories of the first phase – more truly, the first battle – of the Meuse-Argonne, and a proof that when purged and refined by experience the American army could produce leadership and staff work worthy of the gallant sacrifice of the fighting troops – the American nation in arms.

Épilogue

Every anniversary of the Armistice kindles emotions and memories such as no other day in the year has at present the power to do. For those who shared in the experiences of those four and a quarter years of struggle the commemoration does not stale with repetition. But the mood in which it is commemorated has undergone subtle changes. On the original Armistice itself the dominant note was a sigh of relief, of infinite volume, most restrained among those who had the most direct cause for relief, most exuberant, perhaps, among those who least appreciated the relief.

The earlier anniversaries were dominated by two opposite emotions. On the one hand grief, a keener sense, now that the storm had passed, of the vacant places in our midst. On the other hand, triumph, flamboyant only in rare cases, but nevertheless a heightened sense of victory, that the enemy had been laid low. That mood again has passed.

Armistice Day has become a commemoration instead of a celebration. The passage of time has refined and blended the earlier emotions, so that, without losing sense of the personal loss and quiet thankfulness that as a people we proved our continued power to meet a crisis graver than any in past annals, we are today conscious, above all, of the general effects on the world and on civilization. In this mood of reflection we are more ready to recognize both the achievements and the point of view of our late enemies, and perhaps all the more because we realize that both the causes and the course of war are determined by the folly and the frailty rather than by the deliberate evil of human nature.

The war has become history, and can be viewed in the perspective of history. For good it has deepened our sense of fellowship and community of interest, whether inside the nation or between nations. But, for good or bad, it has shattered our faith in idols, our hero-worshipping belief that great men are different clay from common men. Leaders are still necessary, perhaps more necessary, but our awakened realization of their common humanity is a safeguard against either expecting from them or trusting in them too much. It has been for the benefit both of history and of future generations that the past decade has seen such a flood of evidence and revelations, of documents and memoirs. That most of the actors are still alive provides an invaluable check in sifting the evidence, while the historians themselves have been so immersed in the atmosphere of war that they have a certain immunity from the abstract theorizing which an historian in his cloistered study fifty years later so easily contracts. We know nearly all that is to be known. The one drawback is that the flood has been so huge that only the student has been able to cope with its investigation.

What caused that astonishingly sudden collapse and surrender of Germany which, as by a miracle, so it seemed, lifted the nightmare load of war from Europe? To arrive at a satisfactory answer it is not sufficient to analyse the hectic weeks of negotiation and military success which preceded November 11th. Even in the military sphere we need to go back to August 8th, the day which filled the German command with the conviction of defeat, and to July 18th, which witnessed the visible turning of the tide. And if we go back thither we must go back further, to March 21st, for the decline of Germany's military power is not explicable without reference to the consummation of that military effort, and consumption of her military resources, in the great series of offensives which opened in the spring of 1918.

We ought, however, to go back further still. Indeed, if the historian of the future has to select one day as decisive for the outcome of the World War he will probably choose August 2nd, 1914 – before the war, for England, had yet begun – when Mr Winston Churchill, at 1.25 AM, sent the order to mobilize the British Navy. That Navy was to win no Trafalgar, but it was to do more than any other factor towards winning the war for the Allies. For the Navy was the instrument of the blockade, and as the fog of war disperses in the clearer light of these post-war years that blockade is seen to assume larger and larger proportions, to be more and more clearly the decisive agency in the struggle. Like those 'jackets' which used to be applied in American jails to refractory prisoners, as it was progressively tightened so did it first cramp the prisoner's movements and then stifle his breathing, while the tighter it became and the longer it continued the less became the prisoner's power of resistance and the more demoralizing the sense of constriction.

Helplessness induces hopelessness, and history attests that loss of hope and not loss of lives is what decides the issue of war. No historian would underrate the direct effect of the semi-starvation of the German people in causing the final collapse of the 'home front'. But leaving aside the question of how far the revolution caused the military defeat, instead of vice versa, the intangible all-pervading factor of the blockade intrudes into every consideration of the military situation.

This, during the last year of the war, is studded with 'ifs'. If Germany, instead of throwing all her military resources into a series of tremendous offensives in 1918, had stayed on the defensive in the west, while consolidating her gains in the east, could she have averted defeat? Militarily there seems little doubt that she could. In the light of the experience of 1915, when the Allies had 145 divisions in the west to Germany's 100, and when the German trench systems were a frail and shallow bulwark compared with those of 1918, it is difficult to see that the Allies could have breached it, even if they had waited until the inflowing tide of American man power had restored to them the relative numerical superiority that they had enjoyed in 1915.

And if so, in face of the accumulating cost of vain assaults, would they not eventually have inclined towards a compromise peace? A peace, peradventure, which, in return for the relinquishment of Belgium and Northern France, might have conceded to Germany part or the whole of her gains in the east. Yet as we ask the question, and militarily find an optimistic answer difficult, the factor of the command of the sea comes to mind. For it was the stranglehold of the British Navy which, in default of a serious peace move, constrained Germany to carry out that *felo de se* offensive of 1918. She was dogged by the spectre of slow enfeeblement ending in eventual collapse.

Perhaps if she had adopted such a war policy of defence in the west, offence in the east, after the Marne in 1914, or even, after 1915, continued the policy which she had that year temporarily adopted, her prospects might have been brighter and her story different; for, on the one hand, she could have consummated unquestionably the dream of 'Mittel-Europa', and on the other, the blockade was still a loose grip, and could hardly have been drawn effectively tight so long as the United States remained outside the conflict. But in 1918 the best chance had passed.

Another big 'if', often mooted, is the question whether even in the autumn of 1918 Germany could have avoided capitulation. Would the fighting front have collapsed if the war had gone on after November 11th? Was capitulation inevitable, or could the German armies have made good their retreat and stood firm on their own frontiers? German opinion largely says 'yes' to the latter question, and blames the surrender on the 'home front'. Many open-minded and diligent students of the war among the Allies are inclined to agree that it was possible from a military point of view. But again the naval aspect intervenes. Even if the German armies, and the German people, roused to a supreme effort in visible defence of their own soil, had managed to hold the Allies at bay, the end could only have been postponed. The most that history is likely to concede is that they might have held on long enough, tightening their belts, for the Allies, already weary, to sicken of the effort, and thus concede more favourable terms than those of Versailles.

Having disposed of the 'ifs', having emphasized the fundamental cause of the Armistice – Britain's sea power, her historic weapon, the deadliest weapon which any nation has wielded throughout history – let us turn to examine the immediate causes of the Armistice. How did victory come? Here military action bulks large. Other factors contributed, apart from the naval. If we do not accept entirely, we should not discount unduly the unwilling tribute paid by the Germans to the effectiveness of Allied, and especially of British, propaganda. In the later stages of the war it was skilfully directed and intensively developed.

If now, when passions are stilled, the memory of some of the 'facts' that were exploited is disturbing to our sense of fair play and lies uneasily on the stomach, we realize equally that such forms of propaganda neither stimulated our own people nor discouraged the enemy. It was the kernel of essential truth upon the bigger issues which was digested by the German people and, by leading them to question both the honesty of their leadership and the hope of success, weakened the will to continued sacrifice.

Nevertheless, though we should recognize the value of the more discriminating propaganda, its effect was rather in supplementing and completing the military successes than in paving the way for them, as German spokesmen have often contended. There is significant evidence on this point to be found in the memoirs of Prince Max of Baden, a man whose high-minded patriotism and sincerity command the respect of both friend and foe, and whose book is one of the most valuable of the war memoirs yet published. Unintentionally, and unconsciously, he shows in casual passages, easily missed, that when German arms were temporarily in the ascendant moderation was forgotten in exultation, even among the more sober.

In March, 1918, he quotes even a pacifist as exuberantly crying – 'Never worry! ... What an experience! ... World dominion.' And another representative of moderate opinion 'let the cat out of the bag' in saying meditatively – 'It would seem that we needn't say no to Briey and Longwy' – revealing that intoxication of spirit which, more fundamentally than any ill intention, was responsible for Germany's war guilt.

In face of such widespread intoxication, propaganda could only be secondary to military action. Thus we are left with the sure conclusion that the success of the Allied armies was chief among the immediate causes of Germany's capitulation on November 11th.

That conclusion does not necessarily, or even naturally, imply that at the moment of the Armistice the German armies were on the brink of collapse. Nor that the Armistice was a mistaken concession – as some among the Allies, usually those whose fighting was done with their tongue, were so loud in proclaiming at the time.

Rather does the record of the last 'hundred days', when thoroughly sifted, confirm the immemorial lesson of history – that the true aim in war is the mind of the enemy command and Government, not the bodies of their troops, that the balance between victory and defeat turns on mental impressions and only indirectly on physical blows. That in war, as Napoleon said and Foch endorsed, 'it is the man, not men, who counts'.

The reiteration of this great truth is to be found in the war's last phase. Great as was the stimulus and visible success of the tide-turning battle on the Marne in July, Ludendorff was still planning and preparing fresh offensives thereafter. If he was chagrined, he does not appear to have been so disillusioned as he had been after his own outwardly successful attack on the Lys in April.

But the Fourth Army surprise attack before Amiens on August 8th was a dislocating moral blow. Prince Max put August 8th in its true light psychologically, when he defined it as 'the turning point'. Even so, to develop the conviction of failure into the conviction of hopelessness required to compel surrender, something more was needed. It came not from the Western Front, but from a despised 'side-show' – Salonika, long condemned by Allied military opinion and scornfully ridiculed by the Germans as their 'largest internment camp'. With Bulgaria's collapse the back gate to Austria, as well as to Turkey, and through Austria to Germany, lay ajar.

The immediate issue of the war was decided on September 29th, decided in the mind of the German Command. Ludendorff and his associates had then 'cracked', and the sound went echoing backwards until it had resounded throughout the whole of Germany. Nothing could catch it or stop it. The Command might recover its nerve, the actual military position might improve, but the moral impression, as ever in war, was decisive.

Yet, let us once again emphasize that the fundamental causes of the decision are more various than the acts which immediately produced it.

The truth is that no one cause was, or could be, decisive. The Western Front, the Balkan front, the tank, the blockade and propaganda have all been claimed as the cause of victory. All claims are justified, none is wholly right, although the blockade ranks first and began first. In this warfare between nations victory was a cumulative effect, to which all weapons – military, economic, and psychological – contributed. Victory came, and could only come through the utilization and combination of all the resources existing in a modern nation, and the dividend of success depended on the way in which these manifold activities were coordinated.

It is even more futile to ask which country won the war. France did not win the war, but unless she had held the fort while the forces of Britain were preparing and those of America still a dream the release of civilization from this nightmare of militarism would have been impossible. Britain did not win the war, but without her command of the sea, her financial support, and her army, to take over the main burden of the struggle from 1916 onwards, defeat would have been inevitable. The United States did not win the war, but without their economic aid to ease the strain, without the arrival of their troops to turn the numerical balance, and, above all, without the moral tonic which their coming gave, victory would have been impossible. And let us not forget how many times Russia had sacrificed herself to save her allies; preparing the way for their ultimate victory as surely as for her own downfall. Finally, whatever be the verdict of history on her policy, unstinted tribute is due to the incomparable endurance and skill with which Germany more than held her own for four years against superior numbers – an epic of military and human achievement.

Bibliography

The appended list is, of course, far from a complete list of the books which have been read or consulted during the fifteen years since the war. Its purpose is to indicate those of main historical significance. It comprises those sources from which facts or quotations have been drawn for use herein, or which have directly helped in forming one's picture of the war. During these years one has also been privileged to see a number of documents, British and foreign, which have not yet been published or utilized, and to gather the personal evidence of those who participated in critical actions and in the taking of important decisions. Such sources, where they have contributed to the narrative, are referred to as either 'Unpublished Documents' or 'Personal Evidence'. Although it is not yet possible to give a fuller identification, all such sources have been recorded and privately catalogued for the eventual use of historical students.

In concluding this preface to the Bibliography I take the opportunity to acknowledge the great debt which all serious students of the war owe to the *Army Quarterly*, and especially its 'Notes on Foreign War Books'. This feature during the past ten years has been invaluable as a signpost and searchlight amid the vast and confusing mass of material that has been published. No periodical, military or historical, in any country has kept or marked so clear a track for students of the war.

Books published since 1930 are listed separately on pages 485–90, save in the case of a few continuing volumes of books published earlier.

CHAPTER I

ORIGINS

J. W. Headlam-Morley, *The Outbreak of War. Foreign Office Documents* (1926)

G. P. Gooch and H. Temperley, *British Documents on the Origins of the War*, vols i–v (1927)

Haldane (Viscount), *Before the War* (1920)

Grey of Fallodon (Viscount), *Twenty-Five Years, 1892–1916* (1925)

G. Buchanan, *My Mission to Russia* (1923)

H. Wickham Steed, *Through Thirty Years, 1892–1922* (1924)

R. W. Seton-Watson, *Sarajevo* (1926)

G. P. Gooch, *Recent Revelations of European Diplomacy* (1927)

H. W. Wilson, *The War Guilt* (1928)

B. Hendrick, *The Life and Letters of W. H. Page* (1922–5)

P. Renouvin, *Les Origines Immédiates de la Guerre* (1925)

R. Poincaré, *Au Service de la France*, vols i–iv (1926–7)

M. Paléologue, *An Ambassador's Memoirs* (Eng trans 1923–5)

German Foreign Office, *Die Grosse Politik der Europäischen Kabinette, 1871–1914* (1926) (Eng selection and trans in 4 vols *German Diplomatic Documents, 1871–1914*, 1928–)

K. Kautsky, M. Montgelas and W. Schücking, *Die Deutschen Dokumente zum Kriegsausbruch* (1919) (Eng trans 1924)

A. von Tirpitz, *Memoirs* (Eng trans 1919)

The Kaiser's Letters to the Tsar (Eng trans 1920)

M. Montgelas, *The Case for the Central Powers* (Eng trans 1925)

K. Lichnowsky, *My Mission to London, 1912–1914* (1918)

Generaloberst Helmuth von Moltke. Erinnerungen–Briefe–Dokumente 1877–1916 (1923)

W. von Schoen, *The Memoirs of an Ambassador* (Eng trans 1922)

Diplomatische Aktenstücke zur Vorgeschichte des Krieges, 1914 (1919) (Eng trans *Austrian Red Book*, 1920)

Conrad von Hötzendorf, *Aus meiner Dienstzeit*, vols i–iv (1922–5)

Czernin, *In the World War* (Eng trans 1920)

How the War began in 1914, being the diary of the Russian Foreign Office ... July, 1914 ... published by the Russian Soviet Government (Eng trans 1925)

S. Sazonov, *Fateful Years, 1909–1916* (Eng trans 1927)

Un Livre Noir, diplomatie d'avant guerre d'après les documents des archives russes (1922-3)

CHAPTERS II-VII

GENERAL

W. S. Churchill, *The World Crisis*, 4 vols (1923-7)

John Buchan, *A History of the Great War*, 4 vols (1921)

Oxford and Asquith (Earl of), *Memories and Reflections* (1928)

G. Arthur, *Life of Lord Kitchener*, vol iii (1920)

Esher (Viscount), *The Tragedy of Lord Kitchener* (1921)

C. à C. Repington, *The First World War, 1914-1918*, 2 vols (1920)

W. R. Robertson, *From Private to Field Marshal* (1921)
  Soldiers and Statesmen, 1914-1918 (1926)

Beaverbrook (Lord), *Politicians and the War, 1914-1916* (1928)

N. Macready, *Annals of an Active Life* (1926)

C. E. Callwell, *Experiences of a Dug-Out, 1914-1918* (1921)

C. P. Lucas, *The Empire at War*, 3 vols [covers war effort of Dominions and Colonies]

Royal Engineers' Institute, *The Work of the R.E. in the European War, 1914-1919*, 9 vols (1921-7)

War Office, *Statistics of the Military Effort of the British Empire, 1914-1920* (1922)

R. van Overstraeten, *Des Principes de la Guerre*, vol ii [vol ii covers World War]

C. Seymour, *The Intimate Papers of Colonel House*, 4 vols (1926-8)

J. W. Gerard, *My Four Years in Germany* (1927) [USA ambassador]

E. Ludendorff, *Urkunden der Obersten Heeresleitung, 1916-1918* (1920)

Kuhl, *Der Deutsche Generalstab in Vorbereitung und Durchführung des Weltkrieges* (1920) [French condensed trans my Douchy, *Le Grand État-Major Allemand avant et pendant la Guerre Mondiale*]

M. Erzberger, *Erlebnisse im Weltkrieg* (1921) [French trans *Souvenirs de guerre*]

J. V. Bredt, *Die Belgische Neutralität und der Schlieffensche Feldzugsplan* (1929) [excellent summary in *Army Quarterly*, July 1929]

E. von Falkenhayn, *General Headquarters, 1914-1916 and its Critical Decisions* (Eng trans 1919)

Stürgkh (Graf), *Im deutschen Grossen Hauptquartier* (1921) [intimate impressions and pen-portraits by the Austrian military representative]

Zwehl, *Erich von Falkenhayn* (1925) [contains extracts from diary]

Groener, *Das Testament des Grafen Schlieffen* (1927)

H. von Hentig, *Psychologische Strategie des Grossen Krieges* (1927) [criticism, usually acute, of the German war policy and strategy]

L. Gehre, *Die deutsche Kraftverteilung während des Weltkrieges* (1928) [gives location of all German divisions on 15th and last day of every month]

Bauer, *Der Grosse Krieg in Feld und Heimat* (1922) [intimate revelations of the German Supreme Command during the war]

M. Schwarte, *Der Grosse Krieg, 1914–1918*, 11 vols (1921–)

Buat, *L'Armée Allemande pendant la Guerre de 1914–1918* (1920)

WESTERN FRONT

J. E. Edmonds, *Military Operations, France and Belgium*, vols i–v (1922–32) [*British Official History*, vol i–ii, 1914; iii–iv, 1915; v, 1916]

The Despatches of Lord French, 1914–1915 (1917)

French (Viscount), *1914* (1919) [a record of his command, distinguished by inaccuracy]

J. H. Boraston (Ed.), *Sir D. Haig's Despatches, 1915–1919* (1919)

G. A. B. Dewar and J. H. Boraston, *Sir Douglas Haig's Command, 1915–1918* (1922)

H. L. Smith-Dorrien, *Memories of Forty-Eight Years' Service* (1925) [covers, if with extreme reserve, his service as corps and army commander in the first phase]

C. E. Callwell, *Field-Marshal Sir Henry Wilson*, 2 vols (1927) [extracts from an amazingly unreserved diary, 1914–19]

F. Maurice, *The Life of General Lord Rawlinson of Trent* (1928) [covers the whole war]

J. Charteris, *Field-Marshal Earl Haig* (1929)

Huguet, *Britain and the War* (Eng trans 1928) [impressions of French representative at British GHQ, 1914–15]

C. E. W. Bean, *The Australian Imperial Force in France, 1916* (1929) [Australian Official History]

J. Monash, *The Australian Victories in France in 1918* (1920)

A. W. Currie, *Canadian Corps Operations during 1918* (1920)

A. A. Montgomery, *The Story of the Fourth Army* (1920) [for last half of 1918 campaign]

A. de Schrÿver, *La Bataille de Liége* (1922) [by the Chief of Staff of the fortress]

Deguise, *La Defense de la Position Fortifiée d'Anvers en 1914* (1921) [by the Belgian commander]

E. Menzel, *La Vérité sur l'Évacuation d'Anvers en 1914* (1925)

C. Merzbach, *La Vérité sur la Défense de Namur en 1914* (1927)

Duvivier and Herbiet, *Du rôle de l'Armée de Champagne et des Forteresses Belges en 1914* (1929) [effect in detaining German forces]

Les Armées Françaises dans la Grande Guerre, Tome I, vol ii (covers operations up to eve of the Marne, 1914); Tome VII, vol i (covers period June 18th–September 25th, 1928) [French Official History]

B. E. Palat, *La Grande Guerre sur le Front Occidental*, 14 vols (1921–30)

P. Renouvin, *Les Formes du Gouvernement de Guerre* (1929) [relations between Government and commanders in France]

R. Poincaré, *Au service de la France*, vol v, *L'Invasion, 1914* (1929)

Lanrezac, *Le Plan de Campagne Français et le Premier Mois de Guerre* (1920)

V. Margueritte, *Au bord du Gouffre* (1920) [French plan for 1914]

F. Engerand, *La Bataille de la Frontière (août, 1914) Briey* (1920) [French plan for 1914]

Percin. *1914 Les Erreurs du Haut Commandement* (1922) [French plan for 1914]

Tanant, *La Troisième Armée dans la Bataille. Souvenirs d'un Chef d'État-Major* (1928) [special light on the opening battles of 1914]

Toussan, *Historique des Corps de Cavallerie commandé par le Général Conneau du 14 août 1914 au 2 mars 1917* (1924)

E. Valarché, *La Bataille de Guise* (1928)

A. Grouard, *La Conduite de la Guerre jusqu' à la Bataille de la Marne* (1922) [an acute criticism by a famous military critic who gave the French General Staff an unheeded warning of the German plan]

Camon, *L'Effondrement du Plan Allemand en Septembre 1914* (1925)

Mermeix, *Joffre–1er Crise du Commandement*
Le Commandement Unique

Rousset, *La Bataille de l'Aisne* [Nivelle offensive, 1917]

P. Painlevé, *Comment j'ai nommé Foch et Pétain* (1924)

Laure, *Au 3ième Bureau du troisième G.O.C. 1917–1919* (1922)

L. Madelin, *La Bataille de France* [1918 campaign]

Koeltz, *L'Offensive Allemande de 1918* (1928)

Jean de Pierrefeu, *G.Q.G. Secteur I*, 2 vols (1921)
    Plutarque a Menti (1923)

N. Domège, *En Marge de Plutarque*

Mordacq, *Le Commandement Unique. Comment il fut réalisé*
    La Vérité sur l'Armistice (1929)

Reichsarchiv, *Der Weltkrieg 1914–1918*, vols i, iii, v, vi (1924–29)
    [German Official History, covers 1914]; vii and viii [cover 1915]

Reichsarchiv, *Antwerpen, 1914* (1921) [German Official Monograph on
    siege]

Reichsarchiv, *Ypres, 1914* [German Official Monograph, Eng trans
    1919]

Crown Prince Rupprecht of Bavaria, *Mein Kriegstagebuch*, 3 vols
    (1928)

Krafft von Delmensingen, *Die Führung des Kronprinzen Rupprecht
    von Bayern auf dem linken deutschen Heeresflügel bis zur Schlacht
    in Lothringen im August, 1914* (1925) [light on opening battles in
    Lorraine]

Die Schlacht in Lothringen, (1929) [Bavarian Official History]

German Ex-Crown Prince, *Meine Erinnerungen aus Deutschlands Hel-
    denkampf* (1923)

*Generaloberst Helmuth von Moltke. Erinnerungen – Briefe – Doku-
    mente 1877–1916* (1923)

W. Foerster, *Graf Schlieffen und der Weltkrieg* (1920)

Kluck, *The March on Paris, 1914* (Eng trans 1920)

Army Quarterly, October, 1921, *General Ludendorff on the German
    Plan of Campaign, August, 1914* [extract from letter]

The Memoirs of Prince Max of Baden (Eng trans 1928) [especially for
    light on last phase of war]

Final Report of Gen. J. J. Pershing (1919)

First Army Report (printed 1923)

Shipley Thomas, *History of the American Expeditionary Force* (1920)

R. L. Bullard, *Personalities and Reminiscences of the War* (1925)

J. G. Harbord, *Leaves from a War Diary* (1926)

J. W. Thomason, *Fix Bayonets* (1927)

J. T. Dickman, *The Great Crusade* (1927)

Hunter Liggett, *Commanding an American Army* (1925)
    A.E.F. (1928)

T. M. Johnson, *Without Censor* (1928)

T. C. Lonergan, *It might have been lost* (1929) [extracts from British

Official documents dealing with Pershing's struggle to preserve the national unity of the AEF]

RUSSIAN FRONT
(See also Chapter III, Scene 2)

Reichsarchiv, *Der Weltkrieg, 1914–1918*, vol ii (1924); vol v (1929) [German Official History, covers 1914]

E. Ludendorff, *My War Memories* (Eng trans 1920)

P. von Hindenburg, *Out of my life* (Eng trans 1920)

A. von Cramon, *Quatre Ans au G.Q.G. Austro-Hongrois* (French trans. 1922)

M. Hoffmann, *The War of Lost Opportunities* (Eng trans 1924)
  War Diaries and other Papers (Eng trans 1929)

Russian Historical Commission, *La Grande Guerre. Relation de l'État-Major Russe* (French trans 1927)

Conrad von Hötzendorf, *Aus meiner Dienstzeit*, vols iv–v (1925–6) [covers 1914 campaign]

François, *Gorlice, 1915* (1922) [the 1915 breakthrough]

A. Arz, *Zur Geschichte des Grossen Krieges, 1914–1918* [memoirs of Conrad's successor]

J. E. Edmonds in *Army Quarterly*, July, 1921, *The Austrian Plan of Campaign, 1914, and its development*

K. F. Novak, *Der Weg zur Katastrophe* (1920) (French trans) [Conrad's evidence]

Buat, *Hindenburg et Ludendorff Stratèges* (1923)

Camon, *Ludendorff sur le Front Russe 1914–1915* (1926)

Y. Danilov, *La Russie dans la Guerre Mondiale, 1914–1917* (French trans 1927)

Sukhomlinov, *Erinnerungen* (1924)

B. Gourko, *Russia in 1914–1917* (Eng trans 1918)

A. Knox, *With the Russian Army, 1914–1917* (1921)
  Hindenburg's Second Offensive in Poland (in *Army Quarterly*, July, 1921) [Lodz]

C. E. Callwell, *Experiences of a Dug-Out, 1914–1918* (1921)

C. Maynard, *The Murmansk Venture* (1928)

ITALIAN FRONT

L. Cadorna, *La Guerra alla fronte Italiana* (1921)

Capello, *Note di Guerra* (1920–21)

Vigano, *La Nostra Guerra* (1921)

A. Tosti, *La Guerra Italo–Austriaca, 1915–1918* (1925)

Kuntz, *La Psychologie du G.Q.G. Italien sous le Général Cadorna* (1923)

A. Krauss, *Die Ursachen unserer Niederlage* (1921)

A. Arz, *Zur Geschichte des Grossen Krieges, 1914–1918* (1924) [covers 1917 and 1918]

A. von Cramon, *Quatre Ans au G.Q.G. Austro–Hongrois* (French trans 1922) [the chief German representative]

Kerchnawe, *Der Zusammenbruch der Oester–Ungar: Wehrmacht im Herbst* (1921) [Austrian documents]

J. F. Gathorne-Hardy in *Army Quarterly*, October, 1921, *A Summary of the Campaign in Italy and an Account of the Battle of Vittorio Veneto* [by the British Chief of Staff]

R. H. Beadon in *Army Quarterly*, Jan, 1925, *An Operation of War*, [British move to Italy after Caporetto]

BALKAN FRONT

Wolfgang Foerster, *Graf Schlieffen und der Weltkrieg*, Part III (1921)

O. Landfried, *Der Endkampf in Macedonien, 1918* (1925)

Nedeff, *Les Opérations en Macédoine. L'Épopée de Doiran, 1915–1918* (1927)

Feyler, *La Campagne de Macédoine*, vol i, 1915–16; vol ii, 1917–18 [from Serbian and Greek sources]

Jouinot-Gambetta, *Uskub ou du Rôle de la Cavalerie d'Afrique dans la Victoire* (1920) [final breakthrough]

Robert David, *Le Drame Ignoré de l'Armée d'Orient* (1928) [especially political side]

Les Armées Françaises dans la Grande Guerre, Tome VIII, vol i (1928)

Œhmichen, *Essai sur la Doctrine de Guerre des Coalitions. La Direction de la Guerre* (Nov, 1914–Mars, 1917) (1927) [Joffre's influence on Salonika campaign]

Sarrail, *Mon Commandement en Orient, 1916–1918* (1920)

L. Villari, *The Macedonian Campaign* (1922)

THE DARDANELLES
(See Chapter V, Scenes 1 and 2)

PALESTINE
(Including Egypt and Arabia)

G. MacMunn and C. Falls, *Military Operations Egypt and Palestine* (1928) [British Official History]

C. E. W. Bean, *Official History of Australia in the War*, vol i.

H. S. Gullet, *Official History of Australia in the War*, vol vii (1923)

A. P. Wavell, *The Palestine Campaigns* (1928)

R. M. P. Preston, *The Desert Mounted Corps* (1921)

T. E. Lawrence, *Revolt in the Desert*

T. E. Lawrence in *Army Quarterly*, October, 1920, *The Evolution of a Revolt*

W. T. Massey, *The Desert Campaigns* (1918)

M. Bowman-Manifold, *An Outline of the Egyptian and Palestine Campaigns* (1922)

G. E. Badcock, *History of the Transport Services of the E.E.F.*

Army, Navy and Air Force Gazette, 18th June, 1927

Reichsarchiv, *Yilderim* (1925)

Kress von Kressenstein, *Zwischen Kaukasus und Sinai* (1922) [covers the period 1915–17]

Liman von Sanders, *Five Years in Turkey* (Eng trans 1928) [covers 1918]

Rafael de Nogales, *Vier Jahren unter dem Halbmond* (1926)

MESOPOTAMIAN FRONT

F. J. Moberley, *The Mesopotomia Campaign, 1914–1918*, vols i–iv (1923–7) [British Official History]

Report of the Commission on Mesopotamia (1917)

C. V. F. Townshend, *My Campaign in Mesopotamia* (1920)

Erroll Sherson, *Townshend of Chitral and Kut* (1928)

Keisling, *Mit Feldmarshall von der Goltz Pascha in Mesopotamien und Persien* (1922)

Rafael de Nogales, *Vier Jahre unter dem Halbmond* (1926)

Schraudenbach, *Muharebe* (1926)

Gleich, *Vom Balkan nach Bagdad* (1922) [light on siege of Kut]

R. H. Dewing, *Army Quarterly*, January, April, July, 1927, *Some Aspects of Maude's Campaign in Mesopotamia*
Edmund Candler, *The Long Road to Baghdad*
L. C. Dunsterville, *The Adventures of Dunsterforce* (1921)
W. Marshall, *Memories of Four Fronts* (1929)
C. E. Callwell, *Life of Sir Stanley Maude* (1920)

NAVAL

J. S. Corbett, *History of the Great War* (*Naval Operations*) vols i–iii (1920–21)
H. Newbolt, *History of the Great War* (*Naval Operations*) vol iv (1928)
C. E. Fayle, *Seaborne Trade*, 3 vols (1920–)
A. Laurens, *Précis d'Histoire de la Guerre Navale* (1929)
W. S. Churchill, *The World Crisis*, 4 vols (1923–7)
Jellicoe (Viscount), *The Grand Fleet, 1914–1916* (1919)
J. E. T. Harper, *The Truth about Jutland* (1927)
G. Campbell, *My Mystery Ships* (1928)
W. S. Sims, *The Victory at Sea* (1920)
R. Scheer, *Germany's High Seas Fleet in the World War* (Eng trans 1920)
G. von Hase, *Kiel and Jutland* (Eng trans 1926)

AIR

W. A. Raleigh, *The War in the Air*, vol i (1922) (Official History)
H. A. Jones, *The War in the Air*, vol ii (1928); vol vii (1930) (Official History)
C. F. Snowden-Gamble, *The Story of a North Sea Air Station* (1928)
A. Rawlinson, *The Defence of London* (1923)
E. B. Ashmore, *Air Defence* (1929)
E. A. Lehmann, *The Zeppelins* (Eng trans 1928)
H. Ritter, *Der Luftkrieg* (1926)
Keller, *Die Heutige Wehrlosigkeit Deutschlands im Lichte seiner Verteidigung gegen Fliegerangriffe im Kriege, 1914–1918* (1926) [German Air Defence Organization]

PRESS AND PROPAGANDA

E. T. Cook, *The Press in War-Time* (1920)
C. Stuart, *Secrets of Crewe House* (1920)
N. Lytton, *The Press and the General Staff* (1921)
C. E. Callwell, *Experiences of a Dug-Out, 1914–1918* (1921)
H. D. Lasswell, *Propaganda Technique in the World War* (1926)

ECONOMIC AND HOME FRONT

M. Consett, *The Triumph of Unarmed Forces, 1914–1918* (1921)
R. H. Gretton, *A Modern History of the English People, 1910–22* (1929)
A. Hallays, *L'Opinion Allemande pendant la Guerre, 1914–1918* (1923)

CHAPTER IV

SCENE 1. THE MARNE

J. E. Edmonds, *Military Operations. France and Belgium*, vol i (British Official History)
Reichsarchiv, *Der Weltkrieg, 1914–1918*, vols iii and iv (1926) (German Official History)
Kluck, *The March on Paris, 1914* (Eng trans 1920)
J. E. Edmonds in *Army Quarterly*, January, 1921, *The Scapegoat of the Battle of the Marne*
Militär-Wochenblatt, 18th September, 1920 [court of inquiry on Col Hentsch's rôle]
M. von Poseck, *Die deutsche Kavallerie in Belgien und Frankreich, 1914* (1922)
Baumgarten-Crusius, *Marneschlacht, 1914* (1919)
  Deutsche Heerführung im Marnefeldzug, 1914 (1921) [fuller extracts from Col Hentsch's report]
Bülow, *Mein Bericht zur Marneschlacht* (1920) (French trans)
Zwehl, *Maubeuge-Aisne-Verdun* (1921)
Helfferich, *Weltkrieg*, vol ii
Tappen, *Bis zur Marneschlacht*
François, *Marneschlacht und Tannenberg* (1920)
Foerster, *Graf Schlieffen und der Weltkrieg*, Part I (1920)

Kuhl, *Der Marnefeldzug, 1914* (1920) (French trans)

Crown Prince Rupprecht of Bavaria, *Mein Kriegstagebuch* (1928)

German Ex-Crown Prince, *Der Marnefeldzug, 1914* (1927)

Hausen, *Souvenirs de la Campagne de la Marne en 1914* (French trans 1922) [Saxon Third Army commander]

Reichsarchiv, *Das Marnedrama, 1914* (1928–9) [German Official Monographs, in five parts. Extensive summary in *Army Quarterly*, July, 1928, January, April, October, 1929, January, 1930]

Müller-Loebnitz, *Die Sendung des Oberstleutnants Hentsch* (1922) [official account of Hentsch's mission]

Generaloberst von Moltke, Erinnerungen–Briefe–Dokumente, 1877–1916 (1923)

Palat, *La Victoire de la Marne* (1921)

Dubail, *Journal du Campagne*, vol i, 1ere Armée

J. Charbonneau, *La Bataille des Frontières et la Bataille de la Marne vues par un Chef de Section* (1929)

Mémoires du Maréchal Galliéni Défense de Paris (25 août–sept 11 1914) (1926)

Clergerie and Delahaye d'Anglemont, *Le Rôle du Gouvernement Militaire de Paris de 1 au 12 septembre, 1914* (1920)

Marius—Ary le Blond, *Galliéni Parle* (1920)

Les Armées Françaises dans la Grande Guerre, Tome I, vol ii (1927) (French Official History)

Toussan, *Historique des corps de cavallerie commandés par le Général Conneau du 14 août au 2 mars, 1917* (1924)

J. de Pierrefeu, *Plutarque a menti* (1922)

Hirschauer and Klein, *Paris en État de Défense, 1914* (1928)

H. Carré, *La Véritable Histoire des Taxis de la Marne* (1921)

Boëlle, *Le 4e corps d'Armée sur l'Ourcq* (1925) [light on Maunoury's part]

Dubois, *Deux ans de Commandement sur le Front de France, 1914–1916* (1920) [light on Foch's part]

Bujac, *Le Général Eydoux et le XI Corps d'Armée* (1925) [light on Foch's part]

de Castelli, *Le VIIIe Corps en Lorraine août–octobre, 1914* (1926) [light on French right wing and on loss of St Mihiel]

Army Quarterly, October, 1922, *Another Legend of the Marne, 1914*

Private Evidence

CHAPTER IV

SCENE 2. TANNENBERG

Reichsarchiv, *Tannenberg* (1927) [German Official Monograph]
E. Ludendorff, *My War Memories* (Eng trans 1920)
P. von Hindenburg, *Out of my Life* (Eng trans 1920)
Army Quarterly, October, 1921, *An Echo of Tannenberg*
H. von François, *Marneschlacht und Tannenberg* (1920)
    Tannenberg (1926)
Y. Danilov, *La Russie dans la Guerre Mondiale* (French trans 1927)
M. Hoffmann, *The War of Lost Opportunities* (Eng trans 1924)
    Tannenberg wie es wirklich war (1927)
    War Diaries and other Papers (Eng trans 1929)
E. Ironside, *Tannenberg* (1925)
Russian Historical Commission, *La Grande Guerre. Relation de l'État-Major Russe* (French trans 1927)
Noskov, *Militär Wochenblatt* 1st August, 1926 [a Russian view]
A. Smirnoff in *Army Quarterly*, April, 1926, *A New Light upon the Invasion of East Prussia by the Russians in August, 1914*

CHAPTER V

SCENES 1 and 2. THE DARDANELLES

C. F. Aspinall-Oglander, *Military Operations, Gallipoli*, vol i (1929) (British Official History)
The Final Report of the Dardanelles Commission (1919)
Ian Hamilton, *A Gallipoli Diary*, 2 vols (1920)
C. E. Callwell, *Experiences of a Dug-Out, 1914–1918* (1921)
J. Masefield, *Gallipoli* (1923)
Wester Wemyss (Lord), *The Navy in the Dardanelles Campaign* (1924)
E. Ashmead-Bartlett, *The Uncensored Dardanelles* (1927)
W. Marshall, *Memories of Four Fronts* (1929)
Compton Mackenzie, *Gallipoli Memories* (1929)
Liman von Sanders, *Five Years in Turkey* (Eng trans 1928)
H. Kannengiesser, *The Campaign in Gallipoli* (Eng trans 1928)
Reichsarchiv, *Dardanellen, 1915* (1927)

Turkish Official History, *Campagne des Dardanelles* (1924) [extensive summary in *Army Quarterly*, January and April, 1926]

Army Quarterly, October, 1929, *The First Turkish Reinforcements at Suvla, August 7th–9th, 1915* [from Turkish sources]

The Times, February 14th, 1925, *The Suvla Bay Failure. New Evidence*

S. Sazonov, *Fateful Years, 1909–1916* (Eng trans 1927) [shows Russian attitude]

Les Armées Françaises dans la Grande Guerre, Tome VIII, vol i (1928) (French Official History)

Private Evidence

CHAPTER V

SCENE 3. THE GAS CLOUD AT YPRES

J. E. Edmonds, *Military Operations. France and Belgium, 1915*, vol iii

Les Armées Françaises dans la Grande Guerre, Tome III (1927)

Huguet, *Britain and the War*

C. E. Callwell, *Field-Marshal Sir Henry Wilson*, vol i

Volonté (Paris) April 25th, 1929, [account of Gen Ferry's warning]

Hanslian and Bergendorff, *Der Chemische Krieg*, (1925)

Falkenhayn, *General Headquarters, etc*

Unpublished Documents

Private Evidence

CHAPTER V

SCENE 4. LOOS

J. E. Edmonds, *Military Operations. France and Belgium, 1915*, vol iv

Les Armées Françaises dans la Grande Guerre, Tome III (1927)

Army Quarterly, July, 1924, *The Fight for Hill 70* [from German sources]

Crown Prince Rupprecht of Bavaria, *Mein Kriegstagebuch* (1928)

Palat, Vol ix. *Les Offensives de 1915*

Huguet, *Britain and the War*

Oxford and Asquith, *Memories and Reflections*

Maurice, *The Life of General Lord Rawlinson of Trent*

J. Charteris, *Field-Marshal Earl Haig*

Private Evidence

CHAPTER VI

SCENE 1. VERDUN

Reichsarchiv, *Die Tragödie von Verdun, 1916* (1926–9) (German Official)

Wolfgang Foerster, *Graf Schlieffen und der Weltkrieg*, Part III (1921)

German Ex-Crown Prince, *Memoirs*

Crown Prince Rupprecht, *Mein Kriegstagebuch*

Zwehl, *Maubeuge-Aisne-Verdun*

Ludwig Gehre, *Die deutsche Kraftverteilung während des Weltkrieges* (1928)

de Thomasson, *Les Préliminaires de Verdun, août, 1915–février 1916* (1921) [contains numerous documents]

Pétain, *La Bataille de Verdun* (1929)

J. Poirier, *La Bataille de Verdun* (1922)

A. Grasset, *Verdun, le Premier Choc à la 72e Division* (1926)

B. E. Palat, *La Ruée sur Verdun* (1925)

CHAPTER VI

SCENE 2. BRUSILOV OFFENSIVE

For sources see RUSSIAN FRONT

CHAPTER VI. SCENE 3. THE SOMME

C. E. W. Bean, *The Australian Imperial Force in France, 1916* (1929) [Australian Official History]

J. Charteris, *Life of Field-Marshal Earl Haig*

Maurice, *Life of Lord Rawlinson of Trent*

Dewar and Boraston, *Sir Douglas Haig's Command*

J. F. C. Fuller, *Tanks in the Great War*

Army Quarterly, January and July, 1924, *The German Defence during the Battle of the Somme* (July 1st)

Army Quarterly, January, 1925, *Mametz Wood and Contalmaison 9th–10th July, 1916*

Army Quarterly, October, 1925, *Delville Wood, 14th–19th July, 1916*

Army Quarterly, October, 1926, *The German Defence of Bernafoy and Trônes, 2nd–14th of July, 1916*

Palat, *Bataille de la Somme*

Schwarte, *Der Grosse Krieg*, vol ii

Reichsarchiv, *Somme-Nord 1 Theil* [July 13th]
   Somme-Nord 2 Theil [July 14th–31st]

Rupprecht, *Mein Kriegstagebuch*

Constantin Hierl, *Der Weltkrieg in Umrissen* (1927) [German methods of defence]

Unpublished Documents

Private Evidence

CHAPTER VI

SCENE 4. THE GROWING PAINS OF THE TANK

C. and A. Williams-Ellis, *The Tank Corps* (1919)

A. Stern, *Tanks, 1914–1918. The Log Book of a Pioneer* (1919)

J. F. C. Fuller, *Tanks in the Great War* (1920)

D. G. Browne, *The Tank in Action* (1920)

E. D. Swinton, *Tanks* [Encyclopaedia Britannica, 1922]

W. S. Churchill, *The World Crisis*

Evidence given before the Royal Commission on Awards to Inventors

Evidence given in the case of Bentley v The Crown, 1925

Unpublished Documents

Private Evidence

CHAPTER VI

SCENE 5. RUMANIA SWALLOWED

For sources see RUSSIAN FRONT, also

E. von Falkenhayn, *Der Feldzug der 9 Armée gegen die Rumanen und Russen, 1916–1917*, 2 vols (1921)

M. Sturdza, *Avec l'Armée Roumaine, 1916–1918*

CHAPTER VI

SCENE 6. THE CAPTURE OF BAGHDAD

For sources see MESOPOTAMIAN FRONT

CHAPTER VI

SCENE 7. JUTLAND

The Admiralty, *Official Documents and Despatches, Battle of Jutland* (1920)
J. S. Corbett, *History of the Great War (Naval Operations)* (1921)
Jellicoe (Viscount), *The Grand Fleet, 1914–1916* (1919)
C. Bellairs, *The Battle of Jutland* (1920)
R. Bacon, *The Jutland Scandal* (1925)
H. W. Wilson, *Battleships in Action* (1926)
J. E. T. Harper, *The Truth about Jutland* (1927)
W. S. Churchill, *The World Crisis, 1916–1918*, Part I (1927)
R. Bacon, *Mr Churchill and Jutland* (1927) [in *The World Crisis: A Criticism*]
H. S. Altham, *Jutland* [Encyclopaedia Britannica]
R. Scheer, *Germany's High Seas Fleet in the World War* (Eng trans 1920)
G. von Hase, *Kiel and Jutland* (Eng trans 1926)

CHAPTER VII

SCENES 1–4. ARRAS, MESSINES, PASSCHENDAELE, CAMBRAI

B. E. Palat, *La Grande Guerre sur le Front Occidental*, vol xii (1927)
Rousset, *La Bataille de l'Aisne*
R. Normand, *Déstructions et Dévastations au Course des Guerres* (1929)
W. S. Churchill, *The World Crisis*
Dewar and Boraston, *Sir Douglas Haig's Command*
J. F. C. Fuller, *Tanks in the Great War* (1920)
Reichsarchiv, *Flanders, 1917* (1919)

E. Ludendorff, *My War Memories*
Rupprecht, *Mein Kreigstagebuch*
C. E. Callwell, *Field-Marshal Sir Henry Wilson*
F. Maurice, *The Life of General Lord Rawlinson of Trent*
Laure, *Au 3ième Bureau du troisième G.Q.G.*
Mermeix, *Nivelle et Painlevé–2e Crise du Commandement*
P. Painlevé, *Comment j'ai nommé Foch et Pétain* (1924)
Unpublished Documents
Private Evidence

CHAPTER VII

SCENE 5. CAPORETTO

For sources see ITALIAN FRONT

Also Private Evidence

CHAPTER VII

SCENE 1. THE FIRST BREAKTHROUGH

E. Ludendorff, *My War Memories*
Rupprecht, *Mein Kriegstagebuch*
Wolfgang Foerster, *Graf Schlieffen und der Weltkrieg*, Part III
Albrecht Philip, *Ursachen des deutschen militärischen Zusammenbruch, 1918* (1925) [summary of Parliamentary inquiry]
Kuhl, *Entstehung, Durchführung und Zusammenbruch der Offensive von 1918* (1928)
Schwertfeger, *Die politischen und militärischen Verantwortlichkeiten im Verlaufe der Offensive von 1918* (1928)
Bruchmüller, *Die deutsche Artillerie in den Durchbruchschlachten des Weltkrieges* (1921)
Joachim, *Die Vorbereitung des deutschen Heeres für die Grosse Schlacht in Frankreich im Frühjahr 1918* (1927)
Fehr, *Die Märzoffensive 1918 an der Westfront* (1921) [reveals Wetzell's influence on Ludendorff's strategy]
Kuhl, *Der deutsche Generalstab*
German Ex-Crown Prince, *Memoirs*

M. Erzberger, *Erlebnisse im Weltkrieg*

E. Gugelmeier, *Das Schwarze Jahr* (1917) [food conditions]

Rudolf Binding, *A Fatalist at War* (Eng trans 1928)

Laure, *Au 3ième Bureau du troisième G.Q.G.*

Koeltz, *La Bataille de France, 21 mars–5 avril, 1918*
   L'Offensive Allemande de 1918

L. Madelin, *La Bataille de France*

Dewar and Boraston, *Sir Douglas Haig's Command*

C. E. Callwell, *Field Marshal Sir Henry Wilson*, vol ii

F. Maurice, *The Life of General Lord Rawlinson of Trent*

C. Falls, in *Nineteenth Century*, Oct–Nov 1921

C. à C. Repington, *The First World War, 1914–1918*, vol ii

J. Charteris, *Field Marshal Earl Haig*

Seymour, *The Intimate Papers of Colonel House*, vol. iii

Unpublished Documents

Private Evidence

CHAPTER VIII

SCENE 2. THE BREAKTHROUGH IN FLANDERS

Additional:

*La Bataille des Flandres d'après le journal de marche et les archives de
   la IVe Armée Allemande (9–30 avril, 1918)* (1925) [French trans
   of captured documents]

Unpublished Documents

CHAPTER VIII

SCENE 3. THE BREAKTHROUGH TO THE MARNE

Additional:

Unpublished Documents

Personal Evidence

CHAPTER VIII

SCENE 4. THE SECOND BATTLE OF THE MARNE

Additional:
Les Armées Françaises dans la Grande Guerre, Tome VII, vol i
(French Official History)
Zwehl, *Die Schlachten im Sommer, 1918* (1922)
Private Evidence

CHAPTER VIII

SCENE 5. AUGUST 8th

Additional:
A. A. Montgomery, *The Story of the Fourth Army*
J. Monash, *The Australian Victories in 1918*
M. Daille, *La Bataille de Montdidier* (1922) [French share]
C. Falls in *Army Quarterly*, July, 1928, *An Aspect of the Battle of
Amiens, 1918* [French cooperation]
Unpublished Documents
Personal Evidence

CHAPTER VIII

SCENES 7–8. ST MIHIEL AND MEUSE-ARGONNE

Final Report of Gen. John J. Pershing
First Army Report
Frederick Palmer, *Our Greatest Battle* (1919)
R. L. Bullard, *Personalities and Reminiscences of the War*
Hunter Liggett, *Commanding an American Army*
A.E.F.
T. M. Johnson, *Without Censor*
J. G. Harbord, *Leaves from a War Diary*
J. T. Dickman, *The Great Crusade*
Wellmann, *Das I. Reserve-Korps in der letzten Schlacht* (1925)
Passaga, *Le Calvaire de Verdun* (1928)
Personal Evidence

ADDITIONAL. 1930–34

ORIGINS

Bülow (Prince von) *Memoirs* (Eng trans 1931)

Österreich-Ungarns Aussenpolitik von der Bosnischen Krise 1908 bis zum Kriegsausbruch 1914, 8 vols [Austro-Hungarian diplomatic papers]

Beyens, *Deux Années à Berlin, 1912–1914* (1932)

GENERAL

The War Memoirs of David Lloyd George, vols. i and ii (1933); iii and iv (1934)

C. Addison, *Four and a Half Years* (1934)

F. J. Moberly, *History of the Great War (Military Operations) Togoland and the Cameroons 1914–1916* (1931)

M. Paléologue, *Une Prélude à l'Invasion de las Belgique* (1933)

A. Neimann, *Kaiser und Heer* (1930) [an apologia which throws light on the Kaiser's influence on pre-war plans and war-time operations]

Schäfer, *Generalstab und Admiralstab* (1931)

Kuhl, *Der Weltkrieg, 1914–1918, dem deutschen Volk dargestellt* (1929). [précis in *Army Quarterly*, April 1930]

J. J. Pershing, *My Experiences in the World War* (1931)

Peyton C. March, *The Nation at War* (1932)

L. S. Viereck, *The Strangest Friendship in History—Woodrow Wilson and Colonel House* (1932)

C. Seymour, *American Diplomacy during the World War* (1934) [a most able and important summary of old and new evidence]

WESTERN FRONT

The Memoirs of Marshal Foch (Eng trans 1931)

Liddell Hart, *Foch—The Man of Orleans* (1931)

The Memoirs of Marshal Joffre (Eng trans 1932)

E. L. Spears, *Liaison, 1914* (1930)

J. Charteris, *At G.H.Q.* (1931)

C. B. Baker-Carr, *From Chauffeur to Brigadier* (1930)

Hubert Gough, *The Fifth Army* (1931)

C. E. W. Bean, *The Australian Imperial Force in France, vol. IV, 1917* (1933)

J. Fabry, *Joffre et son Destin* (1932)

G. Galliéni and P. B. Gheusi, *Les Carnets de Galliéni* (1932)

Les Armées Françaises dans la Grand Guerre. Tome II [covers the first phase of the deadlock, Nov 1914–May 1915, and reveals the fiasco of Joffre's attempt to stage a great offensive in Dec 1914]
Tome IV, vol i [covers Feb–May 1916]

Mordacq, *Pouvait-on signer l'Armistice à Berlin* (1930) *Le Ministère Clemenceau. Journal d'un témoin* (1932)

General XXX, *La Crise du commandement unique. Le conflit Clemenceau, Foch, Haig, Pétain* (1931)

R. Poincaré, *Au service de la France*, vols vi, vii [1915]; and viii [1916] 1930–32)

Herbillon, *Du général en chef au gouvernement. Souvenirs d'une officier de liaison* (1930)

E. Mayer, *Nos Chefs de 1914*

F. Gazin, *La Cavalerie Française dans la Guerre Mondiale, 1914–1918* (1930)

Castelli, *Cinq Journées au 8e Corps* (1931) [deals with five critical episodes in 1914 when part of the French First Army]

Lucas, *Le 10e Corps à la Bataille de Charleroi* (1931)

J. Delmas, *Mes hommes au feu* (1931) [illuminating sidelights on the blundering French advance into Lorraine]
L'Infanterie de la Victoire, 1918 (1932)

M. Caracciolo, *Le truppe Italiene in Francia*

P. Azan, *Les Belges sur l'Yser* (1930) [sheds some interesting light on Joffre's efforts to persuade King Albert to quit the coast for an inland advance in Oct 1914]

Galet, *Albert, King of the Belgians, in the Great War* (Eng trans 1931) [most important evidence on 1914]

Historical Section, Belgian General Staff, *La Défense de la Position Fortifiée de Namur en août, 1914* (1931)

A. Cerf, *La Guerre aux frontières du Jura* [some light on the possibilities of a German move through Switzerland]

Der Waffenstillstand, 1918–1919 (1931) [German Armistice documents, in 3 vols]

W. Foerster, *Aus der Gedankenwerkstatt des Deutschen Generalstabes*

(1931) [a comparative study of the influence of Schlieffen and Moltke]

Poseck, *The German Cavalry in Belgium and France, 1914* [Eng trans in US]

RUSSIAN FRONT

Army Quarterly, April and July 1931, *The Lemberg Campaign*

W. S. Churchill, *The World Crisis. The Eastern Front* (1931)

A. A. Brusilov, *A Soldier's Notebook, 1914–1918* (1931)

Danilov, *Grossfürst Nikolai Nikolajewitsch, Sein Leben und Wirken* (1931)

L. Trotsky, *The History of the Russian Revolution. Vol I* (Eng trans 1932)

Reicharsarchiv, *Gorlice* (1930) [German Official Monograph]

Österreich-Ungarns letzter Krieg, 1914–18 [Austrian Official History, vol i (1930) covers 1914; vol ii (1932) and vol iii (1933) cover 1915]

ITALIAN FRONT

L'Esercito Italiano nella Grande Guerra (1927) [Italian Official History, Vol i, preliminary. Vol ii, 1915]

L. Villari, *The War on the Italian Front* (1931)

BALKAN FRONT

C. Falls, *Military Operations; Macedonia. Vol I* (1933) [British Official History]

Cordonnier, *Ai-je trahi Sarrail?* (1932)

Pétin, *Le Drame Roumain, 1916–1918* (1933)

Österreich-Ungarns letzter Krieg, 1914–1918 [Austrian Official History, vol i (1929–30) Parts I and V]

PALESTINE

Liddell Hart, *'T. E. Lawrence'–In Arabia and After* (1934)

E. Brémond, *Le Hedjaz dans la Guerre Mondiale* (1932)

A. H. Burne, in *The Fighting Forces*, April 1932–Feb 1933, *Notes on the Palestine Campaign*

NAVAL

H. Newbolt, *History of the Great War (Naval Operations)*, vol. v (1931)
[the Submarine Campaign and its frustration]
L. Guichard, *The Naval Blockade, 1914–1918* (Eng trans 1930)
A. Laurens, *Le Commandement Naval en Méditerranée pendant la Guerre de 1914–1918* (1933)

AIR

J. Poirier, *Les bombardements de Paris, 1914–1918* (1930)
C. F. Snowden Gamble, *The Air Weapon* (1931)
P. R. C. Groves, *Behind the Smoke Screen* (1-34) [important revelations on the misuse of air power in the war]

ECONOMIC AND HOME FRONT

W. Beveridge, *Food Control in War Time* (1928)
Landwehr, *Hunger die Erschöpfungsjahre der Mittelmächte, 1917–1918* (1931) [details of the famine-stricken state of Austria-Hungary]
Kohn and Mayendorff, *The Cost of the War to Russia* (1933)

THE MARNE

Liddell Hart, *Foch–The Man of Orleans* (1931)
    The British Way in Warfare (Chapter iii) (1932).
G. Lestien, *L'Action du Général Foch à la Bataille de la Marne* (1930).
Muller, *Joffre et la Marne* (1931) [important evidence from Joffre's aide-de-camp which goes far to confirm, by admission, previously disputed claims as to Galliéni's influence]
E. Valarché, *Le Combat du Petit Morin ... au 10e Corps d'Armée*
Koeltz, *L'armée von Kluck à la Bataille de la Marne* (1932)
A. H. Burne, in *The Cavalry Journal*, 1934, *The German Cavalry on the Marne* [an able analysis of the German evidence, bringing out the opportunities missed by the Allies]

TANNENBERG

W. Elze, Tannenberg [prints many documents, drawn from the German archives, which are not given in the official history]

THE DARDANELLES

C. F. Aspinall-Oglander, *Military Operations, Gallipoli, Vol II* (1932) [Official History]

THE GAS CLOUD AT YPRES

Les Armées Françaises dans la Grande Guerre. Tome II [this is worth comparative study, as an example of how official historians may falsify history on patriotic grounds]
Mordacq, *Le Drame de l'Yser. Surprise des gaz, Avril, 1915* (1933) [honest unofficial history by the commander of a brigade on the spot]

VERDUN

R. Poincaré, *Au service de la France, Vol VIII. Verdun 1916* (1932)
Paquet, *Verdun, Janvier-Février 1916. Le rôle de la Photographie et de l'Observation terrestre* (1930)
J. Rouquerol, *La Drame de Douaumont, 21 février-24 octobre, 1916*
H. Wendt, *Verdun, 1916* (1932) [reconciles the French and German accounts]

THE SOMME

J. E. Edmonds, *Military Operations. France and Belgium, 1916* (1932) [covers the launching of the Somme offensive]
Army Quarterly, July 1933, *The Somme: 15th of September, 1916*
January 1934, *The Capture of Thiepval, 20th of September, 1916*

THE GROWING PAINS OF THE TANK

E. D. Swinton, *Eyewitness* (1932)
R. Mortier, *Les Chars d'assaut. Comment ils furent realisés.* [sheds light on some French experiments in 1915 towards an armoured trench-crossing vehicle]

ARRAS, MESSINES, PASSCHENDAELE, CAMBRAI

C. E. W. Bean, *The Australian Imperial Force in France, Vol IV, 1917* (1933)
J. Charteris, *At G.H.Q.* (1931)
Hubert Gough, *The Fifth Army* (1931)
Army Quarterly, July 1930, *Cambrai: The Action of the German 107th Division*
Reichsarchiv (Official Monographs), *Die Tankschlacht bei Cambrai, 1917* (1929)
  Die Osterschlacht bei Arras, 1917 (1930)

THE FIRST BREAKTHROUGH

Liddell Hart, *Foch – The Man of Orleans* (1931)
Hubert Gough, *The Fifth Army* (1931)
H. Rowan-Robinson, *Belated Comments on a Great Event* (1932)
Thierry d'Argenlieu, *La Bataille de l'Avre* [covers the operations of Debeney's army, which came up to the aid of the British]

THE BREAKTHROUGH TO THE MARNE

Reichsarchiv, *Deutsche Siege, 1918*
  Das Verdringen der 7 Armee über Ailette, Aisne, Vesle und Ourcq bis zur Marne: 27 Mai bis 13 Juni [German Official Monograph]
  Wachsende Schwierigkeiten, 1918 [covers the ineffectual attacks early in June between the Marne and Somme salients]

THE SECOND BATTLE OF THE MARNE

Reichsarchiv, *Der letzte deutsche Angriff. Reims 1918*
  Schicksalswende. Von der Marne dis zur Vesle, 1918 [German official monographs]

AUGUST 8th

Grasset, *Montdidier, le 8 août 1918 à la 42e Division* (1931)
Reichsarchiv, *Die Katastrophe des 8 August, 1918* (1932) [German Official Monograph]

Index

Index

GENERAL

Index

FACTORS

Sir Basil Liddell Hart
History of the Second World War £14.00

First published in the year after his death in 1970, Liddell Hart's classic history of the Second World War is the work of a leading military analyst, but also of a compassionate and uniquely original thinker. Sir Basil Liddell Hart was the author of more than thirty books and a world renowned lecturer in strategy and tactics; a man of whom *The Economist* said: 'he is not simply a prophet and a critic but a historian of great rank'.

'The greatest British military thinker of this century' THE SOLDIER

'A work of great length and great learning, illuminated by flashes of insight . . . full of brilliant stretegic analysis' A. J. P. TAYLOR

'Unlikely to be surpassed' SUNDAY TELEGRAPH

'The book has the mark of the author's genius – a lucidity and insight such as no other military writer can match . . . it will long be read with profit and enjoyment by all interested in the military art' THE ARMY QUARTERLY

'Remarkably good . . . a mine of accurate information'
EVENING STANDARD

Peter Padfield
Himmler: Reichsführer SS £12.99

'Padfield is a writer of great power. The scenes he paints . . . are as graphic and horrible as our imaginations can grasp, a hell on earth more terrible than any mediaeval artist or Calvinist theologian could depict'
DONALD CAMERON WATT, SUNDAY TIMES

'Peter Padfield writes with massive authority and lucidity . . . his catalogue of Himmler's evil is mind-numbing'
RICHARD HELLER, MAIL ON SUNDAY

'Mr Padfield has convincingly sifted the evidence while steering clear of the pitfalls . . . a grippingly repulsive tale'
GILES MACDONOUGH, FINANCIAL TIMES

'The research is vast and impeccable' DAN VAN DER VAT, GUARDIAN

'Clear writing and much detail bring sharply to life the horrors of Nazi rule'
RICHARD LAMB, SPECTATOR

'We have no excuse for not knowing about Himmler after Padfield's thorough, conscientious and compulsively readable investigation'
A. L. ROWSE, SUNDAY TELEGRAPH

'Padfield writes vividly . . . The story is a chilling reminder of what happens when fanatics get their hold on the instruments of state power'
RICHARD OVERY, OBSERVER

All Pan Books are available at your local bookshop or newsagent, or can be ordered direct from the publisher. Indicate the number of copies required and fill in the form below.

Send to: Macmillan General Books C.S.
              Book Service By Post
              PO Box 29, Douglas I-O-M
              IM99 1BQ

or phone: 01624 675137, quoting title, author and credit card number.

or fax: 01624 670923, quoting title, author, and credit card number.

or Internet: http://www.bookpost.co.uk

Please enclose a remittance* to the value of the cover price plus 75 pence per book for post and packing. Overseas customers please allow £1.00 per copy for post and packing.

*Payment may be made in sterling by UK personal cheque, Eurocheque, postal order, sterling draft or international money order, made payable to Book Service By Post.

Alternatively by Access/Visa/MasterCard

Card No.

Expiry Date

Signature

Applicable only in the UK and BFPO addresses.

While every effort is made to keep prices low, it is sometimes necessary to increase prices at short notice. Pan Books reserve the right to show on covers and charge new retail prices which may differ from those advertised in the text or elsewhere.

NAME AND ADDRESS IN BLOCK CAPITAL LETTERS PLEASE

Name

Address

8/95

Please allow 28 days for delivery.
Please tick box if you do not wish to receive any additional information. ☐